MONUMENTS OF GRASS

~

BOOK ONE – EXILE

MONUMENTS OF GRASS

An American Romance

~

BOOK ONE – EXILE

1756

*   *   *

BRENDAN FRAIN

Monuments of Grass: Exile

2nd (revised) edition © Brendan Frain 2025

ISBN: 978-1-7640051-0-4 (paperback)

ISBN: 978-1-7640051-7-3 (ebook)

Book design and typesetting by Typography Studio

Published by Brendan Frain

A catalogue record for this
book is available from the
National Library of Australia

For Sat, beloved wife
I authored the books; you authored me.

Introduction

IN 18TH CENTURY ENGLAND penal transportation to the American Colonies was a common means of punishment for a variety of criminal offenses. If the convicted felon survived the often-horrific conditions of the voyage, he or she would be sold into indentured servitude, i.e. unpaid labour, upon landing. The more able-bodied were sold to back-breaking field work on tobacco or rice plantations for the duration of their sentence.

The 'New World' that awaited British migrants, both voluntary and involuntary, consisted of 13 English Colonies strung along the Atlantic coast of North America. Excluding indigenous peoples and slaves, the population of the 13 colonies at the period of the novel was roughly 1.5 million. America itself was a battleground for three European empires: Great Britain, France, and Spain. France laid claim to an immense territory extending east from Canada and the Great Lakes region to the territory west of the Mississippi including Louisiana and to the mouth of the Mississippi in the Gulf of Mexico. The vast region was known as New France. Spain laid claim to the southwest part of America including what is present-day Florida. (See Map 1, following).

The huge stretches of land beyond the thinly-populated French settlements and military outposts were inhabited by indigenous tribes, some of whom sided with France and others with Britain when the simmering rivalries between the colonial powers over land and resources erupted in the French-Indian War (1754–1763). The war was the American theatre of a global conflict involving the great European powers led by Great Britain and Prussia on one side and France, Russia and, later, Spain, on the other.

It is this bloody conflict, marked by savageries on both sides, that Boundless and his companion Mose ride into on their journey from Colonial Maryland through the Shenandoah Valley and on through the Allegheny Mountains. (Map 2, following).

The ridges and valleys of the Appalachian Mountains (at the time, commonly called the Alleghenies) formed a natural barrier to westward expansion. Nevertheless, despite hostility from the indigenous populations and the considerable physical hardships involved, many settlers risked the dangers in their determination to claim the abundant land west of the mountains. Their journey took them along the Great Philadelphia Wagon Road. The road followed an old Indian Road and ran for 800 miles from Philadelphia, Pennsylvania to Augusta, Georgia. A section of the road ran the 200-mile length of the Shenandoah Valley in Westen Virginia.

In 1750 the physician and explorer Thomas Walker encountered a 'notch' or gap (later called the Cumberland Gap) enabling passage across the Allegheny Mountains. It is the search for this gap—and the paradisal bounty to which it was gateway—which prompts the epic 'jaunt' of Boundless and Mose beginning in Chapter 28.

Maps

Two maps follow. The first shows America at the time of the novel. Readers will note the vast extent of French land claims compared to the British colonies strung out along the Atlantic seaboard. New Spain was also a major colonial power at the time with claims to the Southwest and southern parts of America, including modern-day Texas, New Mexico, and Florida.

The second map shows the Great Wagon Road from its beginnings in Philadelphia to its terminus in Augusta, Georgia 800 miles distant. On the map, readers can trace the route of the Wagon Road as it heads south-westwards from Maryland through the Shenandoah Valley towns of Winchester and Staunton and towards the James River. The map shows the Allegheny Mountains flanking the wagon road west of the Shenandoah Valley. Near Big Lick (Roanoke) an old buffalo trace later known as the Wilderness Road branches off in a westward direction. It is this road which takes Boundless and Mose through the mountains to Cumberland Gap (also shown). The base of the Gap rises approximately 300 feet (90 m) above the valley floor.

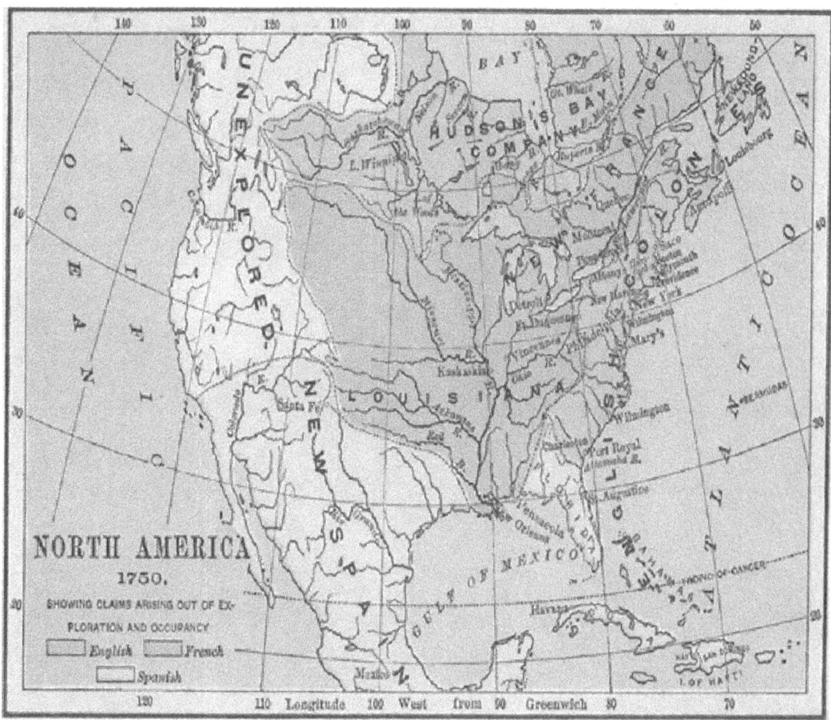

Map 1: North America in 1750 showing the French, Spanish and British claims.

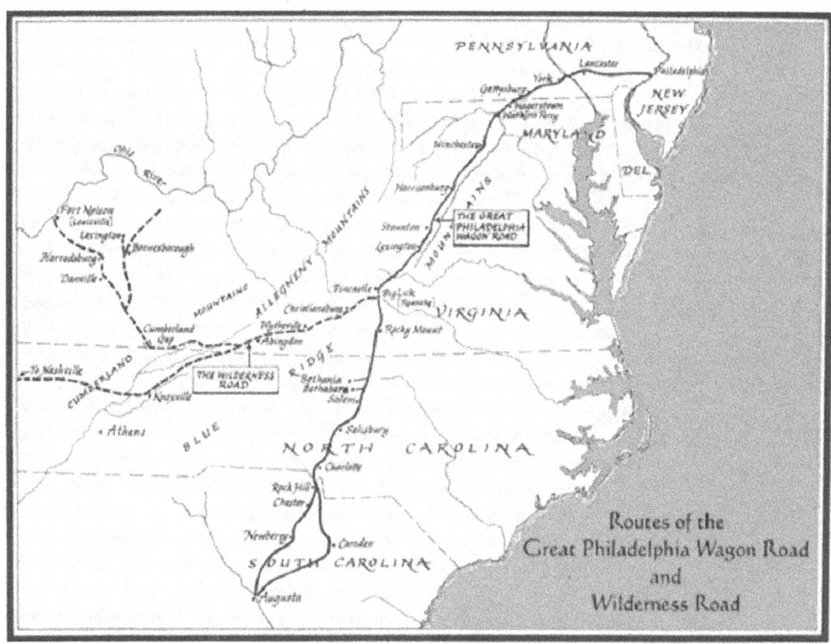

Map 2: The Great Wagon Road from Philadelphia. The Wilderness Road splits off near Roanoke, Virginia (Big Lick) where it leads through the Allegheny Mountains to Cumberland Gap.

Contents

*   *   *

DAWN

T HE FIRST, PRIMAL LIGHT broke over the earth. They had started off in darkness, loading the body onto the backboard by the light of a lantern, the wagon and its cargo shrouded in gloom. She was anxious, impatient to get going. Ira was under the wagon, inspecting the axle by lantern light. Boundary was pacing back and forth, as anxious and fretful as herself. The plain wooden coffin sat on the backboard. Tears came to her eyes. *That a frail wood box could hold him!*

'Did you put the shovels on?' Ira squeezed out from under the wagon.

'I did. We should get going.' Boundary's voice betrayed his agitation.

Ira helped her up onto the seat, her brother squeezing in beside her. 'Har!' Her husband flicked the whip and the horses started forward. She turned to see as the coffin slid against the side.

Within minutes they were on the road. The dawn air was cold and she shivered, pulling the buffalo robe tighter around her shoulders. Where was the snow? she wondered.

'Leastways the earth won't be too hard,' said Ira, as if guessing her thoughts.

She held onto the seat as the wagon lurched and bumped over the dirt track. They passed the turn-off leading to town, the rocking motion abruptly smoothing as they embarked on the tarred road that led to the rock. She glanced toward the town, her thoughts leaping to the schoolhouse. *He would be there in a few hours, standing by the door, his eyes anxious for her arrival.* She sighed, casting the tormenting notion from her mind.

'You alright, Am?' Ira reached for her hand. 'It won't be long,' he said.

The gloom began to lift as they neared the rock. Her eyes searched for it, straining to see though the semi-darkness. Along the eastern sky, a thin red line streaked the horizon. 'Thank God for the late sunrise,' she thought, her mind projecting ahead to when Trust workers would arrive to finish preparations for the great event Lomax had planned.

'Remember to turn-off to the homestead,' Boundary said, leaning across her to talk to Ira.

Her husband nodded, his bare hands gripping the reins. *He doesn't feel the cold. Not like his ma.*

'I see it.' Boundary's voice was sombre with the announcement. And there it was, a dark shape against the pearling light. She clutched the seat as Ira turned off the road and onto the grass—the smooth ride once again giving way to bumps and lurches. She glanced back at the coffin as it bounced on the backboard. *We should have tied it down. It's disrespectful.*

A light gleamed at the foot of the rock. 'There'll be a watchman,' she cautioned Ira.

'At least,' said Boundary. 'Lomax is nervous as a cat of what that crazy Preacher will do.'

Ira took a wide turn making sure they approached from the lee or grass side. They passed the deserted farmhouse and tears came to her eyes. The corral was empty, the barn door shut. She saw herself shrieking with laughter as she dashed across the yard, her ma and pa looking on, their faces young and vital. *It's a shame Boundary doesn't want it. Jube would have.* The wagon lurched as it hit a rut and she turned her gaze back to the rock. A flush of light revealed the head of the great beast as it stared into the gloom. *What is it looking at?* She tried to remember if her pa had ever said.

'I 'spect she's looking for her kin,' her ma had said when she asked. 'It must get mighty lonesome all by herself.'

What made her think it was a 'she'? she wondered, the thought occurring to her for the first time.

They hit another rut and the coffin banged against the bed. 'Careful!' She clutched Ira's arm.

They entered the darkness beneath the massive rock, Ira cautious lest any sentries be alerted by the noise. 'They won't hear past the rock,' she had assured him.

'Whoa!' He pulled the horses to a halt. Boundary got down and turned to assist her. She stepped carefully in the long dress. She retied the laces of her bonnet as Ira and Boundary whispered together in the gloom. It was getting lighter, the eastern sky now flushed a pale white. 'Where is it?' Ira asked.

'Hold on.' Amity took the lantern and walked over to the rock. Holding up the lantern she squinted to see. And then she found the scratches, her fingers running over the cold, hard stone. 'Here!'

She watched as they took down the coffin and carried it over the grass, setting it down before going back for the spades. She remembered, with a start, that she was standing on the graves of her mother and Half Moon. She stepped back, an apologetic murmur on her lips. 'Sorry, ma.'

It was now light enough to see clearly as Boundary tested the earth with the spade. 'Here?' He glanced at her for confirmation.

'Wait.' She paced out a few steps from the last of the scratched crosses. 'Yes.'

Boundary used the spade to etch out a rough plot in the withered grass as Ira watched. Then the two began to dig, facing each other as they stabbed the spades into the cold earth. 'It's hard!' grunted Boundary.

'Not as hard as its gonna get!'

She watched, her thoughts roaming back to the day they had summoned her to the homestead. Boundary was already there, standing outside, his face distraught. 'It was Joe Parson that found him,' he said. 'Joe said the horse was jest cropping the grass. That's what he saw first, the horse. Pa was jest lying there, under a blanket. Joe reckons it was lucky some critter hadn't got at him.'

She had winced at the words.

'It was peaceful, Am. He just passed away.' Boundary took her hand.

'I want to see him.' She tugged her hand away. He didn't protest, just followed her in the door.

Their father was laid out on the bed, his face ashen, his arms by his side. 'Pa!' She burst into tears.

He looked so fragile, she remembered now. *Like a child, but with an old face.*

'Is that deep enough?' Ira's voice broke the silence. He was looking at her.

Why does he have to ask? Doesn't he know? Both men were standing hip-deep in the trench.

'I guess it is,' said Ira, answering himself. He scrambled out of the trench, Boundary following.

It was now almost full light, a cold breeze blowing up out of the grass. She watched as they struggled to manoeuvre the casket into the grave. She thought she heard a noise and turned, anxious lest a watchman had discovered them.

Ira had brought along her father's Sharps, setting it in the back alongside the coffin. *We ought to have buried it with him*, it occurred to her. *Ira would no doubt think it foolish, the waste of a fine gun.* 'He shot all those buffalo, with this?' He had said admiringly, running his fingers along the barrel.

The casket was in the grave and they began spading dirt on top. She watched, too numb for tears.

She heard a cawing noise and looked up at the rock. A crow had alighted on the summit. It strutted up and down uttering harsh cries. For a moment she fancied it was Half Moon come back to observe, the bird half-lifting its wings as it cocked its head to stare down at her. She remembered a chant the woman had taught her. 'It will bring you good things,' Half Moon had promised.

'What does it mean?'

'It means many things.'

'You never answer direct!'

The bird cawed again, loudly, and she half-smiled through her grief. *I hear you, Aunty.*

'Are you ready, Am?' Her brother scuffed over the dirt to make the disturbance less visible.

'What if someone sees it?' She grimaced at the evidence of upturned earth.

'In a few hours it won't matter. No one will notice.' Ira used the spade to further smooth the dirt.

Boundary plucked a few handfuls of grass and scattered them on top. 'They'll think maybe it was some critter,' he said. 'See?'

He pointed to the scratched cross. 'It's lined up.'

'Did you bring the bible?' Her husband remembered to ask.

'No need. I memoried a verse ma liked,' she said as Ira and her brother removed their hats and bowed their heads. 'Pa never did care much.'

The wind blew against her, raising up the fresh dirt and grass as she licked her lips and recited the words.

'The voice said, Cry. And he said, What shall I cry? All flesh is grass, and all the goodliness thereof is as the flower of the field: The grass withereth, the flower fadeth: because the spirit of the Lord bloweth upon it: surely the people are like unto grass.'

She stopped, her voice choked with grief. Boundary glanced up. 'It's alright, Am.'

'The grass withereth, the flower fadeth: but the word of our God shall stand for ever.'

She stood in silence, tears running down her face. Boundary wiped his eyes, staring at the flattened earth.

'We'd better get going.' Ira picked up the spades and placed them back on the wagon. 'We don't want anyone to come by.'

They set off, the lightened wagon trundling over the grass. Grasping the seat Amity glanced back, barely able to discern the fresh plot in the grass. The sun was now fully risen, its shine bathing the buffalo in glorious light.

Fresh tears rolled down her cheeks and she stifled a sob.

Goodbye, Pa. I'll miss you to bits.

EXILE

The grasslands of the wilderness overflow;
the hills are clothed with gladness

—PSALM 65:12

Caught Black-Handed

THEY CAME FOR HIM at cock-crow. Roughly shaking him from sleep, the warders delivered him through the dungeons to the flight of steps that led up into the Old Court. A small cell stood next to the steps and he was confined there, along with a counterfeiter, a thief, a highwayman and a dozen other felons.

The warder shoved him into the cell. 'Wait there!'

Sitting on the hard bench, he waited for several hours—starting up in expectation each time the door opened. As the hours passed, the other accused were taken out one by one and led upstairs. Bored, in spite of his anxiety, he took the folded paper from his pocket—reading through his defence for what seemed the hundredth time. Whenever footsteps approached, he thrust it back into his pocket. Hungry and thirsty, he asked for water.

The warder gave a mocking laugh. 'Mayhap a mug of ale?'

Late in the morning, he overheard one warder complain to another that Tory pressmen had swept the surrounding laneways and taverns for hirelings to attend the court. 'It be for the printer,' the man said. 'And they be half of them so stewed they know not their own names.' He cocked an ear as a roar of laughter sounded from above. 'Hark! They treat the Court as a stinking cesspit.'

Hours passed and the printer fought to stay alert. Fatigued and malnourished from months of confinement in the bowels of Newgate Prison, his senses had grown heavy. When finally summonsed, he was slumped in a corner, fast asleep.

'Wake, thou blackguard!' The warder escorted him up the steps to the Chamber. Halfway up, they were stopped by a court bailiff who descended to meet them.

'Art thou Boundless McLennan, printer?' The man peered at a sheet of paper in his hand, reading it by the light of a lantern attached to the wall. Raised voices and laughter sounded through the open door to the courthouse.

'I am.'

The bailiff beckoned to the warder. 'Fetch him up.'

THE BRIGHTNESS OF THE Chamber was dazzling after the dim light of the cell. Wondering if he were yet asleep and dreaming, he held up a hand to shield his eyes as the spring sunshine poured in through two, high-arched windows. The tiered galleries were crowded with noisy, boisterous spectators who briefly silenced as they turned their eyes on the latest object of their curiosity.

'Walk!' The bailiff, now joined by another, poked him.

He was directed past a double row of benches occupied by the unruly mob of drunks, wastrels and prostitutes conscripted from the surrounding streets and taverns. The motley greeted him with a broadside of whistles, curses and jeers as he was escorted past.

'Hanging for such as thou!'

'Nay. Chop his neck!'

The bailiffs hurried him forward as the mob subjected him to a shower of spit and vulgar abuse. A slatternly woman with a weeping boil on the side of her nose thrust her face at him as he passed. 'Thou dunce! Thou pizzle-pot!' The screeched insults were greeted with hoots of laughter by her bawdy confederates before she was rudely thrust aside by a bailiff.

Boundless was led to the enclosed dock. 'Stand there!'

He blinked as a reflector suspended above the dock threw sunlight from the arched windows directly into his eyes. Opposite the dock, the four city magistrates sat behind a raised, wood-panelled dais. The justices seemed indifferent to the bedlam all around them, sipping brandy or dozing in the stifling warmth. Beneath the heavy, powdered wigs, their flushed faces gleamed with perspiration. Three held up nosegays to block the humid stench of the Chamber. Sprigs of rue adorned the dais as a precaution against gaol fever—a recurrence of the sickness an ever-present dread since the last deadly outbreak.

Below the dais, the bewigged prosecutors sat around a green baize table, waiting for the next case to be called. The clerk of the court occupied a high desk to one side of the table. Witnesses for the various trials sat in a large stall situated to the right of the dock.

An adjoining stall housed the members of the jury. The jurors, looking bored and indifferent, played cards as they lounged on the wood benches. One or two were fast asleep, their heads lolling back against the wood panelling, their mouths slack as they snored.

Boundless panted for breath, feeling faint in the closeted air and the overpowering stench of sweat, perfume, and unwashed bodies. He searched the crowded galleries, feeling as if he was in a bearpit, the focus of all eyes.

'Boundless!' A young man, flourishing a soft-brimmed hat to catch his attention, leaned down from the gallery to shout his name. 'Boundless! Up here!'

He glanced up, relieved to spot a familiar face amidst the noisy throng of spectators. 'Joshua!'

Joshua Lively leaned perilously far over the gallery rail as he called out encouragement. A green ribbon—symbol of the Reformist Movement— was pinned to the lapel of his wool coat, of the same rustic plainness as Boundless' own. 'We stand as one!' he called between cupped hands.

Taking courage from the defiant Lively, Boundless picked out the faces of other supporters in the adjoining galleries. All wore the plain brown coats and beige neckties of the Reformists and their sympathisers. A man he recognised as the pamphleteer Joseph Wainwright caught his eye. Wainwright held up a fistful of green ribbons. 'To adorn the Temple of Justice!' With the cry, he tossed the ribbons high into the air. As they floated down they were snatched at and trampled beneath the spiteful feet of the inebriated hirelings seated below, who now turned their vitriol on each other.

One drunken wastrel wearing a heavily soiled frockcoat took the opportunity to perch precariously atop the wooden bench and shout blood-curdling threats at a love rival. 'Deceiving dog! Abductor of all that is most sacred!' He shook a fist at the object of his wrath—a one-eyed thief who sat with a slovenly woman sprawled on his lap.

'Thou arse-boil! Thou fart-pillow! Purse-filching magpie!' All at once, the aggrieved fellow's legs folded under him, and he tumbled backwards to roars of laughter.

A high-pitched scream caused heads to turn. A Whig and a Tory had come to blows. The two rolled on the floor, punching and gouging as bailiffs rushed to intervene. To shouts of glee, the enraged Tory promptly rounded on the bailiffs, landing several blows as he was dragged kicking and shouting from the Chamber.

Boundless muttered in disbelief at the chaotic scenes, half convinced he had been ushered into a lunatic asylum. To add to the impression, another drunk strutted up and down, bellowing for recognition from the mocking galleries as he insisted upon his kingly status.

The magistrates sipped brandy and gossiped with one another, ignoring the disorder taking placing under their noses. Seated between the four city magistrates was the High Court Justice selected by the Crown to preside over the trial. He was busily making dispositions on a previous case, scribbling notes on a sheet before handing it to a page.

'Justice Mallory—a most vile creature!' Joshua Lively's warning came to Boundless as he studied the Justice, searching for some clue as to the man's disposition in the fleshy jowls and scowling impatience as he despatched the page. 'The villain is as conducive to bribes as any whore in the street,' continued Joshua. 'It is rumoured his wife cuckolds him with half the court.'

IT WAS SIX MONTHS earlier. The two were huddled in The Cock and Hoop, their favourite city tavern, to commiserate over the fate of Henry Fry, an outspoken Reformist recently condemned by the very same judge. 'Five years transportation,' Joshua groaned in frustration. 'At this rate, we must all reconvene in Virginia.'

Glancing around to ensure they were not being observed, Boundless surreptitiously lifted a corner of the broadsheet to reveal a copy of the banned pamphlet. 'Every word of it true,' he whispered.

'Caution, I pray you.' Joshua glanced at a man seated on a nearby bench. 'There are spies and informers everywhere.' He lowered his voice. 'Are you still intent on publishing your own tract?'

'I am. The more voices raised, the harder it will be to silence us.' Boundless slid the inflammatory pamphlet back under the broadsheet. 'Where be our rights when there is no liberty of speech and no freedom to say so?'

'True, and yet I solemnly urge you to reconsider.' Joshua leaned in closer, his voice urgent. 'The time is not right for another such provocation. Our enemies pick their targets. Well-disposed Whigs are preoccupied with France, and each other, and will not support us in the event of a trial. The nest of vipers that infest the court are aware of this and press their advantage. Publishing now would put you at great hazard.'

'I say only what must be said.'

With another glance around, Joshua leaned in to shield the conversation. 'A philosophical argument in favour of free speech might pass unnoticed. But a direct attack on the government, the clergy, *and* the monarchy is foolhardy.'

'But necessary, since these are the instruments that censor and suppress us.' Boundless hesitated, searching his companion's face. 'But I can depend on you—in the event that the authorities take action?'

'You doubt it? I only urge prudence, moderation and, above all, *delay*.'

'You give me too much credit. Do you think that they—the authorities—will take such notice of a little broadsheet?'

'Nay. Rather a brass trumpet, say, in the glorious struggle!' Lively's voice grew sombre. 'But we do not need another martyr in this war, Boundless, only more soldiers. I fear that if you publish now, the government will seek to make an example of you—especially coming so close upon the heels of poor Fry.'

Boundless drank from the tankard and wiped his mouth, a bold sureness coursing through his veins. 'Fear not, Joshua. I shall be careful. And popular opinion, if not yet the times, be on our side.'

'Ever the impatient one!' Joshua shook his head admiringly.

'But caution, I pray you. They will strike at any perceived danger.'

The warning proved prophetic. Just three days after publication, he was identified as the author of the offending broadsheet. Following an attempt to flee the city, he was betrayed—by whom, he never discovered—and charged under the same onerous law of seditious libel used against the unfortunate Fry.

Dragged from his hiding place beneath a bale of hay, he was hauled off to Newgate to await trial and unceremoniously dumped in a foul dungeon whose stench brought tears to his eyes. Abandoned there among those deemed heretics, traitors, or murderers, he feared being left to rot. To his immense relief, Joshua Lively discovered where he was being held and visited three days later.

'What news?' He begged before Joshua had the chance to sit down. His companion had bribed the warder to allow them the use of a small, private room off the main dungeon.

Joshua set down a cloth bag on the stool. 'I have brought paper and ink and some food. If they try to take it away, tell them that Fleming'—he named the notoriously corrupt head keep—'has vouched for it.'

'And the trial?'

'Posted for next month.'

'Is it Mallory?'

'The very same.'

'Then I am done for!' Boundless moaned with despair.

'Take courage.' Joshua laid a hand on his arm. 'You shall be our very own Cato. There is such great public interest in the case that the villain must surely refrain from outright bullying of the jury. And their conscience be our best defence.'

'*Their conscience be our best defence.*' The words returned to him as he surveyed the jurors in whom Joshua placed such faith—and who had so signally betrayed that faith in the case of Fry. The twelve men yawned with boredom as they lounged on the hard benches. The jury foreman had one leg flung carelessly over the rail, leaning his head back in his linked hands. Boundless tightened his lips as his eyes took in the fellow's blue coat. In the adjoining stall, witnesses—some of whom he recognised as germane to his own case—sat gossiping about the trial and their own testimony. One of them glanced up, a frown crossing his face as he exchanged stares.

What a sight I must present! He brushed the front of his stained jacket and tugged at the collar of his linen shirt. Both garments were soiled with the stink and mire of the dungeon. He smoothed his greasy hair, worn clubbed back in the 'natural' style favoured by the young idealists, and forced himself to remain calm. He pressed a hand to his coat pocket, only partly reassured by the feel of the manuscript secreted there.

'Gentlemen!' A page boy dressed in a taffeta waistcoat and poplin breeches climbed onto a stool beside the clerk's desk. In his hand he clutched a brass handbell, which he shook with great enthusiasm. 'Gentlemen! I beg you, come to order!' He shook the bell again.

As the noise began to diminish, Justice Mallory, a scowl on his face, rapped the dais with a brass paperweight. 'Silence!' Holding a pair of hinged spectacles up to his eyes, he barked his annoyance. 'I shall summons the very first man that displeases me!'

When the Chamber did not quiet to his satisfaction, Mallory glared at the noisy benches. 'Do you hear me? The very first man!' The chatter died to a murmur as he glanced at the prosecutors seated below the dais. 'Gentlemen. What cause?'

A prosecutor rose up on tiptoe to whisper the particulars of the case. The judge clutched a silk handkerchief to his nose as he listened. At one point he glanced at Boundless, his eyes narrowing behind the scented cloth.

'As you say, Mr Blackwall.' He gestured with the handkerchief. 'Let the charge be read.'

The clerk of the Court, an elderly man with a bent, arthritic posture, rose stiffly from his chair. 'M'luds—' The fellow stopped to adjust the spectacles on his nose before continuing. 'The accused, one Boundless McLennan, printer—'

'And Jacobite!' The quip drew laughter.

'Be warned!' The judge directed a venomous stare. 'Pray continue, Mr Seaforth.'

'Thank you, m'lud … *printer*, being nineteen years of age and residing at Potter Street in the City of London, is charged—Your pardon, gentlemen!'

Racked by a violent bout of coughing, the clerk pressed a cloth against his mouth. He then guzzled thirstily from a glass of water as the spectators tittered in amusement. 'Pardon, all ...' He bobbed to the magistrates then, as if remiss, bobbed again.

The chief justice muttered with impatience. 'Get on with it!'

'Pardon ... with seditious libel. Wherein he did knowingly print a most scandalous broadsheet casting altogether false and noxious assertions against the person of His Majesty and members of the cler—cler—*Atishoo!*' Seized by a spasmic fit, the clerk collapsed into his chair, where he wheezed and spluttered to howls of laughter.

Scowling at the noise, the judge turned to the prosecutor. 'Mr Blackwall?'

'The plea, m'lud?'

Clucking with annoyance, the judge peered through the spectacles at Boundless. 'Well? How does the accused plead?'

'Not guilty.' Despite the pounding of his heart, Boundless tried to make his voice firm.

The plea drew immediate hisses and cries of 'Upstart!'

'Be warned—for once and for all!' The justice subjected the assembly to an intimidating glare. A magistrate to his right bent to whisper in his ear. Nodding in reply, Mallory frowned at Boundless. 'Does the accused admit to printing the broadsheet in question?' 'I do.'

'And writing it as well?' intervened a second magistrate.

'Aye. And writing it.'

'Are you of the Scottish?' enquired a third.

'I claim that distinction, sir.'

'And where, pray, did you learn the printing trade?' asked the same magistrate.

'In Edinburgh. My father—'

'Your father is not on trial here! Mr Blackwall, the case, if you please.'

'Indeed, m'lud.' The prosecutor tugged at his bourse hair wig while ostentatiously studying the broadsheet in his hand. To the captivation of the spectators, he shook his head and murmured sorrowfully to himself several times. At length, he raised his head to speak.

'My lords. Gentlemen of the jury. The defendant stands accused of writing—as just now plainly acknowledged—*printing*, and circulating a most calumnious and seditious libel of several parts.' He held up the broadsheet to view, turning handsomely to present it to all corners of the Chamber. 'The proof be upon the page.' The courtroom was hushed as, pursing his lips, he proceeded to read from the offending sheet.

'The libel of the first part is entitled "*Animadversions on Clergy, and the Institution of Religion.*" The prosecutor raised his gaze to the jury. 'Gentlemen. This *bawd sheet* doth wantonly and scandalously cast varied and indecent aspersions on the clergy, after the manner of the French.' He glanced severely down his nose at a stifled guffaw from a juror.

'The libel of the second part ... entitled "*Reflections upon the True and Proper Nature of Government,*" doth speak most brazenly and unrestrainedly in preferment of Republicanism. *Republicanism*, gentlemen, and the disburdenment of monarchy!'

'Such be treason!' a voice cried.

A gaunt, scholarly-looking magistrate leaned forward.

'Doubtless,' he explained to the jury, 'the gilded idealism of youth. Perhaps influenced by the so-called Empirics or, if not them, then, of a certainty, the Tribe of Deists.' He glanced at Boundless as if seeking approbation for the remark.

'Quite so m'lud.' The prosecutor acknowledged the interpolation with a bow. 'If I may be permitted?' He returned to the broadsheet. 'I shall quote the offensive words—though, indeed, it pains me to do so.' He cast a disapproving glance at Boundless.

"The statute concerning libel be a concoction of the privileged, a folderol which no man of sense can take as anything other than bad law and bad government." Blackwall stopped and raised his eyes to peer at Boundless. After several seconds, he returned to the broadsheet and resumed reading from it.

"The plain intent—I quote, gentlemen—is to mask corrupt dealings among those charged with high public office. Such odious corruption—such odious corruption—cannot and ought not be protected by a law whose sole purpose is to suppress free and truthful reporting.'

He looked up. 'The learned printer presumes to dictate the law,' he mocked. 'With all his ink-stained arrogance.' The remark drew sniggers from the jury.

Blackwall returned to reading, losing his place. "What madness is this—a law which protects malfeasance by declaring its exposure a crime!"

The words drew gasps from the spectators and alarmed glances from the bench. Alerted to his blunder, Blackwall sought hastily to extricate himself while studiously avoiding the baleful stare of the judge.

'The law be a *concoction*—such be the defendant's very words, from his own hand. And there we have the kernel of the matter, gentlemen.' The prosecutor paused to take a sip of water. 'And what is the accused's defence for such scandalous libel? Some presumed and entirely spurious notion of "liberty of speech." The scathing inflection drew murmurs. 'Or, mayhap, "liberty of the press?" Whichever ox he drives upon the day. A fable, nevertheless, which has the sole intent and purpose to blacken and defame the character and reputation of public men. Indeed, the accused doth freely admit his allegiance to the party of "Free Speechers", the so-called Reformists.' He raised an eyebrow to the court, as if begging their indulgence for such presumption.

'Those *Mohawks*'—the hissed word drew gasps—'whose banditries are as a pestilence to public order and sound government.'

Blackwall bent forward, leaning both hands on the desk as his eyes raked the jurors. 'Gentlemen of the jury, the nub of the case is before you. The charge you have heard. Witnesses you shall have.' He sat down.

'M'luds. Do you wish to examine the accused?' The judge turned to his fellow magistrates.

'Ahem.' The last magistrate on the row, who had so far remained silent, picked up a sheet of paper. 'I have contributory matter, Sir William. This concerns the subject of the so-called Agitators.' The word drew jeers as he held up the sheet for Boundless to see. 'Do you own to it?' he asked.

'What do you say it is?' interrupted a second judge.

'Beg pardon, Sir Geoffrey.' The magistrate read from the pamphlet. "The Glorious Project." That being the title. It undoubtedly has some reference or allusion.'

'Perhaps to the great perturbations of the last century?' speculated the scholarly magistrate.

'Indeed, Sir John. To which is added a sub: "Political and Popular Suffrage Achieved through the Engine of the Printing Press."

He looked at Boundless. 'Well? Do you own to it?'

'I do, sir, most certainly.'

'Do you, indeed?' The magistrate looked greatly surprised at the admission.

'What does it purport?' asked the second magistrate, looking befuddled.

'I believe,' said the first, 'that it refers to the goal of political ferment. An incitement to riotous and unlawful behaviour.'

'Not so! It merely sets forth the argument for liberty of the press.'

'Silence!' Mallory fixed his eyes on Boundless. 'You are not here to argue with the learned magistrate. You are here to answer each charge as directed, no more and no less.' With a warning frown, he signalled the magistrate. 'Pray continue, Sir Robert.'

'He declares to it.' The named magistrate raised the sheet for the benefit of the jury.

'Further, gentlemen?'

No more questions being forthcoming, the judge turned to the prosecutor. 'We shall hear the witnesses. Mr Blackwall?'

A delay now followed as the prosecutor consulted with the clerk. After a brief, whispered conferral, the former glanced up at the dais. 'We are ready to proceed, m'lud.'

Blackwall motioned to a plump, middle-aged matron dressed in a black dress, woollen shawl and white lace cap. The woman rose to her feet, hands crossed importantly on her ample stomach.

'Mrs Fisher?—Nay, *Bishop*, beg pardon. Pray, madam, tell the court— what was the effect upon you, a respectable wife and mother, of reading the broadsheet in question?'

The woman drew the shawl around her shoulders. 'I was shaken, sir. Indeed, I was—to hear such bad words.'

'Hear?' interjected the scholarly magistrate.

'Mr Bishop, sir, read them to me.'

'And you say the words had such an effect upon you?'

'Indeed they did, sir.' The woman trembled and turned pale. 'Mercy!' She sank back onto the bench, heaving for breath. The sight sparked mirth among the spectators as a second female fanned the woman's cheeks with an apron.

Another witness, a wheelwright, was asked to stand. Prompted by the prosecutor, he testified to seeing Boundless with ink-stained hands shortly before coming upon a copy of the handbill freshly tacked to the door of a bakery.

'One might infer that the accused was caught *black-handed*,' quipped the scholarly magistrate.

'Oh, most excellent, sir!' The jury foreman clapped his hands as the jest flew around the courtroom to gales of laughter.

'On your heads, gentlemen! Mr Blackwall, pray continue.'

The next witness, a clergyman, swore on oath to have received the offending broadsheet directly from the hands of the accused. 'He did thrust it at me, whether I would or no,' he declared.

'A damnable lie!' Shocked at the falsehood, Boundless gripped the rail.

'A most blatant perjury!' shouted Joshua Lively from the gallery.

'Hold tongue!' The judge's features mottled with anger beneath the judicial wig. 'Be warned—for once and all!'

A fishmonger was up next. In a blustery voice he testified to the 'wicked' nature of the tract while expressing pious concern for its effect on young and unformed minds. 'It was his very design,' he accused, turning to stare at Boundless. The spectators gasped at such depravity.

'But I know of a certainty that the dunce cannot even read!' Boundless' outraged protest drew howls of laughter—whether aimed at him or the indignant fishmonger, he could not tell.

'Hold tongue, I say!' The judge banged the brass paperweight.

A wave of dizziness swept over Boundless, and he held fast to the dock, taking deep breaths in the stifling air and recalling Joshua's warning in the tavern. '*Your provincial nature in these matters will do you great harm, Boundless. Do you suppose that our enemies shall quibble over niceties?*'

The final witness, a grey-headed tavern owner dressed in ill-fitting breeches and a buff waistcoat with pewter buttons, expounded at length on his horror at finding copies of the handbill lying freely around the premises. 'My wife had obtained a copy and was studying the words. It seemed as if she were a person unknown to me,' he said, the claim drawing a puzzled glance from the prosecutor.

A pause followed as the jurors debated the evidence. Huddled together on the benches, they spared Boundless the occasional glance as they bent forward to consult with a witness. Their deliberations concluded, they sat back and looked to the judge, who appeared to have dozed off.

'M'lud?' The prosecutor coughed.

'A moment!' Rearranging his wig, the judge conferred with a fellow magistrate before glancing at Boundless. 'Well? Do you have anything to say for yourself?'

Wishing desperately for a glass of water, Boundless took a steadying breath, 'I do. But my defence rests not on disproving clear and outrageous falsehoods, but on the grounds of natural justice, as you shall hear.'

'Speak up, if you please.' The scholarly magistrate held up a trumpet to his ear.

'With the court's indulgence.' Drawing the crumpled manuscript from his pocket, Boundless smoothed it against the dock. Taking a deep breath, he began to read, his voice strained from nerves and lack of water.

'Let it be declared—freely and without equivocation—that liberty of speech is the natural right of free-born men.' He glanced up to gauge the effect of his opening words. 'And it follows, as the child to the man, that free speech extends to free print. And as such, it ought not be abridged without just and reasonable cause. Indeed, it may be asserted, with the evidence of both reason and morals, that the Original Author of the Book of Nature—'

'What does he say?' the magistrate with the horn demanded. 'Author? Which author?'

Perplexed, the judge turned to the prosecutor for enlightenment. 'What means this?'

Blackwall half-rose from his chair. 'M'lud. I believe that the accused wishes to make his defence to the charges.'

'Does he, by God? Then why don't he?' The judge stared at Boundless. 'Do you wish to impeach the witnesses against you?'

'I wish to plead, as my defence, the unjustness of the law under which I am charged.'

'The unjustness of the law?' The judge's eyes bulged. 'Do you presume to challenge the law?'

'I do, sir. And if the court will grant—'

'Silence! Do you or *don't you* intend to interrogate the witnesses?'

'Let the printer speak!' a voice shouted from the gallery.

'What noise is this?' The judge directed a glowering look up at the spectators. He cocked his head as the scholarly magistrate leaned across to whisper in his ear. He listened for a moment, a thunderous frown on his face.

'Nay, Sir John. It is not for such as him to expound upon the merits of the law.' He turned to the jury. 'Mark that the accused declines to enter a defence. The case be on its merits.'

'Indeed, such is *not* the case! I *do* make defence. My defence be that the law is unjust.'

'We would hear the defence!' a woman interjected, drawing "ayes" of approval.

'Give the printer leave to speak!' called out a man as the volatile sentiments of the spectators swung in favour of the accused.

'Damn me if I don't summons the very next man to speak!' His face crimson beneath the heavy wig, Mallory glared around the Chamber. When the mutterings had died down, he held up his spectacles to fix the jurors a severe gaze. 'Gentlemen of the jury, I shall make it plain. Wrong words, wrongly spoke are matters for the law to rule upon, whatever their provenance. Where the words are *printed*, as is the case before you, the harm to persons is doubled and permanent. That is the matter of libel. *Sedition* is the deliberate application of such harm to the Crown, Parliament or Church.' He paused to bury his nose in the scented handkerchief. Taking a deep inhalation, he continued. 'You have heard a number of most proper and respectable persons testify as to the injury wrought by the words of the accused. You have heard, moreover, the accused freely admit to being the author of the words in question. You have heard him, further, reject the opportunity to examine the witnesses—Nay!' He waved away Boundless' attempted protest. 'A fact from which you may draw the necessary inference.'

'Put into a nutshell, m'lud,' praised the jury foreman.

'You have heard, moreover, the accused presume to mask such shocking and gratuitous libels under the cloak of liberty and freedom of the press. Indeed, he doth shamelessly and grossly attempt to challenge the very law of seditious libel under which he is served.'

Justice Mallory presented the jurors with a piercing look. 'Gentlemen do not be deceived. *The law is not on trial!*' He paused to allow this to sink in. 'The single question before you is whether the witnesses spoke truthfully under oath. I leave, gentlemen of the jury, the matter of the verdict to your good conscience, severally and all.'

As the jury whispered, Boundless turned to glance despairingly up at the gallery. A grim-faced Joshua shook his head.

Within minutes the jurors sat back in the stalls, the blue-coated foreman indicating that the deliberations were concluded.

'How say ye? Have ye found a verdict?' demanded Mallory.

The foreman stifled a yawn as he rose to his feet. 'Guilty, m'lud.' The bald pronouncement was greeted by a chorus of dismay from the packed galleries.

Stunned at the way events had unfolded, Boundless stared at the jurors, too speechless to protest. One juror winked at him, a smirk on his face.

Clearing his throat, Boundless found his voice. 'What justice is this? I have not yet made a defence, as is my right, under law. I *must* be allowed to speak.'

'Must you, indeed!'

'I do, as is my lawful right. I demand—'

'You demand, do you?' The judge turned an astonished look upon his fellow magistrates. 'Hark, gentlemen. The voice of gutter privilege!'

'I am allowed, nay, *required*, to enter a defence.'

'Allow him to speak!' a voice demanded as other voices rose in support.

'If the words be true, where then be the libel?' a man cried out boldly. The Reformist catchphrase was greeted with cheers, and shouts of 'huzzah!' filled the courtroom.

'Arrest the man that spoke!' The judge pointed at the culprit.

A commotion broke out as two bailiffs attempted to climb the stairs to the gallery only to be forcibly rebuffed by those standing there.

As the disturbance spread, the judge held a hurried conference with his fellow magistrates. 'Are we decided, gentlemen?' He took up the quill pen and jotted on the sheet in front of him. Raising his hinged spectacles, he peered at Boundless. 'The accused is to be transported to the Virginia Plantations as a King's Passenger for a period of not less than ten years.'

The pronouncement was greeted by a collective gasp.

'An outrage!' Joshua's furious denunciation rang throughout the Chamber.

Following a shocked silence, the aroused spectators let fly with a storm of boos, whistles and insults. They were joined in their protests by the drunken hirelings—now thoroughly confused as to their purpose.

Surprised and alarmed at the violently altered mood of the Chamber, the jurors sought hasty refuge beneath the benches as a hail of rotten vegetables—once intended for the accused—rained down on their heads.

Stunned at the severity of the judgement, Boundless stood speechless in the dock, his dazed mind largely uncomprehending of the protests erupting around him.

Additional bailiffs rushed into the room as the uproar grew. The magistrates hurriedly abandoned the Chamber scooping up their papers as they fled. The elderly clerk made to follow when a half-eaten apple struck him on the skull. With loud cries of, 'I am wounded!' he took cover under the prosecutor's table.

Chaos broke out as the Reformists among the onlookers turned their anger on the gloating Tories. Women screamed and fights broke out as the Tories answered in kind. The volatile 'benchers' took advantage of the uproar to launch an assault on the despised bailiffs. The brawls quickly brought in other combatants as the fighting spread to all corners of the courtroom.

'Where now be English justice?' Joshua Lively pounded the wood-panelled gallery with his fist. Others followed his example—pounding and kicking to create a thunderous protest that drowned out the shouts and whistles of the bailiffs as reinforcements hurried into the Chamber.

Amidst the turmoil, Boundless felt rough hands seize him.

'Unhand me! I demand to speak!' He clung to the rail as the hands tried to drag him from the dock. 'I have the right to a defence!'

A voice snarled in his ear. 'That be sufficient from out thy gob!'

Next moment a baton struck him across the skull, and he fell limply between the warders. As the furious protests reverberated in his ears, he was dragged dazed and bleeding from the riotous Chamber.

2

Newgate

STUPEFIED BY THE FORCE of the blow, Boundless was dragged back to Newgate where he was thrown, shocked and feverish, onto a stinking straw mattress.

'Thou'll not be dancing this night, I'll be bound!' The head keep placed a wooden slops bucket on the floor. 'Thou'll not be griping up thy guts and stinking up the cell, norwise.' He turned and gestured threateningly at a group of prisoners who watched listlessly from their chains. 'Take heed!'

Left barely senseless on the bedding, Boundless moaned in anguish at the throbbing in his head. His guts heaved and he scarcely had time to turn over before convulsing into the bucket. Wiping his mouth with his sleeve, he closed his eyes, gasping for breath before losing consciousness.

When he opened his eyes again, night had blackened the sky outside the single small aperture high up the wall. His head pounded as if his skull might split. Gingerly, he touched the swollen bruise on his scalp, relieved to feel no fresh blood on his fingers. He tried to sleep again, but remained sorely awake, his mind tormented by images of the trial.

The gross fabrications of the clergyman, in particular, had shocked him. 'How is it possible?' he lamented, astonished at such perfidy. Sudden remembrance of the sentence caused him to moan in revulsion. Half-remarked accounts of the horrors of penal servitude haunted him as he lay on the straw mattress. He flung an arm over his face as if to block from thought the dreadful images conjured by the words. He remained in that position, profoundly desolate, until shock and exhaustion overtook him and he slipped by degrees into a fitful slumber.

He was awakened by a hand gripping him by the shoulder. Through the slit window, faint rays of daylight illuminated the gloomy recesses of the cell. A gaoler loomed above him holding up a lantern. 'You have a gentleman visitor.' The man set down the lamp.

He pulled himself up into a sitting position, wincing at the stabbing pain in his head.

'Boundless!' Joshua Lively stepped into the dungeon. He carried a large, paper-wrapped bundle under one arm. An oath left his lips as he took in Boundless' fevered appearance. The gaoler, whom he had bribed to allow the early morning visit, returned with a small wooden stool.

'Be thou quick!' the man warned and left them alone.

'My dear fellow!' Joshua embraced him. Feeling Boundless wince, he stepped back. Picking up the lantern, he exclaimed in dismay as he caught sight of the bruised and swollen scalp. He held the lantern closer muttering with disgust. 'Savages!' He sat down on the stool.

'What news of my sentence?' Boundless looked at his friend in desperation, his eyes haunted in the dim lantern light.

'You do not know?' Joshua stared in surprise. 'Did you not hear the damnable magistrate?'

'Indulge me!'

Joshua shook his head, a helpless look on his face. 'You are to be transported to the plantations, as a King's Passenger. And once there you are to be sold into indentured servitude for the prescribed period of ten years.'

'Then I am done for!' Despairing, Boundless put his head in his hands.

'This is not finished. Be of stout heart, I pray you.' Joshua's eyes were full of sympathy.

'My poor parents. Had they been alive to witness …' Boundless choked, unable to finish.

'I promise you Boundless. We—your friends in the movement—are determined to appeal the outrageous verdict. Have no doubt but that we will succeed—at least in reducing the barbaric sentence. Do you wish me to convey a letter to our friends?'

'I have neither quill nor paper. The keep—the other one—has taken them from me.'

'Then I shall return tomorrow with both, and a large pot of ink. Aye, and ointment for that fine bruise. In the meantime, I have brought food and wine.'

Joshua picked up the paper-wrapped bundle. 'And this from your friends,' he said, lowering his voice and glancing around at the shadows. 'They ask that you do not forget them.' Undoing the string, he tugged a heavy woollen greatcoat from the parcel.

Perplexed, Boundless took the gift, uncertain what to make of it.

Joshua again looked around to see if anyone was listening. The other occupants of the cell were snoring on bags of straw or slumped listlessly against the walls. 'The *lining*,' he whispered.

Feeling the wool fibres, Boundless felt a row of hard metal coins beneath his fingers. He looked up in confusion. 'Twenty-five guineas.' Joshua leaned in closer, his voice barely audible. 'A gift from your friends and supporters. They are legal tender in the colonies. Guard them carefully. They will be useful as bribes.'

In spite of his despair, tears sprang to Boundless' eyes. 'Thank my comrades, each one of them.' He folded the coat on his lap. 'Assure them that I shall one day return and repay their generosity.'

'What is with this "return"? We shall strive, with might and main, to see it doesn't come to that.'

'But if it does?'

'Then you shall indeed return one day, I am certain.' Joshua studied him, anxious to bring some cheer to his comrade. 'I recall when you first found your way into our little circle. You had such highland fire!'

Boundless murmured disconsolately. 'That fire, I fear, has been doused.'

'Not a single spark! You shall yet leave your mark on the world. I am certain of it.'

The guard stepped back into the cell. 'Thou must go!' He jerked a thumb at Joshua and stood in the doorway, waiting.

'Farewell, friend.' Joshua placed a hand on his shoulder. 'I shall return tomorrow with the writing instruments and food. Do not despair. Augustus Tyson has, this very day, printed a tract against the monstrous verdict. And there are more. A Mr Arthur Magnuson composes a treatise against the laws of libel and calls for their amendment.'

'Quickly!' hissed the gaoler. 'The day watch steps forth.'

'Until tomorrow, dear friend!'

THE FOLLOWING MORNING, HE was awakened from a troubled sleep by the feel of cold iron against his skin. He started up in alarm. 'What means this?' Starlight gleamed through the aperture in the wall.

In the lantern light a watchman glared threateningly. 'Move not a limb,' he warned. Setting down the lantern, he secured the leg irons and jerked Boundless to his feet. 'Stand there!'

Still dazed from sleep, Boundless stared in horror at the shackles. For a moment he wondered if he was dreaming. A glance at the scowling watchman told him otherwise. 'Where am I to be taken?'

'Where dost thou think, fool! Thou be bound for the plantations as a guest of His Majesty.'

'So soon? It cannot be! I must advise my friends.'

'Dost thou think the King's ship waits on thee, or thy friends?' The watchman let out a mocking laugh.

'Come, whelp!' A second watchman approached, bearing a lantern in one hand and dragging a shackled boy by the other. The boy, a child barely past the age of ten, struggled to keep pace in the heavy chains.

'Move!' The first watchman shoved Boundless forward.

Shuffling clumsily in the leg irons, he was propelled through a maze of narrow passageways. Several times he stumbled and narrowly avoided braining himself on the jagged stone walls. The way was lit by flaring torches held by the watchmen, their flames casting shadows in the cold gloom.

Within the space of ten minutes, he found himself shivering in the pre-dawn cold outside the main gates of the prison. Grateful for the wool greatcoat, he clutched it around him. A prison cart stood in the cobbled street, the horse standing patiently in the traces. Breath steamed from its nostrils in the chill air.

'Good morrow!' The driver climbed down from the seat to exchange rude pleasantries with the watchmen.

Beside Boundless, the boy, clad only in a tattered linen shirt and worn breeches, shook uncontrollably. 'Come here, laddie.' He placed an arm around the boy's thin shoulders, hugging him to his side in an attempt to warm the slender frame.

'Save thy snivelling for the ship!' The watchman dragged the boy from his grasp and thrust him towards the cart. He turned to Boundless. 'And thou!'

A cold rain began to fall as he climbed into the cage beside the weeping boy.

'Now may'st thou bawl thine eyes from out thy socks!' The watchman slammed shut the cage door and locked it.

'Hi-yup, old Jenny!' said the driver and shook the reins. The cart set off in the chill darkness, the watchmen walking alongside.

THEY ARRIVED AT BLACKFRIARS in drizzling rain. There they were escorted from the prison cart and taken down the dismal steps to the river, a watchman holding up a lantern to light the way. A lighter was waiting at the foot of the steps and he and the young boy, accompanied by the two watchmen, were taken on board. As the waterman navigated the river in the darkness, Boundless sat shivering on the hard seat, his mind numbed with dread of what lay ahead. The exhausted boy leaned against him, trembling violently from the cold. He opened the greatcoat and tucked it around the boy, warming him against his own body. The only sounds came from the oars and the rough banter of the watchmen as they discussed favourite taverns and the pleasures of different types of ale.

The sky had lightened by the time they reached Blackwall. Stepping awkwardly in the shackles, he ascended a flight of steps to the semi-darkness of the quay. The shriek of gulls sounded in his ears. A gusting wind blew cold rain across the wharf. On the dock, a group of soldiers lounged at a table outside a tavern. They glanced up without interest as he and the tearful boy were led across the wharf to where a three-masted bark was tied to the dock. In the grey light, he saw the name *Patience* inscribed in gold lettering on the stern.

In spite of the early hour, the area around the ship hummed with industry. Merchants and clerks huddled in conversation next to rows of goods stacked on the dockside for export to the colonies. A gentleman in a cocked hat stood smoking a long clay pipe as labourers filed up and down the ship's gangway bearing crates of tea and Chinese porcelain. Above the deck of the ship, a large crate dangled from a pulley as it was lowered on-board.

'Your ship is ready, good sirs.' The first watchman blew on his hands, cheerful now that the task was almost done, and a hot kettle awaited.

A moist wind blew in from the river, causing Boundless to shiver in spite of the greatcoat. He glanced at the trembling boy, concerned for his welfare. The second watchman walked to the foot of the ramp and hailed an officer.

'Two transports!' He held out a sheaf of documents. The officer nodded and made an entry in a log.

'You be bound to the Pennsylvania for your penance,' said the watchman as he returned.

'Move thy shanks!' The first watchman pushed the weeping boy towards the ship.

'Please, sir. Allow me to go home to mother!' The boy sobbed in terror. 'I want to be good! I do not mean to be wicked.'

'Thou'll go, likest or not!' The watchman pinched the frantic boy by the neck.

'Be tender with him!' Boundless started forward in protest.

The strong arm of the second watchman held him back. 'Fetch the whoreson on board, for God's sake!' The man watched his companion drag the sobbing and pleading boy up the gangway. 'Your turn!' He gave Boundless a hard shove, and he started up the ramp, his feet dragging in the heavy chains. A squall blew in from the river, drenching him. On the quay, the merchants took shelter in the lee of a small hut.

'Move! I shan't be late for my kettle because of thee, laggard legs!' Cursing, the watchman struck him across the shoulders with a cudgel.

Reaching the top of the gangway Boundless glanced back at the huddled merchants and raised his chained hands in despair. 'Remember me!' he cried. One of the merchants looked up.

'Art thou a block?' A forceful shove sent him sprawling onto the deck of the ship.

The noise of wind and rain mingled with the cry of gulls in his ears. He was hauled roughly to his feet. In a daze, he was dragged along the deck to an open hatch. 'Down below,' a gruff voice commanded. 'Grip the steps or break thy neck.'

Clinging to a support, he descended the steep stairs into the darkness of the hold. No sooner had his head lowered below the level of the deck than he was assailed by a foul stench of vomit and excrement. He clung to the steps, trying desperately to suck in the fresh air from above.

'Get below!'

He inched down the steps as if descending into hell itself, the stench threatening to overwhelm his senses. The deckhand followed, pressing a perfumed cloth to his mouth and nose.

The blackness of the hold was illuminated by a single lantern screwed to the timbers. From the surrounding gloom, a chorus of moans and wails caused his hair to stand on end.

The deckhand gripped his arm. 'This way,' he said, his voice muffled by the cloth.

'Sit!'

A rough hand grasped his right wrist and secured it to an iron ring bolted into the timber, pinning it to the wall. Without another word, the deckhand left him alone in the darkness and made his way back to the ladder.

Blinking, he tried to peer through the gloom. Rays of light came in through holes bored in the deck planks, their faint illumination seeming only to increase the darkness. The humid, fetid stench was so overpowering that he felt he must vomit or be rendered insensible by the fumes. He tried to avoid inhaling the rank odours by burying his nose in the sleeve of his coat. Around him, he made out the dim forms of men and women. Some were chained, like himself, to the side timbers. A continual lamentation of cries and sobs rose from the darkness. The noise of such wretched misery made his skin crawl. A man beside him groaned feverishly while calling out piteously for water. Further in the darkness, a woman's voice uttered a keening wail that resonated through the blackness with a profound note of mingled terror and grief.

'Laddie?' he called out. 'Laddie. Are ye there?' He listened for a reply but heard nothing above the cries and groans of the afflicted. He shifted on the hard deck, scarcely able to credit the horror of his surroundings. A cold, stark misery engulfed his soul. *I am surely in the very pit of Hell.*

3

The Patience

EXHAUSTED, HE FELL INTO a fitful slumber, only to be awakened by the noise of the ship raising anchor. The steady rocking of the quayside was replaced by a sudden pitching motion that caused the iron ring around his wrist to rub agonisingly against the bone.

'We be underway,' a voice called out from the gloom. 'Farewell, old London!'

That night they put in at Gravesend, the ship riding at anchor until dawn. Early next morning, they left on the tide, arriving at Margate shortly before midnight. He was drifting in and out of sleep when brought awake by the sound of curses. Two crewmen passed by, lifting the body of a woman between them. A third crewman followed, holding up a lantern. In the gloom he saw her passed up the stairs to waiting hands.

'She be for the deep,' a voice said from the darkness. Straining his ears, Boundless heard the sound of a splash as the body was cast overboard.

The motion of the vessel changed once again as they left the protection of the land, sailing between the coasts of England and France. Adverse winds buffeted the ship, increasing the suffering of those in the hold. At times, he feared the iron ring would saw through the bones of his wrist, such was the pitching of the deck. He tried to alleviate the pain by stuffing his handkerchief into the narrow gap between iron and skin. But the cloth became dislodged by the constant motion and the chafing friction began again until the flesh was rubbed raw and bleeding.

He overheard one crewman announce to another that the *Patience* would anchor that night off Portsmouth. 'What is the day?' someone called out.

'The eighth day of April,' the deckhand answered. 'If it be of aught concern to thee.'

They sat at anchor for three days awaiting a gale to take them across the Solent to Cowes on the Isle of Wight. On the eleventh of April, the wind shifted to a favourable quarter. But halfway across, the gales turned contrary once more and blew them back to anchor. An epidemic of sea-sickness caused by the violent rocking of the ship rendered so noisome a stench that he began to think of death as a welcome release from his torment.

The following day, the vessel took advantage of a favourable wind to put in at Cowes just before sunset. Two days later, the ship raised sail and turned windward to Yarmouth, making very little headway before a gale blew the vessel all the way back to Cowes. Around nine o'clock on the morning of the third day of lying at Cowes, a strong north-westerly blew up, the gale blowing them all the way past Yarmouth, through the Needles and into the Channel. As the winds changed westerly once again, they sat off Portland for the night, riding at anchor in 40 fathoms of water.

He had now been confined to the hold for two weeks—fourteen days and nights of unrelenting torture. Despair had numbed his soul, and he hardly registered the intervals between day and night or port and open water.

On the morning of the twentieth of April, the wind being little more than a breeze, they tacked along the coast to Plymouth, putting into harbour late in the afternoon. They sat there for two days taking on their last supplies before the Atlantic crossing. Listening to the sound of barrels being trundled across the deck, he dreamed of slipping his chains and stealing unobserved from the hold to mingle with the shore labourers as they made their way back down the ramp. The thought was so seductive that he fell asleep in his chains.

Hours later he was jolted awake by shouted commands from above as the *Patience* was towed from its berth. A short time later, the vessel let slip the tow ropes and heeled, fully rigged, into the freshening wind.

'Westward ho!' a voice cried.

A man further along the hold hauled himself to a sitting position. His voice was hoarse for want of water. 'Next stop be Pennsylvanny!'

AS THE SHIP EMBARKED on the great, roiling tides of the North Atlantic, the pitching of the deck increased, compounding the torment in the hold. The stench from shit, piss and vomit grew ever more unendurable. Two of the transports died from dysentery, their bodies lifted up the stairs for despatch. A day later, another perished from fever and sickness. The crew seemed to grow more anxious with each death, redoubling their inspections of the captives and bringing down extra rations of food and water.

Unable to stomach the thought of eating, he refused the meagre ration of heavily salted beef or pork. But he drank thirstily from the water ladled out from a bucket several times a day by deckhands heavily masked with neckerchiefs.

In spite of his fatigue, the continual tug of the fetter and the motion of the hard, bouncing deck kept him from sleep. He suffered a bout of sickness, throwing up next to where he lay, the stench adding further to his distress. The fumes from the hold seemed to have seeped into his skin—the compounded odours so foully oppressive that they seemed an inducement to insanity. A plague of lice infested the hold and he scratched continuously as the creatures burrowed into his skin. In a moment of black despair, he wondered if he might not go mad before the voyage was even properly begun. Around him, the snores of his fellow prisoners were interspersed with piteous cries and groans as though the terrors of the voyage pursued them even in sleep.

One night, exhausted to the point of desperation, he awoke from a feverish dream to glimpse rats scurrying about in the darkness. He moaned in horror, kicking out in desperation as one of the loathsome creatures scuttled across his leg.

To maintain sanity, he recalled tracts of verse learned by heart in childhood. Exhausting these, he silently repeated his favourite passages from *Essays Moral and Political*. One sleepless night was spent composing a damning indictment of the evils of bond slavery. In a half-delirium, he railed against magistrates, the monarchy, restraints upon speech and the general decay of morals. In the intervals when not whipping the judiciary, his thoughts were ravaged by fears of what further degradations awaited in store once his servitude began. He dozed intermittently, only to be jolted back to awareness by a sudden plunging motion of the deck and the agonising pull of the ring. With a groan, he eased his body to relieve the pressure on the painful sores afflicting his thighs and buttocks. But no sooner had he found relief in one position than the cramping soreness started in another.

Night and day ceased to have meaning in the permanent gloom of the hold, the hours joining together in unendurable torment. The prevailing misery was punctuated by repeated cries and shrieks as a sort of madness took hold among the despairing captives. The groans and sobs of the afflicted merged into a devil's chorus so that he scarce could tell whether the worst torment was from the heaving of the deck or the feverish cries of the sick and dying. The poor ventilation produced a stifling heat which compounded the suffering of the thirsty men and women. The crew became ever more vigilant, taking a lantern around several times a day to study the faces of the chained captives. Occasionally, they released a particular prisoner, dragging the afflicted soul above deck to be inspected by the ship's surgeon for signs of fever.

As conditions worsened and more prisoners perished, the ship's surgeon himself descended into the hold, moving from one prisoner to the next, muttering to himself and thumbing snuff into his nostrils. The master's mate accompanied him with a lantern, bending down to illuminate the face of each convict as the surgeon examined the captive for signs of sickness. Several times the surgeon turned and spoke in a sharp voice, seemingly to urge the mate to some course of action.

'It is the open air or the shroud,' he insisted. 'Else shall you lose the entire value of the cargo.'

A day after this visit, Boundless was roused from a dreamless slumber by the agonising pull of the fetter against his wrist. To his surprise, a deckhand unbolted the clasp, allowing his nerveless hand to drop to the deck. Even more surprisingly, the deckhand then bent down and removed the shackles around his legs, cursing the difficulty of the task. As he rubbed his stiff and bruised limbs, a voice shouted through the hatch opening. 'All bodies up on deck! The master would speak with ye.'

Bewildered by this unexpected turn of events, he climbed unsteadily to his feet, wincing at the aching cramp in his limbs. In the glow of lamps hoisted by the several deckhands, he saw, for the first time, the drawn faces of his fellow captives. Many seemed as stunned as himself by the sudden release from bondage; some, unable to move, remained slumped in the same position where they had been confined.

'To thy feet!' A deckhand pulled at one of the recumbent bodies.

Boundless limped to the foot of the stairs, desperate to climb out of the hold. A woman ahead of him slowly raised herself up the steps, tearfully thanking her captors for this bounty. When his turn came, he ascended slowly, his limbs excruciatingly tender from the weeks of confinement. When fully emerged into the daylight, he sank to his knees, dazzled by the brightness of the sky.

'You! Stand there!' A deckhand pointed to a space on the deck.

HE STOOD IN A line with his fellow captives, overcome by the light and noise of the open deck. A gust of wind blew moist, salt-laden air across his face, and he gulped the draught deep into his lungs. Dizzy and nauseous, he stumbled against the man next to him. He murmured an apology, realising as he did so that the words were the first he had spoken to another soul since boarding the ship.

More captives emerged onto the deck—each one blinking tearfully in the fresh salt air. To his eyes most seemed no more than sticks clad in rags and so thickly infested with lice that they could be scraped off the skin. In all, some thirty transports emerged from the hold to take their place on deck.

He searched for the young boy and spotted him hovering next to a bent, shawl-clad woman.

'Pay heed!' A brutish-looking man in a wide-brimmed hat made from tarred sailcloth stood before them. His broad face was disfigured by a squashed nose and a deep scar running from scalp to jaw. His hair was pulled into a long pigtail tied with ribbon. A length of knotted rope was coiled around one fist. He slapped the end against his palm as he surveyed the transports, a ferocious hostility in his gaze.

'That be Mr Queezley, the bosun,' someone behind Boundless whispered. 'A most fearsome man. Stay well clear of him.'

'Stand in line, thou blockhead!' The bosun shoved one unfortunate back into place. 'Give ear to the master.'

'Be at ease, ladies and gentlemen.' A man in his mid-forties, slim and erect in a long, dark-blue coat with brass buttons and white facings stood on the quarterdeck to address them.

'I am Mr Addison, the ship's master.' The man spoke slowly and firmly above the fluttering of the sails and the loud creaking of the cordage. 'Your chains have been removed and you are allowed to move freely about the main deck during the day. I urge you to do so as long as you do not interfere with the workings of the ship. Fresh air and exercise is the surest defence against fever, dysentery, and lice. At night you will be returned to the hold to sleep. I expect each man and woman to observe the strictest moral character at all times. If not, I shall flog the culprit and consign him to the hold where he shall remain chained for the remainder of the voyage. Is that understood?'

In the silence that followed the only sound was the snapping of the sails and the racking coughs of a consumptive transport.

The master glanced at the bosun. 'Mr Queezley. Allow them the freedom to move about, if you please.'

'Aye, aye, sir.' As the master walked away, Queezley turned to the transports, a snarling belligerence on his face. 'Walk as will,' he said. 'But the man or woman that obstructs my crew shall feel my lash.' He swung the knotted rope menacingly. 'Be thou sharp,' he said, before walking away.

The transports remained in place, looking at each other as if uncertain what to do next. Then, slowly, as if released from a spell, they began to mill about on the crowded deck. Some hastened to the gunnels to breathe in the salt gusts, while others embraced with tears and sobs of relief.

'Huzzah!' said one man, his voice bold in spite of his unkempt, malnourished frame. 'We are free of that stinking hold!' He leaned over the side and spat into the wind.

A moment later deckhands began separating the transports into two groups, shepherding one to the starboard side where they were designated the 'starboard party' and warned to stay on that side. The 'larboard party' was given a similar warning and strictly forbidden to congregate in groups so as not to impede the crew. 'Else feel Mr Queezley's kiss!' said one deckhand to a guffaw from his mate.

PROFOUNDLY THANKFUL TO BE free of the pestilential hold, Boundless leaned out into the wind, his face pleasingly numbed by the stinging gale. The sky was overcast, the wind wet and blustery, yet he thought he had never seen so fine a day. Thanks to the greatcoat, he was well protected against the elements. The coat was soiled and foul-smelling from the hold yet warm and comforting in its woollen thickness. He put a hand in the pocket to feel the hard outlines of the coins sewn into the lining. 'God bless thee, Joshua,' he murmured, as his spirits revived in the salt breeze.

Based on the limited pacing allowed him, he estimated the vessel at slightly more than 100 feet in length and approximately 30 feet across the beam. Apart from the raised quarterdeck, the deck was flat and even for the length of the ship. The forecastle marked the limit of their freedom of movement. The space was occupied by a pair of tethered goats and a dozen or more large pens full of caged hens, chickens, and pigs.

A bowsprit projected from the bow, the spar anchoring several forestays. Indeed, the vessel seemed festooned in cordage—the masts, sails and sides a spider's web of rigging. The deck was overshadowed by the acreage of billowing sails, the voluminous canvas snapping and whipping in the wind. A longboat, a third of the size of the *Patience* itself, sat in a cradle in the ship's waist. A smaller skiff was nestled within the larger boat. A third vessel, a jolly boat, was stowed alongside the longboat.

Altogether unfamiliar with ships, he was amazed at the sheer noise that attended the progress of the vessel. The constant creak of cordage was attended by the hiss of wind and spray, and, above all, the dull, muted thunder of the sails. He watched a young deckhand—no older than a boy—climb the rigging. The operation struck him as perilous in the extreme. Clinging to a rope or spar as the vessel bounced and dipped, the boy untangled a fouled line in response to the shouted commands of the mate.

For the whole of that first day, he stayed close to the side, hanging to a shroud as he adjusted to the roll and pitch of the deck. Space for movement was narrow and impeded by the masts and rigging. The constant bounce of the ship also discouraged free movement, as did the actions of the crew as they went about their duties. He gave careful room to Queezley, the latter not hesitating to lash out with the rope whenever an unfortunate man or woman hindered his passage. He averted his gaze whenever the fellow cast a threatening glance in his direction, instinct warning against the slightest challenge to the brute's authority.

As evening fell, the transports were gathered up once again and returned to the hold. Queezley stood by the open hatch to supervise the operation.

'Thy bald pate shall not see old England again.' The bosun gave a gloating smile as a gnarled old man cast a final, despondent gaze at the horizon before taking his turn to descend the steps.

Boundless followed the man down the steps into the dark hold—a wave of nausea engulfing him as the familiar, fetid stench once again assailed his nose. In the gloom he made out a row of cargo crates stacked in one corner. He lurched towards these, determined to find what unspoiled deck space he could in which to sleep. He sat down with his back against a crate, drawing the folds of the greatcoat around him. A woman settled down next to him, spreading a cape under her as she lay down.

'Good night to you, sir,' she said softly, the sentiment so incongruous that tears sprang to his eyes.

OVER THE NEXT WEEK, he found his sea legs, thankful to be largely unaffected by the debilitating bouts of seasickness that plagued so many of his fellow convicts. Suddenly consumed by hunger, he eagerly swallowed the daily rations of hard biscuits, dried peas and salted beef. Something of his natural vigour returned as his body habituated to the ceaseless motion of the deck and the gusting salt spray. He developed a keen interest in the operations of the vessel, memorising the names of the various sails and observing the deckhands as they went about their tasks. He learned to anticipate certain whistles and commands as the men raced to reef or shake out canvas in the ever-shifting gales. He gazed upwards with held breath as the sailors ascended the rigging to dance lightly from rope to rope at the dizzying heights of the main topgallant. The skill and bravery of the sun-browned sailors caused him to temporarily forget his misery as he marvelled at their sure-footedness and cat-like movements amidst the acres of billowing sail.

One afternoon, the transports were ordered back to the hold an hour early, while the sky was still light in the west. Frustrated by the decision, Boundless' mood was further soured by the discovery of another man in his usual spot. Stretched out in the gloomiest corner of the hold, he gradually fell into a broken slumber. He was awakened two hours later by the tolling of the watch bell. He lay still in the darkness, forgetting for the moment where he was as his senses accommodated to the groan of the ship's timbers and the feel of the hard planking beneath him.

Unable to return to sleep, he lay wretchedly awake, enduring the groans and snores of those around him. Something itched his skin and he scratched vigorously to dislodge the ever-present lice. He felt his pinched ribs and tried to remember the last time he had eaten a full meal. A bleak misery at his fate induced a profound despair that caused him to wonder if death was not preferable to such waking torment. He pictured the grey, restless sea just beyond the timber wall and imagined plunging into its fathomless depths and putting an end to his torment. An instinctive horror at such a nameless fate caused him to shudder. *Who would mourn me? Who even note my passing?* An old woman huddled nearby cried out in her sleep as if beseeching some unseen presence. He turned on his side, wincing at the soreness in his back.

After what seemed an eternity of wakeful torment, he was possessed by a consuming urge to escape the loathsome, choking stench of the hold. He climbed unsteadily to his feet, resolved to risk a lashing in preference to the horrors of lying awake amidst such misery. In the dim glow of the lantern, he felt his way towards the hatch stairs.

Several times he stepped on huddled forms in the darkness. Muttering apologies, he groped his way past. Gaining the foot of the stairs, he stood for a moment, gazing up at the starry heavens framed by the open hatch. He started up the steps, his fear of discovery overtaken by an insatiable urge to stand on deck and breathe freely in the night air.

THE DECK WAS DESERTED as he emerged from the hold. The only sounds came from the steady creak of the rigging and the crash of waves against the sides. Grasping the shrouds, he inhaled deeply, relishing the starlit breeze. For a brief moment, he almost forgot his despair in gratitude for the fresh salt air and the reprieve from the noisome stench of the hold. He was preparing to make his way back when, to his alarm, a watchman chose that moment to round the mizzen mast.

The man halted in surprise as he caught sight of Boundless. 'Who be you, then?' He held up a lantern, his illuminated face full of suspicion.

'Sir. I could not endure that hellish dungeon but a moment longer. This is but a brief respite, I beg you.' The watchman studied him in the lantern light, his expression softening as he read the desperation in Boundless' face.

'Mind your business, then,' he said, after a long pause. 'Mr Queezley 'ull flay ye alive if he finds ye. Aye, and me an' all.' The man glanced around the deck to make sure no one was watching or listening. 'There be a space by the jolly boat where a body might lie unobserved.' He pointed to the recess in front of the main mast where the ship's boats were stowed. 'No one will bother you there—as long as you stay hidden.' With that the watchman lowered the lantern and continued his rounds.

Boundless stayed rooted to the deck for a few moments, feeling like a man reprieved on the very steps of the gallows. The unexpected sympathy of the deckhand brought tears to his eyes, his terror at being discovered replaced by a profound and aching gratitude that left him trembling. Leaning over the side, he turned his face to the drenching salt spray, savouring the sharp air while overcome with emotion.

The blaze from the bright, distant stars deepened the profound gloom over the water. White-fringed waves splashed against the side and retreated into the infinite darkness. He shrank into the warmth of the greatcoat, his thoughts temporarily diverted as he contemplated the odds for a man lost overboard in that vast, limitless flood.

After some time, weariness began to overtake him, and he made his way to the short ladder leading down to the boats. Squeezing in between the jolly boat and the wall he found a small, concealed space with sufficient planking for a man to sit up or lie down. He sat huddled in the thick coat with his knees drawn up to his chest in the narrow spot. For a time he was conscious only of the crashing of the waves and the luffing of the sails. But slowly, a profound exhaustion claimed him. His head dropped to his knees, and he fell soundly asleep.

Storm at Sea

DAY AFTER DAY, THE ship ploughed through heavy seas, the wind whipping the topsails as cold squalls lashed the deck. The drenching spray and buffeting winds heaped further torment on the dejected transports. Alone or with a single companion, they clung to their tiny patch of deck, ever ready to dodge a curse or a blow from the aggressive Queezley. Apart from a voluble sheep thief on his second transport, the dispirited prisoners rarely spoke to one another, acknowledging each other with barely a nod if at all.

One afternoon, Boundless was hanging onto the shrouds, his head nodding sleepily in spite of the whipping spray, when he heard a commotion behind him. The noise was followed by a shouted curse and a cry of pain. He turned to see Queezley standing over a man—a forger sentenced to six-years penal servitude—who lay curled up on the deck. The man had thrown up his arms to defend his head as Queezley rained down blows with the knotted rope.

'Thou whoreson!' Enraged, the bosun grabbed and pinned the man's wrists with one huge hand while swinging the rope with the other. 'I'll flay thy bones, thou grizzled gut-lick!' Queezley brutally lashed the cowering man, drawing back his arm to swing the rope again and again. 'Bear my mark, thou stink-pot!'

'Mr Queezley!' The master's voice rang out from the quarterdeck. 'Mr Queezley!'

Queezley turned in a fury. Seeing the person of the master, he stopped short, snarling with rage and panting for breath.

'What is the meaning of this?' The master's voice was sharp. He motioned for two deckhands to assist the trembling forger to his feet. The man leaned unsteadily, as though he might keel over from shock and nausea. His ashen face was bloodied with livid welts and bruises.

'Beg pardon, sir, but he wantonly interfered with my duties.' Queezley had removed his cap, revealing that the top of his head was quite bald.

'You men, assist him to the surgeon. The rest of you, return to your duties.' The master regarded the bosun with a severe gaze. 'Mr Queezley.

I do not wish to see a repetition of this. Understand me well.' His voice carried a steely edge.

'Aye, aye, sir.' Queezley touched a finger to his brow. Turning, he scowled at the open-mouthed transports.

'Make way, thou crabbish gawks!' He barged past as they hastily stepped aside.

The crew seemed perturbed by the beating, discussing it in muted voices with several muttering glances cast at the bosun. Queezley himself seemed invigorated by the incident, radiating satisfaction as he barked orders or bullied the young 'spar rats' as they climbed the rigging at his command.

'That brute will feed us all to the fishes afore we reach land,' a fellow transport—a defrocked priest—grumbled in Boundless' ear.

Three weeks out to sea, an old woman transported for stealing a shoulder of ham died in a pool of vomit in the hold. Her death caused consternation among the officers as the cause was established by the ship's surgeon. 'And I tell you, it is *not* gaol fever,' he argued within earshot of Boundless as another man, a morose individual in a top hat whom he had first taken to be one of several passengers, badgered him for the cause. 'The cause is a flux in the blood, compounded by the effects of exhaustion and seasickness.'

Lowering his voice, the surgeon whispered something in the other man's ear. The top-hatted man nodded, and the surgeon stooped again over the corpse. 'The natural infirmities of age,' he announced in a loud voice, looking around to ensure he was heard.

The woman's body was unceremoniously dropped over the side, the defrocked priest murmuring a prayer as the body sank swiftly from sight.

A day later, a gaunt, despairing youth, whom Boundless had previously tried to engage in conversation, climbed up on the gunwale and, without a word, jumped down into the waves. The suicide provoked little comment apart from a remark of one woman that the youth was 'full up to the guts' with the torments of life aboard ship. 'He was used to beer and skittles,' she said to no one in particular.

Boundless turned and bumped into the young lad from Newgate. 'Hello laddie,' he said, shocked at the boy's emaciated appearance. 'Do you remember me?'

Already thin when first encountered, the boy now resembled a spectre, his frame so wasted through sickness and starvation that the rags hung from his body. He grimaced incessantly, like a lunatic, his head wobbling on his thin neck. His face was deathly pale, made more so by an ugly welt that had swollen the skin under one eye.

'I am pleased to see you,' said Boundless, trying to conceal his alarm at the boy's appearance. 'I thought you had dropped over the side. How did you come by that mark under your eye?'

He lifted the boy's bone-thin wrist to inspect the blistered sores left by the fetter. 'The wound should be bound. Has the surgeon examined you? Would you like me to intercede with the crew on your behalf?'

'Nay!' The boy pulled his hand away, his shrill cry drawing the attention of other transports.

'Hush now! As you wish, laddie. But you must try and remain in good spirits. You are young and agile and may hope to see your mother again. Do you know your letters?'

The boy gnashed his teeth and mumbled, the words making no sense.

'Perhaps I could teach you. Would you like that? No matter. Eat your food and stay out of mischief. Who knows? You may find a kind master when we land. Do you hear?'

'Make path!' Queezley pushed through the group of transports. His ferocious stare fell on the boy. 'Thou be the cause, thou snivelling bilge rat!'

The boy turned ashen, his slight frame trembling with such fright that Boundless feared he might faint to the deck.

'Thou pop-eyed fool!' With a threatening look, Queezley brushed past.

Boundless heard a transport mutter in disgust and looked down to see that the boy had pissed himself with fear. Taking him by the arm, he felt the scant flesh tremble beneath his fingers.

'Stay out of his way and he shall have no cause to harm ye.'

'Sir?' The boy blinked as if greatly puzzled to suddenly find Boundless in front of him.

'Do you not remember me? We met back at Newgate. When we land, perhaps you may ask someone to send word of your whereabouts to your mother. Until then, come and tell me if anyone offers you harm. Will you promise?'

The boy looked down as if only just aware of despoiling himself.

'Would you like to stay by me—on the deck? We can be friends, and be vigilant for one another?'

Just then a squall lashed the deck and the transports hastened to find cover. The boy slipped from Boundless's grasp and darted away along the deck. The rain grew heavier, and Boundless took shelter under the mainsail together with a thin, sourish individual clad in a patch-work coat. The man gazed mournfully at him before sniffing at the rain sweeping the deck.

'We be drowned in weather, day and night,' he complained.

Boundless glimpsed the boy through the driving rain as he edged along the gunnels, clinging to the side to keep from being blown away by the gale.

'The whelp lacks the sense to shelter his head,' said the man, following his gaze.

Queezley appeared through the rain, a thunderous look on his face as though offended by the weather. The boy shrank against the side as the bosun stalked past, a look of abject terror in his posture.

THE RAIN CONTINUED ALL that day and into the next, increasing in intensity with each passing hour. As the waves grew higher and water crashed over the gunnels, the few transports still above deck fled below in a panic. Boundless remained at the aft shroud in spite of the drenching spray, preferring an honest soaking to the foul stench of the hold. At dusk, the air glowed with an eerie radiance that drew alarmed glances from the crew. As the sun disappeared, the winds increased to gale force, buffeting the ship on all sides. The crew rushed to reduce the sail as the taut canvas shook with a noise like drum taps. Fearful to let go of the shrouds, Boundless felt the wind tear at his clothes as if to rip them from his body.

The vessel tossed helplessly amidst mountainous waves that threatened to swamp her at any moment. The wind howled like a demented soul, the gale snapping the yardage and lashing the deck with spray. His position was now perilous in the extreme, and he clung to the shrouds in fear of his life.

The frightened deckhands had roped themselves to a line for safety, their bodies bent almost double beneath the gusting winds as they struggled to secure the lanyards. Boundless felt his grip weakening as his frozen hands threatened to slip from their purchase on the shroud. Water foamed across the deck and soaked his feet. He heard a faint cry and glanced up to see a deckhand standing over the hold. The man signalled urgently and pointed to the closed hatch. 'Below!' he shouted, his voice barely audible above the shrieking winds.

'I dare not!' He clung to the shroud as a gust of wind threatened to pluck him up into the air and sweep him into the raging seas.

'Below, for your life!' The deckhand fought to pull open the cover. 'Below!' he shouted, dragging open the hatch.

Releasing his hold on the shroud, Boundless lunged across the deck. For an instant he feared he was lost as he slipped in the swirling water.

Next moment, he tumbled head-first into the hold, throwing out his arms to protect himself. He lay dazed in the fetid darkness, the breath knocked out of him by the fall. Above, the hatch cover slammed shut and he heard a bolt slide into place.

He got to his feet, badly shaken and soaked to the bone. In the darkness, wails of fear sounded above the shuddering groan of the ship's timbers. By the dull glow cast by the lamp, he glimpsed his fellow transports, their features contorted with dread.

'Are we lost?' An elderly man, his face white with panic, clutched his arm. 'Are we certain lost?'

He extricated himself from the man's grip as an immense crack of thunder sounded from above. The noise reverberated with ear-splitting intensity through the confines of the hold. A woman screamed and the lantern blew out, leaving the hold in pitch darkness. The thunder rumbled with a noise like that of a massed battery of cannon. Dreadful shrieks and wails sounded through the darkness. A flash of lightning illuminated the deck lights. He felt someone clutch his hand.

'O, help me, sir! I'm feared of drowning!'

In the black gloom, he recognised the young boy, his voice shrill with panic. He placed an arm around the terrified boy and murmured reassurances as another burst of thunder shook the air. The noise was followed by an intense flash of lightning. The terrified captives clung to one another, beseeching God's mercy.

'All shall perish!' a voice wailed as other voices rose in fear and lamentation. The desperate prayers and cries of the transports joined with the grumble of thunder in a devil's refrain that threatened to unseat reason amidst the foul, overpowering stench of vomit, sweat and excrement.

All night long, the ship was battered unmercifully as thunder tore apart the heavens. Lightning bolts seared the darkness. Water came in through the deck lights and leaks in the timber, swilling back and forth along the planks.

As the storm raged, Boundless clutched the petrified boy, certain that the next wave would be the one to send them all to perdition. The boy, exhausted by fear and panic, fell asleep in his arms as he sat braced between a crate and the side of the hold. A woman laid hold of his arm, burying her head in his coat sleeve as she moaned in fear. *Surely, the ship cannot withstand another minute of this.* He closed his eyes, fearful that the vessel would capsize while they were bolted below deck.

Shortly before dawn, the shrieking winds at last abated and the ship steadied in its passage. Those transports not exhausted into slumber offered prayers of gratitude and clutched one another in tearful relief. Boundless heard the sound of a bolt as the hatch cover was opened. A gust of cold air blew through the opening. Faint, greyish light filtered the darkness of the hold. Gently disentangling himself from the sleeping boy, he eased his bruised and cramped limbs. He groped his way to the stairs, careful not to step on bodies in the dim light. Holding onto the steps, he took a moment to steady himself while breathing in the cold air from above. He climbed the steps, his entire body stiff, and emerged from the hold.

In the half-light of dawn, the aft deck was all but deserted. Several large cargo crates had torn away from their ropes and lay smashed against the sides. A cask of wine lay on the planks, the staves splintered into pieces. A lanyard, torn from its bolt, swung freely in the breeze. Straw ticks, sacks of tea and fragments of bone china were scattered along the length of the wet deck, the scene resembling the sack of some great house. He heard voices as a gang of deckhands began to clear the debris, the men talking in muted tones.

Pale yellow rays suffused the horizon. Thunder rumbled faintly in the distance. He gazed out over the grey, foaming sea, profoundly astonished to be alive. The stench of the hold rushed up from his bowels to his throat and he vomited over the side.

He clung to the backstay as half-forgotten words came back to his ears. *'For the living know that they shall die: but the dead know not any thing, neither have they any more a reward; for the memory of them is forgotten.'* For a moment he was back in the dim Scottish parlour, listening as his father intoned the verse, his finger tracing the lines. Rain pelted the windowpane and coals smouldered in the grate. *'Also their love, and their hatred, and their envy, is now perished; neither have they any more a portion for ever in any thing that is done under the sun.'*

The memory induced a profound and oppressive melancholy that weighed heavily on his soul as dawn light silvered the immense, fluxing tide.

IN THE AFTERMATH OF the savage storm, the transports grew ever more dejected. Several refused to eat or come up out of the hold, lying listlessly in place. Alarmed at the potential loss of cargo, the master instructed the crew to double the meagre rations while insisting that each transport spend at least one hour per day on deck. One woman was dragged up by force, spitting curses as the crew lashed her to the shrouds for the allotted hour. The surgeon subjected the transports to a daily inspection, searching for signs of disease as the men and women stood passively in line.

'All is well!' he called up to the master, seeking to reassure the crew.

One morning, Boundless was standing at his accustomed station opposite the mizzenmast when he saw a deckhand, heavily masked with a neckerchief, climb the steps from the hold. The man resembled a footpad or highwayman. After a moment he recognised the figure from the block-like frame and bullish walk.

What the deuce was Queezley doing down there? he wondered, it being common knowledge that the feared overseer avoided the stinking hold like the plague.

He had dismissed the matter from his mind and was watching a sailor toe his way along the upper topsail spar when a squall swept the deck. Several of the transports hastened below to avoid the rain. Boundless had just returned to his place opposite the mast—having sheltered beneath the mainsail—when a dreadful shriek rent the air.

The master's mate, who was standing nearby, rushed towards the hatch from where the scream had issued. 'Let pass!' he shouted, knocking a transport to the deck in his haste.

On instinct, Boundless followed, the awful scream releasing some dire premonition that made him hasten to follow the mate down the steps.

'God's blood!' The mate halted at the foot of the ladder. Tugging a rag from his pocket, he pressed it to his mouth. With his other hand, he took the lantern down from its hook and made his way to the furthest recess of the hold. Boundless followed closely behind, pressing his nose into his sleeve.

'Stand aside!' The mate pushed his way through a group of transports. They were gathered in front of the narrow cavity between the stacked crates and the ship's timbers, speaking in hushed tones. It was the same space where he had taken refuge from the violent shaking of the ship during the storm.

'I said stand aside!' The mate held up the lantern and shone the beam into the cavity. 'Christ preserve us!'

Coming up behind the mate, Boundless caught his breath in horror.

The body of the young boy hung suspended from a rope secured to an overhead beam. In the dim lantern light, the boy's face was dreadfully white, his tongue protruding grotesquely from his mouth. The body swung back and forth to the creaking of the ship. Behind Boundless, a woman began to wail, her cries adding to the horror of the discovery.

Handing the lantern to a transport, the mate took out a clasp knife. Hurriedly he sawed through the rope. 'Take the weight,' he ordered, glancing at Boundless.

Boundless hoisted the body in his arms, surprised at the lightness. *No more than a sack of tea.* The boy's head slumped against his neck; the cold flesh pressed against his own.

'Set him down,' commanded the mate as he finished severing the rope. He watched Boundless lay the pale, anguished form on the deck. 'Who is he?'

'Jack,' said someone behind. 'Jack of Newgate.'

'Did ye know the lad?' asked the mate, looking at Boundless.

'By sight only. He sorrowed for his mother.'

'Well, Jack o' Newgate. Thou'll be for the deep.' The words, roughly spoken, were yet tinged with sympathy.

The mate went to remove the knot from the boy's throat. He paused and whistled in surprise. 'The lad had salt water in him. This knot be expertly tied.'

Instantly, Boundless' suspicions leapt to the surface. 'Mr Queezley had it in for the lad,' he said.

The mate gave a humourless laugh. 'The fellow has it in for all of God's creation!'

'Sir, you mistake my point. I saw Mr Queezley come up out of the hold—just before the boy was discovered.'

The mate gave a sharp glance. 'What do you say?'

'I saw Mr Queezley come up out of the hold. Just before—'

'Do you wish to make a charge against the man?' The mate's voice was edged.

'You yourself complimented the knot. Do you think the boy tied it himself?'

The mate stared at the lifeless body for a long moment.

'No, I do not,' he said, his voice softening. 'But neither do I have the proof that your words imply and require. It might equally have been one of these,' he said, motioning to the transports gathered behind them.

The boy's shirt had rucked up out of his breeches and the mate tugged it up further, uttering an oath as he did so.

Peering in the dim lantern light, Boundless exclaimed in revulsion at sight of the bloodied welts criss-crossing the boy's back. 'There be your proof!'

The mate did not reply. His face grim, he pulled down the boy's shirt to cover the welts.

'Surely, the captain must be told. The man cannot be allowed—'

'Say nothing.' The mate's voice hardened. 'The lad is at peace now.

Mr Queezley will get what he deserves, one way or another. Nothing!' he warned, as Boundless opened his mouth to protest. 'The master is a fair man, but he will demand proof—especially in a matter such as this. Proof you do not have. Mr Queezley will refer a charge against you, and it will go ill with you for the remainder of the voyage. Do you wish for that?' He stared at Boundless, his eyes narrowed in the light cast by the lantern. 'No? A wise decision.' He bent to pick up the small corpse.

'Sir, by your leave.' Boundless scooped the slender body into his arms.

The mate stood up. 'Remember, not a word,' he warned, 'for your own safety. Mr Queezley, if he has done this, shall be held to account by a higher judge.'

On deck, a small group of transports watched in silence as the boy was wrapped in sailcloth. A sailor added a chunk of iron before sewing up the shroud. The defrocked priest mumbled a prayer as the slender form was laid atop a plank suspended over the gunnels. At a nod from the mate the plank was swivelled and tipped. The body slid off the end, dropping like a stone to the waves. A woman wept, her sobs blending with the wind and the fluttering sails.

'Clear the deck!' Queezley's voice rang out as he harried the transports away from the side.

Several times in the succeeding days, Boundless felt certain he sighted the boy darting about the deck, the fleeting figure casting fearful, haunted looks as he disappeared around the mast. He developed a passionate loathing for the person of Queezley, watching with burning contempt as the man stalked the deck, bullying deckhand and transport alike. He wished heartily that a wave might break over the side and scoop the miscreant out to sea. His mind was only turned from dwelling on the sorrowful event by the occasion of another death.

IN THE DAYS FOLLOWING the gale, the first mate was overheard to complain that the storm had blown them off course. As the words were circulated among the transports, opinion varied as to whether they were east or west of the desired passage.

'We now be headed to the Timbuktu,' a convicted sheep stealer claimed, swearing 'certain knowledge' of the fact.

In a bid to make up time, the master ordered the crew to fly every square inch of canvas. In this they were assisted by a spell of fine weather, the blue skies and warm breezes lifting the spirits of crew and transports alike.

One morning, as Boundless hastened to his customary station, a cry from the upper topsail alerted him to some commotion in the water. Shading his eyes, he stared at where several dolphins breasted the waves to race alongside the ship. Their silver fins flashed in the sunlight. For a quarter-hour the crew attempted to gaff or bait the creatures, succeeding only in wounding one with the fizgig.

'Who can count the dust of Jacob, and the number of the fourth part of Israel?'

Boundless turned to see where a transport—a man he recognised from a single brief conversation—had clambered up onto the gunnels.

The fellow leaned perilously out into the gusting wind—one hand clutching the shrouds, the other outflung, pointing at the horizon. A woman screamed, alerting the crew to the sight.

'I will rescue you from bondage, and will redeem you with an outstretched arm and with great judgments!' The man cried before he released his hold and dropped into the churning waves. He bobbed up once, a wild look on his face and arms uplifted as though in supplication. A moment later he vanished beneath the swell.

Transports and crew congregated at the spot, searching the waves for any glimpse of the drowned man.

'Stand aside, damn ye!' The bosun stormed up, a snarl on his face. He laid into the shocked transports with the knotted rope, drawing cries of pain.

'Do not hinder my passage! God's blood if I don't flay the next man that jumps!'

The usual constrained silence between the transports was broken by this latest death, gossip and rumour the currency of newfound fellowship.

'He was lunatic in the head,' a man confided, as he and Boundless stood together beside the waist gangway. 'I knew him well.' The man, a notorious procurer, fished a scrap of paper out of his pocket. 'The last words he ever wrote.'

Boundless stared at the scribbled words, barely able to decipher the hand. *Number shall replenish the exhausted soul.*

'What does it mean?'

The man made a scoffing sound. 'He was mad, always. And the storm broke his senses.' He pocketed the paper. 'He was a gentleman though, before falling on hard times, and a great one for chapter and verse. For the good it did him.' He glanced at Boundless. 'Be you for bond or convict?' he asked.

'Beg pardon?'

'I stand here for procurement, thieving, and false possession of goods,' the man said blandly. 'This be my third time to the Plantations. I served four years in Maryland the first, and seven in Virginia, the second.' He conveyed the information with all the nonchalance of a discussion of the weather. 'But a portion of these be here willingly.'

He indicated a group of four or five individuals whom Boundless had taken as passengers. 'They sold themselves for the cost of passage. Others be kidnapped from the streets, like as not. And others, like the lad who necked himself, sold into bondage.'

'Sold?'

'Aye. By his mother. I knew her once. A nasty shrew with a liking for none but herself. Bless her black heart!'

Boundless stared at the informant, unable to form words.

The other man eyed him appraisingly. 'You might fetch five or six pounds. You've a strong young body, fit for labour. Come, friend, no need to look so downhearted. It ain't so bad as some of these sack-faces would have it. Why, I'm minded to stay on this time and save Old England the bother of shipping me out again.

What say you?'

'What will happen to us—when we make landfall?'

The man picked his teeth with a fingernail. 'Auctioned,' he said, 'to the highest bidder. Be sure to look fit and willing. Who knows but a fine lady might take a fancy to your jib?' he joked, and winked.

This bantering prophecy of his fate did little to alter Boundless' mood as he gazed out over the side. In his mind he saw Newgate Jack as he watched, with fearful eyes, for the bosun. He brooded on a conceit of the slender body as it rolled and turned on the seabed, a plaything for darting fish and every motion of the passing tide. Despair confined him to the spot long after the jesting thief had drifted off in search of more convivial companions.

The sun sank and he heard, as from a distance, the tolling of the watch bell. Moments later his fellow transports trudged past, seeming like mournful ghosts in the twilight. A few met his glance, their faces haggard and despairing as they returned to the pestilential gloom of the hold. Rousing himself from the torpor that held him to the spot, he took refuge in the concealed space beside the jolly boat. He remained there until certain that the fearsome Queezley had retired for the night. Only then did he cautiously re-emerge to the darkening sky and the frowning forbearance of the First Watch.

5

Some Unexpected Advice

HE WAS SEATED BESIDE the longboat, his legs dangling over the timber wall, when a deckhand climbed down the few steps to the boat recess. The man looked around and, seeing him, came over and sat alongside. The unusual familiarity took him by surprise. The man said nothing beyond offering a brief nod to acknowledge his presence. Taking out a tinder box, he fired up a pipe and sat back against the side wall. After some time puffing on the pipe, he took out a whale's tooth from his jacket pocket and began pricking the surface with the point of a sharp knife.

Uncertain whether to introduce himself or attempt to strike up a conversation, Boundless stole several curious glances as the man painstakingly imprinted a series of dots on the smooth, rounded tooth.

'Scrimmy.' The sailor glanced up with a grin. 'It keeps the auld hands busy.' The man, a grizzled veteran of the seas with a lean, weathered face and bushy eyebrows, spoke with a strong brogue. Boundless said nothing as he watched the sailor patiently prick at the ivory with the knife. They continued sitting in companionable silence until the watch bell sounded and the man was called back to duty.

The next day, when the deckhand came off watch, he resumed his position alongside Boundless and again fished out the tooth. 'It passes the time,' he said, etching a line with the knife. This went on for some time until the sailor suddenly set aside the tooth and extended his hand. 'Fearghal Bonny,' he said.

Taken aback at the overture, he took the sailor's hard, calloused hand in his own. 'Boundless McLennan,' he said, wondering if such intercourse was permitted. He looked around to see whether anyone had witnessed the handshake.

Bonny grinned as he resumed working the object. 'Mr Queezley be taking his food,' he said. 'Those be soft gentleman's hands,' he teased.

Boundless examined his fingers. 'Printer's hands,' he replied.

Bonny raised his eyebrows. 'Why then?' he said and blew particles of ivory from the tooth.

Over the next few days, the grizzled deckhand struck up a friendly banter, openly asking Boundless about the crime for which he was being transported. When he briefly explained the circumstances of his summons and trial, the Irishman's face darkened.

'They be all the same,' he said. 'Powdered divils with nary a jack of sense nor a dram of guts.' He dug angrily at the bone for a moment. 'Still,' he continued, in a mollified voice, 'You at least be in fortune to ship with Master Addison. Although stiff as auld boots, he be an honest and decent fellow. Not like Master Taylor.' He shook his head in disgust. 'That whoreson would have ye shackled in the hold the entire passage. And mayhap all to perish from the plague.'

'Do you mean gaol fever?' he asked, repeating the term he had overheard the surgeon use. 'Is that what killed the old woman?'

'Like as not.' Bonny's voice was sombre. 'Three voyages ago it perished all the transports, and half the crew as well. It is the reason the master is so keen on giving ye fresh air.'

They sat idly for a few minutes, Bonny minutely pricking the whale tooth with the point of the knife. Noting his interest, the Irishman held out the tooth. 'See for yourself,' he said.

Taking the object, Boundless squinted at the clustered dots. At first, he could discern no shape or pattern. But then, miraculously, or so it seemed, the outline of some creature—a large fish—began to emerge from the cluster of pinpricks.

'What is it?' He asked, tracing the pinpricks with his finger.

'That, boyo, be a right whale. There be the spout. Doubtless 'twill be clearer when rubbed,' said Bonny, taking back the bone. 'Rubbed?'

'Aye. With ink.' The Irishman grinned. 'Something you'd be after knowing about.'

The next day, Boundless waited for his new acquaintance to join him again following the end of the afternoon watch. After being distracted by a brief but heated row between two of the transports, he looked up to see Bonny approach. Sitting down, the sailor at once produced the whale tooth and, without saying a word, handed it to him.

The pricked dots had been rubbed with ink and transformed into a detailed depiction of a floating whale. The scrimshaw showed in clear detail the great fish and the surrounding shades of sea and sky.

'It is a wondrous effect,' he said admiringly, handing back the object.

Pleased at his reaction, the sailor waved back the scrim. 'Keep it.'

As he started to protest, Bonny closed his fingers around the object.

'Save it as a keepsake of the passage,' he said. 'Not that you'll be wishing to remember.' He studied Boundless for a moment. 'I could teach ye,' he said, 'to scrim.'

Surprised by the offer, he immediately agreed. 'I look forward to it and thank you.'

Over the next few days, the two men struck up a friendship of sorts, the sailor tutoring Boundless in the art of scrimshawing while skilfully drawing forth the full circumstances of his exile.

'It appears ye staked the wrong card, Mr McLennan,' Bonny said after Boundless told of his move to London and early engagement with the Reformists. He puffed on a short cob pipe, his gaze on Boundless.

'Wrong card?'

'You oughtn't to waste good salt on rotted fish.' Bonny's voice was unsympathetic. 'Are ye a believing man?'

'I was raised on the Book,' Boundless answered, his voice cautious.

'So were we all—mercy upon us!' The Irishman ruminated for a moment. 'There be other things,' he said, as he indicated over his shoulder with the pipe, 'to put faith in.'

'The sea?' suggested Boundless, puzzled whether the Irishman referred to some notion of pantheism.

'Aye. Why not? The sea, the wind … this.' Bonny held up the scrimshaw.

Boundless furrowed his brow, uncertain of the other's meaning. 'You mean you believe in those things?' he asked. 'As in animism?'

'As in themselves. They have no need of titles. They be as they are.'

'As in being natural things?' ventured Boundless.

'We be all of us natural things.' Bonny puffed on the pipe. 'All of us,' he repeated. He put away the scrim and stood up as the watch bell sounded.

'Work is the only true faith.' He winked. 'Even for heretics.' With a laugh, he walked away.

IT WAS TWO DAYS before he saw the deckhand again. Bonny approached to where he was sitting and sat down. Taking out a pouch of tobacco, the Irishman filled the pipe and contentedly smoked a full bowl before saying a word.

'Mark this.' He handed a flat whale bone to Boundless. 'It be auld Dublin. Or it will be, when done. That be the waterfront,' he said. 'And the foinest tavern you could wish.' He pointed to a cluster of etched lines and pricked dots.

Boundless marvelled anew at the other man's skill. 'I see it,' he said, observing how precisely the many individual knife pricks added together to create the scene. At that moment, he saw, passing above the boat storage where they sat, a top-hatted gentlemen he had noticed many times before. The man held fast to the brim of his hat against the gusting wind.

'Is that gentleman a passenger?'

'That scallyface?' Bonny snorted. 'That be Mr Bainstone. He is the gentleman that will sell all of youse on to your new masters and keep the ink of each transaction.'

'So, it is true, then. We are to be sold on landing?'

'Aye. As soon as we land in Pennsylvanny. That means a tobacco farm, like as not, unless you've carpentry or some other wanted trade.'

A sudden gravity invaded the Irishman's jovial tone. He glanced around again to make certain they were not being overheard. 'But if it was meself, I'd be wishin' to sort out me own fate.'

Boundless hesitated, wary of stepping into dangerous waters. 'You mean ...'

'I mean what I mean. 'Course, that's me.' The Irishman eyed him. 'There's craturs that take what comes—if ye be that sort?'

'No. I had rather be master of my own fate, like yourself.'

Bonny nodded. 'Well then, if we're of a mind.' He gave another look around. 'If I was so-minded I'd take me chances on the wharf. If ye be fetched to the Virginny plantations it becomes harder to *shake loose*, if that be your desire.'

Bonny glanced around again, his voice low and confiding. 'There'll be gads of people rousting about dockside: merchants, gentlemen from the plantations, sailors, soldiers, labourers, slaves. It be a lunatic house. A clever boyo might take that as a chance to slip away. Disappear into the crowd—if ye take my drift.'

Mr Bainstone returned along the deck and Bonny stood up. 'That be enough for today,' he said in a loud voice. With a tip of his finger to the clerk, he headed for the aft deck.

BOUNDLESS PONDERED THE IRISHMAN'S words for the remainder of the day, his mind in turmoil. Although he had schemed to make an escape, the notion had been little more than a fanciful balm against the horrors of the voyage. Now, for the first time, he gave the prospect serious thought as the seed planted by Bonny took root in fertile soil. *'I'd take me chances on the wharf. A clever boyo might take the chance to slip away.'*

He saw himself plunge into the crowd, only for the vigilant Queezley, suspecting his intention, to pounce and seize him amid curses and cutting lashes from the knotted rope. The knowledge that, even should he escape, recapture would mean hanging, sharpened his fears—the hanged boy leaping into his thoughts. And should he not attempt to escape at the wharf? He imagined himself sold and transported to the wild interior, cut off from the anonymity of the town and with only savages for neighbours. *Where then would I escape to—even if it were possible?* Confounded by both prospects, he secreted himself in the narrow recess as the last dog watch sounded.

For hours he looked up at the stars, his mind busily conjecturing one escape plan after another. Finally abandoning the idea of sleep, he sat up and pulled the scrimshaw from his pocket. He studied the object by starlight as the sails shook overhead and the ship rose and plunged in the waves. He traced the outline of the whale, taking pleasure in the simple artistry that rendered the living contours of the creature against the hardness of the bone. The object gratified him in a way that he was unable to account for. Returning the bone to his pocket, he pulled out his own apprentice scrim— of the ship itself as it ploughed through the waves. Under the Irishman's patient tutelage, the deck and sails were already distinct against the background of wavy seas. He rubbed a finger across the etching, feeling the sheen of beeswax and hearing Bonny's rich brogue in his head. '*Stick to the partikulars, boyo. The partikulars make up the scrim.*' Still clutching the object, he lolled his head back against the wall and closed his eyes.

The Irishman had promised to ink the novice scrim and he proved as good as his word, handing back the rubbed object a few days later.

'Ye've a gift for it, friend. I ruined many a yard of good whalebone afore I caught the art of it.'

Boundless studied the finished scrim, greatly pleased with the effect. 'The ink makes it come alive,' he said, rubbing his thumb over the picture.

'Aye. But the dots hold the ink. It's the tiny *partikulars*, boyo ... mind the ink. It be still a midge damp.'

He made a rueful face as he gazed at the faint black smudge on his thumb. *I had thought my ink days over.*

6

———

A Smudge on the Horizon

Five weeks into the long voyage, a heron landed on the deck, certain indication—a deckhand assured all within earshot—that landfall was at hand. The heron was followed a day later by a small flock of tropic birds, the size of pigeons. They circled the vessel before flying off into the distance. The sky was daily blue, and the water colour itself seemed changed to suit. Clumps of grass and gulfweed floated by on the tide and several fishing vessels were sighted in the distance. An abundance of dolphins leapt and splashed around the vessel and the crew succeeded in landing a fine specimen. Boundless watched as the men manhandled the creature onto the deck and despatched it with several sharp blows from a spike as it thrashed about. The creature, so iridescent in the water, at once changed hue to a light-grey colour, losing its gleaming lustre seemingly in the moment of death.

The imminence of landfall provoked excitement among crew and transports alike. It became a diversion to stand by the rail to claim the honour of first sight of shore. On the afternoon of the 28th of May the crew took a sounding but were unable to strike ground. Towards dusk, spirits were raised by a strong nor'easter that increased their speed to seven knots per hour, the increase maintained throughout the night. The following day a duck flew overhead; the fowl heralded as a sure sign that land was close by.

'No more than thirty leagues, I'll wager,' the ship's carpenter was heard to declare.

The crew were now taking soundings every four hours as a mood of expectation spread among the transports that the harrowing ordeal of the voyage would soon be over. The knowledge of what lay ahead seemed not to dampen their revived spirits as they wagered on the hour and minute of first sight of land.

At twelve o'clock on the 30th of May, the crew took a sounding at twenty-five fathoms. The number, when announced, drew cheers as the shore watch redoubled and every speck on the horizon was pronounced landfall.

Birds of different species winged by the mast or dashed into the water to feed upon fish driven to the surface by the numerous dolphins.

Boundless had fallen asleep in the warm sunshine, his back against the side, when he was startled awake by a hand vigorously shaking him by the shoulder. At first, he feared someone was trying to steal the treasure trove hidden in the greatcoat. He reacted fiercely, gripping the excited face looming above him by the throat.

'Land!' With a hoarse shout, the man pointed to the horizon.

Standing at the gunnel, Boundless searched the distance, but could see nothing other than the heaving tide.

'D'ye not see?' His companion gripped him by the shoulder. 'It be the New World!'

Screwing up his eyes, he gradually made out a smudge on the horizon. Unlike earlier, false portents, it remained solid and distinct as the minutes passed. As the smudge extended and more land appeared, a mood of joyous relief, almost jubilation, spread among the transports.

''Tis deliverance from our trials!' proclaimed one spindly old man. The crew were also affected, the men hurrying with cheerful purpose to carry out orders.

Although profoundly relieved at the prospect of landfall, he was beset by fresh anxieties as the likelihood of passing from misery to servitude loomed ever larger in his mind. *As land approaches, so does my bondage.*

As the crew bustled to trim the sheets, the nugget of opportunity offered up by Bonny glimmered ever more richly in his thoughts. Sea birds flocked and shrieked overhead as he contemplated the distant point of land, his mind in flux. Recalling Bonny's advice to avoid his former occupation and to disguise himself in order to evade discovery, he pondered how best to achieve this in the event he escaped. *If this indeed be a New World, then I must needs be a new man.*

By three o'clock that afternoon, the *Patience* stood within a league of the shore. A cape was prominent on the larboard bow, and the subject of much speculation as the officers discussed their possible whereabouts. The master attempted to hail a small fishing boat, but the craft rebuffed all attempts at contact, causing great frustration among those on board.

They stood off the cape until the next morning, the exhausted transports bemoaning the delay. At 11 o'clock on the 1st of June, the *Patience* ventured within a half-league of the headland. Boundless overheard the mate describe it as 'Cape Henlopen, of a certainty.' To their joy, a pilot boat was seen approaching shortly afterwards. The pilot came on board to confirm the name of the cape amidst much backslapping and handshaking among the crew. The pilot had brought with him a peck of fresh apples, which he distributed among the crew and transports alike. The fruit—following weeks of heavily salted meat—seemed the most delicious taste of his life as Boundless slowly and carefully savoured each bite.

Aided by a constant wind, they sailed past the cape and entered the mouth of a broad estuary, proceeding under a full head of sail, the salt spray hissing as the vessel dipped and bounced on the tide.

Within the hour the spacious inlet narrowed to form a sizeable river lined with impenetrable green woods on either shore.

'Why, this be the Delaware,' a deckhand answered a transport who asked its name.

As league after league of dense green vegetation fell away behind them, he fancied that the vessel had strayed into a *terra incognita* of trees and water where no civilisation was to be found. Gossip among the transports of bloodthirsty Aboriginals who inhabited the dark woods and practiced the cruellest tortures, played upon his mind as the ship progressed within cannon-shot of the trees.

They continued upriver, passing patches of cleared land amidst the trees. As the channel narrowed further, they came within sight of a fine stone mansion surrounded by fields full of tall, green plants. A solitary figure waved a greeting, receiving hollers and shouts in return. Soon after this, they observed several log houses and a sawmill.

Around 6 o'clock, they passed within hailing distance of two sea-going ships lying at anchor, waiting for the wind to change. The crew hailed them with shouts and whistles as they sailed by. By nightfall, the *Patience* had proceeded some fifty miles upriver. The ship hove to just offshore, the crew congratulating each other that, come the morrow, they would be drinking in the taverns of Philadelphia.

He dozed off by the jolly boat, greatly relieved that this was to be his last night aboard the ship, while yet consumed with apprehension for what the next day might bring.

Three hours after casting off on the morning tide, they came upon the town of New Castle. The jolly boat was put into the water and three passengers and a quantity of cargo rowed to shore. Boundless leaned over the side as the ship swung at anchor, marvelling at the clear translucence of the water. A school of fish with plump bodies and silvery scales darted to and fro beneath the keel.

'That be the Delaware fish,' said a voice. He glanced up to see Bonny gazing down at the water. 'They be foine eating,' the Irishman added.

'They seem in abundance,' he replied, glad of the opportunity to speak to the amiable deckhand.

'These be spawned already. In season they lie so thick in the water ye could boot across their backs to the shore.' Seeing his sceptical look, Bonny laughed. 'I didn't believe it either, at first,' he said. 'But doubtless you will see it with your own eyes.'

With a glance around the deck, Boundless lowered his voice to cautiously remind the Irishman of their prior conversation. 'I have hopes to make it possible,' he said, risking the admission.

Bonny leaned back against the gunnel to survey any who ventured near. 'Seize the moment when it comes,' he said softly. 'Once ye be fetched away from the landing, opportunities will be scarce and the owners vigilant. It is best done before ye pass into their hands. Godspeed, boyo.' He moved away as a deckhand approached.

An hour later they were underway again, the wind remaining favourable and the day gloriously warm. They were hailed by the occupants of a shallop, which drew alongside with the intention of selling fresh milk and vegetables to the crew. Boundless took the opportunity to observe, close at hand, his first colonials.

The two boatmen cut fine figures, he concluded, as they energetically bargained with the deckhands while holding up baskets of apples, eggs and greens to show. The purchases were passed up in a wicker basket attached to a long pole while the boatman skilfully maintained his balance.

These be the New World Englishmen, Boundless reflected, studying the occupants as curiously as he might a zoological specimen under glass.

NOW THAT THE LONG and dangerous journey was nearing an end, the transports became all at once voluble and companionable with one another, solicitously enquiring after each other's health or stopping a companion-by-circumstance to offer sympathies and consolation.

'I shall nay die until I feast eyes on old Glasgwegie agin,' a thin, stooped woman declared to everyone within earshot. 'I shall nay die until.'

Observing the piteous state of his fellow transports, Boundless reflected on his own dishevelled appearance and soiled clothes. He fingered the straggly beard on his chin, bleakly amused as he considered the spectacle he must present to a prospective master. *They shall think they have purchased a chimney sweep.*

The wind and salt air had diminished the tribe of lice inhabiting his skin and clothes but he still scratched constantly to remove more of the vermin. He held out an arm to examine the scars left by the iron fetter. The action drew a ghastly smile from a man nearby who raised his own scarred wrist in a gruesome show of camaraderie.

They passed the township of Chester, and he heard a deckhand announce that 'Old Philly' lay under ten miles distant. 'We shall be there afore supper,' he added confidently.

But as if to confound that prediction, the wind fell away and they were forced to cast anchor opposite a small cluster of houses. The unexpected delay drew loud groans as the transports were returned to the hold—dejected to be spending one more night in the foul enclosure.

He took his accustomed spot beside the jolly boat and tried to make himself comfortable, drawing the greatcoat around him. But agitation over the coming day kept him from sleep. In a fit of desperation, he conceived the notion of slipping overboard and swimming to land, there to cast himself on the mercy of any person he might encounter. But the fear of detection and his own uncertain swimming skills caused him to quickly abandon the wild scheme. *And who knows but that any man I chance upon might not hand me over to the authorities for reward?* His fingers felt for the gold guineas sewn into the coat lining. 'Thou shall be my warrant,' he murmured and fell into a restless slumber.

At 8 o'clock the following morning, the *Patience* sailed on the rising tide, the sun sparkling on the water. They had been underway for little more than two hours, the river becoming busier by the minute with vessels of every description, when a voice shouted down from the rigging.

'Old Philly, off the port bow!'

The transports flocked to stare as the port came into view. A flotilla of lighters, ketches, cutters, tenders, scows, and barges ferried back and forth between the landing and a veritable fleet of masted ships anchored out in the river. Beyond the vessels, they glimpsed a cluster of buildings lining the wharf. Boundless exclaimed in surprise at the number of sea-going ships at anchor.

A man next to Boundless exclaimed in wonder. 'Blessed if she ain't as busy as old London herself!'

ENTERING THE CONGESTED WATERS of the port, the *Patience* hove to behind the line of anchored vessels. The longboat was lowered, and the crew stood on the yards to reef and furl the sails. The ship sat idly for an hour before a coaster approached bearing the harbour pilot, who climbed aboard and engaged in discussion with the master and first mate as they conferred around a chart.

After an interminable wait, lines were passed to the longboat. Shortly thereafter, the vessel began to move forward, tugged by the longboat and assisted only by the topgallants. They were towed to within hailing distance of the anchored ships, passing between a pair of large merchantmen double or triple the tonnage of the *Patience*.

The transports vied with each other to 'shout' the ensigns of England, Holland, Spain, France, Finland and Sweden as they fluttered in the breeze. A murmur arose as the *Patience* drew abreast of a great-masted ship of the line. Bristling with cannon, the warship rode at anchor alongside a smaller frigate, both vessels flying the red, white and blue union flag as jacks.

As the *Patience* cleared the line of ships, the landing came into full, unobstructed view. A jumble of cranes, warehouses, piers, slipways, ramps, and quays lined a broad concourse. A tall steeple rose in the distance, its height drawing much comment. A great number of wagons, carts, drays and coaches rumbled along the stones of the wharf. The clatter of wheels and *clip-clop* of hooves were deafening to ears accustomed only to the crack of canvas and the crash of waves. Sailors, porters, merchants, tradesmen and dock workers thronged the causeway or busied themselves around the berthed ships.

Starved for diversion after the long, arduous voyage, the transports drank in the wonders presented to their eyes and ears as the ship floated within touching distance of the landing. Cries of astonishment greeted each new scene as though it were a novelty in a playhouse. Men and women poked one another to witness such ordinary sights as harried officials, shouting foremen, snorting draught horses, busy tradesmen, or porters, shouting for passage as they pushed handcarts along the crowded quay.

Exclamations arose as the transports witnessed four Blacks, naked from the waist up and bound in chains, being ushered along the cobbles by a man armed with a musket and accompanied by two ferocious hounds.

The sight induced a sombre hush as relief at journey's end was replaced by fresh fears of what fate awaited them on the landing. 'May God pity us,' a woman said, her voice quavering with fear.

The topgallants were furled as the *Patience* came to a dead stop opposite a vacant berth. Hawsers were thrown from the longboat to labourers waiting on the quay. The lines were tied off and the ship slowly winched into the dock. A small crowd of port officials, merchants and porters gathered to await the arrival, their numbers swelled by curious spectators.

'Port ho!' A voice cried out as the ship bumped up against the wharf.

A liveried official shook a handbell. 'Welcome, the *Patience!*'

The announcement brought huzzahs and applause from those standing on the wharf. A work gang manoeuvred a large ramp up against the side of the vessel.

'Ahoy, mateys!' A gaunt individual in an outlandishly tall hat and tattered yellow coat hopped up on a bollard to welcome the arrivals. Arms spread, he resembled a giant parrot as he balanced precariously on the support. Doffing his hat, he made an elaborate bow, one lanky leg suspended in the air behind him.

'Tumble, thou gizzle-stick!' The remark—shouted by a youth among the spectators—drew laughter. The merriment increased as the gangly man lost balance and was forced to jump down from the bollard.

'Ready the transports!' Queezley's voice roared out above the noise. In response, three or four deckhands pushed the transports into a line. Boundless waited in place, his nerves on edge. He looked around for Bonny but did not see him.

Two deckhands approached bearing a crate full of the hated shackles. The deckhands began to sort the manacles while gossiping cheerfully about the wenches waiting on shore. Boundless watched with mounting despair, bitterly resigned to the failure of his hopes.

'Stand to order!' The ship's master appeared on the quarter deck, hands clasped behind him. 'What are those?' He nodded towards the shackles laid out on the deck.

'Beg pardon, sir.' Queezley touched a hand to his forehead. 'They be for on shore,' he said, 'to prevent absconding.'

'And where, Mr Queezley, do you propose that they should abscond to? Put them away.'

Unable to hide his displeasure, the bosun turned and shook his head at the waiting deckhands.

As the shackles were placed back in the chest, Boundless felt an immense weight lift from his mind. *'Tis an omen*, he told himself, jubilant at the reprieve.

The master was joined on the foredeck by the top-hatted Mr Bainstone carrying a small chest under his arm. The two spoke briefly before the master cleared his throat for attention.

'Ladies and gentlemen.' He raised his voice to be heard above the noise of industry carrying from the quay. 'Before you lies the city of Philadelphia. It is here that you will be consigned to serve out your lawful sentence or fulfil the terms of your bond. Be warned. The penalty for escape or unlawful return to England is death by hanging.'

It seemed to Boundless that the master stared straight into his eyes before continuing. 'Mr Bainstone'—he indicated the clerk—'has the papers of indenture. You will be required to make your mark upon disposal. Those of you here for crimes committed would do well to remember throughout your time of servitude that you are here to pay penance for those crimes.'

His voice softened as he contemplated the drawn, dispirited faces before him. 'Be faithful and honest servants. Though damned, we must needs act as though saved.' He contemplated the transports for a moment, his gaze melancholy. 'Mr Queezley. Take charge,' he said, his voice becoming brusque once more.

By pretending to take a stone from his shoe as the transports shuffled towards the ramp, Boundless managed to position himself at the back of the line, behind an old woman and her younger female companion. Led by the bosun and shepherded by six deckhands, three on either side, they proceeded down the ramp and onto the wharf. His legs buckled as he stood on firm ground once again after almost three months aboard ship.

'God be blessed!' The old lady wept on her companion's shoulder.

AS THEY PRESSED THROUGH the waiting merchants, they were besieged by demands for news.

'What goods do ye carry?'

'Is there a trunk for Mr Pearson?'

'What word of the *Lark*, or the *Prospect?*'

'What news of England?'

'Hold back!' Shouting for clearance, Queezley and the deckhands created a pathway. 'Keep to the line!' The flanking deckhands stretched their arms to ward off any intercourse between the transports and the crowd of officials and workers congesting the quayside.

In spite of his feverish anxiety to escape, Boundless was astonished at the multiplicity of exotic faces milling around the quay. Europeans, Negroes, Asiatics, and other races he could not hazard to guess at hurried back and forth to a constant cacophony of whistles, shouts and hails. Several coasters and barges were discharging or taking on passengers and cargo at the same time. The result was a confusing melee of people and goods as clerks and travellers vied for space and attention amidst a throng of officials, porters, departing and disembarking passengers, and well-wishers gathered to greet or farewell the latter.

The noise and activity seemed to overwhelm the dazed transports after so many solitary days at sea. A bonded youth, so thin his clothes barely stayed on his body, turned to all and sundry, his eyes wide. 'Such a clamour as I never did hear!' Through the noise rose the sound of fifes and drums accompanied by cheers and 'huzzahs!' The crowd parted to allow passage for thirty or forty men, marching in double column, each with a musket against his shoulder. They were dressed in green and scarlet uniforms and cocked hats. The cheers grew louder as the column passed by. The men were preceded by a military officer on a white horse. He held his drawn sabre against his shoulder, his eyes straight ahead. A youth carrying the union flag preceded the column and another followed, carrying the same flag. The onlookers yelled and whooped, breaking forward to clap the men on the shoulder as they marched by.

'Hooray for the militia!'

'Kill the heathen savages!'

'And the murderous French!'

The column continued by, drums rapping and fifes piping a rousing, martial air.

Mr Bainstone appeared, the chest under his arm. The transports were stopped in place as the clerk insisted on a fresh count. 'Fifteen … sixteen …' He went down the line, tapping each person on the shoulder as he went. Finishing with Boundless, the man murmured to himself. 'Nine lost.' He signalled the bosun. 'Advance if you will, Mr Queezley.'

Passers-by turned curious eyes as they continued across the landing. Queezley kept vigilant watch, stalking back and forth to bully and prod the men and women to stay in line. He shoved one tardy transport in the ribs. 'Stay the pace!' Incensed at the same laggard, he lashed out with the rope, striking the man's face and raising a welt. The man gave a cry of pain and clutched his cheek.

The clerk called out in displeasure. 'Mr Queezley! Do you injure the goods?'

Boundless lingered near the back, anxious to take advantage of any lapse in the vigilant scrutiny of the deckhands.

They were led away from the teeming wharf towards an open patch of grass. His eyes darted this way and that as he searched for any opportunity to flee. Several half-chances passed him by and he cursed his indecision. His anxiety increased as they left the landing behind. They stopped to regroup near a tavern. Merchants in frock coats idled in conversation, smoking and drinking as they turned to observe. Nearby, a crowd of buyers surrounded an auction platform. A man dressed in a buff-coloured frockcoat and wide-brimmed hat stood on a box to exhort the spectators in a booming voice.

'Gentlemen! Gentlemen! Make free with your purses! Such fine specimens you never did see!' At his signal, a young Negro in chains was led up onto the platform by two burly men armed with truncheons. The Negro stood with bowed head as the auctioneer loudly extolled his strength and reliability for service—'field or domestic!'—to the buyers. Behind the platform, a line of shackled slaves awaited their turn. A few of the women suckled babies at their bare breasts, their eyes darting to the faces of the eager bidders.

'Move!' barked Queezley. Mr Bainstone had gone ahead, stopping at where a table and chair were set up under a tree. A handful of men lounged beneath the tree or sat in the grass awaiting their arrival. Boundless hung back, more desperate than ever to slip away into the thinning crowd. The line stopped moving and he bumped into the man ahead of him. A few yards in front, the old woman had collapsed, whether from illness or distress. She lay prostrate, insensible to the shouts of the crew who shouted for her to get back to her feet. Her companion knelt beside her, beseeching the escort for patience as she rubbed the old woman's arm. The deckhand beside him hurried forward to assist as Queezley charged back down the line to investigate the cause of the delay.

'Get to thy feet, thou damned fussock!'

Loudly berating the distraught woman, the bosun forcefully dragged her to her feet. 'Dost thou think to jilt with tears?'

At that moment, a man driving a hand cart piled high with goods pushed through the transports and blocked Boundless' view of the drama taking place ahead. He saw the chance and seized it. With pounding heart, he stepped away from the line, walking closely behind the man as if companion to him. He followed as the tradesman headed back towards the landing, his nerves tense for the hue and cry of pursuit. The tradesman called out to clear passage and he followed, expecting hands to seize him at any moment.

HE REACHED THE WHARF without incident, scarcely able to credit his luck. Abandoning the tradesman, he immersed himself in the crowd, his heart pounding. Not daring to look back, he hurried towards the row of customs houses at the back of the landing. In his rush to clear the wharf, he collided with a porter, knocking the man to the ground. Assisting the indignant fellow to his feet, he muttered an apology and hurried on.

As he stood back to allow an equipage to pass, he heard a sharp cry. He risked a glance behind. For a moment he saw nothing and then, through the crowd, he glimpsed Queezley—the bosun turning urgently in every direction for sight of the fugitive. At that moment the two men locked eyes. Queezley's mouth dropped open in astonished rage. Raising a whistle to his lips, he emitted a long, piercing blast.

'Hold, thou villain! Stop him, I say!'

As whistle blasts pierced the air behind him, he turned and fled. Startled looks were cast in his direction. Shouts and cries sounded in his wake. Reaching a row of freight sheds, he found his path obstructed by a slow-moving line of freight wagons. He darted between—in his haste narrowly avoiding being trampled beneath the horses. His carelessness drew a string of oaths from the startled driver. Heaving for breath, aware of nothing save the frantic pounding in his chest, he fled along a winding brick lane as he made good his escape from the wharf.

7

A New Companion and a Curious Beast

A S HE HURRIED THROUGH the streets, people turned to stare, alarmed by his dishevelled appearance and furtive air. He pressed on, eyes downcast, fearful lest someone accost him and demand his purpose. Away from the vicinity of the wharf he passed an alley leading off from the main street. He slumped, exhausted, against the brick wall, his chest heaving. Under the heavy greatcoat, his coarse, linen shirt was soaked with sweat. In the distance, he heard faint shouts, and he held his breath as his ears strained for the shrill cry of pursuit. The shouts faded and he took a deep breath to calm his fraught nerves. The certainty that, if caught, he was a hanged man weighed oppressively on his mind. He heard footsteps coming towards him and braced in readiness. To his relief, the footsteps continued on past the alley.

A noisy tavern at the top of the lane caught his attention. He stared at the hostelry, torn between a desire to seek refuge from exposure on the streets and the fear of discovery. He felt through the pocket of the coat for the treasure trove sewn into the wool lining, relieved by the touch. Glancing around to make certain he was unobserved, he slit the lining with his thumbnail and retrieved three of the guineas, silently blessing Joshua Lively and his Reformist colleagues for their foresight. He made his way up the laneway towards the tavern. Somewhere, a dog barked, and he glanced over his shoulder.

The door to the tavern pushed open. Two men wearing leather aprons emerged, chuckling at some jest. One held open the door. 'Enter, friend. The libations be true and the fire warm.'

The interior was dimly lit and thick with smoke. Merchants, dock workers, deckhands and tradesmen sat around a dozen long tables noisily enjoying dinner. Boys went from table to table carrying trenchers heaped with meat or balancing jugs of wine and cider. His mouth watering at the pungent smells, Boundless squeezed into a space at one end of the nearest bench.

'Gentlemen,' he said, mumbling pleasantries to the row of bewigged merchants seated at the table.

A boy set a wooden trencher piled with thick slices of hot pork in front of him. 'Grub's a shilling,' he shrilled before hurrying on to the next table. Ravenous after the meagre shipboard rations, he choked back a large mouthful of the juicy flesh, barely swallowing before reaching for the next as he gorged on the feast. The elderly merchant seated opposite looked on, nodding as he choked back another mouthful. Turning to a neighbour the man winked. 'What sayest thou he finishes the pig?'

The man continued to gaze approvingly as Boundless pushed mouthful after mouthful of the pork into his mouth. A youth set a mug of lime punch before him. He paused only to take swallows from the mug, aware of the stares of those at the table, but too consumed with appetite to care. At length, his stomach rebelled at the plenitude, and he felt the food rise in his gorge. He took another draught of punch and sat back, his stomach swollen. He gave a loud belch and muttered an apology.

The merchant studied him over a long-stemmed clay pipe.

'Where might thee be from, friend?'

'From Lon—Scotland,' he answered.

'Thou'll be one of the new arrivals, then.' The merchant looked to his neighbours for confirmation. 'More and more each day,' he said, and sucked on the pipe.

'What news, friend, of England?' A ruddy-faced man further down the table leaned forward with the question.

'All is well,' answered Boundless, trying his best to appear convivial, but acutely conscious of his dishevelled state. 'The ports are busy and 'tis said the country prospers.'

The merchant opposite removed the pipe from his mouth. 'Any particular news, sir, of the shipping trade? A vessel from Liverpool, *Swallow*, is two weeks past due and we are anxious for her safety.' A murmur of agreement came from the other men around the table.

'I beg pardon, but I am unacquainted with the vessel.'

The merchant nodded. 'Providence may yet deliver her,' he said solemnly.

Suddenly apprehensive, Boundless glanced at the door and rose to his feet. 'My apologies, sirs,' he said, bowing, 'I have business to attend. By your leave.'

The elderly merchant lifted the pipe in acknowledgement as Boundless went off in search of the host. He found the latter standing behind the counter engaged in earnest conversation with a patron. The tavern keeper, a gaunt figure with pock-marked cheeks, broke off the conversation as Boundless approached. 'That will be one shilling and tuppence, fine sir,' he said.

Boundless raised an eyebrow. 'Indeed? I was told the cost was a shilling.'

'That would be the ordinary, friend. The other is tuppence more.' The tavern keeper indicated a wooden board over his shoulder that listed the prices. 'You had the cider, did you not?'

'I did not. I had the punch.'

'Aye. That will be the difference. One shilling and tuppence, if you please.' The tavern keeper held out his hand.

Boundless handed over one of the precious guineas. 'Might I trouble you for a bed?' he asked, glancing at the board.

The man tested the coin between his teeth. 'One shilling for a shared bed and sixpence extra for a hearty breakfast. Milk, bread and fish.' Seeing Boundless hesitate, he added, 'No stinking mush here.'

'Deduct it from the guinea, if you please.'

The host rummaged through a leather purse around his waist for change. 'Be you from these parts, Mr … ?' he asked, his eyes bright and inquisitive as he took in Boundless' appearance.

'Lively,' answered Boundless, hesitating but a moment. 'Mr Joshua Lively. And as to your question, I am newly arrived to these parts.'

'Where be you from, then?' the tavern keeper asked as he counted the change onto his palm. 'Where do you say?' He glanced up before turning his attention back to the coins.

'From Scotland. Lately arrived from the Port of Liverpool.'

'Liverpool, you say?' The man handed over the change. 'Liverpool? You will find the finest bed in all of Philadelphia right up those stairs, Mr Lively,' he said, and indicated a narrow stairway.

Fingering the whiskers on his chin, he regarded Boundless, a shrewd look in his eyes. 'May I interest you in company, fine sir?' he asked. 'Mary!' He turned and snapped his fingers at a remarkably thin, dour-faced woman watching from the kitchen doorway. 'Mr Lively, sir, I have the honour to present a most delectable morsel for your pleasure.'

The listening patron guffawed, drawing a hard glance from the host. 'I do warrant you full sat—'

'I beg pardon, but, of a certainty, no,' declared Boundless, shocked by the offer. The woman watched without expression as he backed away from the bar towards the stairs. 'I thank you for your hospitality,' he said, and proffered a slight bow. The tavern keeper stared, his bright eyes following as Boundless ascended the staircase.

THE CEILING OF THE small bedchamber was so steeply pitched that he was forced to bend his head to enter. The only light came from a narrow window overlooking the street. The room was furnished with a single large mattress stuffed with straw. It was topped with three linen bags crammed with rags. A stained, heavily patched sheet was the only cover. He sat down on a stool to remove his shoes, noticing the papery thinness of the leather soles. Sated by the heavy meal, he lay back on the lumpy mattress, tucking the greatcoat under his body.

In spite of his exhaustion, he remained wakeful and alert, distracted by the noise and laughter emanating from the tavern below. Suspicious of the villainous-looking host, he strained to hear any discordant noise above the roars of merriment. In fancy, he saw the surly tavern keeper glance up at the ceiling as he signalled his confederate to creep up the stairs to rob and plunder. Or might not the villain, suspecting his fugitive status, send a boy to fetch a watchman in anticipation of a reward?

Overwrought with nerves and fatigue, he imagined the door bursting open to reveal a mob of vengeful pursuers as they rushed forwards to apprehend him. He fought to stay awake as a loud creak came from the stairway. But despite his fearful vigilance, he was unable to keep his eyes open and fell quickly into a profound and dreamless sleep.

HE AWOKE TO THE rasping snores of a drunken tradesman sprawled next to him on the bed. A haggard-looking woman with a heavily rouged face was asleep next to the man. Instinctively, he groped for the store of guineas. A grateful sigh escaped his lips as he felt the comforting hardness of the coins. The memory of yesterday's events swept vividly to mind, and, for an instant, he felt the coarse fibres of the hangman's rope constrict his throat as the terror of apprehension returned. It was entirely probable, he told himself, that the authorities were searching for him—perhaps combing the streets and taverns even at this hour.

A faint grey light illuminated the bedchamber. Minutes ticked by as he stared up at the ceiling. *It be best to flee to the margins of the city. Away from the port.* He sat up, his head groggy from the unaccustomed feast. Some advice Bonny had offered on board ship came to mind. *I must alter my appearance.* Fixed on this purpose, he tugged on his shoes, noting again the worn-through soles. With a glance at his snoring bed mates, he made his way downstairs.

IN THE HALF-LIGHT, THE tavern was empty. A sleepy serving girl looked up as he descended the stairs. Yawning, she got up to stoke a copper kettle that rested on the smouldering embers of the fire. He made his way over to a table by the window and sat there in the shadows, his eyes darting through the glass to observe the darkened street. The girl brought him a trencher of salted herring along with a bowl of bread and milk. She set down a mug of beer, which he drank from thirstily.

'Do you have tea?' he asked.

The girl nodded, her face still sleepy. She returned with the large copper kettle, holding it by a flannel rag wrapped around the handle. Lifting it with both hands, she filled the mug with hot, steaming tea. 'A hearty appetite, sir,' she yawned.

He had just started to eat the fish, scooping it up with his fingers, when he heard the tavern door open. A youth about the same age as Boundless entered. The youth was dressed in a navy-blue gabardine coat, linen shirt and canvas breeches. A knitted wool cap was pulled down on his head of the type worn by the sailors aboard the *Patience*. Bidding a cheerful good morrow to the serving girl, he crossed to the hearth where he selected a taper from a brass bowl. He held the taper to the glowing embers of the fire and then transferred it to the pipe in his mouth—puffing the tobacco to flame. Drawing on the pipe, he eyed each of the empty tables in turn, as if debating the merits of each. When his gaze alighted on Boundless sitting in the shadows, he gave a start, clearly surprised to find another patron at so early an hour. Taking the pipe from his mouth he approached.

'Good morrow, sir.' He proffered a half-bow. Beneath the wool cap, his stringy blond hair was pulled into a tail by a black ribbon. 'Theodore Humpflinger begs permission to sit with you, friend, if I might be so bold?' His manner, like his speech, was suffused with a diffident courtesy.

Swallowing a mouthful of bread, Boundless rose to his feet. 'Mr Joshua Lively, sir. At your service. And I should be most glad of the company.' He indicated the chair opposite.

Pleased by this response, the youth sat down. 'Pray, Mr Lively, continue with your breakfast, sir.' He observed Boundless with mild blue eyes over the pipe. 'That fish has almost certainly lost the contest,' he remarked, nodding at the trencher. He put the pipe back in his mouth and stared contentedly out the window, sending a fragrant cloud of tobacco smoke into the air.

'Woulds't thou choose beer or cider, sir?' The young girl approached the table and placed a mug in front of the young man. 'Cider, if you please.' Humpflinger answered. As the girl departed, he swivelled in the chair. 'Tea!' he called out. 'Tea! Of a certainty.'

Boundless finished the last scrap of bread while studying his companion. 'Your occupation, Mr Humpflinger?' he asked. 'If I might be so bold as to enquire?'

'Certainly, friend. You behold, before you, a boatman.' The youth drew on the pipe as he considered this reply. 'Although, in strictest truth, I might, with equal veracity, have answered "cooper"—a trade of which I have passing knowledge.' He puffed thoughtfully. 'Passing knowledge,' he murmured. 'But as matters stand, boatman—in sum and in short.'

'Ah!' Humpflinger hummed with pleasure as the serving girl returned, watching as she poured tea from the steaming kettle into his mug. 'India tea,' he said happily. He tapped the mug with the pipe stem. 'A most excellent choice.'

'And you are employed here—in the port?' enquired Boundless.

'Alas no. "Alas" because then would my journey be happily ended even before it were begun. The fact of the matter is that I am, of this moment, making the journey south to rendezvous with a vessel for the purpose of my employment. And yourself, friend?'

'A traveller, but lately arrived and looking for honest occupation.'

'Why then, you be in the very place! Philly has plenty of work for willing hands. Of course, you might not choose to make your abode here. They say 'tis a bawdy and ill-mannered town and with oft-times a terrible stench from the marshes. Although, the whole of the matter and the entirety of the argument is that others swear as to its salubrious air.'

Thus, fairly acquitted on both sides of the case, the youth mused contentedly on the pipe.

'What sorts of occupations might be recommended, Mr Humpflinger?' Boundless asked, glancing through the window at a passer-by. The sky had begun to lighten, casting light into the tavern.

Humpflinger reflected for a moment. 'There is field work—strictly to be avoided at all costs. Most of the cropping is done by slaves. An unpleasant task, I assure you. In the town itself there is much work in the trades—brickmaking, carpentry, chandlery, ropemaking, tanning and the like. And, of course, being a port, there is call for all sorts of labour concerning the ships.' Humpflinger took a sip of tea, nodding at the taste.

'Mind,' he continued, warming to the topic, 'An adventurous man might also seek his fortune in the outer colonies. Virginia, for example, is said to be exceedingly blessed in both tobacco and furs. Why, you might even set out for the Ohio country to hunt for buff—if you be willing to risk being murdered by savages. Every year there be young bucks setting off for the purpose.

But as for old Phil, why—there be sufficient work and plenty right here. A man might meet a respectable employer simply by walking down the street.'

Something his companion said, struck Boundless. 'What are buff?' he asked.

'Buff?' Humpflinger looked surprised at the question. 'Why, they be no more or less than … buffaloes.' He took a swallow of tea. Seeing Boundless' puzzled frown, he expounded upon the definition. 'Buffaloes …' He paused, searching for the right words, '… be a cross between a cow and a bear. Or, more judiciously, between a mule and a beaver.' He drew on the pipe. 'With horns.'

Boundless tried hard to picture such an exotic beast. 'How tall does it stand?'

Humpflinger ruminated on the question, and then, with alacrity, leapt to his feet. 'This height, to a certainty.' He extended an arm out straight from his shoulder.

'Naturally, it depends on which part is being measured. But, fair to say, tall as a man—though not so tall as a bear standing on its hinds, generally.' Humpflinger sat back down to cross his legs and draw reflectively on the pipe.

'And what do they do, these buffaloes?'

'Do?' Humpflinger looked nonplussed at the question. 'Why, they generally don't *do* much of anything but stand there and chew the grass.'

'But their meat is valuable?'

'To the squaw, sir.'

'Squaw?'

'Beg pardon. Savages—of the female variety.'

'So why then do these young bucks you speak of go to the trouble of travelling out to the … Ohio, as you say, to hunt them?'

'In a word, fur.' The young man looked pleased at such concision.

'It is of much value?'

'Value?' Humpflinger blinked at the question. 'Why, the hide be as thick as several blankets. A coat made of buff wool will keep you alive in the middle of the severest cold. For hardiness, they say, it has no equal. It keeps out thunder, snow, rain, wind, ice … most anything.' Humpflinger pondered the list. 'Most anything.'

The girl returned, holding up the copper kettle. 'Woulds't thou take more tea, sirs?'

'A finger!' Humpflinger crooked his little finger to indicate. 'Just the one,' he cautioned, peering into the mug as she poured. 'Halt! Most excellent,' he pronounced happily. 'A veritable finger's worth.'

As the girl left, Boundless heard the tavern door open and looked up to see a group of four men enter. 'Do you think that perhaps I might find occupation on this boat of yours, Mr Humpflinger?' He asked, his eyes dwelling on the men as they sat down at a table.

'Occupation?' Humpflinger gave the notion thought while ruminating on the dark tea. 'I suppose I could put in a word with Captain Taysick on your behalf.' He brightened. 'Indeed—why not! And I shall have a companion to travel with.' He picked up the tea and set it down again. 'Did I mention that the boat is in Maryland? It requires better than three day's travel.'

'So much the better.' Boundless drained the mug, greatly relieved at the prospect of departing Philadelphia.

'You may wish, though, to dress in more customary attire. I fear your coat—worthy though it be—may prove cumbersome to the requirements of a boat.'

'In which case, might you be so good as to direct me to a provisioner of such clothing, Mr Humpflinger?'

'Why, I shall do better, friend. I shall escort you there myself. The Maryland packet does not sail until tomorrow. And the haberdasher does not open for some hours yet. What say I guide you through the town until then? Philly be a fine old place, with many pleasing prospects.'

'I should be glad of it, Mr Humpflinger.'

'Theodore, or Theo, if it pleases.'

'It does. And Joshua, by return.'

Humpflinger beamed. 'Shall we depart?'

Boundless stood up. 'I shall consider myself in your debt, Mr—Theo!' With another glance at the seated men, he accompanied his new-found companion from the tavern.

Unpeeling the Onion

ONCE OUTSIDE, HUMPFLINGER LED the way along a narrow, cobbled street. He set a brisk pace and Boundless soon began to perspire in the humid air, taking off the greatcoat and holding it over his arm as they proceeded. 'What street is this?' he asked as they passed an inn.

'This be Front Street. And that is the Blue Anchor tavern, a fine watering place.'

'We are following the path of the river?'

'We are indeed. My ambition is to take you along the river to the woods and fields that border the city. And from thence, by a circular route, to proceed back to the town again. Thus, viewing the town first from the outside and from thence, by degrees, the *inside* as we return to the port—much as one would unpeel an orange. Or, if you prefer, the layers of an onion. Is such a course satisfactory to you?'

'Indeed. I am most eager to become acquainted with the colony.'

Shortly after passing the tavern, they came to a broad creek crossed by a stone bridge. As they crossed over the waterway, a foul stench met their noses. 'The tanneries.' Humpflinger pointed to a row of buildings further along the creek. 'And the slaughterhouses,' he added as the odorous whiff grew stronger. 'Hold thy nose,' he advised, taking out a neckerchief to clutch to his face.

As they continued, Boundless switched the greatcoat to his other arm. 'Is it not remarkably warm?' he asked.

'With luck, the wind may shift and blow in from the river.'

'But is it always so inclement?' Boundless asked, suddenly homesick for the wet, grey mists of his native land.

'Along the Delaware the winds will generally give relief, but deeper inland the heat can be something fierce.' In his first concession to the warmth, Humpflinger removed his cap and stuffed it into his jacket pocket.

They continued their passage in the muggy heat of the New World. Boundless stopped to wipe his brow with a soiled handkerchief, sweat trickling down his neck in the hot sun. A cloud of mites swarmed around his face, and he swatted vigorously as he proceeded, irritated by the troublesome insects. His companion gave no heed to the swarms, seemingly lost in thought.

They proceeded along a shaded street lined by a ship repair yard, a cordage factory, some warehouses, and the fenced premises of a wainwright. The yards were opening for the day's business. Tradesmen dressed in leather aprons touched a finger to their straw hats or called out a greeting as the companions strolled by. The day was growing hotter, and Boundless transferred the heavy greatcoat back to the first arm, wishing he might slake his thirst.

Humpflinger evidently had the same thought as he detoured towards an iron pump standing amidst a patch of weeds. 'Cup your hands, Joshua,' he instructed, pumping the handle.

Boundless did so, drinking gratefully from the cool water. He returned the favour as Humpflinger drank thirstily and splashed water onto the back of his neck.

Refreshed, they resumed walking along a brick thoroughfare partly overgrown with grass and lined with small manufactories. 'There is much industry,' Boundless remarked as they passed, by his calculation, a fourth carpentry shop within the space of ten minutes.

'The ships require much in the way of supplies. But there is also great demand from the town and from the northern and southern colonies. A skilled joiner may command a handsome salary and will be much in demand.'

They stood aside as a freight wagon creaked past, transporting a cargo of unvarnished chairs and stools. 'They will be bound for export like as not—whether to the north or south,' said Humpflinger, touching his forehead in response to the driver's raised whip.

Walking past a brick factory, they left behind the rows of commercial premises and came into full view of the Delaware. Boundless stopped to draw breath—regretting the loss of shade as they emerged into the bright sunlight. In the middle of the river a square-rigger proceeded downriver under full canvas. The billowing sails reflected in the sunlight as the ship dipped gracefully on the glittering tide. Even as he admired the fluttering jib and taut staysails, he was oppressed by a vivid image of the *Patience* and the wretchedness of the manacled transports in its dark, oppressive hold. The reminder drew a shiver in spite of the humid air.

'They carry tobacco and food back to the mother country,' said Humpflinger, following his gaze. 'And return slaves and manufactories to the colonies.'

Leaving the yards behind, they followed the path where it ran along the grassy margin of the river. Boundless sweated profusely from the unaccustomed exercise after so long at sea. To his relief, a freshening breeze from the river gave succour from the pestilential mites. A man poling a shallop close in-shore hailed them, the two companions turning to watch as the boat traversed slowly upriver. The deck was heaped with loose sheaves of corn, turnips and beetroots. A woman in a linen cap and dark-grey cape sat perched on top of the turnips, nursing a baby at her breast. She looked steadily in their direction as the boat poled slowly upstream towards the port.

As they came abreast of a battery Humpflinger called a halt. 'I had intended us to walk as far south as the point,' he said. 'It lies two miles further along the river. However, given the heat of the day, it might be wise to proceed directly to the second leg of the journey, which is to our east.' He pointed in the direction.

'Second leg?'

'To the point being one; and from thence across to the Schuylkill being the second. East to Cob's Creek, third, and north to the ferry, the fourth. And, from thence, through the city and back to the landing.

'Indeed, I had thought the tour impromptu, but I see now it has four legs and an onion for a head.' Boundless smiled in spite of his discomfort in the humid air.

Humpflinger acknowledged the quip—by his face and manner taking not the least offence. 'It is a route I have walked before. It provides a perspective on the town and surrounds. Is it too far? The whole I calculate at twelve miles—the amended whole.'

'Pray continue, friend. I need the exercise. I have been cramped on board ship for too long. The fresh air, although exceedingly warm, is a tonic, I assure you. You are very well acquainted with the countryside, Theo,' he said as they struck away from the Delaware and followed a footpath through the grass. 'Did you say you were from the city?'

'I hail from Concord—in the New Hampshire colony.'

'What brought you, then, to Philadelphia?'

'I was apprenticed to a trade. The labour didn't sit with me. So, I ran away to see more of the world.'

Boundless nodded. 'We have it in common. It was why I took myself off to London.'

'Once here,' continued Humpflinger, 'I found hire with a wheelwright on Front Street, near the port. On free days I walked around the city to better acquaint myself with its environs.'

'And how did you come to find occupation as a boatman—in Maryland?'

'A chance meeting, much like our own, which took me to a colony I was eager to see. After two years on the boat, Captain Taysick gave me leave to visit my parents and I am now on the return.'

'Your parents did not try to prevent you leaving again?'

'My father did not see the point.'

Thus, engrossed in conversation, they arrived at the river, crossing numerous small creeks and freshets along the way.

'The Schuylkill,' said Humpflinger as they paused to take in the broad flow. 'It runs north to south and bounds Philadelphia to the west as does the Delaware to the east.'

'And the name again?'

'*Sku-kill*. After the Dutch. Come. The ferry is but a half- mile north.'

'*Skool-kill*' Boundless repeated, following after.

They had barely proceeded—following a wagon path parallel to the river shore—when Humpflinger hurried to the water's edge. 'Ahoy!' He waved his arms energetically to attract the attention of a man poling a skiff upstream. He carried on a brief, shouted conversation with the boatman. 'He will take us across for a shilling each,' he said, turning to Boundless. Cupping his hands to his mouth he called out across the water. 'A shilling, both!'

'A shilling sixpence!' came the shouted reply.

'Done!' Humpflinger turned to Boundless. ''Twill save us the distance to the ferry, and sixpence into the bargain.'

The man poled the skiff to the bank and they climbed aboard, the small craft rocking perilously as they took up position on the planks. The boatman waited as the two companions pooled together pennies to make up the required fare.

'Hold tight!' Pocketing the coins their pilot shoved off against the bank. Standing skilfully athwart the planks he poled the small vessel out into the stream.

'We be obliged, friend,' said Theodore, introducing himself and Boundless.

'Good morrow to ye,' the man answered. 'I be Joseph of Went's Farm.'

'Just Joseph?'

'Aye.'

Humpflinger cast a covert glance at Boundless. 'Joseph the Just,' he whispered.

A quarter way across, the man dispensed with the pole, swapping it for a pair of oars. Sitting down on a small thwart, he energetically paddled the skiff the remaining distance to the far shore. Without a word, Joseph set them down on the bank before pulling out into the stream again.

'Good morrow to you, friend Joseph!' Humpflinger called cheerily as the man turned the skiff to point upstream.

JOKING AT THE FELLOW'S laconic demeanour, they headed in a north-west direction, following a track where it wound through the grass. Boundless estimated they had been walking for the best part of two hours. The heat was intense, and he hung the coat around his neck to block the sun. But after a few minutes, the weight was so uncomfortable he transferred it back to his arm again. He gave thanks for a warm breeze blowing across the grass, which drove the small, distracting midges from his face.

They were now in open country, the town behind them. To their left, a bank of woods extended to the distance. He gazed at the trees while recalling the scores of leagues of impenetrable forest seen from the ship. *Who knows if it might not hold all of Scotland, and half of England besides?*

'What is that noise?' He stopped to listen to the sound—a crackling, rustling noise.

'They be locusts,' said Humpflinger, after a moment's pause. 'They set up a whistling and a chirping and will not stop until the summer turns.'

'Locusts?' Bemused by the image of Egyptian pyramids that popped into his head, Boundless wiped his brow as they pressed on. The breeze grew stronger and warmer, fanning his cheeks and making him thirsty again. He licked his dry lips, desirous of another swallow of water. Directly ahead, a stone tower stood atop a prominence. Humpflinger led directly towards the structure, taking leave of the path to strike out through the tall grass.

Following his companion, Boundless climbed to the top of the rise, the heavy greatcoat ever more burdensome. The fortified stone tower, long fallen into disrepair, loomed above them. 'I see you already have your ruins.' He gazed up at the gun slits hacked into the rough stone.

'A defence against the savages—or perhaps the Dutch.' Humpflinger looked up at the tower. 'Unless it were built against the French—or the Swedes.'

'So many nations?'

'The land is much fought over. Even the savages, it is said, slaughter whole tribes over hunting rights to the woods. And now England and France make war on each other on the western borders.'

'We saw militia march by on the wharf. I did not know we were at war with the French.'

'The colonies of England and France be forever at each other's throats over land rights and trade with the Indians. Now France has sent troops into the Ohio River country to build forts. We send our own troops in return. War was formally declared two years past, but in truth, the fighting broke out long before. And both sides have their Indian allies.'

At the mention, Boundless cast an apprehensive glance at the distant woods. 'And the Indians leave the colony in peace?'

Humpflinger sighed. 'At one time there were excellent relations between us. But since the fighting started, both Indian and French raiding parties have wreaked havoc on the frontier settlements. They burn homesteads and murder the occupants or take them as captives. The Assembly has voted to raise a militia and make war on the Indians in return. They have offered a bounty on every Indian scalp. Who knows how it will all end?'

'But Philadelphia itself is not threatened?'

'The Indians are peaceful near to the town. The fiercer tribes keep to the deep woods or stay further to the southeast where the game is more bountiful. Those allied to the French—the Shawnee and Delaware—are the most dangerous. But, for the moment, they confine themselves to wanton slaughter and plunder on the borders. We are quite safe, I assure you. As long as we do not stray beyond the confines of these farms.'

The prominence gave a grand view of the country before them. The port and the buildings of the town lay behind and to their right. Ahead, a patchwork of cultivated pastures was dotted with farmhouses and square-shaped barns.

'Cob's Creek.' Humpflinger pointed to where the broad expanse of meadowlands was cut by a waterway. 'It runs north for a considerable distance and discharges into the Delaware. Those mills you see are for snuff and wood. And that one in the distance, for grain. At harvest 'tis said the mills can barely keep abreast of the quantity of corn. Much of it is exported to England and the other colonies. The quality is said to be excellent and to exceed any produced in Europe. Our path continues there … along the Chester road.'

Boundless shaded his eyes to glimpse where a line of fence posts marked the road as it wound alongside a series of planted fields. Tiny, white-clad figures could be seen moving about the fields as they tended crops of flax, beans, squash, corn, and tobacco. The scene struck him as one of bucolic tranquillity. 'I had but little notion the colonies were so well advanced in wealth and trade,' he admitted as they recommenced the tour.

'The bolder philosophers claim that these lands, once properly brought under the till, will furnish sufficient for the wants of all of Europe. It is already claimed that tobacco from the Virginias is of such quantity that the price will be halved by next year.'

'And Virginia lies to the south?'

'It does.' Humpflinger extended an arm to indicate the woods and marshes to their left. 'And beyond those woods lies our destination on the morrow.'

'Three days, you say?'

'If fortune holds. Four, if not. It be a considerable distance—downriver and across the Chesapeake.'

'Chesapeake?'

'Aye. We proceed down the Delaware to Willington and from thence across a point of land to the Elk. From there we passage by boat downriver and so into the bay and across to the Patty-papsco.'

'The names are most agreeable to the ear, are they not? I have not heard the like.'

Humpflinger considered the point as he led off once more. 'They are, I believe, savage names. Or Dutch, mayhap. Or some squeezing together of several of the European and Indian tongues.'

'Patty-*paps*co …' Boundless sounded the name on his tongue. 'Stirring names, nevertheless.'

They continued in the humid heat, Boundless now experiencing extreme thirst. Humpflinger offered to take a turn carrying the coat, but Boundless declined, feeling it his responsibility. They had lost the path, and the ground beneath their feet was rough and uneven. The dry, withered grass brushed against their legs as they walked. Cutting across in a straight line, they came upon the Chester Road and the row of fence posts seen from the rise. As they emerged from the grass to stand on the road, they found themselves facing a handsome stone farmhouse. The building stood well back from the road in front of an embankment thickly crowned with trees.

'The ferry lies but two miles north-east,' said Humpflinger, leading the way along the dusty thoroughfare. They walked slowly in the heat, following the road where it led past a group of men and women tending a field of tobacco plants. Small children worked alongside the adults as they toiled among the fertile rows. As they drew abreast of the field workers, Humpflinger stopped to lean on the fence, fanning himself with his neckerchief. 'Perhaps a short breather is in order?'

'Agreed!' panted Boundless, winded by the long walk and parched for water. From the close-up vantage, he saw that the workers were Negroes, men and women alike dressed in white smocks and wearing straw hats against the sun. 'They are slaves?' he guessed, frowning.

'Aye. Field slaves. Friend!' Humpflinger hailed the nearest figure, the same desire for water evidently on his mind.

'Yes, massa?' A Negro straightened up at the hail and approached the fence.

The man was strongly built and about fifty years of age. His face was smooth, the perspiration running down his face and throat into a strip of cloth tied about his neck. As he approached, he gave off a rank smell that sharply recalled to Boundless, the stench of the ship's hold. The man halted at the fence, his face impassive. A large scar, freshly healed, ran down one cheek.

'Might we trouble you for some water, friend?' Humpflinger spoke in his usual amiable manner, as if seeking for directions in the city.

'Yes, suh. Water, suh.' The words were spoken so thickly Boundless could scarcely detect the meaning.

'Samuel!' The Negro turned and motioned to a younger man. He pointed to a wooden box protected from the sun by a hempen cloth. The young man, bare from the waist up, took a clay jug covered with a damp cloth from the box. As he bent over to retrieve the jug, Boundless saw a row of whiplash marks criss-crossing the black skin.

The youth approached the fence, handing the jug to the older man, who passed it to Humpflinger. They took turns drinking, draining the jug.

'Morning, massah!' The youth flashed a grin at Boundless and then, as if remembering his place, dropped his gaze, the grin vanishing from his face.

An old woman approached bearing another jug, which she handed to Boundless without a word. Her face was drawn and tired and she seemed to be suffering in the heat. 'Sis down, Mamma,' the older man said. 'Sis down.'

Boundless drank the warm water gratefully. He took a second long swallow before wiping his mouth and handing back the jug to the man, who waited in silence.

'I thank you, friend,' he said, unable to turn his eyes from the vivid scar disfiguring the man's face.

The latter nodded expressionlessly. 'Massah, suh,' he said, taking the jug.

After a few more minutes of rest, they resumed their journey, continuing the post road as slave children watched from behind the fence, running to keep pace as they walked. A young girl with tight black curls held out her hand through the rails, calling out something, her childish words indecipherable.

They walked silently for some minutes. Several times Boundless made as if to speak, but each time held his tongue. 'That mark—on the fellow's face—what was it?' he asked finally.

'The brand of an iron—as a warning to others. The fellow must have tried to escape.'

'It is contrary to morals!' The words burst from Boundles' mouth.

Humpflinger nodded, showing no surprise at the outburst. They walked on in the heat until Boundless again broke the silence. 'It does not trouble you?' he asked, glancing at his companion.

'Trouble me?' Humpflinger looked surprised. 'I am accustomed to it. The plantations could not exist without slavery.'

'Indeed. The indentures, too, are treated in such a manner?'

Humpflinger scratched an insect bite on his cheek. 'Much depends on the master.'

'There is a contradiction, is there not, between what the city purports to represent—the brotherhood of men—and the institution of slavery?'

Humpflinger spent a few minutes mulling the proposition before answering.

'There be many opposed,' he said, 'especially the Quakerish that founded the colony. Equally, many maintain it is God's will and essential to the workings of the plantations and therefore to the prosperity of the whole.'

'And your own opinion? By what right does one man enslave his fellow?'

His companion considered the question with furrowed brow. 'Why, I might deem it right by natural law. Although in truth, I could, with equal merit, claim the contrary.'

'And the question causes no tension—between the proponents of either case?'

'It does,' Humpflinger acknowledged soberly. 'Oftentimes considerable.'

They walked on in companionable silence, following the broad wagon road where it swung in towards the river. They passed by a large barn, a tanning yard, a blacksmith and a ropemaker's yard. They paused at the latter to refresh themselves with a large draught of water from a well standing in the yard. Thanking the proprietor, they continued on their way, stepping aside to allow a wagon to pass.

'Good morrow, friends!' The driver raised a battered hat. Two small children clung to the back of the wagon, their bodies bouncing up and down with the motion of the backboard.

'At harvest 'tis said fifty or more wagons convey grain along this road,' Humpflinger remarked. In the distance, the gleaming waters of the Schuylkill River marked their destination.

'Shall we be forced to wait for Joseph Sixpence and his boat?'

Humpflinger chuckled at the question. 'Nay. There is a ferry to take us across. And there is an inn where we may take dinner.'

Their route took them past several houses standing alongside the road. Dogs on ropes leapt and barked, and children ran out to stare as they walked by. A two-storey house made of fieldstone with a slate roof, prominent windows, and a wooden door caught Boundless' eye. A weathered signboard beside the road proclaimed *The Chester Meeting House.*

'That be one of several where the local Quakers meet to worship,' said Humpflinger. 'There be others at Merion, Frankfurt, Fairhill, and Germantown.'

'It is a fine-looking house,' Boundless said, admiring its sturdy appearance.

'They say that the women, and even the children, may preach as the spirit moves them.'

'They—Quakers—have great influence in the colony?'

'Considerable, yet not so much as before. There be a large population of Germans in Germantown, and they bring with them Moravians, Pietists, Anabaptists, Lutherans, and Calvinists. They sometimes oppose the Quakers, although they share common ground on the question of slavery. The Methodists and Baptists also oppose it.'

'It be a wonder there are any left in favour.'

'There be also Papists, Newlightmen, Anglicans, Presbyterians, Seventhdaymen, Hugenots, Mennonites, Jews and—for all I know—a Turk or two.'

Boundless shook his head in surprise. 'Such a diverse mix for so small a colony?'

'And not to include the Indians, who have their own beliefs.'

Boundless was about to pursue the latter topic when Humpflinger continued. 'It is the legacy of good old William Penn, the founder of the colony. He gave licence to all men to practice freely their faiths without let or hindrance, Indians included.'

'Such broad-mindedness is most uncommon. And most refreshing.'

'To speak of refreshments, we are arrived,' said Humpflinger.

The river stretched barely fifty yards ahead. A ferry boat, moored to a short pier, rocked on the current. A dozen houses and shops lined the road leading to the ferry. A cooling breeze had sprung up and Boundless passed the greatcoat to the other arm. He was ravenously hungry as well as thirsty, his throat parched from the long walk.

'By zooks, but I could murder a yard of ale!'

'Like minds, Joshua. And a bowl of stew to settle our bellies.' Humpflinger stopped outside a tavern. 'I have eaten here several times and can vouch for the table.'

The tavern, housed in a brick building, was small and nondescript. A wooden board hung above the door proclaimed *The Traveller's Haven*. An awning of painted cloth hung over the door. Inside, it was cool and dim, two small windows providing the only light.

A plump, middle-aged woman wearing a homespun dress and a yarn apron around her middle stood behind the small counter in an alcove in the corner of the room.

'That be the Widow Conley,' Humpflinger whispered as they took seats at one of the two tables in the hostelry. The other table was occupied by a bewigged man dressed in a wool coat with wooden buttons. He was smoking a long-stemmed pipe and looked up as they entered, nodding a welcome.

'Gentlemen, what be your pleasure?' the widow asked, in a cordial yet firm voice. 'There be the bill of fare.' She pointed to a plank board.

'First, good mistress, two tankards of your finest ale,' said Humpflinger, loosening the collar of his shirt.

'I can heartily recommend the fish pie,' said the other patron. 'Baked with shad freshly jumped from the stream this morning.'

The widow set down the tankards on the table. 'The fish pie, if it pleases,' said Humpflinger after a nod from Boundless.

'You are visitors to our city?' the other man guessed. 'Elijah Greenwood,' he added, introducing himself. 'Purveyor of fine cloths and bespoke gentlemen's fashions.'

In turn, Humpflinger introduced himself and Boundless. 'I am taking my companion on a tour of the city and its surrounds.'

'Capital.' The merchant nodded vigorously. 'And your opinion, so far, Mr Lively?'

'Entirely favourable, I assure you, sir. Although the climate be exceedingly warm.'

'Hellish, more like.' Greenwood took a swallow of ale. ''Tis the only blot on the Athens of mankind—in my humble opinion, sir.'

'Athens?'

'Indeed. Gentlemen, with your permission?' Greenwood half-rose as if to join them, waiting on their invitation.

'By all means.' Humpflinger pushed out a third chair at the table.

'Capital!' Transferring his tankard and pipe, the merchant sat down, pulling back as the Widow Conley arrived bearing the dish of fish pie and two trenchers. 'You shall not regret the pie, friends. I have had it twice this week.'

'Three times,' said the widow.

'As witness!' With a pleased chuckle, Greenwood sat back in the chair. He took a sip of ale as he watched Boundless and Humpflinger tuck into the pie.

'Any news of the war, gentlemen?' he said.

'The Delawares continue to wreak havoc in the backwoods,' said Humpflinger.

The merchant sighed. 'The *Gazette* reports that the entire country between the head of the Potomac and the Upper Delaware is reduced to ashes, and all those not fled have been slaughtered or taken captive.' He shuddered. 'Death would be a greater mercy. The times are bloody, and hazardous for trade. Pray the fighting stays far from Philadelphia. But come, gentlemen. Enough of war. Let us speak of more pleasant things.'

'You are born in the city, Mr Greenwood?' asked Boundless between mouthfuls.

'Born and bred, sir. And witness to its growth. Just this morning I was taking a turn along the new 7th Street, admiring the many vacant lots for sale. And on every corner new buildings have sprung up. Soon, I have no doubt, we will fulfil Mr Penn's intention and expand all the way to the Schuylkill. Indeed,' he continued as Boundless and Humpflinger conspired to demolish the pie, 'but a week past I heard Mr Morris declare to the Assembly that the number of domiciles within the city had surpassed 2,500 and the number of persons to exceed 15,000. Imagine! It is barely credible for a city scarcely as old as its most venerable resident.'

Humpflinger made an agreeable sound around a mouthful of fish. 'As you say, friend.'

Greenwood wet his lips with ale before proudly expounding the wonders of his natal city. 'The shops overflow with commodities of every kind—from my own stock of fine French linens and English worsted to congestibles from every corner of the world. The market is famous for the quality and variety of its butchered meats and tanned leathers. The trades flourish and mechanics are in demand everywhere one looks.—Did I over-praise the pie, gentlemen?'

'You did not. And the bare dish be testimony.' Boundless wiped his lips with his sleeve. 'I am quite recovered from our jaunt,' he said, looking at his companion. 'What say you, Theo?'

'Ballasted and fitted-out,' agreed Humpflinger, swallowing the last of his ale. 'Another?' he suggested, setting down the tankard.

They happily drank another mug, listening as Mr Greenwood waxed lyrical about the quality of Madeira and port available to the discerning buyer in the shops and taverns. 'You sit, gentlemen, in the greatest and most prosperous city in all the thirteen colonies. Upon my word!'

'You called it the 'Athens of Mankind'?' said Boundless, returning to the phrase.

'Words not, alas, my own, friend. But those of a verse extolling the merits of our noble founder.' Wetting his lips, Greenwood gazed up at the roof: '*Europe shall mourn her tragic fate declined/And Philadelphia prove the Athens of all Mankind*.'

'Bravo, friend, and excellently spoke.' Humpflinger raised his tankard.

Greenwood acknowledged the gesture with a gratified smile. 'The words come naturally to all as love their city.' He fixed an eye on Boundless. 'If you wish to make your fortune, friend, why you have come to the very Xandu of the world. Wealth and the pursuit of profits be the watchword of every merchant and man of business. We have such a quantity of stock companies and foreign investments as to astonish a London banker. I have spoke of the Spanish and Portuguese wines. But consider …' He tugged a folded newspaper from the voluminous pocket of his coat. 'Consider,' he repeated, pulling a pair of hinged spectacles from his vest pocket. He struggled to unfold them with his mouth and one hand while holding the paper with the other. 'Dithers!'

'Pray consider,' he said a third time, peering at the print and reading: '*The ships do bring spices, sugar, tea, coffee, rice, rum, molasses, fine china; Dutch and English clothes, leather, linen, stuffs, silks, damask, velvet. And many thousands of slaves*.' The *Gazette* itself!' He held up the newspaper as warrant. 'And more, gentlemen, more!'

Greenwood balanced his spectacles to continue reading: '*We send out to the grateful world, fruit, flour, corn, tobacco, honey, skins, furs, flax and linseed; fine cut lumber; horses; and wild animals*.' Putting down the paper, he considered Boundless and Theodore with solemn intent. 'Is it not, gentlemen, a most comprehensive list?'

'Indeed,' said Boundless, assenting to the magnificence of the New Athens. 'And how is it administered? Being a new arrival, I am unfamiliar with the workings of colonial governance.'

'On sound principles, sir. Principles forged in the purest mind that ever set foot upon these shores. I speak of Penn, gentlemen, William Penn.'

'And Mr Penn's arrangement?'

'As stands, a governor and representative assembly—elected by freemen as set forth by the founder himself in *The Frame of Government*. I see you are unfamiliar with the work, friend? It is our founding charter and a most worthy document. In its pages, Mr Penn set forth the mechanisms by which the colony is to be governed. In brief, we stand firmly established on three unshakeable rights: of liberty, of popular government, and of justice—that being the right to free and fair trial by a jury of one's peers.'

'And where does the colony stand on the question of slavery?' asked Boundary.

Greenwood carefully took off his spectacles at the question. 'Ah, yes, the great question,' he murmured. 'Well, friend, as a practical man I own to three slaves in my possession. Well treated, mind you, and they want for nothing in the way of comforts.'

'Excepting their liberty, is it not so?'

Greenwood tutted at the objection. 'Without their labour the entire thirteen colonies would be at peril. There are not so many freemen as is necessary to perform all the duties necessary to maintain the colony. The plantations, for instance, would collapse without the labour slaves provide. Who would nourish the seeds or cultivate the plants or harvest the crop?' He paused as if for answer. 'Slavery is a most necessary contribution to our prosperity. Regrettable as it might be in its excesses. However, I do concede that were the colonies ever to dispense with the practice, then Pennsylvania would lead the way.'

'Pardon, but I am not clear. Are you for or against the institution?'

'In morals, against. In commerce, for.'

'But is your commerce not governed by morals?'

'In principle, friend, yes. But in practice, principles must sometimes give way to necessity.' Greenwood stood to his feet. 'A most pleasant and edifying diversion, gentlemen. Now I must return to the cares of business. I bid you good morrow.' So saying, he touched his cane to his hat and departed the inn.

Humpflinger called out a farewell before turning to Boundless.

'An eccentric opinion, do you not think?'

'Did I press him too hard on the matter of slavery?'

'Not an ounce. The colony is half-mad on the question. Entire households be at odds with one another. But come.' Humpflinger pushed back his chair. 'Are you ready to unpeel the onion?'

9

The Athens of Mankind

REFRESHED FOLLOWING THE MEAL, they took their leave to walk the short distance to the ferry. 'We do not depart until the quarter-hour,' said the boatman as they approached.

After paying the toll, they lingered on the bank while a wagon and team of horses was led onto the deck. The boat was long and narrow, flat-bottomed and with hinged doors at either end. Coils of rope and lengths of chain were stacked along the sides.

They began pacing up and down the grass to pass the time. 'To take Mr Greenwood at his word, this Pennsylvania seems exceedingly well-governed,' remarked Boundless, his imagination stirred by the conversation and Greenwood's description of Penn's charter. 'Is it not a marvellous thing—to found a colony and to set forth its principles so firmly and with such originality?'

Humpflinger nodded. 'My father once met with Mr Penn. He called him a great and pious man. The only time I ever heard him use the words.'

They passed by a small house, Humpflinger looking back to admire a maid as she hung washing from a line. They reached an oak tree and rounded it to head back to the ferry. Boundless tugged his collar to loosen it as he ruminated on Mr Greenwood's revelations. The conversation, together with his own vivid impressions of the New World—formed in the space of barely twenty-four hours—left him questioning his former assumptions about the colonies, about which, he now realised, he knew very little, and, indeed, his knowledge of things in general. He glanced up at the noise of a barking dog while struggling to sort the stream of thoughts and observations that tumbled through his mind. The irony that Pennsylvania was founded on rights barely tolerated in the mother country struck him as both sharp and poignant. *Had this Mr Penn the misfortune to declare his principles in England he might well have found himself standing alongside me in the dock.* He pondered the notion, his mind a whirl of impressions.

'I confess, Theo,' he said, after walking for some minutes in rueful contemplation, 'That I feel like a man who has spent the better part of his life staring down the wrong end of a spy glass.'

'Indeed? In what respect?'

'Why, with respect to … not simply the play, but the *stage*. Aye, and the theatre itself, its size and dimensions. Seen from here, every question takes on a new and original aspect, as if the formulations and expectations of the Old Word are being—pardon, *recast* in the furnace of the new. The weight and *feel* of things—I express myself badly—the import and consequence of questions, great questions, are being answered afresh and declared in a manner that is as bold as it is original.'

He swapped the heavy coat to his other arm as he grappled to express his thoughts, his latent political sentiments fired by all he had seen and witnessed since his fraught arrival to the shores of Pennsylvania. 'It truly *is* a New World,' he concluded, his voice animated in spite of fatigue. 'New in every join.' He glanced at his companion, 'Pardon. I show myself a fool in every respect.'

'Not at all, Joshua, I assure you. Your observations, as a newcomer to these shores, are most refreshing.'

They were interrupted by a whistle blast from the ferry. Hurrying back, they took their place on board as the boatman untied the hawser and prepared to depart. The wind had dropped, and the broad river sparkled in the sunshine.

'How wide is it at this point?' Boundless asked a deck hand.

'A half mile, less or more,' came the response.

The crew of four used poles to push off from the bank before taking up long paddles to stroke the ferry through the water. Boundless walked to the front, shading his eyes to catch sight of the town as Humpflinger fell into conversation with the wagon driver.

'We must walk almost an hour back to the Delaware to begin our inspection,' said Humpflinger, coming up beside him.

Reaching the 'Delaware side' of the river they walked off the ferry and onto the grassy bank. A footpath turned into a dirt road, the surface scored with wagon tracks, and they followed this. It was now well past noon and they had been walking for the better part of five hours. Boundless was beginning to feel greatly fatigued from the heat and exertion. The refreshment afforded by the beer and pie had worn off and he once again felt plagued by thirst.

Humpflinger strode effortlessly ahead. 'This is Market Street,' he announced, gesturing to indicate the road upon which they walked. 'It will lead us back to the port, with some diversions along the way.'

As they drew nearer the town, they were overtaken by freight wagons and sundry other conveyances. Two men on horseback plodded toward them, the riders lifting their hats in greeting. Passing beyond the ruins of an old stone wall they entered into the outlying streets of the city. Other pedestrians walked ahead or behind as the tranquillity of the country gave way to the hurly-burly of the town. '7th Street,' said Humpflinger, stopping at an intersection. He pointed to the left, and a row of empty lots for sale. One lot contained a newly constructed three-storey tenement. A large sign proclaimed rooms to let. 'Those must be the ones Mr Greenwood spoke of.'

Houses built of brick or stone and roofed with cedar shingles now lined both sides of the street. Some reached up to four storeys and had balconies attached. A foul stench arose from the refuse piled in the street and Boundless pulled up his neckerchief to cover his nose and mouth. Atop one, particularly odorous pile, lay a dead cat, its stiff body crawling with maggots. To his relief, water pumps were situated at the numerous cross-alleys that intersected the street. At the corner of 6th Street, he took refuge from the burning sun in the shade of a buttonwood tree as he waited for Humpflinger to drink. Across the intersection a new building was rising from a vacant lot—the fifth such construction along the thoroughfare. The sounds of hammering and sawing and the rumble of carts delivering bricks to the site carried above the sounds of the street.

'The streets seem very regular,' remarked Boundless as they resumed walking. 'They seem uniformly laid out—at angles to one another.'

'The entire town is laid out like the squares on a checkerboard. The east-west streets are named after trees, and the north-south thoroughfares numbered.'

'Indeed? A most practical scheme.' Boundless deliberated over the arrangement as they continued, much taken by the logic.

Their progress was interrupted by the passage of a funeral cortege. They stood to one side as four stout men, followed by a group of mourners, bore a coffin across the pavers. Humpflinger bowed his head as the mourners filed after the coffin. It was carried through the gates of a churchyard and into the doors of the church.

An elderly priest comforted a group of black-clad women gathered on the church steps—the darkness of the interior a stark contrast with the blazing sunshine outside. To the side of the church stood a graveyard, the several rows of headstones partially overgrown by grass. The sound of a hymn rose from the interior as the priest escorted the women inside.

THEY CONTINUED INTO THE town Boundless perspiring freely in the heat. '5th Street,' announced Humpflinger, turning a corner. They heard a sudden noise of shouts and jeers. Exchanging surprised glances they quickened their steps, crossing a thoroughfare past a signpost announcing 'Chestnut Street'. Before them, a spacious square, was occupied by an angry crowd gathered in front of an imposing, red-brick mansion. The protestors shook fists and shouted demands at whomever was inside. A line of militiamen, with bayonets fixed, stood guard in front of the building. Several heads were poked out of upstairs windows gazing down on the mob who, in turn, hollered up insults.

'Goodness!' said Humpflinger. He led the way into the square past a formal garden of ornamental flower beds fenced by iron railings and planted with hawthorn. A scattering of large chestnut trees shaded the grass clearing in front of the mansion.

As they stood on the fringes of the incensed crowd a woman turned to them, her face suffused with anger. 'Gentlemen, join us!' she urged. 'My entire family were slaughtered by the savages—my daughter made captive. And all the while the cursed Assembly sits on its hands and does nothing to protect us!'

'They are as bad as the French!' a man shouted, to angry cries.

'These people are all from the borders?' asked Humpflinger.

'Aye,' another man answered, his brow beetled with wrath. 'All driven from our homes by merciless heathen—whipped on by the French, who burn and torture wantonly while our governor drinks wine and sits behind his fine desk!'

The words roused those standing nearby to greater fury. Yelling and shaking their fists, they pressed forward, causing the nervous guards to raise bayonets.

'Come, Boundless. Let us depart. I fear this may turn to violence.'

As he followed his companion, Boundless turned to stare back at the building. In spite of the noisy crowd that besieged it, he was much taken by its singular elegance. He shaded his eyes to take in the whole, gazing up at where the tiered façade culminated in a cupola and spire. 'Upon my word, that is as handsome a building as my eyes have seen. What say you, Theo?' It took him a moment to realise his companion was no longer by his side, the latter having continued up the street to a small tavern, where he stood peering in through the window.

'That is where the governor resides, no doubt?' he asked, hurrying to join his friend.

'Reside? No. It is the State House where he meets with the Assembly to discuss the affairs of the colony. The people you saw have fled the backwoods with their lives and precious little else. The city is full of such. They depend on charity and are reduced to sleeping on the streets. They are enraged because the Assembly seems powerless to halt the depredations of the Indians.'

'And what is your opinion?'

'The Assembly cannot find agreement amongst themselves as to the time of day, much less halt the Indian attacks. Mayhap the mob will force them to take action. But it is the same in Virginia. Everywhere the authorities sit in disarray while the savages slaughter entire settlements. Philadelphia has raised a regiment, and so has Virginia. But still the savages raid with impunity, driven on by the French, as the man rightly claimed.'

'The city contains much to surprise,' he said as they continued and the cries of protest fell behind them.

'We be original in some respects, I venture,' agreed Humpflinger as they strolled side by side. 'No doubt in part because we must cut freshly from whole cloth, lacking the pattern.

'Nevertheless, such industry and originality as I see all around me gives the colony great credit.'

Boundless' favourable impressions were reinforced as they continued along a row of houses, each one a uniform two and a half storeys high. Marble sills, white ornamental trims and long, rectangular windows set into the brickwork lent a pleasing, shared symmetry to the dwellings. The harmonious effect was counterpointed by coloured, panelled shutters unique to each house. Pausing to admire the brickwork, he took in the distinctive red and black alternation of stretchers and headers.

'They be reminiscent of dwellings in the finer parts of London,' he said, tracing his fingers over the bricks. 'Although the London houses be not so colourful nor so well met to their neighbours. Is this brickwork peculiar to the Pennsylvania colony?'

'It is very common,' said Humpflinger. He gazed into the distance, an absent look in his eye. 'I should like to visit London one day,' he murmured. 'And take tea with a duke.'

Boundless smiled at the guileless sincerity in his companion's voice. 'They are not as obliging as yourself, Theodore,' he said, laying a fond hand on his companion's shoulder. 'Nor a half so amiable a person, I assure you.'

RETURNING TO MARKET STREET, they were prevented from crossing by a man holding a staff in one hand and dressed in a blue, knee-length coat adorned with brass buttons.

'If you please, gentlemen!' The man held out the ivory-tipped staff. Within moments a richly appointed coach-and-four rumbled slowly past accompanied by two liveried footmen walking alongside. Through a gap in the curtained window, Boundless glimpsed a fashionably gowned, heavily rouged lady fanning herself in the heat.

'Proceed, gentlemen, with much thanks,' said the man, lowering the staff.

He was still gazing after the equipage when Humpflinger tugged his sleeve. 'This way.'

A short distance ahead, a striking church loomed above the tree-lined street. Standing in the shadow of the edifice, they gazed up at the towering frontage and high-arched windows. A gleaming white belfry rose resplendently above a red-brick façade to support a wood steeple where it soared into the blue sky.

'A splendid building,' he said, admiration in his voice.

Humpflinger craned his neck, a puzzled look on his face. 'I do not remember the steeple being part of the church the last time I was in the city.'

'Pardon sir,' he said, accosting a passer-by. 'But when was the steeple added?'

'Why, no more than three year ago,' answered the man—a mechanic, by his clothing. 'It was finished thanks to a public lottery organised by Mr Franklin.'

'Is it permissible to go inside—and to climb to the tower height, at least?' asked Boundless.

The man looked doubtful. 'There, I cannot assist,' he said. 'But,' he continued, proudly. 'I can say with certainty it is the tallest building in all the colonies. The steeple itself is said to rise to two hundred feet.'

'Which denomination is it?'

The man looked surprised. 'Why, Church of England, of course.'

'It is somewhat similar in appearance to the State House, is it not?' he remarked to Humpflinger as the man continued on his way. He stood back to gaze up at the masonry. 'It is truly a fine building. But not so handsome, in my estimation, as the other.'

'You do not think so? The brickwork is particularly fine.'

'I speak from bias. The other being testament to man's ability to govern himself based on knowledge and reason.'

Humpflinger appeared not to have heard, absorbed as he was in the figure of a pretty girl who passed by carrying a basket full of cut flowers.

They continued into the heart of the town, the streets becoming congested with people and conveyances. Indeed, the thoroughfare soon became so busy that Boundless was forced to tread closely upon the heels of his companion for fear of losing him in the crowd. Carts and wagons rumbled along the pavers, the drivers calling out to alert pedestrians as they shook the reins. Boys darted between the conveyances to play hoops, their sharp cries and laughter rising above the clop of hooves and the clatter of the wheels. Tradesmen in leather aprons mingled with serving girls, shopkeepers, farmers, chimney sweeps, matrons and slaves.

Fascinated by the variety of persons and dress, Boundless looked everywhere at once, drinking in the colonial sights and sounds. A man walked by wearing a soft, wide-brimmed hat and dressed entirely in what appeared to be deerskin. He had no sooner taken his eyes from this exotic sight than he was forced to give way to a sweating, round-faced Negro who navigated passage while balancing a carved, ornamental table on his head.

'Do my eyes deceive me or are the Negroes very nearly equal to the English population in number?' he asked, surprised at the number of black faces.

'It may be so,' acknowledged his companion. 'Many are freedmen and work in the trades. Others are still in bondage but allowed to wander freely as domestics or trusted servants. Ah! The market.'

Boundless followed his companion into a brick hall full of market stalls. A thousand smells and odours assailed his nose as they strolled past vendors offering a great profusion of meats, cheeses, fowl, vegetables, fish, skins, furs and imported spices. Humpflinger lingered several times to point to some colonial delicacy or to listen with amusement to the strident claims of competing vendors. In a cleared space between the stalls a slave auction was in progress. A half-dozen Negroes were paraded back and forth for the discernment of prospective buyers. A little further on they come across a preacher standing on a wooden box as he exhorted a knot of witnesses to observe the Sabbath.

Diverted by the sound of a fiddle, Humpflinger darted off to investigate, calling for Boundless to follow. They emerged into a side street to find a throng of spectators standing in the shade of a willow. Before them a small boy vigorously stepped and toed on a wooden plank laid across the stones. The boy's father stood nearby, scraping out a jig as the onlookers called out humorous jibes or tossed the occasional penny. At each toss, the boy stooped to retrieve the coin while hardly breaking step. Laughter went up as a tiny monkey, attached to the fiddler's waist by a rope, gambolled and tumbled, apparently at the behest of the music.

Continuing up the busy street they came upon a coffee house where a group of men were gathered around an elderly merchant as he read aloud from a newspaper. The merchant interrupted his reading to exclaim in disgust as those around him shook their heads and muttered. A man turned to Boundless, his face pinched with disapproval. 'It be one impost after another,' he complained.

'What news of the war?' a man called out to the reader.

'They say the French are again stirring up the tribes,' the reader answered, the assertion sparking much comment and discussion.

'Come, Joshua,' said Humpflinger, heading off once again. 'I propose that we find your haberdasher, and then retire to a good old tavern. What say you?'

They resumed their progress towards the riverfront, engaged in a discussion on the respective merits of colonial and English ales, both men feeling the effects of their long perambulation. Cutting up a cross street, they came across a drunken man lying fast asleep against a wall. Humpflinger paused and signalled to Boundless to do likewise. 'A heathen—a tame one,' he said, in reply to Boundless' inquisitive look. 'There be a fair number in the town. They beg during the day and get drunk in the gin houses by night.'

The sprawled sleeper wore a felt hat twined about with a gaudy array of coloured ribbons and stuck feathers. Greasy black hair fell in lank strands from beneath the hat brim. Two brown, naked legs stuck out from under a threadbare blanket the sleeper had drawn about himself. In one hand he clutched an empty bottle of spirits as he snored, oblivious to the hum of the nearby streets.

'So, this be the New World Aboriginal?' Boundless stared at the sleeping figure, perplexed at the contrast between the pitiful creature in front of him and the fearsome savages discussed in hushed tones aboard the *Patience*. 'He strikes me as neither fierce nor painted.'

'The wild ones, I assure you, be considerably different and, as such, to be avoided at all costs. Though not, perhaps, so different as to altogether confound similarity.'

Their attention was drawn by a shout from further up the narrow street. Pedestrians stood aside to allow passage to a procession of Negroes. The two-dozen men, women and children were yoked together at the waist by a single rope that yoked them in file. The Negroes stared straight ahead as they drew level, their eyes set on the distance. Some of the women carried infants at their breasts. One man turned to look directly at Boundless as he shuffled past, his eyes large in his head. An overseer with a musket under one arm ushered the line through the street. Two more armed men brought up the rear.

'New slaves from the Indies,' remarked Humpflinger. 'To be sold at the market and shipped to the southern plantations, like as not.'

Boundless gazed after the slaves as they passed, a sharp jolt of fellow feeling rousing both pity and anger in his breast. Around him, the street had resumed its usual activity, the strollers and tradesmen going about their business. Humpflinger had walked some distance ahead, stopping to look back for Boundless as he was about to turn a corner. He hurried after, the stark reminder of his own prescribed fate clouding his mood and hardening his resolve to leave the colony behind as soon as was humanly possible.

10

A New Man

A s they drew nearer to the landing, the streets inclined downwards, becoming more random and congested—the regulated squares of the upper town disappearing amidst a profusion of alleys and by-ways that branched off from the main thoroughfare. A breeze had sprung up, carrying with it the smell of salt and tar. Through a gap in the buildings, he glimpsed the topmasts of ships anchored in the river. The sight inspired vigilance and a sense of apprehension as he covertly inspected the faces of individuals coming towards them. A group of sailors emerged, laughing and jostling, from the doorway of a tavern. They turned to admire a passing servant girl before starting off in the same direction as themselves.

More sailors issued from another tavern, and he averted his gaze, fearful lest any were from the *Patience*.

'Where now be our destination?' he asked, made anxious by the presence of the noisy, bantering deckhands.

'We are bound directly to the haberdasher off Elfreth's Alley.'

'And is it very much further?'

'Very near, Joshua. Very near.'

They passed by a group of redcoats lolling around a wooden bench. One used the seat as a footstool as he scraped mud from his boot with a bayonet. The man looked up in his direction, the idle glance increasing his sense of alarm.

Humpflinger had stopped at a crossroads to look up and down the various laneways. 'The saltbox,' he said, pointing to where a large, painted sign hung above a wooden shopfront: *Abercrombie and Sons, Outfitters and Purveyors of Quality Goods and Clothing*. They proceeded along the street towards the store, his companion nodding to sundry individuals as they passed by. 'Good morrow,' he called out amiably to one and all.

'With your permission, Joshua, I shall wait for you here.' Humpflinger seated himself on a wooden bench across from the shop. 'Tell them that you be engaged to man a riverboat. They will fit you out in the proper fashion.' Fishing a tinderbox and a twist of tobacco from his pocket, he settled comfortably back against the bench. At that moment he seemed, to Boundless, the most contented man in all the world.

When, a quarter-hour later, Boundless emerged to present himself for inspection, he found that his companion had dozed off, his head slumped onto his arm. He shook him gently by the shoulder. 'What be your opinion, Theo?'

Humpflinger yawned and blinked as Boundless stretched out his arms to display the sleeves of the coat. The garment, made of blue gabardine, reached down to his knees. Beneath it, he wore a bleached linen shirt, tied with a beige neckerchief around the collar.

The assemblage was continued by loose-fitting trousers sewn from sailcloth, and a pair of new, square-toed leather shoes topped with brass buckles. A knitted wool hat, similar to Humpflinger's own, completed the transformation. He had transferred the precious gold coins to a soft, deer-skin pouch that hung from his neck by a leather cord, the pouch tucked safely inside the shirt.

'Do I pass muster?' he asked, his expression one of mingled pride and embarrassment.

'Splendid, Joshua, quite splendid,' praised Humpflinger, scrutinising him from head to toe. 'Indeed, you stand as the very emblem of a boatman. All that you lack is an oar.'

Boundless fingered his lank hair and wispy beard. 'A shave before supper?'

A half-hour later, he stared at his reflection in the looking glass provided by the barber. The change in appearance, from escaped felon to tonsured colonial, was so complete that he hardly knew himself. It was probable, he calculated, that the fearsome Queezley himself could pass him by in the street and be none the wiser for it. ''Tis true,' he said to his reflected self, 'that clothes do indeed make the man.'

THEY RETRACED THEIR STEPS through the streets, Boundless carrying his old clothes bundled under one arm. Refreshed by the shave and confident in the anonymity afforded by his new dress, he felt optimistic for the first time since his arrival in the colony. Relaxing his former vigilance, he cheerfully returned the nods of passers-by, eagerly looking forward to a hearty meal and a pitcher of ale.

He stopped suddenly as they passed by a brickworks. 'A moment,' he said.

A fire burned in a kiln in the deserted yard. Walking up to the kiln he consigned his former clothes to the flames, piece by piece, until he was left with only the greatcoat. He was about to toss in this garment when he muttered to himself. Rummaging through the pockets he rescued two objects before heaping it, too, onto the flames. As the coat smouldered into flame, he watched with the melancholy realisation that the last remaining connection to his former life was consuming to smoke and ashes.

'Did you forget to remove something?' Humpflinger asked, curious about the objects Boundless had retrieved from the greatcoat pocket.

Boundless glanced down at the objects in his hand. 'These two,' he said, handing the scrimshaws to his companion.

Humpflinger examined the artefacts with expressions of admiration, much as Boundless himself had done on first being shown the skill aboard the *Patience*.

'This one is mine,' said Boundless, embarrassed by the pleasure he took in acknowledging his creation. 'The other is by the sailor who taught me the method.'

Humpflinger handed back the objects. 'They are fine examples of the art. I have encountered it before but rarely in such picturesque detail.'

'Take this one—as a token of friendship. It was, and remains, my first attempt at the skill.'

As Humpflinger started to protest, Boundless closed his companion's fingers around the object. 'I insist, my dear Theodore. And what is more, I would be obliged if you would join me as my guest in the consumption of a very large beefsteak.'

'Indeed, Joshua, I should be most pleased. Aye, and I know the very tavern.'

THE TWO SPENT THE remainder of the afternoon cementing their friendship as they dined and drank at a port-side tavern. Around them, the tables were crowded with fishermen, coopers, sailors, dock workers, shipwrights, tanners, and brick makers, all feasting heartily on trenchers of ham, venison, salt shad, pepper pot soup, and roasted pigeon, washed down with jugs of punch, cider and ale. Buoyed by his impending departure and the prospect of employment, Boundless feasted and drank freely, enjoying the rough intimacy of the crowd and the convivial fellowship of his companion.

During the course of the evening, he quizzed Humpflinger on every aspect of the manners and customs of the New World. He noted with admiration his companion's frankness in voicing his opinions, Humpflinger seemingly indifferent to the censure of others in the noisy tavern.

'Your colonial manners be original in many respects,' Boundless acknowledged, following a minute comparison of dining habits and the preferred order of fare. 'Although the over-abundance of hot peppers in the diet is surely not to be commended.'

The conversation then turned to conventions between males and females—Boundless taking the occasion to remark upon the manners of colonial women. 'I have observed that your Philadelphia women seem most high-spirited,' he said, recalling a fresh-faced girl in a blue bonnet who had boldly returned his glance in the street.

Humpflinger puffed on his pipe as he considered the question. 'Why, they be natural,' he answered after giving it some thought.

Boundless laughed. 'Why, so they are! *Natural!*'

He paused to allow a serving boy to refill the cider jug. 'And what of England? Be it benevolent or harsh in its governance?'

'Generally, in most matters, Parliament lets us be,' answered Humpflinger, waving aside the offer of another trencher of pork. 'But in the manner of taxation and regulation, it be a sore vexation to many. Nevertheless, as is truly said, the Redcoats protect us from the French—and the savages.'

'But is there no unhappiness with rule by a parliament so distant? Colonial Englishmen strike me as altogether more ... *independent* in their relations with authority.'

'I cannot say of a certainty. There is great sentiment in favour of the Crown generally throughout the colonies; although, in truth, there has been some talk this past year of native government.'

'As is right and proper.' Boundless raised the tankard. 'A toast!' he proclaimed boldly. 'To native rule!' Several of the men seated nearby raised mugs—whether out of sympathy or convivial good spirits he could not tell. He drained the tankard, feeling merry and a little light-headed.

'You, yourself, Theodore, are most natural!' he declared, deciding, in the warm cider-glow, that colonial Englishmen were of a type far superior to their cautious, island-bred cousins. 'Come, friend, another glass!'

The two stumbled out from the tavern well past the supper hour, swearing vows of eternal friendship as they staggered, arm-in-arm, through the streets. After some confusion as to direction, they found their way to Humpflinger's lodgings in a nearby hostelry. Declining his companion's suggestion of one more tankard 'to see them safely through the night,' Boundless threw himself down on the shared bed. Immediately, his head began to spin. He groaned in misery. 'Are we on board ship?' He groped for the chamber pot. 'Theo—Mr Humpflinger, how fares your head?' He turned to his companion only to find him fast asleep, breathing as peacefully as a new-born babe.

11

A Babble of Tongues

EARLY NEXT MORNING, THE two sat in sober silence as they shared a breakfast of cold pork, boiled eggs, milk and bread next to the smouldering embers of the fire. Barely able to swallow a mouthful, Boundless winced at the throbbing in his head while fervently wishing he could retire back to the warm bed. He sipped at the strong tea, closing his eyes as a dizzying wave of nausea swept over him.

Opposite, Humpflinger did no more than peck at the food, taking up a chunk of pork and setting it down again. Wrapping up the pork in a strip of cloth, he pocketed it for later in the day, advising Boundless to do the same. He toyed with the pipe but, unusually, thrust it back in his pocket. Following a glance out the window at the lightening sky, he rose slowly to his feet. 'It is time to proceed,' he announced—his sombre tone indicating that he, too, was heavily influenced by the lingering effects of the cider.

The dawn air was chill and damp as they made their way through the streets. Boundless shivered and drew the gabardine jacket tightly around his body whilst ruefully recalling the discarded greatcoat. The exercise and the fresh air had the advantage at least, he conceded, of dulling the brain to the effects of the cider and he slowly began to feel more alive as they continued through the deserted streets.

It was still barely half-light when they arrived at the river and began a search for their vessel. The port was largely silent, the various wharfs deserted save for the occasional glow of a watchman's lantern. The berthed ships rocked gently on the rippling tide, the only sound the creak of the hawsers or the splash of waves against the wharf. Boundless kept watch for the *Patience*, trying to remember where it was berthed. As they rounded a storage shed, he sighted the vessel tied up to the wharf. The ship seemed innocuous in the morning calm, the empty deck and tidy rigging giving no indication of the misery it transported. His eyes detected no sign of activity on board. Nevertheless, he experienced a twinge of anxiety and increased his pace.

They arrived at a two-masted, square-rigged vessel, approximately seventy feet in length. Humpflinger led the way on board, doffing his hat to a group of passengers huddled at the rail. Following a brief conversation with a deckhand, he turned to Boundless. 'Bid you farewell to Philadelphia, Joshua. We leave on the tide.'

As Humpflinger resumed talking to the deck hand, Boundless made his way to the gunnels to gaze at the *Patience* where it swung gently against the hawser. A light appeared on the deck. Wretched memories filled his thoughts as he watched the solitary, moving light. The unendurable stench of the hold invaded his nose and his stomach tightened in response. He pondered the fate of his fellow captives—imagining them consigned to yet further misery, whether on a distant plantation or in the bowels of the city. An image of Queezley staring wrathfully across the crowded wharf caused him to shiver. *How chance doth dictate our lives*, he pondered, giving fervent thanks for his deliverance.

Above, a deckhand clung to the yards as he loosened a sheet. He looked up, briefly envious of the purposeful labour. He glanced at his hands in the half-light, reflecting that they were now entirely free of ink for the first time since he was a boy. He was still sunk in contemplation of the fact as early light silvered the sky.

'We lack the wind.' Humpflinger appeared beside him at the rail. 'We shall have to draw out into the channel and hope to pick up a favourable gale.'

A small boat was lowered over the side. Boundless watched as the crew let down a kedge anchor and several hundred feet of rope into the boat. The crew rowed away into the semi-darkness. After some time, those on board heard a hail and saw a lantern swing through the gloom. Immediately, the deckhands began to wind the capstan, hauling in the line. By this method they arrived at where the anchor had been dropped several hundred yards away. When they were directly over the hawser, they winched up the anchor and swung it aboard the small boat to repeat the procedure. Following half-a-dozen such repetitions they cleared the line of anchored vessels, using the foresail to maintain position.

Boundless felt a breeze against his neck as the small boat was taken back on board. 'Wind ho!' a voice sang out.

As the vessel turned its bow to the mid-stream channel, he crossed to the port side to catch a last glimpse of the *Patience*. Unable to sight her past the dark bulk of an anchored Dutchman, he returned to his spot. The sky was now a pale white with flushes of pink. Above him, the sails shook into place as sheets were tightened in the freshening breeze. The deck thrummed beneath his feet. He leaned over the side to catch the wind on his face as the port slipped behind and the journey downriver began.

MORNING LIGHT BURST GLORIOUSLY over the water as they proceeded downstream under the influence of a strong following gale. He stood in the bow, taking a lively interest in the operations of the ship. Impressed by the ability of the voluminous mainsail to command the wind, he watched closely as the busy crew expertly worked the sheets to keep the ship fairly skimming over the waves. Now that his head had cleared from the previous night's overindulgence, a sense of reckless freedom surged through him. His heart leapt with the flap of the topsail and the sturdy bounce of the ship beneath his feet. 'Such rare moods be the final grace of last night's spirits.' He heard Joshua Lively pronounce the words in his ear and smiled at the memory.

Seven and a half hours after leaving port, the vessel turned away from the Delaware and into the mouth of a river—'The Christina,' a passenger remarked of the tributary. Beating against the wind, they proceeded upriver for just over a mile before reaching the settlement of Wilmington, their destination. They put in alongside a projecting bank of rock which served as a wharf. A large *bateau* was tied up next to the rock. The small settlement consisted of a few dozen stone and wood houses, 'We shall rest here for the night,' said Humpflinger, leading the way to the single tavern. 'The food is to be commended, and there is a large fireplace for sleeping.'

The food proved as good as Humpflinger's opinion of it, and Boundless soon found himself making up for the deprivations of the morning as he feasted on trenchers of beefsteak, cured bacon and boiled pigeon. To his surprise, the people around him spoke in a tongue he was entirely unfamiliar with, his ears catching only the occasional word of English.

'Swedish,' explained Humpflinger around a mouthful of ham. 'They be original to these parts.'

After dining, they sat at a bench outside the tavern idly gazing at the river while Humpflinger smoked a pipe. At one point, he nudged Boundless to indicate a group of quaintly dressed men and women descending from a barge at the rock wharf. 'Moravians,' he said. 'They inhabit the upper river and generally keep to themselves.'

Boundless watched the group as they passed by on their way to a waiting wagon. The men chatted animatedly, stopping to exchange a few words with the tavern owner. 'This be a strange and bounteous country,' he said as he observed the conversation. 'Abundant in tongues as well as in fish and game.'

'You will not hear much of English spoken beyond this point. You are more likely to encounter the Dutch, Swedish, German—or heathen.'

'And the Aboriginals—do they share the one speech?'

'Far from it. 'Tis said the heathen speeches be as various and divergent as the tongues of Europe.'

'Is such a multitude of tongues not a cause of great confusion?'

Humpflinger yawned. 'People use hand signs to communicate with each other.' Settling back in the chair, he closed his eyes. Boundless followed suit a few minutes later, still wondering at the babble of colonial tongues.

THE REMAINDER OF THE day was spent preparing for the next stage of the journey. Humpflinger, who was well acquainted with the passage, having traversed it twice previously, advised that the route would be through the woods to the Elk River, some eighteen miles distant. 'Foot is preferable to wagon, and faster. Not to mention easier on the bones. But Mr Jameson insists on taking a cart for the return.'

'Return?'

'Aye. He accompanies us only as far as the river—where he will fetch back passengers and cargo.'

'Through the woods, you said? Are we likely to encounter any of the wild inhabitants?'

Humpflinger shook his head. 'They are mostly driven from the area. The ones that remain are peaceful.'

They strolled through the streets to a trading post where, under the tutelage of his more experienced companion, Boundless purchased a pair of deerskin moccasins, a leather jerkin, a jack knife and a spare wide-brimmed hat made of felt. Completing his transition to colonial man, he further purchased a blanket roll to wrap himself in at night or in cold weather; a wooden canteen to carry ale; and a large knapsack made of tanned cowhide and with a leather strap to carry all the additions. Taking Humpflinger's advice, he purchased a flintlock pistol together with a quantity of black powder, a powder horn and a handful of lead balls. He weighed the pistol in his hand, grasping the butt and pointing it into the distance.

'One is as well to be prepared,' said Humpflinger, watching. 'Thieves and footpads be as dangerous, or more so, than the heathen.'

'I am barely familiar with the weapon,' Boundless admitted, putting it into the knapsack. 'A foe might stand safest directly in front of the muzzle.'

'The noise alone will frighten the wits of any lurking scoundrel. A walk along the river before dining?'

Over a long, leisurely supper Humpflinger described the companions who would join them on the morrow. 'They are fine fellows and able boatmen. In truth, I had expected to find them already waiting. With luck they will arrive from New York by tomorrow's packet.'

Next morning, after the two had finished breakfast, Humpflinger went to speak to the inn keep. He returned carrying a heavy canvas sack over one shoulder. 'Provisions,' he said. 'Cuts of pork, cold beans, corn mush, and some hasty pudding. That should carry us through until we reach the Elk where a boat will be waiting.'

'And the expense?' asked Boundless, keenly aware of his dwindling supply of coins.

'The inn keep will add it to our bill. Be sure to fill the canteen with ale before we leave.' He passed an empty sack to Boundless. 'Let us divide the provisions. It will make it easier on the road.'

They went outside to a fine, sunny morning. The packet not yet being arrived, they took a stroll around the village, stopping to converse with a farmer who spoke some English. 'He confirms that the heathen in these parts be either friendly or gone,' said Humpflinger having asked the question to reassure Boundless. They returned to the tavern to see a sloop berthed at the rock wharf alongside the ferryboat.

'They have arrived!' said Humpflinger. 'Come, Joshua. Meet your sterling boatmates.'

12

A Passage Through the Woods

JOSHUA LED THE WAY back to the tavern where three men stood conversing around a sturdy, two-wheeled cart. A pair of oxen stood in the yoke.

'Why,' said one, looking up, 'Here be Humpflinger!'

'Gracious! At last. Good old Theo!' Clearly pleased to make reacquaintance, the men gathered around to pump Humpflinger's hand and clap his shoulder.

'Good morrow, friends!' called Humpflinger, vigorously shaking hands.

'And who be this?' One of the men looked at Boundless.

'An honest man and, God willing, a member of our merry crew. Mr Lively, I present for your dubious edification—Mr Thompson. Mr Cassidy. And Mr Jameson. Pirates all.'

The men laughed at his description. 'Aye, and peerless rogues!' they added as they shook hands with Boundless.

Humpflinger looked around. 'Where is Mr Turlington?'

'Inside, with the inn keep. But come, Theo, sit down, and tell us what adventures since last we met?'

Boundless sat down in the dry grass to listen as his new companions bantered about taverns or wagered on the prospect of fine weather for the passage through the woods. They seem fine, decent fellows, he thought, greatly liking the informality of colonial manners. After a short wait a fourth man—Turlington, he guessed, came out of the tavern, chewing on a chicken bone.

'Where the blazes is Harry?' he asked, frowning, as he approached and surveyed the waiting faces.

'Pickled in rum like as not,' said one of the men to guffaws.

Turlington flung away the chicken bone. 'Cap'n Taysick will be best pleased,' he said, shaking his head.

'Then all the more room for Mr Lively,' said one of the men, indicating Boundless. 'A born oarsman, according to Admiral Humpflinger,' he said, the description drawing laughter.

'Pleased to make acquaintance.' Turlington wiped his hand on his shirt before shaking hands with Boundless.

'Shall we wait for Harry at least?'

Turlington glanced up at the sky. 'No use to wait. Harry can make his own way, if he chooses. Is every man set?'

Jameson walked to the oxen and took hold of a leather strap around the neck of the largest. 'Hup, Betsy,' he said, tugging on the strap. 'Hup, now!'

BOUNDLESS WALKED BEHIND WITH the others as the cart trundled along the dusty track the short distance to the ferryboat. The sun was already hot, and he mopped his brow, thankful for the river breeze that kept the mites at bay.

'Good morrow, gentlemen! Fine day for a crossing.' The ferryman set aside the rope he was coiling.

'Five for the passage,' said Turlington.

'And the cart?'

'As you plainly see, friend. As you see.'

As Turlington paid the boatman, Boundless joined the others in tugging and pulling the oxen on board. The beasts were clearly reluctant to enter the boat, bellowing and grunting as the men bullied and cajoled them forwards.

'Stand, for mercy's sake!' Cassidy—a stout fellow wearing a yellow necktie and brown, felt hat, leaned against the cart, perspiration running down his face.

As he waited for the ferrymen to get the craft underway, Boundless took up position in the front of the vessel. The shallow draught boat was flat-bottomed and square-ended at both stern and bow. It had a small, makeshift sail. A boatman stood on either side of the vessel, each man holding a long wooden pole. Boundless unbuttoned his new coat to enjoy the light breeze blowing across the water. The opposite shore was densely wooded, and he could see no opening of any kind through the trees.

'Heave away!' cried the boatman, he and his companion using the poles to push the boat away from the bank. As it caught the current, they exchanged the poles for paddles and raised the small sail.

'The fellow has agreed to drop us off three miles downriver, for an extra thruppence apiece,' said Turlington. 'It will save us a good half-day's walk.'

'What about the road?' protested Cassidy.

'He swears there is a path that cuts through the woods and back to the road.'

Turlington collected the money, Cassidy grumbling that he should have held out for half the amount. 'These fellows will rob you blind,' he complained, handing over the three pence.

AS THEY CUT ACROSS the current, the bow swung constantly down-stream in spite of the boatmen's energetic efforts to drive the vessel toward shore. Taking in the sail, they redoubled their efforts with the paddles—to little avail as the ferry continued to drift downstream.

'There be the mark!' said Turlington, pointing to the trees.

Straining to see, Boundless glimpsed a strip of cloth fluttering from a stake driven into the ground.

The ferry continued to drift, drawing an exasperated groan from Cassidy. 'We are well south of the mark,' he complained. 'A half-mile by my reckoning.'

'Taken,' said Thompson. 'Any settlement to include last night's stake on the origin of punch in the bowl.'

Cassidy harrumphed. 'You shall receive full payment. Whether on the present stake or by other means.'

Despite the strenuous efforts of the paddlers to put into shore, the boat continued to drift downriver.

'A *good* half-mile,' affirmed Cassidy.

'The wager was a half-mile, I remind you.'

'At the *minimum*. Additional distance reinforces the stake.'

'Not so. The wager be a half-mile. Less or more gives the stake to me.'

'Upon my word! He tinkers with the pot to suit his own ends.' Frowning with umbrage, Cassidy appealed to his companions.

'The wager is foolish on both sides,' ruled Turlington. 'How to acquit it unless you have the exact measure, half-mile or no. Is it not so?'

''Twas not meant as an actual wager—only for the gullible to take it so,' argued Cassidy.

'The sum was struck,' insisted Thompson. 'You shall not escape on a quibble.'

'Brace!'

Before Cassidy could reply, the vessel shuddered against the muddy bottom and came to a halt against the bank. One of the ferrymen leapt onto the grass to steady the boat as it sat, half in water, and half on land. The hinged bow was let down, forming a ramp for the ox cart.

'The path is a half-mile back that way,' said the ferryman, pointing. 'Look for the flag.'

'A half-mile! There you have it,' crowed Cassidy. 'On the word of our good pilot.'

'A half-mile, or further?' demanded Thompson of the ferryman. 'He presses the case unfairly!'

'To blazes with your gambles! I declare the wager null and void,' Turlington interrupted. 'I do not intend to walk all the way to the Elk listening to such palaver. Skit! Ye fine ladies!' He urged the yoke forwards with vigorous flicks of a cane switch. 'Shoulder to the wheel!' he ordered as the oxen struggled to manoeuvre the heavy cart up the grassy incline.

Once the cart was safely situated on the shore, the companions shoved the boat off the bank to begin its return journey. Boundless slipped as he did so, taking in water in both shoes.

'Get used to it.' Humpflinger laughed at his look of annoyance. ''Tis stock-in-trade for our profession.'

'Aye. Those feet shall nary be dry from now on,' said Thompson, shaking the water from his own shoe. 'Wet socks and cold toes—what say you, Mr Cassidy?'

'And fingers, Mr Thompson. Toes and fingers, all. And fortunate if we are not drowned into the bargain.'

'Are we well, boys?' asked Turlington. 'We must strike back along the shore afore we find the road. I judge it less than a half-mile.'

Thompson flashed a looked of triumph at Cassidy, who shook his head.

'Haul away, old Bets!' Jameson flicked the oxen, and they set off along the grassy margin of the woods.

Boundless could see no signs of a track in the overgrown grass. He was wondering how they might enter the woods when they spotted the staked flag. Turlington directed the oxen towards the trees. 'This way, boys,' he said in a confident voice. The cart lumbered forwards to where a faint path led into the woods.

'I wager we sleep on board two nights from today,' said Thompson as they entered the dense canopy.

'Not two but three, surely,' said Cassidy.

'Last time it was three,' agreed Humpflinger.

'But we did not have the extra passage down the river.'

'And thus, did not have to fight our way back to the road. A shilling on it,' challenged Cassidy with a glance at Thompson.

'Taken! And stipended to the punch bowl.'

IN THE BRIGHT SUNLIGHT, the oxen plodded slowly along the forest trail, the men walking alongside or behind the cart. Boundless glanced around at the tall, mossy trees, feeling a sense of trespass as they ventured deeper into the lush, primeval growth. He turned to look for the river, but it had already vanished from sight. Twittering birdsong came from the surrounding foliage but, try as he might, he was unable to catch a glimpse of the singers. The thick, green shade made him uneasy as his fancy conjured up fierce savages lurking in the thicket. He imagined the cruel faces as they noiselessly shadowed the companions' every step. To take his mind from the notion, he speculated on how ancient the gnarled trees might be, calculating that they had lain unmolested—save for their savage denizens—since the infancy of the earth. The thought was sobering, and he reached out to hold the side of the cart as they proceeded.

The day was humid, and the cart trundled slowly over the uneven trail. The men walked alongside, yarning and swapping tales of the river. Boundless found himself pestered by mites, which sorely tried his patience. The insects swarmed above the sweating necks and flanks of the oxen as they plodded along. His companions seemed largely indifferent to the infestatious clouds, occasionally swatting a few but otherwise ignoring the pests.

The path was exceedingly rough and liberally sown with tree roots and fallen trunks. The companions were constantly called to clear the ground in advance of the cart or to put their shoulders to the conveyance to assist the oxen over a troublesome root.

Progress was slow and intermittent, and Boundless estimated they had covered but two miles in the several hours since leaving the ferry. He thought of announcing the fact but held silent, cautious of inadvertently sparking a wager between Cassidy and Thompson.

They stopped at a creek to water the oxen and take a short rest. The men refilled the emptied canteens from the clear waters of the stream—with much joshing over the dangers of the practice. Humpflinger alone seemed unperturbed by the prospect of drinking creek water for the remainder of the journey, swallowing an entire bottle at once. 'It does no harm to the oxen,' he pointed out to his companions as they bemoaned the insufficient quantities of ale they had brought with them.

As the sun climbed higher in the sky, Boundless was grateful for the shade afforded by the dense, overhanging canopy. To his relief, the insect pestilence diminished as they ventured further into the shaded woods.

For the better part of an hour, progress was halted by a tree fallen across the path. Sweating, and taking turns, they used axes to cut the trunk before hauling it out of the way so that the cart could continue. He took off his coat and rolled up his shirt sleeves as he panted from the exertion. After allowing a brief halt to recover their breath, Turlington signalled for them to start forwards again.

The portage through the wilderness—so remarkably different to his previous experience of turnpikes, towns and domesticated landscapes, induced a sense of phantasy as he walked and stumbled alongside the cart. Indeed, the contrast between his late life in London and this encounter with the primeval forests of the New World struck him as so remarkable as to surpass comprehension. He pictured the Cock and Hoop and the raucous, opinionated circle of friends nightly gathered there. *What would those friends make of the untutored rustic, Humpflinger?* he wondered, glancing ahead to where the latter yarned cheerfully with his companions. He felt a surge of affection for the artless nature of the young colonial—so perfectly at ease in the wilderness. In an imaginary epistle to London, he praised the youth's unaffected simplicity and unassuming equality towards all and sundry, whether freeman or slave. *Where others act out of Christian principle, he acts out of nature,* he mused, watching as Humpflinger hurried to assist Thompson in clearing a root.

Thoughts of his former friends stayed on his mind as he trudged behind the cart. What, he wondered, would they be doing at this very instant? *Whatever it may be,* he reflected, *It would be hard put to match with this adventure and these fine fellows.* The gulf between the primal forest and the stifling lanes and squalid byways around Clerkenwell Street, home to the tiny, airless print rooms where he spent long days sorting and inking type, struck him as both comic and tragic. He would not, he decided—and the realisation surprised him—exchange the one for the other for all the wealth of India. The confounding notion that his former life had been but prologue to this one, teased and perplexed him as he walked along behind the cart.

His foot caught on a knot of grass and he tripped and fell, throwing out his hands to save himself.

'Are you all right, Mr Lively?'

'I am, thank you,' he said, scrambling to his feet. 'Pray continue.'

SHORTLY BEFORE NOON TURLINGTON called a halt. 'Time for dinner, gentlemen!' They were stopped beside a bubbling creek that skirted a large clearing, which contained the remnants of fire-blackened pits—evidence that it had been used for such purposes before. One of the party was already setting up a fire to boil water for coffee while others rummaged through the stores for the pork and beans.

'How far are we to our destination, Mr Jameson?' he asked, addressing the most reticent member of the party, as he assisted the latter to unyoke the oxen.

Jameson squinted up at the sky as if the answer might be found there. 'Roughly one-quarter,' he said. 'We should reach the one-third mark afore dark.'

'You are from England, friend?'

'Aye. I was indentured as a lad and despatched here. I took a great liking to the country and stayed on rather than face the voyage home.' Jameson unbuckled a leather trace and threw it to the ground.

'And you do not miss your loved ones—nor England itself?'

'No sir, I do not. I have taken a colonial as a wife and am blessed with a fine son and daughter. I be now a Pennsylvanian.'

Boundless lingered on the man's answer as he ate his warmed pork and beans and, later, as he lay sprawled in the shade as the party smoked pipes or drank boiled tea. 'A Pennsylvanian,' he repeated, savouring the term. He made up his mind there and then to adopt it as a designation should his identity ever be questioned.

HE WAS HALF-DOZING IN the shade of a hickory tree when he heard a sharp cry. Fearful of attack by savages, he jumped to his feet, searching the nearby woods for the source of the alarm.

'Pigeon!' a voice whooped, greatly increasing his confusion.

'What is it?' he shouted to Humpflinger, who had armed himself with the flintlock and was busily pouring powder down the barrel. 'Is it savages?'

Flummoxed as to the source of the danger, he rushed to fetch his pistol from the cart. At that moment he heard an odd noise, as of fluttering sails.

He glanced up as the noise increased. To his astonishment he saw the sky darken as an immense flock of birds flew low overhead. So great was their number that, within minutes, the clearing was cast into shade as though a great cloud passed above. The air filled with a mighty thrumming sound as the draught caused by the beating wings shook the branches of the trees. The oxen bellowed in fright and Jameson ran to secure the beasts.

He saw his companions stand a few paces apart to fire haphazardly at the feathered torrent. Cassidy held a pistol at arm's length as though to touch the whirring cloud. As soon as they fired, they reloaded and fired again—the cooing crescendo and fluttering thunder of wings drowning out the crack of the firearms. Remembering his own weapon, he primed the pistol and fired blindly upwards. Pigeons were falling all around him as though it rained birds—whether from the fire of his companions or some other cause he could not guess. The great mass of birds now eclipsed the sun and the entire sky—individual birds lost amidst the noisy, shimmering whole. After a second shot, he let the pistol hang limply by his side, content to simply gawk at the staggering abundance.

The companions became accustomed to the false twilight as they hitched the cart and resumed their journey under the twittering shade of the vast armada. They had travelled for three hours and were preparing to make camp for the night before the last of the flock passed overhead and the rustling of wings abruptly ceased. Whether through skill or chance, the scattered fusillades had succeeded in bringing down dozens of birds—it being near impossible to miss hitting the enormous flock, and the men plucked a plentiful supply for supper. He picked up a specimen in his hands, studying the blue head and reddish breast. It looked little different, he observed, from its English counterpart, save in its coppery hue and stupefying bounty.

'I see no evidence of shot on this bird,' he said to Turlington.

The other man nodded. 'The flocks be so numerous that oftentimes they collide or simply fall from the sky in exhaustion.'

Humpflinger had already plucked and bled six of the birds and set them on spits to roast. 'What do you make of our native birdlife, Joshua?' he asked, an anticipatory smile on his face as he turned the spits.

'I never saw the like,' Boundless confessed. 'The sight surpassed my wildest and most reckless fancy. I still scarce believe it.'

Humpflinger lit his pipe from the fire and reflected on the stem. 'They be a common sight in these parts. Hunting parties are reputed to kill 50,000 or more in a day for food or sport.'

'So many?'

''Tis said their numbers are so vast they do not even notice the absence. I have shot and eaten them since I was a boy.'

'Europe, and perhaps the world, has nothing of the like, I am certain.' Boundless shook his head, still nonplussed at the spectacle.

'The savages consider them a great delicacy and roast them in hot coals. We use them in pies or stews or burnt over the fire like this—' Humpflinger indicated the roasting birds.

The flesh of the cooked fowl, seasoned with salt, tasted little different from the English or, indeed, Scottish pigeons he was used to save perhaps for a gamier taste which he attributed to the arboreal wilderness. The party consumed two dozen of the pigeons, gorging themselves on the flesh while throwing aside any portion less than a mouthful. After the feast, Cassidy, or 'Cass' as his companions referred to him, stoked up the fire even though the evening was warm and humid and the sky still light. 'It comforts,' he said to the watching Boundless.

'Will it not signal our presence?' asked Boundless, still apprehensive of savages.

'Pshaw!' Cassidy waved a hand. 'No heathen worth the salt stays around these woods.—Too close to civilised folk. You have more to fear from cut-throats or bandits.'

'Sleeping outdoors is a novel experience for me,' he admitted as he watched Humpflinger brush away some dirt and stones before lying down in the grass.

'The ground here is soft and clean. And the weather dry. You may sleep in the cart if you prefer, but it will go harder on you than the grass.'

He copied his companion, creating a small declivity for himself in the earth and positioning a sack of beans as pillow. Lying down, he realised how tired he was from the long hours of tramping and cutting through the woods. He pulled the blanket up to his chest and slowly relaxed his limbs into the earth as the others began to snore.

A sense of strangeness pervaded his mind as he gazed up at the darkening sky, an effect enhanced by the soft, shadowy twilight. *What would Joshua, or Will, or Gilbert think of my sleeping arrangements?* he pondered, his thoughts returning to his London friends. *They would consider me a raw, untutored colonial.* The thought both pleased and amused him. *And so I am,* he conceded. *A fresh-air man—not mithered with ink or the London gossip but concerned with shooting my supper and making a bed in the wilderness.*

He grimaced at the romanticness of the notion even while fondly recalling the many tavern sessions devoted to arguing man's original nature and how this might be restored through enlightened government. *And here am I, the embodiment of such primal nature,* he reflected, diverted by the thought.

He glanced around at his snoring companions. *These be all natural men, and in the wood surrounds are men far more natural, far more savage.* The idea preoccupied him as he contemplated the desired extent of nature and at what point nature gave way to savagery. He shifted his body on the grass, wincing at some root or obstruction while wryly reflecting on the hard dirt and its resistance to tavern theory. *Ale and pipes, be one school. And the grass and woods be another—the natural empiric.*

He yawned sleepily. Around him, the birds had ceased singing and the woods seemed hushed and pensive. Far overhead, stars glimmered through the twilight as the grey dusk shivered to the call of a roosting owl. He adjusted his head on the sack and, within moments, was fast asleep.

HE AWOKE WITH THE dawn, groggily wondering if true darkness ever diminished this nacreous, American light. Humpflinger was already boiling tea over the fire while the others stretched sleepily or went about collecting the oxen to harness them to the cart.

'Good morrow, Joshua!' Humpflinger handed him a mug of tea, carefully pouring the brown liquid from a pot suspended over the fire.

'A most hearty thanks,' he said. The tea was slightly bitter but, to his mind—seated on the grass, his stiff body softening in the morning warmth—no drink from a London coffee house ever tasted finer. He sipped at the liquid, surprised at the salubrious effects of his open-air sleep and feeling a sharp appetite for the cornmeal mush simmering in the pot. As he enjoyed the hot tea, he gazed around at the dense woods—his senses keenly awake to the twittering birdsong, the misty dawn and the purposeful movements of his companions.

'How much further?' he asked.

Humpflinger had started his first pipe of the day, puffing on it as he stirred the bubbling pot. 'We should be at the river head in two more days—barring a turn in the weather.'

The forecast proved ominously correct as, a little after two hours start into the day's journey, the sun retreated behind a bank of thick, grey cloud and drops of rain began to fall. The men hastily unyoked the oxen and pushed the cart into the shelter of a grove of trees. Unrolling a length of canvas, they stretched it over the open cart, tying it down over the wheels as the heavens opened and the drops of rain quickly gave way to a torrential downpour. He joined Humpflinger under the branches of a huge oak as Cassidy and the others also found shelter beneath the trees.

'It is fortunate we made a good start yesterday,' said Humpflinger as the air turned cooler. 'This deluge will make the road very hard to pull through.'

Huddled in the blanket, his thoughts drifted back to the *Patience* and the terrible storm at sea. The vessel and its miseries seemed already to belong to another world. 'I note the New World is plentiful in rain as well as in roots and pigeons,' he said, trying and failing to peer more than a few yards into the downpour. The surrounding trees had disappeared behind sheets of rain.

'It can be a trial,' acknowledged Humpflinger. He puffed contentedly on his pipe—as seemingly unperturbed by the storm as by everything else. Taking the pipe from his mouth he gestured with the stem. 'That creek we camped at last night will be swelled to a flood by now.'

The rain fell in undiminished fury for the better part of the morning, running in rivulets across the canvas cover and seeping into the sacks of flour and beans as it poured off the sheet. The dry dirt of the forest floor had churned into a mire before the clouds at last parted and a watery sun broke through again.

'It will be hard going the next few miles or so,' observed Cassidy, staring ruefully at the drenched supplies.

Thompson approached with his hand out. 'Here, I surrender the shilling,' he said, handing over the coin. 'Three nights it is,' he acknowledged.

'And four, mayhap.' Cassidy pocketed the coin.

'It was the storm. Or else we had arrived in two.'

'This shilling denies the hypothesis!'

'It is too wet to proceed,' decided Turlington. 'We had best make camp here for the night.'

'Add one more,' said Cassidy, with a triumphant glance at Thompson.

DESPITE A WARM MORNING and a southerly breeze that helped dry the ground, Cassidy's prediction of hard going proved entirely correct. The men sweated and slogged the next few miles, heaving the cart through sucking pools of mud while slipping and falling in the process. The oxen bellowed in protest at the dead weight while straining to pull the cart over the sodden grass. Cassidy gave a shout as his feet went from under him and he took a header into a swamp of liquid mud. 'Upon my soul!' He knelt back on his heels, coated in the brown sludge, his face a mask of exasperation.

'I see that you have turned heathen, Mr Cassidy!' Thompson turned to the rest of the party with a twinkle in his eye.

'Ad—adorned with mud!' spluttered Cassidy as he rose from the mud bath like a splattered tribal deity. The men laughed uproariously as he used his neckerchief to wipe the mud from his face, accepting the merriment in good humour.

After only two miles they made camp in the wet grass—exhausted from their labours. After a supper of cold pigeon, Boundless wrapped himself in his blanket and, unheeding of the damp ground, fell instantly sleep.

LATE IN THE AFTERNOON of the fifth day, they emerged from the trees, wet and tired and coated with mud and dust. Before them, the river glittered brightly in the sunlight. A small trading post stood on the shore, not twenty yards from a wooden jetty. Smoke curled from a pipe projecting from the roof. A pair of tethered horses foraged on the wet grass next to an unhitched wagon.

'Is this the Chesapeake?' asked Boundless, gazing at the river as he removed his hat to wipe the perspiration from his forehead. Behind him the cart sank into a rut and stopped.

Cassidy laughed heartily. 'By your leave, Mr Lively. By your leave, sir,' he apologised, still chuckling. 'But this be the Elk. It flows into the Chesapeake—which be another matter altogether, friend. I assure you.'

'No sign of our boat,' said Humpflinger, looking up and down the river.

Thompson flicked the dried mud from his shoes with a stick. 'Tomorrow, mayhap. Unless it be come and gone, in which case we shall be sitting on our hands for a week.'

Cassidy frowned. 'That rain may have caused us additional harm.'

'Hi-up!' Turlington swatted the nearest ox as it stood blowing and exhausted in the yoke. 'Hi-up, the pair!' The tired oxen bellowed and refused to move. 'But a few yards more!' He flicked the obdurate beasts on the flank, but still the pair stubbornly held ground.

'Lend a hand, boys.' Jameson positioned himself at the back of the cart. The men strained to move the conveyance out of the rut as Turlington set about the oxen with the switch.

'Haul—ye sons of perdition!'

Pushing manfully, the companions propelled the cart over the rut and the last few yards to the post.

'Thank Jesus!' Cassidy mopped his face, his shirt streaked with dried mud. 'May they grow wings and fly you back,' he said to Jameson.

'Best hitch it, then, to the pigeons,' quipped Thompson.

The door to the post opened and a burly, bearded man stepped out onto the porch. The man wore a tattered velvet waistcoat over a hunting shirt of dressed deerskin tied into a breechclout. On his head he wore a felt hat decorated with a feather cockade. His naked lower limbs terminated in a pair of moccasins decorated with coloured ties. To Boundless' bemused eye the man seemed merchant from the waist up and savage from the breechclout down. '*Hei!*' the man called out. '*Hei!*'

Turlington returned the greeting, his reply indecipherable to Boundless.

'That be the Finnish,' said Cassidy, noting his puzzled expression. 'Turlington can speak a few words—which is as well since our host speaks nary a word of English. But the two get along tolerably well in the Swedish.'

They unyoked the exhausted oxen as Turlington huddled in conversation with their host. Boundless walked over to join them, curious to observe the proprietor from a closer vantage. He stood watching as Turlington communicated with an ingenious mixture of Finnish, Swedish, and, opined Thompson, coming to observe, 'A goodly portion of savage.'

'Well, boys,' Turlington, turned to his companions. 'We be in luck. The boat has not yet arrived. It is expected late today or first thing on the morrow.'

'Thank Heaven! At least we sleep under a roof,' said Cassidy, looking tired and out of sorts.

Inside the trading post, a single large room contained a long table and a stone hearth. An iron pot was suspended over a blazing fire in the hearth. The aroma of spiced meat came from the pot, the fragrant smell whetting Boundless' appetite. The companions ate heartily of venison stew and fruit dumpling, washing the repast down with mugs of ale. Reinvigorated by the food and the warm fire, they sipped tankards of punch and beer as they reminisced fondly over the events in the woods. Cassidy's mud bath was the butt of jests, which the man himself took in tired good humour.

Following supper, Boundless joined Cassidy and Thompson on the porch where they went to yarn before turning in for the night. The air was warm and sultry, and mosquitoes swarmed their ears and necks as they sat on the rough wooden chairs to smoke and drink ale. Irritated beyond reason by the vexatious pests, he was about to retire inside the post when the door opened. Their host emerged carrying a bunch of dried knotgrasses which he proceeded to stuff into a basket hanging from the roof. He set light to the grass from a taper, addressing Cassidy in Finnish over his shoulder as he did so.

'I understood not a word,' Cassidy protested. ''Tis a whoreish tongue.'

'He claims it is a heathen remedy for driving off the pests,' said Turlington from the open doorway as the grass began to smoulder.

'Then why does he not say so—in plain English,' demanded Cassidy, settling back in the chair.

'The Elk flows downstream for less than twenty miles before entering into the bay,' said Thompson, for Boundless' benefit.

Turlington nodded at the description. 'From there it be but a short haul across the Bay and up the mouth of the Papsy-O.'

'Let us hope for a gale that will blow us all the way down.' Turlington turned in the doorway to go inside. 'Good night, gentlemen. One and all.'

'Sleep tight!'

Cassidy half-stood from his chair and fanned the smouldering grass with his hand. 'It may be that it as good attracts as repels,' he complained.

'Where be Theodore?' asked Cassidy, looking around.

'Lost in a pipe, I do not doubt,' said Thompson.

The three fell into a contemplative silence as they watched the sun sink into the trees across the river. Boundless marvelled at the vast hush, which seemed to settle over the landscape with the setting sun. He imagined the same cosmic stillness as it descended across all the verdant wilderness between the trading post and the Atlantic.

'Is it true that only a tiny portion of the land is settled, Mr Cassidy?' he asked, breaking the dusk reverie.

Cassidy nodded sombrely, his face shadowed in the twilight. 'They say the hinterlands are vast beyond comprehension. Mr Thompson here has travelled all the way up to the Ohio and claims there be more country remaining west and east than in the whole world put together.'

'Now, Mr Cassidy, not quite,' demurred Thompson. 'But certainly of an extent to challenge the whole of Europe—or so I am given to believe. 'Tis said, mind, that mostly it is fit only for savages or the buffalo.'

Boundless' ears pricked up at the word. 'You are acquainted with the beast, Mr Thompson?'

'Not within shooting range. But I traded many a pelt in my time.'

'He talks about the buffalo, of course,' interjected Cassidy, a sly grin on his face. The remark elicited a loud and prolonged guffaw from Thompson.

The door of the post opened and Humpflinger emerged carrying a flagon of ale. 'My ears are ringing with the Swedish,' he complained, sitting down on the porch floor.

'Finnish,' corrected Cassidy. 'Or a combination of both.'

'As for me, I shall stick to good old English,' grumbled Humpflinger, drawing on the pipe.

'Good old Pennsylvanian English,' agreed Thompson.

'Unless it be of the Virginia variety,' remarked Cassidy, drawing nods from both.

'Mind, I would be curious to learn a heathen tongue,' said Humpflinger over the pipe. 'It would be a spectacle to see the world as it is in heathen.'

'Why, I expect it would look much the same as it is,' hazarded Cassidy. 'What say you, Mr Lively?'

Boundless sipped the ale, mulling the question. 'Undoubtedly savages have different names—and thus precepts—for the animals and such. They may comprehend the world in a way we do not.'

'Indeed,' said Cassidy, conceding the point.

'Of course,' said Thompson, 'the same could with equal merit be said of the Finnish and the Swedish tongues.'

'Which begs the question,' Boundless suggested, enjoying the porch colloquy, 'of how many times the world could bear to be understood so differently.'

'A capital observation,' agreed Cassidy. 'My head spins with only the English notion of things.'

'The Pennsylvanian English notion,' corrected Thompson.

'My head reels of hop notions at present.' Humpflinger rose to his feet. 'I shall turn in, gentlemen, and bid you good night.'

'I, too, am reeling,' said Boundless, rising to join his companion. 'Good night, friends.'

'Sleep well, Mr Lively,' advised Thompson. 'For tomorrow thou shalt feast eyes on the mighty Chesapeake.'

13

A Coat of Native Hue

THE MORNING DAWNED BRIGHT and clear with such a sparkling transparency to the air that—scratching and yawning on the porch—Boundless exclaimed with delight.

'Did you say something, Mr Lively?' Thompson stepped out onto the porch.

'Only that your New World be marvellously original in respect of freshness. London mornings be stale and grey by comparison.'

'Indeed. Although the winters be quite another matter.'

'The boat!' Stepping out to join them, Turlington pointed to the distance.

Shading his eyes, Boundless saw a longboat, the sail from its mast furled in the still air. He counted a crew of four rowers and a helmsman in the craft, plus what appeared to be three passengers.

'Where is that gale that shall blow us down, Mr Turlington?' asked Cassidy, drinking from a mug of tea as he joined them.

'The weather is as contrary as yourself, Cass. It may blow at any moment.'

Twenty minutes later, the longboat bumped up against the dock. The waiting Turlington quickly secured the thrown line. 'Good morrow, friends!' he called out. 'Four for the return.'

The passengers stepped ashore, stretching their legs as they shook hands and conferred with Jameson. 'Two for Wilmington, one for Philadelphia,' a man said, pointing to a companion. He spoke with a very heavy accent, seeming to exhaust his supply of English with the words.

Along with his companions, Boundless assisted the crew to carry several crates and boxes up the grass bank to the waiting proprietor, who ticked off each item against a bill of lading. Following the discharge of goods, the crew loaded several crates as well as a pile of cured deer hides—'on consignment', explained Thompson, before retiring to the post for breakfast.

'What news?' asked Cassidy as Turlington stepped from the post onto the porch after conversing with the men.

'No luck. They be as Finnish as our proprietor.'

'Not a word of English?'

'The steer master, after a fashion.'

'And his opinion?'

'Four or five hours to the mouth, depending on the wind.'

'Say at least that our ship doth wait?'

'It has sat at anchor these past three days—as I can make sense from the man.'

'Ship?' interjected Boundless.

'Aye. Did ye think to cross the Chesapeake in a cockleshell?'

Humpflinger appeared in the doorway. 'A shilling each, friends,' he said. 'For the victuals.'

'Highway robbery!' Cassidy took out his purse. 'What is the feast that warrants a shilling?'

Humpflinger peered into a jute bag he held in his hand.

'Chicken—a half fowl each. Cheese, boiled eggs, bread.'

'A bag for each?' demanded Cassidy.

'Aye. Collect it on handing over the pence.'

Cassidy went inside, grumbling at Finnish rapacity.

Thompson shook his head. 'There goes a man that happily squanders a day's recompense on ale but will quarrel with the devil himself over the price of a boiled egg.'

An hour later, the companions climbed into the longboat, squeezing into the thwarts forward of the mast. 'Farewell, Mr Jameson!' Humpflinger waved as Jameson pushed them away from the dock.

'Next year—or mayhap the one after!' Cassidy called out.

Thompson cupped his hands to his mouth. 'Avoid the mud bath on the way back! It be the sole preserve of Mr Cassidy!'

'Preserve yourself!'

'Settle yourself, Joshua,' advised Humpflinger as the boat drew away from the bank. 'The seat be hard and the hours awful tedious.'

THE MORNING CONTINUED FINE and fair, the current assisting the rowers as they propelled the boat with just the slightest hint of a breeze. They progressed in this fashion for three hours, the helmsman calling a halt at periodic intervals to rest the rowers.

Shifting his buttocks continually on the hard seat, Boundless had fallen into a semi-doze when a shout brought him awake. Looking to the port side he saw two men hail them from the shore.

'Good morrow, friends!'

The boat pulled into the shore as the two passengers, dressed in plain grey coats and leather breeches, picked up a crate of chickens and another of lettuce. 'Good morrow one and all,' said the elder of the pair as they passed the crates to those on board.

'A fine day, sir,' said Boundless, making room as the older man squeezed in beside him.

'I thank, thee, friend. We shan't steal much room. We merely cross the stream,' the man replied, his tone grave and courteous.

The river was almost a thousand yards across at this point. Boundless could see no sign of habitation on the far bank. Pulling strongly against the current, the rowers took the vessel across the channel, putting into shore at a point a mile downstream. He watched the men scramble onto the bank as their cargo was passed ashore.

'Hang tight!' called Cassidy, raising a hand in farewell as they pulled away from the bank.

'Where in God's name are they bound?' Boundless queried Thompson, scanning the deserted shore for signs of a road or a cabin.

'No doubt there is a farm nearby. They will walk there when ready.'

'Even so, the country appears very wild and deserted.'

'It is the same where we are bound, country not fit for horse or wagon.'

The river became wider as they progressed until the far bank threatened to disappear from sight. Boundless gazed at the wide water, speculating if the most ordinary stream in the Americas did not equal the Thames in size and splendour. He was pondering this when the steersman again gave the order to rest, as the fatigued rowers laid up oars and sat sweating in the hot sun.

'What say you we take a turn and give these fellows a respite?' said Thompson, with a wink to Turlington. 'It will speed the journey and give Mr Lively here a practice at the oar. '

'Capital notion!' said Turlington over Cassidy's groaned protest.

'For the love of God, why in blazes would—'

'Come, Mr Cassidy, Christian charity demands.'

'Christian charity, my foot! Do we demand that the passengers, in addition to paying the tariff, also row the vessel? Answer me that—with your charity!'

''Tis just the one turn, Cass. And you may sit out if you wish. We have our four.'

Turlington explained the proposition to the helmsman, gesturing for the rowers to give up their seats. The two conferred for some minutes, the helmsman appearing doubtful.

'He suspects we wish to work the passage,' opined Cassidy. 'Did I not say it was a mistake?'

With a shrug, the helmsman said something to the rowers who showed equal surprise. Finally, one gave a short laugh and gave up his seat, swapping places with Thompson. The other rowers followed, joking with one another in their native tongue as they surrendered the oars. One slapped Boundless on the back as he squeezed past to take his place on the hard wooden seat.

Boundless grasped the oar, surprised at the weight as he flexed it against the rowlock. 'Go gentle,' he said as Humpflinger took the oar on the opposite side. 'I am a novice to the art.'

'Judge how well it agrees with you,' said Humpflinger, pulling at the oar as they got under way again. 'This be an introduction to our employment.'

'The merest handshake!' called Turlington over his shoulder.

A half-hour later they again exchanged positions with the rowers. Boundless winced from the strain in his back and the soreness in his arms as he took his place back in the bow. 'Is this hardship indeed the means by which we are to earn our keep?' he questioned Humpflinger.

'The wind be our dearest friend,' grinned his companion.

'Second only to a strong spine,' said Turlington, perspiring profusely. He took off his jacket. 'Mine is out of the habit,' he said, placing the jacket on the seat beside him.

'Be you well sat, Mr Cassidy?' enquired Thompson of the half-dozing Cassidy.

'Aye—and mock as ye please,' said Cassidy without opening his eyes. 'My conscience be as clear as my back is rested.'

TOWARDS NOON, THEY PULLED alongside a two-masted schooner anchored in the middle of the river. A jolly boat was tied to a short line suspended from the stern. On the shore behind the vessel, Boundless saw several log cabins and what appeared to be a tavern. They transferred to the larger vessel, scrambling up the side by means of a rope Jacob's ladder. Several other passengers were already on board.

'Are they from the settlement?' Boundless asked as Turlington came to stand alongside.

'Aye. They be farmers, or traders come to sell goods.'

They remained at anchor for some time—the ship's master explaining that they waited on a passenger. After a meal of cheese and hard-boiled eggs, the companions settled down to a card game to pass the time. Declining the offer to join in, Boundless inspected the ship, studying the rig and asking questions of an obliging deckhand. As the sun grew hotter, a stout man was seen to emerge from the woods, walking purposefully. He hailed the vessel from the distance, energetically waving his hat while hastening his stride. Shortly thereafter, the man, who appeared to be a farmer, huffed and puffed as he was pulled aboard the ship from a rowboat.

'Good morrow, sirs,' he said, breathing heavily while doffing his hat to all and sundry. 'My apologies, gentlemen. I was delayed by the birth of a calf.'

'Make sail!' the master ordered.

Boundless watched as the crew rigged the sails fore and aft. 'It is a different arrangement to the square rig with which I am familiar,' he said to Thompson who stood alongside. 'Observe how the sails stand parallel not perpendicular to the keel.'

'Square rig or circular, I know not. You have the Jack Tar in you, Mr Lively.'

'Knowledge but lately acquired, I assure you. And as practical as it is useful. The knots, for example'—he pointed to where a deckhand was testing a bowline—'are of a number and complexity to stagger the comprehension. There be such a variety of loops, hitches, splices, bends, plaits and bindings as to astonish the man who has never set foot on board a ship.'

'I had never given the matter much thought. But it be as you say.' Thompson pursed his lips as he watched the deckhand use the bowline to secure a piece of freight. 'Indeed, it be as you say.'

AS THEY GOT UNDERWAY, a stiff wind blew up. The gale filled the sails and lifted the vessel effortlessly over the water.

'If this blow continues we shall be in the bay before the quarter hour is gone,' opined Turlington. As if to give truth to his words, the vessel heeled with the force of the wind.

A short time later, Boundless felt a distinct change in the motion of the ship as the mouth of the river came into view. 'Ready about!' a voice commanded as the deck crew manned the sheet lines. The command was shortly followed by another. 'Helms A-lee!' The sails snapped and spray showered over the side as the tiller was pushed to leeward. The bow swung into the eye of the wind as the ship cleared the bar and entered the tidal waters of the bay.

'Observe, Mr Lively—the Chesapeake!' Cassidy signalled Boundless to join him on the larboard side. He made his way across the deck, ducking to avoid the foresail spar. A shower of salt spray dashed against his face.

'By God, but we are flying!' Cassidy's cheeks were flushed and wet, his face giddy with pleasure as he clutched a stay for balance.

'Better than eight knots, I hazard!' Boundless shouted to make himself heard above the gale. ''Tis a marvellous fast ship!'

The land fell away behind them as the ship careered through the turbulent waters and the crew trimmed the sails. Boundless brushed the salt from his eyes as he took in the vastness of the surrounding waters, unable to tell if they were still within the bay or launched upon the open sea.

'And this be but a finger of the whole!' Cassidy shouted into his ear as though reading his thoughts.

Above the ship, an immense abundance of sea birds thronged the sky, their sharp cries combining with the wind and the hissing spray. Cassidy tugged his shoulder and pointed to where a heron emerged from the waves, a fish clutched in its beak. 'He fishes below the waters!'

'I never saw so many birds! Except for the pigeon!' he corrected as Cassidy strained to hear. Within the space of several minutes, he sighted geese, cormorants, terns, ducks, swallows, ospreys, herons and several species of birds that were unknown to him. Shrieking and cawing the birds plundered the heaving waters—wings folded as they dived beneath the surface to fish. Egrets and gulls swooped and dipped above the waves, their raucous cries filling the air as they harried the fisher-birds for spoils. He glanced around to remark on the sight and saw Humpflinger sitting on the deck fast asleep, his head hung forward on his chest.

DRIVEN ON BY THE strong gale, the vessel proceeded on a south-westerly heading, occasionally coming back within sight of land. The gale diminished in force as the ship made towards a point of land a half-league off the starboard bow. The vessel held steady against the wind as they approached to within a thousand yards of the forested shore. With great skill, the master held the vessel to leeward as the winds veered one way and another. *The ship is built for these waters*, Boundless reflected, admiring the way the rigging allowed the crew to shift tack as quickly as the wind changed course. A sudden shower swept the deck and he saw Cassidy duck for cover beneath the sails.

He positioned himself near the starboard bow as the vessel's tack brought it closer to the densely wooded shore. Sighting smoke rising from a clearing, he saw a cluster of log houses. Excitement gripped him as he realised that he was seeing his first Aboriginal encampment. Numerous bark canoes were drawn up along the shore, and figures could be seen moving about the lodges.

'A heathen village,' said Thompson, coming to stand alongside. 'They be friendly, for the most part. They trade fish and game with the settlements for pots and kettles and such trinkets as catch their fancy.'

Boundless shaded his eyes to better discern the occupants. 'A man could go among them unmolested?'

'I would hesitate to say so with certainty. It would be prudent to go well-armed and as a party. Your savage be notoriously quick to take offence and is reckless when angered.'

'I observed a few specimens in Philadelphia, but they were drunk or tamed, as Mr Humpflinger assures me, and seemed more to be pitied than feared.'

To his surprise, the vessel dropped sail and, a short while later, hove to roughly five-hundred yards offshore opposite a second, larger group of lodges. A small boat was lowered over the side. Minutes later, a man dressed in a military uniform scrambled down into the boat. He was joined by two other men, both dressed in civilian clothes. A half-dozen crates were passed down. The master gave a signal and two crew members proceeded to row the men to shore. 'Emissaries,' said Turlington, coming up to join them. He set his elbows on the rail to watch the progress of the small boat.

'Emissaries?'

'Aye. Ever since the start of this fracas with the French, the authorities worry about the Indian allegiance and send gifts to keep them loyal.'

'But surely, the war is far from here?'

Turlington shrugged. 'The armies, mayhap, but French agents are rumoured to be everywhere, stirring up unrest among the tribes.'

'Nonsense!' Thompson clucked with annoyance. 'The authorities see French spies under their very beds!'

'And you would know, I suppose?' retorted Turlington.

'The heathen be in number along these shores, and very wild in their habits,' said Thompson, ignoring the jibe. 'They be greatly skilled at fishing these waters—which be exceedingly abundant in fish of all kinds. As judge for yourself.' Leaning over the rail, Thompson pointed to the waters beneath the ship.

At first, Boundless could see nothing other than a swirling sandbank. He was about to say as much when he realised that the sandbank was, in fact, a great shoal of fish, twisting and darting beneath the keel. So plentiful were the creatures that he wondered if it might not be possible to reach down and scoop up a rich handful to deposit, flopping and squirming, onto the deck.

'My old father, bless, used to claim that when he was a boy the waters were so thickly populated with fish of all kinds that you could walk across their backs to shore.'

'I have heard the very sentiment before.'

'Then there may be truth to the claim.'

Boundless leaned further over the side as the clear waters yielded up their diverse riches to his gaze. Fish, molluscs, and rays presented themselves in great profusion—the latter gliding above the sandy bottom with propulsive flaps of their wing-like bodies. He glimpsed a large turtle swimming with strokes of its flippers and a swarm of strange, gelatinous creatures floating limply on the tide.

'There be oyster, crab, bass, trout, shark, whale, and goodness knows what else,' said Thompson, moving aside to make way for the awakened Humpflinger. 'All in plentiful abundance. The waters feed both the heathen villages and the colonies south to Jamestown and further, so 'tis said, to New York in the north.'

'I have feasted on fresh-caught lobster from these waters at home in Concord,' confirmed Humpflinger. 'If we had the time we might cast a net and drag in a few dozen.'

'Of what—lobster?' Thompson snorted. 'A pestilent creature!
The turtle be far superior.'

'Each to each, but the lobster be my preference.'

'What say you we sit down out of this wind?' suggested Turlington. 'My skin is salted to a turn.'

The shore boat returned and they got under way again. Seated on the deck, Boundless leaned back against a trunk, half-listening as his companions debated the merits of various fish—Thompson proclaiming the excellence of trout above all contenders while Humpflinger stoutly defended the virtues of the lobster—'boiled and drowned in butter.'

The gale picked up again, a fresh breeze filling the sails as the ship gained momentum. Boundless yawned, feeling sleepy in the salt air. Overhead, the sails whipped and cracked in the wind, sunlight flashing between the billowing sheets. 'I am as Gulliver in Brobdingnag,' he fancied, idly attempting to reconcile the ordered domesticity of his former life with the sprawling light and stupendous bounty of the Americas. Closing his eyes, he pictured his friends gathered around a letter while exclaiming in loud disbelief at the tall tales of their absent Gulliver. 'They would consider me either a liar or a shameless braggart,' he mused, smiling as he imagined their astonishment.

Immersed in this reverie, he fell asleep—to be roused by the hand of Cassidy shaking his shoulder. 'Ready yourself, Mr Lively. We approach the port of Baltimore. I look forward to getting off this squeezebox for an hour. Rise up, Theo! Five minutes to shore!'

YAWNING, BOUNDLESS STOOD AND stretched while gazing at the approaching harbour. The day was still very warm, and he loosened his necktie. The vessel was sailing up an inlet to where it terminated in a sheltered cove overlooked by a redoubt of forested hills. A horseshoe-shaped ring of clouds cast glittering light on the flat water of the cove—the habitation reminding him of a Scottish fishing village. Several fine mansions sat atop the surrounding bluffs. Two dozen or so smaller houses were clustered along the waterfront. On the flat foreshore, four men cast nets into the water—momentarily pausing in the task to gaze at the arriving ship.

They dropped anchor in the middle of the cove. The jolly boat was pulled alongside as the deckhands formed a line to off-load the cargo.

'Passengers first!' shouted a deckhand, assisting the stout gentleman from the woods over the side.

When his turn came, Boundless clambered down the ladder, clinging on tightly as the ship swung on the tide. The boat rocked underfoot as he stepped gingerly to the deck, clutching the side for balance.

'The saints preserve us!' Cassidy tumbled in a heap alongside him as he took a seat on the main thwart. Thompson, Humpflinger and Turlington followed, the small boat rocking perilously at the shifting weight.

'Shore ho!'

At the command, the four rowers began to pull on the oars, slowly propelling the boat towards the flat, grassy landing. Boundless sat with his knees drawn up to his chest, feeling lightheaded in the hot sun. Greatly desirous of a drink, he drained the last few drops of water from the canteen, reminding himself to refill it ashore. The boat ground against the bottom as the rowers splashed into the water to pull the boat up onto the grassy bank.

'Let us walk to ease our legs.' Humpflinger stepped nimbly over the side.

Boundless followed, stepping onto dry land. 'I am perished with thirst, Theo. My canteen is dry.'

'Mine is full.' Humpflinger held out the canteen and Boundless accepted gratefully.

'Aye, and me.' Turlington held out his hand for the canteen after Boundless had taken a swallow.

'You shall be blessed in Heaven, Brother Theodore.' Cassidy accepted the canteen in turn and drank thirstily. 'Drained!' he said, shaking the bottle.

Feeling refreshed by the drink, Boundless followed as his companions struck out from the landing at a brisk pace. A group of a dozen men and women were gathered under the shade of a gnarled beech to await the arrival of the ship. The men were well-dressed in frock coats and breeches, and he supposed them to be gentlemen of leisure or merchants awaiting in-bound goods. The women were dressed in gowns and straw hats and carried parasols against the sun. A slim young man dressed in a finely tailored frock coat, leather boots and tan breeches broke off his conversation to hail the party as they approached.

'Good morrow to you, gentlemen!' he called out breezily, and touched the brim of his straw hat. He had his other hand on the shoulder of a small boy who stared curiously at Boundless. A pretty woman holding an infant smiled happily as she looked up. The young man returned to the conversation, speaking animatedly while drawing laughter from his companions and admiring glances from the young woman.

The companions trod along a dusty street, passing a row of small, framed houses, each occupying its own, rectangular lot. The street ascended a steep bluff, leading up to a brick church. 'It offers a prospect,' said Humpflinger as he and Boundless led the way. Cassidy and Thompson followed at a short distance, vigorously debating the merits of the Baltimore settlement. Turlington lingered to the rear, having stopped to remove a stone from his shoe.

'What be your impression, Mr Lively, as a new arrival, of the town?' puffed Cassidy as he quickened his stride to close the distance between them.

'It hardly resembles a town, so much as a village. I count no more than a dozen or so brick buildings, including the church.'

'Capital observation, Mr Lively!' Thompson beamed, evidently pleased at the assessment. 'Annapolis, I tell you, is its superior in every respect.'

'But what of the harbour?' persisted Cassidy. 'Is it not a perfect haven for ships?'

'It is very well protected. And offers access for a considerable distance.'

'A trump!' crowed Cassidy.

'Now, Cass, we were debating the merits of the town, not the harbour, were we not?'

'A finagle! One might as well consider the sauce apart from the goose. A finagle, is it not?' protested Cassidy.

From their vantage point at the top of the rise, the small habitation displayed that air of pastoral prosperity which Boundless now assumed to be characteristic of colonial settlements. Each mansion stood each on its own expanse of land looking out to the sea. Behind the settlement, and tiered into the distance, rose the omnipresent woods. In the bright sunlight the quiet town seemed the very embodiment of tranquil, rural domesticity.

Cassidy's stomach gave forth a loud growl, drawing laughter from his companions. 'What is the clock?' he said. 'I must needs eat or perish.' Casting around, he spied a small bank overlooking the rise. 'Here be the perfect spot,' he declared. Sitting down, Cassidy pulled the jute sack from the haversack and placed it on the grass beside him as the others followed his example.

'I was concerned that you grow thin about the ribs,' said Thompson, taking out a portion of chicken. Cassidy, busily engaged in eating a boiled egg, snorted in reply.

Boundless ate a mouthful of cheese, enjoying the warm breeze and the respite from the bouncing deck. Beside him, Humpflinger took out the tinderbox and struck a spark, blowing on the char cloth. 'Save a spark,' said Thompson, taking out his own pipe.

'I confess I look with anticipation to working the river again,' said Humpflinger, gazing thoughtfully at the tiny vessel in the cove below. He drew on the pipe. 'Despite of Captain Taysick.'

'He is bound to be anticipating your own dear self, Theo,' said Turlington, drawing a chuckle from Thompson.

'And we bring him a genuine Englishman!' Cassidy winked at Boundless, a jovial mood spreading among the companions as they digested the meal.

'Scotsman.'

'Beg pardon?' Cassidy frowned.

'Our Mr Lively is a Scotsman, are you not?' said Thompson. He raised an eyebrow at Boundless for confirmation.

'Rather, a new-minted Pennsylvanian, if you please.'

Thompson chuckled. 'I stand corrected, sir. A Pennsylvanian man, indeed!'

'A borrowed coat!' objected Cassidy.

'But a coat that fits,' interjected Humpflinger, drawing a smile from Boundless.

'Nevertheless, the native garment be Scottish tartan,' insisted Cassidy.

'Pshaw!' Thompson vigorously dismissed the point. 'The gravamen of the case and the truth of the matter is that our Mr Lively stands before us well *suited* to his preference. He calls *suit* as a Pennsylvanian.'

He turned to Boundless. 'From now on, as to point of origin, it shall be Pennsylvania and Pennsylvania only. Does that sit well with you?' he asked his voice jovial.

'Indeed, it does. It *suits* me well indeed. A Pennsylvanian in all respects—organic and constituted.'

'The question is settled,' declared Thompson.

'On the word of a Virginian!'

'A protest raised by New York—so noted.'

'Overruled by Massachusetts!' Turlington winked at Thompson as he poked Cassidy in the ribs. 'What say you, Mr Humpflinger—will you tip or nay?'

'New Hampshire, sir, stands with Massachusetts.' 'The ayes have it,' ruled Thompson.

'The proposition?' objected Cassidy, his face flushed.

'Indeed, the learned member scores a point,' Thompson conceded with good humour. 'I quite forget. The motion, sir?' he asked, turning to Boundless.

'That this coat—be indissolubly Pennsylvanian, much as the wearer,' Boundless replied, fingering the cloth of his gabardine jacket.

'Naysayers?' asked Thompson, raising an eyebrow at Cassidy.

'Refusal!' the latter stated, his vehemence surprising his companions.

An awkward silence followed, Cassidy looking upset and out of sorts before the silence was broken by Thompson.

'Majority taken as assent!' he declared. 'Motion passed, New York withstanding!'

'Come now, Mr Cassidy.' Turlington placed a hand on the shoulder of the discomfited Cassidy. 'Be of good cheer. A season of honest labour awaits. What say—friends?'

Cassidy coughed. 'Indeed. Friends. Beg pardon all. I fear I have trodden over-heavily on the spirit of the jest.'

'Gone and forgot!' Thompson pointed to where the ship's boat was returning to the shore. 'Make haste, one and all—lest we enjoy the hush of this Baltimore for the rest of the week!'

They returned to the schooner to find the vessel crowded from bow to stern with more than a dozen additional passengers. Chests and trunks occupied seemingly every inch of the deck—men and women perched atop their baggage. Turlington led the way across the congested deck, apologising as he stepped on a foot.

'Dear Jesus!' Cassidy struggled to find space amidst the overflow of goods and travellers.

'Are we not over-laden for such a voyage?' Boundless asked as they found some room in front of the foremast. 'Such a number of people may interfere with the operation of the vessel.'

'Mayhap,' said Turlington. 'But our destination lies just around the point, and the weather is fair. Do you swim? I ask only as a general matter, not to imply danger from the excess of tonnage.'

'A yard or two at most. I have rarely had occasion to practise the skill. Mind, I have never stood on board ship so much as in these past few months.'

Turlington moved to one side to make room for Humpflinger. 'If—and I hasten to add "if", strictly as an observation—if, perchance, one found oneself in the unfortunate position of being cast into the water, it were best to seize hold of the nearest large object—be it cargo, flotsam, or the body of the ship itself, and cling to that as a means of succour. I was once wrecked off the shores of New Hampshire and saved myself by that method.'

'Indeed,' said Boundless, 'I shall remember the advice.'

The vessel slowly got underway, the sides sitting heavily in the water as the crew let loose the sheets and the helmsman positioned the vessel into the breeze. Feeling someone bump against his shoulder, Boundless turned to find the young gentleman from the wharf squeezed alongside.

'Pardon!' he said.

'Mr Carroll, sir, at your service.' The man spoke with a confident, cultured voice and seemed of a most agreeable disposition. 'And may I be permitted to introduce Mrs Carroll?' The man turned and gestured proudly towards the pretty young woman Boundless had seen earlier on the landing. She sat atop a brass-reinforced trunk nursing the infant, the young boy seated beside her.

At the introduction the young woman nodded and smiled. 'Pleased to make acquaintance, sir.' She cradled the infant to her bosom.

'Mind your breeches, Harry,' she pleaded as the young boy twisted and turned on his seat, evidently unhappy at being confined to a single spot.

Boundless introduced himself in turn, careful to point out his starting place in Philadelphia. The young man brightened at the mention and promptly declared his admiration. 'The finest city in all of the colonies!' He glanced to his beaming wife for affirmation.

Charmed anew by the inherent graciousness and ease of colonial manners, Boundless praised in return the pastoral tranquillity of Baltimore, supposing the family to reside there.

'Not so!' The young man dissented with some vigour, much to the amusement of his wife. 'We come for the diversion,' he explained. 'The plantation offers little in the way of polite society. And also,' he added, 'for the purchase. My cargo has already been shipped upriver. We follow at our leisure.'

'Purchase?'

'Pardon, sir. It is a term familiar to the plantations. I meant the auction. In this instance, three fine specimens who should be capable of much hard work.'

The young man grasped hold of the nearest object for balance as a gust of wind rocked the vessel. 'It is a scandal,' he continued. 'We are in the habit of employing white bondsmen, but they are becoming scarce. And those who arrive are increasingly in demand for domestic and trades. Also, they are not so suitable for field work as Blacks. Harry!' He muttered in exasperation as the small boy squirmed free of his mother's restraining hand and rushed forward to fling both arms around his father's legs. He stroked the boy's hair. 'Will you be a good boy?' he asked fondly. 'I should like to climb the mast!'

'Hush now.' The man touched the brim of his hat to Boundless. 'I bid you safe journey, sir.' Steering the boy firmly by the shoulder, he made his way back to his wife.

Boundless felt someone at his elbow as Humpflinger squeezed into the space vacated by the young plantation owner. 'How say, Theo?'

'One day I should wish to own a handsome vessel such as this.' Humpflinger gazed admiringly around the deck. 'There be great demand for boats to convey trade and goods between the settlements.'

'You will make a fine master. I have no doubt.'

'Mind, I confess also a desire to own a small tavern.'

Boundless laughed. 'Then which shall it be? Land or sea?'

Humpflinger gazed back at the small settlement. 'There be equal consideration for both, if truth be told. And who knows but that a third possibility may present itself over time?'

'Wedlock and family, you mean?'

Humpflinger sighed. ''Tis my certain wish. When I have raised sufficient stake to set myself up in the world. And your own hopes, Joshua?'

'I have not given the matter sufficient thought. But it is a desirable prospect—for when I am settled and established in some trade or other.' He gazed at where the young woman sat beside her husband. Taking out a lace handkerchief, she solicitously dabbed a droplet of water from his cheek.

'It would be pleasant to be so bound, would it not?' he said, half to himself.

The voice of the master rang out as the crew close-hauled the sails and the vessel commenced to tack around the point of land which formed the entrance to the harbour. In spite of the fine weather, Boundless experienced misgivings as he observed how closely the over-laden vessel rode to the water. But these misgivings were put to rest as the vessel rounded the point and proceeded in a south-easterly direction, the master making skilful use of a headwind.

In the distance, Boundless spied the mouth of an estuary, which seemed to be their destination. On the port bow, the rolling tide stretched into the distance, the heaving flood undisturbed by either land or sail. *"Tis but a finger of the whole,'* he recalled, wondering if the Chesapeake was not as voluminous as the vast Atlantic itself.

As the wind blew stronger and spray showered over the sides, he found shelter between the aft mast and three barrels lashed together on the deck. He sat there out of the gale, shifting to make space as Thompson squeezed in beside him. Humpflinger joined them as all three sat together in the cramped nook.

'Zounds, but my arse be wedded to the deck!' Groaning, Thompson adjusted his buttocks. 'Do we not have the dice or a deck of cards to pass the time, gentlemen? No? Come then, Mr Lively. Pray entertain us with tales of old England.'

'Do you speak of cards?' Cassidy pushed his way into the confined space, having abandoned an animated discussion with a fellow passenger.

'Who was that?' asked Thompson.

'An opinionated fellow. He has the war won and lost in the same five minutes. If bluster were gold, he might set claim to his opinion.'

'Another?' Thompson feigned a look of amazement.

'Does he have fresh news?' asked Humpflinger.

'Only that which he makes up on the spot.'

'Make room, boys. Not much further,' Turlington added his bulk to the tight space, forcing Boundless to squeeze up tighter against the lashed barrels.

Cassidy eyed the strained rigging, his expression worried. 'This wind be a concern,' he said. He turned to Thompson. 'Do you recall the passage three-year back—'

'Gracious! Harry!'

Their conversation was interrupted as the young woman clutched a hand to her mouth. The small boy had wriggled free from his seat to stand by the gunnels. He turned to his father, eyes shining with excitement. 'Look Father! It's the good old Papsy-co!'

Thompson laughed. 'The lad has sharp eyes. Look you, Mr Lively.' He gestured to the river mouth. 'The liquid turnpike awaits!'

The Patapsco

As they drew closer to the mouth of the river, the vessel began to toss violently in the maelstrom of waves created by the gusting winds and discharging tide.

'Hold tight!' A voice shouted.

The passengers braced themselves, seeking any secure hold as the ship heeled sharply and took on water over the side. Cries of alarm went up as a wave broke across the bow and drenched the frightened travellers. He glimpsed the young woman as she cradled the infant in her arms. The boy clung to her skirt as the husband tried desperately to shelter them from the flung spray. 'Ready about!' The hoarse voice of the master sounded above the gale.

The contrary winds and tides now buffeted the ship with such force that Boundless feared the overloaded vessel must surely capsize. He braced himself for the event—Turlington's advice sounding in his ears. He looked around for Humpflinger but was showered by another breaking wave.

A section of cargo broke loose, the heavy crate sliding along the congested deck. 'God have mercy!' a voice cried.

The vessel was now buffeted by the discharging river on one side and the wind and waves of the Chesapeake on the other. The crew struggled to trim the fore-and-aft sails as the master shouted commands. A large wave hit the vessel broadside, heeling her ever closer to the water. Just as she appeared certain to capsize, a blast of wind drove her across the mud bar and into the river mouth. The deck instantly steadied as the swirling tides fell away in the vessel's wake. Moments later, the ship settled itself as it gained the comparative calm of the inland channel.

'All be well!' shouted the master. 'We sleep in our beds this night!'

The shaken passengers exchanged cries of relief, consoling one another as the deckhands hurried to secure the loose cargo. The young husband murmured tenderly to his wife and stroked her hair as she wept with fright. The boy clung to his side, a shocked look on his face.

'God in Heaven, but that was a close shave!' Cassidy breathed hard, his face pale. He struck Boundless as cutting an almost comical figure, his clothes thoroughly drenched, the hair plastered to his skull.

'Theo, I witnessed you throw the bones. Did you wish us all drowned?' Thompson extended an accusing finger, attempting to inject some levity into the mood of fraught relief.

'Nay sir,' Turlington mopped his wet brow with a handkerchief. 'Our Mr Humpflinger was far too busy at worship, having converted on the spur. I witnessed him praying like a Turk amid the wind and waves. What say you, Theodore?'

'You do me an injustice. My fervent prayers were entirely for your safety, Mr Turlington. I believe they carried us all to salvation.'

'Spoke like a true Turk!'

'What now be your opinion of our gentle Chesapeake, Mr Lively?' asked Turlington, wringing out his handkerchief. 'She is given to playful moods, is she not?'

Struggling out of his coat, Boundless shivered as the breeze blew against his wet shirt. 'I was in a far worse gale once, on the open sea.'

'Indeed? Then you are twice-blessed—to have come through both.'

'I trust that is the last time. I doubt my nerves would stand another.'

'Never fear, boys,' said Cassidy, recovering from his fright. 'From here all is plain sailing, as the adage has it. Now the only danger is perishing from hard work.'

'You be quite safe, Cass, from that affliction, quite safe.' Thompson winked at Boundless as Turlington roared with laughter.

PROPELLED BY THE RESIDUAL gales blowing off the bay, the vessel proceeded upriver at a good rate of knots. The soaked and exhausted travellers took advantage of the broiling sun to dry out their jackets and capes, so that soon every square inch of the deck was festooned with wet clothing. The busy crew restored a semblance of order to the congested ship—using wood buckets to bail out the water where it swilled along the deck.

As they proceeded further up the inlet the wind fell away and the vessel slowed in the water. After the hissing spray and shrieking birdsong of the open bay, the river struck Boundless as unnervingly quiet. Both shores were cloaked in a profusion of green foliage. The creak of the rigging and the fluttering noise of the wind in the sails were the only sounds to disturb the vegetative hush. Leaning over the side he saw a bottom of mud and clay—the water around the ship taking on a murky brown colour distinct from the blue transparency of the bay.

'Well, Mr Lively, what think you of our honest-to-goodness Papsy-co?'

Turlington had taken out a blanket and wrapped it around his shoulders while he waited for his coat to dry.

'It is exceedingly wild-looking. And empty of habitation, as far as I can judge. What is our destination?'

'Elkridge Landing—at the head of the river. There we shall collect our boat, God willing. Unless, mayhap … *Ah—tishhoo!*' Turlington sneezed forcefully. 'Pardon! That soaking will be the death of me. Now, where was I? Ah, the boat. We may well meet with it along the way, as we did the year before last. As for habitations, you shall see them soon enough, by and by. But there!' He pointed over Boundless' shoulder.

Boundless turned to see a three-masted brig approaching downriver, her sails billowing as she travelled under full canvas.

'What is the depth?' he asked, surprised to encounter a sea-going vessel on the turgid stream.

'She will have drawn ten feet or more of water all the way down from the port.'

'Where is she bound?'

'England, like as not, her hold stuffed with tobacco leaf. That be the Jack, I do wager.'

Turlington's eyesight proved correct. As the vessel drew abreast, Boundless spotted the Union Ensign fluttering from the stern. A deck-hand hailed them from the rigging, doffing his cap as he clung to a yard. The master stood on the aft deck, regarding the occupants of the smaller vessel with a solemn face as the brig dipped past.

'Godspeed!' Humpflinger raised an arm, his shirt still damp from the soaking.

Boundless stared at the departing vessel, experiencing a pang as he pictured it dropping anchor off Blackwall, the smoky, noisy city in the background.

The breeze died to a whisper as they progressed further up-river, the giddy speed of the Chesapeake now well behind them. Two miles upstream they came across a flatboat being poled along the shore. Within the space of several minutes they encountered a dozen other vessels—yawls, longboats, canoes, shallops and barges proceeding both up and downstream.

'Where have they all come from?' he asked.

'There are many plantations along the river.' Humpflinger indicated where a barge was being poled out of a side channel. 'And there be numerous creeks and inlets, each leading to a farm or cabin. The water be indispensable for trafficking back and forth between them.'

'In sum, that be our contracted employment,' put in Turlington. 'The collection and conveyance of goods along the river. What say you, Mr Cassidy?'

'Aye. The water be the turnpike and we the coach.' Cassidy took off his hat to fan his face. Under the hat, his thick brown hair was slicked with sweat.

'Handsomely put,' acknowledged Thompson. 'Indeed, we be the stage-coach, Mr Lively. The water be our road and the wind our horses.'

'The oars, more like,' Turlington laughed. 'And we the horses.'

'The oars and the rowers, both, cannot equally be claimed as horses,' objected Cassidy, drawing a perplexed stare from the other man.

Boundless heard a woman's voice and looked up to see the young plantation owner and his wife make their way along the deck for exercise. The boy tagged along behind. He watched her switch the infant from one shoulder to the other, and wondered where they would disembark.

The wind picked up again as they rounded a bend and came upon a break in the forested shore. In the middle of the large clearing stood a trading post. A pair of horses grazed the pasture, their tails twitching at flies. A cart sat in front of the post, its yoke resting on the grass. A wooden jetty projected into the river with a rowboat tied up alongside.

They hove to a short distance from the shore. A deckhand blew a piercing blast on a whistle as a disembarking passenger stood at the side with his baggage. The deckhand blew a second blast. A few moments later, the door of the post opened and a youth hurried down to the wharf. Untying the rowboat, he climbed in and rowed out to the ship.

'We shall lose the wind,' fretted Cassidy. 'Hurry, man!' He continued to mutter under his breath as the rowboat drew alongside. A trunk and several small boxes were lowered over the side, followed shortly by the passenger—the small boat rocking precariously as he sat down on the planks.

No sooner had the rowboat commenced its return journey than the master gave the order to raise sail. 'He is as anxious as yourself, Cass, to preserve the wind,' said Thompson.

The gale freshened as they left the post behind. The unbroken solitude that had accompanied their voyage since first entering the river reasserted itself as they entered a channel bounded on all sides by high bluffs crowned with trees. The imposing heights added to the green hush surrounding the ship as the passengers lowered their voices in unconscious deference.

'An unusual palette.' Boundless pointed to the ochre-coloured clay lying beneath the cliffs.

Thompson unwrapped the blanket from his shoulders. 'It be due to the exceedingly hot sun in these parts. See. My shirt is quite dry.'

Cassidy joined the conversation, looking tired and miserable. 'By God's grace, but I shall be glad when our journey is done. I have gulped enough salt to preserve a hog.'

The three men fell into an idle discussion on the curious ways of the Aboriginals—Thompson advancing the opinion that they were distantly linked to the race of Tartars, although at a loss to explain how that might be. 'Their customs, 'tis said, be similar in many respects, and that both share the same, savage physiognomy.'

Cassidy snorted. 'Balderdash! It has been shown that they are descendants of a race, hitherto unknown, lying far to the west—or perhaps the north, I forget which.'

'That lacks sense. How could they be unknown if we know of them?'

'*Hitherto.* Do you have ears? I said *hitherto.*'

'*Hitherto* might comfortably stretch to encompass all that is now known—'

'I am anxious to examine an Aboriginal at close quarters,' interjected Boundless, keen to avoid another round of quibbles.

'Not too close,' advised Thompson, 'else you may find yourself divested of your scalp.'

'Blast this heat!' Cassidy retreated into the shade of the sail, his face flushed. Opening a canteen, he poured water onto his necktie and dabbed his brow. 'How far to the deuced landing?'

THEY HAD LEFT THE cliffs behind and were proceeding through an area of extremely dense vegetation, the trees so thickly clustered that it was impossible to see a yard beyond the shoreline. Overhead, thin white clouds had begun to form, partly obscuring the sun and promising some relief from the sultry heat.

'Was that not a thriving village this past month?' An elderly gentleman, bundled up in a heavy wool greatcoat despite the hot sun, pointed with great emphasis to the far shore. 'See there!'

In a clearing stood the charred and blackened ruins of over a dozen bark houses. The smashed remnants of pots and dishes scattered across the grass indicated the sudden catastrophe that had overtaken the inhabitants.

'I witnessed it myself,' said a second man, confirming the account. 'Half a hundred heathen or more. But recently migrated, I do believe, from the upper Chesapeake.'

'Not so, sir,' argued the first speaker. 'I had it from a military man on the passage down that they were most certainly Powhatans, from the Virginias.'

A lively discussion broke out among the two as to the identity, and fate, of the inhabitants of the sacked village.

'What could have been the cause?' Boundless asked, as more blackened lodges appeared through the trees.

'The savages constantly make war upon one another. 'Tis their chief sport.' Thompson shaded his eyes to better observe the ruins.

'Or mayhap it were slavers,' suggested Turlington. 'They are said to be active in these parts. I have seen no other sign of villages along the river. Perhaps they are all fled into the forest.'

'Slavers?' asked Boundless.

'Oftentimes they pass through searching for heathens to sell off to the farms or plantations. But the Indians make notoriously poor stock and will run off into the woods at every chance.'

'Your wild savage cannot be domesticated,' said Thompson firmly. 'Being neither as sturdy nor as servile as the African, who can be relied upon to work—'

'It be an abomination to the Almighty! And the wickedness of these colonies!' Cassidy squeezed in beside them, his face showing the strain of the arduous passage.

Thompson glanced at the other passengers. 'Now Cass, your thoughts on the matter are well known. I pray you,' he urged in a low voice, 'confine them for the present time.'

Cassidy looked visibly upset but said nothing.

The burned lodges fell behind them as Boundless made a mental note to pursue the matter with the distressed Cassidy at a more opportune time.

The gale continued to drive them forward, the sacked village soon forgotten as a topic for discussion. Boundless took down his gabardine coat where he had secured it to a spar and found it fully dried.

'Five o' the clock to the landing,' calculated Thompson, holding up a finger to the wind.

'Taken! And add a quarter hour!' Turlington hooked thumbs confidently in the pockets of his coat.

Several other travellers joined in the wager, sums of money pledged on the approximate quarter hour of their arrival. Drops of rain began to fall, followed shortly by a glittering rainbow, the lucent arc drawing gasps of admiration as it spanned the river ahead of the ship.

They made several more stops to let off passengers along the way. Each was farewelled with fond hails and remembrances. 'Many of them be known to each other,' explained Thompson.

Feeling fatigued from the heat, Boundless found a spot at the foot of the mast and sat down. Humpflinger sat across from him, knees drawn up and his head down, fast asleep.

'Sound sense, Theodore,' he said, yawning, and closed his eyes.

WHEN HE AWOKE, HUMPFLINGER was gone. Squinting, he saw him standing at the bow along with half-a-dozen passengers. Easing his cramped limbs, he made his way forward.

'I shall have your shilling yet,' he heard one man say to another as he squeezed into a spot alongside Humpflinger.

'A quarter hour to the port!' a voice called.

The announcement created a stir of excitement, the mood of anticipation heightening as they passed an assemblage of log huts on the shore.

'I see it!' Standing next to his father, the small boy pointed to the distance. The premature claim drew a hoot of laughter from a youth with a broken front tooth. The boy wrinkled his face in dismay.

The ship rounded a point, giving wide berth to a cluster of tree trunks poking up through the water. A series of wooded bluffs came into view, rising above a flat, curving shoreline dotted with buildings. The sight drew muted cheers from the weary travellers.

'I bid it first!' insisted the boy to general amusement.

'Indeed, Harry, you win the laurel!' His father stroked the boy's head. 'D'ye see the house?' he asked, shading his eyes to look.

'There!' The boy pointed to where a handsome stone mansion sat on the topmost bluff, the vantage point affording it a commanding view of the river. The husband turned fondly to his wife. 'Home, dearest.'

She smiled, holding up the infant to look. 'Grandpa and Grandma, too!' She kissed the infant on the cheek.

At the foot of the bluffs, a row of wharves, taverns and sheds marked the landing. Four sea-going vessels rode at anchor in the natural bay formed by the surrounding hills. A line of fishing boats, shallops, sloops and barges lay beached along the flat shore.

Humpflinger buttoned his coat. 'There stands our destination, Joshua. Our long journey is done.'

A GOODLY NUMBER OF people could be seen moving about on the landing—some, it seemed, awaiting their arrival. Numerous piles of freight were stacked on the shore—whether awaiting conveyance to a vessel or transportation further inland, Boundless could not guess.

'I had not expected so much activity so far upriver,' he confessed, bemused once again at the capacity of the colonies to spring forth so much industry from the wilderness.

'The Elk be the main port for all the farms and plantations along the river and further upstream—past the falls. 'Tis said to be busier than Baltimore and Annapolis together,' said Humpflinger, a note of pride in his voice.

'Douse sail!'

The crew rushed to ease off on the mainsheet as the vessel approached the shore.

'We are arrived safely, thank God!' said Cassidy, coming up to join them. 'You are fortunate, Mr Lively. This time last year we were stuck on the river for two whole days due to contrary winds.'

'Aye,' said Turlington. 'And the year before a tempest blew us all the way back down to the river mouth. It was a sore trial after such an arduous journey.'

The ship had slowed to a crawl as the helmsman skilfully guided the vessel towards the one remaining open berth. On the landing, a dozen or so people broke out into cheers and applause. Several called out names and greetings as the gap closed and they spotted loved ones onboard.

'Esmeralda! God bless!' Beside them a short man in a woollen cape waved his stick to a shawl-wrapped woman who tearfully hailed him from the shore.

'Welcome, good souls, welcome!'

Voices called out more greetings as the vessel slowly floated the last few yards to the landing.

'Ready all hands!' With a solid bump, they came up against the wooden pier. A hawser was thrown down from the bow. Dock workers secured the mooring ropes as the vessel came to a stop.

'Grandpa! Grandma!' Before anyone could prevent him, the small boy had scrambled over the side. He hung by his hands for a moment before jumping down to the pier. Picking himself up he dashed into the outstretched arms of an elderly couple, almost bowling the man over in his eagerness.

'Grandpa! I saw the landing first!'

A ramp was carried up to the side of the vessel and secured in place. The sun beat down fiercely as trunks and boxes were passed over the side. The plantation owner stepped nimbly onto the platform and turned to take the infant from his wife. Boundless quickly stepped forward to offer assistance as she gathered her skirts. 'Thank you, kind sir.' She flashed him a grateful smile as she leaned on his arm.

'Come, Constance.' Her husband held out his hand to assist her down the ramp. No sooner was the young woman stood safely on the wharf than the elderly woman flew forward to smother her with tears and kisses.

'We feared you had been wrecked!' she sobbed, stroking the young woman's face.

'Thank God for your safe return!' The elderly man stepped forward to embrace the young couple, liberally bestowing kisses on both.

A FEW MINUTES LATER, Boundless stood on the landing alongside Humpflinger, waiting for their companions to join them. A strong, distinctive odour filled his nose—like musk, or pine, or a combination of both.

'What is that smell?' He turned, puzzled to Humpflinger.

'Tobacco. You will soon enough get used to it.'

'Are we gathered?' Turlington led the way off the wharf, stopping at a freight shed situated at the edge of the landing. 'Let us sit here a moment and collect ourselves,' he said. 'No doubt Captain Taysick will put us to work the moment we are arrived.' So saying, he sat down in the shade of a poplar.

'Then let us collect ourselves for the hour or more.' Cassidy plonked himself down in the grass. 'My head is feverish, I declare.'

Although the sun was well advanced across the sky, the day had grown even hotter. Boundless poured some water from the canteen onto his neckerchief and used it to dampen his forehead. Close by, several men and women sat in chairs under the shade of a wooden awning, awaiting passage. Men in wide-brimmed hats strolled up and down the wharf inspecting the piles of freight. Across the street from the landing, a row of taverns, workshops, yards and offices stood in the shadow of the bluffs. In front of a brick warehouse, a half-dozen Negroes, dressed in trousers and open-collared linen shirts, tended to a line of mules, while others lashed chests and trunks to the backs of the animals.

Boundless searched for a sign of the young woman among the figures milling about the landing. He sighted her across the single, dusty street, surrounded by an effusive welcoming party of friends and relatives. Gossiping animatedly, she and her husband made their way towards a path leading up the side of a bluff. She clutched her straw hat to her head in the warm breeze, the long skirts of her dress blowing back against her body. As she climbed the steep path, she cast frequent glances behind to where the elderly grandmother carried the infant cradled to her bosom.

'She be as pretty as a swallow.'

'Beg pardon?'

Humpflinger stared at where a young maidservant hoisted a small chest into the back of a cart standing in the street. An elderly woman sat on the seat fanning herself.

'She is, indeed,' Boundless concurred, following his companion's gaze. 'Although, if truth be told, a little stout to my taste.'

'A stout woman be a solace to the eye,' averred Humpflinger as he observed the girl laughing heartily at some jest of the driver. 'As sweet as nutmeg,' he added admiringly.

The two watched the girl clamber into the back of the cart and make a place for herself amidst the chests and boxes.

'Har!' the driver shouted and cracked the whip over the pair of oxen.

As the cart trundled off, the girl turned and poked her tongue at her admirer.

'D'ye see!' Humpflinger gaped in astonishment.

Boundless chuckled. 'Your eyes be struck from your head!'

Humpflinger gazed after the cart as it trundled down the street. 'I should count myself fortunate to net such a pretty dove.'

'Despair not, my love-struck Romeo. Mayhap you shall see her again, under more opportune circumstances.'

'I fear not.' Humpflinger gave a despondent sigh. ''Tis the way of things.'

'Shall we proceed, gentlemen?' Turlington walked up with Thompson and Cassidy, their faces red from the sun.

As they set off along the shore, Boundless glanced back at the bluff. The young couple walked arm-in-arm up the steep track, the husband holding a parasol above his wife's head. Ahead of the party, four Blacks toiled under the weight of the family's baggage. The boy darted back and forth between the Blacks and his parents, inexhaustible in his energy. A small brown dog raced down from the summit and leapt into the arms of the boy. A moment later, the party entered a screen of trees and were lost to sight.

'Mr Lively?'

'Coming!' He said, and hastened to catch up with his companions.

15

The Liquid Turnpike

ASSIDY AND THOMPSON LED the way past a line of freight sheds and fishing vessels—the two bickering over some point of astronomy. As he followed, Boundless observed several paths cut into the wooded bluffs above the shore. A pair of Blacks descended backwards down one of the paths, their legs and backs braced against the momentum of a large barrel. A number of similar casks were stacked along the bluffs under the shade of trees. Quickening his pace to catch Humpflinger, he enquired as to the contents.

'Tobacco leaf. That be the main export of these parts.'

'They be in great quantity. Some hundreds, at least.'

''Tis but a fraction.' Humpflinger gestured to the row of casks. 'This be the wealth of the Virginias. And perhaps of the colonies entire. Mind,' he added, 'the trade in furs might, with equal merit, dispute the crown.'

They passed a crab boat pulled up on the muddy shore, the crew hanging out nets and baskets to dry. 'Fish, also,' added Humpflinger, with a glance at the boat. 'Tobacco, fish and furs,' he enumerated.

'The leaf?' said Cassidy, having dropped back to converse. 'Sweet-scented is best. Although Mr Thompson claims to the Orinoco. Both varieties are of much value.' He pursed his lips as he calculated. 'Twelve shillings and sixpence per hundredweight, if I recall.'

'And how much leaf per barrel?' Boundless asked as they passed another line of hogsheads.

'Above 1,000 pounds. Am I not correct, Theodore?'

'I do believe.'

'Let us say, for convenience, ten hundredweight to the hog. And let us round off the sum to six guineas a barrel. Well then—' Cassidy gestured to a hogshead. 'We stride past six guineas. And another, which be 12 guineas in the space of a yard or two. And six again,' he said, nodding to a third barrel.

Cassidy pointed to another dozen hogsheads stacked in a double row. 'Add 72 guineas! At this rate we shall be rich as old Croesus by the time we reach the boat.'

He continued counting as they passed another pyramid of barrels, abandoning the task after scaling them up to Philadelphia millionaires.

'I grow tired of my wealth already,' he confessed, as they stopped alongside a large, roofed structure with open sides. The ground beneath the roof was occupied by piles of crated goods and rows of the ubiquitous hogsheads, stacked one atop the other. A mixed gang of workers carried goods from the shed onto the deck of a single-masted sloop some fifty-five feet in length. The starboard side was already stacked with cargo, the crates and barrels restrained by thick ropes. The name *Egret* was painted on the bow of the boat.

Boundless looked around for Cassidy, who had disappeared.

'Where are the others?' he asked Humpflinger.

'Doubtless renewing acquaintances.'

'The day is but gone! Hop to it!'

On the dock beside the vessel, a short, wiry man with a red cloth wrapped around his head harangued the sweating labourers. 'By the bones! Do you intend to swamp her?' He glared at two men manoeuvring a hogshead along the deck of the boat. 'Such numbskulls! As I swear—By the aftboard!' Furiously, he pointed to a spot further along the deck.

Humpflinger nudged him. 'That noisy jay be Mr Cribble, the foreman. He flaps much, but his efforts be all wind. And that personage over yonder be Cap'n Taysick. Take care with him. He be a rum character—drunk or sober.'

Boundless looked at where a frowning, plump-bellied man in his forties engaged in animated dispute with a merchant dressed in a wig and frockcoat. The captain wore a red livery jacket over dark-blue fustian breeches. On his head he wore a battered cocked hat. A grey stubble clung to his veined cheeks—now flushed crimson as he argued with the other man. The two came close to where he stood, the merchant hovering at Taysick's elbow as he insisted on his case.

'Too much and too late!' he complained, thrusting a bill of some sort under the captain's nose.

'Begone, sir!' Taysick let out a ferocious roar at which the merchant backed off, still flourishing the bill.

'I shall have redress at the courts,' threatened the merchant.

'*Baa! Baa!*' mocked the captain as he watched the affronted merchant depart. Sticking a finger in his mouth, he scraped a tooth. Removing the finger, he jabbed it at a Black toiling under the weight of a heavy chest. 'Drop that trunk at your peril!'

Boundless took his eyes from the captain as he spotted Turlington talking to a sun-browned man in canvas trousers and a sleeveless leather jerkin. The man listened intently, glancing over at Boundless.

He was about to enquire as to the man's identity when Humpflinger forestalled him. 'That be Thomas York, a most agreeable man. With luck, he will commend you to the captain for hire. Come, Joshua.' Humpflinger led the way as Turlington beckoned them both.

'This be Mr Lively.' Turlington gave introductions as they approached. 'Mr Humpflinger, you are already well acquainted with Mr York.'

The sun-browned man stuck out a hand. 'Welcome back, Mr Humpflinger.'

'And you, Mr Lively.' He gave Boundless' hand a firm shake. 'I shall be glad to speak to the cap'n on your behalf. A moment …

Mr York walked over to where the captain was adding a pinch of snuff to his nostrils and spoke in his ear. Captain Taysick turned to stare at Boundless. He said nothing for a long moment, and then gave a curt nod. Mr York raised a thumb.

'Welcome to the crew!' An elated Humpflinger slapped Boundless on the shoulder.

Boundless sighed with relief, immensely pleased to have secured employment. 'I feared I would be stuck rolling casks!'

Humpflinger chuckled. 'And so you shall! Have no fear.' The two went on board the boat to deposit their haversacks.

''Tis a very dependable vessel,' said Humpflinger as Boundless glanced around the deck. The fully decked sloop was twenty feet across the beam. A long tiller extended from the stern in front of a small cabin. Oarlocks were set along the gunnels, the wooden oars stowed along the planks beneath. 'Each is fourteen feet,' said Humpflinger as Boundless bent to examine one. 'The rowing be hard at first, as you have already discovered, but you will quickly accustom to it.'

'But she has a sail; a gaff rig,' said Boundless gesturing to the mast.

Humpflinger smiled. 'Aye, but we ship oars as well as sail. And believe me, we row as much as sail. Oftentimes, it is not worth setting the sail as we stop and go along the shore, picking up and dropping off often within a quarter mile or less. And as you see, there's plenty of flat deck space for hauling cargo or persons.'

'How large is the crew?'

'Sixteen in all. Yourself now included.'

'Everyone takes a turn—to row?'

'Excepting the captain, Mr York and Mr Cribble—also, the cook, Levi Hopkins. We call him "Boiler". Which leaves twelve of us to do the pushing and pulling. But unless we go against the tide, we generally take our places six and six. Six on the oars, and six in relief.'

'There is no shelter from the elements,' observed Boundless, gazing around the open deck.

Humpflinger sighed. 'No, as you shall shortly learn for yourself. Expect to get lashed by wind and rain, and boiled to a turn by the sun, oftentimes within the same day. And there is precious little room to move about, unless the oars are stowed and we proceed under sail. The only open space is up there,' he nodded toward the bow, 'unless, indeed, it also be filled with cargo.'

The boat was already half full, most of the cargo stowed forward of the mast or along the sides behind the rowing benches. As he watched, two Blacks rolled another barrel up the loading ramp and along the deck.

'How much tonnage will she bear?'

'Six, as I remember. And she will travel in less than a yard of water.' Humpflinger glanced back at the wharf. 'But come. Else will Mr Cribble flay yards off us with his tongue.'

As they returned to the wharf, the foreman glared in their direction. 'I see you are returned from your foreign jaunts, Mr Humpflinger. I hope you are well rested from your travels.' He pointed to a mound of hempen sacks, each one stuffed with dried goods. 'Take those aboard and stack them along the sides—if it pleases a gentleman such as yourself.'

His glance fell on Boundless. 'You return bearing gifts, I see. And not just that Irish mope-a-deck Cassidy. Such a privilege it be.' Perhaps you've a mind to stand there, admiring,' he said. His brow furrowed with displeasure.

'Aye, aye, Mr Cribble.' Humpflinger touched a hand to his forehead and sprang to pick up a sack of goods. Boundless quickly followed suit, hoisting a sack up onto his shoulder to follow Humpflinger as he navigated between the piles of cargo to the boat.

'Bend backs, by God! But one hour and the day is lost. Bend to it!'

IT WAS DUSK BEFORE all the cargo was stowed aboard. The deckhands secured the last of the freight as the weary Blacks retired along the path leading up to the heights.

Boundless sat to catch his breath, resting his back against a hogshead. Around him, the deckhands lounged in the grass. 'They look hardy fellows,' he thought, reminded of the sailors on board the *Patience*. The men were dressed alike in canvas trousers, linen shirts and leather jerkins. Their faces were burned brown by the sun. One hand was a boy, no older than twelve or thirteen, he guessed, and seemingly as at home as any of the men.

Captain Taysick walked the deck with Mr York, inspecting the cargo and checking off items against various bills. The breeze ruffled the grey hairs that wisped from under the felt hat as he stepped off the vessel to count the crew. '… eleven, twelve,' he said, looking displeased at the tally. 'Cassidy! Sit still, damn ye!' He cursed and counted again, slowly poking a finger at each recumbent body. 'Fourteen,' he announced. 'Mark, Mr York.'

'We ship tomorrow, boys,' he announced, scratching his neck above the collar of his shirt, his face ill-tempered in the twilight.

'But beware. I shall off-load the first man that displeases me. I will not abide fighting, drunkenness or thieving.'

Humpflinger leaned forward to whisper in Boundless' ear. 'Excepting for himself—who excels at all three!'

The captain scratched behind his ear as if recalling some thought or other. Unable to summon the errant notion, he beckoned the foreman. 'Mr Cribble. Allow each man a jig of rum. I shall be on board if needed.'

'Come, Joshua, time for grub.' A cheerful Humpflinger led the way across the dusty grass to where the cook stirred a large iron pot suspended above a crackling fire. They sat down on a patch of grass.

'I confess I scarcely know whether I am the more famished or fatigued,' said Boundless, sore after the unaccustomed lifting and carrying.

Humpflinger fiddled with the tinderbox. 'You shall feast on fine beef-steak, and plenty of it. And after, sleep soundly like a newborn lamb.'

'Where is the ale, for God's sake!' Cassidy joined them, struggling out of his coat. 'I see the drunken sot has not mended his character,' he said as he sat down.

'Aye. And he was most pleased to enquire after your health, also,' rejoined Humpflinger.

'Ha!' Cassidy stared around. 'The ale?' he demanded.

Four bowls of stew, a jigger of rum and two tankards of ale later, Boundless loosened his breeches and reclined lazily in the grass, sated and sleepy as the sun sank behind the ridge. Cassidy and Thompson had fallen into animated debate over the distance in nautical miles between Elk Ridge and Baltimore, each man vigorously disputing the other's estimate. Barely able to keep his eyes open, he half-listened to Cassidy's blustering enumeration of each landing point as he drifted off into an exhausted sleep.

He awoke to the sounds of men moving about. Sitting up, he winced at the stiffness in his back. Humpflinger slept soundly under a tree, his hat pulled down over his eyes. The sky was dull and overcast, and the morning air unseasonably chill. The men lined up for breakfast, holding out wooden bowls as the cook doled out copious ladles of porridge. Within minutes, the entire camp was astir as Captain Taysick groggily emerged from his sleeping position aboard the boat to vigorously scratch himself, his hair in disarray.

'Mr York, fetch me my breakfast aboard. One half-bowl.' Spotting an arriving barge, the Captain walked off to discuss river conditions with the master.

Following breakfast, they cast off from the wharf, using the oars to propel the *Egret* out to mid-channel. There they lay at ease to give passage to a ship under full canvas.

'Way ho!' a voice shouted. The clouds parted and a brilliant burst of sunshine illuminated the flat, brown river.

'Hoist sail!'

Moments later the ship jerked forwards as the mainsail filled with wind and they started back down the river.

THE SLOOP HELD TO the mid-channel as the cool morning gave way to the humid heat of day—the vessel splashing through the water under sail. Boundless observed the other deckhands closely, copying their actions and making himself useful by testing the cargo ropes for tautness and assisting with the sail when required. His companions seemed well-practised to the rhythms and necessities of the vessel, going about their tasks without fuss or instruction as the breeze drove them along at a good rate. Captain Taysick sat at the tiller, one leg flung over the gunnel, the other manoeuvring the long arm with careless ease as he kept them to the wind.

Within a mile, he brought the vessel over to the starboard shore where a group of men sat in the grass awaiting their arrival.

'How do, boys?'

The men got to their feet as the captain held the boat just offshore. A deckhand threw a line, and the men hauled the boat in close to the bank.

'That tea chest and the marked crates for the Dowson plantation.' Mr York pointed to the cargo as it was lifted ashore.

'And brood hens for the Cutler house,' a man on shore responded, handing a cage full of fluttering hens to Turlington.

At that moment, a youth from the shore party—perched with one foot on the bank and the other against the side of the boat—lost balance and fell into the water. His companions roared with laughter as the discomfited youth scrambled to his feet, his clothes dripping wet, and his drenched hair plastered to his face.

'Zounds! He has a fish in his pocket!' Cassidy roared with laughter as the chagrined youth pressed water from his hair.

'Mr Cassidy! Kindly save your Irish antics for the tavern.' Scowling at the disturbance, Cribble scolded the crew back to work. 'Stand ready!' he shouted as Captain Taysick looked on.

The next landing was across the river, a quarter mile further downstream. The boat put in alongside a small dock to off-load several casks and the caged hens. Two passengers climbed on board, bringing with them a goat on a rope leash. The men paid a sum to Taysick, who deposited the coins in a leather purse strapped to his waist. The men stood in the stern, gossiping with a deckhand while the goat lay curled at their feet like a pet dog.

Boundless noticed a dozen barrels standing in the shade of the trees and queried Thompson if they were to be taken on board.

'They are for the return passage. The cap'n likes a full boat, up and downstream.'

Enjoying a favourable wind, the *Egret* crossed back over the river to set the two men and the goat down on the overgrown bank. 'We shall rest our backs this day, God willing,' predicted Turlington with a glance at the sky.

'Now he has pointed the bone,' groaned Cassidy. 'Ready your backs, boys, of a certainty.'

The superstition proved well founded as, midafternoon, the wind fell away, and they took to the oars with much joshing and feigned protests from the crew. Copying his companions, Boundless set the oar in the oarlock and took his place on the hard wooden seat behind Humpflinger who sat in front. The long oar felt heavy and awkward in Boundless' hands.

'Keep smoothly,' said Humpflinger. 'Don't dig too deep. And lean with the oar. 'Twill go better once we build up a surge.'

'One! Two! Three! Haul away!'

Cribble called out the time, beating a stick against a keg as the crew dipped oars into the water. To Boundless' mortification, he missed the water entirely with the first stroke, nearly unseating himself into the man behind—an action which did not escape the sharp eye of the foreman.

'Do you joust at air, Mr Lively? Mercy! The whole river to aim at, and he dips at clouds! Where did you find this popinjay, Mr Humpflinger? In the same penny-jar as yon Mr Cassidy, I'll be bound! Give way together! One! Two! Three! Smartly now. Smartly!'

To his relief, he managed the next stroke, and the one after, although losing the pace and drawing an irritable look from Cribble.

'One-two-THREE! Mr Lively. *Three*, sir. Not four, nor five, nor sixes by sevens.'

'Harden your backs into it, ye fish-faced slack-a-beds!' Cassidy called out in the voice of the foreman, causing a pink-cheeked lad—the youngest of the crew—to miss the stroke in merriment. 'I see your tongue be as free as ever, Mr Cassidy. Perhaps you'd be so good as to show Mr Lively by example?'

To Boundless' surprise, Cassidy proved to possess a fine singing voice, the Irishman 'breaking out a shantee' as he heaved at the oar.

> *You must make me a fine Holland shirt,*
> *Blow, blow, blow, ye winds, blow, And not*
> *have in it a stitch of needlework.*
> *Blow, ye winds that arise, blow, blow.*

'Careful the stroke, Mr Cassidy! Keep to the time, thou jitter-head!'

'Belay the noise!' The peevish voice of the captain brought a halt to the spirited banter. Notwithstanding, several comic quips from Cassidy delivered *sotto voce* were sufficient to keep the pot of glee at a simmering boil over the next half mile.

The initial good spirits gave way to exhaustion as the crew put in a second hour at the oars—the men sweating profusely as the wind dropped away to a whisper and the sun beat down. Boundless was certain his back would break, or his arms fall off from the exertion as they propelled the heavily laden vessel downstream in the slack current. After a further hour of slow progress, Captain Taysick gave up in disgust.

'Lay-to for the day,' he said, to gasps of relief from the exhausted rowers.

After securing the boat, the men flung themselves down in the grass to rest as the cook stoked the fire. Boundless found a tall hickory and sat with his back against the trunk, wincing as he felt the soreness in his spine. He examined his hands, frowning at the raw blisters.

'They will harden to the oars.' Humpflinger sat down beside him. 'You must prick them to salve the skin. And wrap a wet rag around them tomorrow at the oar. With God's grace, the wind may rise overnight.'

'My back is broke,' Thompson stepped gingerly about the grass. 'I could use another—one that bends and relieves. Thusly!' He made a bobbing motion—drawing laughter as he bobbed off to relieve himself in the trees.

Following a supper of boiled fowl and freshly baked bread, the men sat quietly in the gathering dusk. Boundless leaned against a tree, enjoying the mild air and relief after the day's toil as the fire spluttered in the twilight. Several of the men were already snoring in the darkness when Cribble approached.

'Ahh! The two imports. Your turn at watch.' Cribble jerked a thumb at Boundless and Humpflinger.

'Aye, aye, sir.'

The pair walked a short distance from the fire to a fallen log where they sat facing the dense woods, muskets cradled in their arms. The trees were cloaked in darkness, making it impossible to see beyond the nearest one.

Boundless stared apprehensively to where his ears perceived a rustling in the undergrowth. 'If a savage should rush out, surely he would overwhelm us before we fired the musket?'

'No doubt,' replied Humpflinger, dreamily smoking his pipe. 'No doubt.'

Boundless chuckled. 'Are you thinking of your pretty young dove?'

'I shall never see her again.' Humpflinger sighed heavily.

'Who knows? You may encounter her when we come again to the port.'

Humpflinger nodded. 'Mayhap,' he said, his tone indicating otherwise. 'And if not, there shall be other lasses—both comely and stout.'

Boundless sat in silence beside his companion, sunk in thoughts of the young plantation wife. His mind watched again as she wended her way uphill, one hand clutching her straw hat to her head, the other smoothed against her skirts. He dwelt on the smiling warmth of her features and his last glimpse of her as she passed into the trees. He sat thus until the end of the watch, lost in contemplation, the wooded shore dark and silent under the starry skies.

MID-MORNING, A MILD GALE blew up and the crew enjoyed a welcome reprieve as they raised the sail. Boundless had no sooner settled down against a cask than he heard an urgent summons.

'Joshua! Come see your authentic savage!'

He hurried to join is companion on the starboard bow. 'See yonder!' Humpflinger pointed downstream.

At first, he could see nothing but the empty river. Then, in the shadows of the bank, he spied a bark canoe floating motionless in the shallows. Two Aboriginals sat in the craft, peering into the water. The Indians spared not a single glance for the vessel as it drew near, so intently did they observe the still water beneath the canoe. They were strong of limb, their foreheads daubed with red dye under a coxcomb of jet-black hair. Both wore breech clouts, their coppery-coloured torsos and limbs exposed to the humid air.

As the *Egret* drew abreast, one gave a brief glance. His companion darted a lance into the water, uttering a shrill, ululating cry as he withdrew a large, wriggling fish. The other immediately brained the fish with a club.

'Which tribe are they?' he asked, staring as the canoe fell away behind the boat.

'I do not know. Mayhap they be Massawomecks, who are reputed to hunt these parts.'

'Not so,' interjected Thompson, who had come alongside to observe. 'I have it on a certainty that the Massecks were slaughtered to a man these ten years past.'

'Then what are they?'

'Nanticoke, perhaps, or Conestoga.' Thompson hawed dismissively. 'One savage be as good, or bad, as another.'

Although Boundless kept a sharp eye out for the remainder of the day, he was disappointed in his desire to encounter more of the Aboriginals. He lamented the fact to Humpflinger, who nodded.

'Last year there were two or three villages observable from the shore. But it may be they do not care for the presence of so many farms and plantations and have withdrawn to the deeper woods.'

'Have you ever been to a village?'

'Once only. When I first came to these parts, I worked on a barge for some months. One day, the master led four of us a half mile into the forest and there we came across a village of more than fifty lodges. They wished to trade for sugar, tobacco, coffee and pots and pans of all sorts.'

'They were peaceful, then?'

'Fearsome, more like—to my mind. The chief man carried a club more terrible than any I should ever wish to see again. We kept our muskets primed and would allow only three or four savages at a time to inspect our goods. There was an awful reek of bear grease and hordes of flies everywhere. The devilish, painted faces and fiendish expressions made a fearful impression on me. I could hardly sleep peacefully for a week to think back on it.'

Boundless mulled over the account as he went about his tasks, picturing the two Aboriginals in the canoe, hearing again the harsh cry of triumph as they held aloft the speared fish. He shivered, suddenly glad for the sanctuary of the boat.

16

Captain Taysick

THE FOLLOWING DAY, THEY left the main channel and proceeded a half mile up a creek to where four crates of freshly picked apples sat in a clearing. A note was pinned to the crates requesting that they be delivered to a plantation downriver. A fifth crate was added as payment, along with a basket of freshly baked bread.

As they returned to the river and raised the sail, Boundless watched as the cook trailed a line over the side. 'Hooray!' he shouted, immediately hauling in a large bass. He repeated the action several times, drawing in perch and shad with ease. Turning from the line, he produced a small hand net, which he dipped into the water. With the single scoop he retrieved a bulging and promiscuous sackful of herring, shad, alewife and eel. Reaching into the net, he tossed out the eel and a small crab.

'Would ye take a turn?' he asked, noticing Boundless' interest.

Accepting the invitation, Boundless scooped the net through the water and soon captured a trout. Surprised by the quick return, he deposited the fish on the deck. It flopped and wriggled before the cook seized it by the tail and smacked the head sharply against the deck. Whistling, he began to gut the catch, tossing the entrails over the side.

'I hope thou hast belly for the finny tribe,' he said. 'For ye shall soon stomach as much as old Jonah himself.'

Late the next morning, they stopped at a wharf as a single passenger appeared from out the surrounding woods, accompanied by a farewell party of four women. The man, dressed in sober garb and carrying a bible under one arm, shook hands with Thompson, whom he appeared to recognise.

'Who is the preacher?' Boundless asked as they got underway again.

'Reverend Stokes.' Thompson watched the man settle himself in the bow and open the Bible on his lap. 'He is attached to the Wormley plantation, but oft times ships up and down the river to minister to the other habitations along the valley. He is reputed to be a fine speaker.'

Following a turn at the oars, Boundless made his way forward to where the clergyman was seated with eyes closed as if asleep or in prayer. He opened them at Boundless' approach. 'Good morrow, friend.' His voice was deep and pleasant. A small pair of spectacles were pinched on his nose. 'This wind be contrary to our purpose, is it not?'

'It is indeed.' Boundless eyed the reverend curiously. 'By your voice, sir, I should place you at London or thereabouts?'

The clergyman brightened at the estimate. 'Indeed! A most accurate judgement. I lay humble claim to both that city and a Divinity from the Oxford College. And yourself, friend? By your speech I should put you at Glasgow or the Edinburgh? Come, sit by me.'

They fell into amiable conversation, Reverend Stokes proving intimately knowledgeable of the wild inhabitants along the river.

'The villages you sometimes see,' he explained, 'are heathens of the Susquehannock nation, with a few Nanticokes thrown in for good measure.'

'Their names be altogether strange.'

'No more so than their ways, I fear.'

'Is it true that they consume human flesh?' asked Boundless, alluding to the lurid tales told by the men as they gossiped around the campfire at night.

'The cannibalistics—mostly Algonquians—I assure you, have all been chased away further into the woods. The ones that remain follow the cross, for the most part.'

'They are Christian?' Boundless' eyes widened.

'Oft-times when it suits, or they can wrest some advantage from it. I refer to trade, of course.' The pastor pursed his lips as he gave consideration to the question. 'A savage, sir, cannot generally be relied upon as to disposition. They are childish creatures, given to murderous thoughts one moment and remarkable civility the next. Christian by word, but heathen by nature. But come,' he continued agreeably. 'How do you, a Scotsman, and a recent one I'll wager, come to find yourself here, on this wild river?'

'In great part, I confess, for the adventure of it.'

'But you do not strike me as a natural boatman like the others? Surely, you have some longer prospect in view?'

'For the present, I am content to learn more of these colonies.'

'But beyond that, sir?' The clergyman fixed him a keen glance.

'I have no certain goal—beyond, perhaps, an ambition to one day impress myself upon the notice of the world.'

'How so?' persisted the reverend, his interest seemingly genuine.

'As to the means, I cannot say.' The bald admission irked Boundless. He glanced back to where Thompson and the others were resting at the oars.

'Perhaps, sir, you are in want of a calling?'

'No doubt it be a matter of settling on a course.'

'Then let this be your guide.' The pastor held up the Bible. 'In it you shall find the answers you seek.'

'Indeed, there be many sources of wisdom.'

"Get thee out of thy country, and from thy kindred, and from thy father's house, unto a land that I will shew thee." Reverend Stoke's eyes gleamed with the quotation as he regarded Boundless. 'Friend, are ye of the true Christian faith?'

'I was so raised. I have since found inspiration in many different authors.'

'Mr. Lively—your turn!' Thompson signalled from aft, summoning him back to the oar.

He got to his feet, thankful for once, to be so summoned. 'Beg pardon. But I am needed at the oar.'

'Be warned, friend! Man is of no more account than particles of grass or the leaves that drop down from the trees. His time is but a breath, his end certain!' The clergyman's voice rose behind Boundless as he made his way back to the oars.

'Did he convert you?' Thompson grinned as Boundless took his place by the oarlock.

'He left me as he found me.'

'Which is?'

'A true heathen, in all respects.'

Thompson laughed heartily. 'Then, Mr. Lively, you be safely ensconced among the members of your tribe.'

At the next wharf the reverend disembarked into the welcoming arms of a group of eager women. Before setting off, the reverend proffered Boundless a courteous bow.

Boundless turned to Thompson. 'It is strange, is it not, to find an Oxford Divine in so savage a place?'

'Like as not, he has some reason to be here other than to preach.'

Thompson watched as Reverend Stokes disappeared into the woods along with his escorts. 'The outer fringes of the colonies be a good place to hide from debtors or the law.'

'You say? He strikes me as a decent enough fellow—although rather full of the sound of his own voice.'

'Oft-times it is the decent who be in most need of refuge.'

'By my oath! Do ye stand there jabbering while the boat is adrift on the tide?' The irate voice of Cribble terminated the conversation and they returned to work.

HE WAS LYING AGAINST a sack of onions, awaiting his turn to row, when he was distracted by a loud whoop. Captain Taysick stood on the starboard side staring intently at the shore, Cribble and York by his side.

'Mr York. The flintlock, if you please.' A murmur of anticipation went up from the crew as the captain held out his hand for the weapon.

Curious, Boundless moved to the side to better observe. Following one man's pointed finger he saw where a magnificent elk stood in the shallows under the shade of the overhanging trees. Three or four deckhands joined them, exclaiming at the size of the elk.

'Those horns must be a yard on either side!'

'Hush now! You'll scare off the beast afore the cap'n gets off a shot.'

Armed with the flintlock, the captain steadied himself and took aim. The musket gave a loud *crack* as white smoke rose from the pan. The ball struck the water a good six yards from where the elk drank from the stream. The miss drew groans from the men.

Taysick ground his teeth in annoyance as Mr York prepared the musket for a second attempt.

'Hold steady, damn ye!' Taking the reloaded gun, he took careful aim. The gun discharged in an explosion of powder—the ball whizzing harmlessly into the trees. 'Confound the beast! Once more!'

'To the left, sir,' Mr York advised as he handed back the reloaded musket. 'The wind blows from starboard.'

At the third shot the elk gave a startled roar. A cheer went up from the men. 'A hit! Bloodied on the flank,' declared Cribble. The captain handed the flintlock to Mr York and took out the spyglass.

'Confirmed. Bloodied on the quarter.' He snapped the glass shut as the elk shook itself and disappeared into the foliage. 'Keep the flintlock at the ready, Mr York.'

Several more times that day the weapon was called into service as the captain fired at a bear glimpsed through the trees, at an eagle as it alighted on a floating log, and even at a large fish as it swam alongside the boat.

'He be in a rare mood, today,' said Thompson as Taysick threw back his head to swallow from a flask, the flintlock cradled under his arm.

By the afternoon, the captain was hopelessly drunk. He sat sprawled in the stern as Mr York remonstrated with him to surrender the flintlock. Loudly and belligerently, he refused, tugging back the gun as the other man tried to wrest it from his grasp. Mr York gave up the attempt as Taysick began to snore loudly, the flintlock still cradled in his arms.

'Behold the man!' Cassidy nudged Boundless as Mr York gently prised the weapon from the captain's grasp.

'Does he get puked often?'

'Several times in the month. Last year, he fired off the musket in his stupors and sent a ball clear through the hat of a travelling parson.' Thompson guffawed at the memory. 'The man kicked up such a ruckus. It were a sight!'

'God forbid he should take it into his head to practise his skills on the crew,' said Humpflinger.

'Hark! The Leviathan stirs.'

Taysick slowly sat up, a befuddled look on his face. Flushed and dishevelled, he made as if to stand before thinking better of the manoeuvre. With a shuddering groan, he fell back onto the deck and commenced to snore thunderously once more.

AS THE SLOW DAYS of ferrying up and down the river turned to weeks and then months, Boundless became acquainted with every creek and side channel and the names of all the farms and plantations along the water-road.

'Wurtzer Farm!' he called out as they rounded a point.

'Augusta Plantation,' he murmured to himself as they came in sight of a prominent bluff above the Landing.

Once or twice a month, they left the river to convey passengers to Baltimore—the captain handling the dangerous Chesapeake tides with seemingly indifferent ease.

'Whatever his personal faults, he be a master mariner,' Boundless conceded to Turlington as they made camp onshore after navigating the sand and mud bars into the river mouth.

'It is said he was master of a merchantman before the drink got the better of him. 'Tis rumoured he ran aground while afflicted and lost the entire cargo, for which he was publicly disgraced. But you, yourself, Mr Lively, are no sprat. I confess I had some doubts as to your ability to turn a hand so quickly. Based entirely, I assure you, on my own lack-study as a freshling.'

Boundless laughed, pleased with the compliment. ''Tis the plenitude of fish in the pot!'

'Indeed! It *angles* a body the right way.'

THEY WERE ON THEIR way to Harrison's Wharf to pick up some cargo when, just before noon, they collided with a floating log.

The collision drew a string of voluble curses from the captain as he poured blame on the youngest member of the crew for the mishap. The boy stood crestfallen as he was subjected to a tongue lashing of such severity that it warranted the intervention of Mr York.

The mate unintentionally stoked Taysick's ire by pointing to the side planking where the seams had sprung apart as a result of the collision. As Mr York attempted to placate him, the captain fulminated at the damage, heaping curses on the log, the boat, and the river itself before once again pointing an accusing finger at the white-faced boy.

'Such a poor excuse for a lookout as I never did see! Put in, put in, Mr Cribble!' he commanded, snapping his fingers.

'Here, Cap'n?'

'At the cove, you dolt!'

The boat put in at the shallow cove a half-mile downstream as the men commiserated with the sniffling boy. Winking and patting him in consolation, they whispered scandalous allegations against the captain and his nativity. So spectacular and inventive were the accounts that the boy eventually laughed through his tears, the tongue-lashing forgotten in the joshing sympathy of his shipmates. Seated at the tiller, Captain Taysick ran the vessel up onto the bank, effectively beaching the hull.

'Everybody off,' ordered Mr York.

'Thanks to you, bonny lad, we get a holiday,' said Cassidy, rubbing the boy's head.

THE DAY WAS EXCEEDINGLY bright and temperate, cheering the men's spirits even further. They were raised again when the captain grudgingly announced a few hours 'release' as the ship's carpenter prepared to caulk the seams. Armed with the musket, he then took off into the woods in search of something to shoot.

Turlington took full advantage of the unexpected respite to organise a game of Ring Taw, the men fashioning a makeshift ring in the grass and collecting pebbles for marbles. Declining to join in, Boundless sat under the shade of a box tree to watch as the crew wagered noisily on each hit. After a few minutes he yawned, his eyes growing heavy in the languid air.

He awoke to a burst of laughter. Cassidy and Turlington were bent over with merriment. An ebullient Thompson backslapped the abashed Humpflinger as Cassidy chortled and tried helplessly to speak. The others roared with laughter—the Herculean labours of the river temporarily forgotten. An exuberant *whoop* went up from the gamesters as Cassidy and a second man promptly rough-housed, each trying to unfoot the other.

'Tuppence on New York!' shouted Thompson.

Mr Cribble ended the revels by sending the young deckhand to summon them back to the ship. 'Where is the captain?' asked Mr York, looking around as they returned.

'I heard him talk of visiting Skelton's Farm, after shooting,' said Boiler.

At the mention, Mr York glanced at Cribble and shook his head. 'Wait here, lads,' he said, and took off into the woods.

'Well, I for one am happy to take another sabbatical,' said Cassidy. He hopped up onto the gunnels and dangled his legs over the side.

'You be very Christian when it comes to work,' said Cribble. 'Why, I believe you would happily become a Seventh-Day Sabbatical, if such a thing were possible.' With a scowl in Cassidy's direction, he went to check the caulking.

Cassidy pulled a comical face. 'If taverns were churches, that apple-head would stand the most pious fellow in Maryland.'

'A sixpence that we visit Baltimore again before the month is out. What say, Enoch? Will you take the wager?' Cassidy's face wrinkled into a frown as Thompson made no reply. 'Are you paralytic, that you do not answer?'

'Hold oar, Cass, I was thinking.' Thompson scratched behind his ear. 'Was it at the Mermaid or the Fox that we had that splendid tansy—the one you gulped three helpings of?' He glanced at Turlington for assistance.

'The Mermaid,' said the latter. 'And it was the best I ever ate.'

'The price of eggs, Mr Thompson,' said Cassidy, his voice sour.

'Baltimore?' Thompson ruminated for a moment. 'It is true we proceed there more often than in the past.'

'And the better for it,' opined Turlington. 'I grow sick of canoeing up and down this river. I welcome the tides and the bracing air.'

'Not to mention the sails.'

'Aye. The sails also. My backbone is worn to a nub with towing and oaring.'

'And you, Mr Lively. How does your back fare after so much to-ing and fro-ing?'

'I am the stronger for it.'

'A noble answer. See Cass, how the newest amongst us finds gold among the dross?'

'Hush! He thinks of his beloved.'

'Is it true, Cass? Do you still pine for your beauteous, black-haired girl?'

'Which girl is this?' said Turlington. 'I spoke as to the generality.'

'Nay, but he hankers for a particular biscuit—a serving wench in New York who stole his heart the night afore we left.'

'Pshaw! Mock as ye will. I would swap all of this—aye, and gladly, too, for a pleasant cabin by the shore with a winsome wife to come home to.'

'Ha! What would you do with a wife?'

'I would settle down, as befits a man. Raise crops and grow fat in winter. All warm by the fire. And no more of this blasted boat business.'

Thompson shook his head. 'Heaven help us. A cabin on the seashore!'

Cass snorted. 'Who said *sea*shore? I said *shore*, thou rattle brain. Might it not be the shore of a stream, or a creek, mayhap, such as by Skelton's Farm? And what of yourself. Do you intend to play the glad goat for ever?'

'As long as I have horns—for that way I cannot be horned. But, by and by, I shall succumb to the contagion—if only to keep you company in your domestic woes.'

Turlington laughed. 'And what say you, Theo?'

'He has his eye set on a sweet peach up by the Landing, do you not?' teased Thompson.

'A wife is a pleasant thing. So long as she be stout and of merry temper.'

'Then are we all married and settled save Mr Lively and yourself, Harry,' said Thompson as eyes turned to Turlington.

'I remain content as a confirmed and rusted bachelor. I take ale as a wife and the tavern as hearth.'

'Then are you married and quit a dozen times within the week!'

'In truth. I had rather make a fortune than find a wife.'

'D'ye hear, Cass? Treasure before matrimony.'

'Fiddle! A warm fire, a mug of tea and a round of hot, buttered toast be worth more than all the treasure of the world.'

'And to speak of buttered toast, here shanks our noble lord and master.'

Heads turned to follow Thompson's gaze. Captain Taysick staggered towards them over the grass, supported by Mr York on one side and a slave on the other. As they watched, he slumped between the two, only to be hauled upright again and half-carried, half-dragged towards the ship.

'God in Heaven! Sozzled by noon! Rest, good gentlemen, we sail no more this day.'

ONE BRIGHT DECEMBER MORNING, six months after joining the boat, Boundless sensed an air of anticipation among the crew and questioned Humpflinger as to the cause.

'This afternoon the cap'n will make half payment of our wages for the year. The men will settle debts and, if experience be a guide, fall over themselves to lose it all over again at cards.'

Boundless waited eagerly in line before supper to receive £20 against the yearly sum of £40 due all 'apprentice' crew members. To his dismay, the eagerly awaited payment consisted of one silver Spanish coin, a paper bill of credit redeemable for ten Maryland shillings, and a promissory note for 100 lbs of tobacco to be handed over 'at the satisfactory culmination of twelve months' service'.

'What am I to do with this … *miscellany*?' he complained to Turlington, who looked at him in surprise.

'Why, the tobacco be exchangeable for any goods you desire. ''Tis as sure as the Spanish.'

'I had rather the latter. At least it will fit in my pocket.'

The payment created high spirits among the crew and gave rise to much bantering good humour about taverns and wenches. As Humpflinger predicted, it also sparked an immediate upsurge in card-playing and impromptu wagers on everything from the weather to the time and date of the captain's next whisky splurge.

'Four royals against any taker that he be guzzled by the Sabbath!' Cassidy challenged, several of the crew immediately taking him up on the offer.

THE UNSEASONABLY WARM WEATHER had given way to a month of cold days and colder nights, a light sprinkling of snow greeting them one morning as they awoke. But the exertion of rowing proved so warming that often Boundless rowed in shirt sleeves, his breath wreathing in the sharp air. He was now well accustomed to the strain of pulling the heavy oar and kept time with practised ease, his back and arms developing new strength and the blisters on his hands callused over with rough, dry skin.

'Does the captain observe Christmas?' he asked Thompson one afternoon as they sat at oar.

His companion laughed. 'Any day that celebrates the consumption of grog be a religion to him. In that respect, he be a true adherent to all the faiths.'

After several more stops and a detour up a side channel where the creek was so narrow that they had no option but to get out and tow the boat, they tied up for the night at a small island in the middle of the stream. For supper, they feasted on turkey and rabbit, received from a local farmer in payment for passage. The night air was chill and Boundless slept close to the fire, snugly wrapped in a blanket.

The following day, they came upon his favourite section of the channel—a wide, placid stretch of water where the view up and down river was unrestricted for almost a mile in either direction.

Around noon, they put into shore within sight of the only farmhouse visible from the river. Four individuals waited on the grassy bank, seated in the shade of a beech tree. Three of the four were Blacks. The fourth person was the overseer, a gaunt individual clothed in a woollen jacket and cocked hat. He carried a flintlock in his arms. At the approach of the boat, the man stood to his feet. 'Three hands for the Emry house!' he called through cupped hands. He roused the seated slaves and ushered them towards the boat. 'Hi-up!'

The Negroes wore canvas pants, cut at the knee, and tattered, homespun shirts. Each had a straw hat on his head and carried a canteen slung across one shoulder. They walked barefooted through the grass despite the cool weather. Stepping on board, they looked to the overseer, who shepherded them forward to a spot by the leeboard. There they sat on the deck, their eyes wide as they stared about them. The overseer sat across from the captives, perched atop a chest. Unbuttoning his jacket, he took out a ramrod and a scrap of cloth and began to clean the muzzle of the flintlock.

'Cast off!' commanded Mr York.

Boundless pulled at the oar, his eyes returning again and again to where the three Blacks sat silently side by side. One of the men had a weeping sore below his left eye.

'They look new to the country,' he said to Turlington, who rowed alongside him.

'Do they?' Turlington eyed the slaves. 'Mayhap.'

'They seem hard used by.'

'They be well suited to field work.'

'You do not think it an abomination?'

'Unlike Cass, I do not bother my head with such things.' Turlington grunted as he leaned into the oar. 'Besides, 'tis truly said that the wealth of the colony rides upon their backs. If they did not seed the crops, till the fields and harvest the plants who would? Certainly not I.'

'Nevertheless, it be a great evil.'

Turlington seemed surprised at the remark. 'Well now,' he said, pulling on the oar.

THE NEGROES WERE LED off the boat at the second stop along the river—the overseer handing them over to the care of a short, sunburned man who stood bareheaded in the sunshine. The two men talked for a while as the new owner paid the agreed price. The three purchases waited passively to one side.

'Go!' The sunburned man motioned his new possessions to proceed. A grizzled 'house Black' in a linen smock positioned himself at the front of the party and set off on the path towards the woods. The sunburned man brought up the rear, turning to wave to the overseer, who had climbed back aboard the boat.

'Out the oars!' Mr York's voice boomed in the stillness. 'Cheerly now, lads!'

A Wild and Savage Air

THE TEDIUM OF WORKING back and forth up and down the river was relieved by the captain's frequent bouts of intoxication. During one such fit, he insisted on racing the crew of a flatboat—wagering half the cargo on the outcome before falling to the deck in a dead faint. On several other occasions, he took up position with the flintlock and engaged in shooting contests with assorted passengers. 'A shilling on the fowl!' he cried, sighting on a fish-eagle as it alighted on a floating branch. Two of the passengers took him up on the wager, discharging pistols and flintlocks in succession without success. Taysick then made the attempt, the ball harmlessly striking the water a dozen yards from the bird.

'Bring her about!' he cried, furious at the miss. As the crew took to the oars, Mr York manoeuvred the boat closer to the branch. The three men held fire until the bird flapped up from the branch as the boat approached. Amid several puffs of gunpowder, it fell back to the river with a splash.

'Mine, sir, mine!' insisted the captain as each of the shooters claimed credit for the shot.

Within days of the wager, the captain tippled so much rum that he fell from the boat and had to be dragged, spluttering and gasping, back on board.

'A penny to a pound he forgets the splashing by the morrow!' Cassidy offered as the captain was close-hauled along the deck to his makeshift bed in the stern.

The day following the incident, they awoke to rain and drab skies. The weather continued cool all morning as they rowed a short distance up a creek to deliver two pigs and a firkin of wine. In the afternoon, they put ashore to disembark a farmhand and collect a crate of preserves. The captain, bareheaded and unshaven, his eyes red-rimmed and his manner surly from his latest bout of intemperance, lashed the men unmercifully, cursing volubly at the least infraction that caught his eye.

'Such a motley I never saw!' he thundered, a wrathful expression on his face.

They had barely cast off again when they heard a holler. A thinly built individual rapidly descended the path from a small bluff above the landing.

Behind him, a large, florid-faced man in an unbuttoned shirt gave chase. The thin man reached the foot of the bluff and hastened towards the boat, barely a dozen yards in front of his heavy-set pursuer.

'Make way!' warned Mr York.

Boundless stepped back from the side as the fleeing man splashed through the water and grasped hold of the rail, pulling himself up nimbly over the side and onto the deck.

'Make haste, boys! Make haste!' The fugitive picked himself up to glance back at where his stout pursuer had stopped to catch breath. 'Thou fat-bellied lack-wind! Thou fart in a gale!' He hurled a series of taunts and insults as the boat pulled away from the shore. The florid-faced man, still gasping for breath, shook a fist and shouted curses at his mocking quarry.

To Boundless' surprise, the older crew members gave the new arrival short shrift, barely concealing their annoyance at his presence. The man was bare headed, his unruly hair tangled into a pigtail tied with a fibre of hemp. His face was sharp—a thin nose offset by narrow eyes and a smudge of a mouth. He wore a dirty linen shirt and tattered canvas trousers—both garments seemingly his sole possessions in the world, apart from a knife sheathed at his waist and a deck of cards he pulled from his pocket. Through the open collar of his shirt the design of a mermaid could be seen inked on his chest. The newcomer made himself comfortable in a spot next to the mast. Seemingly unconcerned by the muttering looks of the crew, he whistled jauntily while shuffling the deck of cards.

'Who is our new passenger?' Boundless asked at the first opportunity. 'If I had not recently encountered a heathen with my own eyes, I should mistake him for the very article. He has a wild and savage air about him.'

Thompson flashed an irritable glance at where the man sat cross-legged on the deck, laying out the cards in front of him. 'That, Mr Lively, be Mercer Dowell—no honest passenger, but a thorough-going rascal. A notorious sharper and drunk. We had best abandoned him to whoever it was pursued him. A bilked farmer no doubt, or some cuckolded husband. The villain will have half the crew's wages before we have gone another week. I advise you to steer well clear of the fellow. He has been on furlough in these parts—doubtless there is a card game ashore. He uses the boat to work passage from one end of the river to the next, staying only so long as to relieve the crew of their hard-won wages and then on to pluck the next chicken. The men are not pleased to see him as half of them are indentured to him for their next wage. It is a great wonder that the captain allows him aboard.' Thompson lowered his voice. 'But, in truth, not altogether surprising. He is rumoured to be heavily in debt himself to the scoundrel and works it off by allowing free passage.'

Boundless covertly studied the new arrival as the wind picked up and they raised sail. The fellow had a mocking, volatile look about him that bespoke caution. His occasional laughs were devoid of humour, rather resembling barks as he summarily relieved the only other passenger—a sheepish youth travelling between plantations—of his single coin. He determined to follow Thompson's advice and give the fellow a wide berth.

THE FOLLOWING DAY, THEY reached a creek near the mouth of the river and spent several hours unloading cargo and taking fresh goods aboard before the captain gave the command to turn around the boat.

'Now 'tis all to do again,' quipped Thompson as the boat tacked across the river. They proceeded upstream along the windward shore, a wind from the bay buffeting the sail. Before dusk, they had put in twice to off-load cargo or pick up passengers. To Boundless' pleasure, Mr York commended him on his quick handling of the sail as the wind continued to blow strongly.

In the afternoon, they journeyed up an inlet, taking to the oars as the wind fell away again. With scarcely an hour of daylight remaining, Taysick gave the order to pull into shore. There they encountered a party of men awaiting the arrival of a barge. The men refused the captain's invitation to board the boat instead.

'Master Williams would never forgive,' said one, the name seeming to irritate Taysick. Muttering at all such 'featherheads', he returned to the boat.

Following supper, the men lounged about on the grass, bored and listless. In spite of his sinister reputation, several succumbed to Dowell's invitation to take a 'harmless turn' with the cards.

'Now you shall see the wolf fleece the lamb,' Thompson predicted, as a young farmhand, bound for the upper river, shouted with glee over a winning hand.

'See with the evidence of your eyes? 'Tis I that am paupered!' Dowell complained loudly in a voice that yet rejected commiseration. Grudgingly, he handed over a coin to the beaming youth.

''Tis his stratagem,' Thompson muttered. 'By short losses he draws them in.'

Several other men, whether out of boredom or a desperation to reduce their debt, slowly joined in the game. Boundless glanced at the stern where Captain Taysick and Mr York were engaged in conversation, the former occasionally looking up to watch the game, a calculating expression on his face.

'Pshaw!' A deckhand threw down his cards in disgust and stalked off as Dowell quickly pocketed the small pile of coins on the deck.

'That man will work the remainder of the trip for no wages.' Humpflinger sat down beside Boundless.

'You do well to keep your money in your pocket, Theodore.'

Humpflinger gave a rueful grimace. 'Experience, my friend, be a hard master.'

AFTER NO MORE THAN a week on board, Dowell had not only extracted the coins from the pockets of the more gullible members of the crew, but also a lien on their future wages, much to the anger of the older deckhands. Veiled threats and loathing glances were cast in the direction of the card sharp as he fleeced yet another despairing victim. 'Why does the captain allow it?' Boundless asked, as Dowell grinned and pocketed the winnings.

''Tis whispered the villain credits him with a third of the takings,' said Humpflinger, 'to ease his own indebtedness. If true, 'tis scandalous behaviour and will only end badly.'

Several passengers taken aboard also fell victim to the sharp, in spite of warnings from Mr York and members of the crew.

'You would think they would beware him by reputation,' said Boundless as an elegantly dressed young man in a cape and leather shoes sat down on his trunk. The obliging Dowell laid out several cards on a barrel head.

'He baits the lure to suit the fish. Observe how he feigns reluctance—as if drawn into the game against his judgement. I witnessed that same sprat lose ten pounds to Dowell not two year ago. Either his memory is lost or he fancies the chance to win back his pot.' Thompson scowled as the young man immediately won a turn and Dowell threw down his cards in frustration. 'Now is the game afoot.'

THE DAY WAS FINE and hazy with a gentle mist on the river and a mild headwind. In the midafternoon, as they sailed close to the shore, they were hailed by a loud 'Halloo!' from the thickly wooded heights. The shout was followed by the discharge of a musket and a puff of white smoke. The men scrambled to their feet and scanned the bluffs for signs of the hailer.

'Over there!' Mr York pointed to a small prominence overhanging the river directly ahead.

Boundless squinted, finally glimpsing through the trees a figure waving and hollering to catch their attention.

'It's Fesky!' whooped one of the boys. 'Hey, Fesk, you old coot!'

'Who is that?' Boundless looked to Turlington for explanation.

'Fur trapper,' the latter said, grasping the foresail sheet.

'Heave to!' commanded Taysick as the crew leapt to trim the mainsail and jib in tight. The boat swung towards the low bluff under the influence of the tiller, the captain expertly balancing the sails and rudder as the boat came to a stop in the water.

'Get ready, boys!' shouted Mr York. 'Mind your heads!'

As the boat floated to a halt beneath the bluff, a bundle of furs sailed over the mast and landed on the deck with a thud. It was followed by a second bundle and then a third. A fourth bundle descended on a rope with a flintlock sticking out along with a pan handle. Once this bundle had been safely deposited on board, the owner himself tumbled agilely to the deck to the cheers of the crew.

'Mighty appreciate it, boys!' The trapper picked himself up, grinning as several of the men crowded around to shake hands and clap him on the back. He raised a hand to Taysick, who nodded and gave the command to raise the windward jib sheet.

Boundless eyed the new arrival with avid curiosity, undecided if he had ever beheld such an eccentric figure. The trapper was small in stature but lean and weathered, with a wiry look to his frame that bespoke energy and strength. He was clothed in an exotic costume of furs and patched buckskin, which from certain points caused him to resemble a bear or some other wild creature alighted on the deck. The bearish effect was compounded by an unkempt beard streaked with grey.

As the crew pressed forward to ply him with questions, the trapper removed his fur cap to reveal a lock of long, greyish black hair pulled into a tail and tied with a strip of buckskin. The man conducted himself with a free and independent air that complemented his woodland garb as he gossiped and bantered with the gawking deckhands.

'Back to your duties!' snapped an irritable Captain Taysick as the trapper good-naturedly waved off more questions from the crew. He knelt down to check the bundles, fishing out a metal flask from one roll.

'The whisky ain't broke! Thank perdition!' Raising the flask to his lips he took a long swallow.

'Where are you headed, Fesk?' asked a deckhand.

'Elk Ridge, boys, if ye be going that far. I've a mind for some heathen society.'

The reply drew admiring laughter. 'Good old Fesk!' cracked a veteran deckhand. 'Ain't he just like himself!'

As the boat tied up at a wharf to await a shipment of tobacco, the men again flocked around the trapper, pressing for accounts of his adventures. In between copious swallows of whisky, he regaled their interest with tales of wild jinks and hair-raising escapades among the savages. Boundless listened avidly, intrigued by the man's fearless manner and open disdain for all forms of authority—a theme evident from the fellow's colourful boasts of outwitting officious bureaucrats and grasping merchants alike.

As the general fuss over the trapper's arrival died down and the men turned to other diversions, Boundless approached the man to introduce himself.

'Pleased to meet you, Mr Lively.' The trapper grasped Boundless' hand in a grip so strong it made him wince.

'Mr Fesky, sir,' he began, only for the trapper cut him off.

'Fesk'll do. I left the "Mister" behind a ways ago.'

The trapper sat cross-legged with his back against the side of the boat as he searched his haversack.

'Ha!' With the exclamation, he withdrew a short clay pipe, a tinderbox and a pouch of tobacco. Breaking off a twist of tobacco, he stuffed it in his mouth.

'I see you eyeing those pelts, young fella,' he said, as he opened the tinderbox. 'Take a look, if it fancies ye.'

'Indeed, it does. I thank you.' Boundless fingered the soft, dark pelts, caressing their supple thickness. 'Which creatures are they from?'

Fesky didn't answer for a moment, absorbed in the tinderbox. Carefully positioning the box away from the wind, he struck sparks with the flint onto the char cloth. Nursing the spark, he transferred the glowing embers to a frayed twist of jute, then, shielding the smouldering jute against the pipe bowl, he sucked the tobacco to flame. Sitting back with a satisfied air, he exhaled a puff of smoke.

'By Glory, but that's a taste! My baccy got wet crossing the river a week back. First pipe since that woeful day.' He closed his eyes to savour the draw. 'Fine leaf, it is, too,' he murmured. He still had the plug of tobacco in his mouth, chewing around it as he smoked the pipe.

'The pelts? Mink, otter and muskrat, mostly, with a relish of squirrel and fox. I had a wolf but lost the pelt to a savage, which was a trial. Wolf be getting devilish scarce around these parts.' He lifted himself up and spat a stream of tobacco juice over the side. 'Guess I'll have to cut further west,' he grumbled. 'Maybe go back to hunting buff. Leastways *they* ain't running out.'

'You have hunted buffalo?' Boundless paused in his examination of the pelts.

'Hunt? Why, I used shoot a dozen afore breakfast! There's no meat like buff. It thickens the hide and grows hair on the chest.'

'What does a buffalo look like, exactly? I have heard accounts, but they differ in part.'

Fesky eyed him suspiciously. 'You ain't never seen a buff? A picture, even?'

'I assure you, sir—the animal is unknown to me, apart from what I have heard from my companions.'

Fesky snorted. 'Them bowlegs? They acquaint us much with the buff as a bride with a parson!'

Convinced of the genuineness of Boundless' interest, he tugged a large knife from a sheath around his waist.

'Lookee here.' Sweeping a handful of dried mud and dust from the deck of the boat, he heaped it into a pile in front of him. Chewing vigorously on the tobacco plug, he spat a squirt of juice into the dirt and mixed the two with the knife. He repeated the action, patting the moistened dirt into a square. Using the point of the knife he then delicately sifted the grains to produce a silhouette of an animal that might have been a cow or a stag. Frowning at the result, he scrubbed over the image and started again, squirting more tobacco juice into the mix and adding more dirt.

'That be a buff,' he grunted, and sat back, satisfied with his efforts.

Boundless studied the mud scrim, careful to murmur appreciation in justice to the effort.

'Do they—buffalo—inhabit these parts?'

'One time. Not here, exactly, but up around Pennsylvanny and further west.'

Fesky squeezed his chin, considering the reply. 'Course, they be awful hard to find nowadays. The farmers and settlers between them have jest about shot them all to hell. Mind, they are said to be in abundance the other side of the mountains—out beyond the French country.'

'Is the beast as plentiful as is reputed?'

'You ever seen a pigeon flock? Those big ones that block out the sun?'

'I have.' said Boundless, pleased to be able to claim this much knowledge.

'Well, buff are like that.'

'As many as the pigeon!' His eyes widened in disbelief.

Fesky nodded sagely. 'More. 'Tis said that their numbers be so great west of the mountains that their passage shakes the earth.' He lifted himself and spat a stream of tobacco juice over the side. 'Course, the claim is by repute, only.'

Eager for more knowledge of the wondrous creature, Boundless pestered the trapper for details of its habits, disposition, and enemies, adding more questions as each was answered. The trapper answered patiently each time until finally waving a hand in exasperation.

'There ain't no more! That's it. I'm wore out. I ain't talked so much in a year!'

Taking another swallow from the flask of whisky, the pulled his fur hat over his eyes, giving every appearance of going to sleep.

As Boundless took his turn in line to roll six tobacco hogsheads on board, he went over the conversation in his mind. Disappointed that he would not have the chance to see the animal roaming the nearby woods, he reflected on the vast numbers Fesky had claimed to lie beyond the mountains. Accustomed only to the small bands of deer roaming the Scottish Highlands, he tried to imagine a creature so bountiful as to defy comprehension. 'Balderdash!' he muttered, frowning with the suspicion that the trapper was taking humour at his expense.

WITH THE CARGO OF hogsheads lashed in place, the boat put out from the landing, headed for the Fincastle plantation a mile downstream. To general groans from the crew, the wind, which had driven them to the wharf, changed quarter and then died away entirely. 'Out the oars!' shouted Mr Cribble. 'Jump to it!'

Boundless took his place behind Humpflinger as the boat drifted almost to a halt in the slack tide. 'Row dry!' Mr Cribble directed an annoyed glance at him as he splashed the oar in the water.

'Beg pardon!' Flushed, he pulled back on the oar as Cassidy broke into giggles behind him.

'Stow the japes, Mr Cassidy! Bend backs to it!'

They rowed for the better part of an hour until they reached their destination. Panting, they waited at the oars as a farmer and two Blacks came on board—the latter struggling to carry a large trunk between them. They set out once more, angling in a line across the river to a small dock on the far side. Midway across they passed by a barge rowing in the opposite direction.

'Ahoy!' A man stood up in the stern of the vessel, waving his cap.

'It's old Pearson, boys!' someone shouted, leading a cheer in return.

'He rowed with us last year,' said Humpflinger, grunting as he pulled on the oar. He glanced around before continuing in a low voice. 'He and the captain fell out over a wager and the poor fellow was abandoned to the shore. I am glad to see him well.'

Relieved at the oar, Boundless made his way back to the side where Fesky was engaged in an animated argument with a passenger—a cooper taken aboard at the previous landing. The cooper, who imbibed freely from a canteen of his own, insisted that the price of pelts had declined, despite the scarcity of beaver.

'A handsome pelt would fetch no more than two shillings in Philadelphia, friend, I assure you. Or a half crown at most. I have but lately had the pleasure of visiting the city where I purchased this very hat.' The cooper took off his felt hat to illustrate the point.

'Then you were duped! Each beaver be worth six shillings or more,' Fesky argued. 'A beaver pelt be as good as a Pennsylvania pound.' That commodity rates held a fluid credit in the valuation seemed not to deter him in the least when the loquacious cooper seized on this fact.

'Pshaw to your reckoning!' snapped Fesky. 'Why, I could walk into a Philadelphia tavern, throw a pelt on the table and require the finest service. And no man dare refuse me, afore God!'

'What in blazes does that have to do with the price of fish?' demanded the cooper.

Fesky spat a stream of tobacco over the side. 'Away with ye! Give me space to drink my whisky in peace.'

After another turn at the oars, Boundless took up position midship where Fesky sat with his head slumped on his chest. The trapper had fallen fast asleep, one hand resting on a bundle of furs, the other lying in the lap of his soiled leggings. Further along the deck, Dowell sat out of the wind, engaged in a hand of cards with the cooper and another passenger.

'I'll wager both will be relieved of the shoes on their feet before we are called back to the oars.' Humpflinger squeezed into the space beside Boundless, glancing at the somnolent trapper. 'Hark, he sleeps like a foundling babe.'

'But is he not a most original character, Theodore?'

'Aye. That he is. Those furs shall fetch a pretty penny.'

'Are there many more like him—on the river?'

'At one time.'

'But no more?'

'They follow the beaver. As the animal is perished out of stock so, too, the catcher must find fresh stores.' Humpflinger took out his pipe. 'You admire him, Joshua?'

'I do. I confess. Such as he feed and clothe themselves from the creatures of the field. They are beholden to no man and exist without benefit of society. Are they not the truest type of the original Adam?'

Humpflinger nodded over the pipe. 'Mayhap. Although to live like a savage is more than I could bear.' He gazed soberly at the silent, surrounding wilderness. 'It be a hard and perilous occupation, make no mistake.'

Boundless fell silent, contemplating the thick green forest from whence Fesky had emerged. That a nature existed so bountiful that meat and fish were plentiful to hand and beefsteak and venison an everyday affair struck him as a miracle beyond reckoning. Perhaps Adam himself, he mused, had never encountered such a stupendous abundance as was commonly found in every stream, branch and field of this New World.

'Adam was naked,' he murmured to himself, 'but such as Fesky comport themselves in the finest leather.'

'What do you say?'

'I was remarking upon his sturdy garments.'

'That be called buckskin.' Humpflinger nodded towards the trapper's leggings. 'It must be cured and tanned to a turn. But it will outlast wool or linen.'

A loud curse interrupted their conversation. The cooper had climbed to his feet, loudly berating the hand. Flinging down the cards, he made his way along the deck, flushed with temper.

'He still has his shoes,' Boundless noted, as the man pushed by, stepping over the sleeping Fesky.

'Aye. But empty pockets, I'll be bound.' Humpflinger knocked the tobacco from his pipe and stood up. 'I must piss before we are called back to the oars.'

Fesky gave a shuddering snore, his breath interrupted for a moment before he fell asleep again.

On impulse, Boundless knelt by the trapper—glancing at the sleeper before closely examining the bundle of pelts. He ran his fingers through the fur, marvelling at the dense softness. Sensing he was being watched, he glanced up to find Dowell looking down at him.

'Pretty though, ain't they?' The gambler stared insolently, a wolfish smile on his lips.

'Ain't you got some greenhorn to filch?' Fesky lifted his hat, giving the gambler a hard stare.

'A fellow is just taking a look.' Dowell held up his hands, professing innocence. 'Where's the harm in that?'

'None. If he has an invite.' Fesky's voice was sharp, his eyes narrowed. 'Suppose I invited myself?'

'Do you mean to have words?' Fesky's voice held an unmistakeable edge.

A venomous look passed over Dowell's face. Then, as if reconsidering, he licked his lips and broke off his gaze to glance carelessly about the deck.

'Ha! I ain't that particular about a bunch of mouldy old furs. I guess there's better to see somewheres else.'

'Then you'd best go find it.'

The gambler gave an exaggerated stretch and yawn before slowly moving off along the deck.

Fesky watched him go. 'That there is a snake, absolute and certain. Mind him, Mr Lively. He has such a stench of poison to him as befouls the air.'

18

A Justified Murder

L ATE ONE AFTERNOON, THEY put into shore for the night. The stretch was wild, without any sign of habitation. After building a fire and cooking supper, the men lazed around or went for exploratory strolls into the thickly wooded hinterland. Boundless joined Humpflinger and Thompson on one such walk, marvelling at the congestion of trees and the tangled canopy of branches that soared overhead. The solitude was broken only by birdsong or the occasional rustle of a deer or some other animal in the undergrowth. Several times, he stopped to try to catch a glimpse of the river behind them, concerned lest they become lost and swallowed up by the wilderness.

'This be fine timber for cutting.' Thompson's voice was loud in the pristine hush. 'What say you, Mr Humpflinger?'

Humpflinger was crouched down, examining a growth of large mushrooms among the ferns. 'The heathen, so it is claimed, eat these plants. They are said to be poisonous to all but savages.' He poked the mushrooms with a stick.

Mention of the word 'savage' set Boundless' mind racing on the hazards of encountering a party of Indians in the green twilight of the woods. He glanced around at the gigantic trunks, supposing the glade was so thickly wooded it could hide an ambuscade of savages without the least suspicion of their presence. Thompson, evidently, had the same thought—the latter starting as a twig snapped somewhere in the undergrowth. In the lengthening shadows, the forest hush seemed pregnant with danger.

'Mayhap we should return to the fire,' Boundless suggested.

'Agreed!' Without more ado, Thompson set off in that direction.

'Mr Fesky has a bracing way with the language,' Boundless remarked as they retraced their steps through the undergrowth.

'Ohio English, Mr Lively,' said Thompson, visibly relaxing as the river came back into sight. 'One-quart Presbyterian and three quarts savage. It be the *braggadocio* of the frontier. Now, where is the wretched camp?'

A card game was in progress as they returned to the fire. Four or five men were gathered around a blanket spread with cards and coins. Fesky reclined against a fallen log, watching the game while smoking a pipe. Dowell was evidently on a rare losing streak—muttering with anger as a man opposite whooped at a winning hand.

'I'll have my wages back, if you please!' The man scooped a pile of coins to his side of the blanket.

'Do you play another?' challenged Dowell, his voice fierce as if daring the man to refuse.

'No fear!' his rival chortled. 'You shall not have back what I have only just reclaimed.' His companions guffawed and slapped the grinning man on the back as he pocketed the coins.

'You see the game?' Thompson whispered in Boundless' ear. 'The villain pretends to lose only to draw the men in deeper. But they are on to his tricks.'

'Any man among you with the fortitude?' Dowell glared at the men in turn. His eyes fell on Boundless. 'Come, friend, turn a hand,' he said, his tone dark and inviting.

Boundless shook his head. 'Cards and I be no friends.'

'A wise decision, Mr Lively.' Thompson laid a hand on his shoulder. He turned to Dowell. 'You shall not pluck another chicken this night, *friend*,' he said.

Dowell swore and flung down the deck. 'I guess I'm to be blamed for enduring the contrariness of all *plugtails* who refuse to give a man a fair turn to shake his fortune for the better!'

As the sharp glowered and complained, the men drifted off to find sleeping spots under the trees. Boundless and Humpflinger elected to stay close to the fire, aware of the chilliness of dawn. As he lay under the blanket, listening to the snap and pop of the burning logs, Boundless turned to gaze at the anchored *Egret* and, beyond it, the river. The water glittered in the bright moonlight, the ripple of the tide a soothing *slush* above the crackle of the fire. Across the river the line of woods presented a dark and impenetrable shade. He shivered at the thought of being lost in such a maze, far removed from the comfort of open ground. He was dwelling on the thought when his eyes closed and he drifted off to sleep.

HE AWAKENED TO A hand tugging stealthily at the deerskin pouch around his neck. Still groggy with sleep, he was dimly aware of the cold feel of a knife blade against his skin. Instinctively, he groped for the hand holding the knife, a sharp sense of peril penetrating his drowsiness. A voice cursed and he felt the unknown assailant's breath against his face.

'Help! Thief!' he cried, his heart pounding with shock and fear. Others around him stirred at the disturbance. 'Help!' He twisted his head as a hand clawed at his eyes.

Now fully awake, he saw Dowell's face gleam above him in the moonlight, a murderous snarl on the gambler's lips. As his assailant attempted to wrench back the knife, Boundless clung on desperately, not daring to breathe in the intensity of the struggle. Dowell swore and elbowed him sharply across the nose, the pain almost causing him to loosen his grip on the knife hand. The grim and silent struggle continued, both men gasping for breath as they fought for the advantage.

Cries of alarm came from the aroused crew and Dowell seemed to hesitate. Seizing the advantage, Boundless twisted the knife and thrust upwards, sticking the blade deep into the ribs of his assailant. Dowell gave a strangled gasp. For a moment he glared at Boundless with maddened eyes. Then, uttering a groan, he slumped forward onto his intended victim.

'Break them apart!' Humpflinger was on his feet, dragging Boundless from beneath Dowell. 'Are you hurt, Joshua? Did he cut you?' He knelt beside Boundless, his face anxious in the gloom.

'No. I do not think so.' Badly shaken, he was assisted to his feet. Someone ignited a torch from the glowing embers of the campfire and held it up in the darkness as the men bent over the limp body of the assailant.

'He's about done for,' Fesky announced, kneeling to peer at the fatally wounded gambler. He looked up at Boundless. 'You done saved yourself, young fella. I 'spect he was after that coin pouch around your neck. I caught him admiring it earlier today.'

They heard a gurgling sound from Dowell, followed by a drawn-out moan. 'He's breathed his last,' a man said, hovering over the sharp.

Fesky thrust a canteen of whisky into Boundless' hand. 'Take a swallow. It will settle the nerves.'

White-faced and trembling from shock, Boundless swallowed from the canteen, gasping as the raw whisky burned his throat. His hand shook uncontrollably as he handed back the canteen.

'Get some sleep, friend.' Fesky slapped him on the shoulder. 'He sure as fire ain't going nowhere.' He motioned at the corpse.

'Do not take it over-hard, Joshua.' Humpflinger laid a hand on his arm. 'The villain is justly repaid for what he intended to you.'

'He would else have murdered me,' Boundless protested, feeling faint. For the first time he noticed the blood soaking his shirt. A wave of nausea engulfed him and he thought his legs might collapse beneath him.

'What is the hullabaloo?' Cribble shouldered his way through the deck-hands, a lantern in his hand, his face cross in the reflected light. Leaning down, he held the lantern above the dead man. He swore an oath as he caught sight of the knife still embedded between the ribs.

'What ho! Murder! We have an assassin among us!'

Holding up the lantern, Cribble looked around and caught sight of Boundless' dazed expression.

'You!' he cried accusingly. 'I 'spected you'd be trouble when we took you on board!'

'It weren't him, Mr Cribble,' Humpflinger protested. 'The fault was entirely Dowell's.'

'It was indeed,' Thompson insisted. 'Mr Lively was defending for his life.'

Several of the surrounding crew strongly voiced their assent. Taken aback at this show of unity, Cribble gestured at the body. 'Stow him until daylight,' he snapped. 'The captain will want a full account.' With a last, threatening glare at Boundless, he turned on his heel and stalked off to the boat.

Humpflinger and several of the deckhands immediately gathered around to voice sympathy. 'Do not concern yourself, Joshua. The men will swear to your account. It was self-defence, was it not?' Humpflinger asked, turning to the men.

'Without a doubt,' Cassidy asserted. 'Does anyone say to the contrary?'

'There be none to say what is not true,' Thompson said, as murmurs of agreement came from the crew.

Cassidy made a motion with his hand. 'The matter be plain as day. Have no fear, Mr Lively. The entire crew is of a mind on this.'

'Why did he do it?' Boundless implored, clutching Humpflinger's hand.

'It was his nature,' Humpflinger said soothingly. 'Try to sleep. We will sort this matter in the morning.'

Boundless lay down in the grass, his limbs trembling as he tried to come to terms with the horror of what had happened. After a sleepless half hour, the notion struck him that Dowell might not be dead after all. He sat up in fright. The gambler lay stretched out by the smouldering fire. The hairs stood up on Boundless' neck as he fancied he saw the thin chest rise and fall in the moonlight.

He lay back down, shielding an arm over his eyes to block the violent event from his thoughts. Unable to sleep, he re-enacted the desperate strug-gle again and again in his mind as a sense of unreality overtook him. He pictured, with vivid fright, Dowell sitting astride him, a murderous gleam in his eyes, the knife raised to strike a fatal blow. He moaned in horror, still muttering as he fell asleep from shock and exhaustion.

'WAKE UP!' A MAN'S voice was loud in his ear. A hand shook him by the shoulder. 'The cap'n would speak with ye.'

Opening his eyes, he was momentarily dazed before being seized by a fresh sensation of horror as the events of the previous night flooded back. He glanced towards the fire where the body of the dead man lay under a blanket. Light bathed the sky above the trees. The men were seated around the coffee pot, talking quietly. One or two glanced at him as he sat up and looked away again.

Humpflinger approached, holding a mug of hot tea. 'Drink this, Joshua,' he said, kneeling.

Boundless was about to take the mug when he glanced down at his shirt, recoiling at the sight of the dried blood. 'I must change my shirt,' he said, his voice thick. He climbed to his feet.

'The cap'n!', warned Humpflinger, moving to stand alongside him.

Captain Taysick approached over the grass accompanied by Mr Cribble and Mr York. Looking grim, he advanced towards Dowell's body. Bending down, he pulled the blanket aside to stare, briefly, at the dead man's face. He straightened up and raked the gathered crew with his glance.

'Where is the man that did this?'

Cribble whispered in his ear and nodded in the direction of Boundless.

Taysick fixed him a bloodshot stare. 'This was by your hand?'

'He gave me no choice in the matter. He tried to rob and murder me.' Boundless licked his dry lips, his heart thumping in his chest.

'He lost heavily at cards and wished to relieve Mr Lively of his purse by way of recompense,' said Humpflinger. 'Mr Lively did only what he must to defend his person.'

'The man was a thief and a cut-throat,' Cassidy added to murmurs of agreement.

'Be that the case? Justified murder? So say you all?' The captain swept the surrounding men with his gaze.

'It is. We be of one mind,' said Turlington. 'Mr Lively acted only to save his person. The facts speak for themselves.'

Taysick scratched his chin, his face sickly pale under the stubble as he considered the shrouded corpse. 'Doubtless the deed discharged many a debt,' he remarked sourly. The spidery veins stood out in his cheeks, the tip of his nose flushed and dripping in the cool morning air. He considered a moment longer, the breeze ruffling the thin hair on his head.

'You will be surrendered to the magistrate at Elk Ridge,' he declared brusquely, glancing at Boundless. 'For such action as he deems fit.'

Humpflinger uttered a protest. 'It was justified! We are all witness!'

'The law is the law!' Captain Taysick held up a hand to quell the protests. In the silence that followed, he made a rasping sound in his throat and spat into the grass. Looking deathly pale, he pulled out a silk handkerchief and dabbed at his mouth.

'I shall mention the opinion of the crew to the magistrate. Each of you may be called upon to offer evidence.' He gazed at the body as if deliberating whether to add further to this pronouncement.

'Bury the corpse,' he said briskly. 'We leave within the half hour.' Turning on his heel, he strode back to the boat.

The men gathered around Boundless, offering fresh sympathies. Fesky, who had observed the scene unfold, came over and clapped Boundless on the shoulder. 'That snake belly was full of bile. Judge yourself to have performed the world a service, Mr Lively.'

Following breakfast, Boundless watched, lethargic and ashen faced, as the men dug a trench and interred the corpse. He had been unable to take any food, fearing he might instantly vomit. He watched, his emotions drained, as a final spadeful of dirt was tossed onto the grave.

No one spoke following the interment, the men merely marking the spot with a simple cross. Either from a sense of sardonic humour, or misplaced piety, one of the crew pinned a playing card to the cross, before burying the pack in the freshly turned earth.

'Come, Joshua, we are ready to depart.' Humpflinger laid a hand on his shoulder.

Boundless nodded, staring at the grave for a moment before turning away and following his companion back to the boat. Once on board, he stood by the side, staring at the solitary mound of earth as the oars stroked the cold water and the boat pulled away from the deserted shore.

THE MEN'S SYMPATHY OVER the affair was evident in the many expressions of fellowship offered him over the course of the day. But the incident left him severely shaken, robbing him of both appetite and his normally keen observation of the passing shoreline. Several times, he gazed at the spot on deck where, just the day before, the dead man had engaged in a card game or complained loudly of his ill turn of luck. In fancy, he saw Dowell glance up at him—only this time the glance was tinged with reproof and regret. Feeling light-headed, he sat on the side of the boat, holding onto the forestay as the vessel dipped in the stream.

His spirits remained low for the remainder of the day, even as the weather continued clear and mild, the sunlight glancing off the limpid waters of the river. He was manoeuvring a keg into place when his captain's declaration sprang suddenly to mind—it having been temporarily forgotten in his anguish over the fatal struggle: *'You will be surrendered to the magistrate at Elk Ridge.'*

As the full import of the words struck home, his listless mood gave way to a sense of alarm. There would undoubtedly be an inquest. Of a certainty, this would involve a check into his person—and perhaps the prospect of being sent back to Philadelphia for trial or further investigation. He forgot to breathe as the terrifying prospect of exposure exorcised all other thoughts from his mind. *It would mean certain hanging—whether for murder or escape.*

'Which way be your thoughts tending, Mr Lively?'

He looked up to find Fesky standing beside him.

'I was thinking over the captain's promise to hand me to the authorities in Elk Ridge,' he admitted.

'And not liking it?' Fesky fixed him a shrewd look.

He could only shrug, the truth of his feelings written on his face.

'If it was me,' the trapper said, spitting over the side and lowering his voice, 'I'd skip this darn rowboat at the very next landing and damnation to the magistrate. That thief and scoundrel wouldn't warrant a minute of time explaining myself.'

He studied the trapper—wary of the conversation but drawn to the man's frank and honest manner.

'And where would you go—if it were you that was … responsible?'

'There are but three ways.' Fesky folded his arms and leaned his hip on the rail as he considered the possibilities. 'South to the Virginias. East to Philly and New York. Or west to the Ohio.'

'And your own determination—if faced with such a predicament?'

'East and south would bring notices—posters, bulletins and the such. In which case inland, to the Ohio, would be the path a prudent man would follow. It would be an amazement for anyone to bother you there.'

Boundless drummed his fingers on the gunnel, wondering if this wasn't all a hideous nightmare. 'There is much to consider.'

'There ain't but the one thing to consider—the damn magistrate!'

Making a wry face at the trapper's rude perspicacity, he fell silent for a moment.

'Suppose a body … *skipped*, as you say, this boat and elected a return to Philadelphia. Would not the passage itself be a risk? The captain would be certain to raise a hue and cry. And who knows, but several days might pass before a ship bound for Phil—'

'Pshaw! Who mentioned *ship*? Did I? Such a way is a certainty to get caught. Word will fly before you—have you not seen how quickly news travels up and down the river?'

'Then how in the name of the goose to reach Philadelphia, if not by ship?'

'The way lies before you.' Fesky gestured to the shore.

Nonplussed, Boundless stared at the impenetrable tangle of trees along the bank. 'The woods? You mean *walk*?' He stared at the trapper as if the latter had taken leave of his senses.

'Philadelphia ain't so far. I've trod the path myself. I could sketch you a track to the Indian Path. The road will then take you to Baltimore—and all the way east to Philly.'

Boundless' mouth dropped open in astonishment. 'I am—I remind you, a novice to these woods. The way is unknown to me, the distance far, the peril—'

'Fiddle the way! Just point your nose. And if you don't care to walk, then buy a horse and ride the distance.'

Exasperated by the trapper's laconic dismissal of every difficulty, he shook his head. 'I must think on it.'

'Not too long,' warned Fesky. 'Else that sot of a captain will have you fetched back to the Landing afore you can strike a spark.'

FOR THE REMAINDER OF the day, Boundless avoided company, throwing himself into the operations of the boat to forestall questions or attempts at conversation from his solicitous companions. He performed his tasks by rote, his mind going over and over Fesky's advice. A memory of the courtroom at the Old Bailey came suddenly to mind—the justice condemning him with a malicious glance even as his friends protested his innocence.

To perdition with all magistrates! he swore to himself, his mind made up on the instant.

'Friends, would you take the air with me?' he asked his companions that evening as they waited for supper.

The companions strolled away from the boat as he revealed his conversation with Fesky, adding his determination to take the trapper's advice and abandon the boat.

'I believe it the only prudent course,' he said, without revealing his reason.

Thompson objected at once. 'I have severe doubts, Mr Lively. You would be a wanted man. Stealing away would be seen as an admission of guilt. Besides which, the entire crew is willing to testify on your behalf. What need have you to flee?'

'Mr Thompson is correct—and I say that with the greatest reluctance,' agreed Cassidy. 'A few days inconvenience in the watch house and the matter is behind you for good. What say you, Theo?'

Eyes turned to Humpflinger, who had followed the conversation carefully as he considered the various points of view. 'One matter may follow another,' he now observed soberly, 'as an innocent stream may lead to rapids.'

In spite of his anxiety, Boundless was unable to suppress a smile as he gazed at the guileless but perspicacious face of his friend.

'Well said, my dear Theo,' he said softly.

'Ah! There is a matter to the matter?' Thompson spoke up with surprising alacrity. 'Why then, that entirely changes the prospect,' he continued. 'In which case, Mr Lively, you would be well put upon to follow Fesky's advice.'

The remarks drew a frown upon Cassidy, who had missed the inference entirely. 'Upon my soul!' he spluttered with annoyance. 'Is this a conversation in the savage tongue? Mr Lively, what—'

Thompson interrupted. 'Do you recall that incident with the saloon keep some years ago in Williamsburg?'

'Why, yes. But what does that black-hearted villain have to do with the present situation?'

'He said one thing, Cass, and you another … ?' Thompson frowned at his companion's obtuseness. 'Think, man. The incident with the cards—was it not tacked onto a trumped-up charge of fraud?'

'Ah!' Understanding dawned on Cassidy's face as he drew forth Thompson's meaning. 'Indeed, Mr Lively. Apologies for my denseness. If the case be indeed anything like the Williamsburg, then I urge you to follow Fesky's good advice.'

'Gentlemen, my heartfelt thanks for this understanding.' Boundless' voice thickened with emotion at the simple loyalty of his companions. 'Even if it means we must part.'

'Nature has a way of putting things back together again, Joshua,' said Humpflinger quietly. 'Who knows but we shall be having a fine old reminisce in Philly a year hence?'

In the distance came the ring of a spoon on the iron cooking pot and a shout of 'Grub up!'

'We will speak more after supper.' Boundless threw an affectionate arm around Humpflinger's shoulders as they started back towards the fire.

After they had eaten, Boundless took Fesky to one side, plying the trapper with questions while his companions listened, occasionally interjecting with opinion or advice.

'I am determined, Fesky, to follow your suggestion and make my own way back to Philadelphia—at a distance from the authorities. As to the manner, I place myself in your hands.'

Fesky sucked on the pipe, gazing at the fire. Boundless was about to speak again, imagining that the trapper had forgotten or ignored the request, when Fesky replied.

'Our next landing, if I'm not mistaken, is by the Point?'

The trapper looked to Thompson for confirmation, his manner indicating that he had merely been mulling over the answer. 'The land thereabouts be mostly flat and passable for travel on horseback. You can purchase an animal at the post. From the Point, head north a mile or so until you come across a well-marked Indian path through the woods. Follow that trail east to Baltimore—no more than a long day's ride. Two, if you must. The trail will take you past Baltimore and on to the York Post Road. Take the road north until you reach York. From there, take the Lancaster Pike east all the way to Philadelphia. There are taverns along the way where you can buy corn for the horse and, mayhap, a bed and supper for yourself.'

'And the distance?' asked Boundless, highly dubious at the prospect.

Fesky considered. 'To Balt no more than a day's ride. York, add … three … mayhap four days—'

'—Five, surely,' protested Cassidy. 'It must be a very considerable distance.'

'*Four* days,' repeated Fesky, with a frown at Cassidy. 'Calculating you have no aversion to long hours in the saddle?' He cocked an eyebrow at Boundless, who shook his head.

'Well, then—*barring interruptions*—Baltimore in one day, York in four. From thence to Philadelphia?' He counted on his fingers. '—Eight more.'

'So there you have it—thirteen days, Mr Lively, give or take,' summed up Thompson.

'So far?' he said, his mind reeling at the prospect.

'These woods be infernal for a man alone on horseback,' objected Cassidy. 'There are said to be numerous cut-throats lying in wait for solitary travellers.'

'There will be farms, remember,' said Turlington, 'and fellow travellers once Mr Lively reaches the York turnpike.'

'Pshaw! A turnpike, is it now?'

'You can sell the horse in Philadelphia and regain your expense,' said Thompson.

Perplexed, Boundless looked to Humpflinger for advice. 'Theodore?'

Humpflinger drew reflectively on the pipe. 'The way be long and difficult, Joshua, make no mistake. It be best you fell in with another traveller, quickly, to avoid the cut-throats Mr Cassidy rightly warns of.' He puffed on the pipe. 'Albeit the hazards of the road are uncertain, the danger of apprehension by ship's passage, be greater still, I fear.'

'The matter in a nutshell!' Thompson looked at Boundless. 'What say you, Mr Lively?'

'My head is a-whirl with directions. You say I should proceed north on the Indian path—'

'North and then east. It takes a turn.'

'—to Baltimore. And from thence to the Post Road?' Fesky nodded.

'And suppose I miss this Post Road?'

'Keep heading east—until you strike the Susskyhanna River. Follow that north to the Pike. You cannot get lost so long as you follow the stream.'

'And so onto the Lancaster Pike?'

'And follow that east to Philadelphia.'

'And the post has horses for sale?'

'I can confirm,' said Thompson. 'I myself admired two or three in the enclosure on our last visit.'

Boundless fell silent for a long moment, his mind plagued by doubts. He felt the eyes of his companions on him as he wrestled with his thoughts. At length, he gave a heartfelt sigh. 'Then the matter is decided. Gentlemen, my thanks for your forbearance.'

'Wait, the need for provisions!' said Cassidy as a host of other questions and opinions quickly followed—so many that Humpflinger intervened.

'Gentlemen, enough!' he said firmly, holding up his hands. 'Our friend has more than sufficient to think on. Come, Joshua, let us sleep on the matter.'

HE LAY DOWN TO sleep, his mind overwhelmed with fears and uncertainties. But gradually, a determined calm quietened his fears as his resolve to abandon the boat at the next landing hardened. *There is no other course*, he told himself, the image of the hangman's rope pushing aside any lingering doubts. The fact he would have to forsake his outstanding wages for the trip annoyed him greatly. So distracted was he by the forfeiture that it was only just before he fell asleep that he remembered the body lying buried in the grass on the same shoreline where he slept.

THEY PUT IN AT the Point shortly after midmorning of the following day. Boundless exchanged a glance of silent understanding with Humpflinger as the boat bumped up against the dock. Three waiting passengers lounged on chairs in the shade of the trees. Crates of corn and sacks of onions were stacked on the wharf to be taken on board. Two horses grazed the pasture beside the trading post. A clutch of hens squawked loudly in a pen next to a cow tethered in the grass. A man sat on a rocking chair on the porch, his feet up on the rail, a pipe in his mouth as he watched half-a-dozen deckhands pass the sacks of onions from one hand to another.

Boundless retrieved his haversack from the stern, pretending to rummage inside for a pipe. He looked around for Captain Taysick and saw him deep in conversation with a passenger. Mr York and Mr Cribble stood on the shore supervising the exchange of cargo. He removed his shoe, pretending to dig for a stone as he scanned the open ground around the landing for a place of concealment. A large box elder grew some two hundred yards back from the landing, its massive trunk offering ample shade for refuge. Tugging his shoe back on, he made towards it, glancing over his shoulder to make certain he was unobserved. Now that his departure from the boat was imminent, he was afflicted by a severe bout of anxiety at the prospect of abandoning his only surety.

After the cargo was secured on board, his companions unobtrusively made their way over to the elder tree, seemingly stretching their legs as they awaited the signal to reboard.

'Godspeed, Mr Lively.' Glancing around to make certain they were unobserved, Cassidy held out his hand. 'It has been a most pleasant journey in your company. I hope with all my heart to meet with you again.'

The obvious sincerity in the man's voice moved him as he fervently returned the handshake. 'If at all possible, Mr Cassidy, we shall yet share a fine beefsteak and a yard of Philadelphia ale.'

Thompson and Turlington wished him similarly heartfelt farewells, assuring him of their continued friendship. 'We are comrades, all,' said Thompson, holding on to his hand.

Fesky slapped him on the shoulder. 'The path lies that way.' He pointed towards the thick woods. 'Remember, it will take you to the Baltimore road. Travel well, young fella. And keep your eyes wide open.'

Humpflinger stepped up last to offer his hand. 'Farewell, Joshua.' His face was solemn, his eyes moistening. 'I wish you Godspeed.'

'Farewell, dear friend!' Overcome with emotion, Boundless clasped his companion in a warm embrace. 'You were my first and best guide to this New World, for which service, my deepest thanks. If we should never meet again, I swear I shall never forget your true and generous friendship.'

'Nor I you, Joshua, I assure you. But we shall most certainly meet again. I return to Philadelphia twelve months from this one. Leave word for me in the same lodging house. We shall have a fine old yarn over rum and ale.'

The two stood for a moment, regarding each other with undisguised affection.

'All on board!' Cribble's voice sounded from the wharf.

'Quickly, Theodore. You must go!'

Boundless stepped back into the shade of the tree as Humpflinger returned to the boat where Mr York stood waiting to release the line. 'Cast off!'

The crew began to row the boat away from the wharf. From his place of concealment, he saw Humpflinger raise a surreptitious hand in farewell.

'Godspeed, dear friend,' he murmured, tears springing to his eyes. A feeling of desolation overtook him as he watched the boat recede from the landing. Within minutes, it had entered the mid-channel where the wind caught the sail and propelled it forwards—the vessel seeming to glide over the water in the glorious morning light. He watched it proceed upstream, the deckhands now dark, indistinguishable shapes in the bright sunlight. Within the space of a few minutes, the vessel disappeared around a bend in the river, leaving him alone and friendless on the shore.

19

The Baltimore Road

WITH HEAVY HEART, HE turned away from the river, eyes misty with the burden of departed friends. Two barefooted and starved-looking ragamuffin boys were gawking at him.

'Were you hidin', mister?' asked one.

'No. Is the post open?'

'Why wouldn't it be?' asked the other, his thin face squirreling with suspicion.

'Never mind.' He made his way past the gawking waifs to the post, anxious to secure a mount and be on his way as soon as possible. Despite Fesky's assurances that the boat would not turn back once there was an alert that he was missing—'it saves the cap'n one more headache,' the trapper had insisted—he wished to take no chances on the captain's choleric temper. Bracing himself for whatever might lie ahead, he pushed open the door to the post.

Inside, he discovered a room with a counter, a table and chairs, and a shelf full of bottles.

'Welcome friend! A most hearty and Christian welcome!' A bareheaded man observed him keenly from behind the wooden counter. He wore a threadbare black waistcoat over a homespun shirt. Long whiskery sideboards ran down his cheeks and disappeared into the grey stubble beneath his chin. The man's voice was at once bluff and ingratiating as he stepped around the counter to offer his hand.

'Charles Wilkes, proprietor of this humble establishment. At your service, friend.'

'Lively, sir. Mr Joshua Lively.' He shook the proffered hand.

'Fine weather!' The proprietor revealed blackened teeth as his eyes busily inspected Boundless from head to toe.

'Indeed. I understand, sir, that you trade in horses. If so, I wish to purchase a mount suitable for riding to Baltimore.'

'Baltimore! Ain't that tub you jest stepped off of headed back to Baltimore?'

'On the return, perhaps. But I have pressing business there that will not wait.'

'A horse, you say?' The proprietor put a hand to his jaw, stroking the skin as he studied Boundless' shoes. 'Come, friend! What say you to a glass of rum?'

'Pardon, but I had sooner—'

'A single swallow!' From beneath the counter, the proprietor produced a small, brown bottle and two glasses. 'Finest Indies cane!' Wiping a glass on his shirt sleeve, he poured a careful measure for Boundless and a more generous one for himself. 'Of great benefit to digestion and the general constitution.' He raised the glass in a toast. 'Your rude good health, sir!' Draining the glass in a single gulp, he smacked his lips. 'By God! A taste to relish! Say you?' He poured himself another. 'Now, I believe you asked about a horse, Mr—?'

'Lively. Joshua Lively.' Boundless took a sip of the liquor, grimacing at the taste.

'Mr Lively, indeed sir. I have a fine animal grazing out back. At a fair and reasonable price. The frisky brown mare,' he said, gesturing to the open door.

Boundless stepped out to gaze at the horse where it fed in the grass alongside a handsome black stallion. 'And the other?'

'Spoken for, sir. Promised to a gentleman of an old and cherished family. But ye be a judge of horseflesh, I can plainly see. Then you will agree that the mare is a rare specimen. Fully broken and gentle as a lamb. Spirited, yet eager to please. It grieves me to part with her.'

The two small boys were sat on the porch, trading a twist of tobacco back and forth. They stopped chatting to stare, mouths agape. Considering their stares impertinent, Boundless frowned and stepped back inside the store.

'I shall need provisions, also.'

'Goods of every description!'

The proprietor rubbed his hands and led the way into the adjoining room. 'Merchandise to suit every taste!' He gestured proudly at the stocked shelves as though inviting Boundless to take his pick.

The shelves were full to overflowing with lanterns, canteens, knives, powder horns, oils, ointments and tinderboxes. Coils of rope, leather harnesses and horsehair whips hung from pegs. A pair of saddles sat on the floor alongside barrels heaped with cornmeal, salt, beans, sugar and flour. Hempen sacks of coffee and tobacco leaned against the wall. One corner appeared to be given over to haberdashery—coats, jackets, shirts, breeches, leather shoes, cocked hats and waistcoats sat in piles. The emporium was completed by two spinning wheels, a tape loom and half-a-dozen unpainted stools.

'Finest quality merchandise—at an honest price as my name be Charles Wilkes. What be your pleasure, friend?'

From his jacket pocket, Boundless pulled the sheet of paper upon which he had written Fesky's list of necessities. As he studied the items, he experienced a fresh rush of anxiety as to the wisdom of his decision to abandon the boat. Beset by doubt he, stared at the list.

'You shall need a saddle and harness for the mare,' Wilkes prompted, his eyes shrewd and appraising.

He mumbled a reply.

'Beg pardon?'

'Yes.' Boundless took a determined breath. 'To which add a good quality pan, straw hat, a thick blanket—'

'Jest the one?' The proprietor blew dust off a rolled blanket as he pulled it from a shelf. 'It gets mighty cold of a night.'

'One will suffice. A tinderbox. Two pounds of cornmeal. One pound of salted pork. Tea. A pot for boiling water. Beer for the canteen. Fresh biscuits—if you have any. All, in sufficient quantity for three or four days.'

'And as to payment, friend, if I might enquire the means?'

Reaching into his pocket, Boundless took out the promissory note and paper bill of credit, carefully unfolding both on the counter.

'No sir!' The proprietor's face hardened, his manner rigid on the instant. 'Solid coin only—be it Spanish, Dutch, Maryland or English.'

'But the notes are redeemable and perfectly sound! The tobacco alone, I am reliably informed—'

'Pshaw!' Wilkes waved a hand in disdain. 'A note is one thing—tobacco in the hand another, is it not? As for the Maryland, it's worth wanes and waxes by the hour. No, friend. Coin or none.' Turning his back as though the matter was concluded, he began to briskly re-arrange items on the shelf.

Taken aback at this unexpected turn, Boundless hesitated.

'English coin will suffice?'

'Happily, friend, happily.' The proprietor's affable manner at once returned. 'May I see the list, friend?' He held out his hand.

Reluctantly, Boundless handed it over.

'Finely written! And itemised to a turn.' The proprietor studied the list for a moment and then, humming to himself, began to pluck various items from the shelves to set on the counter.

Boundless watched for a moment and then turned his back to pull the leather pouch from inside his shirt. He tapped several guinea coins into his palm. He counted them twice, nervous at the probable expense of the transaction. His fears increased when he turned to see the amount of supplies stacked along the counter.

'Those seem very considerable quantities,' he protested, suspicious that the man was gulling him.

Wilkes gave a look of amazement. 'Baltimore ain't around the corner! Not by any man's reckoning. Why, I can hardly think of all that a traveller requires to venture off alone into the woods.' He stopped as if struck by a thought. 'I do not see a weapon, Mr Lively?'

'I have a reliable pistol.' Boundless gestured to the haversack.

'Pistol!' The proprietor's eyes grew wide. 'You will need sharper teeth, friend—considerable sharp should you have the misfortune to encounter a band of savages or a bunch of cut-throats on the road. I would fail in my duty, sir, as a Christian man, did I not furnish you sufficiently with the wherewithal to ensure your safety. Upon my word!'

Reaching down, the proprietor lifted a flintlock from under the counter.

'An English musket, sir, produced for these colonies and renowned for its accuracy. I should hold on to it for myself—a man must be prepared to defend his property and person. But your need, Mr Lively, be greater. I can part with it out of Christian charity, although in truth it sorrows me to do so.'

The musket was long and slender, with a dark, oiled stock and elegant firing mechanism.

'The barrel seems rather long,' said Boundless, dubious of the weapon.

'Heft it, sir,' Wilkes urged. 'Finest beechwood stock.'

Still reluctant, Boundless lifted the musket, pointing the long barrel out the open door.

'A peerless gun. Tried and proven from the Massachusetts to Georgia. And a sleeve, friend, for protection from the elements.' The proprietor set a deerskin sleeve on the counter.

Boundless pulled back the hammer, mindful of Fesky's admonition on the necessity of a reliable gun. The hammer cocked into place, and he drew back the frizzen to inspect the pan. Placing the butt on the floor, he peered down the barrel as the proprietor watched. Frowning, he held up the piece to examine the date stamped on the plate.

'Finest workmanship throughout,' praised the proprietor. 'Dependable springs, and most reliable lock.'

'What is the bore?' asked Boundless, doing his best to sound knowledgeable.

'She will take a .50 calibre ball. Standard to these parts, and more than sufficient for deer or fowl.'

Boundless laid the weapon back on the counter. 'If it be an honest price, you may add it to the tally.'

'And shot, sir, and powder! What use a musket without a horn full of power? I will throw in some tow wadding as a gift.'

Boundless nodded, resigned to the expense. 'The powder and shot as well.'

As the proprietor bustled about, Boundless walked to the door to stare at the mare where she chewed the grass.

'Done, sir,' he heard Wilkes say behind him. 'And the tally, for your convenience.' He handed Boundless back his list with the cost added to each item, and several other items added in.

His suspicion of being gulled increased as he studied the bill under the hovering gaze of the proprietor.

'Four pounds for the saddle!' He looked up in shock. 'And the musket—five pounds?' He gasped in astonishment as he read further. 'Ten pounds! Is the mare priced by the leg!' He muttered in disbelief, now fully convinced that the man was a scoundrel.

'Nay, but you do impugn me, sir!' The proprietor gazed reproachfully. 'Upon my soul, those prices be as just as any along the length and breadth of the river. But come, friend, let us not quarrel over trifles.'

Wilkes turned and picked up a small jute bag from the shelf behind him.

'A quarter bag of cane sugar. Yours friend, at no extra charge. Not a penny extra! As plain proof of honest dealing.' He set the bag down squarely on the counter. 'What say you? Shall we shake on it, as gentlemen?'

'Four pounds for the musket, and ten shillings to be knocked off the price of the mare.' He thrust his hands into his coat pockets, determined not to budge from the offer.

'Four pounds and ten shillings for the musket. The mare I cannot haggle upon. I would rather save her for my own use—so peerless an animal and so sturdy in her ways. But witness—as further token of plain and honest dealing ...'

Turning, the proprietor took a thick, leather-bound volume from the shelf behind him. 'Yours sir—at a single shilling. One shilling!'

Curious, in spite of his agitation, Boundless took the volume in his hand and opened the cover. 'What is it?'

'Why, a nautical log, friend. Tendered to me by a seafarer down on his luck. Printed in London and only used for the first dozen or so pages. A treasure, sir, not to be passed over lightly.'

Boundless turned the pages, feeling the stiff paper between his fingers.

The log contained two hundred or more pages. The top-left margin of each was occupied by a small box containing several columns for recording wind direction, vessel speed and weather conditions. The remainder of the page was left blank for estimations of reckoning, observations on progress, and sundry other notations relating to the passage.

'It is fine workmanship,' he conceded. 'But what need have I—'

'And the instruments!' The proprietor placed a flat wooden case on the counter. He opened the case to reveal a compartment containing three quill pens and a small, embedded ink-well made of brass and set into the wood.

'Does it contain ink?' asked Boundless, struck by the cleverness and economy of the case.

'Observe.' With a flourish, the proprietor carefully unscrewed the cap from the inkwell. He held the case up under Boundless' nose so that he might smell the ink. Boundless took a deep inhale suddenly dizzy as the years of labouring over a press came rushing back.

'Sterling, friend, sterling,' prompted the proprietor. 'And all for a single extra shilling. As token, sir, of honest Christian dealing. What say you?'

'I am paupered,' he muttered. He rubbed the grain leather of the log, debating with himself. After some further moments of indecision, he gave out a heavy sigh. 'Very well.' He counted out sixteen of his precious coins under the eagle eye of the proprietor.

The proprietor's eyes lit up at the sight of the gold guineas. 'English stamp!' He held one up and peered at the face. 'Good old King George,' he said. He studied the reverse crown and rubbed a finger around the milled edge. Satisfied as to authenticity, he tapped the coin on the counter. 'True as a bell!'

Now that the transaction was completed, Wilkes' mood of amiable good fellowship redoubled. 'What say we round up the tally with two bottles of this fine Indies rum?' He held up the small dark bottle for inspection.

Boundless shook his head, impatient to be gone.

'You two!' Wilkes glared past Boundless to where the two young urchins stood watching from the doorway. 'Don't stand there gawking like ticks on a flea! Saddle the gentleman's horse.'

Boundless watched as the two boys picked up the heavy harness between them and struggled to carry it out the door.

'The mare!' Wilkes called after them. He shook his head sadly. 'I keep them around for the intertainment.'

'The Baltimore road?' Boundless reminded him.

'The road? Simple as day!' The proprietor led the way out the door.

'See that trail?' He pointed to a dusty path leading away from the clearing towards the woods. 'Keep to it all the way to Baltimore. It heads inland for a ways to skirt the creeks, but is generally well marked. If you've a doubt, jest give the mare her head. She can find the way better than a brown savage.'

He followed Boundless to where the mare stood saddled and waiting.

'A wondrous animal! It grieves me to part with her. A most sterling horse. Strong as a bull, yet gentle as a lamb.'

Boundless examined the mare critically, uncertain of her quality, but wishing to appear knowledgeable in such matters. 'She is sound?'

'As a judge, friend. As a judge. She will carry you to Baltimore safely. Aye, and back again, should you wish.'

Far from convinced of the man's sincerity, he inspected the animal at length, feeling her hind quarters and running a hand over her withers.

'She'll live off grass?' he asked.

'She'll feast on it. But she'll eat most anything. Apples, turnips, carrots, cornbread, even the bark from trees if she gets hungry enough.'

The proprietor snapped his fingers at the two urchins. 'You two hopple-heads—run and fetch the gentleman's tack. A boat,' he said, shading his eyes and turning to gaze at the river.

Boundless turned in alarm. 'What kind?' He held a hand above his eyes, anxious lest Captain Taysick had returned to find him. He sighed with relief as he made out the shape of a barge coming down the river.

The urchins returned with his supplies and set them down in the grass.

'Fix them to the mare! Such jackanapes.'

The boys leapt to the task, expertly securing the supplies to the mare as he watched, deeply regretting his unfamiliarity with riding a saddle.

'What is she called?' he asked, running his hand over the mare's neck. The skin was warm and moist with sweat. He felt her tremble beneath his touch.

'Bessie, by rights. But she'll answer to 'bout anything you wish.' 'Does she buck?' he asked as the mare shied away from the boys.

'Only if she's feeling right!' The elder of the two piped up. The younger stifled a guffaw.

The proprietor shot a venomous glance. 'Hark now! Ye peck-eyed jimkins! Help the gentleman into the saddle.'

Chastened, the elder boy held the bridle and steadied the mare for him to mount. Boundless gripped the saddle and clumsily placed one leg in the stirrup. The mare stepped sideways, and he hopped after as the younger boy sniggered.

Instantly, the proprietor rounded on the offender, cuffing him across the ear. 'Lend a back—you turtle-necked gape!'

Grimacing and rubbing his ear, the boy offered his shoulder as Boundless climbed awkwardly into the saddle.

'How far would you calculate—to Baltimore?' he asked, perched stiffly atop the mare.

The proprietor scratched his chin. 'Far, I reckon. Don't forget the gun.' He handed up the musket.

Boundless strung it across his back, the long barrel projecting above his shoulder. He took a deep breath and looked around at the surrounding woods, feeling momentarily light-headed in the bright sunlight. The proprietor looked up at him expectantly. The boys stood off to one side, their scrunched faces watchful as they nudged one another and whispered, hands over their mouths.

'This way, you say?' He pointed to the woods.

The proprietor nodded.

Feeling acutely self-conscious, he pushed his heels against the mare's flank. 'Forward!'

To his mortification, the mare stood stock still, dropping her head to nuzzle the grass. The boys guffawed into their hands.

'Forward!' He jerked the reins. The mare whinnied in protest but remained in place.

'Skit now!' Stepping forward, the proprietor slapped her hard on the rump. With a snort she started forwards—the abrupt motion almost unseating Boundless.

'She'll go fine once she gets a taste for it,' the proprietor called out. 'Why, I should hardly be surprised if she took it into her head to trot all the way to Balty!'

The mare plodded off as Boundless clung tightly to the reins with one hand, and to the saddle horn with the other, fearful lest he topple off at any moment and snap his neck.

'I bid you farewell!' he called over his shoulder while swaying awkwardly in the saddle.

'Watch out for murderous savages!' the younger boy piped up, drawing a chortle from the other.

'Keep a sharp eye!' called out Wilkes. 'Remember. Jest allow her the rein!'

At the sound of the proprietor's voice, the mare attempted to turn back. 'Skit!' He kicked her in the sides. The mare snorted but, to his relief, continued onwards. He heard the proprietor call out something but dared not turn to enquire. Before him, the dusty path wound over a small hillock and continued across the sunny clearing before disappearing into the hushed and shadowy woods.

A Wilderness of Trees

AFTER FOLLOWING THE TRAIL for two hours, he began to suspect that the entire New World was comprised of trees. Thick trunks of beech, maple, poplar, oak, hickory and pine hemmed in the path on all sides. The overarching branches created a permanent twilight of dusky shade punctuated by brilliant shafts of sunlight. The combination of the musket and his inept horsemanship soon proved so cumbersome an arrangement—the long barrel continually fouling against the branches—that he was forced to dismount and tie the weapon to the side of the mare before continuing.

Birds screeched incessantly in the dense foliage, seeming, to his nervous annoyance, to signal his general progress through the wood. He started suspiciously at rustlings in the thick undergrowth—the dread of some bloodthirsty heathen springing from ambush to dash out his brains with a hatchet never far from his mind. So fearful did he become of the prospect as he navigated deeper into the wilderness, that he deliberated whether to untie and load the flintlock. Deciding that the thick foliage made carrying, let alone discharging the weapon, next to impossible, he decided against the precaution. *'Twould pose a greater danger to myself or the mare than to any lurking savage.*

He ventured ever deeper into the shaded woods, frequently bending his head to avoid being brained by an overhanging branch. He drank thirstily from the canteen full of ale—stopping only when the bottle was almost drained. Coming upon a creek, he dismounted to allow the mare to drink. Remembering Humpflinger's indifference to the perils of drinking water, he filled the spare canteen from the stream and took a long swallow before continuing.

Unused to riding, he stopped frequently to climb down and walk the mare, taking the opportunity to rest both himself and the horse while nursing his stiff body. 'I thought the oaring had toughened my spine,' he groaned, as pain shot through his back. The strain of keeping upright in the saddle gradually caused him to slump further and further forward until he was resting on the mare's neck. 'I had rather row ten-mile,' he told himself, wincing at the soreness in his hips.

In late afternoon, the mare stopped suddenly—jolting him out of a half-slumber. He sat upright in alarm.

'Who goes!'

Hurriedly tugging the unloaded pistol from his coat pocket, he trained the weapon on the dense undergrowth. A bird flew up from the thicket and his heart leapt into his mouth. After a nervous interlude, he put it away. *If it were a savage I would doubtless be brained already.* Twisting in the saddle, he was confounded to discover that the trail had disappeared. 'Where the devil is it?' he said aloud. Cursing his inattentiveness, he pressed his heels into the flanks of the mare. 'Skit!' He jerked on the reins, forcing her head up from the grass. To his relief, she started forward, although whinnying in protest.

After ten minutes, he climbed down from the mare and tethered her to a bush. Proceeding in a circle, he vigilantly scanned the ground, but could find nothing to suggest the missing trail. Coming across his own tracks again he muttered in frustration—utterly perplexed as to the whereabouts of the path.

Removing his hat, he scratched his damp hair, debating whether to press on or turn back to try to recover the way. Deciding the latter would be a vain endeavour, he untied the horse and started forwards again, berating his own carelessness. *'Jest give the mare her head.'* The words of the proprietor grated in his ears as the mare plodded on without purpose or direction.

As darkness gathered, he stopped to make camp—disturbed at the prospect of spending a night in the trackless woods. The mare was sweating and breathing heavily in spite of the walking pace. He led her to a small creek to drink—staring suspiciously at the dim foliage as the birds fell silent. The night air was chill, but he decided against a fire for fear of alerting any nearby Indians to his presence. He ate half of the salt pork and three of the hardtack biscuits. Still hungry, he scooped a handful of cornmeal and chewed on it, sharing it with the mare. He loaded the pistol and set it at half-cock. He then wrapped the blanket around him and lay down, folding the pistol across his chest. As he drifted off to sleep—fatigued despite his vigilance—he heard a twig snap in the undergrowth. He sat up in fright and levelled the pistol.

'Step forth!' After a minute's strained attention, he lay down again. 'It is no use, I shall not sleep,' he muttered even as he fell into an exhausted slumber.

BY LATE MORNING THE next day, he was forced to admit that he was utterly lost. There is nothing for it but to continue, he told himself, propelling the resistant mare forwards with a sharp kick. When hunger began to bite, he reached behind him and took out the remaining pork from the saddle bags—Fesky's caution to 'stock overmuch' sounding in his ears.

He ate hungrily, promising himself a hearty meal of cornmeal mush for supper. For the next several hours, he continued in an easterly direction, alternately riding and walking alongside the mare. Towards dusk he made camp for the night—sore, hungry and profoundly discouraged. 'I am as lost as a man can be,' he acknowledged tiredly. 'I might be in Hades for all that I know.'

Unpacking the supplies, he was horrified to discover the much-anticipated cornmeal was missing. He searched without success while racking his brains to recall whether he had securely retied the hempen sack that morning. He boiled a pot of black tea and drank the liquid sweetened with a pinch of cane sugar to stave off the hunger pangs while bitterly upset with himself. Thoroughly miserable, he tried to sleep as the lost cornmeal played on his mind.

The next day his hunger was so acute that he went through the supplies, finding a few grains of cornmeal and chewing on these as he rode. Tormented by thoughts of food, he diverted himself by composing a letter to *The Rambler* describing the instincts and habits of horses as compared to those of men. As the mare plodded slowly through the woods, he minutely catalogued the points of similarity and difference between the two species. Absorbed in the disquisition, he concluded, with a flourish, that 'apart from raiment and habitation, it may, with justice, be observed that the gift of language is the principal difference between ourselves and the equine order.' A passing shower of rain brought him back to attentiveness and he sheltered beneath a pine until the rain had stopped.

Resolved to try his luck at hunting, he made camp by a bubbling creek while it was yet full daylight. Tying the mare to a branch, he collected sticks for a fire and readied the musket, pushing aside his severe doubts over his ability with the weapon. Laying it on the ground, he readied the powder horn, lead ball, wadding and ramrod. He tried to recall the loading procedure—demonstrated by Humpflinger on the pistol. Angling the musket stock on the ground he inserted the ramrod in the muzzle and began to saw it up and down, uncertain of the reason beyond a vague recollection of the necessity of cleansing the bore. Unplugging the powder horn, he sifted a measure of black powder down the muzzle, adding a few additional grains for insurance. He knocked the stock on the grass to seat the powder. Next, he took a portion of wadding and placed it on the muzzle. He set a lead ball on top and, using the palm of his hand, pressed both down into the mouth of the barrel. Using the ramrod, he pushed the projectile down the barrel until it made secure contact with the powder. Remembering Humpflinger's admonition to properly 'seat' the powder and ball, he tamped it a second time. Still uncertain whether or not the ball might roll out of the barrel, he added a second pinch of wadding on top, pushing it down with the ramrod. Setting the hammer at half-cock he opened the frizzen. He uncorked the powder horn and tapped a small measure of powder into the flash pan and closed the frizzen. With the weapon thus prepared, he felt a small glow of reassurance.

'I shall be back, anon.' He patted the mare and set off into the surrounding woods, stepping as noiselessly as possible through the foliage. Every few yards, he turned to ensure he retained the direction of the encampment. Coming across a small clearing, he set the musket to full-cock and took cover behind a chokeberry bush.

After an hour of silent surveillance, he grew increasingly impatient—having sighted nothing other than squirrels and birds. He had no sooner set down the musket to drink from the canteen than he heard a rustling in the bushes. A branch snapped and his heart pounded as he levelled the musket. Next moment a large black bear emerged from the foliage, nose to the ground as it foraged for berries.

Trying to ignore the trembling in his hands, he trained the musket on the creature. Plagued with indecision he took his finger from the trigger— the fear of wounding, or more likely, missing the shot and thus enraging the beast overcoming his acute hunger. Nervously, he watched the bear root in the grass for insects—too afraid to risk easing his cramped limbs. To his relief, it lingered for no more than a minute before wandering back into the bushes—snuffling and grunting as it made its way through the undergrowth.

Composing himself, he settled back to continue the watch. Within the space of a quarter hour, his persistence was rewarded as a small deer stepped forth from the bushes. The animal advanced timidly into the clearing, stopping every few yards to test the air.

Hardly daring to breathe, he sighted the flintlock on the deer's frontquarters, judging the heart to be in that spot. As the creature lowered its head to feed, he pulled the trigger. A bright flash of sparks and a puff of white smoke broke the silence as the powder in the pan ignited and the musket misfired. The startled deer bounded off into the bushes, its white tail flashing.

Vehemently cursing his ill-luck, he held up the musket to stare at the still-smouldering grains in the pan. Next moment the powder in the muzzle ignited with a tremendous *crack* that caused him to drop the weapon in fright as the ball flew into the trees.

'Perdition!'

He resumed breathing, pale with the realisation he might have shot himself. Roundly berating both the musket and the proprietor who sold it to him, he prepared the weapon a second time, carefully cleaning the bore and ensuring that the wadded ball sat securely atop the powder. The sun had begun to set and he changed position to get a better view of the clearing.

Rain began to fall and he gave up the hunt in disgust. To his consternation, he was unable to determine the way back to the camp—the changed position and dusky light confusing his senses. Attempting to retrace his steps in the twilight, he suppressed a growing anxiety as he became increasingly uncertain of the way. He tried first one direction and then the other, straining to spot his tracks in the gloom. Finally, he halted, utterly flummoxed as to his whereabouts. As he stood there, he heard a neigh followed by a whinny.

'Thank God!' Overcome with relief, he followed the sounds back to the camp.

'No supper this night, good Bess,' he said, stroking her mane. Attempting to light a fire, he found that the wood he had collected was wet from the rain. After a further, fumbling attempt, he abandoned the task. Famished and miserable, he wrapped himself in the blanket and lay down under the branches of a tree. 'If I fail to find a path—any path, on the morrow,' he decided, 'then I shall strive to make my way back to the post'. He turned restlessly on the damp ground, enduring the triple miseries of cold, starvation and despair. Nearby, the mare nickered and whinnied her unhappiness. 'I am sorry for the corn,' he murmured tiredly.

NEXT MORNING, HE SADDLED the mare as soon as it was light enough to travel. He set off in an easterly direction, increasingly agitated at the absence of any resemblance to a trail. The mare's whistling breath added to his concern as he noted her listless manner. He thought back bitterly on the proprietor and his fulsome assurances as to the sterling worth of the animal.

'Scoundrel!' The outburst provoked a shriek of birdsong from the surrounding trees. Fatigued and hungry, he continued at a slow walk, scanning the ground for the elusive path. Eventually, he dozed off in the saddle. He awoke to find the mare stopped and cropping the leaves of a shrub. 'Would that I could stomach the same!' His belly began to growl, and he took a swallow of water.

He made camp early and collected enough twigs to build a fire—fatalistically indifferent to the prospect of attracting any savage denizens of the woods. Unable to sleep, he stared up at the stars, distracted by the pop and crackle of the burning wood. A burning branch crumbled, and fiery sparks flew up into the surrounding darkness, the tiny fires extinguishing against the stars. The irony of escaping death on the ocean only to perish from starvation in the limitless woods struck him as stark evidence of the heavens' indifference to human fate. The nobilities of art or ambition were, he decided, mere wisps, like the trajectory of a firefly against the encompassing dark. He lay brooding in this fashion for some hours, half-slumbering, half-awake while despairing of the morrow.

The embers still glowed in the morning chill when he awoke, shivering beneath a layer of dew and blown leaves. Mist rose from the trees. The mare neighed where he had tethered her. In spite of the cold, and in spite of his hunger and exhaustion, he was surprised to feel himself keenly alive in the verdant air. The feeling of well-being inspired him to optimism as he saddled the mare.

'Who knows, but today our luck may change, Bess.' He stroked her muzzle as she pushed her nose into his armpit.

It took but an hour in the saddle for the morning euphoria to wear thin and vanish. The sweeping branches that hindered his path—knocking his brains if he forgot to duck—the endless vale of trees, the interplay of sunlight and shade, all conspired to reduce him to a fretful, exhausted *'thing aboard a horse'* as he plodded slowly through the undergrowth. The hunger pangs gnawing his stomach were now so sharp he feared he might topple from the saddle with starvation and fatigue.

'I am heartily sorry for you, Bess,' he said, despairingly. 'You deserve better than to perish in these infernal glades.'

The prospect that some future traveller might stumble across his bones and wonder at their provenance compounded his gloomy temper as he continued, indifferent to whichever direction the mare chose.

Early in the afternoon, he stopped suddenly in the midst of a grove of scarlet oaks, scarce able to believe his eyes. A few short yards ahead, the flattened earth gave unmistakeable evidence of a path! He urged the mare forward to investigate, filled with elation as he studied the ground.

The trail wound between the trees—the path smooth and distinct in the sunlit woods.

He shook the reins—fervently hoping he had at last found the Indian path Fesky had spoken of. After an hour of steady progress, fresh doubts began to plague him. 'Mayhap it leads directly to a savage encampment,' he told himself, greatly concerned at the prospect. Dismounting, he took out the pistol and carried it in his hand as he followed the trail on foot to rest the mare. A mile later, exasperated with carrying the heavy firearm, he tucked it back in the blanket tied to the saddle.

His ears picked up the sound of moving water. He halted, unable to determine the source. The mare pulled her head and whinnied. He let go the reins and followed. Minutes later, he found himself on the banks of a flat, slow-moving river, some fifty yards across. Stumped at this latest obstacle, he turned around, realising that the path had vanished once again. 'Where the blazes did it go?' He scanned left and right as the mare drank thirstily from the river. Unable to find it, he reasoned that it must continue across the river. 'Mayhap it is the very Baltimore road,' he told himself.

Climbing back into the saddle, he urged the mare forward into the stream. She was reluctant to enter, refusing to advance beyond the bank in spite of his threats and cajolements. Finally, snorting in protest, she stepped into the water. Midway across, the water reached the level of his shoes. It had also, he realised, drenched the musket in its deerskin sheath beneath the stirrups. His heart sinking at this carelessness, he continued across, chanting words of praise and encouragement to the mare.

To his great relief, she soon gained the shallows beneath the far bank, and scrambled up onto the shore. He sat down in the shade as the mare drank her fill. As he waited, listening to birdsong and watching the play of light and shadow on the water, he day-dreamed that he had just forded a gentle English stream, and that the potential terrors of the surrounding woods were but a mirage. Memories of a childhood picnic on the slopes of Arthur's Seat came to mind and he salivated at the recollection of boiled chicken and raisin pudding. Mounting the mare, he kicked her into motion. 'Skit, Bess!'

By late afternoon, the trail had vanished once again. He circled his tracks for a quarter-hour in a vain search, his agitation rising as he scanned the ground without success. Finally, retracing his steps for a half mile, he found where the path disappeared into the thick undergrowth. 'How in Jupiter am I supposed to follow there?'

Greatly put out at this latest setback, he prodded the mare forwards. Her neck was slicked with sweat. Increasingly concerned at her laboured breath, he dismounted and led her through the dense foliage. He felt a spasm in his stomach and irritably turned his mind away from thoughts of the missing cornmeal. 'I must hunt, or starve,' he told himself, gloomy at the prospect. He tripped on a tree root and startled the mare. 'Sorry,' he mumbled. Cursing at his misfortune he continued, despairing of ever finding a path from out the trackless woods.

Mose

THE NEXT MORNING, HE had travelled for little more than an hour when the surrounding trees suddenly fell away and he found himself positioned on the edge of a clearing. Between himself and the next line of woods stretched a half mile or more of open space. He was surveying the spot when, to his astonishment, he beheld a lone horseman emerge from the woods to his left. The solitary figure led a mule with a deer draped across its back as he proceeded at a leisurely pace across the clearing. Overcome with relief, he nevertheless held position, a sense of caution rooting him to the shade. The figure drew abreast of where he sat concealed, and he heard the faint sound of singing—the stranger bellowing out a tune as though without a care in the world.

Making up his mind on the instant, he urged the mare out from under the trees. 'Ahoy!' Taking off his hat he, waved it furiously in the air. 'Ahoy!'

The rider stopped to stare in his direction, seemingly as astonished as himself by the encounter.

'Skit!' Whipping the reins, he kicked the mare into a trot. Unaccustomed to the gait, he bounced dangerously in the saddle as he closed the distance between himself and the stranger, who had stopped to await him, a musket held across his lap.

'I bid you—sir … Good morrow!' he called out as he approached. Panting for breath, his every bone shaking, he reined the winded mare to a halt. She was blowing heavily, her withers trembling as vapour rose up from her neck in waves.

The man—clad from head to toe in hides—regarded him with undisguised suspicion. Through narrowed eyes, he glanced from Boundless to the woods behind him and then back at Boundless again 'Where in *tar* did you spring from?'

Boundless wiped his mouth, suddenly acutely conscious of the spectacle his dishevelled figure must present on top of his unexpected appearance.

'Pardon, sir. I did not mean … My mare … has lost the path. I am most anxious to find the road to Baltimore.'

'Balty-more!' The other man's face wrinkled in amazement. 'By all the— Why, I had planned and schemed from the instant when you stepped out from those trees that you might purpose to murder me or, mayhap, share a drink of whisky—' He paused. 'Do you *have* any whisky?'

'Whisky?' It was Boundless' turn to be confused. 'I have nought but water.'

'That be a confoundment. I've a powerful thirst for whisky.' The man scratched his cheek—his keen eyes taking in the winded mare and the pale, drawn expression on Boundless' face. 'Ye seem a mite pinched, young fella.'

'That I am.' Too exhausted to speak further, he sat slumped in the saddle, a wave of tiredness rendering him temporarily mute. 'No wonder. You are nearer to Philadelphia than Baltimore.'

'You say?' Boundless opened his eyes wide in astonishment.

'As good as. The Suskyhanna be but a day's ride that way.' The stranger pointed to the east. 'And acrost it, Philly—mayhap another ten days or so.'

Boundless was still digesting this information when the hunter jerked the rope tether on the mule and kicked the horse into motion. 'Hie thee, Jack!' Turning his head, he looked back at Boundless. 'Follow on, young fellow.'

'Sir! I beg pardon?'

'I've a cottage up ahead. Follow on if ye wish for a bowl of venison. Balty-more?' The man shook his head. 'Balty-more!'

HE PLODDED ALONG BEHIND the eccentric figure, his relief at the miraculous encounter overtaken by a giddy sensation at the prospect of food. He eyed the bloody deer carcass draped across the mule, wandering if this might be dinner. His mouth salivated at the prospect. As they proceeded across the clearing, he strained to listen as the stranger conversed freely— whether with himself, his horse or the open air, he was unable to determine.

'Do ye sing, friend?' the hunter asked over his shoulder.

'Sing? I fear not. I have not the voice for it.'

'That be a sore misfortune. A sore misfortune. A man that can carry a tune is worth a passel of furs.'

A squawking sound caught the hunter's attention, and he glanced up. 'Black-bellied ducks,' he said, squinting at the wildfowl as they flapped overhead. 'They sit easy in the belly ... Did ye say you can sing?'

'Pardon, but no. I have not the voice.'

'A misfortune to be certain. What say you, Jack?'

In this manner they proceeded across the clearing and into the trees— the hunter maintaining his nonchalant air as the woods closed in around them. To Boundless' surprise, the man seemed indifferent to any threat from wild beasts or savages. For some time, they followed the path of a small creek where it trickled through the trees. Exhausted from his travails, Boundless was dozing off in the saddle when the stranger called a halt.

'Whoa, Jack.'

They were stopped in a small clearing. Before them, the creek bubbled across a bed of rocks to disgorge in a large pool before continuing into the forest. A row of wooden tubs stood in the grass. A dozen or so pelts hung from the pine branches. More hides were stretched across a line of wooden frames set at intervals in the clearing. A tiny hut or smokehouse stood in the shade of the pines. A second hut stood nearby. Looking around for a habitation, he caught sight of a cabin partly hidden in the trees. The hovel seemed scarcely tall enough to contain a man standing upright.

'Set yourself down, friend. That's if you've a mind to eat.' The hunter dismounted with agile ease. 'Stand, thou sweet,' he said to the mule.

Climbing down from the saddle, Boundless leaned against the mare—too tired to bother with unstrapping the harness.

'Come.' Leading the way to the cabin, the hunter opened the unlocked door and stepped inside.

Bending his head to follow, Boundless was immediately assailed by such a rancid stench of grease, smoke, hides, and roasted meat as to make the gorge rose in his throat. For a moment, he lost his nerve and wondered if he had ventured into the lair of a cannibal.

Holding his sleeve to his nose, he glanced around the habitation. The primitive dwelling consisted of little more than a confined space and a fireplace constructed from loose stones. Numerous furs and pelts lay in untidy heaps on the dirt floor. Snares dangled from the roof and a skinned rabbit hung from a length of rope. A large iron pot hung in the open fireplace above the smouldering embers of a fire. There were no windows—the only light coming through the open door. A chair, a small makeshift table, and a stool were the only furnishings.

The hunter was on his knees fiddling with a tinderbox. He quickly struck a spark which he nursed to a flame and transferred to a grease lantern propped on a packing case. 'And lo, there was light!' Getting to his feet, he fussed with hanging the lantern from a long nail stuck at an angle into the wall.

Observing his host properly for the first time, Boundless calculated the man to be around fifty years of age. The weathered face and blue eyes were framed by an unkempt grey beard that flowed down onto his chest. The sleeves and front of his worn buckskin jacket and breeches were heavily soiled with grease and stained dark with blood.

The lantern hung to his satisfaction, the man turned to face Boundless, holding out his hand.

'Mose van Zeke, friend—trapper of these woods and sovereign of this here nimble dwelling.'

Boundless took the proffered hand—hesitating briefly. 'Jo—Boundless McLennan, sir. At your service.'

'We don't exercise on formality in these woods, young fellow. "Mose" be my preferred title and all in all. Or "Trapper Mose" if we be standing on ceremony.'

Mose took a long leather apron hanging from a peg and hung it around his neck. 'Where do you hail from?'

'Philadelphia. Although of late, I have been travelling in these parts. And you, yourself, Mr—*Mose*. Be you from these parts? Your name suggests the Dutch country.'

'Dutch?' The trapper's amiable manner changed on the instant. 'I dare any man say so!' The blue eyes flashed with scorn.

'I beg pardon,' said Boundless hastily. 'I assure you that I intended no offence.'

The trapper chuckled, his face crinkling with humour. 'Nay. I do but jest with thee, friend, meaning no harm but the jape. 'Tis but my way. The sterling truth is I be a son of Virginny—born and bred as any man could be.'

The mule whinnied loudly from the clearing. 'I haven't the time to warble, friend. The danged mule is vexed, and the carcass won't wait. Anon, good William. Anon!' He hurried from the cabin, Boundless following.

The trapper attempted to untie the deer as the mule uttered a snort and backed away. 'Stand idle, thou misbegotten son of Lucifer!' Freeing the deer, Mose hefted it across his shoulder. He aimed a foot at the mule. 'Git now! Shoo!'

'I must hang this fellow,' he said. 'I had my eye on a second, but there was fresh heathen sign on the ground, and they be a mite testy of late—ever since they got kicked out of the woods along the Chesapeake.'

'Heathens? Are they a danger?'

'They likely won't come this way, have no fear on that account. They be Mattaponi and have a quarrel with the Pamunkey who hunt these woods and with whom I am on generally good terms. Unhitch the stock, if ye please. Beware the mule. The cussed critter bites—in between kicks.' With that warning, Mose headed off toward one of the two small huts.

Boundless had just removed the saddle from Bess when his host returned.

'Now, where was I? … the Pamunkey! Why they fell out, I've not a notion. Savages will generally dispute over the least offence. One day they will feast and drink in good fellowship, the next they be at each other's throats. It makes for hair-raising entertainment, if you be partial to such. Indeed, hair-raising. I could tell you a tale of such. By Glory! They'd as soon flay a body as share a carcass. I speak from certain knowledge.' He paused, plucking his chin as if to consider the disputatious ways of the savage.

'Certain knowledge,' he mumbled, seemingly deep in thought before turning to Boundless.

'Ye might water and feed the stock while I make a start on the pot. You will find a bag of oats in the cabin. Best serve Jack first—else will he fuss and jig-jangle to beat the darned mule.'

WHEN BOUNDLESS RETURNED TO the cabin, he found his host seated on a stump stirring beans, corn, salt and wild onions into the bubbling pot. The rabbit that had hung from the roof was gone and he presumed it was in the pot. The trapper had removed his fur cap. Long grey locks hung freely over his neck. The locks, together with the full, bushy beard, gave him the appearance of a half-wild forest creature or venerable sage—Boundless was uncertain which—as the trapper fussed with the pot, raising the spoon to taste the stew.

'How hungry are you, young fella? You look about ready to chaw the pot.' Grimacing at the taste, Mose threw more salt into the mix.

'It has been two whole days or more,' Boundless admitted. A feeling of famishment wrenched his insides as the aroma of boiled meat tantalised his nose. His stomach growled and he mumbled an apology, now desperate to eat.

'Two days! That's jest working up an appetite. The savage oft times eats but once every several days. I myself have fasted—unwillingly, mind—for five or more days at a stretch.' Mose stirred the broth and set down the spoon. 'It will boil a mite longer. It's time to get acquaint. Proper acquaint, I mean.'

Fishing a pipe from one pocket and a twist of tobacco from the other, he filled the bowl. He offered the plug to Boundless, who shook his head. The trapper raised an eyebrow. 'Neither chaw nor smoke?'

'Neither. Pardon—my belly thunders from hunger.'

Drawing a puff of smoke, the trapper studied him over the pipe. 'Now, what in the blazes brought you to these woods in search of Baltimore?'

'Baltimore is but a milestone. I am intended for Philadelphia.'

'And how'd you get lost?'

'I lost sight of the trail. I was perhaps over-reliant on the mare to find the way.'

'The mare?' The trapper's eyes widened.

Discomforted, Boundless cleared his throat. 'I was given to understand, by the seller, that she was—through much repetition—familiar with the passage.'

'By Solomon's nose!' Mose threw back his head and cackled with glee. 'And did you prod her on?' His eyes twinkled with humour. 'And still she trod the wrong path? Nay, but a tale to relish!' He took a draw on the pipe but erupted into laughter again, convulsing with smoke. 'The mare!'

'Pardon,' said Boundless, anxious to change the subject, 'but you mind me of a certain trapper I had occasion to meet on board the boat that brought me to these parts. A Mr Fesky.'

'Fesky!' Mose blinked in astonishment. 'That old muskrat? I heared he was dead—drowned in the creek!'

'I assure you, sir, he is very much alive. I spoke to him not four days past.'

'I ain't heard that name mentioned in more than five year—and that be Gospel truth. And still alive?' Mose shook his head, profoundly bemused by the revelation. 'The Lord moves in wondrous ways, 'tis true. See how He joins us all!'

'You were intimate friends?'

'As young bucks we shot buffalo together—up near the Ohio.' Mose poked the fire under the pot, still registering the import of the news. 'Wondrous are the ways, and that be a fact.'

'You hunted the buffalo?' Boundless sat up, rubbing his tired eyes. 'A most remarkable creature—so I am told.'

Mose tested the stew again, wrinkling his nose at the taste. 'Buff? They be what they are. 'Course, they be hard to find nowadays.' He stirred the pot, his face thoughtful. 'The truth of the matter is I can't recall seeing one these past ten year or more.' He mulled on the fact as he smoked the pipe.

'I should be very glad to see one with my own eyes.'

'Why then, judge for yourself.' Mose nodded towards a pile of furs in the corner. 'That robe on top. The tawny one.'

Boundless picked up the topmost fur, inspecting it with unrestrained curiosity. The robe was larger than a blanket, and soft and cool to the touch. He hefted it in his hands, exclaiming in surprise at the weight. The hair was dark-coloured—almost black along the edges, while lightening to a bleached brown tint in the centre. Holding it to his nose, he inhaled a dark, musky smell of hide and smoke. He ran his fingers across the fine hairs, marvelling at the dense softness. Suddenly aware of Mose's scrutiny, he coughed with embarrassment and set down the robe. 'A most handsome fur, indeed.'

'You handle it well,' said Mose, approvingly. 'A good buff hide is a powerful thing. The savages worship the critter, and that's a fact. I shot that fine specimen almost 20-year ago. It keeps me warm on the wintriest night.' He held the spoon up to his mouth. 'Supper invites!'

To Boundless' famished palate, the stewed rabbit tasted as sumptuous as the finest meal from his favourite London tavern. He gulped three heaped bowls in quick succession, fishing out the chunks of meat with his fingers before tipping the bowl to swallow the thin, salty broth. Mose ate from the pot—dipping the spoon and testing each portion for hotness before swallowing. The trapper proved a surprisingly dainty eater, tossing into the fire any morsel that did not agree with him and chewing slowly and carefully those that did.

'I am greatly in your debt, sir,' said Boundless, declining the offer of a fourth bowl. He wiped the grease from his mouth with the sleeve of his jacket as he savoured his first full stomach in four days.

'That was a mighty appetite,' approved Mose as he removed the pot from the flames and set it on the hearth. 'You are welcome to rest here for the night. You can find the trail on the morrow. The truth is I should be glad of some Christian company and a good yarn. Jack is a dependable listener, but he don't say overmuch. What say you?'

'Accepted, sir, with many thanks,' said Boundless, enormously relieved at the offer.

Mose warmed his hands over the fire. 'These old bones feel the chill. Hark!' He cocked his head as a gust of wind rattled the door. 'Windy March,' he said. 'And then cometh April showers, and then May, meek and mild.'

Boundless studied the trapper, curious as to his history. The man's wiry frame seemed scraped to the bone by years of tireless striving amidst the wilderness. *He is a hardy fellow,* he observed to himself, *to live thusly at his years.* Above the crackling of the flames, he heard the hoot of an owl. 'This be a lonesome spot,' he said.

Mose nodded slowly. 'It is. Awful so, at times. You say you came here from a boat?'

'I did. I was a deckhand.'

'And your occupation—afore the boat?'

'Printer.'

Mose raised an eyebrow. 'Then you can read?'

'I can.'

Mose pondered this. 'A most useful skill.'

'I believe you mentioned coming here from Virginia?'

'Aye. More than thirty years ago.'

'You have family there?'

The trapper remained silent a moment before answering.

'They all be departed. God bless their souls.'

'I am heartily sorry for it.'

'And your own kin?'

'Departed also.'

'And no other issue—no brother or sister?'

'To my regret, no.'

'Ah! 'Tis a hard thing—to be alone in the world.' The trapper reflected on this. 'A hard thing,' he repeated, studying Boundless over the pipe. 'Do you have news of the war?'

'The war?' Boundless shook his head. 'I confess I had entirely forgot it.'

Mose shook burnt tobacco from the pipe. 'I expect it will be won or lost without interference from us.' He stood and walked on stiff legs to the open door. Sticking out his head, he peered into the gathering dusk.

'Goodnight, old Jack! And you, sweet William! Adieu my friends, until the morrow.' Closing the door, he lifted the bar into place. 'That mule be a trial,' he muttered. 'Only I don't say so—to spare his delicate feelings.'

Boundless suppressed a yawn, his stomach heavily replete with the meal. 'Pardon.' He yawned again.

Mose knelt to rummage among a pile of utensils. 'Found and found!' He held up a leather canteen. 'Whisky!' he said. 'The trapper's dearest friend.' Casting around further, he produced two cups, both missing the handle. Handing one to Boundless, he poured out a generous measure. 'A mite overpowering, but tolerable for the most part.' He raised the cup in a toast. 'To full bellies, dry powder, and a well stocked fire!'

'Amen.' Boundless winced at the taste of the potent brew.

'It gets so you don't mind the sting. I get it from a Mr Gottschalk over at the trading post. Where he obtains it, I tremble to think.'

Mose refilled his pipe, a thoughtful look on his face. 'It be a rare pleasure to yarn with a fellow Christian. 'Course, there's Mr Gottschalk every three month or so, but he be sorely limited in the ways of conversation. 'Tis in the way of merchants to weigh and charge by the pound. A word here, a "well-met" there—weighed and costed, by gar!' He puffed on the pipe, his blue eyes curious through the smoke. 'You seem partial to the buffalo, friend.'

'I have heard of nothing but the creature since arriving in the colonies.'

Stretching out his legs, Boundless rested his back against a sack of salt. The effects of his travails in the woods, together with the whisky and the stew, combined to produce a sudden, overpowering fatigue.

'Pardon,' he said, yawning and struggling to keep his eyes open, wishing only to sleep.

Mose appeared not to notice, staring into the flames as he smoked.

Boundless yawned again as the warmth of the whisky and the heat of the fire spread throughout his limbs.

'Is it not most warm?' he murmured. His head sank back and his eyes closed as the hiss and crackle of the burning logs sounded in his ears.

An Interlude in the Woods

H E AWOKE TO FIND daylight streaming through chinks in the cabin walls. He sat up in some befuddlement—staring around before recollecting where he was. The cabin was empty, the door ajar. Getting to his feet, he stretched, feeling refreshed from the sound night's sleep. In the morning light, the cabin appeared larger than the day before. The heaped piles of skins and the stink of tanned hides mixed with the smell of wood smoke to give the impression of an artisan's workshop as much as a rude cottage.

Scratching at tick bites, he stepped outside. The sky was lightly overcast. A cool breeze blew against his cheek. The mare snickered to see him and tugged at where he had tied her to a branch. 'Good morrow, Bess,' he said, looking around for his host.

At that moment, Mose emerged from the surrounding trees bearing an armful of branches. 'I see that you are awake.' The trapper was bare headed, his lank, grey hair wisping in the wind.

'I am, sir, and fully rested, thanks entirely to your kind hospitality.' He eyed the slate-grey sky. 'I trust that the weather will hold?'

'I feel a storm in my bones.' Mose set down the branches. 'The horses need watering.'

Untethering the horses, Boundary led them to the creek. While the animals drank, he gazed around at the thick woods. Birds twittered loudly in the foliage. He searched for some evidence of the path that had brought them to the cabin but could find none. The mare nuzzled his shoulder, and he stroked her neck. A gust of wind stirred the branches, and he glanced at the grey clouds overhead. 'The weather is contrary,' he said on returning to the cabin.

Mose grunted. 'But set the one way only.' He held out a bowl full of the previous night's stew. 'Whatever the weather brings, this will keep you tight until supper.'

Accepting the bowl with grateful thanks, Boundless wondered if he should offer the trapper a coin as payment, but dismissed the thought, fearful of offending his host. His hospitality is genuine and seeks no recompense, he told himself. He sat down on the stool and began to eat.

Mose picked at his portion. 'If you are set on chancing the weather, I'll point you to where you can pick up the trace to the York Road. It be a distance, though. I calculate you have overshot the mark by two days. And the trail runs through some rough country.'

'Say at least that it is clearly marked?'

'Not so as that winded nag of yours could read it. But you should have little trouble so long as you keep pointed the right way. Once you are on the Lancaster Pike, the road is signposted to Philly. You can take that venison.' He indicated the smoked tenderloin he had brought into the cabin. 'It will give supper for tonight.'

'Again, sir, I am heavily in your debt.' Boundless scooped another chunk of rabbit, humbled at the generosity of the trapper. 'Winded?' He glanced up as the meaning struck him. 'The mare. You said she is winded?'

'D'ye not hear the rattle she makes? She may fetch you to York, but she'll scrape to get by.'

'Then I must sell her?'

'For meat, mayhap. You can purchase a better horse at York.'

Boundless stared frowningly at the floor, his suspicions of the post trader confirmed.

Mose looked out through the open door. 'If you wait but an hour or two, you may float to Philly.'

'It may not rain at all. I have seen it often on the river—a grey morning giving way to a bright afternoon.' Swallowing a last mouthful, he set down the bowl, impatient to be on his way. 'A thousand thanks for your hospitality, friend. I wish only for the opportunity to repay the kindness.'

Mose gave him an odd look. 'Who can tell but that we may both advantage the other and share the road as fellow travellers one day?'

'Indeed.'

'Why, if you change your mind on Philly—'

'Pardon, but I must take my leave lest the weather change.' He rose to his feet.

Even as he spoke, a shadow obscured the light from the doorway. Going outside, he found the sun entirely disappeared behind a mass of clouds. The wind had grown stronger, shaking the branches. Remembering the fraught passage through the flooded woods to the Elk River, he hesitated to saddle the mare.

'You'd be advised to study the weather,' cautioned Mose as he eyed the swollen clouds. The mare stepped skittishly at a change in the air. Without warning, a loud crack of thunder rent the clouds directly overhead. In an instant, the heavens opened and a drenching rain swept across the small clearing.

'Take heed!' Mose scurried back to the shelter of the cabin.

Boundless quickly followed suit, already soaked through to the skin. Together with Mose, he stood in the open doorway peering out at the torrential downpour. A flash of lightning split the clouds followed shortly by a crash of thunder.

'Thou shan't travel this day, friend. The road will be awash with mud. Mud and torrents.'

The storm continued without let-up, rain pelting the roof. Mose tacked up a square of canvas as the deluge dripped through chinks in the logs. 'Mayhap we must join old Noah on the Ark!' Drops of water leaked onto the fire, sizzling against the burning logs.

'Will the creek flood?'

'Do ducks fly! Do store keeps rob and filch!' Mose picked up a log and placed it on the fire. 'Two by two,' he murmured as he studied the roof for more leaks. 'We shall proceed in two by two. Two of every kind.'

Mose resumed his seat by the fire, shivering at the sudden change in temperature. 'By gar,' he muttered to himself. A thought appeared to strike him and he pulled a tattered haversack to him and rummaged through the contents.

'Eureek!' He flourished a pack of playing cards. ''Twill pass the time,' he said, and in spite of Boundless' loathing for the pastime, cajoled him into a game of All Fours.

'A trick!' Mose threw down a hand. 'Again, friend,' he crowed, gleeful at the triumph. 'One more turn afore we drown.' He distributed the cards, humming as he studied the hand. 'A trump, or I be a Turk!'

Several hours later, as Mose basted a leg of venison, Boundless peered out the door at where the horses shivered under the trees. The rain sheeted down so intensely that he could scarcely see across the clearing. The creek had swollen to three times its size and water lapped around the tubs on the bank. 'Tomorrow is certainly lost, and mayhap the day after, as well,' he conceded, bitterly disappointed.

'To sop the flood!' Mose thrust a bowl—heaped with pink, juicy cuts of meat—into his hand. Boundless picked morosely at the meal as he contemplated the prospect of confinement to the tiny cabin for a further two or three days. 'Nay. But be merry.' Mose speared a portion of meat on the point of his knife. 'Think—you be under shelter with a blazing fire and a full belly. Would ye prefer to drown in the naked woods?'

This reminder of his good fortune sobered Boundless considerably as the truth of the trapper's words sliced through his disappointment.

'Indeed. You speak sense. A prudent man resigns himself to that which he must endure.'

'Endure with whisky!' Mose hunted around for the canteen. Finding it beneath a fur, he poured a measure for each. 'To old Noah and the Flood!' He raised the glass and swallowed at a gulp.

Towards dusk, the rain eased, pit-pattering gently on the roof. Mose stood at the door to peer out at the flooded glade. 'Jakes if the tubs ain't floated!' Agitated, he held up the lantern. 'D'ye see them?' He held the lantern higher, searching the creek bank. 'By jinks if that ain't them over there—ship-wrecked under the pine!'

Lowering the lantern, he shivered and stepped away from the door. 'Come inside! Another sup to keep the damp from our vitals.'

Boundless lingered by the door, looking out at the flooded grass, a resigned look on his face. 'I do not think I shall see York this week.'

'This week? Mayhap not this side of Creation!'

IN THE AFTERMATH OF the storm, the air turned warm and sticky even as the grass remained soaked with the overflow from the creek. The following morning Boundless stood in the doorway cursing his luck as another faint rumble of thunder sounded on the horizon.

'Patience, friend, patience,' said Mose, coming up beside him to squint at the swollen creek. 'Who knows but the sky will clear tomorrow, and the ground dry out within the week?'

His eagerness to be on his way was further confounded when he discovered a swelling on the leg of the mare. He summoned Mose for assistance, watching anxiously as the trapper raised the injured leg for inspection.

'She has harmed above the joint.' Mose felt around the bruise. 'She must have ricked it on the trail. Or else was spooked by the storm. With luck it be only a swelling and the bone beneath is unhurt.'

'It will heal—of itself?'

'Aye. Time is the only cure. You must hobble her so that she does not place too much weight on the knee.'

'How long—for it to mend?'

'How long? A week—two, to be certain. It is not advisable to travel her. She will pull up lame after a few hours and you will have to shoot her and walk the remainder.'

'Is there a post nearby where I might buy another?'

'Gottschalk's. But that be a fair walk through the woods.' Mose fixed Boundless with the same, ruminative look he had given him the day before. 'You would be wise to stay here until she recovers her health.'

For a moment, it occurred to him that he might ask to borrow the trapper's horse to ride to the trading post in order to purchase another. The thought that he might well get lost again—even if his host agreed to the proposal—increased his sense of frustration. 'It seems I am defeated,' he conceded.

'For the moment only. Philly will still be there in a month.'

'But if I am to stay I must either pay you for your troubles or earn my keep.'

Mose pinched his lower lip as he considered this. 'Can you hunt or lay a snare?'

'Neither I am sorry to say.'

'Butcher, then. Surely, you have butchered afore?'

'A pig, only.'

'And never tanned?' Mose looked surprised at the admission. 'Say, then, that you have at least skinned?'

He shook his head. 'I am afraid not.'

'Can you use an axe, at least—to cut firewood?'

'That I can.'

'Then, by hookery, we are saved!' Mose scratched his chin. 'The wood is over-wet for now. Mayhap we'll butcher the buck.' He led the way to the smoke hut. 'Perish the rain,' he grumbled, stepping around a large puddle in the grass. 'Why don't it all fall in the creek!'

Pulling open the door, Mose revealed a small, windowless space with a sloped roof. The inside was heavy with the smell of smoke. The walls were blackened with tar and grease. A firepit stood in the middle of the dirt floor. A long, crudely fashioned bench held various smoked portions of meat and a bucket of salt. The gutted buck hung from a rope fastened to a beam. A pool of blood was soaked into the dirt beneath the carcass.

'Take the fellow,' said Mose, 'and I'll show you how to skin him. Save your clothes.' He pointed to where a leather apron hung on a peg.

Boundless hung the apron around his neck and tied the sides. The garment reached from his neck to his toes. Mose nodded approvingly. 'Fetch him to the small pine down by the creek. You will find rope tied to the branch. String him up while I fetch the knives.'

Boundless took down the buck, feeling as he did so the weight of the hanged boy against his body. He found the rope loops Mose had described secured to the branch of a young white oak. Before hanging the deer, he examined it, finding a wound above the chest wall. The coat was reddish-brown. The belly and throat were white, as was the underside of the tail. He ran his fingers through the short, wiry hairs before feeling the antlers—small and spike-like in appearance. The gutted carcass weighed no more than sixty or seventy pounds. He had just finished hanging it when Mose returned, carrying a rawhide bag.

'Gadzooks! Head down!'

Embarrassed, he took down the buck and hung it again. It dangled in place, its hide a mottled brown as it swayed in the breeze.

Mose bent over the hemp sack, pulling out a big-bladed knife and a handsaw. A gust of wind blew the scent of wet pine from the forest. He stood up and breathed in. 'D'ye smell it? 'Tis Nature's incense.'

'I have smelt little else ever since I abandoned the boat.'

Mose frowned as he inserted the knife point under the skin of the rear leg. 'A fine fellow,' he said, 'Though a mite small. Observe the cuts.' He ran the blade under the skin toward the knee joint. 'Stop afore that.' He tapped a dark spot just under the knuckle. 'It will spoil the meat.' He repeated the cuts on the other hind leg, huffing as he narrated in between cuts. 'The aim is to … *strip* the hide. With the least … *harm* to the skin.' He turned his attention to the front legs, pulling them apart. 'Take the knee joint as mark.' Inserting the knife tip, he ran the blade up under the skin toward the chest. 'Follow the white—up to the brisket.' After incising the skin, he handed the knife to Boundless. 'Try your hand at the other leg.' Boundless imitated the method, surprised at how easily the skin yielded to the sharp knife. 'All the way up,' said Mose, watching closely.

Taking back the knife, Mose began to peel away the skin away from the hind quarters. 'Where it sticks, use the knife to cut the threads.' He demonstrated by severing some membranes. 'D'ye see?' A splatter of rain fell and he glanced up. 'Lucky you chose to stay, else would you be soaked as a fish. What did ye mean, *abandoned* the boat?'

'A turn of phrase. "Left it," I meant.'

The severed hide hung down around the hind parts of the deer. 'Watch.' Mose took a handful of skin and began to tug it down around the carcass. 'First one side, then the other. Work your way round.' The skin made a sound like tearing paper as it came away. 'Give it a turn,' he said, stepping back.

Boundless tugged the hide down the sides, exposing the marbled fat beneath.

'Use the knife—cut the threads.' Mose muttered approval as Boundless severed the connective tissue. Taking over, he worked the skin all the way down until it hung about the head of the buck like a partly divested cloak.

'Hand me the saw.' Mose sawed most of the way through the neck bones. Then, grasping hold of the head, he wrenched it between his hands, snapping it off. 'The consumption to be wished!' He held up the fresh, bloody cape, the head still attached. 'This be the value of the animal, and what the fine ladies in Philadelphia pay for. It will make a fine leather. Feel.'

'What is it worth?' The skin felt slightly warm beneath Boundless' fingers, like a removed glove.

'It will fetch a pretty shilling or two—or a bottle of molasses rum if you prefer. How now, Horatio.' Mose laid the wet pelt in the grass. 'Stay there, good sir. You say you've never butchered?'

'As I said, a pig, only.'

Mose tapped the skinned, dangling carcass. 'The method is the same each time. Start by taking off the shoulders.' Mose bent to make the cuts. 'She hangs low,' he said, and fussed with the rope, untying the loops and pulling the rope higher. 'Now, where in tar—The shoulder! Make the cut around the blade. Like so ...'

Boundless bent in closer to observe as Mose sawed through the meat. 'Next, sever the joint.' In a moment, the shoulder was cleanly despatched. 'Now the other ...' Mose repeated the procedure, talking through each stroke of the knife.

'Pull the leg away to see the join. Some folk like to chop off the legs first.' Wrenching the shoulder free, he passed it to Boundless.

'Lay that on the hide.'

The deer now dangled half its previous length.

Mose bent down and scrubbed the knife blade in the grass.

'D'ye see the method?'

'I do.'

Mose stood up and twisted the carcass slightly. Holding the buck steady with one hand, he pricked the meat either side of the spine. 'These be the tenderloins. The heathen admire them so much they chew them right off the carcass.' He traced down the spine with the tip of the knife. 'Find the rib bone and—'

'Where—the rib bone?'

'Put your finger there. D'ye feel?'

Boundless nodded, pressing into the meat to feel the knob of bone.

'Take that as your mark. Cut back to the spine.' Mose made a lateral cut in the meat next to the ham. 'D'ye follow?' He ran the knife lightly down the spine. 'And then a second cut here—to the neck. Samewise to the first. Those be the marks.' He inserted the tip of the knife along the back bone. 'Work it in … Like this. *Wriggle* the blade. Be it *wriggle* or *wiggle*?'

'I believe either would—'

'—Under the meat and work it down to the mark. It will come away.' Mose demonstrated, peeling away the meat.

'Shoo!' He flicked the knife at a persistent fly. 'Did ye say *wiggle*?'

'I said—'

'Judge!' Mose held up the bloody tenderloin. The meat was dark red and threaded with tendrils of fat. 'A peerless cut. 'Twill make a fine roast or half-a-dozen chops, as ye prefer.'

Handing over the warm knife, he watched as Boundless attempted to replicate the cuts on the other side of the spine.

'Here?'

'Aye. Dig the point in … until ye strike rib. Run it down. Use the other hand—the idle one, to strip away the meat.' Finishing the cuts, Boundless held up the severed meat, pleased with the effort.

'Set it on the hide.' Mose ran his fingers down the exposed lattice of bones. 'These be the ribs—my favourite meat. We come to them by and by.'

Holding out a hand for the knife, Mose began slicing meat away from the neck bones.

'A bit scraggy, but useful for soups or what-have-you.' He held out a hand. 'The saw.' He tapped the carcass with the blade. 'Next, we take off the hinds. They remove without fuss.'

So saying, he sawed around the joint, breathing heavily as he did so.

'The sock. See?' Pulling away the leg he revealed the white ball socket. He looked around. 'Where in *perdition* is the deuced hatchet? In the hut,' he answered himself.

When Boundless returned with the hatchet, he found Mose grumbling to himself, seemingly incensed at the 'contrariness' of a preacher he had once encountered.

'A witless fellow,' he muttered. He sawed around the socket, waving away the hatchet. 'A mix of Baptist and some other, and a disgrace to *both*. A wretch fearsome in his ignorance!' Snapping off the bone he set the severed quarter down on the skin. 'Pompous? By gar, but the word is too thin!' He sliced meat from the ribs, slashing the preacher with each stroke.

'A nose beaked like a fish hook, and a queer, sideways gait like a ...' He paused, unable to think of a word. 'Like a *pigeon!*'

Mose halted his fulminations to untie the remaining hind. Laying the carcass in the grass, he handed the knife to Boundless. 'Do the other limb the same.'

He watched critically as Boundless imitated the cuts on the other hind.

'*Pull* the leg—out from the socket. '... A face to sour milk and a tongue to curdle cheese!'

Boundless severed the limb, perplexed at his new companion's propensity to jump from thread to thread as though all conversations were of the same ball of wool.

'Such gibberish deserved hanging. There is much meat on that part. I never saw him again but the one time,' he said, further entangling and cross-stitching the conversational threads. 'Lay it there—on top.'

The quartered carcass lay in the grass on top of the removed skin. 'Rest a spell.'

Mose sat on a small log. 'Your first butchering,' he said, 'apart from the vaunted pig?'

'Aye.' Boundless stared at the bloody, dismembered carcass, trying to reconcile it to the live buck.

Mose took out a pipe and put it into his mouth without lighting it. 'I butchered my first at the age of six. Six or seven. If I were heathen I would chant a prayer over this specimen.'

'I have heard said that they are animists, and worship stones and trees, as well as animals?'

'They be less particular than we as to creed. They hold everything to be an equal part of creation.'

'There is much to commend in such a view. Fesky claimed that certain tribes worship the bear, others the wolf. Is it true?'

'I have heard it said. Mind, whether it be the one God for either, or but a fragment, I could not say.'

'A fragment of God?' Boundless pondered the phrase.

'The longer I live in these woods, the more I incline to their beliefs. But not entire. It be a disputatious point—where heathen belief touches upon our own.' The trapper motioned the pipe at the pile of freshly butchered meat. 'This be a communion, whether to the Indians or ourselves, as Christian folk.'

Boundless studied the trapper, uncertain whether his companion spoke from genuine piety or was indulging in fancy.

Mose frowned as he considered the point. 'Mayhap old Adam was a Pamunky, and these woods his Garden.' He inhaled on the notion.

AFTER A BRIEF REST, they picked up the hide with the butchered parts on top and carried it between them to the smokehouse.

'Lay out the parts on the bench.'

Mose selected a thin-bladed knife from the bag of tools. 'First things first—as the groom said to the bride.' Chuckling at his own joke, he began deboning the portions, peppering the task with homilies and advice. 'Save that bone for soup … sharpen the knife every ten minutes or so … that be the middle steak, peerless with gravy … that part could double for veal … the rounded portion? As good as the best beefsteak … save the scraps for stew. Where is the filleting knife?' He looked around. 'The small fellow … with the thin blade.'

When he had finished, some thirty pounds of trimmed meat lay in a line along the bench. Wiping an arm across his forehead, Mose searched around.

'The tub,' he said, pointing to the object.

The tub was the sawed-off section of a barrel with holes cut into the sides and bottom. As Boundless dragged it to the bench, Mose cut open a sack of salt. He shook a generous amount into the tub. 'Lay the meat on top. Ye've at least salted afore?'

'Aye. Mostly pork. Mother liked to add sugar.'

'As we will, in time. Tip in some more.'

After all the meat had been layered in salt, Mose gripped the tub and shook it. 'That will keep until the smoke. It gets hard on the back. Are ye a churchgoer?'

'I am afraid not.'

'No matter. There is better scripture in the wind and trees. Fetch that bucket and follow.'

In the shade of the pines, a log, smoothed of its bark, sat suspended atop two cross-ties. Mose draped the freshly removed skin across the log. 'The scrape beam.'

'What are we doing?'

'We must scrape it clean and then salt to cure it. Mr Gottschalk be pernickety about the quality.' Using his fingers, Mose pulled lumps of white fat from the bloody hide. 'For tallow,' he said, and tossed the globules into the wood bucket. 'We can boil it later and have ourselves a dozen candles courtesy of Mr Buck.'

Selecting a large, flat-bladed knife, he began to scalp away the clotted fat and pieces of wet, pink tissue. 'Keep the edge. Scrape it down to the skin. There's lots of meat on it still. I once saw a starving Pamunkey boil and eat the skin entire.'

He handed over the knife and watched closely as Boundless imitated the method.

'Not so deep as to nick the skin … do not let it ruck … use your body to hold it tight against the log … Slice the blade … smoothly! Like so …' He took back the knife to demonstrate.

'Your heathen will use a shell, bone or sharp stone to scrape off the issue. Remember that if you ever find yourself short of a knife.'

Mose watched for a further minute or two before disappearing back inside the tanning shed. He returned bearing a long bone, knuckled at each end, the middle part bevelled to a sharp edge.

'This is a bone tool I got from a Lenape hunter.' He demonstrated by using both hands to push the bone across the skin. 'But scraping is hard work. The knife blade is better.' He stood back to watch as Boundless resumed fleshing.

After scraping for a further ten minutes, Boundless halted to rest his back. The front of the leather apron was greasy with fat, blood and tissue, the stench of blood cloying in his nose.

'Turn it to do the edges,' said Mose as he took up the knife again. '*Scrape it*—don't woo it! What is that air? He hummed a bar. Deuced if I can remember—'Twas my father's favourite.' He began to sing in a thin, reedy voice.

'Five years served I, under Master Guy
In the land of Virginny-o—

Keep it tight … scrape that spot again. Let me see.' Mose held up the bloody skin for inspection. Laying it back down, he spent a few minutes fussing over parts, pulling it tight over the beam to scrape away any membranous residue.

'What about the other side—the hair side?'

'We use a different method, as ye shall see.'

Picking up the fleshed hide, Mose led the way to the tanning hut. Inside were half-a-dozen tubs, identical to the ones standing by the creek. A powerful stink of smoke and ash filled the air. A bench, similar to the one in the smoke house, occupied one side. 'Lay it there.' Mose picked up a wooden pail full of salt. 'Stretch it out so that it is even.' He tipped the salt onto the skin, heaping the white grains in a pile. He then began to smooth the salt with his hands, pressing it into every inch of the skin. 'It must cover entire,' he said as Boundless joined in. 'Work it into the edges. Don't stint! More!' Boundless tipped the pail. 'More!—as the virgin chanted to the groom.'

It took the entire pail and half of a second before the salt was layered to Mose's satisfaction.

'Twill stop the putrefaction,' he said, smoothing the grains. 'You must cover every scrap, else will it spoil.' He stood back. 'We repeat the business in a day or so.'

'What about the hair?'

'We will soak it off with lye, in time. Some, we leave to the tannery.'

As Mose busied himself refilling the salt pail, Boundless wandered around the hut inspecting the contents of the various tubs and pails. 'These are soaking?' he asked, peering at one tub. The tub contained a hide, submerged in a grey fluid.

'Aye. For buckskin.'

'What is in there?'

'Wood ash and water compounded. It loosens the hair. But if you ever lack a tub, soak it in a running stream. The Indians follow that method. Where in the name of Abe—' He cast about on the floor of the hut before picking up a short stick.

'It is deer, also?' he asked as Mose stirred the hide.

'It is. A fine, friendly fellow. I brought him down by yonder creek as he stepped up to drink.'

'They are all deer?'

'Half, mayhap.' Mose pointed to a dried skin. 'A racoon I caught sniffing around this house. And that top pelt—over there,' he pointed to a pile of cured hides. 'A muskrat. Snared not 100 yards from here.' He went around the other tubs, stirring and poking the contents. He took out a skin and tugged a clump of hair from the surface. 'This fellow is ripe for the plucking.'

Using the stick, he carried the soaked skin down to the creek where he immersed it in the water. 'The lye will burn,' he explained. 'It must be washed off first.' Dunking and wringing the skin he fetched it back to the scrape log. 'Judge for yourself,' he said.

Curious as to the effectiveness of the lye, Boundless experimented with pulling out several clumps of the wet hair. 'It comes away easily.'

'For buckskin, we must shave the fellow bald. Hair and grain both— down to the hide. We want the pure skin only.' Mose picked up the fleshing bone and began to shave away the hair in sure, bold strokes. After a while, he handed the bone to Boundless. 'Keep the edge. Oft times it is easier with the fingers.' He pulled at a resistant knot of hair to demonstrate.

When the hide had been scraped and plucked clean of hair, Boundless stood aside as Mose examined the result. 'D'ye see the grain?' He pointed to a speckled patch. 'It will refuse the tan. Hand me the bone.' He began to scrape the area. When finished, he held it up again, surveying several holes. 'They will need thread.' He tugged at one.

Boundless felt the wet skin between his fingers. 'Is there more to the method?'

'More? Why, we ain't fetched the half of it! Take it to the crick, to rinse and stretch.' Mose chuckled. 'By jinks, there be method and *yards* of it still to come.'

Boundless submerged the skin in the creek, creasing his brow in annoyance. 'The fellow perversely mistakes my meaning.' He took it out to wring it dry before repeating the process. Mose came to sit on a log to watch. Smoking a pipe, he offered instruction. 'It will need to be worked before we lay on the tan. Twist it *hard* … pull around the sides … it won't tear … drown it again.'

Following a quarter hour of washing and squeezing, Boundless flexed his fingers. 'It is most tiring. Is this your daily round?'

'Add in tanning, hunting, snaring and smoking.'

'Is it not a hard life—in such a lonesome spot?'

'It would go easier if I had a Suskyhannock squaw to share the labour. But such don't suit a Christian man, as I claim to be. Although the bachelor life has its severities.' Kneeling, he spread the washed hide and dug at the edges with the knife point.

'What are you doing?'

'How else are we to tie it to the frame? Fetch me those leather thongs. "*When that I was weary, weary, weary-o!*"'

The afternoon was warm and humid. They returned to the cabin for a dinner of cold pork and warm cornbread Mose had left baking in the embers of the fire. After eating, they went back outside to sit on a log as a stiff breeze kept the insects at bay. Mose smoked a 'digestive' pipe and imbibed from a canteen of ale. He held out the canteen to Boundless, who shook his head.

'Are ye certain? A libation after dinner be most natural.' Mose puffed on the pipe.

'What will you do with the hides?'

'After salting and drying, I pass them on to Mr Gottschalk at the post.'

'Pass them on?'

'Barter them for goods. Whisky also, and tobacco.'

'And Mr Gottschalk?'

'Will consign them to a merchant in Lancaster—a Mr Potts, I believe. He, in turn, sells them to a house in Philadelphia—to be tanned and sold as leather or buckskin. What will you do there?'

'Where?'

'Philly.'

'Find work—mayhap on a boat.'

'There is work here, aplenty—as you can see.'

'You are the woodsman, Mose. I am merely a … stranded fish.'

Mose dug burnt tobacco from the pipe bowl as he considered this. Then, tucking the pipe away, he stood to his feet. 'Are ye fit to continue?'

OVER THE NEXT SEVERAL days, the ground dried out quickly under a hot, cloudless sky, the sun's fierce heat penetrating even the cool shade of the woods. The humid air brought out dense clouds of insects, the buzzing pests driving Boundless to distraction. The air within the cabin became so stifling that both men took to sleeping outside on the grass, enduring the mosquitoes for the sake of the night breeze. Twice each day, he checked the mare, eager to see if her swollen foot had reduced, but she continued to favour the leg as he led her to water, causing him growing concern as to whether she would ever make a full recovery.

'A watched pot,' said Mose, coming to observe as Boundless walked her around the grass.

'Is there ointment I can apply, or a bandage, perhaps?'

'Fresh air the ointment, and time the bandage. Patience. She will gait naturally when she is able. The firewood is low. There be the axe. It needs sharpening first.'

AS HE WAITED FOR Bess to show signs of improvement, he busied himself with whatever chores Mose set him, determined to pay for his keep. He found the scraping and fleshing a messy, distasteful business, one which caused him to reflect sourly on his earlier admiration for the independent life of a trapper. 'He works hard for his free supper,' he thought, watching Mose make his way to the tanning hut, a sack of salt under his arm. The list of tasks that required daily, sometimes hourly, attention struck him as improbable for one man, even one as redoubtable as his host. 'Theo was right. It is indeed an arduous life.'

One afternoon, they were standing by the creek when Mose suddenly cocked his head and looked at the trees. Next moment, he hurried back to the cabin, leaving Boundless baffled and not a little alarmed at his companion's behaviour. Mose soon returned bearing the musket. Putting a finger to his lips, he bid Boundless follow him into the line of trees. Hardly had they entered the shadowy undergrowth than Mose raised a cautionary hand. He stepped behind a tree, motioning for Boundless to do the same. They heard the cracking of a twig as a large whitetail buck stepped from the surrounding foliage. Before Boundless could fully take in the animal, Mose had lifted the musket and fired. The buck took half a step and tumbled to the dirt.

Delighted at his good fortune, Mose stood over the kill, a gleeful expression on his face. 'The fellow most obligingly presented himself to us. Why, a few more steps and he had wandered straight into the smokehouse!'

Boundless bent down to examine the kill. 'A fine shot—straight through the heart. The buck's eyes were wide open as though in shock. The broad antlers stood proudly out from the head.

'My belly is growling for a good steak. Help me turn him over.'

Taking out the big knife he wore around his waist, Mose leaned over to tap the deer on the chest. 'This is the brisket. Feel.'

Boundless placed his finger on the spot, feeling the bone beneath the skin.

'That be your beacon. Trace the knife up the belly—nicely.' He demonstrated, inserting the knife point and slicing the skin up the belly to the sternum. Working his way back down the belly Mose tapped the fur. 'The gut is under here. Be careful not to nick it.'

Hooking his fingers, Boundless lifted the skin and slit the belly down to the pelvis. The greyish gut bulged out through the cut. He splayed the hams farther apart.

'Cut out the stalk and balls.'

He did so, holding up the bloody parts for inspection.

Mose nodded approval. 'Then tie off the fundament or else spoil the meat.' Demonstrating, he tied the tract with a length of sinew he pulled from his pouch.

'Some hunters like to start with the privies. Fesky always swore by that method. Next, we fish out the insides.'

Using both hands, Mose levered the big knife up through the rib cage, grunting as he broke through the bones. Pulling the sides apart he showed the glistening innards.

'Two halves,' he said, indicating the chest and abdomen. 'The heart and lungs here—and the gut and kidney there. Some fancy the heart, but I don't care for the taste. The Indians, however, waste nothing and will eat every morsel. He reached inside the chest. 'Take out the gorge first, afore the organs.'

The buck soon lay eviscerated in the grass, the bloody porridge of gut and entrails lying alongside. Mose wiped the knife.

'Git now!' He barked at the mule as it wandered over to examine the entrails. 'You'll find a shovel just inside the door. Bury them over by the trees.'

Boundless edged the bloody entrails onto the shovel and carried it carefully to the edge of the clearing.

'Dig them deep! There's all kinds of critters that will claw them up.'

By the time he had finished, Mose had skinned the deer and started to flesh the bloody hide. Not bothering with the scrape log, the trapper quickly shaved off the bloodiest clumps of fat and meat before passing it to Boundless.

'Lay this in the creek. Use rocks to weigh it down.'

Taking the hide down to the creek, Boundless dunked it several times, washing away the gore. The water was cool, in spite of the summer heat, and he glimpsed a fish dart in the shadows. Submerging the skin under the water, he heaped several rocks on top, watching as the ends rose in the current.

THE NEXT MORNING, HE returned from gathering firewood to find Mose standing in the stream, bent over and muttering to himself as he scoured the creek bed. A brass kettle sat on a small fire that burned in a nearby fire pit.

'What are you looking for?'

Mose made no answer but poked among the rocks, grumbling and cursing all the while. 'Jinks if I didn't toss it back in error. An absence of mind. A severe mis—Ah! Lost but found!' He straightened up in triumph, a small flat rock clutched in his hand. 'Fetch me that fellow's head.'

Guessing 'that fellow' to be the buck Mose had shot the day before, Boundless retrieved the head from where it sat in the tanning hut. He held it in his hands for a moment, gazing at the voluminous black eyes. 'I have seen such mounted on many a wall,' he reflected, carrying it down to the creek.

Kneeling beside the head, Mose lifted it by the antlers and began to shave the fur from the back of the skull. 'The rock—if you'll oblige.' He struck the edge of the rock against the exposed area of skull, striking it several times until the skull began to crack. Using his fingers he pried apart the smashed bone. He held it up to show the grey-pinkish brain nestled within. 'The yolk,' he said. '—Alas poor fool. I 'member him well. What is the line?'

'Yorrick, I believe.'

'Yorrick!' Mose wiped his brow. 'Fesky had the damnable habit of reciting it every time he oped a skull.'

Boundless watched curiously as Mose fingered the brain from the skull—any trace of squeamishness subsumed in his interest at what his companion intended.

'What are you doing?'

'Making the tan—to dress the hide. I learned this skill from the Nanticoke. The heathen waste nothing of the creature.' He scooped the brain into a wooden bowl, crumbling the larger pieces with his fingers.

'Fetch me that kettle. Lift it by the rag … pour it in the bowl.' He watched the hot water mix with the brain.

'Enough.' Mose touched a finger to the pottage. 'Jinks!' He blew on the finger. Leaning to the side he scooped up a handful of creek water and added it to the bowl. Taking up the rock, he began to mash the brains.

'Mash so it is like porridge.' Setting aside the rock, he worked the sludge with his fingers, smoothing and pressing until it resembled a thick, grey mush.

'The hide, if ye please.'

Boundless retrieved the damp hide from where it hung from a pine branch.

'Lay it out on the grass.'

Mose gave a last stir to the grey slurry, pronouncing it 'sound as a mouse.' He scooped a large handful and began to work it into the stiff rawhide. 'It must soak in—every inch. It will soften to buckskin.'

Boundless scooped a handful of the slurry, imitating Mose by rubbing it into the hide. 'You will trade it—when tanned?'

'Not this fellow. I am in need of a second shirt. Tip the remainder back into the bucket.'

Holding up the hide, they drained the excess into the wooden pail. Mose added the remaining tan from the bowl, half filling the pail. 'Put in the hide,' he said. He immersed the hide in the brain liquid, pressing down until it was completely covered.

'Let it soak. Time for a pipe.'

A FEW MORNINGS LATER, Mose summoned him to the tanning hut. He joined the trapper with some reluctance, expecting to scrape or tan another hide. Instead, Mose selected an already tanned hide from among a dozen stretched on drying frames.

'Since you will not smoke a pipe, you'd best learn how to smoke a hide—if you are to be of use.' Taking the awl and thread, Mose sat down and sewed the hide into a 'bag', open at one end.

Boundless watched, trying to anticipate the process, and failing. 'Why one end and not the other?'

'The smoke goes in here.' Mose held up the open end. 'And collects up here. Hand me that length of buckskin.'

Taking the awl again, Mose tacked the length to the open end of the deerskin. 'This is the skirt which holds it down over the fire. D'ye see?'

Giving the buckskin to Boundless to carry, Mose walked to a second, smaller fire pit. He touched his toe to a pile of rotted wood. 'We use the bark to make the fire. You will find a tubful in the hut should ye need more.'

Kneeling, he began to build the fire, laying pine branches beneath as 'coals' before piling the bark on top. 'Smother the pine with the bark.'

Boundless took a handful of the bark, crumbling the pieces over the pine as Mose had done. The wood felt rotted and slightly damp.

'Fetch the hanger.' Mose pointed to a wooden frame. 'Hang the hide from it.' He blew on the fire. 'We do not want flame, but smoke.'

Standing up, Mose stood back to watch smoke rise up from the smouldering bark. 'You can use most any wood, but I hanker for the cotton. It gives a pleasing colour.' He held his hand over the fire. 'Not too hot. We want to smoke, not cook it.' He chuckled to himself. 'By gar if old Fesky didn't cook a hide once and blame it on an innocent squaw.'

'When do we place the hide over it?'

'Once she sends up sufficient smoke. Watch.' Mose positioned the tripod over the pit, manoeuvring the white deerskin so that the open end circled the small fire. 'Now we must make a chimney. Fetch those stones, if you will.'

Mose weighed down the skirt with the stones so that the hide formed a funnel over the fire.

'The smoke will colour it?'

'Aye. And preserve it against the wet.' Mose tugged at his shirt to make the point. 'When wet, it dries a mite stiff but softens again with handling. Else—without the smoke—it would turn back to rawhide. Watch the fire and turn her inside out when smudged on the one side.'

Boundless watched for some minutes, surprised at the volume of smoke pouring out of the hide. Concerned lest it catch fire, he tugged at the skirt, moving it away from the smoking embers. To his growing interest, the hide began to change colour as the smoke permeated the pores.

'Instead of gawking, there's wood that needs chopping,' said Mose, passing by.

He went to fetch the axe, muttering to himself. 'I may as well have stayed on the landing and found work as an indenture in a tobacco field, for the fellow orders me about like a slave.'

After the buckskin was turned inside out and fully 'coloured', he took it down. He forgot his annoyance at Mose as he marvelled at the rich yellow tint and the soft, supple feel of the cloth. He pressed it to his nose, inhaling the smell of smoke.

'You must air it,' said Mose, coming up to inspect the cloth. 'Drape it over the drying frame so that the colour sets.'

Over the next few days Boundless made several attempts to smoke some 'scrap hides', under the watchful tutelage of the trapper. After 'over-smoking' the first, and setting fire to the second, he was in possession of two smoked buckskins. He hung them to air before joining Mose in scraping several small muskrat hides.

After two days, he took the buckskins down and washed each in the creek before wringing and hanging them up to dry. A day later he inspected the cloth, pleased with the smell and the feel. *But a short while ago you clothed an animal. You were then a wet and bloody hide. And now you be a cloth as soft as linen. And perhaps one day you shall clothe me.* Ruminating on the thought, he fetched the buckskins back to the cabin.

The following day he accompanied Mose back to the tanning hut. The trapper went first to a fresh hide they had salted the day before.

'Mark where the salt has turned pink.'

Taking the hide outside, he shook off the loose, damp salt. He then laid it flat across the bench. At his signal, Boundless heaped fresh salt onto the skin.

'Plenty of it! Look for the wet parts.'

Mose turned to the tanning tubs. Taking up a stick, he fished out various hides for inspection.

'Not you, friend,' he said, placing the first back in the tub. 'Nor you,' he said to a second. Moving onto a third tub, he lifted out a deer hide.

'Behold, and I do marvel at thee! Drunk in every pore. Witness.'

He held up the dripping hide for Boundless to examine before immersing it in a tub of fresh creek water, stirring the hide for a few minutes, 'to get out the burn'. Picking it up, he squeezed out the excess tan.

Kicking the tub to one side, he draped the soaked buckskin across a short, horizontal beam. He began to twist the buckskin from the bottom, plying it into a tight coil.

'The stick—over there.' Using the stick, Mose twisted the hide further, tightening it to squeeze out every drop of moisture.

Satisfied, he rolled the hide and stood it against the wall.

'You leave it to dry?'

'To drink in the tan.'

THE NEXT MORNING, MOSE unrolled the damp hide and laid it on the bench. Scooping a handful of the remaining tan, he began to supple the gelatinous pulp into the hide, working it vigorously into the skin.

Boundless joined in, the two working side by side until the hide felt soft and pliable. To his surprise, Mose placed it back in the tub, stirring until it was thoroughly saturated with the mix.

'You will soak it again?'

'Aye. And maybe a third time, too. The brain needs to get into every speck of the cloth.'

An hour later, Boundless took the tanned hide down to the creek where he repeated the washing and wringing of the previous day. After a quarter hour of this process, he sat down in the grass, breathing heavily. Mose, who had come down to watch, picked up the hide and ran it around in his hands. 'It will make a fine shirt.'

'A linen shirt—bought from the store—would save considerable labour.'

Mose stared in astonishment. After a moment he guffawed, shaking his head. 'D'ye send for the apothecary when you must bandage a finger? Fetch it back to the hut. Tomorrow, you can tie it to the frame for stretching.' He walked away, chuckling.

BEFORE RETIRING FOR THE night, Boundless fed and watered the live-stock, taking the opportunity to examine the mare. She walked with a distinct hobbling motion, whinnying as he stroked her mane. 'Get well quickly, Bess,' he urged, fondling her ears. 'This skinning and tanning be a tiresome, stinking business.'

Mose's voice sounded from within the cabin. 'Where in *creation* is the Applejack!' A moment later, a loud whoop signalled discovery of the liquor.

The fellow would drink a distillery dry. He looked around at the surrounding pines, now disappearing in shadow and sighed. ''Tis a lonely spot. One I am best quit of as soon as possible.' He winced as he flexed his fingers, his hands and wrists sore from working the hides. He stood there for some minutes, tired and immersed in self-pity as he inwardly railed against thunderstorms, lost paths, and rapacious store keeps.

'D'ye intend to stand watch all night?' Mose's voice bellowed from inside.

With a despairing look around in the fading light, Boundless dragged his steps back to the cabin.

A Hunt

TWO MONTHS AFTER HIS arrival in the woods, his skin and clothes so stank of smoke, grease, lye and ash that he fancied he himself was in danger of becoming leathered. He had salted, stretched, washed, brained and smoked hides until heartily sick of the business. To add to his concern, the mare showed scant signs of improvement, still favouring the injured leg as she walked.

'Give her two more weeks and judge again,' advised Mose.

'She steps easy, in spite of the knock,' he insisted.

'Put an ear to her lungs. 'Tis not the foot that will miscarry, but the wind.'

Doubtful, Boundless put an ear to the mare's chest. 'I can hear nothing untoward.'

'Not now. But ride her a mite and see. Do you wish her to break down two miles into the woods?'

'Perhaps a slight rasp,' Boundless conceded. Taking off the saddle, he watered the mare and brushed her coat. But a week more, he promised himself. Seven days.

The next morning, Mose surprised him by inviting him along on a hunt.

'But I can hardly load a musket, let alone hit a target,' he said. 'And I am not at all sure of the weapon, truth be told.'

'Hand me the piece.'

Setting the stock on the floor, Mose peered down the muzzle. 'A smoothbore. And clogged with powder into the bargain. You say you shot at a bear? A deer? A mercy that it didn't blow up in your face.' He pulled back the hammer and examined the flint, making a noise of astonishment. 'D'ye see the flint? Dull as a parson! And the spark hole? Fouled is too honest a word. The stock is remade—but not well.' He returned to his inspection of the hammer. Setting it at full cock, he was about to pull the trigger when the hammer slipped and struck the steel. 'By the saints! It does not lock!'

Boundless muttered at the confirmation of his suspicions. 'The man that sold it to me was a thorough-going scoundrel.' Mose took down a musket where it was pegged to the wall. 'You can use my second. A Pennsylvania rifle. It shoots true, and three times as far as yon cobble-stick.'

Boundless stood up to handle the weapon. In length it was even longer than the musket, the tip of the barrel level with his chin. He drew it up to aim, pleased at the balance. The butt stock sat securely against his shoulder, the weapon surprising him with its balance despite the near four-foot barrel. The stock was burnished with use, the flint sharp to the touch. He pulled back the hammer, contrasting the strong pull with that of the smoothbore. 'A fine weapon,' he said admiringly as he fingered a brass plate on the stock. 'What is this?'

'You do not know? That is the patch box. Open it.'

Boundless did so, swivelling the plate and revealing some linen patches inside.

'Show me how you load the gun.' Mose placed a powder horn on the table and took a handful of lead balls from a bucket.

Setting the butt on the floor, Boundless set the hammer to half-cock. He then took the plug out of the powder horn. Under the watchful eye of his companion, he made to pour powder into the muzzle.

'You do not have a measure?' At his blank look, Mose retrieved the leather pouch he wore around his shoulder to hunt. He took from it a small brass powder measure.

'You must measure or else lose a hand.' He watched Boundless pour powder into the measure and prepare to tip it down the muzzle.

'Hold! Put the plug back in the horn first—unless you wish to spill out the powder.'

Boundless tapped the butt stock on the floor, as he had seen others do to tamp the powder. The trapper nodded and handed him the patch of greased cloth.

'Set this on top of the muzzle, place a ball on top. If you are short of wadding, use grass in a pinch. Fesky used swear by chawed tobacco.'

Boundless set the ramrod atop the patch and ball and pushed, surprised at the resistance compared to the musket.

'Hold.' Mose stood up and extricated the patch before trimming it with his knife. 'Now, again.' He sat down.

Boundless pushed the ramrod down the barrel, seating the ball and patch atop the powder.

'Do not ram over-hard. Firm is sufficient. See the line?' Mose pointed to a scratch on the ramrod. 'Take that as a mark.'

He opened the powder horn and prepared to sift grains into the flash pan.

Mose interrupted his arm. 'Do not pour from the horn. Use the measure.

Horn to measure. Measure to gun. Follow each step, exact. 'Tis all in the method.'

Boundless sifted a smidgen of black powder from the measure into the flash pan. Mose squinted at the result. 'Not overmuch. Sufficient grains only. Too much and it will crowd the spark hole; too little and it will squib.'

Boundless closed the frizzen over the powder and looked at Mose.

'Prick the spark hole.' Mose handed over a feather from the pouch. He watched Boundless insert the quill end into the vent.

'Wriggle it about. *Wriggle* or *wiggle*, again?'

'Blow powder out of the pan between shots. And swab the bore every second or third shot, else will the powder foul the barrel.'

Setting down the gun, Boundless sighed, 'I have a great deal to learn it seems—even before I shoot the piece.'

'It will come, by and by.' Mose pulled the leather pouch over his shoulder. 'Are ye set to hunt?'

'I am, indeed.'

'D'ye have a knife?'

'A jack knife, only.'

''Twill not do for hunting. Take the butchering knife.'

Mose watched Boundless tuck it into the sash around his waist. 'You must make yourself a belt and pouch if you are to hunt these woods.' He briefly checked his own long rifle before looping the powder horn around his neck. 'Come then, to arms!'

THE LATE SPRING MORNING was fresh and warm—the absence of winged pests a balm that raised his spirits. Mose hummed a sprightly tune as he led them past the creek and into the woods. Boundless breathed deeply in the salubrious air, fancying that it gusted all the ingested smoke and gore from his lungs. A half mile past the creek, they halted at a stream-let as Mose motioned for silence—the *bonhomie* of the pipe replaced by the keen air of the hunter.

'See there.' The trapper pointed to a cluster of hoof prints in the mud. 'Whitetail. And still fresh.'

Boundless briefly studied the prints, setting the concave hollows to memory.

Mose set off again, moving quietly and cautiously through the under-growth. Boundless followed at his heels, doing his best to avoid stepping on twigs and praying not to embarrass himself. Ahead, Mose had gone into a crouch, hiding behind a shrub. He signalled Boundless to do the same.

'Where?' he whispered, kneeling beside the trapper, unable to see anything in the dense brush.

'Patience.' Mose motioned to a leafy white oak not twenty yards distant. 'Let him come to us.'

Boundless set the musket at full cock, wincing at the sound. He searched the surrounding undergrowth but still could see nothing.

'I do not—'

'Shush! Make ready!'

At that moment a buck stepped out of the bushes and began to chew on the leaves of the oak. Heart pounding, Boundless trained the long barrel on the deer. He hesitated to take the shot, breathing purposefully to control his nerves.

'While we yet draw breath,' Mose whispered beside him.

The musket went off with a sharp retort. White smoke puffed into the air as the ball whizzed into the branches of the oak. The startled buck leapt away into the bushes.

'Thunder!' Crestfallen, he mumbled an apology.

Mose seemed undeterred by the miss. 'Nay but be of good cheer. Why, I 'spect you'll roundly slaughter the next specimen.'

A short distance further on they chanced upon a black bear as it browsed the forest floor.

'A fine coat! He is yours to bring down.'

Holding his breath, Boundless levelled the flintlock. The bear ambled forwards and he resighted the long barrel, his hand trembling. To his horror, the musket discharged suddenly as he prepared to pull the trigger. With a loud grunt, the bear loped, unscathed, back into the trees.

'Perish the thing!' He examined the pan, furious at the mishap.

'Check the spark hole. Use the feather to clear it. And swab the barrel.'

They set off once more through the trees. A short distance further through the woods, Mose signalled a halt. Ahead, Boundless saw a wild turkey feeding on acorns.

'A plump specimen,' said Mose, his voice low. 'But let us get closer.'

Using the thick foliage as cover, they advanced to within twenty yards.

'Are you set?' whispered Mose. 'Take the wing as mark.'

Boundless carefully aimed the flintlock, choosing a point where the wing met the body. The turkey constantly moved about, bobbing its head, and he murmured in frustration. Holding his breath, he fired. The bark splintered from a pine as the intended target flew off into the branches.

'I shall starve 'ere I hit the mark,' he grumbled, dejected at the third miss.

'Did ye learn to oar afore ye sat in the boat?' Mose unslung the canteen and took a swallow of beer. 'The bird was a difficult shot, and for practice only. Be of good cheer. The day is afore us.'

Several more fruitless attempts followed, each one causing Boundless greater annoyance than the last. 'I am thankful for your patience and good humour,' he said as Mose called another halt to imbibe more of the beer.

'It takes but the join of hand and eye. Once found, the skill becomes nature.'

They set off on a circuitous route back to the cabin, Boundless berating himself for his crass ineptitude. 'Suppose I were attacked by a savage? I should be scalped and dead ere I set the cock!'

He was still scolding himself when Mose suddenly raised a hand. They were in a deep part of the woods, the lattice of sunlight barely penetrating the dusky shade. He squinted at the trees but could see nothing. 'What?' he whispered.

For answer, Mose placed a hand on his shoulder and pointed to the shadows beneath an herbaceous vine some 100 yards distant. Squinting at the spot, he saw a doe browsing the leaves. Mose noiselessly led the way to a chokeberry bush and knelt behind it. Boundless followed, stepping gingerly. A small clearing lay ahead of them.

'She will come this way,' said Mose, his voice barely audible.

Boundless levelled the musket in anticipation, his mouth dry with tension. The doe finished nibbling the leaves and advanced tentatively to the edge of the clearing. She paused to sniff the air, one leg raised in readiness for flight. She seemed nervous of the open space and retreated back into the shade, eyes darting, ears pricked for the least sound. Mose laid a restraining hand on his arm. '*Wait!*' he hissed.

The doe now advanced again, her limbs quivering as she put one foot cautiously before the other and entered the glade. 'Free your breath,' Mose whispered. 'Stay calm. Fix the sight on the chest …'

The explosion shattered the peace of the woods. Boundless held his breath as the doe stumbled a few steps before collapsing to the grass.

Mose whooped and clapped him on the shoulder. 'The seal is broke! Afore God, but I shall make a marksman of ye yet.'

Boundless walked forwards to stand over the doe. She lay as if stunned, her eyes open. 'She is still alive!' The doe made a soft, wheezing sound and kicked her legs.

'Then *finish* her.'

As the doe struggled to rise, he threw himself on top of her. She thrashed in terror as he locked an arm around her neck and groped for the knife. Eyes bulging, she snorted and kicked wildly. He hung on, smothering her with his body as she squirmed desperately beneath him.

'Beware the hooves!' As if in a dream he heard the shout.

Wrenching back the head, he dragged the knife blade across the throat. He felt the doe shudder and convulse. Warm blood flowed between his fingers. He held on tightly as she gave a hoarse, gargling sound and lay still.

Shocked and breathless, he looked up to see Mose holding his sides with mirth.

'By the bones!' Convulsed with laughter, the trapper spluttered and wheezed as he pointed helplessly to the deer. Wiping his eyes, he brought himself under control.

'The musket ...' he said, chuckling. 'The musket ... not the knife! The blood will taint the meat.' Shaking his head, he wiped his eyes again. 'Lord, but that was worth climbing out of bed for!'

Chagrined, Boundless stood to his feet, his shirt and breeches caked with blood and dirt. 'I feared she would escape,' he protested, his breath coming in pants. 'I had no time to reload the gun.'

'No matter.' Composing himself, Mose stood over the doe. 'Never walk up on a creature unless you be certain it has expired. If that was a buff, it would have kicked you as far as Baltimore.' He nudged the doe with his foot. 'D'ye see where the shot went in?'

Boundless knelt to see, panting and dishevelled from the contest. 'Here, above the brisket—almost on the neck,' he said, flushed with pride at the kill.

'Aye. You missed the vitals. T'was why she tried to dance.' Mose chuckled. 'By gar! but it was a sight to relish.'

Breathily heavily, Boundless sat down in the grass. 'She had a powerful kick.'

The deer lay on its side, its head lolled onto the grass. Flies alighted on the throat and flew off again to return a moment later. 'She must stand three feet at the shoulder,' he said. 'How heavy, do you think?'

'Short of a hundredweight, but not by much.' Mose slapped him on the shoulder. 'A fine first kill—even without the fandango. But we have no time to stand and chaw. The flies will make a meal of her—if the sun doesn't boil her first.'

'You wish me to dress her?'

'Dress her! If I wished you to *dress* her, I should have fetched a gown or a pair of britches. I wish you to *gut* her.' Mose handed him the big knife. 'You saw me with the buck but yesterday?'

'Aye.' He rolled up his shirt sleeves as he tried to recall the method. Standing between the back legs, he splayed them apart. Inserting the knife point at the base of the ribcage, he sliced up the warm, white belly toward the breastbone. Turning the knife, he cut through the muscle, careful to avoid the intestines. Gripping the knife with both hands, he sawed upwards, breaking the ribs. He glanced up at Mose, who nodded.

Kneeling, he reached into the sundered doe, groping the soft, moist innards. Fumbling for the windpipe, he felt the heat of the just-vanished life beneath his fingers.

'So delicate! Poke around! D'ye feel the pipe—where it is sewed to the throat?'

'I have it.' He cut the tract, pulling it out, along with the entrails. His extracted arm glistened with blood and grease. Wiping his hand on the grass, he tugged his collar loose, sweating profusely in the sun. Then, shifting position, he cut away the skin and fur over the gut, hooking two fingers to lift the skin, as he had seen Mose do.

'Good. Now the privies.'

He dug around the back passage, feeling the knife strike against the pelvic bone. Cutting out the udder, he held it up. 'It has milk,' he said. He hesitated before tossing it to the grass. He then sawed through the exposed pelvis with the knife. Breaking the bone, he splayed the legs further apart.

'Free the belly wall.' Mose pointed to the stretched muscle partitioning the heart and lungs from the stomach.

Panting and wiping the sweat from his eyes, he sawed through the fibrous tendons sewing the muscle to the chest wall. 'Blasted flies!' He flicked the air with the knife.

Reaching in with both hands, he pulled the swollen gut free of the deer. The bulbous bag slid onto the grass amidst a sludge of scarlet-blue entrails. Blood had pooled in the hollowed-out cavity. 'Roll her onto her belly. Let her bleed.'

He stood up, breathing heavily from the exertion. The discarded entrails were black with buzzing flies. The hollowed-out doe lay spreadeagled on the grass, her head resting daintily on one front leg as if asleep. An image of the gaffed dolphin lying on the deck of the *Patience*, ebbed of life and colour, came to mind as he observed the slender form.

'Let her drain for a minute or so,' said Mose. 'You've kilt us a fine dinner.'

After a few minutes rest, Boundless bent down and humped the doe onto his shoulders. As Mose followed with the muskets, he started off through the trees, the prize slung limply across his back.

What Mighty Prospects Await the Eye!

BACK AT THE CABIN, he stripped the doe of its skin, tugging the hide down past her head as the slender form swung delicately, almost demurely, from the frame. He then hung it up to cool. Elated at his first kill, he returned to the carcass an hour later, butchering it under Mose's guidance. They cut steaks from the loin and pan-fried them over the fire. He savoured the taste, declaring the meat 'succulent' and the best he'd ever tasted.

Mose nodded, his mouth full. 'The meat you shoot yourself is always finest.'

After, still basking in triumph, he joined Mose for a 'libation', drinking two mugs of whisky. He gave a long yawn, thoroughly sated on a full belly. The fire blazed, despite the warm evening. He leaned back against a stump he had dragged into the cabin for the purpose. Mose sat on the only chair, smoking and sipping whisky in-between gazing into the fire. 'Are ye still bound on heading off for Baltimore?'

'Philadelphia. As soon as the mare is recovered.'

Mose smoked on this for a while. 'You say you are new to the country?' He held out the canteen of whisky.

He shook his head. 'I have not the head for it.'

'I had not, the once, but persevered.'

'I am—' He yawned. 'As you say, new to the country. Scarce a year.'

'What then do you know of these colonies? I speak as to extent and bearing.'

'Bearing?'

'Aye. The size and generality of all. The entire baker's dozen.'

'In truth, beyond the names of most, between little and else. Why do you ask?'

Mose made no answer but fumbled behind him. Failing to find whatever it was he expected, he got down on his knees to rummage through the detritus on the floor. 'Where in the name of *Hezekiah*!' ... Crawling to the corner, he peeked under a hide, grumbling to himself. After further rummaging among the hides and pelts he knelt back in triumph. 'Lost but now found!' He declared, holding up a deerskin pouch. 'The parchment, if it pleases.' Still on his knees, he pointed to a square of tanned hide lying on the floor.

Boundless passed the hide, surprised to note that it did indeed have the feel of stiff parchment. His curiosity piqued, he watched Mose position it flat on the floor. The trapper fished out a stub of charcoal from the pouch. Shifting position, he hovered it above the hide, his manner frowningly intent.

'Do you intend to sketch?'

For answer, the trapper drew a smudged line across the bottom third of the patch of hide. 'Here be the thirteen—' He marked 13 Xs on the hide. He glanced up to check that Boundless understood.

'The thirteen colonies?'

'Aye.'

'And where are we—Maryland?'

'Thereabouts.' Mose tapped the middle of the row of Xs.

Boundless pointed to the hide. 'And there, the Atlantic?'

'Even so.'

'And this part?' Boundless gestured to the unmapped portion of the hide.

'Land claimed by both the French and Indians. But the *nub* of the matter, be these mountains, the Alleghenies.' Mose drew a squiggly line and inscribed it with several inverted Vs a few inches above the row of colonies. 'These be the line of mountains that flank us to the west.'

'Alle-*ghen*ies?'

'Aye. The word is Indian. They—the mountains, act as a mighty wall, partitioning the country east and west.' Mose reached for the canteen to top up his whisky. 'More than thirty years ago—up in the Ohio country, I made camp with a Frenchie, a most obliging fellow. Over buffalo rib, he fell to yarning about such and such, finishing with a claim to have crossed over said mountains.' He tapped the hide. 'Moreover, he claimed intimate knowledge of the country.—Where in *perdition!*' Muttering, he cast about for the tobacco pouch. Finding it, he poked his fingers inside and began to stuff the pipe bowl.

'And?'

'*And.* Here was one who had *crost* those mountains. Crost them with a tale to tell. A tale of sights and marvels the like of which staggers the comprehension. I see his face before me even now, as if it were but yesterday.' A gust of wind rattled the door and raised sparks in the fireplace.

'Tales of what?'

'Tales of endless grassy plains—so vast as to encompass half the given earth.' Mose stared into the flames, his voice rapt as if transcribing from the very lips of the long-ago Frenchman. 'Of rivers *latitudinous* as the sea. Of *incredulous* mountains that are as giants to the piffling Alleghenies. Of beaver to every crick and stream. And buffalo in numbers so great as to madden the senses.'

'Ha! A liar or a drunk no doubt!'

Mose turned on Boundless, his expression fierce. 'Not so! He was an honest fellow and swore most solemnly as to the truth of his account.'

Grudgingly impressed—whether at the claims or Moses's conviction of their authenticity, Boundless picked up the hide map and studied the lines.

'And no Englishman has set foot there—beyond the mountains?'

'If so, they have yet to speak of it. The heights be formidable and divide all the way to Virginny and points south.'

'The buffalo—in his account, were of such number?'

'So stupendous that Jehovah Himself could not count the heads!'

Boundless searched his mind as he pondered the phrase. 'It is peculiar, but I recall Fesky vouching a similar claim.'

'He did?' Mose's face lit up with triumph. 'There you have it—buff beyond measure of counting!' He jabbed the burning logs with a stick, raising a fresh shower of sparks. Reaching for the whisky, he poured himself a generous measure. Filling another cup, he held it out to Boundless. ''Twill ward off the cold.'

He sipped the whisky while seeing in his mind the redoubtable Thompson sit back in the twilight to prop up his feet while declaiming of hinterlands 'as vast as the whole world together.'

'Nigh on a year ago, at Mr Gottschalk's, I fell into conversation with a merchant from Carolina. The man, a rascal, no doubt, but an honest one— by which I mean the truth of his deceit was writ clearly on his face—attested that, some few years back a certain Mr—whose name I cannot now recall, stumbled upon a notch across the mountains.'

'Notch?'

'Aye. A way across. Where is the stub?' Mose took back the map. With furrowed brow, he inserted an X between the arrowhead mountains. 'Thusly.' He sat back. 'What say you?'

'As to which point? There be so many to the tale I am stuck full of pins.'

'Do you not see what is plain before you?'

'I confess I am perplexed.'

'Long have I prayed to see such sights—to set eyes on such bounty. All I lacked for the venture was a trusty companion.' Mose fixed him a hopeful gaze. 'And now Providence has led you to my very door.'

'Me!' Boundless laughed, astonished. 'Impossible! I am intended to Philadelphia.'

'Pshaw! On a winded nag fit only for the pasture!' Picking up a stick of firewood, Mose snapped it in two and threw it onto the fire. 'Is Philadelphia such a prize that it cannot wait? Why, I 'spect you are planning to hitch up with the first curly-haired filly that takes your eye.'

'Balderdash!'

Mose tamped more tobacco into the bowl. Drawing it to flame, he studied Boundless. 'I know not how you stand in the world. And nor should I hazard to guess. But a young spark wishing to make his way could use a stake. And there's no finer or quicker way to turn a stake than to trade in beaver pelts. Why, never mind that danged old mare! In six months you'd be fixed to ride to Philadelphia in a coach and four!'

Boundless snickered at the vision conjured up. 'Aye. In tattered breeches and worn-out soles! And as for hunting the beaver—if that be your point, why I can as well lay a snare as bake a cake.'

'I could teach ye.'

'And gladly would I learn—but not at the cost of travelling to those deuced mountains of yours.'

'Did ye not come all this way from England for the adventure?'

'I *came* … No matter. I had as soon ride to the mountains as to the moon.'

Mose grunted, a look of severe disappointment on his face. 'At your age I should not have hesitated.'

'You be far more independent and accomplished than me—at any age.' Boundless shook his head. 'Philadelphia is my destination. You shall have to wait on some other companion.'

Looking greatly put-out, Mose picked up the canteen and shook it. 'Empty!'

THREE OR FOUR TIMES a week, Mose returned from checking his trap lines with a hare, squirrel, woodchuck or quail slung over his shoulder. 'A musket will fetch you a deer—if you be fortunate. A well-laid snare will catch you dinner several times a week,' he said one morning a few days after their conversation. So saying, he led off into the woods, biding Boundless follow.

He did so, glancing at the thick brush that hemmed in the path. 'Does the prospect of encountering Indians ever concern you?' he asked Mose.

'There be room enough in the woods for all. I am more cautious of stumbling onto a bear.' Mose stopped and crouched beside a bush. Brushing aside some grass and twigs, he revealed a loop made from braided sinew hidden beneath. 'This is a simple snare, one favoured by the heathen. The loop runs to that tree.'

Boundless bent to examine the loop. 'How do you remember where you placed it?'

Mose looked perplexed at the question. 'I mark it by the bush.'

Boundless made a rueful face. 'I can scarce tell one plant from another.'

'They be as various as people. The heathen have names for each one.'

They continued through the trees, coming upon a dead possum crushed beneath a log. Thinking the occurrence the result of an unhappy accident, he remarked upon the fact, to be met by an indignant snort.

'Accident! D'ye not see the trap? And the bait?'

Bending, Boundless saw a scrap of meat caught in the paws. 'This is a different snare—not a loop, like the other?'

'Aye. A drop. It is tiresome to make but useful for catching possums, muskrat or beaver. But your best bet is the simple loop.'

They made the round of the traps, Mose commenting on the various kinds and the animals suited to each. 'There be several. The loop, the drop, the cage, the spring. But the first two are best and easiest.'

Back at the clearing, he cleaned and skinned the possum while Mose watched, occasionally correcting his hand. Taking off the leather apron, he glanced down at his shirt, now heavily soiled with accumulated grease and blood. Going to the cabin, he changed to his one spare shirt. Holding the soiled shirt across his arm, he made his way to the tanning hut. He emerged holding an empty tub which he carried to the creek. Filling the tub with water, he knelt in the grass to scrub the worn shirt.

Mose came over to join him, sitting on a log and taking out his pipe. Lighting it, he puffed on the tobacco, regarding Boundless through the smoke. 'You say you hanker to see buffalo? Where will you find one in Philadelphia? If you wish to acquaint yourself with the beast, then you must venture across the mountains to the grassy plains where you shall see so many as to doubt your eyes.'

'I say it plain. I am bound to Philadelphia—as soon as the mare is fit to travel.' He vigorously scrubbed a patch of blood.

''Tis a great pity.' Mose smoked in silence, lost in thought. A few moments later he spoke again.

'You will scrub clean through the threads. That shirt will fall apart within the month.'

'By which time, I trust, I shall be safely arrived in Philadelphia.'

'What will you do there that you cannot do here, just as well?'

'Buy a clean shirt and breeches, for one.' Exasperated at finding a new tear in the shirt, Boundless dunked the garment back under water.

'Aye. And filch and scrape and hither and thither at the pleasure of some harping wind-bellows to the tune of a shilling a week.' Mose snorted at the prospect.

Boundless held up the soaked shirt, vexed at the conversation. 'Truly, I prefer the plain and simple routine of my former occupation. It had not so many parts to it—nor a tenth so many guts!'

'Will a boat fetch you supper or a good, buckskin suit? A drowning, only!'

Boundless wrung the shirt, suspecting what was to come next.

'Is it not a shame to grovel and thumb at the behest of some spindly backed *flossamer* when you might eat and clothe yourself for free? A hunter's is the purest life there is. You'd be beholden to no man. Think of it—the great, western plains with nought but grass from sky to sky.'

'Aye. And *savages*. And flies. And wild beasts. And God knows what other hazard that may befall a man.'

'Pshaw! Do you wish to die in bed surrounded by candles and choking on soot?'

'I *wish* to stop this endless palavering about mountains and plains and buffalo fables and—'

'Fables!' Mose stiffened with outrage. '*Fables,* by gar!' He got to his feet, his face creased with annoyance.

He watched the trapper stomp off, spluttering and hawing. Regretting his intemperance, he stared into the stained water of the tub. For a moment, he indulged a fanciful vision of the near depleted pouch under his shirt bulging with gold from the sale of beaver pelts. He pictured his London friends gathered around him in the tavern—admiration infusing their faces as he repaid debts and dispensed largesse from a seemingly bottomless purse.

Hearing an exclamation, he looked up to see Mose emerge from the tanning hut an empty salt sack under one arm. The trapper stalked past to the cabin, muttering to himself. 'Such be your fables!'

For the remainder of the afternoon, a strained silence existed between them. Putting the mended shirt aside, he collected wood from the log pile.

Bundling the firewood in his arms, he emerged to find Mose crouching over the fire pit recasting lead balls that he had retrieved from his kills. *The man is a manufactory to himself.* He walked up to the trapper. 'I am heartily sorry we quarrelled.'

Mose grimaced. 'Accept my apologies, too. I be so taken up with the western scheme that it inflates my senses.'

'Who knows, but that you may meet a suitable companion at the trading post.'

'Aye.' Mose tapped a lead ball from the mould. 'Let us take supper and speak no more about it.'

A FEW DAYS LATER, Mose declared the time was ripe to visit the trading post. 'Tomorrow I intend to fetch the hides to Mr Gottschalk's.'

'Where is your Mr Gottschalk to be found?'

'His post lies on the Susskyhanna, a day's ride east of here.'

'Fesky mentioned it.'

'He has traded hides—and barbs, with Mr Gottschalk of old.'

The next morning, he helped Mose tie the hides to the mule. 'Twenty-three … Twenty-four,' said Mose, counting. The sky was slate-coloured, the sun hidden behind a cloud.

'They make a fine cargo.' Mose tightened a strap. 'Doubtless Gottschalk will strive to snip the value, but I am on to his tricks.' He climbed into the saddle. 'I shall return on the morrow. Keep a sharp eye and scrape that last skin. Hup, Jack!' He headed off, the mule plodding behind on a rope bridle. "How long, dear Saviour, O how long shall this bright hour delay?" He half-turned in the saddle. 'Farewell, friend! Guard the door. And easy on the prime! "O how long ere the promised day?"

Following his companion's departure, Boundless took the musket and strolled off into the woods to practice his shooting skills. Several hunting forays with Mose subsequent to bringing down the doe had done little to improve his aim and the trapper had frowned on the suggestion he try his hand at hitting a marked target.

'Powder and lead cost money. Practice on a bird or a deer—something that carries flesh or a pelt.'

Conscious of the trapper's parsimony, he had given him the wherewithal from his store of coins and credit notes to purchase powder and balls on his behalf as well as to make a contribution to the cost of his keep.

'He will accept the Maryland and the Spanish, only' said Mose, handing back the promissory note.

'How in blazes then am I to discharge this?'

'Hang on to it. Mayhap Gottschalk knows of a merchant. I will ask him.'

And what am I to do with a hundredweight of tobacco? he wondered as he strolled through the woods, musket across his shoulder. He walked on, bemused at the varied and seemingly endless chain of notes, coins, commodities and bartering that formed the colonial economy. *One may trade from a pelt up to a shirt, and back again.* He was pondering the fact when he heard a rustle in the trees.

At once he halted, pulling the hammer to full cock. After a long moment, he lowered the firearm and continued, angry at himself for his fears. He started humming—in imitation of Mose, to signal his disdain of any peering eyes. Perhaps that is why he does it, he speculated. He start to sing, softly at first and then lustily as he shouldered the musket and fell into a march step. "Hark now the drums beat up again, for all true soldier gentlemen!"

After three unsuccessful attempts at catching a deer, he bagged a wild turkey, striking it in the wing as it attempted to flee. He proceeded back to the cabin, greatly pleased with both the shot and the catch. 'Twill make a handsome dinner and supper.' he congratulated himself. He bled and plucked the bird, his thoughts turning briefly to the astonishing armada of passenger pigeons encountered on the way to the Elk. He ate part of the fowl, salting the remainder. He fed the mare some oats and inspected the fore joint, pleased to note that the swelling was gone. 'The leg is sound.' The observation caused him to reflect as he pictured Mose arguing the wonders of the western plains in an attempt to postpone his departure. *He seeks, by degrees, to delay me and thus seduce me to his foolish scheme. He is fixed on the mad venture and will not rest until he inveigles me to partner him. Well, he shall have but poor luck!*

As evening came on, he built up the fire, determined to announce his intention to depart immediately on Mose's return. I shall leave before the week is out, he promised himself. He placed a pot of mush on the embers of the fire, checked to make sure that the door was securely barred, and stretched down to sleep. Bundling the buffalo robe as a pillow, he imagined his return to Front Street. *I shall stink like—if not resemble—your actual trapper.* The conceit amused him as he fell asleep.

Two days later he had just returned from cutting firewood when he heard a cheery hail. Moment later, Mose emerged from the woods. Behind him he towed the mule, laden with goods. 'We be set for the flood!' he cried as he drew rein in front of the cabin. 'Stand, good Jack.' Climbing down from the saddle, he eased his back by walking stiff legged up and down. 'William doth bring gifts for all,' he said, gesturing to the cargo that burdened the back of the mule.

Boundless helped carry the provisions inside. In addition to jute sacks of sugar, salt, beans, oats, onions, carrots, turnips and flour, the supplies included a firkin of whisky, two more of cider, two of beer and two of whisky. 'Hides paid for all of this?' he asked.

'They did. I sounded Mr Gottschalk on the tobacco note and he made mention of a gentleman who may be willing to redeem it for coin.'

'Where is this gentleman now?'

'Away in Baltimore, at last report. But is pledged to return within the twelve-month.'

He held his tongue, remarking instead upon the quantity of liquor. 'Deuced if you don't have enough to fill a tub,' he said, untying a sack of beans from the mule.

'With luck, and temperance, sufficient to carry us through to winter.'

Boundless took frowning note of the sentence as he shouldered the sack of beans.

After they had finished unloading the mule, he unsaddled the stallion and led both animals to the creek. The day was well advanced, the air drenched with moisture. He heard a grumble of thunder—signal that another summer storm was on its way. He stooped to inspect the mare once more, satisfying himself that the doubts raised by Mose as to her fitness was yet one more stratagem to delay his departure. Another rumble sounded in the distance, and he prayed that any storm would pass them by. *A deluge may yet spoil my plans.*

The threatened thunderstorm never came about, the over-moist air instead discharging a steady stream of rain that persisted into the evening. Dispirited, he watched the downpour from the cabin doorway. Mose had made himself comfortable, lighting a pipe and pouring whisky from one of the newly refilled canteens.

'Come, comrade, a sup!' The trapper was in celebratory mood, evidently pleased with the return on the hides. He handed Boundless an unfamiliar mug liberally filled with whisky.

'A part of the trade?' Boundless examined the cracked glaze on the earthenware mug.

'The pair of them—at the price of that muskrat you shot the week afore last.'

He marvelled anew at his companion's encyclopaedic knowledge of the provenance and destiny of each and every fur. From pelt to mug, he mused. From Mr Muskrat to …Z The conceit failed him and he drank the whisky, the raw liquid setting fire to his throat. He grimaced at the potent taste.

'I prefer the cider.'

'By gar, but it kicks!' agreed Mose. He wiped his mouth. 'The cider, by all means. The second bottle to the left,' he said, pointing to the row of canteens hanging on the wall. He poured himself another shot of whisky, smacking his lips as he downed it. 'I freely confess a shameful weakness for the concoction. I see you busied yourself with the axe,' he said, picking up a split log to add to the already blazing fire. 'It be hotter than Hades. But the flames do comfort and this rain cools the air.' He leaned back in the chair, a look of great satisfaction on his face. 'It minds me of your first night in this habitation. Nigh on three month ago.'

'Four, headed on five.'

Mose gave a look of astonishment. 'You say! Lord, but the time doth fly.' He mulled the proposition for some minutes. 'The heathen mark time by the passage of the sun or the shape of the moon or the tide in the bay. And out on the plains there is buffalo time. Time when they follow the fresh grass and time when they follow the wind south.' He pondered this, seemingly beguiled by the notion. 'Out on the plains there is no yesterday and no tomorrow, only the God-given day itself.'

'But you haven't been to the plains.'

'I know the heathen, do I not? And the buffalo! Do you imagine they are different there than here?'

It was on the tip of his tongue to argue that there were no buffalo 'here', but desisted, sipping on the cider instead, gratified by the sweet taste after the whisky. 'Your Mr Gottschalk is a provisioner of some worth.' He tipped more of the beverage into the mug.

Mose leaned forward, holding out his own mug. 'Do not spare me.'

The two sipped in companionable silence listening to the rain drumming on the roof and the snap and pop of the burning wood. Mose puffed out a steady stream of smoke, his expression pronouncing him to be in expansive, good humour. 'This rain gives me a hankering for the sound of verse or the words of some reputable author.' He ruminated for a moment before brightening. '*Still was the night! Serene and bright when all men sleeping lay. Soul, take ease! Sorrow hast thou in store! In Adam's fall, we sinned all! Thy life to mend, this Book attend! A dog will bite a thief at night! A stream …*' He stopped, a confused look on his face. 'I had it by heart.' He frowned, scratching his cheek.

He mulled the mystery for a moment before chuckling. 'Ah! But mother was a fierce one with the stick. She stripped yards of hide afore I could quote her favourite lines to her satisfaction. Father never cared a jot one way or the other—so as long as I did my chores. But mother insisted that I memorise whole scads of Job and the Psalms. God bless her overworked stick! She had some scraps of education and tried to learn me to write—in the ashes of the fireplace. I learned to scratch my own name, the months of the year and the numbers one to ten afore she broke the stick. I tried hard but hadn't the head for letters.'

'Indeed? Even so, I estimate you to be a man of immense natural arts. Gladly would I swap a yard of tracts and broadsheets for a tenth of your woodland skills.'

Mose pondered this. 'Mayhap. But that which I know I memoried. All the art be in that.' He picked up the canteen and shook it. 'The cider has expired.' He pointed to the hung canteens. 'Third to the left, if it pleases. The whisky.'

Boundless filled both mugs, judging the moment right. 'Mose, I must—'

'Surely, an educated man like yourself must know bushels of fine words?'

'In a moment. But first—'

'Come! The minutes fly by!'

With a sigh of frustration he itched his neck, thinking. A passage came to him and he cleared his throat.

What cannot Praise effect in Mighty Minds,
When Flattery Sooths, and when Ambition Blinds!
Desire of Power, on Earth a Vitious Weed,
Yet, sprung from High, is of Celestial Seed:
In God 'tis Glory: And when men Aspire,
'Tis but a Spark too much of Heavenly Fire.
Th'Ambitious Youth, too covetous of Fame,
Too full of Angel's Metal in his Frame,
Unwarily was led from Virtues ways;
Made Drunk with Honour, and Debauch'd with Praise.

Mose slapped his knee, hooting with admiration. 'By old St. Thomas! It doth rhyme a treat.' Inspired, he flung out a declamatory arm. "*Turn ye! And take your journey. And go to the mount of the Armorites, and unto all the places nigh thereto. To the plains! To the hills! To the valleys! And in the west, and by the seaside! Even to the land of the Canaanites, and unto Lebanon! Unto the great river, the Ohphrates—*"

He choked suddenly, grimacing as he coughed up smoke and spittle. 'By the bones, but I ain't quoted so in many a year! I got it when but a boy, at my mammy's knee. And it comes to me now—after all these years.'

Taking a swallow of whisky, he gazed into the fire, a forlorn look on his face. 'I fetched up here but yesterday, or so it seems, fresh-sprung from Virginny. I was but a stripling—in the glory of my days. I—he—could leap into the saddle at a single bound. Or bend a green sapling with his—my—own two hands. And now these same bones do creak and hinge and caterwaul to every gust of wind.' He grumbled with disgust and spat into the flames.

'You be sprightly still. I scarce can keep step.'

'Pshaw! I be like yonder mare—hobbled in all my joints. Age be a hard thing. When I was a boy the world seemed budding in step. Oh, but I was full of schemes and fancies!'

'Of which sort?'

'Why, for one, I was bound and determined to ride clear across to the French country and back again.'

'How is it you've waited so long to explore beyond the mountains? I should have thought that you might have done so long ago?'

'Ah, but that I had such foresight!' Mose stared at the burning logs as though once again seated across from the mysterious Frenchman and caught up once more in his exotic yarns. 'A young man thinks the world awaits his pleasure—infinitely so. The plain fact is that the world stays young, but bones do grow old apace. Mark the world, young Boundless. Mark it so that it remembers ye. Else is all forgot.'

A drop of rain leaked through the roof and dropped, sizzling, into the fire. Boundless cocked an ear—listening as the rain continued to fall. *The woods will be flooded.* His head began to spin and he poured himself another whisky while recalling Cassidy's admonition to 'drink yet one dram more' as safeguard against 'the fits' of sobriety. He emptied the canteen, pouring also into Mose's cup. The trapper drew on the pipe, his face thoughtful.

'A penny for your thoughts,' probed Boundless.

'I was dwelling that mayhap I waited too long—in the hopes that a trusty companion, such as yourself, might happen along with whom to share the burdens of such a venture. The journey is long and hazardous. And now I fear I may die afore I get the chance.' Mose vented a doleful stream of smoke.

'A toast!' Boundless raised the cup, determined to keep his companion *from going back to the mountains.* 'To the eternal *sup-lime.*'

'So say.' Mose leaned forward to again refill the cup even as Boundless tried to shield it with his hand.

'No more. I am flooded to the gunnels—'

'A tot only. To your health.' Mose splashed liquor into the cup. 'To Providence! May she think kindly of us and remember our poor names.'

Unthinkingly, Boundless tipped back the mug. 'Ye Gods!' His face soured in disgust.

'Nay. But bear it the while. It improves with fortitude.'

As the fire crackled and burned, he drank liberally of the whisky, no longer sensible to its taste. The eyes felt heavy in his head, and the room began to spin.

Mose poked the logs, fixing him a sideways look. 'Truly, a man might think himself blessed to have the opportunity of such a grand venture.'

'Venture?' He grimaced, wondering if the whisky had made him dull.

'Do you not see the adventure before you—what mighty prospects await the eye! I would—d'ye have sense?'

'Pardon.' He wiped his mouth, his head reeling from the effects of the whisky.

'We might journey through the mountains in spring, afore—'

He groaned in protest as the trapper's meaning struck through the fog in his brain. 'What in God's name have *I* to do with your blessed mountains? I am forsworn … To Phila-*delphi*. I have—' He belched, whisky fumes rising in his throat, 'Hopes of employment.'

'Hopes! A slender meal to batten on.' Mose glanced up at the roof. 'Hark. The deluge has ended. We shall not drown this day.' He splashed the last of the canteen into Boundless' cup, waving aside his weak protests. 'To a boon companion and new-born son of Maryland!'

Thus anointed, he swallowed at a gulp, marvelling at how the liquor had gained in taste. 'Why, I do confess I am tit—*tip*-addled!

I am bowz'd to the gills. Barkeep, another—if you please!'

Mose raised his mug, eyeing Boundless. 'To the westwards passage!'

'The westwards passage!'

HE AWOKE WITH A start—a dizzying sensation in his head. Beside him, Mose snored mightily, head sunk to his chest. The depleted fire glowed in the darkness. He sat up, gasping as the cabin whirled about him. He felt his belly gripe and placed a hand there. 'I must make a shit,' he mumbled, greatly annoyed at the inconvenience. Climbing unsteadily to his feet, he lurched towards the door, cursing as he stumbled over a snare in the darkness. He unbarred the door, striking his head against the lintel. 'Mercy!'

Outside, the night air was chill and cloudless. Moonshine flooded the small glade and silvered the dark woods. Shivering, he sucked in his breath and made his way over the swampy grass toward the trees. The ground was cold and sodden underfoot and one shoe stuck in the mire. He gasped as his bare foot sank into the mud. Precariously perched on one leg, he tugged the muddied shoe back onto his foot. From where she was hobbled beneath the tree, the mare whinnied and shook her neck.

'Soothly Bess! Soothly!' He placed a finger to his lips.

Inside a grove of pines, he found a fallen log and pulled down his breeches. Around him, the trees silvered into various shades of gloom. Holding up his shirt tail, he crouched over the log and emptied his bowels. The cold air revived his dull senses and he looked up at where the golden orb shimmered brilliantly against a backdrop of deepest night. The more distant stars glittered like costly jewels. He shivered, feeling suddenly naked and vulnerable before the eyes of the universe. Tugging a scrap of cloth from his pocket he cleaned himself and pulled up his breeches.

Trembling from the night chill, he made his way back across the sodden grass. Pulling the door shut behind him, he paused to adjust to the darkness. The interior was warm and breathy with wood smoke. Mose now lay stretched out beside the glowing embers, snoring fit to shake the walls. As he groped his way towards the hearth, his hand fell upon the buffalo fur. He picked it up, nuzzling the soft warmth against his cheek. 'Thou shalt keep me from perishing,' he slurred. He spread the robe on the dirt floor—almost tumbling into the fire as he did so. The hide smelled of smoke and ash and something he could not place. The whisky rose sickeningly in his gorge and his head began to spin. Burying his face in the dense fur, he fought the urge to toss up his guts. Mose snored thunderously beside him. He moaned in despair as the evening came back to mind. 'What foolishness did I pledge?' He was still trying to recall the events of the night even as the stink of buffalo filled his nose and he fell insensibly asleep.

Light filtered through cracks in the log walls. He pressed his fists against his eyes as an ache clamped his head in a vice. Beside him, Mose gasped and sputtered in sleep. He sat up, moaning in torment as the pounding ache inside his head threatened to split his skull asunder. He crawled on his knees to the door—barely gaining the outside before puking up his guts in the cold, wet mud. Groaning piteously, he pressed his forehead into the soaked grass. 'May I turn Turk if I ever again touch a single drop!' Cold water dripped onto his neck from the cabin roof. He heard the mare snort and snicker at the hobble.

'Anon, Bess! Anon.'

His face ashen, he remained propped on his hands and knees, not daring to risk standing up. He felt his guts heave, and he spewed again, gasping in anguish. 'The damn whisky was poisoned!' He gave a dry heave, his belly churning. With a heartfelt groan, he winced at the aching in his head.

Crawling on hands and knees to the creek, he splashed water on his face. His guts convulsed and he shivered in distress. 'I am surely ruined!' Unable to get up, he rested for a moment. He briefly fell asleep in the position before collapsing onto his side and waking himself with a start. Slowly, gingerly, he stood to his feet. He remained in place, swaying to one side as the sick rose again in his throat.

In spite of his sore distemper, he managed to stoke the fire and water the horses before Mose awoke an hour later.

The trapper sat up with a deep, shuddering groan. 'What in the name of Creation did you strike me with?' His face was a deathly white mask, the grey hair falling untidily about his neck. In the morning light, he presented a strangely forlorn appearance.

Boundless sat slumped against the wall, exhausted from the compounded effects of his labours and the lingering influence of the whisky. 'Do not trouble. The horses have been watered.'

'Dang the horses! What have they to do but eat from God's plate?'

'There is fresh, boiled tea to be had, if I can find the leaves.'

Mose moaned and hung his head in his hands. Slowly, he raised his eyes to stare at a small jute bag sitting on a shelf. He pointed a finger, refusing to speak.

25

A Suit of Buckskin

SIX MONTHS AFTER HIS arrival at the cabin, he admitted to himself that his haste to put distance between himself and the frowning figure of Captain Taysick had lost its former urgency. Day by day, the flat, brown river and the incident that had caused him to flee the boat grew ever more remote amidst the encompassing silence of the woods. At times he half-convinced himself that he had dreamed the fatal encounter with—deuced if he could recall the fellow's name!—the desperate struggle and its fatal consequence no longer haunting him. Slowly, the voices of his former companions faded against the chatter of birdsong, the trickle of the creek and the swishing of the wind through the pines. 'Unless *this* be the dream' he mused, diverting himself from the skin he was scraping.

Since the drunken revels of a month before, neither man had mentioned the westwards venture, an unspoken pact allowing time for each to collect his thoughts before again broaching the subject. But in spite of their attempts to skirt the vexatious topic, it sat, unspoken, between them as they hunted the woods or cured skins or butchered meat. Each kept his own counsel, a shared reluctance to lay open the question, allowing both to maintain whatever private hopes or trepidations they harboured as a result of the whisky feast.

Although wishing to distance the preposterous scheme, and all that it implied, from his thoughts, he annoyed himself by frequently revisiting the proposition, like a skunk sniffing around a lure. Vexed with himself for whatever rash pledges he might have voiced while in his cups, he yet harboured a faint hope that Mose's silence on the subject meant he had either forgotten the drunken toast or dismissed it as of no consequence. Several times—determined to discover the trapper's cogitations on the question—he was on the brink of raising the matter. But each time, an instinctive caution bade him bite his tongue. 'To speak is to commit— one way or the other,' he counselled himself. While cleaning the musket, he soberly considered the immense risks of such a perilous journey. 'We could be slaughtered—or worse—by Indians. Devoured by wild beasts. Perish from floods or get hanged by the French.' Such a venture is lunacy, he firmly decided.

But such was his contrary mind on the matter that within the hour he chided his own hesitation. 'I set out from Scotland to see the world,' he reproached himself. 'Am I now to abandon that ambition through cowardice? After all, there is risk in Philadelphia as well—for a twice-wanted man in particular. And who is to say but that Theo and the others might not digress into other plans—or meet with some pressing matter of their own?' The enticing prospect of securing a fortune in beaver pelts further coloured his conjectures. "*Beaver pelts—why, they be as precious as gold!*" The words echoed in his mind as he found himself returning, again and again, to the audacious proposal. 'I would be able to repay my friends,' he reasoned, 'and advance myself in these colonies.' Dwelling on the thought, a sudden horror of pauperism so affected his senses that he all but blurted out his explicit agreement to Mose.

At night, the tantalising words of the unknown Frenchman returned to perplex him further and prevent him from sleep. "*Staggering mountains and grassy meadows so vast as to encompass half the given world!*" He stared up at the roof listening to Mose's rasping snores as his mind grappled with the fantastical vistas conjured up by the words. He turned on his side, his sleepless thoughts beset by jostling images of wind-blown horizons, endless plains, and turbulent rivers vast as the sea. Groaning in frustration, he pressed a hand over his ear to block out the sound of Mose's snores.

"You can't count buff!" Fesky looked shocked at the notion. "Ain't nobody—never. You ever seen a pigeon flock? Those big ones that block out the sun? Well, buff are like that. Only there's more of them, in my estimation."

'As many as the pigeon?'

Fesky nodded sagely. "More."

Mose remained obdurately silent—whether through second thoughts or through thinking an agreement had been reached, Boundless could not hazard to guess. *He will speak when he is ready,* he told himself. *Perhaps sober reflection has changed his mind and he is embarrassed to speak of it.* As the days passed, his companion's continuing silence only served to deepen his conviction that the trapper had privately abandoned the foolhardy scheme. Vastly relieved, he pushed the contentious topic from his thoughts, determined to waste no more energy on the matter. *Let things be as they are.*

He took to visiting a nearby river, whose pebble-strewn depths contained a variety of perch, walleye, catfish, pickerel and chub. He smoked a goodly portion of the catch, pounding the dried fish and mixing it with elderberries as Mose had taught him.

THE DAYS BECAME MISTY and the ground sodden underfoot as leaves carpeted the forest floor. Game became harder to find. Showers of rain compounded the difficulties occasioned by the scarcity of whitetail—'our daily bread', as Mose termed the deer. They frequently resorted to snared rabbit, muskrat and squirrel as substitutes. Twice, Boundless had a pheasant in his sights and both times, much to his chagrin, failed to hit the elusive quarry. 'My skill comes and goes with the weather,' he complained to Mose.

Determined to make a regular contribution to the cook pot, he ventured into the woods several times on his own. But in spite of his single-minded application, the outcome of each hunt remained uncertain—a snapped twig, a sudden shift in the wind or simple mischance too often frustrating the pursuit. 'Each hunt be a hit-or-miss affair,' he reflected, the daily mishaps a sober reminder of the thin line between sufficiency and starvation amidst nature's plenitude. Even the vastly experienced Mose, he noted, was not immune to such misfortunes.

'By gar!' The trapper spat in disgust as the whitetail they had stalked for the better part of the morning took fright at some invisible alarm and bounded off into the trees. 'But an instant more and I should have claimed him for the pot!' His companion's good humour was only restored later that afternoon when he brought down a quail with an expert shot. 'The next volley be yours,' he said, stooping to pick up the bird.

A sudden cloudburst interrupted the hunt. As they sheltered under a tree, Mose showed the use of pitch-pine for starting a fire. 'It will light even when wet.' He pulled away a layer of bark to reveal the dark, sticky resin. 'You can use the bark to make cord. Avoid those turnips like the plague.' He pointed to a growth of whitish toadstools clustered at the base of a tree. 'One time I near perished from gobbling the devils.'

Although still prone to the occasional misfire and spectacular failures, he slowly began to achieve some mastery over the flintlock. Following a week of mild, sunny weather at the beginning of October, he astonished himself by bringing down an elk with a single shot—the feat drawing rare praise from Mose.

'By the bones, but that was a most excellent shot! A Christian man can do no more. No more, friend, what say ye?' Bending over the animal, the trapper pointed to the bloody wound. 'Straight into the heart, I declare.'

'I have seen its like before—on the river,' he exulted, jubilant at the shot. *I should back myself against Captain Taysick!* He held out his arms to estimate the antlers. 'How big, do you think?'

'Too big to carry,' grunted Mose. 'Gut the fellow while I fetch the mule.'

That afternoon he began to clean the hide—a proprietary interest impelling him to take additional care on the task. After scraping and soaking the skin, he immersed it in a tub of lye. Three days later, he fished it out to comb and pluck away the hair.

''Twill make an excellent leather—supple and unblemished,' Mose pronounced on viewing the tanned hide. Taking the skin, he pressed it between his fingers. 'Lenape squaws chaw the hide to soften it. Try it if it takes ye. Though it awful dries the teeth.' He looked Boundless up and down. 'Those clothes be past timely for the thread. Only buckskin will do in these woods.'

He glanced down at his tattered canvas breeches. His homespun shirt and leggings were holed and threadbare and hung loosely over his worn stockings. Both garments were caked with dried blood and dirt despite the apron. 'They were not meant for such hard use,' he acknowledged to himself. He returned to cleaning the hide, ruefully recalling the cost of the items.

The weather turned colder and wetter. When a week of heavy rainfall confined them indoors, Mose declared the foul weather opportune for cutting and sewing.

'This be the civilised part,' he said. Sitting on a hide-covered stump, he instructed Boundless in the arts of 'haberdash', using his own buckskin garments to illustrate. 'This be a whip stitch. Use it on the edges of the garment. And here, the running variety. Use it to join or mend. Use the deer sinew. It is stronger than the thread.'

Determined to replace his threadbare shirt with the buckskin, he practised his sewing skills on several patches of leftover hide, using the bone awl to pierce holes in the fabric before tugging through the thread. After 'running' several lines of stitches, he felt ready to tailor himself a pair of moccasins—his leather shoes having worn through the sole.

'Fetch that wrap paper,' said Mose when consulted on the method. 'Use it to trace your foot.' The trapper hummed on this for a moment before changing his mind. 'I would begin with the leggings, as they are easiest.'

'I have started now,' he objected. He positioned one bare foot on the square of paper and traced around it with the charcoal stub. On Mose's advice, he left a space the width of his thumb between the line and his foot. Next, he measured a line from the toe to the instep for the 'upper shoe' as Mose called it.

'You must draw around the line, using your foot as pattern. Add three inches as a precaution.'

Using the paper as a template, he transferred the markings to the buckskin and cut out the patterns. He ended up with a sole and an upper and back piece—the latter cut to allow four inches in height. After tacking the shoe to test for size, he used a whipstitch to join all three pieces, striving to maintain a consistent pattern. Throughout, Mose sat on the stump, smoking and sipping whisky while proffering words of encouragement and advice.

'If the fit is tight, you can stretch it … I prefer rawhide for the soles. They are the very devil to sew, but a pair will see out a summer. Double up the buckskin—your feet will thank you. Thou might make an honest cobbler if nought else,' he conceded as Boundless stood and flexed his toes in the tight moccasin.

Pleased with the shoes, he turned to the leggings as the gloomy skies and wet weather continued. He selected the tough elk skin for the purpose, following Mose's prescriptions as the trapper puffed out clouds of tobacco smoke.

'Neither too high nor too low,' he cautioned, as Boundless used a length of string to measure his leg. 'Britches are for the parlour … thorns will prick above and below the knee, be you gentleman or thief.'

Taking the length and the circumference of his leg, he transferred the two measurements to the elk skin. Mose drained half a canteen of cider as he watched.

'Cut loosely down to the ankle … and do not be afeared to leave a generous seam. You can restitch and recut as needs be … I'm minded of when I made my own first pair …'

As wind and rain gusted against the roof, the trapper meandered into a smoke-laden soliloquy that drifted back to his childhood days and fierce contests with a neighbouring boy. 'By jinks but we did whale on each other!' He tamped the tobacco, his face curious. 'What the deuce happened to him? And to Tom and poor Edward?' He puffed on the mystery, occasionally muttering to himself before falling into a doze, the pipe still clenched firmly in his mouth.

Boundless worked on, bringing the two sides together and testing the fit of the first legging. He stitched the seam, adding three inches for the upper limb. Piercing holes with the awl, he threaded leather ties into the garment. 'They will keep up better than a garter,' advised Mose, rubbing his eyes as he awoke. 'I copied the method from the Indians.'

With the first legging finished, he started on the second, abandoning the sewing as his eyes grew weary. 'My fingers are numb from the needle,' he complained, flexing his hand. 'Would it not be simpler to purchase a pair from your Mr Gottschalk?'

'Pshaw! Mr Gottschalk will claim six hides for the privilege of swapping two. You have the one done. 'Tis nothing to do the other.'

'On the morrow. My fingers are worn to the bone.' Boundless sat and stretched out his legs. 'This life be an arduous one. What other occupation calls for a man to both feed and clothe himself from scratch?'

'True.' Mose used a splinter from the fire to light the grease lantern. 'But no other man on the face of the earth be as independent of merchants, bosses, and shopkeeps. The savages excepted, of course.' He paused over the lantern. ''Tis said that the Lenape claim we pass from this life into another. If so, I should not mind returning as a heathen.'

Boundless raised an eyebrow. 'You surprise me. Your savage has no arts. Nor civility, nor polite society. In reasoning, he is reputed to be hardly above a child.'

'Nay. You be overly harsh. The Indians worship their own gods and observe their own laws. They make firm and honest friends and keep to their word. They trade among themselves—and with both us and the French. They negotiate and make treaties. Aye—and maintain them as good or better than us.'

'And the arts of reading and writing?'

'They have their music—of flutes and drums. They ornament their clothes. They make the finest skins. What else?' Mose knitted his brow. 'They shoot with a bow better than we do a musket. They be brave and skilful fighters.'

Boundless yawned, sleep tugging at him. 'It may be as you say,' he conceded. 'But one lifetime in these woods is surely sufficient.'

FLUMMOXED BY THE SKILLS required to set a snare, he took advantage of a break in the weather to apply himself assiduously to the method. He laid several loops in the hope of catching rabbits, squirrels, quail or woodchucks. He experimented with different methods—to his delight, catching a mink with fish oil and claiming a turkey through a deadfall log. 'Mose is right,' he reflected, resetting the snare. 'It is easier to trap than hunt a creature.'

One morning, he found, to his pleasure, that he had snared a muskrat and hare in successive traps. He cut up the hare for the pot, becoming absorbed in the cuts and the configuration of the bones. Finished, he took the skin down to the creek to wash away the blood. The day was dull and pregnant with rain. A stiff breeze rustled the branches. Kneeling, he was dunking the shirt when he caught sight of his reflection against the clouds. The image made him pause as he peered at his vaporous self in the blood-stained water. 'I am become a natural man,' he thought, the notion recalling the romantic speculations of his London friends. After a moment, he brisked the ghostly image, suddenly impatient at *tavern notions* of Aboriginals.

In the afternoon, he cut more firewood, leaving it in the smokehouse to dry. He had no sooner closed the door behind him than the heavens opened once again, a cold, drenching rain soaking him as he hastened back to the warmth of the cabin.

'The proof is in the pudding,' remarked Mose as Boundless held up the finished leggings for the latter's inspection late in the evening.

Sitting on the stool, he wrapped the buckskin around his legs. 'It feels like a leather apron for each limb.' Standing, he walked stiff-legged back and forth, tugging at the thongs to loosen the fit. The bottom end of the legging fell over his foot and he reached for the scissors, intending to trim it.

'Split it,' advised Mose. 'And tie the two ends around your ankle or under the foot. They will help keep it in place.'

Equipped with the leggings and moccasins, he turned his ambition to making a shirt. Before attempting the task, he rummaged in the haversack and took out the nautical log and the wooden case containing the quill pens and ink. Opening the small brass inkwell, he dipped the tip of one finger to test the ink.

Mose leaned in to examine the case. 'Three quills—and the ink, also?'

'Purchased from the same villain who sold me the mare.'

Mose took the case, holding it carefully. 'A noble case for a noble art,' he said, praising the economical workmanship. Boundless watched as his companion set the case down, reverential in his handling of the object.

'You may use the quills any time you wish.'

'It is not for such as me.' Mose murmured the reply.

'I could help you practise—as you did me, with the musket.'

'They claim the pen is mightier ...' Mose pondered this. 'And perhaps it is,' he said, 'perhaps it is.'

Unscrewing the ink, Boundless dipped a quill. Using his own shirt as a pattern, he drew two illustrations in the log, diagramming the parts of each. Mose watched, his face perplexed. 'If you could ink the shirt to wear t'would be one thing. But you must cut your actual hide.'

'But to see it thus laid out helps me to think.'

'What is there to think about? The hides lie there before you. Simply measure, cut and sew.'

'As you say. But I know now that there are four parts.'

'Parts?'

'The arms or sleeves being one. The neck, another. The sides a third—there being two sides or seams, thus, four.'

'A child might see the same by looking.'

'Mayhap. But it helps to see things clearly in the mind before venturing on a task. Did you not draw a map to represent the passage to the western plains?' He silently cursed himself as soon as he made the comparison. To his relief, Mose did not take up on the opening. Instead, stumped for an answer, the trapper furrowed his brow and stared into the fire.

The next day, Boundless fetched the three remaining buckskins. Holding the first against his body, he used the charcoal stub to mark the neck and shoulders as Mose watched.

'The skin is wrinkled. You must damp and press it first—afore the measure.'

After doing this, he held up the skin again, surprised to discover that the charcoal marks had shifted sufficiently to require re-marking. Laying the skin on the floor, he cut out the neck and then down the sides in a straight line. He overlaid a second skin against the first and was about to cut out the neck when an exclamation from Mose prevented him.

'What! Do you need a collar front and back? Where be your sketches now?'

Annoyed at his own obtuseness, Boundless muttered an acknowledgement. He then tailored the edges of the second skin to match the first. He tacked the sides with a baste stitch—stopping every quarter hour to flex his cramped fingers. 'Never again shall I scorn the art of haberdashery,' he vowed, before going outside to breathe some fresh air.

A LASHING RAIN PENNED them in the cabin all the next day and he returned to the half-finished shirt. Donning the stitched buckskin, he inspected the garment where it hung loosely about his body. He took it off, shaking his head. 'A grotesquerie—fit only for a giant to wear. And a waste of good buckskin into the bargain.'

Mose glanced up from the cooking pot. 'Do not compare it to your present shirt. Buckskin needs room and space to air.' He tugged at the sides of his own shirt. 'There will be some tightening as it wears.'

He took out the basting stitches and recut the buckskin, taking in two inches on either side. Following Mose's advice, he used a pin to tack each side before pulling the skin over his head again. 'Better,' he said, tugging at the sides.

'Hold, I will mark the sleeves,' said Mose. He did so, allowing a generous 'drop' for each arm as Boundless held out his hands. He then looped the string around the upper arm. 'Take twice the measure,' he advised, playing out the loop.

Armed with the new measurements, he painstakingly whipstitched the sides together. It was evening before he had finished. He tried on the sleeveless shirt once more before setting it aside.

The following day, he cut four rectangles from the third hide to serve as sleeves. After joining the sides, he stitched them to the shirt, growing both weary and impatient of the task.

It was late afternoon before he threaded the last stitch and cut the thread. 'Done—for good or evil.' He held up the finished garment for inspection. The shirt seemed monstrously large, the arms voluminous and the length too great. 'It will drop to my ankles,' he complained, disappointed at the fit.

'Ye cannot say until it is tried,' said Mose, abandoning his own repairs to look.

Boundless tugged the garment over his head, tying the ends into a breechclout. He then stepped into the leggings, lacing the ties around his breeches. Sitting on the stump, he pulled the moccasins onto his feet, wincing at the tightness. Thus outfitted in the buckskin, he stood and stretched out his arms. 'What say you?' he asked. He flexed his arms, pleased at the feel of the buckskin against his skin. 'The devil take me if I ever again wear homespun!'

'The sides hang like the pantaloons on a Turk.'

'They shall have to suffice.'

'The collar looks tight.'

'Then I shall shrink my neck.' He glanced down at himself. 'Deuced if I mightn't pass for a true woodsman—almost like yourself!'

Mose scratched his cheek. 'Solomon in all his glory.' He looked around for the whisky canteen. 'For baptals,' he said, and held out a mug.

THE VARIABLE OCTOBER WEATHER continued into November, a succession of grey, damp days followed by a week of scattered sunshine. In the interregnum between showers, the ground dried rapidly and it was possible to walk through the woods without drawing down a cold spray of rain from every jarred branch.

On a misty day, he accompanied Mose through the woods to check the line of traps. They went from snare to snare without success, Mose remaining good-humoured in spite of the empty lures. 'I do love most this time of year,' he said, glancing up at the whitish-blue sky. He began to hum, a sure sign that he was in good spirits. He halted before the next snare, pointing to the prints around it. 'A fox. The fellow has grown wise to the snare. We must move it else will he gobble up whatever he finds there.'

They checked several more before Mose gave a grunt of satisfaction at sighting a rabbit caught in one of the loops. The animal had exhausted itself in trying to escape and lay passively on the grass as they approached. Mose glanced around at the soft earth. 'There was a second one with it.' He pointed to a set of prints. 'Fortune dictated that this fellow be caught and that his companion escape. Had I a placed a second loop mayhap we had secured both.'

'The man that chases two rabbits catches none.'

'What is that?'

'A saying. From where, I cannot remember. One of the classical authors, I think.'

'There is truth to it.' Mose crouched to snap the neck of the rabbit. 'It would grieve me to ride to the western plains with an uncivilised man.'

He stared at the trapper's back, too surprised to speak. Mose lingered over the rabbit, his posture expectant. After a long moment during which he seemed braced—whether for refusal or correction, he slowly stood up. 'This fellow is for the pot,' he said, and headed back to the cabin.

Boundless followed, his mind a whirl of conflicting thoughts. *It is best to correct him now. Before the notion takes hold.* He opened his mouth to speak, but closed it again, confused as to his own mind.

'Roasted or stewed?' Mose asked the question over his shoulder.

'Either' he said, after a pause. And so, the moment was lost.

In the days following, Mose seemed invigorated, adopting a cheerful air and whistling tunelessly as he went about his tasks. Frequently he stopped to remark upon some commonplace sight or other, praising the ordinaries of each day as though witnessed for the first time.

'Mark the nip!' he said, inhaling as the wind rushed the scent of pine to his nose.

'Hi-yup old Jack!' he said to the horse, joshing its neck while marvelling at how sturdily the stallion performed all that was asked of him.

'A man that can fill his own belly is beholden to no one,' he declared on shooting a whitetail.

One afternoon, the trapper stood over a snare looking at the body of a muskrat. 'Acrost the mountains I'll learn ye how to trap beaver. These trifles be but the taster.' Freeing the muskrat, he handed it to Boundless. 'This be but the poor relation, the impoverished cousin to his fat kinfolk out on the plains. Why, come the summer you will be trimming your hat with beaver wool.'

Such comments now fell daily from the trapper's lips as if to mortar in place the tacit covenant. 'Wait until you taste buffalo rib,' he said, on serving up a portion of deer.

'Beaver coat is like no other—as you shall soon judge for yourself,' Mose remarked on another day when Boundless complimented the quality of a mink.

'You must aim true—a big grizzly or buffalo won't fall so easily out on the plains,' he cautioned, just as Boundless jerked the barrel and struck a whitetail on the rump.

In spite of such opportunities to rebut, Boundless held his tongue. *I should speak,* he chastised himself. *But to what purpose? I hardly know my own mind.*

And thus, slowly, silently, he sank deeper into the buffalo morass.

26

An Avalanche of Fowl

ONE COLD DECEMBER MORNING, nine months since his arrival in the woods, he opened the door to find frost on every surface. He broke a skin of ice over the creek to water the horses, exceedingly pleased at the way the soft buckskin kept him warm in the wintry air. 'If Humpflinger should see me,' he thought, recalling with a pang his erstwhile companion.

With the threat of snow in the air, they stayed close to the cabin. Mose lit a fire in the fire pit and showed him how to cast musket balls from an ingot of lead. 'Use these to build the flame.' He handed Boundless a leather bellows, and watched as the latter pumped them. 'More wind,' he said as the lead in the pan slowly began to melt.

Tilting the pan, Mose poured the melted alloy into the mould. An instant later he tapped the lead ball out onto a rock. 'It be still hot as blazes,' he cautioned, picking up the ball with a pair of tongs. Dropping the ball into a pail of water, he swilled it for a few moments before fishing it out with his fingers. The lead had formed into a round ball with a tiny spike protruding from the surface. He trimmed the spike with his knife and held up the finished round for inspection. 'A bit light, for buffalo. We shall have to choose our shots.'

'Do you cast all your own shot?'

'Whenever I can. One time a companion and I ran out of lead while being pestered by a bunch of Delawares. We melted our pewter mugs afore we ran the devils off.'

'For shot?'

'What?'

'You melted the pewter to make shot?'

'Did I not just say so?'

THE NEXT MORNING, WHITE flakes drifted across the clearing. The fall grew heavier towards evening. Boundless looked out the following day to find the ground covered with a layer of snow. He stood in the doorway, momentarily lost in thought as the powdery whiteness glittered under a bright blue sky. Behind him, Mose fiddled with the tinderbox.

'Close the confounded door. D'ye wish to perish us?'

After breakfast, they saddled the horses, and set out through the woods to hunt. Although clear and sunny, the day was chill, and he wore his gabardine jacket over the buckskin. In front of him, Mose was wrapped in a cape made up of a patchwork of hides, the collar trimmed with rabbit fur. He congratulated himself again on the new garments, gratified at the way the tough elk hide leggings deflected branches and thorns.

They rode for the better part of two hours, Mose venturing beyond the usual hunting grounds into country new to Boundless. The mare's breath steamed in the cold air as they plodded through the hushed woods. The sky continued bright and clear, the sunlight streaming through the branches. He was enjoying the ride—the mare responding easily to his touch—when he heard a warning hiss from Mose. The trapper had reined to a halt on the edge of a clearing.

'What is it?' Expecting to sight a deer, he nudged the mare alongside as Mose raised a hand in caution. Directly ahead, not five-hundred yards distant, three savages were gathered around a bloodied carcass. One Indian hacked into the kill with a hatchet, while his companions stood watch, bows held loosely in their hands as they scrutinised the surrounding woods.

'What are they?' Boundless whispered the words, a cold sensation gripping his stomach.

'They 'mind me of Suskihannocks—'cept they're reputed long vanished from these parts. Nanticoke, mayhap.' Mose had taken out the musket from its deerskin sleeve. 'Are ye primed?' he asked, his voice soft.

'He has seen us!'

One of the savages stared at where they sat in the shadow of the pines. He barked a warning to his companion and notched an arrow to the bow string. The second savage looked in their direction. After a fraught interval, he said something to the first Indian, who slowly lowered the bow.

'They be friendly, by all appearances. Let us go and be Christian. What say you?'

'Is that wise? Why not turn back and give them berth? And there may be others, close by.'

'If we turn back now, they may calculate us enemies next time we meet.'

Holding up the palm of his hand, Mose kicked the chestnut a few steps out from the trees. '*Itetskin!*' His voice rang out loudly in the cold air.

The savage called out in reply, raising a palm in return.

'What does he say?'

'It is generally how heathens in these parts say "hello". They likely mean us no harm but keep your hand on the musket. They be devils for luring folk in close where they can do mischief.'

With that, Mose nudged the stallion forward. 'Keep your eyes sharp,' he warned over his shoulder. 'They can loose an arrow quicker than a body could cock a musket.'

Boundless followed, the musket held loosely across his body, his thumb on the hammer. As if sensing his apprehension, the mare snorted and pulled against the rein. The Indians made no motion as they approached. The third looked up from where he knelt beside the bloody carcass of a bear. Bright red blood stained the snow.

Mose halted around ten yards from the party. '*Bonjour!*'

Boundless was keenly aware of the cold air against his cheeks and the sun sparkling on the fresh snow. He noted the steam rising from the bloodied entrails of the dead bear and the puffed breath of the kneeling savage—his every sense unnaturally heightened as though dreaming the tableau.

'*Winquipim!*' Mose pointed to the carcass.

The nearest savage uttered words that were unintelligible to Boundless' ears. The Indian was dressed only in deerskin shirt and breeches in spite of the cold. His dark face was daubed with streaks of coloured dye. The teeth or claws of various animals hung from around his neck. A pair of fox paws were fastened to one shoulder of his shirt. His hair was completely shorn save for a single, greased lock decorated with a tuft of feathers that hung down over his shoulder. The savages resembled those he had encountered on the river, although subtly different in a manner he could not place. The faces of all three were pock-marked—the scars adding to their savage demeanour.

'*Meetsee!*' The kneeling savage glanced directly at Boundless—the blood on his face and mouth evidence he had been eating from the freshly slaughtered kill. Laughing and showing sharpened teeth, he held up a bloodied organ—the raw flesh steaming in the chill air. '*Meetsee!*' He gestured for Boundless to join him.

'He's inviting you to take a chaw,' Mose advised. 'It be considered polite to accept.'

'Damn'd if I will!'

'Then keep an eye on that short one.' Mose climbed down from the saddle, careful to position the horse between himself and the savages. '*Sisk-y-ro!*'

He advanced towards the kneeling savage, the musket cradled in his arms. Leaning down, he accepted the proffered organ with one hand.

'*Sisk-y-ro!*' He took a bite of the bloody organ. '*Merci! Bon! Good!*' He nodded vigorously as he chewed.

In his absorption in the scene, Boundless forgot Mose's warning to keep his eyes on the short savage. Alarmed at a movement from the Indian, he squinted in the bright sun to discern if he intended harm. The savage showed him no interest, instead watching Mose as the latter belched and rubbed his stomach to show his appreciation of the meat.

'*Merci!*' Mose nodded vigorously, his lips and beard bloodied from the organ. He said something and gestured toward the trees. The kneeling savage responded in like fashion, his voice guttural as he extended an arm to indicate the far line of woods. To Boundless' ears, the savage's speech resembled short, accented barks or grunts.

'*Nah-kehmean!*' Mose returned to his horse. '*Adieu!*' He climbed back into the saddle.

They edged the horses sideways away from the Indians and headed back into the woods. As they gained the shelter of the trees, Boundless glanced back at where the Indians had resumed butchering the carcass.

'Were they as you thought?' he asked, his voice strained from the encounter.

'They were Conestoga, sure as fire,' said Mose, sounding bemused. 'I supposed they were chased out of these woods long ago. It appears our friends back there be a hunting party. They are skittish about meeting up with the Pocomoke—who sometimes hunt these woods and whom you'd be wise to avoid.' He turned in the saddle for a last glimpse. 'A long time back, when I first came to these woods, they were plentiful as rabbits. But 'tis rumoured the pox killed most, and war and strife did for the rest. I hazard I haven't seen one these dozen years.'

'You speak their tongue?'

'Ha! A mish-mash of tongues, more like. I generally try Nanticoke or Pamunkey or whatever heathen comes to mind.'

'They were fierce-looking specimens.' Boundless let out a deep breath, relieved that the encounter was behind them.

'That liver was a mite sour.' Mose leant from the saddle to spit into the snow. 'The deuced bear was full of bile.'

AS THE DAYS GREW ever shorter and colder, he found 'winter Mose' a variable companion. Bouts of long-windedness brought forth loquacious opinions on various subjects, which were interspersed with brooding silences where he did little, except stare into the fire and smoke or sip whisky—of which he seemed to have an unending supply despite his daily indulgence.

Boundless learned to chart these moods, noting his companion's slow-ripening good cheer as they set out in the mornings to trap or hunt—the trapper regaling him with stories of his adventurous youth—against the brooding, evening silences that presaged some change of temperament. For often, as the day wore on and the wind rose, or the skies darkened, his companion slumped into a black introspection, grunting in response to questions or responding curtly when an answer was required. Infrequently, these moods were coloured by periods of intense agitation during which the trapper strode restlessly to and from the cabin all the while muttering that it was 'past the hour' to start out for the western plains. 'By jinks, but I wisht it were spring!' he exclaimed as a cold north wind rattled the door.

Boundless' concern at such vagaries of humour were dispelled by the many days when the trapper was talkative and forthcoming, garrulously instructing in every aspect of woodland lore, and teaching the names and habits of every kind of plant and animal along with their various uses.

'Pull the cattail to kindle a fire,' he advised, lecturing on the plant. 'You can throw it in the pot and eat it if your belly's tight. You'll find them along water or where blackbirds gather. You can chaw the needles if you are hungry,' he said, breaking off a handful of white pine needles and putting them in his mouth. 'If you've a toothache, plug on this,' he said, peeling back a section of willow bark. 'The leaves, also.'

'By the bones if you ain't a woodsman already!' he pronounced on another occasion as Boundless demonstrated his growing skills by skinning a muskrat with a dozen quick flicks of the knife. 'Only the fellow's bald,' he grunted on closer inspection of the fur.

Whenever inclement weather restricted their activities to the vicinity of the cabin, they used the time to cure hides, mend clothes, cast shot or preserve food. On the occasions they were pent-up for the entire day by wet weather, they retired to their separate thoughts—a tacit understanding granting each other this much privacy.

To pass the time, Boundless took to making entries in the log, recording the different kinds of snares and drawing sketches to illustrate. He made a list of plants, identifying the useful properties of each. He noted the weather and the creatures hunted or trapped that day, offering opinions on the merits of the various skins or the taste of the meat.

Once or twice, Mose peered over his shoulder, the trapper regarding the inked illustrations with grunts of curiosity or scepticism. 'That fellow is over-long in the tail,' he said of a deer. 'What is that? A muskrat? Such a creature resembles none ever seen in these parts. Mayhap you dreamed the animal. That is the fetlock of the mare? As true as I stand here.'

Feeling increasingly joined—nay, *obligated*—to the western venture, Boundless took to riding the mare an hour each day to improve his horsemanship. A nearby clearing provided a convenient spot to practise the canter and trot. Once, feeling overly confident, he whipped the mare into a short gallop, clinging on for dear life as he bounced about in the saddle. 'God's Blood!' he breathed, hauling the winded mare up short. *Pray that we walk all the way to wherever the blazes it is we are headed.* He dismounted, concerned once more at the laboured breathing issuing from the mare.

When he returned to the cabin he found Mose jovial with whisky—the trapper doing his best to inveigle him into sharing a canteen. He refused, instead taking the flintlock apart to clean the bore and grease the lock. 'It is the most elegant mechanism I ever saw,' he declared, peering at the removed lock in the light of the fire. He pulled back the hammer. 'Simple, yet ingenious.'

'Put away the gun and quote me a line.'

'I am tired, and to bed.'

'As you will.' The trapper drank straight from the canteen, belching as he stared into the fire.

Boundless lay down under the buffalo robe as his companion mumbled to himself and fumbled to light the pipe. *What am I promised to?* he wondered for the hundredth time. Filled with foreboding, he heard Mose curse as he dropped the canteen. *I am pledged to the godforsaken plains with a drunkard as guide. Why do I not say something? Why do I not insist on an immediate return to Philadelphia?* He reproached himself in such manner until he fell asleep.

He opened his eyes sometime later to see the trapper still hunched over the dying fire, muttering and shaking his head while grasping the canteen. He tugged the buffalo robe up under his chin, despairing of the future.

HE WAS SITTING INSIDE the cabin door sewing up holes in some buckskin when he heard a joyous whoop. Going outside to investigate, he found Mose gazing up at the wintry blue sky. 'Look yonder!'

Overhead, a formation of several thousand geese passaged across the sky, their shrill, chattering cries sounding clearly through the cold air. The flock was followed by a second of similar size, the birds strung out across the sky in a wavering line.

'There be a marsh about a day's ride where they set down to drink. 'Tis easy sport.' Mose's face glowed with anticipation. 'They be so thick on the ground a man could knock them over the head. Why waste good shot?' He chuckled at the notion.

The birds flew overhead all day, the flights of geese interspersed with smaller flocks of ducks. Several times Mose halted whatever he was doing to glance up at the sky, his features flushed with pleasure. 'By jinks if I ain't in the mood for a goose!' He was still brimming at the prospect of 'fowl for supper, fowl for breakfast, and fowl for in between' as darkness fell.

'Make certain you swab the bore,' he advised, as Boundless rechecked the musket and pistol. ''Tis a test of skill to shoot a bird on the wing. But on the ground, they gather so thickly that a flung stone might just as easily secure one.'

THEY SET OUT FOR the marshes at first light, each of them carrying a pound of pemmican in his saddlebag, along with ample supplies of powder and swan shot. The light snow had all but vanished following several days of mild weather, and the trail was firm, although sodden with wet leaves. He had fashioned himself a hat out of muskrat fur, like the one Mose wore, and tugged it down around his ears as he followed his companion through the trees. They headed in a southerly direction at a walking pace. He kept a close eye on the mare as she huffed in the cold air.

After riding for two or three hours, Boundless smelt salt on the breeze and assumed that they were nearing the Chesapeake. 'We are near,' confirmed Mose.

The dry ground gave way to a soft marsh, the horses splashing through shallow water. The air filled with a loud twittering noise that reminded Boundless of the incessant shrill of locusts in the woods around Philadelphia.

Fording a creek, they entered upon a vast swamp heavily populated by what seemed millions of birds, each fighting and squabbling for food and resting spots. So great was the profusion that it seemed to Boundless' eyes as if the abundance of all of nature was gathered there. More fowl appeared by the minute as fresh flocks arrived to join those already feeding in the waterlogged grass.

Mose pointed at the squawking multitudes. 'Black-head ... Mallard ... Gadwall. And over there—a pintail. A green wing. See the bluebill! And there ...' Frowning, he scratched his cheek. 'A longtail, mayhap. Come!' He kicked Jack forward, eager to claim the spoils. After a short distance, he dismounted on a grassy hillock. 'Pour your powder, friend—for a banquet awaits!'

The feeding birds proved so easy to shoot that Boundless soon abandoned the musket to improve his use of the pistol. Spoiled for choice, he shot through the body, unconcerned with eating the fowl. At first, it proved difficult, if not impossible, for him to take a bird from the air. But, encouraged by Mose, he learned to lead the bird and to shoot smoothly and expectantly. In this manner, he eventually brought down six or seven on the wing. Growing in ambition and confidence, he shot one swan as it flapped its wings for flight. 'By Harry, knocked him with the pistol!' he shouted, turning to see if Mose had witnessed the feat. He stood and fired until the barrel was too hot to touch, moving from each pile of fresh carcasses to a new vantage point.

Over the course of the day, he shot well over one hundred fowl and would have shot more for the sport only for the need to retrieve the shot at Mose's urging. The latter contented himself with occasional shots at departing or arriving birds, scorning the ground shot as too feeble.

They took two dozen of the birds home to brine, Mose giving assurances that the natural larder would remain full for a month or more. ''Twill replenish daily,' he said.

Back at the cabin, the trapper showed Boundless how to slice the skin and remove the legs and wings before cutting along the keel bone to extract the dark-coloured flesh.

'Make sure you cut out and save the shot,' he said, digging the small nail-like shot from the breast of a swan. They salted the meat and left it overnight in a tub for brining on the morrow.

'It were best to hang this fellow for a day or two.' Mose held up a plump goose. 'But my belly aches for him.' In a pot, he mixed onions, pepper, salt, dried berries, grease, and wild herbs. He took the plucked goose and stuffed the mixture in the cavity, sewing it up with sinew. He then impaled the bird on a spit above the fire, placing a smaller, long-handled pan beneath to catch the fat. For the next three hours, the two went about their sewing and repairing, each keeping an eye on the dripping pan so as to baste the roasting bird with the melted fat. Mose licked his lips as he turned the spit. 'By gar if my teeth aint a-shakin'!'

Boundless was so hungry that he took to chewing on the pemmican as he waited for the goose to roast. Finally, Mose pronounced it 'done to a turn' and pulled the fowl off the spit, setting it down on a split log for carving.

'What be your opinion?' he asked, as Boundless took a first mouthful of the feast.

'Fit for a king's table! The flesh be as fine any I have eaten.' He ate hungrily, relishing the fowl.

'Hang fire on that judgement until ye feast of the buffalo. Their meat be of the rarest taste.'

TWO WEEKS LATER, THEY rode out to the marsh again. On this occasion, they were joined by a goodly number of savages who emerged from the surrounding woods to take advantage of the natural bounty. The Indians cast nets of woven grass, nettle fibres and bark to trap dozens of fowl at a time, the men skilfully creeping up on the feeding birds to fling the nets. Young boys then bludgeoned the fluttering captives with sticks and cudgels, all the while uttering shrieks of triumph. The dead birds were strung on long poles which the hunters balanced across their shoulders as they returned to the woods with their quarry.

From a distance, the Indians appeared, to Boundless' untutored eye, cousin to those he had beheld fishing along the banks of the Chesapeake, or those he and Mose had encountered, recently, in the woods. The men of one tribe had shaved half their heads, retaining a single lock on one side. Others had tonsured their hair into a coxcomb, while some wore combed locks down their backs. All were liberally festooned with dyes and painted marks.

Throughout the week, other groups appeared from the woods—some with heads almost completely shaved, others almost as bald save for a thin strip along the crown. Observing some unspoken truce, the different parties stayed well clear of each other as they continued to harvest the birds—their combined efforts seemingly making no impression on the enormous flocks.

'What tribes are those?' Boundless asked, as a fresh band of hunters emerged from the woods.

Mose glanced at the newcomers. 'Powhatans. I broke bread with them several times. A hospitable people.' He looked further along the line of woods. 'And those there be Nanticoke and Lenape.' He pointed at another group. 'Hurons. They be the ones with the bristly heads. Those ones over yonder may be Abenaki—I am uncertain.'

'They do not seem to trouble one another.'

'Why should they? There be enough fowl for the entire heathen nation. They are more concerned with filling their bellies while the bounty lasts.'

They visited the marsh twice more. In spite of the many hunters, each arriving flock appeared as unwary as the one before—their inexhaustible numbers seeming to lull them into safety. Indeed, so profligate were the flapping, squawking multitudes that Boundless scarce knew where to point the pistol. He fired until his arm hurt, at one point firing with his left hand for variety. Mose seemed not to mind the continual shooting so long as he retrieved the carcass to dig out the lead. As he dug the shot out of a duck, he saw small boys among the Indians dash out from the wet grass to seize the bloodied birds by the neck before disappearing back into the marsh.

'I do believe you are taking charge of that pistol,' Mose remarked as they rode back through the woods following one visit. A dozen of the choicest fowl lay strung to their saddles.

'My hand is sore from the firing.'

'Tomorrow, mayhap, try your hand at taking one with a round ball from higher in the air.'

'A waste of shot, I fear.'

'Nay, but I'll wager the odds. Your eye is good, and your hand steady.'

'If you say,' he conceded, greatly pleased with the compliment.

SLOWLY, THE GLOOMY SKIES and cold, precipitous days gave way to mild, southerly breezes that ushered in March. The ground began to harden, the grass slowly drying underfoot as the game grew plentiful once again. He welcomed the milder days and the sharp light that heralded spring. His well-worn buckskin shirt and leggings were moulded to his body after he had restitched the sleeves and sides. Over the winter, he had fashioned a pair of buckskin trousers as well as several additional pairs of moccasins, coming to prefer a higher-cut shoe with a rawhide sole to better protect his feet. He had adopted Mose's habit of wearing a deerskin pouch to hold sundries such as tow, tools for the musket, a cartridge box, extra flints, and a fishing line.

It was now routine for him to venture into the woods alone to bring down a deer and to gut and butcher the carcass, salt the meat and cure the skin unaided. But in spite of his growing proficiency with the musket, his uncertain riding skills left him feeling more and more nervous as spring approached and a likely departure date for the west. Mose made regular allusions to the expedition—as much to gauge his state of mind, he suspected, as anything else.

'What month is it?' his companion asked one day. 'The ground will be dry all the way to the mountains,' he observed on another. 'Why, I 'spect there will be game aplenty, on both sides of the notch,' he said on yet another.

The last comment was spoken with one eye on Boundless' reaction, which finally provoked the latter to speak. 'You forget, I am still a tyro to these buckskin ways.'

To his great surprise, Mose, after a long silence, gave a small nod, as if giving assent to the objection. The trapper said nothing, going off to the smoke house to take down a loin for supper.

Later that day, Mose paused from rubbing the loin with his own concoction of sugar, wild berries, morel mushrooms and onion. 'I have been dwelling on the matter,' he said, itching his cheek. He regarded Boundless, a thoughtful look on his face.

'I had intended to depart within the month. But am willing to postpone until late April. Do you—if I agree to this delay—give me your solemn word to accompany me?'

It was Boundless' turn to hesitate. *He considers the question still afloat!* Amazed at the fact, he stared at his companion. *There may be yet an escape from this foolishness!* That he effectively broached, then foundered, then sunk the vessel of Good Hope with his next utterance hardly betokened him, so relieved was he at the postponement, 'I give you my solemn word.'

Mose spat into his hand. 'Then shake on it!'

He took the proffered hand. 'Indeed,' was all he managed—his commitment to the enterprise thus sealed by a simple handshake.

IN THE DAYS AND weeks that followed, he had cause to regret his over-hasty pledge, berating himself for the ease with which the promise had tumbled from his lips. *But does not that fact, of itself, signify a deeper wish— to undertake this outlandish venture?*

As the myriad of potential pitfalls crowded in upon him, he wavered yet again. *Mayhap I shall have the good fortune to fall upon my musket and shoot myself!* Glum with the knowledge that he was irrevocably committed to the mad scheme, he headed back to the cabin.

Mose's disappointment at the temporary 'dashment' of his great project was made manifest in his immediate recourse to whisky, spending most of the succeeding weeks either insensibly drunk or spending days at a time at the trading post. *He rides off with hides and returns with nought but more whisky!* In between bouts of intemperance, the trapper drove Boundless to the point of exasperation with his insistence that he 'ride, ride and then ride some more.'

Nevertheless, he admitted, with some pride, that his hunting and riding skills had improved markedly over the winter. He now rode for two hours a day as his comfort in the saddle increased. He grew accustomed—and indifferent to—the mare's laboured breath and sweaty fatigue as he urged her to now trot, now canter, now gallop—in short bursts, until contemptuous of his former nervousness in the saddle. 'Tis but a matter of deciding who will be master,' he reflected, kicking the mare into a different stride.

When not riding, he spent hours in the woods hunting or laying snares, often tracking animals for considerable distances merely for the opportunity to practise the skill. And, insensibly, his confidence in the western venture, and his own ability to undertake it, increased to the point that he no longer tortured himself with doubts. *I can ride and shoot almost the equal of Mose,* he reflected one night, his former fears replaced by a new eagerness to see the buffalo in its rumoured plenitude.

His growing proficiency did not escape the eye of his companion, who seemed content to turn over the bulk of the hunting and trapping responsibilities to Boundless and to occupy himself with scraping and curing.

Since the advent of milder weather, Mose had rarely mentioned the western expedition, seemingly preoccupied with his own thoughts. Even when Boundless stumbled across the hide map and looked at it with renewed curiosity and interest, the trapper only nodded when presented with the sketch.

Mayhap he has changed his mind, Boundless pondered. *As the venture draws daily near, he broods on it and mayhap sees more clearly its great hazards and pitfalls.* To his surprise, the notion brought on a pang of disappointment.

AS THE BLUSTERY SKIES of March gave way to April, with few words or hints from Mose, who seemed half-drowned in whisky, Boundless turned his thoughts again to the future. *If he has abandoned all thoughts of the hazardous enterprise, I shall continue my journey to Philadelphia. Who knows, but perhaps he will give me a share of the furs, as stake?*

One fine spring day, he knelt beside the stream to fill the canteens. Catching sight of his bearded reflection in the water, it occurred to him that thirteen months had passed since his arrival in the woods. The realisation came as a jolt, and his mind drifted back to when he stood, gaunt and bedraggled, on the deck of the *Patience*, striving to catch sight of the New World in the distance.

Returning from the stream, the canteens strung about his shoulders, he found Mose, hands on hips, staring up at the pale, late-afternoon sky.

'What is it?' Boundless glanced up, half-anticipating a fresh avalanche of ducks.

'Are ye in the mood to venture forth?' Mose's features were serene in the pale, luminescent light.

'To where?'

'Why, to the western plains,' said Mose, as if surprised at the question.

'So soon?'

'One or two weeks, no more.'

Boundless stood silent, his thoughts so mixed that he could not tell his own mind.

Mose started back to the cabin. Reaching the doorway, he turned, his face exultant in the greenish light. 'By God's grace we shall stand this year on the buffalo plains!'

27

The Trading Post

As THE BLUE SKIES of April flowered into a glorious spring, Mose conducted himself with a new sprightliness, the doleful visages of winter giving way to joshing good humour as the mountains beckoned. He had forsworn whisky, to a degree, abandoning its consumption during the day to resume hunting and raise his tally of hides for the trading post.

'Mark that, Mr Gottschalk!' he exclaimed, gleeful at bringing down a buck. When a flight of swallows passed overhead, their twittering calls echoing through the air, he looked up, his face brightening at the sight. 'Such be the pilgrims of spring!' He shaded his eyes, following the birds as they flew west. 'And where birds do lead, horses and men may follow.'

One fine spring morning, Boundless was seated on a stump, flexing a new pair of moccasins when Mose stepped outside to join him. He carried a stool in one hand and a shirt in the other. 'I do feel in my bones that the time is nigh,' he said, sitting down on the stool. 'The ground is dry, the weather warm. A mite drier, a mite warmer. And so forth—by *mites!*' Mose chortled, his face alight with mischief.

'Someone be in a merry good temper. The fine weather, no doubt?'

'Nay, it be the power of roaming. A body in motion is a thing that cannot be at rest. D'ye see?'

Mose took up the buckskin shirt, holding an awl and thread between his fingers. 'It is a thing unheard of. Why, it goes against the laws of God and Nature.' He set down the shirt to mine the conceit.

'Did you ever see a duck drop on the wing? No, nor I. Such a thing cannot be. It stands to reason and common sense. Or a man dancing?' His face crinkled with humour. 'Remember old Mose when, years hence, you feel a chill you cannot shake no matter how deep you burrow beneath the sheets. Why, at such a moment, fling aside the covers and leap up and *prance!*' Taking up the shirt again, he chuckled at the notion.

Boundless shook his head, amused at his companion's high spirits. *He itches to set forth. No more than I,* he admitted, acknowledging his own quickening sense of adventure as the siren lure of the buffalo grew stronger with each passing day. Now resigned, if not yet fully reconciled, to the 'grand excursion', as he thought of it, he greeted the warmer weather with a growing sense of anticipation. If, on occasion, he was given pause by a fresh doubt, it dispelled like mist before the dazzling, totemic creature that rose up, rock-like, to defy every instinct of caution and self preservation. *After all, it will not come to me.*

He pulled on the moccasins, frowning at some residual tightness. He walked up and down the grass to loosen them further, while listening to Mose warble over the shirt.

'*One morning, one morning, one morning in May, I spied a young lady all on the high way. All on the high way.*'

Mose stopped singing and set down the shirt. 'Gadzooks, but we must make a list—for Mr Gottschalk!' He squinted at the creek. 'Rum, cider and whisky—a firkin of each. Tobacco. Beans. Flour, oats for the horses—a bushel to start. Powder and shot in plenty—we may not have time to cast our own. Awls. A supply of threads. Five pounds of salt. The same of sugar. Did I mention oats? Volatile Drops. Two shovels and a pick-axe—mine be hovering on ruin.'

'A moment, I cannot keep track.' Boundless went into the cabin and returned with the ink case and the log. Carefully placing the inkwell in the grass, he dipped a quill. 'Fire away!'

'Hemp rope—two hundred feet in four coils of fifty feet each. Six woollen blankets—they be useful for trade. A dozen gunnysacks. Did I say oats? A bell mare—'

'Pardon?'

'To lead the mules. And to serve as spare lest anything happen to the horses. Mr Gottschalk has a practised animal in his paddock. Where the deuce was I? Rum, whisky. Two mules … six wicker baskets—two to each mule.'

'*Two* mules?' Boundless looked up in dismay, conscious of his own limited ability to sustain such expense. 'So many?'

'Three, including William. We must pack all our supplies—tools, tack, food, powder, shot and sundry items, as well as oats for the horses. Add to which we shall be blessed if we don't lose one or two on the way. Mr Gottschalk has lately acquired a fine Spanish pacer that will fetch you safely to the plains. You may swap that winded nag of yours. Old Gottschalk is overly fond of horses. He will turn her out to pasture. Who knows but she has a foal or two in her, yet. Add five pounds of tea and three straw hats with broad brims—one for spare. Add two pair of good wool socks. And a curry comb.'

Boundless eyed the burgeoning list. 'The expense will be very considerable.'

'Aye. Old Gottschalk will charge to the last penny.'

'Does he still object to notes of credit?'

'He does.'

'Then I am but a poor partner in the venture.' Reaching inside his shirt, he tugged open the coin pouch and tipped the remaining four guineas into his hand. 'To replace the mare alone will all but impoverish me.'

'Wait but an instant.' Mose disappeared back inside the cabin. He emerged holding a small, hinged chest under his arm. He handed the chest to Boundless, a note of pride in his voice. 'Judge how well provisioned we be for capital.'

Boundless opened the lid. Inside was a jumble of papers and coins. With a glance at Mose for permission, he sifted through the contents, noting coins of English, Spanish, Dutch and Portuguese provenance as well as tokens, tobacco notes and various paper issuances from the colonies of Massachusetts, Pennsylvania and New York. 'It be a great variety of tender,' he said.

Mose nodded, his gaze sanguine. 'Each issue authentic and tenderable, from Maine to the Carolinas. Let no man say aught to the contrary.'

'Why then, you be a man of some fortune.' Boundless handed back the chest, impressed at the trove yet harbouring doubt as to the trust of the miscellaneous *specie*. 'I mistook all of your trades for barter.'

'A squirrel must set aside acorns for the winter, and a fisherman mend his nets. Where I may, I sell as well as barter. This treasure be the result.' Mose closed the lid on the box. 'The quantum shall meet all our expenses and more, the costs of which I willingly bear in return for your partnership in the venture—and on pledge of repayment as means allow. Does that sit well with ye?'

'I cannot allow—'

'There be pelts and hides in abundance west of the mountains. We shall divide our catch, less my recompense.'

'Nevertheless, I must—'

'Accept—say!' Mose stuck out his hand.

'On pledge of repayment.' With a fatalistic sigh, he shook the extended hand.

A WEEK LATER, THEY loaded the bulk of the skins onto the mule, securing the excess to the horses, and started out for the trading post. They followed a trace through the woods, travelling in a north-westerly direction with the wind at their backs. They kept to the trace all morning, Mose leading with a nonchalant assurance, even where the trail seemed to disappear in the foliage. Following a halt for the animals to drink, Boundless took a turn at riding in front as he tried to pick out the faint trail.

'To the right, look to your right,' chided Mose as Boundless stopped to survey the ground. The trapper pointed to barely discernible marks in the soft earth. 'The prints be your plain sign.'

They made camp for the night, dining on jerk and pemmican. Next morning, they continued, Boundless again leading the way. In the afternoon, he halted at the sound of flowing water.

'The Susskyhanna?' he asked, twisting in the saddle to pinpoint the source.

'The very same.' Mose plodded past to take the lead. A short time later, they emerged from the trees onto the banks of a wide river. 'The post lies but a few miles further upstream.' Mose pointed north.

'And downstream?'

'The Chesapeake, in time.'

They followed the river for the best part of an hour. Towards noon they came within sight of a large, strongly built dwelling situated on the riverbank. Chickens and hens pecked the ground in front of a fenced enclosure. A sow and several small piglets rooted in the dirt. Three horses and several mules could be glimpsed in a paddock behind the post. Two men sat on the porch smoking, their feet up on the rail.

'See there.' Mose pointed to the horses. 'The Spanish Bay will be the prize that will fetch ye to the mountains.'

As they rode up to the post, a pair of leashed dogs barked and growled. The curs stood stiff-legged in the dirt, hackles raised.

'Hold peace now!' One of the two men lounging on the porch spat a stream of tobacco juice at the barking dogs.

'Braddock's ghost! It be old Mose!' said the second man, rising slowly to his feet. 'How you be, Mose?'

Mose reined to a halt in front of the porch. 'In the doldrums for seeing such scoundrels as yourselves.'

The man laughed, coming down off the porch. 'You find yourself a partner, Mose?' He scratched his shirtfront as he looked at Boundless.

'This here be Mr McLennan,' said Mose, climbing down from the saddle. 'A one-hundred-percenter, late of Philadelphia or thereabouts.'

'Gentlemen.' Boundless touched a hand to his fur hat.

'He's got Philly manners. Perhaps he can civilise you, Mose. What do you reckon, Frank?'

'Hard task,' said the seated man. 'Pleased to meet you, Mr McLennan. I be Frank Worley, and that disreputable specimen over there be my boon companion, Lucius Vintuck, late of New York society.'

The other man snorted. 'Society yerself!'

The two men—whose clothes and appearance indicated to Boundless that they were hunters and trappers like Mose—*and like himself!*—looked up as the door opened and a short, thin man with slicked back hair stepped out onto the porch.

'Good morrow, sirs,' he said, drying his hands on a dirty linen apron around his waist. 'I see it is you, Mose. And a fine cargo of hides, I've no doubt. And you bring a comrade?' He eyed Boundless with curiosity.

'As witness!' said the lounging man, drawing a guffaw from his companion. 'Mr McLennan be a learned wig.' He winked at Boundless. 'Careful what you charge, Mr Gottschalk, or you shall feel the sting of the magistrate.'

The proprietor bristled at the remark, drawing himself up to his full height. 'Indeed! I welcome the full inspection of the most learned judge in Philadelphia. Let no man say that Jakob Gottschalk ever filched a single penny!'

'Come, friend, we do but tweak thy beard,' the taller of the two men said soothingly.

'You be an honest man, good proprietor, of that I have no doubt,' said his companion.

'We be here to trade, Mr Gottschalk. Indeed, to strip your shelves bare.' Mose proceeded up the steps to shake the proprietor by the hand. 'But first, a yard of your finest ale for two cracked throats!'

The proprietor held open the door. 'At your service, Mose. And you, Mr McLennan, you be most welcome, sir!' He bowed his head as Boundless passed.

Inside, the post was pleasantly warm—a huge fire blazing on the hearth. The spacious interior contained a small dining area set off from the main room. Barrels of flour, salt, sugar and other commodities competed for space with lamps, harness, nails, knives, coils of rope, candles, hats, coats and sundry other goods. A union flag was tacked to one wall.

'Gentlemen.' Gottschalk placed two pewter tankards on the counter. 'To honest trade!' He poured himself a small measure of punch. 'Sit, gentlemen, sit!'

He ushered Mose and Boundless towards the single, long table. The two men were already seated and smoking pipes, a look of anticipation on their faces.

'A hand of cards, Mose? Or a game of the goose?'

'It is business that brings us here,' said Mose. 'Gaming will do for another day.' He turned to Boundless. 'Mr McLennan, the sheet if you will.'

Boundless handed the log to the proprietor. 'The requirements are listed on the tabbed page.'

'Why, a handsome ledger, sir.' Gottschalk rubbed the brown leather cover. 'Fine stitching.' He opened to the tabbed page and studied the list, raising his eyebrows at the quantities. 'Upon my word!' He ran his finger up and down the listed items. 'These provisions greatly exceed your usual requirements, Mose. A horse. *Two* mules! And the bell mare also! Why, that alone is most unusual and near depletes my entire stock.' He glanced at Mose for explanation as the latter drained his tankard.

'An expedition, good proprietor.' Mose wiped his lips with his sleeves. 'Across the Alleghenies,' he said, a note of satisfaction in his voice.

'You say!' Gottschalk looked astonished at the announcement.

'By hookery!' said the tall hunter. His companion seemed equally nonplussed, his mouth dropped open.

'Indeed. This be most unexpected news. The Alleghenies.' Gottschalk scratched his head at the notion. 'I have known you fifteen or more years, Mose, with scarcely a thought that you harboured such a lofty ambition. Indeed, that be all the way to the French country.' He scrunched up his face as though calculating the distance.

'*And lo, he went into a far country, away from the face of his brother, Jacob.* That be from the Bible, Mr Gottschalk, although in the Moravian you may be unfamiliar with the quote.'

'Indeed! I trust I am as good a son of Maryland as any here present. My sainted mother, bless her memory, would answer you like for like, line for line. But I have neither the reading nor the memory. I am grieved that my deficiency pains you, sir. Greatly sorrowed.' Using the hem of his apron, Gottschalk vigorously wiped the counter, his face a picture of displeasure.

'Come, my good fellow, I meant no offence,' said a genial Mose. 'If I don't practise on my scripture every once in a while, it entirely slips my mind.'

''Tis true,' said Boundless, further smoothing the proprietor's ruffled feathers. 'He recites at will and without intent or malice.'

'Then no injury taken, where none be intended.' Mollified, Gottschalk cleared his throat before picking up the list to study it again. 'It shall be majority coin or good Maryland paper only,' he warned, glancing up from the log. 'I have skins enough delivered by these two gentlemen.' He indicated a large pile in the corner.

'Majority coin and paper it shall be,' said Mose grandly, tapping the purse beneath his shirt. 'Or tobacco notes, if you prefer. All as genuine and honest as the king himself!'

Gottschalk considered this for a moment and then turned away to tend to the roasting beefsteak, the aroma of which filled the room. 'The Moravian? I have hardly a word of it,' he grumbled, turning the spit.

'The Alleghenies? Deuced if you say.' The tall man glanced at his companion, who looked equally dumbstruck.

'I do. The Alleghenies—and points beyond.'

'Say again—the Alleghenies?' The other man squinted at Mose, who seemed much contented with the surprise his announcement had aroused.

'Bother the Alleghenies! You say, "points beyond"? You do not mean *acrost* the mountains, surely?'

'I do.' Mose winked at Boundless and took another swallow of ale.

The man sat dumbfounded, looking from Mose to Boundless and back again.

'And you, Mr McLennan?' asked his companion.

'I, too,' said Boundless, unable to resist a smile at the incredulous look on the other's face.

'You pull our leg.'

'Not so, friend. Upon my word.'

'Well smoke and double-smoke! It remains to ask *why*,' declared the tall man. 'Why in God's name would any man want to journey such a distance? It makes no sense. And for what? Why, barren deserts and godforsaken hills aswarm with savages.'

His companion nodded solemnly. ''Tis true. I have it on authority that the French country be overrun with savage Indians and terrible, wild creatures that feast on men and horses alike. The Frenchies consider it worthless and stay only to cause annoyance and in hope of securing favourable trade terms from the heathen.'

'It is fact,' his partner put in as Mose made a scoffing sound. 'There be no game to speak of only warlike savages and foaming rivers that bear no fish fit to eat.'

'It is a fool's errand,' averred his companion. 'If the French don't shoot you, then the savages will scalp your hair.'

'Balderdash!' Mose dismissed the arguments with an airy wave of his hand. 'I have it on certain oath that there be rich, grassy plains and majestic mountains—bathed in snow nine months of the year. And deer, beaver and buffalo to torment the senses. What d'ye say to that?'

The two trappers exchanged dubious glances. 'On what authority?' challenged one.

'The word of an honest man. A man, unlike yourselves, who has stood upon the plains with his own two feet.'

'A Frenchie? Hah!'

'What say you, Mr McLennan? Are you party to this nonsense?'

'I am. And I do believe—within bounds, that the country be as Mose has described.'

'Have you not heard that we are at war?' objected the tall trapper. 'The French will hang you—if the savages don't scalp you first.'

'Scalp you first,' agreed his companion. 'Why you must be set on going down the Valley Pike?' At a nod from Mose, he continued. 'Well then, you will be stepping into the fire. The Pike is overrun with Shawnee, scalping and murdering from one end to the other.'

'Scalping and murdering ...' echoed his companion.

'Pshaw! Are ye frightened of a few Shawnee?'

'A few? No! Hundreds, yes!'

'Not to mention the French,' his companion put in.

As the trappers recited the dangers in store, Boundless listened with growing alarm. 'Perhaps, Mose, it would be prudent to wait until—'

'Gentlemen!' The proprietor returned bearing another jug of beer. 'I for one, envy you, Mose.' He placed the jug on the table. 'I had a boat laid by, but a week since, and I do recall a fine conversation with a Mr Luddock, late of Augusta, who spoke most glowingly of the Carolina colony and the wondrous fertility of the soil. On every plot and acre, hogsheads of tobacco—hogsheads by the thousand! A man is to be envied, sir, to witness for himself such prosperity.'

'They head *west*, to cross the mountains, not *south* to your Carolina.'

'Across the mountains?' Gottschalk looked befuddled. 'Why, what is there *across* the mountains?'

'The very subject, good proprietor, of this congress. Have you not ears?'

'Indeed, I should hope I do. And passing good ones, at that.' The proprietor flicked the cloth in annoyance.

'Frank here meant no offence but to exercise his tongue.'

'A tongue which starves for a morsel of that roasting beefsteak!'

'To our most excellent proprietor!' Mose raised his tankard in the air.

'And beefsteak!'

'And bountiful plates!'

AFTER FEASTING ON THE beefsteak, squash, pickled fruits and cinnamon pudding, Mose doused his post-prandial pipe and rose to his feet.

'Suffice! There is business to be done,' he said, waving off yet another question from his inquisitive dining companions. 'Boundless—if you be ready. And you, Mr Gottschalk?' The proprietor came around from behind the counter. 'Proceed, fine friends. I am ready and willing. But remember, hides in the minority. The majority to be in coin or warrantable paper.'

Boundless followed Mose outside, where the trapper began to untie the ropes that held the cargo of hides. 'Peace, sweet William! Stand, good mule!' Mose glanced at the post door and then at Boundless. 'Now the merry tribulations begin. Observe, the wiles and lures of your Moravian trader.'

A few minutes later, the two comrades returned to the post carrying armfuls of hides, which they spread on the floor for inspection.

'Freshly cured and ready for the tan,' said Mose, kneeling to display a skin.

The other men gathered around to watch as Gottschalk leaned down to feel the hide between his hands. 'Deer,' he said, disappointment in his voice. 'I could use a good fur, Mose—a beaver pelt would be more welcome.'

'Beaver!' Mose snorted dismissively. 'Jest find me a beaver!' He turned to the watching men.

'There be none,' the tall one agreed. He looked at his companion. 'How long has it been, Frank?'

'A time, Lucius,' agreed Frank. 'Two year or more since we last snared one.'

'I have but this morning purchased the wealth of these two gentlemen.' Gottschalk gestured to the hides piled in the corner. 'My quota is full for the month.'

'There is a boat due by shortly is there not?' enquired Frank, with a meaningful glance to Mose, who turned to Gottschalk.

'Then what better time to purchase?'

'Even so, I am replete with hides. Honest coin, however, be another matter.'

'I told you, did I not? I be ready to part with coin as well—to buy up stock and goods aplenty.'

The proprietor mulled over this as he inspected the hides.

'An excellent leather!' Mose raised his voice in protest as Gottschalk made to place a hide on the 'secondary' pile. 'What say?' he demanded of the watching trappers.

'A fine specimen,' Lucius insisted. 'Come, Mr Gottschalk. Admit the worth.'

''Twill make a handsome shirt,' agreed Frank.

Unmoved, Gottschalk placed the hide among the seconds. 'Fair is as fair be,' he said, taking up another hide. Pursing his lips, he considered the unsmoked skin before setting it to one side. He continued sorting—turning a deaf ear to Mose's grumbles, until the hides were stacked in three separate piles. Finished, he got to his feet.

'A moment,' he said, returning to the counter and picking up a small, leather-bound journal. Dipping a quill, he made some notes while calling out the tally to Mose. 'Twenty buckskins—twelve smoked. Four bear. Six— pardon, seven fox. Thirteen muskrat—'

'Fourteen.'

'Fourteen?' Gottschalk looked up, frowning.

'Placed there by your own hand.' Mose held up each skin as he counted aloud. 'Fourteen,' he said.

'I'll not quibble … fourteen.'

'Where be the quibble? Fourteen is fourteen, is it not?'

'Fourteen is fourteen,' agreed Lucius. 'Counted by your own hand.'

'Seven squirrel,' said Gottschalk. 'Correct? And twelve rabbit. Five mink. Eight fisher. And two wolf.' He looked up from the journal. 'Are we in agreement?'

'I'll not *quibble*. Assign a worth.'

'Then sit … if you please.' Gottschalk gestured to the table. 'Let us agree an honest exchange.'

Over a fresh tankard of beer, Boundless watched Mose and the proprietor haggle over the value of the hides—each vigorously disputing the other's estimate. The bartering was accompanied by frequent appeals to the watching trappers, who arbitrated several points, invariably coming down on the side of Mose. At one point, the latter threw up his hands in anger. 'By the bones, if I won't fire the entire cargo afore I accept less than their true worth!' His fellow trappers muttered in sympathy.

'More ale?' the trader asked genially, seemingly unfazed by the outburst. 'And you, Mr McLennan, what is your opinion, sir?' he asked, seeking to draw Boundless into the exchange.

'I am afraid I have none,' answered Boundless, receiving an approving nod from Mose. 'Mose here is the only envoy as the proper owner of these hides.'

'And dying of thirst in the nonce.' Mose raised his empty tankard.

After protracted haggling and further threats from Mose to 'fire the bunch', negotiations were quickly and amicably concluded, both men shaking hands to seal the trade.

'Witnessed by the Philadelphia wig!' quipped Lucius.

The proprietor went to the counter and took out a ledger in which he entered the particulars of the transaction, copying from Boundless' logbook.

'That be two mules, the bell mare, three pound of butter, two sacks of flour, five pounds of beans, the same quantity of sugar—salt, drops, a barrel of powder, ten pound of lead shot, a firkin of whisky—and one of cider. Two felt and three straw hats. Tack and articles as listed, assorted sundries—to be named, and a jar of biscuits. The cost of the bell mare, the sugar, flour, butter, powder and lead shot to be struck against the worth of the skins.' He looked at Mose. 'Have I said fairly and as agreed?'

'Only to mention two hearty suppers, the ale, and a bed by the fire.'

'That be a marked addition to the tally—four shillings worth.'

'It be his final trade, Mr Gottschalk.'

'A farewell 'ere he fly for the mountains.'

Grumbling, the proprietor made a notation in the ledger. 'Let no man—wig or other, say that Jakob Gottschalk treated him unfairly.' He glanced around at the shelves. 'Some of these goods be in short supply. But I have a boat arriving within the week.'

Mose tugged at his beard, considering. 'A week? Then have the goods—all and entire—set aside for ten days hence. Ten days, no more.'

'I shall require full payment as security.'

'Half now, and half thence.'

'The animals to be held as well?'

'Aye. After we have looked at their teeth.' This draw laughter from the other men.

'Then the cost of keep to be added to the invoice.'

'Keep! Do they sleep on straw mattresses?' The objection brought guffaws.

'Oats, sir, and the labour of watering and feeding. Unless you propose to leave Mr McLennan behind to carry out those duties?'

''Tis a wonder you do not charge the cost of grass!'

Gottschalk bent under the counter to retrieve a small brass object.

'A spyglass, gentleman. Single draw and made in London.' He pulled open the tube to demonstrate. 'I had it from the boat master himself. Invaluable for spying landmarks or lurking savages alike.'

'These eyes be sufficient.' Mose picked up the object and turned it in his hands. 'Mayhap I could relieve you of it for an honest price.'

'Are we concluded our business, gentlemen?'

'Indeed, there is yet one more item,' said Boundless. 'I wish to barter my mare for the bay outside in the paddock.'

The proprietor raised an eyebrow. 'Is your own horse not to your liking, Mr McLennan?'

'She be a bit slow on the hoof—for such a long journey.'

The proprietor leaned on the counter. 'The bay has a gentle temper, yet hardy and dependable.'

'What is the breed?'

'A Spanish cross. Gelded. More than that, I cannot say.'

'And the name?'

'Buck, or Buckshot. He answers to both.'

'May I inspect him?'

'By all means, friend. By all means.' The proprietor held open the door and pointed to where the bay stood in the grass.

'Lead on,' said Mose.

Following an extended inspection of the horse, which Mose declared to be 'in passable fettle', Boundless walked over to where Gottschalk was casting a critical eye over the saddled mare.

'A fine mount, Mr Gottschalk. I am loathe to part with her.'

'You are certain she is sound?'

'As sound as she is hale.'

Gottschalk pressed his ear to the mare's chest. 'Her breath rattles,' he observed, suspicion in his voice.

'Pshaw!' Mose slapped dirt from his hands. 'She rode here dragging the mule—who tarried at every step.'

The proprietor squinted doubtfully at the mare. 'I should like to see her pace.'

'The day wears on, Mr Gottschalk. By jinks but my mouth is dry!'

Gottschalk bent to inspect a pastern, a frown on his face. 'Her foreleg sits at an angle, does it not?'

'The mules, friend. For secured notes and coin. Time presses.'

Gottschalk scratched his lip. 'You agree to take two mules and the bell mare?'

'The entire four-legged cargo. Now, do we shake hands upon it?'

'I shall package the sum.'

'The gelding as distinct, if you please,' Boundless insisted, ignoring a frown from Mose.

'Five pound,' Gottschalk offered.

'Four.'

'Four pound, ten shillings. I cannot release him for less.'

'And the mare—in part-credit?'

Gottschalk looked the mare up and down. Muttering to himself, he bent down to prod the foreleg. 'I have honest doubts as to—'

'The day passes.' Mose stamped impatiently. 'Say yea or nay, afore I perish from thirst.'

With a sigh, Gottschalk stood up. 'I shall take your word on her soundness, Mr McLennan. To one half the value.' 'Then done!' Boundless extended his hand.

'You will take him now?'

Boundless felt an elbow in his back. 'In ten days. With the other provisions.'

'The mules, Mr Gottschalk, 'ere we expire on the spot!'

With a lingering look at the mare, the proprietor led the way around the post.

'Well bid,' Mose whispered in his ear.

'Come Bitsy!' Putting his fingers to his lips Gottschalk gave a sharp whistle. A sorrel-coloured mare snorted and trotted over to where he stood. The mules followed closely behind as if drawn by an invisible thread.

'Observe!' The proprietor beamed as the mare sidled up to his touch. 'The mules and her be old friends. Did I not promise as much?'

'She seems a mite long in the tooth.'

'Scarce twelve years! Upon my word.'

'That first mule—the lop-eared one, hitches in the left hind.'

'Come now, Mose. I know you of old,' Gottschalk scolded. 'You shall not knock me. The price be fair and reasonable and remains the same, in spite of your quips and cavils.'

Mose sighed, as though greatly put upon. 'Very well. Hold them all for the ten days. Come—a drink by the fire, to seal the purchase.' Boundless lingered to pass water as Mose and the proprietor returned to the post. Pulling down his buckskin breeches, he relieved himself while staring at the river, his thoughts following it downstream where it flowed into the Chesapeake. As he mounted the steps to the post, he heard the sound of raised voices and a vigorous debate from within. The air inside was thick with pipe smoke and the aroma of spiced beefsteak.

'And I vouch there be nought but stony plains and barren hills!' Frank slapped the table to echoes of agreement from his companion.

'Are we still on the same point?' asked Boundless, taking a seat.

'And travelled over and over! Come, a turn of trump.' Mose signalled Gottschalk. 'The cards, if you will!'

'What news of the war?' Boundless asked, remembering suddenly.

'As bad as could be,' said Lucius.

Frank nodded solemnly. 'There was an awful massacre up by Lake George.'

'A bloody business. Hundreds of women and children scalped and slaughtered.'

'Women and children?' Boundless stared in horror.

'Not even the infants spared.'

'Not a single babe in arms,' echoed Lucius. 'All scalped and tortured, alike.'

Boundless stared out the open door, trying to comprehend such an atrocity.

'When was this?' asked Mose.

'Did ye not hear? It was but seven or eight months ago.'

'I am sure I mentioned it,' said Gottschalk, coming over to shake his head. 'I can scarce forget it. By all accounts, it was a sight to trouble the devil himself.' He shuddered and crossed himself as the table fell into smoke-filled contemplation.

'And what news of operations along the Ohio?' asked Mose, breaking the silence.

'You mean your Alleghenies?' Lucius rubbed his jaw. 'I should advise to stay clear until this quarrel is declared, one way or the other.'

His companion nodded. 'If the French catch you on your little jaunt they will shoot you, sure as hellfire.'

'Where are the blasted cards!'

'Coming, Mose. No need to curse.' Gottschalk hurried back to the counter.

The five men drank and played cards the rest of the afternoon and evening, the games punctuated by lively debates on Indians, the best bait for lures, the incompetence of the colonial administrators in Philadelphia and Virginia, and the virtues of smoothbore as opposed to rifling. Frequent toasts—to King George, Maryland 'fillies', the absent beaver, and 'good old Gottschalk'—brought them to bedtime.

NEXT MORNING, FOLLOWING A hearty breakfast of beer and porridge, they bade farewell to their host.

'I shall look for you in ten days,' said Gottschalk as they sat the horses. 'The livestock to be fed and watered as agreed.'

'See how he indexes the mark! He will no doubt charge credit for each outstanding hour!'

The watching trappers laughed, slapping the affronted Gottschalk on the shoulder.

'Farewell!'

'Keep your hair tight, Mose!'

'And don't get lost in the Alleghenies!'

'Why do we not take the mules, at least, with us?' Boundless asked as they plodded away from the post. And the Spanish as well? Mr Gottschalk may change his mind upon reflection.'

'No sense, seeing as we must ride back this way. And as for the Spanish—why give him the time to acquaint with the mare's constitution? Fear not. Gottschalk drives a hard bargain, but he be true as his word. His reputation depends on it.'

AS A SPRING SHOWER fell, Mose instructed Boundless in the fashioning of a deerskin cape which would, he promised, 'hold out the foulest wind and rain'. The garment consisted of four hides doubled into two sides with holes cut for the head and arms whereby the cape could be draped over the entire upper body. A pair of leather ties secured the sides. Boundless tried on the finished garment, smoothing the hide across his chest. 'It is fine and warm,' he conceded, 'Although a mite cumbersome.'

'At night it will turn as a blanket,' assured Mose.

Boundless eyed the few remaining hides where they lay on the floor. 'Are we to fetch the remainder to Mr Gottschalk?'

'Nay. We must needs make additional buckskin for repairs along the journey. And we could both use second britches, shoes, and jerkins.'

Throughout the days and nights that followed, they cut and sewed until Boundless was heartily sick of the art.

'A stitch in time, friend.' Mose tut-tutted as he reached for the awl. 'Where better for such work? Here—in our familiar little cottage—or out on the windy plains?'

Boundless welcomed the opportunity to leave off sewing to go on a hunt. He shot a small buck and humped the carcass back to the cabin where he butchered it in the grass. After quartering the meat and hanging a portion in the smoke house, he washed in the creek. Drying his hands on his shirt, he lingered to observe a covey of quail rustle through the grass. He stood there for some time, lost in thought. When he returned to the cabin, he found Mose poring over the hide map in the light of the open door.

'I have been studying on our passage.' Mose fumbled among the objects on the floor, muttering to himself as his fingers closed on the stub of charcoal. He poised the stub before drawing a line upwards from the bottom, right-hand corner. 'This be the York Road—three- or four-days ride from Mr Gottschalk's.'

'That would mean doubling back. Could we not continue up the river to the Lancaster Pike? Fesky … …' Boundless paused at Mose's questioning look.

'We could if we were on our own. But the way runs through thick woods that would be a hazard for the pack mules. We can follow the stream north for two miles at best. There is a trace there that will take us back to the York Road.'

'And we follow that to the Pike?'

'Aye. The Wagon Road, some call it. That will take us west to the Valley Pike and draw us all the way across the Virginia country.' Mose drew a horizontal line from right to left across the centre of the buckskin.

'All the way across?'

'Aye. We follow it south-west, across the Patowmack and into the Virginias. By and by we reach the Fluvan—the James River. Past that stream we gain passage to the French and Indian lands across the mountains.'

'Through the famous notch?'

'Through the notch. Once across, it is but a matter of heading west, and so onto the buffalo plains. Thusly and thusly.'

'How far distant do you calculate—to the plains?'

Mose set the hide on his knees. 'Mayhap one thousand miles. Three months and more of travel—depending on the ground, the weather, Indians, the horses.'

Boundless frowned at the charcoal lines. 'But the path is largely unknown, is it not? How shall we find our marks?'

'Do you suppose I have forgotten my own way back to Virginny?'

'But across the mountains?'

'Pshaw! Follow thy nose!'

Boundless sighed and shook his head, torn between admiration for the trapper's gusto and unease at such reckless confidence. His eye returned to the map as he contemplated the distance. The immense figure filled him with equal parts exhilaration and alarm. His long, arduous journey from Edinburgh down to London seemed but a footstep by comparison. And who knows how much more land lies beyond the plains? he reminded himself.

'You have doubts?'

'Over the journey? No. The way, perhaps.'

'This sketch be but a presage. The sun be our true compass.' Mose bent over the map, his face scrunched with deliberation. Slowly and laboriously he printed large, misshapen letters across the bottom: *Mose van Zeke*.

Pleased with the result, he held out the charcoal stub. 'If you will oblige.'

Boundless knelt and wrote his own name in smudgy copperplate beneath that of Mose. He paused for a moment and then added the legend, *Expedition to the Western Plains*, across the bottom.

'What is that?' asked Mose, squinting. 'This light blinds me,' he said irritably.

'*Expedition to the Western Plains*.' Boundless pointed to each word. 'We should add the date—to mark the occasion.' He offered the stub to Mose.

'Your hand be clearer than mine.' Mose leaned over to watch closely as Boundless added the day, month and year, *27th April, 1758*.

'Why did ye add the day?' asked Mose.

'The 27th? That be when our ten days are up with Mr Gottschalk.'

'Then it be true and warranted! This buckskin be our headstone—the origin and keepsake of our journey.' With a triumphant air, Mose took back the hide and rolled it up. 'The way is set forth—the rough places made plain. In but ten days, we commence our passage. A whisky toast, what say ye?'

AS THE NOMINATED DAY approached, Mose's buoyant mood increased to the point of jubilation. Several times, Boundless observed him standing in the grass staring westwards as though he might glimpse the elusive notch.

'But two days to the ten,' he said in reference to the arrangement with Gottschalk. 'Glory be if I didn't lose that fellow twelve year ago,' he exclaimed upon coming across a lost jack knife as he inventoried the contents of the cabin. At various moments, he stopped whatever he was doing to mutter in exasperation as a notion struck him. 'The ropes!' He slapped a hand to his forehead. Still muttering, he went about his business, only to stop a minute later to exclaim, as if thunderstruck. 'Nails!' Frowning and cussing, he abandoned whatever task occupied him to search the cluttered dwelling for said nails.

'When did ye arrive?' he asked, apropos of nothing, as Boundless helped him bundle the supplies.

He stopped to think. 'I calculate thirteen months—give or take a week.'

'How it doth fly.' Mose sighed in bemusement. 'Twas Providence led your footsteps, friend. That and yon near-sighted mare.' He wheezed with laughter at the recollection. 'By jinks, if she had found her proper way to Baltimore then where might you stand now?'

'In Philly, like as not.'

'And thus absent for the adventure of a lifetime.'

On the evening of departure, Mose stood in the emptied cabin, looking around at the bare walls. The snares, tools and lanterns sat on the floor, bundled for the journey. The trapper scratched his chin. 'I believe we are set. As set as we ever shall be.'

Boundless went outside to make a last check of the smokehouse and tanning shed. The smokehouse was emptied—the remaining meat pounded into jerky and pemmican. The shed was similarly bare. He watered the mare, stroking her mane as she drank. 'We must soon part ways, good Bess. But you shall be fed and grassed under the care of Mr Gottschalk, never fear.'

Glancing up at the evening sky, he imagined the sun setting over the Patapsco. 'And farewell also, dear Theo—and all my stout companions. The journey is far, and full of dangers—but I shall return, God willing. Until then, keep me in heart.'

He returned to the cabin where Mose had washed the cooking pot and added it to the store of provisions stacked just inside the door. The trapper gazed fondly at the pot. 'We have endured many a winter together. I had you from Mr Gottschalk, many years ago.' Mose turned at the sound of hooves and a bray from outside.

William had wandered up to the open doorway as if curious at the pile of supplies. 'Hie thee, good fellow,' Mose said, advancing to the door to scratch the mule's cheek. 'Thou be a solid and equal companion in the enterprise.'

He stood absorbed for a moment before turning to look at the empty cabin. 'Nought remains but to load the supplies on the morrow. Let us get a good night's rest, for tomorrow shall be a long day.'

Boundless awoke to the sound of a fly buzzing around the cabin. Daylight shone through the open door. He heard Mose moving about outside. In the morning light the cabin looked bare and diminished minus the usual clutter of skins, snares and bric-a-brac. Yawning, he pulled the buffalo robe around his shoulders and stood in the doorway, blinking in the bright sunshine.

'Are ye bid for a gentle stroll?' Mose's voice sounded cheerfully from the creek where he stood watering the horses. 'Unfurl those tangled limbs young spark! The bright day be upon us.' The jubilance in the trapper's voice left Boundless in no doubt as to his companion's happiness at the prospect of at last setting forth on his long-dreamed-of expedition.

After breakfasting on pemmican, they spent an hour loading the mule with the pots and pans and the remaining quantities of flour and beans. When the mule was loaded to capacity, they transferred the remainder to the horses. 'It will be a mite heavy until we get to Gottschalk's,' said Mose, patting the mule.

Boundless took a deep breath, a momentous feeling in his chest as he climbed atop the mare. Mose stood in the open doorway, his face preoccupied. 'By gar,' he muttered. 'If it ain't the thing.' He checked that the pipe was tucked into the deerskin pouch around his waist and tugged, frowning, at his shirt. Shutting the door for the last time he climbed aboard the stallion.

'Are ye set?'

A south-easterly breeze rustled the pines. The drying frames stood bare and naked in the grass. The wooden tanning tubs sat abandoned beside the creek. Mose regarded the hovel, mixed emotions on his face.

'It has been my home for many a year, ever since I came to these woods. And now, 'tis farewell. *Adieu*, my woodland home! I bequeath thee to the thunderous air and the beasts of the field. Or, mayhap these logs … these walls … these *splendiferous joins* will give shelter to some lost or lonesome soul.'

He stared a moment longer and then jerked the tow rope. 'Hi-yup, old Jack. Follow on, good William. Do not stop afore we reach the mountains!'

Westward Ho!

A S THEY RODE UP, the trading post door opened and the proprietor stepped out onto the porch. 'Good morrow, friends, good morrow!' Gottschalk rubbed the apron between his hands, his usually pained features flushed and animated. 'I had expected you yesterday. But no matter—dinner awaits!' He stood aside as they mounted the porch, bobbing his head, a cheerful expression on his face. 'Your goods be all squarely accounted and await but your hand. Enter, good sirs! Pray, enter!'

Inside the doorway, shovels, axes, trenchers, and coils of rope were piled against the wall. An assortment of gunnysacks, canvas wraps and wool blankets lay alongside. Sundries, perishables, and six large wicker baskets completed the provisions.

'There be your necessities—as promised! But sit, gentlemen. A repast before labour!'

Barely had Boundless sat down than the proprietor thrust a glass of rum into his hands. 'To fond, old comrades!' Gottschalk lifted his glass and swallowed the contents in a single gulp.

Mose raised an eyebrow. 'You be most sociable this day, Mr Gottschalk.'

'And why not? Who knows when, if ever, we shall meet again?' Gottschalk's eyes grew moist. 'Nay, but I am cupped, gentlemen, *cupped.*' He sat down across from Boundless and refilled all three glasses, knocking the bottle as he did so.

'I envy you, sirs. *Envy,* I say—and unashamed to say so. Long have I wished to explore the Carolina colonies, but I remain bound ... alas! ... to this single, solitary spot.' He bowed his head, a sorrowful look on his face.

Mose nudged Boundless, who replied, 'Mayhap you will—'

'My father on his deathbed—his *deathbed*, gentlemen!—made me pledge to maintain the trade. And I do honour that promise. I alone. My two brothers—such villains!—despatched themselves as fast as they were able when the old man died, unable to bear the solitude.' He stared in anguish, his lip trembling. 'Villains, I do say! But here I, Gustavus Jakob Petr Gottschalk, stayed, honest to my word. I alone.' Tears seeped from his eyes.

'A most faithful choice.'

'And a profitable one,' added Mose.

Gottschalk stood unsteadily to his feet. 'I must plate the dinner.'

'Boozled on his own stock!' whispered Mose as their host navigated to the pot.

After stirring and tasting the food, all the while heaving and sighing, Gottschalk returned bearing two heaped trenchers. His progress proved so unsteady that Boundless leapt up to assist.

'Nay, friends. Feast! Be merry to the plate.'

As Boundless spooned the bubbling mix, Gottschalk leaned towards him, his eyes bleary. Draining the glass, the proprietor began to speculate on the whereabouts of an Indian he claimed to have seen skulking in the nearby woods.

'A fearsome-looking fellow!' His eyes bulged at the memory. 'The knave was after the horses, for a certainty. Do not doubt but I had the musket at the cock! But an instant—one step!—and his murderous scalp would even now dangle above the hearth!'

'You are not lonesome, here, Mr Gottschalk—by yourself?'

'As if spoke by the angel!' With a beseeching look, the proprietor grasped Boundless' hand across the table. 'A man sorrows for the graces of a good wife, does he not? But sir, I ask—what woman in her right mind would choose to live in such a desolate wilderness? What woman?'

'Fortune changes daily, sir. Who may tell what the morrow shall bring?'

'True, friend. Truer words were rarely spoken. Witness, Mose, the wisdom.' Overspilling with emotion, Gottschalk dabbed his eyes. 'To Fortune, gentlemen!' He refilled the glasses, slopping rum over the table. 'May she favour us with her grace.'

'I noticed a halfways useful-looking mule added to the harem.' Mose glanced shrewdly at the stricken proprietor. 'I could use a spare.'

'Take her! Take her my old friend, for your long journey. With God's blessing!' Gottschalk bent his head, overcome with sorrow. 'Four pounds!' He raised his head. 'Four pounds and an honest handshake.'

'Three,' Mose proposed flatly. 'And you can throw in the beefsteak and two extra baskets as well.'

'Three then, by God's grace!' Gottschalk looked as though he might burst into tears.

THE COMPANIONS SPENT THE early afternoon sorting the provisions while Gottschalk snored soundly on the porch, his head lolling to one side of the rocking chair. The dry goods—beans, corn, oats, flour, bacon and tea, along with the cider, whisky and ale—were distributed into five piles.

The pots, pans, awls, flints, lead shot, black powder, snares, shovels and pickaxe were consigned to a single mule.

Mose surveyed the gathered piles. 'Jinks, but we could use still another mule. We may have to pack the mare.'

Two wicker baskets were attached to each mule—the baskets secured with a crupper under the tail and clinch ropes around the belly. Dissatisfied with the knots, Mose pulled on the ropes, frowning as the baskets slipped to one side. As they tried different arrangements, Boundless took the opportunity to show off the 'Spanish knot' he had learned from observing idle sailors on board the *Patience*. 'See how one pull anywhere tightens the whole?' he said, demonstrating.

Mose nodded approvingly. 'A most useful knot. I would have saved a yard or two of skin had I known of it earlier. And very timely, since we must tighten the rigging always.'

They loaded the goods, going back and forth between the baskets to ensure an even balance. Mose fussed mightily over the task, constantly adjusting the weight of each basket. 'An unequal load will slip under the belly and tip the creature,' he warned, transferring a hemp sack from one mule to another.

'We shall have to swim rivers,' he said, tightening a strap. 'And the Lord knows what we may encounter in the way of snakes, bears, heathen and highwaymen.'

As the last pack was secured into place, Boundless wiped his face with his sleeve, wondering at the indefatigable energy of his companion as Mose ducked under the neck of a mule to make one last check of the ropes.

Satisfied that the packs were secure and balanced, Mose stood back to observe the effect. The mules looked distinctly unhappy with their lot, snickering in protest at the heavy baskets and binding ropes. The bell mare stood placidly under her light cargo of blankets and the buckskin capes. A brass bell was attached to a leather strap around her neck, the bell tinkling each time she moved.

'Will they manage the weight?'

'Manage? They will carry themselves *and* the mare, if needs be. Be concerned only that the new bride gets along with the grooms.' He went along the train, tugging at each basket. 'I place William here in the lead, since he is the most contrary, and Snuff-Pot, there, second.'

Boundless gazed at the named mule—a refractory animal that had arched and bucked as they secured the baskets. 'A name well-suited.'

'The third—what say you?'

'Whitesock—he has a flash.'

'And thou …' Mose paused at the most recent addition, the most reluctant to stand in line. 'Thou shalt be deemed "Prodigal", for coming late to the feast.' He stepped back to address the train. 'Step together for the love of God and keep the peace with one another.'

'Must we rope them?'

'Lightly only, until they observe their place. They will follow the mare like Mother Goose.' Mose glanced at the sky and wiped his hands on his shirt. 'Are ye shipshape?'

'But a moment.' Boundless walked over to where Bessie rested her head on the paddock rail. 'Goodbye, sweet Bess.' He caressed her muzzle. 'Mr Gottschalk will take good care of you. And there be oats and grass aplenty.' The mare whinnied and shook her neck. 'I hope your successor be half as sterling a companion.'

'Brother Jakob!' Mose shook the snoring Gottschalk. 'Awake! The savages are upon us.'

'Zounds!' Gottschalk started to his feet. 'What ails, friend! What ails?' He glared about wildly.

'Hush now, good proprietor. Do not fret. We wish merely to bid our farewells.' Mose grasped the hand of the befuddled man. 'I bid you all good fortune, Mr Gottschalk. As true and honest a proprietor as ever there was.'

He walked back down the steps and slapped Boundless on the back. 'Are you primed?'

'I am!' He put a foot in the stirrup and swung aboard the Spanish bay. He felt it tremble beneath him. Bessie gave a loud neigh and pushed against the paddock rail, as if expecting to be bridled and saddled at any moment. He touched the brim of his new felt hat.

'Farewell, Mr Gottschalk. Take good care of Bessie.'

Gottschalk staggered to the porch post. '*Dobrou noc,* friends!' Tears ran down his face as he embraced the post. *Dobrou noc!*'

'What gibberish is that?' Mose climbed into the saddle. 'The Good Lord protect us, Jakob. We sail for the mountains!'

'Would that I were going with you!' called out Gottschalk as he clung tearfully to the post. 'Godspeed, dear comrades! Remember your old friend, Jakob Gottschalk! Farewell! May God and all the saints protect you on your journey!'

THEY SET OFF NORTH along the banks of the river, riding slowly to accustom the mules to the pack train. Mose turned constantly to cast an eye over the stock, occasionally leaning to check a strap or rope for tightness. Boundless rode to the rear, adjusting to the pace and feel of the new mount.

'How does he travel?' asked Mose.

'He gaits differently from the mare.' Boundless nudged the bay up alongside, pleased at the instant response and the gelding's eagerness to trot. 'He is sprightly,' he said, restraining the horse.

'See how he follows?' Mose closely observed the most recent addition to the pack train. 'He looks set to trot all the way to the western plains. A fine specimen of the mule tribe. And a bargain at that.'

'Your Mr Gottschalk was the worse for wear.'

'He was quizzed in the head when he got here, no doubt. The woods did the rest.'

'How so?'

'Some folk can't stand to be by themselves. They hanker for society and such. I've seen many a tyro flee back to Philadelphia or New York after scarce a winter in these woods.'

Boundless nodded, thinking back on the over-wrought proprietor. 'This wild country is hard on a man, especially one lacking a wife and family.'

'Nay, but you be the currant that spoils the cake, I do wager.'

'You say? I am, I assure you, disposed to taverns and good company. Indeed, all the pleasures of the town. A solitary life holds no joy for me.'

'Mayhap, but you have the spark to live apart from folk. Why, it be plain as the nose on your face.'

They continued in silence, Boundless contemplating the drunken proprietor and his long, lonely habitude. 'It would be a sore trial to the spirit,' he reflected, staring at the wide, slow-moving river as they plodded alongside. The notion that Mose should mistake him as one suited for such solitude caused him to shake his head in bemusement.

After less than two miles, the open path gave way to woods.

'There be our trace.' Mose indicated a faint trail that led away from the river and into the trees. 'Yip!' He guided the bell mare along the trail, pulling her bridle as the mules unswervingly followed the noise of the tinkling bell. They had no sooner entered the trees than their progress slowed in half as brambles tore at clothes and branches snagged the wicker baskets. Several times they were forced to stop and cut branches to enable the train to pass. The difficulty reminded Boundless of the passage through the woods to the Elk River. After struggling through the trees for three hours, they came across a clearing, and Mose called a halt.

'We make camp here for the night,' he said.

'We have two hours, at least, of daylight,' Boundless objected, frustrated at the clinging thickets. 'I estimate we cannot have travelled further than five miles from Mr Gottschalk's.'

'Mayhap. But we have a long way to go. Why risk overworking the mules at the very start?'

Setting up camp proved a tiresome and time-consuming business. First, they unstrapped and lifted down each of the wicker baskets. They then examined and, if necessary, repacked the baskets before watering the stock. Boundless made a fire as Mose inspected the mules for bruising or injury caused by the heavy baskets rubbing the flesh through the hide covers.

'They are scratched, some,' said Mose. 'The rigging on Snuff-Pot was overtight.'

'Near two hours to make camp,' complained Boundless while chewing on smoked venison. 'At such a rate we shall be fortunate to reach the mountains by next spring.'

Mose puffed reflectively where he sat by the fire. 'This'—he motioned to the baskets sitting on the ground—'will get easier as we find the method. In a week or so the animals will break to the pace. What matter the distance, so long as the journey is begun?'

Boundless held his tongue as he dug several thorns from the leg of his buckskin. Around them, the woods were cast in blackness—the gloom relieved only by the sparks from the fire. He tugged at a particularly resistant thorn.

'How far is the York Road, do you estimate?'

'Five miles, no more.'

'Mayhap it will go easier on the morrow.'

'Mayhap,' Mose replied, his voice giving scant assurance that such would be the case.

IN THE MORNING, IT took almost as long to break camp as it had been to make it. Mose fussed over each rope and basket, paying particular attention to Snuff-Pot, who carried a deep graze on his belly. After examining the injury, he gave the signal to continue. 'It was a branch,' he said, 'rather than the basket.'

Boundless judged that the way seemed easier than the previous day. 'Maybe it's easier because of the bright morning,' he told himself. Nevertheless, he breathed a sigh of relief when they left the thickets and returned to the flowing river.

Towards noon, they came upon a wide creek that flowed across the path.

'Keep an eye on the mules,' said Mose.

He nudged the stallion into the creek while leading the bell mare. The mules seemed reluctant to follow. Leaning down, Mose shook the bell where it hung around the neck of the mare. 'Git, ye hell-bound sinners!' He kept shaking the bell while leading the mare further into the stream. When she was up to her hocks, one of the resistant mules lunged forwards into the water. A moment later, its companions followed.

Bringing up the rear, Boundless felt the bay stiffen as the water swirled up around its girth. He lifted his feet in an effort to keep them dry as the stream rose higher. Ahead, Mose had already emerged onto the dusty bank, turning to watch as the mules scrambled from the water.

'The first creek and a triumph! But a few miles further and we are found on the York Road.'

The 'road' turned out to be little more than a narrow track, rutted and pitted with holes, snags and stumps. They had been following it but a short time when, in the distance, they spied an ox cart, proceeding in their direction. A rider on horseback accompanied the cart.

'Hail, friends!' The driver, a freckled-faced youth with red hair and a friendly, eager expression called out from his seat as the parties converged. The cart was heaped with cabbage and broccoli and several large jars of preserved apples.

The boy's older companion dismounted and stretched his legs. 'Thunder, but my shanks be sore!'

'I'll pay you a half-shilling for six of those pretty apples,' Mose offered, peering into the back of the cart.

'Done!' the man said just as the youth appeared about to wave off the money. 'Henry, fetch the gentleman a half-dozen of the cheeriest of the bunch.' He held out his hand as Mose paid the coins.

'How is the road further north?' asked Boundless.

'Rough as blazes,' the man replied. 'Henry—where are those apples?'

'Coming, Pa.' The youth held up the apples to Mose, who took three and indicated that the other three should go to Boundless.

'There's a big hole a half-mile back,' the man said. 'You'll need to skirt it. And there's a section overrun by the creek. We had the devil's own time getting across.'

Mose nodded, chewing vigorously on the apple. 'Fine fruit,' he said. 'How far to York?'

The man removed his hat to consider. 'Two days. More, if them mules get whipperty. I have no fondness for the animal.'

'Did you see any sign of Indians?' asked Boundless.

The man looked surprised at this. 'Indians?' He shook his head. 'The militia shot up a village a year or so back. They haven't been seen since.'

'Good riddance,' said the son as the father nodded in approval.

'Where are you headed, sirs?' the boy asked.

'The French country,' answered Mose.

The youth looked perplexed. 'Where is that?'

'Across the Alleghanies,' said Boundless. 'The border mountains ... Virginia?' he added in response to the youth's befuddled expression.

'They're headed for Virginny, Pa!'

'I have ears, don't I?' The man squinted at Mose. 'That be an arduous ways.'

'I ain't never met anybody travelling to Virginny!'

'Well, now you have. Two gentlemen of fortune who intend to stand on the great western plains before the year is out!'

'I never!' the youth gasped at the notion.

'Well, Baltimore won't wait.' The man poked his son in the ribs. 'You take a turn on the mare.' He held out the reins. 'I bid you good morrow, gentlemen, and Godspeed.'

'Thank you for the apples,' Boundless called out as the wagon lumbered off.

They continued their journey in good spirits, although covering less than eight miles for the day. Several times they were forced to dismount and lead the animals on foot—the road being mired by deep ruts and stumps. Freshets flooded the path at regular intervals, the animals flinging up wet mud as they splashed through the trickling streams. They made camp while it was yet daylight. Confident of the solitude, they slept the night without standing watch.

Next morning, to Boundless' amusement, the mules appeared to recognise their own particular cargo, standing alongside the baskets while patiently awaiting the load to be lifted onto their backs. 'They are smarter than a horse,' said Mose, observing.

During the course of the day, they encountered more farm carts as well as several groups of men riding together for protection. Each encounter entailed a short visit that involved introductions, an exchange of information on the condition of the road surface in either direction, and a short 'sociable' as Mose termed it.

''Tis the colonial parlour,' he said, gesturing to the grey, luminescent sky and bare horizon as they continued. 'What need have we of teacups and fancy lickings?' He kicked the stallion. 'Skit!'

FOUR DAYS AFTER DEPARTING the post, they found themselves on the margin of a road that ran at right angles to their path. The road, heavily scored with wheel tracks and strewn with mulched leaves, stretched for a considerable distance on either side before vanishing into the trees.

'The Wagon Road,' announced Mose with satisfaction. 'It travels all the way south to the Carolinas. York be but three miles distant that way.' He pointed to the left.

'And the other way?'

'Philadelphia. Near on a hundred mile—as a sagacious mare late of your acquaintance could testify. Come.' He led the way onto the rutted, mossy turnpike.

Boundless hesitated, gazing at the path to the right to where it vanished around a bend in the trees. A soberness coloured his thoughts as he considered that, had he discovered the road when lost in the woods he might, even now, be toasting his woodland adventure in the taverns of the city. '*To Philadelphia from York? No more than eight days.*' Fesky's voice sounded in his mind as he gazed at the deserted thoroughfare.

'Are ye coming?'

He turned left onto the forest road, reflecting on fortune. 'We are little more than the sum of our mishaps and mischances,' he decided. 'A false turn here; a delay there. A chance encounter on the street. These things, more than purpose or design, govern our fates. But a year since I would have travelled this road east in homespun and breeches. I now travel it west in buckskin and furs.' For a moment, he fancied he saw his former self plodding along the road to Philadelphia, all unknowing of hides and scrapes and smoked buckskin.

'Skit!' Thrusting aside the notion, he closed the distance on Mose.

THEY FOLLOWED THE ROAD throughout the morning, passing a dozen farm carts and three persons travelling on foot. They were slowed by a swineherd driving a herd of over 500 pigs to market in Lancaster—a pair of dogs nipping at the flanks of the squealing beasts.

Shortly after noon, they came upon a covered wagon pulled by a team of two oxen. The wagon was the largest he had seen, its peculiar, curved shape reminding him of a boat. The sides and rear of the wagon were festooned with chairs and pots and pans. A group of men, women and children walked alongside the slow-moving conveyance. One young woman carried a babe in her arms.

'Good morrow, all!' He raised his hat as he passed, drawing tired stares in return.

Barely had they left the wagon behind than a collection of houses hove into view as they approached the York settlement. 'Thank the day!' He raised himself in the saddle to relieve the soreness in his hips, back, and buttocks.

The settlement consisted of a single through-street flanked by two-dozen wood and stone houses, a log church and a hostelry. A creek ran behind the houses. Several wagons stood alongside the stream as the drivers watered the livestock. The wagons were of the same large type he had passed on the road. Three or four women knelt next to the stream washing clothes. Nearby, a man banged on a detached wagon wheel with a hammer. He heard a shout and turned to see a dozen militiamen practising arms in the grass. Watched by a group of children, they marched and wheeled, shouldering muskets as they did so.

At the Golden Plough tavern, they purchased additional oats for the horses and ale and beefsteak for themselves. He ate hungrily, famished from the long hours in the saddle. As Mose fell into yarning with a grizzled trapper of his acquaintance, he took the opportunity to stretch his legs and explore the settlement. 'We sleep by the hearth this night,' Mose said as he stood up.

Outside, on the dusty street he tipped his hat to a passer-by. Reaching the end of the street, he came upon a grassy commons containing half-a-dozen wagons drawn up for the night. He sat on the grass in the shade of a red oak, his head bare as he enjoyed the late afternoon sun. On the commons, men and women cooked food or tended the stock in preparation for the next day. Looking up at the noise of an approaching conveyance, he recognised the covered wagon they had passed earlier. The wagon lumbered towards the camp site, the oxen looking greatly fatigued, their sides grimy with sweat and dust.

'Heigh-up!' The driver, a florid man in his fifties, halted the conveyance. A young boy leapt forward to unharness the team as the man climbed stiffly down from the seat. 'A glass of ale, Mary, for the love of God!' he called out to someone behind the wagon.

'Good morrow again!' A youth he recognised from the earlier encounter approached where he sat with his back against the oak, 'Greetings, friend. Where are you bound?' He stood up and held out his hand for the other to shake.

The youth pushed his battered, cocked hat back on his head. 'North Carolina. We intend to farm there. And you, sir?' He eyed Boundless curiously. 'From your appearance, I judge you as a trapper or hunter of some kind?'

Boundless smiled, pleased at the impression. 'But a poor specimen of either, I assure you. I am following my companion to Virginia.'

The youth looked surprised. 'Indeed? Then mayhap we shall cross paths again. My family—' He stopped, distracted by a shout from the wagon driver.

'Joseph! D'ye intend gabbing 'til the moon rises?'

'Coming, Pa!' The youth hurried away. 'Godspeed on the morrow!' he called over his shoulder.

They departed early the next morning while mist was still rising from the grass. The occupants of the wagon lay sleeping, a pair of dogs yawning and snuffling alongside them.

FIVE MILES OUTSIDE OF York, they came to a crossroads where several wagons were camped, and Mose called for a halt. A wood signpost, crudely etched with the words *Nichols Gap*, pointed one way, accompanied by an arrow. A second signpost pointed to the *Monocacy Road*. Wagon tracks scored both paths.

'Hold fire,' said Mose. Dismounting, he went to join a group of men gathered in the grass. He spoke to a tall man for a few minutes before returning. 'This way,' he said, remounting, and pointed to the Nichols Gap road.

'Where does the other road lead?' asked Boundless, glancing at the wagon tracks.

'To Big Pipe Creek and the Monocacy River,' said Mose. ''Tis the road I followed up from Winchester. But the wagon master advises we take the gap road as it is less troublesome. Both roads lead to Winchester.'

'How far is that?'

'A hundred miles or so. Git, Jack!'

They forded a creek and rode west twelve miles before coming upon another crossroads, twenty miles from the first. A sign, nailed to a tree, pointed to *Black Gap Road*.

Mose ignored it, following their present route.

As they continued, the small settlements or single farmhouses along the road provided corn, food and, occasionally, a hospitable bed for the night. This latter display of hospitality impressed Boundless as yet more evidence of colonial helpfulness towards strangers. 'Do they not fear for their safety?' he asked Mose.

'Why should they? The guests are but poor, innocent travellers, such as ourselves.'

Passing a solitary farmhouse, Boundless noticed a wooden sign proclaiming *Welcome to the Town of Marsh Creek*. 'A town of one farmhouse,' he noted, amused at the colonial propensity for humour.

After camping for the night beside a hamlet, they continued next day under fair skies, passing several wagons broke down at the side of the road. 'Good morrow to ye,' said Mose, touching his hat brim as they passed.

'Thank God for the mules,' muttered Boundless as he observed the tired and anxious looks on the faces of the travellers.

THE WEATHER REMAINED MOSTLY fine—although a dry, sunny start was no insurance against a heavy shower later in the day. Such cloudbursts were often followed by rushing water further along the road, an association Boundless quickly noted. At places, the road was hemmed in by dense forest—the trees so thickly congested that they were forced to delay making camp until a clearing presented itself. On occasion, they fell in with other travellers and made common camp, taking turns to keep watch.

One afternoon, they camped beside a creek—retiring from the road early to dress a sore on one of the mules. Shortly before midnight, Boundless was awakened by a crashing noise in the undergrowth. The noise was followed by a horrid roaring sound amid panicked screams from the livestock. Snatching a brand from the fire, Mose hurried to investigate, Boundless following closely behind. As they searched the darkness for the mules, the shrill whinnying increased, accompanied by savage growls that set his nerves on edge.

'Bear!'

By the flare of the torch he saw one of the mules thrashing about on the ground, a dark, growling form clutched fast to its throat.

Beside him, Mose cocked the musket and fired. With a roar of pain the wounded bear let go the mule and rushed off into the bushes. The mule lay on its side, the whites of its eyes rolling in shock. Moving the torch, Boundless saw that the entrails had been ripped from the belly. Stooping over the animal, Mose shook his head.

'Hold the torch steady,' he said, his voice grim. He took out a pistol and, extending, his arm discharged the weapon into the brains of the stricken mule. A grunt came from the darkness and Boundless raised the torch. Although they heard the bear, they could not see it and dared not venture after it into the thick woods. Calming the nervous stock, they lit another fire, keeping watch in case the wounded bear returned. Suspicious of every sudden noise, Boundless kept the musket close to hand, getting no further sleep that night.

In the light of morning, the full extent of the carnage was revealed. The mule's belly and flanks had been torn asunder, the bloody entrails strewn about the grass. 'It is William, as I feared,' said Mose, his voice heavy as he knelt to study the animal. He laid a tender hand on the dead mule's flank. 'By gar, but he was a prince among mule folk. I had him for nigh on ten year. A loyal, if contrary, companion.'

When Mose stood up, he cast a baleful eye on the remaining mules, where they stood alongside the mare. 'Well may ye stutter, ye misbegotten apes! Your companion and better fellow lies here slaughtered and still ye nick and fuss. By God if I don't hand feed you to the next bear that happens along! We will need to apportion the weight.' He grunted with displeasure. 'We shall be exceedingly fortunate not to lose another afore the plains.'

SIX DAYS AFTER LEAVING York, they arrived at the Patowmack River, exiting the woods to see a small stone tavern situated on the banks of the broad stream. A group of men and women were congregated around a line of covered wagons. Out on the water a large, flat-bottomed ferry was crossing the 250-yard-wide river.

Mose halted to survey the scene. 'On the far side be Virginia.' Nudging the stallion, he started forwards, visibly pleased at their progress. '*There was a ship that sailed all on the lowland sea!* Come good Jack, the chorus! *And sink her in the lowland sea!*'

As they rode up to the landing, the men stationed there turned to observe, several raising their hats in greeting.

'Good morrow, friends.' A tall, lean man in a black frockcoat walked up as they dismounted. 'You may have to spend some time on this bank awaiting your turn.' He indicated the line of waiting wagons. 'The boat can carry no more than two conveyances at a time.'

Boundless shook the man's hand. 'Where are you bound for?'

'The Valley of the Shando. There be rich farmland remaining for those willing to claim it.' The man gestured at the waiting families. 'Each of us has hopes of securing a favourable plot. And yourself, sir?'

'Virginia and, from thence, across the mountains,' he answered, feeling somewhat self-conscious at the declaration.

'*Across* the mountains?' The man's face showed surprise at the answer.

'How much is the passage?' asked Mose, indicating the ferry.

'Threepence each, for man and beast, and another sixpence for a wagon.'

'Two shillings threepence, then,' said Mose, frowning at the cost.

'It seems as though half the world is bound along the same road,' remarked Boundless.

The man smiled. 'Penn is getting crowded, and Virginia and Georgia lie half-empty to the south. Three shillings will buy you an acre of farmland in Pennsylvania. The same amount will buy you sixty acres in the Carolinas.'

The man turned as a shout from his companions alerted him to the returning ferry. 'I wish you Godspeed,' he said, re-joining his party.

Boundless wandered up and down the bank as the ferry carried various parties across the river. He saw several more wagons emerge from the woods. each one weighed down with supplies, their axles creaking as they approached.

When their turn arrived, Mose led the chestnut onto the wooden deck. The mare followed, closely trailed by the mules. Boundless and the bay brought up the rear. He herded the animals to one corner of the deck as Mose spoke to the ferryman and paid for the crossing. A family of Moravians introduced themselves as they waited for the ferry to depart.

The ferry cast off from the bank. To his surprise, the polers considered it sufficient to merely launch the ferry into the main channel. From thence they relied on the current to float them to the opposite shore at a point downstream from their departure.

'It be hit and miss, but mostly miss,' laughed one of the polers when asked about the practice.

'And how do you return?'

'The opposite method. We pole back to this side. Then we tow her back up again to where you boarded. We hope, one day, to lay a rope across,' added the man.

Boundless lounged against the wagon, enjoying the brief respite from the saddle. As he gazed at the sunlight on the water, his thoughts drifted back to the Patapsco and the long, idle days putting in at tobacco wharves along that river. A sense of unreality affected him as the two rivers, past and present, flowed into one in the glittering sunlight. He turned to check the horses, half expecting to see Humpflinger grin back at him.

'Virginia!'

He came to with a start, having dozed off. A deckhand threw a rope to a man stationed on shore as the boat bumped up against the bank. 'Let the wagon proceed first!'

Setting off again, they passed by the settler wagons where they were drawn up in a line alongside the road next to a hamlet of several houses and workshops. 'They will wait until they've assembled some twenty or more wagons before proceeding,' said Mose. 'A precaution against Indian attack and also to lend extra hands to clear the road.'

'Would it not be wise to travel with them?'

'Pshaw! And make five mile a day?'

Boundless touched his hat as the man he had spoken to earlier came up to watch them depart.

'God preserve you!' The man raised his hat in the air.

Several small boys followed alongside as they rode—running ahead and whooping to each other.

'Godspeed!' a boy shouted and held up a hand in farewell.

The road re-entered the woods as they left the Patowmack behind. The trail was narrow and mossy and hands had clearly been at work cutting down trees and broadening the way to allow passage for carts or wagons. In several places, the path rose steeply, forcing them to dismount and lead the animals on foot. He marvelled at the thought of the wagons negotiating the same passage.

Descending a twisting defile, they arrived at the banks of a fast-flowing creek cutting across the path. Mose pondered for a moment, studying the flow and trying to ascertain the depth before entering the stream.

'Perhaps we should look for a crossing,' Boundless suggested, not liking the look of the turbulent water.

'Jinks! It ain't but a pond. Hi-yup!' Grasping the tow, Mose nudged the stallion forward into the water. The mare resisted before following, clearly unhappy as she tugged back at the rope. The mules showed no such reluctance, splashing behind each other as they followed. The water rose up to lap around the wicker baskets.

As his turn came, Boundless urged his mount into the stream as the cold water drenched his buckskin leggings. 'Skit!' To his pleasure, the bay showed not the least reluctance to enter the water.

Once safely across, he dismounted to join Mose in inspecting the provisions. 'The blankets are soaked, and so are the corn and beans,' he said, dismay in his voice.

'I expect they'll stay wet half the journey,' answered Mose, his voice bland.

They continued along the road, passing a train of six wagons whose quaintly dressed occupants called out to them in German as they passed.

'Mennonites,' said Mose. '*Viel Glück!*' he called in return, the salutation bringing smiles and similar hails in reply. On several occasions, they stopped and moved aside to allow passage to herds of cattle and pigs bound in the opposite direction.

'I never saw so many pigs at one time,' said Boundless as a large herd of several thousand pigs squealed past, accompanied by several swineherds on foot and a man on horseback. The herd was followed by several wagons, two dray carts and a line of pack horses, the drivers unable to pass the pigs on the narrow path.

'The road is remarkably well-travelled,' he said as they waited for the wagons to go by.

Mose nodded. 'The first time I travelled it there was nary a soul for days on end. And scarcely a farmhouse to be seen.'

'I had quite forgot you had travelled it before.'

In the late afternoon, they stopped at a farm to purchase corn, eggs, flour and two loaves of bread. The German farmer, who spoke passable English, stubbornly refused the offer of a buckskin in exchange for the provisions. A clearly reluctant Mose handed over a handful of copper coins.

'Such clearly outweighs the value of the goods,' he argued, seeking a smoked ham hock and an additional bushel of corn as make-weight. Unable to sway the obdurate German, Mose surprised Boundless by handing over still more coins for a supper of pork, potatoes, sugar peas and cucumber, which they ate with relish. Following supper, the farmer offered them shelter for the night, pointing to the hearth and barring the door behind him as he bid them '*Gute Nacht*'.

THE NEXT MORNING, THEY came upon a wagon stopped by the side of the road as three men repaired a broken axle. A sweating man wearing a shirt with rolled-up sleeves came forward to greet them.

'Beware,' he said, following introductions. 'We have it on the authority of a wounded man that cut-throats infest the road up ahead. The devils lie in wait for innocent travellers to prey upon and murder.'

'See to your weapon,' advised Mose as the two continued after a further exchange of news. 'If we be accosted, look to your right and rear as I shall look to the front.'

Boundless loaded the pistol, holding it in readiness across his lap as they continued.

The rutted track was littered with roots and trunks cut by previous travellers. 'It is a good place for an ambush,' he thought, nervously eyeing the road ahead where it passed within yards of the surrounding trees. The same thought had occurred to Mose, who turned and beckoned Boundless to join him.

'Close the distance. Keep tight,' Mose warned. 'If challenged, be prepared to flee.'

They continued in a state of high vigilance. As they rounded a bend, they came upon a man standing beside a horse. Immediately on seeing them, the man bent and lifted a hoof as though inspecting the animal for injury.

'Stand ready!' Mose set the pistol to full-cock as Boundless followed suit, his mouth suddenly dry.

'Good morrow, friends!' The man straightened as they approached, his manner cheery. 'Mayhap you could assist an honest traveller with a small repair. She buckled a shoe and I must needs remove it.' The man wore a tattered riding coat and cocked hat. The coat was unbuttoned to the waist and his hand rested in his pocket.

Mose reined to a halt. 'You are on your own?' he asked, eyes searching the nearby woods.

'As you see, friend, as you see,' the man said disarmingly. 'Why, they be fine mules. Where be you bound?'

Boundless heard a branch snap behind him even as Mose shouted a warning. The man before them brought out a weapon concealed within his coat. 'Boys!' he shouted.

Next moment the crack of Mose's pistol shattered the silence. The man gave a gargled curse and sank to his knees, blood staining the front of his shirt.

Boundless glimpsed three or four men hurrying through the bushes towards them, muskets in hand. Raising the pistol, he fired. He heard a cry and then a loud retort followed by a puff of white smoke.

'Flee!' Mose whipped the stallion forward.

Another gunshot sounded from behind as Boundless spurred the bay, bent low in the saddle. He heard shouts and a musket ball whizzed over his head. He whipped the horse for several hundred yards, overtaking the mules as he galloped to where Mose had drawn rein. Mose raised himself in the stirrups to scan the road behind them.

'The murderous devils!' The trapper's face was thunderous as he looked back at the frustrated attackers—now safely to their rear. 'I've a half-mind to go back and finish the business!'

Panting, Mose sat back in the saddle. 'The livestock is sound, as are you. Thank God!' He set off again, casting a glance behind. 'They rob and murder innocent folk as they please. Hanging is too good for such as they!'

'That one you struck will not rob again, I fear.'

'Good riddance! Come, let us proceed. Who knows but they have confederates nearby.'

They continued, casting frequent glances backwards. A mile further on, they encountered a convoy of wagons proceeding in the opposite direction. They stopped to confer with the drivers, warning them of the danger ahead. Immediately, seven or eight men, armed with muskets, set off in advance of the wagons with loud promises and threats to 'despatch' the cut-throats if found.

Reassured by this intervention, they continued on their way. Now that the threat had passed, Boundless found time to gauge his own, delayed shock at the incident. 'Yet my hand is steady,' he observed, pleased with the fact. His heart no longer pounded in his chest and his breathing was regular.

'We gave them stiff medicine!' he called out to Mose, who raised a hand in acknowledgement.

They made camp that night in the company of a caravan of wagons, retelling the incident over and over as the alarmed settlers plied them with food and questions.

'Praise be to God that you are safe!' a woman exclaimed while offering tea. 'Surely, Brother Edgar,' she said, turning to address a white-haired elder, 'this be proof of a merciful Providence!'

29

The Shenandoah

THE INCIDENT WAS SLOWLY forgotten as they continued in a south-westerly direction under sunny skies and mild breezes. They shared the road with numerous wagons, drays, carts, and riders on horseback, as well as swineherds and shepherds driving flocks to market. They were forced to ride behind a line of wagons proceeding in the same direction. Several times Mose signalled a halt to increase the distance in an attempt to avoid the mud and dust thrown up by the wheels. ''Tis well named the Wagon Road,' he grumbled.

Families walked alongside the conveyances, the wagons crammed with furniture and household goods. Pots, pans and sundry other items were tied to the frames, the objects bouncing and rattling to the motion of the wheels. Many of the wagons had a cow, goat or flock of sheep in tow, the animals adding to the slow progress of the convoy.

'Hi-yup! Hurry the mules!' Mose kicked the stallion forward as they took advantage of a rare opportunity to overtake the cumbersome wagons. 'Thank the stars we are past!' He ejected a mouthful of spit into the grass.

In addition to being held up by migrant caravans headed south, they were several times forced to yield passage to considerable herds of hogs, horses or cattle being driven north to York and Lancaster. The clouds of dust raised by the animals hung in the air for minutes afterwards, forcing them to pull their neckerchiefs up over their nose and mouth.

They gave similar right-of-way to convoys of carts loaded with agricultural produce headed to the same northern markets. The carts were oftentimes so freighted with grain or vegetables that the team of oxen struggled to pull the load. Smaller dray carts carried cargoes of fruit or chickens or greens, the overloaded conveyances leaving a trail of cabbages or carrots along the road.

They started out early the next morning in order to avoid the 'pestiferous wagons' that held up progress. At the early hour, the road was almost deserted, although they encountered several farm carts and a flock of sheep being shepherded towards York. The morning was warm and the mules in good fettle as they proceeded, both companions enjoying the open road.

Boundless was trailing the mules when he saw Mose rein to a halt on top of a rise. His companion sat there until Boundless joined him.

'The Valley Pike,' said Mose. Ahead, the road descended into a spacious landscape of meadows, pastures, woods and creeks. Mountainous hills flanked the verdant prospect to both the east and west. Mose pointed to where the sun glistened on a winding river in the distance. 'The Shenandoah.'

'*Shenandoah*.' Boundless repeated the word, enjoying the fertile roll of the vowels across the tongue. 'This is unparalleled country, Mose.' He twisted in the saddle to better survey the diverse riches of the landscape, speculating whether they might not, with sufficient cultivation, feed the entire thirteen colonies and more besides. 'Small wonder that settlers should flock here.'

Mose gestured to the east and a line of pine-clad hills, still wrapped in haze in the mid-morning sunlight. 'They be the Blue Ridge Mountains. And those peaks …' he gestured to the west, 'be the Alleghenies.'

'The ones we must cross to reach the plains?'

'Aye. They be higher further south.'

'And this road will take us to your famous notch?'

Mose nodded, seemingly lost in contemplation of the view.

'How far does it go?'

'All the way down to the James River, and from thence to the Carolinas and points beyond. I first travelled up this valley from the Fluvannah country over thirty year ago—a puff-cheeked lad bent on seeing the world.' He gave a heavy sigh. 'I see myself as a boy astride a testy mare—what was her name? Brown Nancy! She kicked and bucked all the way to Pennsylvanny. I near cracked my neck a dozen times.'

'Did you come alone?' he asked, impressed anew at his companion's early independence.

'Pshaw! The Indians would have had my scalp for certain! I rode with Jim Clarkson and his two brothers, along with two or three others whose faces I see, but whose names I cannot now recall.' He gazed at the shining prospect as if witnessing the young boy venturing out into the world. Tears gleamed in his eyes. 'Lord, in Thy Providence.'

Boundless nudged the bay forward. 'Shall we continue?'

'Aye. Winchester is not far. We can eat and rest there.'

As they followed the road into the bounteous valley, it seemed to Boundless that in richness and beauty it far surpassed any that he had encountered previously, in either the old world or the new.

'*The land, once brought properly under the till, will furnish sufficient for the wants of all of Europe.*' The words came back to him as he gazed around at the lush, rolling pastures and abundant creeks. 'It is as pleasing to the eye as it is promising to the belly,' he told himself.

The road led past a tidy house set amidst a grove of chestnuts. His gaze rested on a woman as she hung washing from a line stretched between the trees. His thoughts wandered back to the young woman on the Patapsco and her graceful, bent posture as she ascended the steep track to her home on the crest. He fancied her riding alongside him, catching her breath at the sunlit landscape. The conceit brought a lump to his throat and a feeling of melancholy that lingered throughout the morning.

The valley was populated by farmhouses, taverns, houses, barns and trade shops of every description. Signs advertised bricklayers, cabinetmakers, weavers, rope-makers, carpenters, and auctioneers. They passed a wood mill, a school, and several churches. Oftentimes the inhabitants ventured out as they approached to give greeting, enquire about news along the road or, occasionally, to offer apples or fresh-baked bread for sale.

'I see that commerce flourishes despite the war,' observed Boundless as they pulled aside to give passage to yet another drove of hogs. The hogs were accompanied by three drovers on foot, two of them Blacks.

'How far to Winchester?' Mose called out as the men came close. The two Blacks ignored him, but the third man, perspiring heavily, his clothes caked with mud and dust, stopped.

'Winchester?' He took off his straw hat to think. 'No more than two mile.' He hawked noisily. 'Durn mud! How is the road ahead?'

'Passable, friend. Especially with that multitude breaking the trail.'

Not long after, Mose gestured to where a log bastion loomed over the road a short distance ahead. 'What is that building?' he asked a man proceeding on foot and carrying a live chicken over his shoulder.

'That?' The fellow shifted the chicken from one shoulder to the other. 'Quit it Henrietta!' He shook the squawking fowl by the feet. 'That,' he resumed, 'be Fort Loudon, home of the Virginia regiment.'

'I wonder why he doesn't kill that chicken,' grunted Mose as they continued.

'Mayhap he likes the company and enjoys the squawks.'

Mose frowned. 'Then he be as dull as the chicken.'

THEY FOUND THE APPROACHES to the fort crowded with carts and wagons, the conveyances so numerous they threatened to block the road. Horses and oxen grazed on a wide commons. Women cooked over open fires alongside unyoked wagons while children played in the grass.

'What the deuce is this?' exclaimed Mose, frowning as he looked around. He hailed a passer-by. 'What in tar is going on?'

'You haven't heard?' The man looked surprised. 'The French have stirred up the tribes along the length and breadth of the valley. 'Tis said no house or farm is safe from the devils. Most of these you see here be settlers displaced from their homes. Others wait to journey south but will not dare do so until they are strong enough to withstand the Shawnee.'

'It is that bad?' asked an alarmed Boundless.

'Worse. The Indians run amok scalping and murdering all they can find. We are none of us safe in our beds so long as the war lasts.'

They continued towards the fort, mustering the livestock to prevent them straying amidst the wagons and livestock jostling for room along the street. The open grass adjacent to the fort was occupied by dozens of wagons and carts. Picking their way through the congestion, they found a space where they picketed the mules. In the grass, a group of boys mock-marched up and down with wood pickets for muskets.

'You there!' Mose summoned two of them over. 'Look after the mules and our provisions for an hour or so and I shall pay you two pennies each.'

'Sixpence! Each!'

Mose turned to Boundless, an astonished look on his face. 'By the bones, did you ever meet such shameless whelps?'

With a frown and shake of his head, Mose reluctantly agreed to the price. 'And not a single item of stock to be touched,' he warned. 'It all be counted!'

Remounting, the companions headed for the fort, Mose grumbling about 'milk-tooth thieves, and teat-pirates'. Riding past the redcoats stationed at the gate, they found themselves inside a large square lined with barracks, quarters, barns and workshops.

Immediately on dismounting, they were surrounded by a throng of men shouting for news.

'There is none,' said Mose, testy at the hollered questions. 'We came down from the north. Now make way!'

'Pennsylvania? Well, what in blazes is happening there?' demanded a stout man wearing a stained felt hat.

'There be no Indian attacks?' called out another man, incredulity in his voice.

'Make way!' ordered a testy Mose, pushing his way through.

LEAVING THE DISPUTATIOUS CROWD behind they went in search of a tavern. 'Three shillings!' Mose stared, aghast at a board announcing a 'special' of peppered pork and roasted chicken.

'It be daylight robbery!' he declared. 'The scoundrels take advantage of the misfortune of others.' Still protesting, he pushed open the door and entered the tavern.

As they waited for the food, Boundless paid scant attention to his companion's irascible tirade about 'filches and grope-pockets', his thoughts returning again and again to the conversation with the townsman. '*The Indians run amok, scalping and murdering!*'

'What?' He realised Mose had asked him a question.

'D'y e not think the cost a great scandal?'

'Perish the cost! We have greater matters to concern us. 'Tis foolhardy to ride alone into so much danger as awaits. Let us at least wait for a wagon party to form. We can ride with them for safety.'

Mose's face crinkled with displeasure. 'Did you not hear the fellow say a company of militia has been despatched to defend the farms?'

'Yes, as I heard also that the Indians raid up and down the valley. Two travellers alone would be a tempting prize. Besides, what harm to ride with a wagon party?'

Wagons! We would do nought but fix wheels every half-a-mile.'

'I have no wish to lose my hair.'

'Fie! But a few days to rest the stock and the town will be telling a different tale—of the Indians bloodied and the settlers returning home. See for yourself if I do not speak the truth. Come. Try the fowl.'

Boundless ate in irritable silence, half-minded to abandon the reckless venture altogether. *His foolhardiness will get us scalped!*

Back at the fort, they purchased corn from the suttler and replenished their supply of beans, sugar, tea, and flour.

They paused to watch a company of militia practise drills under the critical eye of a drill sergeant.

'Shoulder arms! Slope arms! Support arms!'

The volunteers proved hopelessly inept, tripping each other in the drill and mixing up the manoeuvres to shouts and curses from the exasperated sergeant.

A fife and drum sounded as a youthful-looking officer dressed in a blue cape and mounted on a white charger entered the gates followed by a column of soldiers on foot. A group of thirty or forty Indians followed the soldiers into the fort. The Indians were clad in breechclouts, their hair tonsured into distinctive quips at the neck.

'Who is that man?' Boundless asked a soldier making his way past.

'Why, that be Colonel Washington. Our commanding officer.'

'And the Indians?'

'Cherokee. They are sided with us, as the Shawnee the French.'

He was still looking at the Indians when Mose turned away. 'Let us return to the camp, 'ere they seek to enlist us.'

FOR SEVERAL DAYS THEY rested under the protective guns of the fort. Boundless took advantage of the respite to record their progress in the log. Sitting against a tree, he penned a brief summary of their journey since leaving York, mentioning the bear attack as well as the encounter with bandits. In the square box set aside for astronomical observations, he noted the weather and the condition of the road. Under the subheading *Progress* he wrote: *10 miles per day.* Thinking back to the congested road since entering the Pike, he put a line through the notation and wrote instead, *avg. 8 miles per day.*

The next day brought fresh alarm as an influx of settlers fleeing the Indians, brought news of bloody raids further south. Tales spread of massacres and dreadful atrocities in the backcountry. The distressed refugees reported that a large force of French troops accompanied by Shawnee allies were laying waste to farms and settlements north of the James River. In response, a company of one hundred soldiers, along with militia and Cherokee reinforcements, was hastily despatched to the sound of fifes and drums.

'Go get 'em, boys!' rang out the cheers and shouts as the local populace gathered to farewell the troops.

'We should travel with them,' Boundless urged Mose, 'for protection.'

'And be drawn into the fighting? We be best to rest a further day. Let the soldier boys clear the road ahead.'

That evening, Boundless wandered among the wagons and the men and women gathered around the campfires. He stopped at several of the fires, squatting to exchange news with the displaced settlers and listening to their stories of Indian predations further south. Most of the informants had fled towns and farms in terror of the Indian raids, and told harrowing tales of murder, torture and kidnappings. 'None be safe!' a woman cried, her features distorted with fear.

'The devils attack in broad daylight and vanish as soon as their blood lust is slaked,' said her husband. 'The militia and the soldiers are hopeless to prevent them or to recover those poor souls taken hostage.'

'Aye. To be tortured with fire and murdered most horribly,' agreed another man.

He reported the conversations to Mose, adding that the refugees still looked frightened to death even in proximity to the fort. 'So terrified that they still insist on mounting guard,' he added, 'in spite of the soldiers.'

Mose added a stick to the fire. 'The Indians be inside their heads,' he said. 'I have seen it before. Get some sleep. We leave at dawn tomorrow.'

Boundless stared. 'You are not the least concerned by what I have just told you?'

'I am more concerned lest the horses, or a mule, break a leg. Good night!'

Boundless laid his head down on a saddle and drew up the blanket, mentally shaking his head at such an obdurate companion. *He will deny any danger until the savages be at our throats.*

The next morning, they rode past the fort while the sun was still rising.

'Keep a sharp eye!' a sentry warned, the words hanging in the air behind them.

30

The Valley Pike

Talk of slaughter and bloodthirsty savages seemed incongruous amidst the beauty of the landscape as they continued under a warm and sunny sky, their contentment spoiled only by numerous clouds of gnats. The mules were fractious after the lay-over, the latest addition, Prodigal, lunging to bite the one in front.

'Step nicely!' Mose leaned in the saddle and grasped the mule by the rigging strap as the lead mule kicked out in reprisal. 'That one will be a trial,' he muttered, letting go the strap.

The road was still populated with wagons, although not nearly so many as before. They sometimes had the road to themselves for a mile or so before encountering another conveyance. The houses and farms, too, became less numerous. Fording a creek, they passed a heavily fortified blockhouse.

'The settlers gather there for protection from the Shawnee,' remarked Mose.

As they proceeded, Boundless cast frequent admiring glances at the rolling peaks to the west. The tallest of them he supposed to lie somewhat below the highest peaks of his native Scotland. *Indeed, they might pass as the Highlands,* he considered, struck by the association. *Mayhap it is the fancy that finds relation between disparate things.* On reflection he dismissed the notion. *Surely, a Chinaman or even a savage, miraculously conveyed between Scotland and these same mountains would observe the likeness? If so, then it must follow that things similar in themselves proceed from like causes.*

Absorbed in the speculation, he almost bumped into Mose as the latter reined to a halt outside a small farmhouse set a few hundred yards back from the road.

'Let us stop and water the stock,' said Mose. 'And mayhap bargain for a plate of food.' As they approached, the door opened and a man stepped out, holding a musket. Behind him, they glimpsed a small boy holding an even smaller girl by the hand.

'We be peaceable travellers,' Mose called out, 'wishing only to pay our respects.'

The man placed the stock of the musket on the ground. 'Then ye be welcome to water.' He nodded towards a well. 'Aye, and a bowl of stew, if it pleases ye. A shilling apiece with bread and pudding thrown in.' He spoke with a strong brogue, his features relaxing as he assessed their intentions.

'I thank ye kindly, friend.' Mose climbed down heavily from the horse. 'It pays to be vigilant,' he added, nodding at the gun slits set into the timber walls.

'The savages come calling from time to time,' said the man, spitting into the grass. 'I must have the boy sleep with the horses in the barn to prevent the thieving Canaanites from running off the stock.'

After eating, and a pipe for Mose, they resumed the journey, farewelling their host as he stood at the door to watch them leave, pipe in hand.

'A prickly sort on his best day, I'll be bound, in spite of his goodly stew,' remarked Boundless as they left the habitation behind.

'He must be on constant guard. The Shawnee resent the settlers worse than they detest spoiled meat.'

'Surely, by staying he puts the lives of his children at risk?'

'These Scotch-Irish be as stubborn as yonder mules. He will not give up his patch of land while the breath remains in his body.'

THE ROAD GREW PROGRESSIVELY rougher as they continued south. At places it was no more than a path three or four feet across, hemmed by thick bushes and growths of oak and chestnut. At others, it rose and fell through bluffs and gullies, sometimes twisting back on itself to avoid a prominent rise or drop. On occasion, it briefly split into two, one path evidently cut for wagons, the other for pack horses. As they proceeded up a steep defile, Boundless marvelled anew at how the large wagons they had passed along the way could navigate such a wilderness. 'Surely, they were better to abandon the wagons for pack trains?' he reasoned.

As if to confirm his doubts, they scrambled up a gorge to come upon a wagon blocking the road. Ahead of it, two other wagons were halted before a large tree fallen across the path. A group of men and women turned to look as they rode up.

'Good morrow friends!' Drawing rein, Mose dismounted, motioning for Boundless to do the same.

Making their way forward to investigate, they came upon half-a-dozen men hacking at the fallen tree with axes. 'It has held us up all morning,' complained a sweating man as they joined the group.

'There is no way around, even for the mules,' said Mose. 'We had best fetch the axes and help.'

Taking turns, the work party attacked the formidable trunk in an attempt to cut it into smaller sections. The day was hot and, after toiling for two hours, they stopped for refreshments, the women bringing salted pork and bread, which the men ate while sitting on the log.

Boundless found himself next to a sanguine German who munched slowly and deliberately, pausing to frown and nod at each question so that he was unsure whether the man understood him or was merely being polite.

A broad-shouldered man wiped his mouth and stood up. 'Let us finish the task, boys.'

'Were you travelling together?' Boundless asked, as he stood atop the log alongside the German.

'Who was?' The man took off his hat to slick back his hair.

'Pardon. I meant were you—the three wagons—travelling together?'

'No. 'Tis the log made us friends.'

They drove deep notches into the trunk, the wood proving surprisingly hard. As he paused for breath, Boundless overheard Mose ask a man about 'the Alleghany Fork'. He posed the same question to his workmate, adding that the putative road led to a pass over the mountains.

'A pass?' The man muttered and shook his head.

IT WAS LATE AFTERNOON before the road was cleared. Exhausted by the effort, the men shook hands and returned to the wagons. The women exchanged fond farewells, expressing the hope that they would 'companion' each other further down the road.

Boundless and Mose were forced to follow the wagons for the better part of an hour until the road widened sufficiently for them to ride around the slow-moving conveyances. Bidding their erstwhile companions farewell, they took their leave.

'Good luck finding that road of yours!' his workmate called out.

'He was no help, then?'

'No. He could not conceive of such a road.'

'No more than the two I asked. We may have to find it on our own.'

The casual declaration, following the hours of strenuous labour, did little to dispel Boundless' growing doubts over the venture and, indeed, to the existence of the pass. He felt a soreness in his shoulder and winced. 'I hope we encounter no more such logs,' he said, rubbing the muscle.

They passed the night at a tavern in company with a handful of other weary travellers. After eating, they sat for an hour listening to rumours and counter-rumours. In one version, the Shawnee were 'whipped' and running for the hills; in another they were advancing up the valley and might fall upon the tavern at any moment.

At length, Mose shook his head and got up to retire for the night, his expression indicating his impatience at the conflicting reports. 'Wake me if the Shawnee should pay a visit.'

FORTY-FIVE MILES SOUTH OF Winchester, they caught up with a solitary wagon proceeding in the same direction. The north fork of the Shenandoah was figured to be a mile ahead, and they rode alongside for a while, Boundless expressing his surprise to the driver at his unaccompanied journey. 'We heard repeatedly of Indian trouble ahead.'

'The hell with the Indians!' snapped the driver, a taciturn young man with several razor cuts on his face.

Beside him, his nervous wife put a hand to her mouth. 'Heaven preserve us!' A small boy peered out from among the bric-a-brac stuffed into the wagon.

Mose cast impatient looks, anxious to ride on. Boundless was about to knee the horse into a trot when the ford came into view. It had rained hard overnight and the crossing, although not overwide, was swollen, the water lapping up to where they stood.

'Ahoy travellers!'

As if sent by Providence, two men rounded a bend in the stream, poling a flatboat.

'They have a ferry!'

'Bother the ferry.' Mose urged the chestnut a few steps into the water. 'It is but a puddle,' he said. 'Why d'ye hesitate?'

Boundless frowned 'Why wet the supplies when we can arrive on the other side safe and dry? I am resolved to take the boat.' Grumbling in protest, Mose called out to the boatmen as they manoeuvred the vessel up onto the bank. 'How much?'

'Four shilling for yourself and the stock. And the same again for the wagon.'

'Four shillings? I had rather take my chances swimming!'

'Then do so. And you, friend?' The boatman turned to the wagon driver.

'How far across is it?'

'Nigh on eight hundred yards.'

'Pshaw!' Mose pointed an accusing finger. 'Five hundred! And a shilling!'

'Three shillings and sixpence. This be the last ferry, I warrant, until ye reach the Carolinas. The Shawnee have driven off all the boats below New Market.'

Boundless removed his hat. 'Did you hear plain enough? The last one, Mose. We shall have ample opportunity to swim.'

Ten minutes later they were on board, alongside the wagon. As the boatmen poled them across, the older of the two complained about Indian activity south of the river.

'Murdering heathen!' He spat into the water. 'They slaughtered a party of innocent travellers not two weeks since. Scotch-Irish from Pennsylvania. All eight of the family horribly scalped and left for the buzzards to feast on.' He became agitated at the memory, volubly denouncing the 'skulking murderers' responsible. So dire were his accounts of the massacre that the woman in the wagon refused to leave the ferry, in spite of the expostulations of her angry husband.

'Boots and all, Hannah! They will be clear back to the mountains by now. I ain't turning back for toffee!'

'We shall be scalped and murdered—like that poor family!' His frightened wife clutched the small boy to her skirts and adamantly refused to leave the ferry. 'We must wait for more wagons to join us or turn back.'

'I shall have to pay the passage twice over!' the husband argued before finally giving in to her demands. 'Have it your way, woman,' he said with bad grace. 'But don't blame me if all the best land is gobbled up afore we arrive!'

Boundless and Mose lingered on the bank watching as the ferry crossed back over the river with the distressed woman on board. Boundless looked at Mose. 'I suppose you are adamant not to follow that wise lady's counsel?'

'If the report even be true. Each rumour gives birth to a thousand offspring, each more terrible than the last. Hi-up, Jack!'

They spent the night in a small settlement seven miles south of the crossing. Five wagons were drawn up close to the houses, the travellers reluctant to venture further on their own.

'We be too fearful,' admitted one wagon driver, when questioned by Mose. 'They say a party of Rangers are headed this way. If so, we will await their arrival before proceeding farther.'

'What news?' asked Boundless, remembering the warnings of the ferry man.

The wagon driver looked glum at the question. 'Some, and all of it bad. Not five miles south of here, a farmhouse was attacked and the occupants badly frightened. They drove off the Indians, but not without some injury to themselves. But ask for yourself. They be resting here now.' He nodded to a nearby wagon. 'Too fearful to go back to their home—and who can blame them?'

'Did you hear of a party of travellers—Scotch-Irish, ambushed and murdered on the road?'

'You say!' The man's eyes bulged from his head. 'Hark!' he called out to a group conversing nearby. 'More butchery!'

The following day, they set out again after breakfast. Shortly after noon, they came upon the burned-out farmhouse mentioned by the wagon driver, the charred timbers offering stark testimony to the violent assault. Boundless stared uneasily at the blackened ruins as he passed. *This is madness! We are riding straight towards the war.*

The country was now exceedingly wild, the path obstructed by thick mud and potholes, or entirely washed away by rain. They saw plentiful evidence of obstacles removed by previous travellers including a giant, partly burnt stump by the side of the road.

'They set fire to it to make it easier to chop,' said Mose.

The occasional inn or farmhouse provided hot food and a bed for the night, each stop providing more alarms about French and Indian depredations with constant warnings to stay vigilant. They passed two blockhouses and encountered several more burned-out farms and homes. They took turns to stand guard at night and, wherever possible, bedded down with the few other travellers on the road.

In the log, Boundless noted that they covered between eight and ten miles a day, stopping every two hours to graze and water the stock.

One morning, they forded a swift-running creek, swimming the horses and mules across while they clung to the stirrups. On the other side they made camp, spreading out the supplies to dry in the hot sun. Mose watched approvingly as Prodigal shook the water from his coat. 'William would have given him a kick or two—as a sign of respect. But by jinks if he don't carry better than the other three put together.'

In the afternoon, they stopped to converse with a packtrain headed north.

'Staunton lies up ahead,' the pack master informed them. 'It holds the last reliable tavern afore North Carolina.'

'I do not recall the town,' said Mose as they continued. 'It must have sprung up since I came this way.'

The remark stayed with Boundless as he pondered a country so new that persons had more lineage than towns.

The Staunton hamlet consisted of a row of houses, one store, and a tavern. They stopped at the latter to eat their evening meal, Mose taking the opportunity to refill the canteens with whisky and beer. After sleeping beside the large hearth, they ate a hearty breakfast of pork, eggs and cornbread the next morning.

'How is the road south of here?' asked Mose of another guest who claimed to have ridden up from the James River.

'Road?' guffawed the man. 'It ain't!'

Boundless recalled the man's laughter as they proceeded. 'Indeed, the fellow was right,' he reflected as the dusty track they had been following all but disappeared amidst a tangle of grass, trees, bluffs and defiles. At times, the path was so choked with brush that he had to stop and search for the passage.

'This way!' Mose rode blithely past, his nonchalant ease at detecting the trail exasperating Boundless.

Fifteen miles from Staunton, they made rendezvous with a party of horsemen banded together for protection and headed north. They held a brief colloquy, conducted from the saddle, to learn that they were 'within fifty miles of the James'.

'Be vigilant,' a portly man with a bulbous nose warned. 'We saw plenty of Indian sign on both sides of the river.'

The sky grew overcast, a cool breeze hinting at rain as they continued. They forded several freshets, Boundless now resigned to permanently wet shoes and leggings. Unwilling to risk running into Indians, they made early camp within the security of a brushworks rampart thrown up by previous travellers. On his watch, Boundless thought his ears detected the faint sound of gunshots. He listened intently but could not hear them again.

Mentioning the fact to Mose next morning, he drew a snort in response.

'You don't think it dangerous to continue?' he insisted, annoyed by his companion's summary dismissal of every sign of danger.

'Who's to say it wasn't the militia driving them off? Let's make a fire and put on some coffee. I doubt the Indians will offer us a cup.'

31

A Deadly Encounter

THEY HAD NOT LONG broken camp when they sighted smoke in the distance. Arming themselves with the muskets, they proceeded cautiously. Emerging from a grove of trees, they saw where the smoke issued from a smouldering farmhouse. An agitated group of heavily armed men stood in the road arguing with one another. The men looked up at their approach.

'Hail, friends,' said Mose, drawing rein. 'What be the ruckus?'

'Indians!' said one, gesturing to the smouldering logs.

'And French!' said another man, spitting in disgust.

'They raided poor Henry last night,' said a third—a gaunt fellow who appeared greatly perturbed. 'The murderous devils killed his boy and took his wife and two daughters.'

A man sat on the grass being consoled by three or four others.

'Did I not say I heard shots?' said Boundless, turning to Mose.

'Did ye say French?' asked Mose, ignoring the point.

'Aye. Two of them directing the raid. Henry heard them gabbing to each other. Fiends!' The man shook with anger as the others muttered and cast anxious looks down the road.

'Will you send for the soldiers?' asked Boundless.

'The savages will be long gone!' The speaker, a youth hardly as tall as the musket he clenched, interrupted, his face pale with distress. 'I say we chase after the murderers!'

The others looked at each other uneasily. 'We don't know the number,' argued one. 'Henry calculated thirty or more.'

'And our own farms be at risk,' added another.

'By God, but I'll go alone if I have to!' declared the hot-headed youth. 'Who rides with me? Think of poor Mrs Morgan,' he challenged as no one stepped forward. 'And Clementine and little Janey!' He stared wildly around the group. Finally, two men agreed, their faces reluctant.

'We are with you,' said one, 'But to steal them back only, if possible, not to fight such a large party.'

'Then why d'ye tarry?' The youth sprang for his horse. Hardly waiting for the other others to follow, he spurred the mount into a gallop. 'Come, if ye be coming!'

The others watched them depart. 'He was awful soft on Clemmie,' said one.

'Let us send to the fort. We must have protection,' insisted the gaunt man. He held up four fingers to Boundless. 'Four raids within the past month!'

In the grass, the sobbing farmer was being assisted to his feet.

'What will happen to the missing women?' Boundless asked as they took their leave of the men, and resumed the journey.

'Enslaved perhaps or adopted into the tribe—especially the younger one—to be ransomed or married off to some buck in the future.'

Boundless murmured in disgust. 'Let us hope they are rescued.'

They continued in a state of high alertness, flintlocks laid across their saddles. Mose stopped several times to scan the country ahead with the spy glass. 'Keep the mules tight,' he said.

The pack slipped on the lead mule, and they stopped to tighten the straps before continuing. Late in the afternoon, Mose raised a hand in warning.

'There!' He pointed to where a flock of buzzards circled above the grass in the distance. 'Be prepared to turn tail and run!'

As they proceeded cautiously towards the spot, Mose raised himself in the saddle to search the surrounding slopes. 'An Indian can hide himself behind a blade of grass,' he warned. 'Look to your weapon.'

'Perhaps it is a wolf kill.' Cocking the musket, Boundless strained to see as they drew nearer the circling birds.

That hope was dashed as they came across the bodies of the would-be rescuers lying in the grass. Each man had been scalped, the hair and skin hacked from their skulls to leave a bloody and grotesque crown in its place. In spite of the disfigurement, he recognised the face of the smitten youth who had urged the pursuit. He lay on his back, a feathered shaft sunk deep into his chest. The grass was flattened on either side, evidence of a fierce struggle. A dead horse lay not far from the men.

He heard Mose curse from where he stared down at the grass.

Hastening to the spot, he saw the bodies of the kidnapped woman and her two daughters lying in the dirt. He moaned with horror at the sight. The mother's throat had been slashed, the front of her grey tunic drenched with blood. Her two daughters lay close by. They looked unharmed at first, as if they might have been sleeping—until he sighted the blood and brains staining the grass beneath their hair, evidence their skulls had been cleaved with a hatchet.

'I thought you said they had been taken for slaves or ransom?' he said, accusing Mose in his distress.

'They were. This shows the savages took fright at the pursuit and slaughtered the women to make their escape.' Mose scratched his beard. 'In trying to save them, the men prompted their deaths, like as not.'

'Are the devils still close by?' Clutching the musket, Boundless scanned the nearby bushes. The mules and bell mare started grazing on the lush grass, unperturbed by the gruesome scene, and seemingly glad of the rest.

'A Shawnee can travel almost as fast afoot as we can on horse—faster, since they know the country. They are probably many miles away by now.'

'And the French—they did nothing to restrain them?'

'There was nothing they could do. The savages have their own way of treating enemies. Our own Indian allies would doubtless do the same if they had the chance. Fetch the shovels. Let us bury these poor souls afore the buzzards get at them.'

The face of the young woman looked curiously peaceful in death, as if surprised by the fact. *The blow was from behind. Perhaps even the savage could not bring himself to strike such beauty and innocence from the front.* Angrily, he dismissed the fancy. *They are cold-blooded butchers, without a shred of feeling!*

They buried the six bodies beside the road, raising prominent crosses over the graves so that relatives and friends could find them. To Mose's disapproval, Boundless insisted on laying the body of the lovelorn youth next to the grave of the eldest daughter.

'Who knows but she saw him riding to her rescue,' he said, arranging the arm of the dead youth. 'Perhaps she hoped she was saved, even at the end.'

He tore a scrap of packing paper and wrote a brief note explaining how they found the bodies and pinned it to the cross above the grave of the hot-headed youth. On each of the other crosses he wrote brief descriptions of the occupants: *mother, eldest daughter, beardless youth, youngest daughter.*

'The families will doubtless dig them up again,' said Mose.

'Then they will know where each of their loved ones lie.'

THEY HAD PROCEEDED BARELY two miles from the spot when they saw four riders approach, escorting a string of mules. They held a brief parlay explaining what had happened. The horsemen readily agreed to report the buried bodies and explain the circumstances of the burial upon reaching Staunton.

'I do believe I know the family,' said the leader, turning to the rider behind him.

'Who?'

'The Morgans.'

His companion looked blank.

'You know, Gordy. The eldest girl—the beauty with the long brown hair.'

'Oh, her! Clemmie. She gave me an apple one time.'

'By Christ, I knew her, too,' said a third.

'Damn savages!' The fourth rider shook his head in disgust. 'We ought kill 'em all!' Leaning, he spat into the grass.

'We are obliged to you for passing on the information,' said Mose. 'Please tender our heartfelt sympathies to the families.'

They rode in silence for the next two hours, each of them harbouring his own thoughts. They were descending a narrow gorge when the stallion neighed suddenly and shied to one side. There followed an anxious few minutes while Mose examined the animal.

''Tis nothing.' He stood up, stretching his back and visibly relieved. 'He spooked at something. What, the good Lord knows. A horse may get something into its head and act the devil if it takes him.'

Exhausted and tetchy from the travails of the day, they made early camp in a grove of mountain laurel with a small gushing spring. Around them, pink blooms rustled in the warm breeze. Walking off with the musket, Mose brought down a wild turkey for supper.

'By jinks, the plumpest specimen I ever saw!' he crowed, holding it up with both hands.

They ate the choicest portions of the bird, rubbing the cooked remains in salt. Mose dug out a square of linen from the supplies and sprinkled more salt on the cloth before carefully wrapping the pieces for later consumption.

Boundless slept badly that night, waking several times to stare up at the stars. '*Clemmie. She gave me an apple one time.*'

THE ROAD—IF, INDEED, IT could be referred to as such—was now almost entirely devoid of traffic. They rode an entire day without seeing another soul. Calculating they were within 'striking distance' of the James, Mose drove the stock as fast as he dared, constrained only by the fear of a horse or mule breaking a leg when scrambling up a bluff or negotiating one of the many tortuous gullies.

Mildly astonished to come upon an occupied farmhouse—the only one they had encountered in two days—they slept there for the night, the nervous inhabitants gladly offering shelter while pestering for details of the Indian raid further north. The windows were tightly shuttered, and the door immediately barred behind them as they entered. Three muskets along with a sack of powder and plenty of shot stood against the wall. The dogs had been brought inside and sprang alert at every sound, having caught the family's alarm.

'We had our own troubles but a week past,' the farmer said over supper while his wife and children listened, wide-eyed. 'The Bohler family not two miles away were attacked but were well fortified and drove off the devils.'

'Did they happen to make mention of Frenchmen among the Indians?' asked Boundless.

'How did you know?' The farmer gaped in astonishment.

''Tis said they have been stirring up the tribes.'

'They be worse than the heathen!' The wife shook her head in dismay.

The next morning as they ate a breakfast of corn mush, the wife approached and, out of earshot of her husband, begged them to stay another night.

'Mr Penshurst must work the fields by day, and we are left alone, with only the door between us and the savages,' she said, her face showing her fear.

Mose shifted uncomfortably. 'We must away, Madam. But fear not, the soldiers will surely arrive to chase the savages away.'

'If they are not fled already,' added Boundless.

The woman gave them a linen bag containing seed cakes and boiled eggs and stood in the door with her children to watch as they rode away.

'Do you think they are in great danger?' asked Boundless, looking back at the wife as she hovered fearfully in the doorway.

'It be hard to say. The valley is long and the Indians know every inch of it. They might strike anywhere at any time.'

The day grew hot, and they stopped to allow the horses to drink. He was rummaging through the saddle bags when he heard an exclamation from Mose. Walking over to where the trapper stood beside the stream, he stared at where Mose pointed to several footprints in the mud. 'Moccasins. They are fresh. We must be vigilant.'

They continued in a state of strained watchfulness, scanning the way ahead while making frequent glances behind. The road had all but disappeared, wheel tracks in the dirt the only indication wagons had passed by. Trees and shrubbery closed in on both sides so that Boundless had to raise an arm, ready to fend off a branch if it whipped back at him.

The bell mare plodded patiently behind the stallion, and he briefly admired her unstinting nature and endurance. *The mules also. They protest overmuch at times but are hardy and dependable.*

At that moment, one of the mules whinnied and Boundless shot a nervous glance at the brush, the thought of ambush constantly on his mind.

After proceeding for another hour, Mose led them off the track and called a halt at the foot of a small bluff.

'A good spot to camp for the night,' he said. A mossy indent in the side of the bluff offered protection against any attack from above or the sides.

They took down the cargo baskets and unsaddled the horses. After a while, he noticed that Mose seemed uneasy, the trapper constantly pausing to listen for some sound or other while casting suspicious glances at the surrounding woods.

'Is something amiss?'

'Mayhap it is nothing.' Mose paused to listen again. 'We had best forgo a fire for tonight. Keep your weaponry close to hand.'

Perturbed at his companion's behaviour, he tethered the stock close to the bluff. The horses seemed spooked, and he wondered if they sensed some danger before dismissing the thought as a product of his own unease.

They chewed on scraps for supper, neither man professing an appetite. As dusk fell the sense of peril increased. A tangible air of menace pervaded the hushed woods. Mose held the flintlock across his lap, his eyes rarely leaving the dense, surrounding thickets. 'Do you think that perhaps we imagined—'

'Shush!' Mose held up a hand for silence.

Boundless strained his ears but could detect nothing other than the hoot of an owl and the screech of a wildcat. 'What is it?' he whispered, his nerves on edge. The surrounding woods lay shrouded in twilight, the air heavy and still.

'Indians will imitate the sounds of a creature to deceive their victims. If they intend mischief, they surprise their quarry at first light, hoping to catch them while sleeping.'

'I am certain that was a wildcat.'

'Mayhap you are right. But savages imitate to the exact note. I suspect danger.' Mose stood up and walked over to where a heavy tree branch lay on the grass.

'Give me a hand,' he said, tugging the log. Together, they wrestled the branch over the grass to the foot of the bluff. 'Gather some brushwood and place it on top. I will keep watch.'

As Mose stood sentinel, Boundless dragged smaller branches over to the log, the hairs on his neck prickling each time he turned his back to the trees. Mose was not satisfied until the rampart was almost three feet high. Darkness had closed in as he took his place alongside the trapper behind the breastworks.

'Ready your weapons,' said Mose. 'We shall get no sleep this night.' The trapper's face was drawn and tense, his eyes constantly probing the woods.

They primed all four muskets and the two pistols, laying the weapons between them on the grass. He saw Mose lay an axe within reach and did the same. This done, they made themselves as comfortable as they could while eyeing the dark trees. A soft, fluting hoot that might have been an owl came from the darkness. The sound was followed by the grunting call of a bear. His sense of imminent peril was now at fever pitch, the apprehension underpinned by a shrill note of fear that he did his best to suppress. Stories of the barbaric cruelty of Indians and the indignities they inflicted on their captives haunted him as he maintained an anxious watch on the dark woods. He gripped the musket tighter, every nerve on edge.

The shrill yip of a coyote sounded, followed shortly by another, the noises seeming ever closer in the darkness of the glade. 'I fear we are at hazard,' he said in a low voice, his eyes never leaving the shadowy trees. Mose nodded, his face grim. The two remained watchfully alert throughout the long night, weapons in hand, their eyes trained on the surrounding darkness.

In spite of the danger, he could not help but close his eyes as dawn approached. He was awakened an instant later by a hand on his shoulder.

'See to your weapons.' Mose whispered in his ear. 'I fear they are all about us.'

He positioned himself behind the rampart, flintlock at the ready. Faint glimmers of light appeared in the sky as he strained to see into the surrounding gloom. He tensed at the whistling chirp of a bird—the sound repeated and echoed on both sides of the glade. In the fraught silence he fancied he could hear his own heart as it pounded in his chest.

Mose, a few feet to his right, chewed on a twig, his rigid posture the only indication of his apprehension.

All at once, a bloodcurdling shriek shattered the hush. The cry hung in the air as the concealed Indians rushed the rampart. A figure loomed in front of Boundless and he fired instinctively, drawing an agonised scream in response. He heard Mose fire both muskets in quick succession. Snatching up the second musket, he discharged it as an Indian attempted to vault the redoubt. The savage fell back with a cry. Another instantly took his place. Seizing the pistol, he shot the man in the face at point blank range. The Indian crashed against the breastworks and lay still. Mose fired again as the savages suddenly melted back to the safety of the woods. Taking advantage of the respite, he reloaded while feverishly scanning the gloom for more enemies.

'They are driven back—for the moment,' said Mose, his voice strained as he poured powder into the muzzle of the flintlock.

They remained crouched behind the makeshift rampart, their eyes trained on the woods as light slowly filtered through the trees. In the greyness, he detected two Indians lying prone before the redoubt. Another had dragged himself to the shelter of a tree where he lay moaning and gasping and calling out for his comrades.

'Take heed!'

Boundless ducked as a volley of arrows flew from out the bushes and buried themselves in the rampart. The volley was followed by loud taunts as the lurking Indians hurled threats and insults in a mix of English and French. It was now light enough to see approximately fifty yards into the woods, but he could not glimpse where the Indians lay concealed in the undergrowth.

'Damn ye! Murdering savages!' he shouted as the taunts continued—the outburst startling the Indians into silence.

'Well chanted! You have put the wind up the devils.'

As if in response, the Indians launched forward once more, seven or eight attackers rushing from the trees with fierce cries. He shot the first as he leapt across the body of a fallen comrade. Taking up the second musket, he felled a second as the man made ready to throw a tomahawk. Beside him, Mose discharged the flintlock as the Indians abruptly abandoned the attack and retreated back into the woods.

He quickly reloaded, his heart thumping in his chest. 'Will they try again?'

'It depends—on their number and their courage.' Mose peered at the livestock as they neighed and whinnied in fear, restrained only by the hobbles from fleeing in panic. 'I fear that poor creature is done for.' One of the mules lay on its side in the grass, a feathered shaft protruding from its ribs. The creature hawed continuously and struggled in vain to get to its feet.

They waited until full daylight for yet another assault, their weapons cocked as they vigilantly scanned the woods. But the Indians appeared to have given up the occasion, lacking the stomach for a third assault.

Towards noon, they emerged cautiously from the rampart, muskets at the ready. Boundless trained the flintlock on each trunk and bush as Mose checked the nearby woods, alert for the least movement.

Satisfied that the attackers had indeed departed, Boundless carefully approached the stricken savage, musket at the ready. The Indian lay slumped against a tree, his eyes closed. The fierce visage was contorted into a grimace of pain. Although fatally wounded, the Indian seemed no less fearsome in repose. A bristly fantail of hair was greased into stiff spikes atop the otherwise shaven head, the locks painted red and yellow. The broad forehead was painted orange and the eyes etched with black dye. A quill was inserted through the nose—the whole combining to present a terrifying appearance. The naked torso was adorned with paw prints inked onto the skin with red and blue dyes.

Uncertain whether or not the Indian had expired, he leaned down for a closer look only to step back in fright as the savage suddenly opened his eyes. The man stared up at him, a look of burning hatred in the fierce gaze. Hurriedly he levelled the musket. 'This one is still alive! What shall we do with him?'

For answer, Mose leaned down and, in one swift motion, sliced the Indian's throat. The savage uttered a strangled sigh as blood and air bubbled from the wound. 'Do you wish to take the hair—as a token?'

At his horrified refusal, Mose stood up, wiping the knife on his sleeve. 'I am glad. It is a practice fit only for heathens. Let us abandon this spot lest they alter their purpose and return.'

The trapper went to examine the stricken mule, ruefully determining that the animal was past help. 'Do not waste your shot. It is poor Whitesock. He is on his last breath.'

Leading the horses through the trees, they hastened to put distance between themselves and the encampment. They rode until late afternoon, stopping only to rest and water the stock while turning frequently to check for any signs of pursuit.

'Doubtless the devils will go in search of easier prey,' Mose concluded, satisfied that the Indians had abandoned any notion of giving chase. He selected a stand of hickory on the banks of a creek for their camp. Hidden in the thickness of the trees, they feasted on cold, salted venison for supper, deciding against a fire in case more Indians were roaming the country.

Now that the immediate danger was past, Boundless was flooded with a sense of giddy relief. Unable to sit still, he stamped back and forth as if to physically discharge the strong emotions coursing through his body.

'That first savage brandished a hatchet with every intention to brain me!' He shook his head in disbelief. 'A narrow escape from murder—by God!'

Sitting down, he leaned against the roots of a tree as Mose struck a spark from the tinder and lit the pipe.

'What would have happened had they managed to capture us?' He voiced the question in spite of fearing the answer.

'They would have sported with us first, no doubt—particularly so as we inflicted mortal hurt on their comrades.' Mose deliberated over the pipe. 'It is better to be dead than taken alive into their hands.'

Boundless shivered at the images conjured by the remark. 'They are truly savages! Without benefit of culture or restraint.'

'They have their savage beliefs. But cruelty is part of their ways. It is common to all the Indian tribes. They are not to be measured by our manners. And yet it is said that they make loyal and steadfast friends and will share food or all that they have with a comrade.'

They fell silent, each reflecting on the averted danger as the moon rose high overhead and an owl hooted from the trees. Mose eventually spoke. 'I will stand first watch. Try to get some sleep.'

He lay with his head pillowed on a rolled-up blanket, staring up at the stars through the overspreading branches. In his mind's eye, he saw the cruel faces of the Indians—their features distorted with bloodlust. Shuddering, he tried to dismiss the picture from his mind. He experienced an immense, overpowering fatigue and closed his eyes, comforted by the sounds of the horses and the hooting owl.

'I will wake ye in two hours,' he heard Mose say. He murmured a reply and fell instantly into the profoundest of sleeps.

The James River

FIFTEEN DAYS AFTER ENTERING the great valley, they had ridden over a hundred and fifty miles and were, according to Mose, 'within spit' of the James River at its southernmost end. The weather was variable, sudden showers succeeded by a blazing sun. The country was hilly, the slopes clothed with dense green woods. Often, they were forced to dismount and lead the stock through some particularly twisted gorge or defile. Indeed, at times the track appeared to vanish altogether, only to resume a hundred yards farther on. At other places it resembled a road once again, the path widening out sufficiently to permit them to ride alongside each other.

The few farmhouses they passed were empty—the inhabitants having fled to the nearest fort or blockhouse. The road was deserted, such was the alarm created by the continuing Indian attacks. The previous day, they had ridden ten miles and encountered only one other party, a homesteader hurrying north with his family to seek refuge at a blockhouse. Two small children crouched in the back of the open cart, their faces white and frightened where they peered out from under a canvas.

'Be on guard!' the farmer warned as he whipped the horses forward again. The cart lurched off, sending a spray of wet mud over the cursing Mose.

They maintained an alert watch, scanning the road ahead and arming the muskets whenever they passed through a spot susceptible to ambush. Once while standing sentry, Boundless thought he detected an Indian crawling stealthily through the bushes towards him, and nervously discharged the musket, earning the wrath of the awakened Mose. After determining the 'Indian' to be a wolf or fox, Mose grumbled mightily before returning to his blanket.

'Zounds, but if the savages didn't know we were here, you have now signalled them!'

Chastened, Boundless privately acknowledged his dread of hearing another blood-curdling shriek erupt from the dark woods, to be then followed by a murderous assault. Each formerly innocent copse or thicket now seemed, to his over-wrought nerves, laden with menace and potentially hiding a party of blood-thirsty Shawnee. By contrast, his stalwart companion appeared fully recovered from the bloody encounter. He glanced at the snoring Mose, admiring the trapper's astonishing equanimity in the aftermath of the attack. 'He treats each hazard as no more unexpected than a change in the weather,' he reflected, determined to adopt some of his companion's stoicism.

The following day, the trail wound through a series of rolling hills. He was beginning to think that the path had been entirely abandoned by travellers when, in the distance, he spied a long train of wagons wending towards them. The wagons were accompanied by armed men riding in front. A train of mules and pack horses brought up the rear along with a herd of pigs and goats.

'By Ezekiel if I don't count thirty carts!' Mose shaded his eyes to squint.

It was another hour before they encountered the first of the wagons as they proceeded slowly down a narrow gorge hemmed in by trees. As the convoy descended toward them, they waited with the pack mules where the trail ran through a stretch of flat, open grass.

The lead horseman held up a hand as he approached. 'Hail, friends!' The man, flanked by five or six companions, all heavily armed, drew rein in the natural commons.

'Good morrow,' replied Mose.

The first wagon turned off the trail and into the grass where it came to a creaking halt. 'Brother Elias, 'tis a good place to stop and mend the wheel,' the driver called out.

'As you will,' the lead rider replied. Turning in the saddle, he shouted a command. 'We rest for a quarter hour! Pass the word!'

Climbing down from his horse, the man invited Boundless and Mose to do the same. Men, women and children gathered as more wagons descended the gorge and came to a stop near the first. The women tended to infant children or sat down in the grass, doubtless glad of the respite from the long, arduous road. Four, strong-looking young men hoisted a corner of the first wagon while another removed the wheel.

A lean man in his forties approached. He wore a broad felt hat above a good-humoured face distinguished by a grey beard and bare upper lip. 'Josiah Hoffman. Wagon master. At your service, friends.'

'Pleased to meet you,' said Boundless, shaking hands. 'Where are you headed?'

'To Lancaster, in the Pennsylvania.'

Another man produced several stools from the back of the wagon. 'Rest yourselves,' invited Hoffman. A stout woman in a severe black dress and plain white cap approached and offered water, which they accepted. Other men and women gathered around, pressing for news of the road ahead. 'Do there be Indians?' one man asked. The others waited in anxious silence for the reply.

'We ran across a bunch a few days back,' replied Mose, 'but nothing since.' The news brought an exchange of glances among the brethren.

Hoffman nodded. 'We lost two good pigs not three nights ago and would doubtless have had to defend ourselves were we not so many. We are two dozen families, and some single men, bound together for protection.'

'You have the road to yourselves. The Indians have almost entirely stopped the traffic.'

The announcement induced murmurs. 'We need not fear,' said Hoffman, half-turning to address the group. 'We are well armed and under God's protection.'

'How is the road ahead?' asked Mose.

'Passable, just, to the James River, although cut by several creeks, all fordable. There is much game, and some pleasant prospects should you be inclined to linger.'

'How many Indians—that attacked you?' asked Boundless.

'We saw only their tracks and heard them yelp in the night. I believe they were after the pigs and sheep rather than scalps.'

'How far have you come?' asked Mose.

'Most from Georgia or South Carolina, others from points along the way.'

'We are seeking a gap—a pass in the Allegheny Mountains, somewhere southwest of here. Are you knowledgeable on such a place?'

Hoffman looked doubtful. He shook his head. 'A pass? I fear not.'

'A notch through the Alleghenies,' Mose pressed. 'To the French country?'

'I heard talk of a hunting party crossing through the mountains some time back.' An elderly man dressed in a stained black frockcoat interjected. 'Brother Samuel. What was that about a pass through the mountains?' He turned to an equally venerable man snoozing against a wagon wheel. 'Samuel Worthington!' he said, his voice sharp.

'Who calls!' The old man started up, rubbing his eyes and drawing chuckles from his companions. 'Are we at hazard?—Eli Went!' He glared accusingly at the speaker. 'I hear your stentorian voice roaring in my ears.'

'Now, Samuel. We have polite company. This gentleman is enquiring about a pass through the mountains. Have you—'

'There be such a pass,' the old man interrupted. Boundless gave Mose a surprised glance as the old man crawled over on hands and knees to join the parley.

'I was saying—'

'You were saying? Ha! What do you know of the country in question, Eli Went, being as you hail from the backwoods of Georgia? What, pray tell?'

The first speaker shook his head. 'Forbear, Brother Samuel,' he said mildly.

The old man shot a scornful look at his companion before turning to Mose. 'I have heard tell of such a pass as you describe. I spoke but a week since to a personage who claimed knowledge of it.'

'Then you know of its location?' Mose sat forward, his face eager.

Worthington contorted his brow as he searched his memory. 'Not I. But I speak of someone who claims such knowledge.'

'Do you intend to share the knowledge, Brother Samuel?' chided the first speaker.

'I do—if asked, Eli Went!'

'Pray tell,' coaxed Boundless.

'Then, since you ask …' The elderly man shot a dire glance at his companion. 'About twenty miles south of here is the James River. D'ye know of it?' He squinted at Mose, who nodded for him to continue.

'It is at the bottom of the valley. You will need to cross it by raft or find a shallow ford.'

'Indeed, we could not find such a ford—to our regret,' interrupted the first speaker, drawing a wrathful glance from the other man.

'As I was *speaking*—before the noise of mules-a-bray!'

The reprimand drew stifled laughter from those gathered around and a sigh from the interlocutor.

'The river lies directly south of here. The road is well marked.'

'Marked, but awful rough in places.'

'*Marked*, to the James River. Two or three days across the river lies a fork—' Here the speaker stopped to glance, as if astonished, at his companion. 'Hark! No quibble? No "*and such and so forth*" to build upon what is already plain?'

'None, good Samuel. Pray continue.'

'*With kind permission!* At the fork we came upon a party of soldiers camped by the road. I spoke to their scout—a most agreeable man, He happened to mention such a pass, for what reason I cannot recall. But he was a merry fellow and greatly knowledgeable of the country.'

'Indeed. I had quite forgotten the redcoats.'

'*Now* who be the sleepy head!'

'Temper, good Samuel. Temper.'

'The soldiers will still be there?'

'No. But the scout—'

'I do now recall! He mentioned a fort—'

'Lord, in Thy forbearance!'

'Peace, Brother Samuel,' rebuked Hoffman. 'These friends await your report.'

'The scout mentioned a fort, under construction, south of a river ... whose name escapes—'

'The New River, I believe he termed it.'

'*The New River*. The scout is stationed at the fort. He will undoubtedly give further directions to this pass you speak of.'

'Do you know how we can reach this river?'

Hoffman took over the account, the elderly man yielding without protest. 'Two or three days south across the James is the fork where we met the soldiers. You will know it in advance as there are two or three big salt licks to the side. The soldiers came down that fork. If Samuel is right, and I see no reason to doubt his account, the fork leads to the river in question. There you will find the fort, and your scout.'

'How did you get the wagons across the river?' asked Boundless.

Hoffman sighed in resignation. 'By God's grace—and immense labour,' he said, to solemn nods from his companions.

Before farewelling the party, they purchased three loaves of corn bread and two dozen macaroons. The seller, a matronly woman, generously added six buttermilk biscuits as a gift for 'fellow pilgrims'.

Taking their leave, they continued along the road, cheered by the encounter. The optimism lasted but an hour before a rainstorm swept down from the hills to leave them cold and shivering beneath the deerskin capes.

The sky had cleared again, and the sun had turned hot by the time they reached the James. The river was wide and flat and sparkling in the sunlight. The banks were steep and heavily wooded except for where the trees had been chopped down along a single short stretch on both sides. Wheel tracks showed where the wagon party had crossed.

'How in the name of God did they get the wagons across?' Boundless shook his head, astounded once again by the ingenuity and sheer audacity of the men and women who travelled such hostile country in wagon trains.

'I do recall there was a ferryboat,' said Mose, 'but the operator must have fled, like everyone else.'

Boundless had dismounted to ease his back and stretch his legs when he heard a whoop from his companion.

'Hi-yup old Jack!'

Turning, he saw, to his astonishment, Mose urge the stallion forward into the stream. 'What in blazes—'

''Tis not so rough!' A moment later, the horse was swimming strongly. Mose paddled furiously alongside, one hand grasping the saddle. Even more astonishingly, the bell mare splashed in after the stallion, closely followed by the mules. Within minutes, the entire train was swimming strongly for the opposite bank.

Boundless watched for a moment, dumbfounded at the impetuosity of his companion. *He will plunge where others fear to step.* Within the space of ten minutes, the stallion had found the bottom and was scrambling up the opposite bank.

Mose hollered across. 'D'ye wait for Judgement Day?'

Shaking his head at such recklessness, Boundless nudged the bay forward into the stream.

Reaching the other side without incident, he found Mose already starting a fire under the shade of a tree. 'We will stay here until we dry out and then start again. Divest yourself of those wet clothes. The sun will dry us in a tick.'

'Was it not foolhardy to drive into the river without so much—'

'We be acrost, ain't we?'

Boundless clucked in annoyance. 'Should we not at least find a more concealed spot?'

'Pshaw! Here we find ourselves, so let us rest in the moment. Who knows, but other travellers may come along to keep us company.'

LATE IN THE AFTERNOON, they started off again, still damp, but anxious to reach the fork the wagon party had mentioned.

To their pleasant surprise, the path flattened into something resembling a 'road' once more as the narrow valley widened to a flat, grassy plain. They made good time, covering fifteen miles in a single day.

Two days after the crossing, they came upon a series of salt licks by the side of the road, and shortly thereafter, came to the fork.

'There she is!' Mose beamed as he halted to survey the road. The right fork led off in a southwest direction. 'This must be where they met the soldiers.'

'Where does that road lead?' Boundless asked, gazing at the left-hand fork.

'Further south, to the Carolinas. Where the brethren hail from.'

'That old fellow was a spark.'

'Fortunate for us that he awoke.'

'Would you have known to take this road?'

'As long as we are headed towards the mountains, how can we get lost?'

'Should we make salt—from the lick?'

'We can buy some at the fort. Skit!' Mose kicked the chestnut forward.

'How far did that fellow say—to the fort?'

'He didn't! Git, you dang sons of Lucifer!'

They made camp a mile beyond the fork as rain started to fall. The rain continued throughout the night, turning the passage into a lake of mud. The next day they covered less than four miles, cursing and struggling as the horses and mules slipped and scrambled in the mire. They passed another cold and miserable night chewing on salt pork and sleeping in the wet as it rained steadily until morning. Drenched and cheerless they recommenced, leading the horses on foot.

'Are we headed in the right direction?' asked Boundless, as they stopped briefly before navigating another ascent.

'You see the mountains, don't you?' Mose, his face drawn and grimy with dirt, waved a tired hand at the distance.

Two days later they halted, soaked and exhausted, on the banks of a swollen stream. 'Is it the New River?' asked Boundless, breathless from the laborious trek.

'What else can it be? The soldier fort cannot be far distant.'

'How in blazes will we cross? It must be a thousand or more yards across.'

Buffeted by the swirling gusts of rain, they studied the turbulent river. The swift-flowing water was muddy, with tree branches and half-submerged logs swept along in its flood.

Boundless glanced to the east, and took in the mountains, the summits concealed in heavy mist.

'We have no choice but to build a raft.' Mose frowned as he said the words, clearly reluctant to undertake so arduous a task in the rain and wind.

'There may be an abandoned one lying along the shore.'

'If the flood hasn't swept all away. You search upstream, I will search down.'

Boundless set off along the muddy riverbank, shrinking further into the deerskin cape as the wind blew rain against his face. He had previously swapped the sodden straw hat for the fur one and now diverted himself from the weather by pondering whether their route could be illustrated by the exchange of hats. 'Straw to Winchester, fur from Staunton ...' Hearing a faint hail from Mose, he turned and headed back along the shore.

He found his companion standing outside an abandoned farmhouse. A note was pinned high up on the door beneath the sheltering eave.

'My eyes can't see in this deuced light,' complained Mose.

Dismounting, Boundless walked up to the door. The note contained four, hurriedly scribbled words: *Injuns! Gone to Fort.*

'They have abandoned the place and taken refuge at the fort.'

'Which one?'

'They did not say.'

'And no mention of a boat? Surely, they must have had one for their own use.' Mose surveyed the riverbank in front of the house. 'Let us search a little further.'

They searched the nearby woods and reeds for any sign of a conveyance. After a few minutes, Mose gave a triumphant cry.

'Found, by zooks!'

Boundless hurried to join him, seeing a flatboat where it lay concealed in the reeds. Two long poles lay inside the boat.

'It is small. We shall have to make several crossings.'

'Pshaw! We need only carry ourselves and the cargo. The animals will swim across.'

'We should wait. Until the rain clears.'

'We have the fortune of this boat. Let us take advantage of it. If we stay, mayhap the Shawnee, or the French, or both, nay chance upon us.' Mose grasped the front of the boat. 'Pull!'

They dragged the boat down to the water, leaving half its length on the bank lest it be carried away on the flood.

'The water looks high.'

'The better to float on!' Brimming with renewed optimism at the discovery, Mose whistled for the stallion. 'Jack!' He walked off along the bank calling out for the horse.

Boundless followed, a sense of foreboding filling him as he contemplated the mist-shrouded hills. Overhead, a weak sun broke through the mass of cloud. 'We may have luck,' he conceded, resigned to his companion's refusal to countenance delay of any sort.

Collecting the stock, they led the animals back along the shore, Mose humming at their good fortune. 'The far shore in a quarter hour,' he predicted cheerfully.

'Why not make camp and wait one more day until the rain clears?'

'And what if it doesn't? Nay, he who delays is confounded!'

A mute protest on his lips, Boundless picked up a sack of beans, glancing up again at the clouded hills.

After unloading the supplies, they unsaddled the horses and took the baskets and rigging from the mules. Boundless checked that the log and ink case were wrapped in oilcloth before stuffing the parcel back in the saddle bag. The cargo sat stacked in the centre of the boat, loosely secured by canvas and tied down with rope. It seemed to Boundless that the level had risen in the time it had taken to load the boat.

'The rain has stopped. Providence smiles upon us!' Grasping the stallion by the mane, Mose led him down to the water.

The stallion reared, clearly spooked by the swirling turbulence. Mose stroked his neck. 'A good swim, Jack, 'tis all.' He steered the snorting animal into the water. 'Swim, boy!' Neighing loudly, the horse splashed into the river. In moments, it was up to its belly. An instant later, it was swimming strongly against the current.

'Skit, Buckshot. Skit!' Boundless urged the bay into the water as Mose cajoled the bell mare. Stubbornly resistant at first, the latter eventually plunged into the muddy flow, whinnying as she lost the bottom. The mules splashed after her, holding their heads high as they kicked in pursuit. In no time, the water closed over their backs as, seemingly undeterred, they kept swimming after the mare.

'They will prosper,' said Mose, watching.

'Are you set?' Boundless stood on the bank ready to push the boat into the water.

Mose walked on board and picked up a pole. 'Cast off!'

'In for a penny,' muttered Boundless, and gave the boat a mighty shove, launching it into the stream. He almost lost his footing as he scrambled aboard, his buckskin trousers soaked with water.

Standing on opposite sides, they propelled the flatboat into the stream, digging the hickory poles against the soft bottom. The strong current took the boat as they poled furiously to keep it pointed at the far shore. Ahead, the stallion was at the three quarter mark, only his head visible above the water. The gelding, the mare, and the mules followed some distance behind.

Pushing manfully, they struggled to keep the boat square to the current as the flood carried them rapidly downstream. Rain began to fall as a freshening wind ruffled the surface. At that moment he lost the bottom, the pole sweeping uselessly through the water.

'The shore lies ahead!' shouted Mose. The mud bank was flat and almost bare of trees.

A drenching shower of rain swept the deck. Boundless glanced up in alarm as the wind began to gust. The peaks were hidden behind a solid mass of cloud.

'The higher ground will be awash!' he shouted, even as a dull rumble of thunder sounded overhead. 'We must hurry!'

He was looking around for something to use as a paddle when he heard a roaring noise and glanced up to see a wall of water surging towards them. He scarcely had time to shout a warning before the wave crashed over the boat and swept him into the river. The shock of the cold water almost paralysed his limbs. As he tumbled under the flood, he felt objects strike his body. He fought to the surface, gasping for air. He heard a faint shout but could see no sign of Mose through the surging wash. He sank again and flailed his arms to catch a breath. He glimpsed the capsized boat being carried away downstream. Gulping air into his lungs, he floun-dered wildly for the shore. He felt mud under his feet and scrambled to stay upright. Wading, exhausted, through the shallows, he collapsed, half-drowned, in the mud.

He lay there for some minutes—too drained to move. A hand tugged his shoulder, and he looked up to see Mose leaning over him, a frantic expression on his face. The trapper was soaked through and hatless—his hair plastered to his head.

'By Christ but we have lost the mules!'

Boundless climbed to his feet, the soaked buckskin heavy and uncom-fortable against his skin. He saw the stallion where it had taken refuge under the line of trees some twenty yards back from the river. The gelding stood alongside, his flanks trembling.

'The mare is missing!'

'We must find the mules,' said Mose, his voice urgent.

Drenched to the skin, they proceeded downstream, searching and calling out for the animals. Further along the shore they found two of the wicker baskets washed up on the mud. A short time later, Boundless spot-ted one of the mules floating motionless in a side-creek. Mose moaned in dismay. 'It be Snuff-Pot,' he said hoarsely.

They proceeded several hundred yards further downstream, coming upon a sodden sack of corn and several other perishables washed up on the bank. A short distance along they came across the drowned carcass of Redcoat in the shallows.

'We are as perished as the Pharaoh and his army!' Distraught at this further loss, Mose pointed to the mule's flanks. 'See where he carried the mark of an arrow—only to perish from the flood!'

They were about to give up in despair of finding the remaining mule when they heard a snicker from the undergrowth. To their great relief, the bell mare emerged from the line of trees, nervous and soaking wet but unharmed. 'Praise the Lord!' Mose hastened to collect the animal.

'Where is Prodigal?'

They searched further along the shore but could find no sign of the missing mule.

As they looked, Boundless was struck suddenly by the extreme peril of their position. He caught Mose by the arm. 'We are unarmed and on foot. We shall be easy slaughter if Indians come along. And we must dry ourselves or catch our death.'

Mose hesitated, reluctant to abandon the search. 'A mite further.'

'Damnation to the mule! We are exposed and defenceless!'

With great reluctance, Mose conceded the point. 'Very well. Let us move into the trees.'

They found a small clearing within the tree cover and began to collect sticks and branches to make a fire. Hands shaking with cold, they hurried to light the pile. Once it was blazing, they rummaged through the scant remnants of the cargo they had managed to retrieve.

'The powder is drowned.' Mose held up a small keg. 'We must dry it and lay out the muskets and pistols as well.'

Taking off their shirts and leggings, they hung them as close to the fire as they dared. Dusk was closing in. Acutely aware of their perilous position, they kept the axes and knives within reach as they sat close to the flames. Neither had an appetite and they sat in silence, the scale of the disaster only now beginning to sink in. Mose wrung water out of a gunny sack, lamenting the loss of the mules—Prodigal in particular, to whom he had grown increasingly attached.

'He may have been kin to Lucifer, by Jove, but I was getting used to his airs and high-handed ways. And poor old Pot! And Whitesock! He deserved a better fate.' He wrung the sack between his hands, grieving the loss. 'Perdition to the cursed river!'

'You were over-anxious to cross!' Boundless' simmering anger boiled over as he contemplated the calamitous loss of mules and cargo. 'Only a fool would have taken such a risk!'

'We are acrost, are we not? That is the main thing.'

'The main thing?' Boundless stared in disbelief. 'We are *defenceless*, half-naked and half-drowned, and at the mercy of any savage that chances along. In addition, we have lost *all three* of the blasted mules!'

'I have suffered worse.' Mose, clad only in his wet breeches, turned his backside to the fire. ''Tis a set-back, no more. Did ye think to ride all this way and not receive some harm? 'Tis a miracle when thought upon.'

'A miracle we didn't drown!'

'We have our scalps, do we not? We have our horses. And what was lost may be replaced at the fort.'

'Replaced! I am heartily glad you think so lightly of our predicament. We shall be fortunate to reach those damned plains of yours with our scalps intact.' He stuck his hands out to the fire, bitterly regretting his foolishness in ever setting forth on so perilous a venture.

Mose rubbed his hands and blew into them. 'By the bones, but I miss my pipe.'

Boundless added branches to the fire, reasoning that any nearby Indians would have spotted the flames already. Unable to sit still due to a mixture of alarm at their predicament and resentment at his partner, he walked out of the firelight. *If I stay I shall surely say something I will regret.*

To try to calm his tumultuous thoughts, he walked down to the star-lit river, amazed at how placidly it flowed under the bright moonlight. 'We might cross now without a care in the world,' he reflected, shaking his head at the thought. The river struck him as emblematic of the entire wild continent: splendid in repose, terrifying in action. Sobered by the thought, he returned to the fire.

He passed a nervous and uncomfortable night. In spite of his exhaustion, he found it difficult to sleep, starting up several times to check that they were not under threat of attack by lurking Indians. To his chagrin, Mose snored peacefully, his damp shirt covering him like a blanket. He moved closer to the fire, brooding on his companion's reckless indifference to all hazards. His doubts over the wisdom of the expedition surfaced again as instances of the trapper's heedless nature came back to perturb him. It was, he concluded, an instance of overweening ambition to set out for the perilously distant plains in the first place. *What have I to do with his madcap schemes? Yet I have myself to blame for allowing myself to be drawn into them, like a fly into a web.*

He lay resentfully in this fashion for the better part of the night as Mose snored mightily alongside him.

33

Fort Chiswell

THE NEXT MORNING, THEY were pulling the stiff moccasins onto their feet when they heard a bray. Boundless looked up, amazed to see Prodigal trotting towards them along the bank.

'By all the saints!' Mose danced on one leg as he pulled on a shoe. 'He has returned—as prophesised! See how he struts and bobs! Thou prodigious mule! Welcome, a thousand times!' The bell mare plodded over, and Mose hooted with delight as she and the mule nuzzled each other.

'See is thy brother alive again! He was lost and is found! Drowned and yet saved!'

Cheered at this unexpected gift, they set off along the mud bank to see what could be salvaged from the disastrous crossing. The remaining wicker baskets, largely emptied of their contents, had washed up on shore and they retrieved these. Continuing the search, they found the shovels, axes, ropes and a pickaxe. What little food they recovered was soaked or spoiled by the water.

Two hours later, clothed in the damp buckskin, they sat the horses and prepared to depart the spot. The mule carried what remained of the cargo while the six empty wicker baskets were tied to the back of the bell mare. Mose had even retrieved his straw hat from a branch sticking up out of the mud. 'It were as a sign,' he chortled. With a glance at the river, he shook the reins. 'Let us find a willing farmhouse and a hearty breakfast. Hup!'

Still angry from the disastrous crossing, Boundless watched in grudging wonderment as his companion chatted gaily to the chestnut or ruminated aloud on what fine breakfast awaited them at the next farmhouse.

'No devilish mush, but pork and beans and eggs aplenty! And a fine feed of oats for thy good self. What say thee, Jack?'

But in spite of the trapper's optimism, farmhouses along the road proved exceedingly scarce. The first they encountered was abandoned. A second lay in blackened ruins. The occupants of a third refused to open the door, an alarmed voice from within demanding that they leave or risk being shot. 'Git now! We got no vittels to spare!'

'Then out of Christian charity, where be the next hamlet or tavern?'

'There ain't none! Move on!' the voice threatened. From within the barred window, a pair of eyes looked out above the muzzle of a flintlock.

'Hold fire! We be on our way.' Grumbling at such rude inhospitality, Mose turned the stallion back to the road. 'Confound the villain. Would a breakfast—handsomely paid for—have put him at risk? The devil take him—and his musket!'

They continued on in silence for a few minutes, digesting the incident. 'The French and Indians, both, have them scared out of their wits,' conceded Mose after a time.

They rode for an hour, slowly drying out under the sun. The trail, mercifully flat from the river, now rose again as they entered a region of tall hills. Dismounting, they led the horses, the solitary mule bringing up the rear. They were forced to walk for two miles before the ground flattened sufficiently to permit riding again. It was late afternoon, and the sun was hot once more. Halting under the trees, Mose indicated they would make camp for the night. They built a fire and chewed on the scant remains of a rabbit shot two days before.

'I will take first watch,' said Mose.

THE MORNING DAWNED BRIGHT and clear, heartening them as they set off again, eyes searching for the fort at every rise in the ground. 'We be a sorry enough sight,' Boundless reflected. 'I never in my life saw so many rivers, creeks and springs.'

Ahead, he heard Mose grumble. 'What harm if the scoundrel passed breakfast through the window?'

The path, now little more than a trace, became increasingly difficult to navigate as they proceeded along the fork. So dense was the surrounding brush that they were forced to walk most of the way, constantly pulling and pushing the protesting stock as they proceeded, with infinite slowness, towards the hoped-for fort. The ground rose steeply as they laboured up the side of a ridge, their bodies whipped and scarred by branches. They were surrounded on every side by high hills that seemed to get higher as they continued.

To add to their labour, the day was hot and cloudless, and they were tormented by mites. Every half hour, they were forced to stop and rest, exhausted from the toil.

Mose halted, sweating, to remove his hat and wipe his slicked brow with the neckerchief. 'By hick and by crick if the cursed path doesn't keep on getting higher!'

'How much further, do you think? I doubt the horses will last another mile.'

'Let us see if we can at least reach the top of this peak.'

To Mose's disappointment, they were forced to abandon the goal as the panting horses simply stopped, refusing to go further.

'For the love of God, let us make camp,' protested Boundless. 'My bones are broke.'

Next morning, under a cool, grey sky, they reached the top of the ridge to behold a valley through which snaked a broad river. The country on all sides appeared exceedingly wild.

Boundless groaned in frustration. 'God in heaven! Where is the dammed fort?' He glanced at Mose who looked equally dismayed. 'Did we miss a turn?'

'Mayhap that wasn't the New River we crossed. Confound it!' Mose tugged the bridle. 'Come, Jack. Another bath awaits!'

Boundless followed, now certain they were doomed to perish in this wilderness of trees and water.

They descended the ridge slowly and tortuously, stopping at one point to use the axes to broaden the path sufficiently to allow them to pass unhindered. It was afternoon before they reached the bottom and were able to mount again and proceed at a walk towards the river.

Two hours later they sat on the shore, staring at the even flow.

'It looks deep,' said Boundless.

'Deep, mayhap, but not so wide. We can swim the horses over.'

Boundless frowned, determined not to give his companion free rein in the matter. 'Patience. We do not wish another disaster. Let us explore a little, first. There may be a ford.'

They rode north along the shore for a mile, coming upon a grove of felled trees. Mose raised an eyebrow. 'We are not the only pilgrims,' he said.

Moments later, they chanced upon a small farmhouse not far from the riverbank. They halted, vastly surprised to discover the dwelling amidst so much wilderness. They observed it for a few minutes, unable to perceive any occupants.

'Is it habited?' asked Boundless, scanning for signs of life.

'Let us find out.' Mose nudged the stallion forwards, stopping a few yards from the house. 'The occupants may have fled.'

At that moment, a wiry, elderly man carrying a bucket walked around the corner of the cabin. Seeing the two travellers, he dropped the bucket in fright.

'Good morrow, friend! Pray, do not be alarmed. We are but two honest gentlemen who would speak with you.'

A youth stepped out from the doorway, holding a musket. Behind him, Boundless saw the pale, frightened face of a grey-haired woman. 'We are innocent travellers, I assure you,' he said, raising his arms.

The youth slowly lowered the musket, his gaze sharp and suspicious.

'Pray, what stream is this?' asked Mose.

'Stream?' The old man frowned. 'Why, the New River, of course. Do not be afeared, son.'

Mose shot a look at Boundless, the same question evidently on both their minds. 'We believed we had crossed the New River some days back,' said Mose.

'Mayhap you did. Doubtless it has forks and streams aplenty.' The old man picked up the bucket, having recovered his composure.

'Come, gentlemen, a parley.'

The farmer proved a welcoming host, inviting them to supper, and providing feed for the horses and mule. Over an excellent meal of pork, fried potatoes and cornmeal pancakes, he pressed for news of events in Philadelphia and points in between. 'We are famished for reports—of any vintage,' he said. When told of the rumoured sightings of French troops along the Valley Pike, he expressed considerable astonishment.

'Lord above, Mother,' he said, looking to his wife. 'Lord above,' he repeated, shaking his head.

'You are some ways from the road,' observed Mose.

'It used to run by here—but shifted downstream some years past. We ought follow it but are used to this spot.'

'You do not fear an attack by Indians?' asked Boundless, the burned house near Staunton still vivid in his mind.

The woman cried out an anguished, 'Oh!', at the question, her face draining of colour. Such was her distress that Boundless felt compelled to apologise for raising the subject.

'Now, now, Mother.' The farmer spoke soothingly, leaning forward to stroke her hand. 'We provide the Shawnee with flour and vegetables as a keep-peace,' he said, with a glance at Boundless. 'And generally try to maintain civil terms. Although their rude ways be a sore trial at times.'

'Savages!' The wife looked fearfully at her husband. 'They will scalp and murder us in our beds!'

'There be no cause for alarm, Mother,' said the youth. He looked worriedly at his father—either sharing in his mother's distress or himself fearful of the Indians.

'We are told there is an army troop nearby,' said Mose, further consoling the wife as well as taking the opportunity to quiz the farmer on the where-abouts of the fort.

'That there be,' confirmed the farmer. 'They have come to build a fort. Their camp lies but a two- or three-day ride across the river. And most welcome they are, too. A fort will provide protection for other settlers to join us. There be a flow of people headed further south for the Carolinas, but none wish to stay and set up home around here, although the land be rich and fertile. Mayhap after this war is finished, things will change.'

He offered a twist of tobacco, which Mose accepted gratefully, his own being lost in the river. 'And now, friends,' the farmer leaned back in his chair. 'What tales of the road?'

They passed the rest of the evening gossiping and eating and taking a turn at cards—the latter to the great delight of the farmer. 'It be a diversion I sorely miss,' he said, turning over a dog-eared card.

As dusk fell, Mose gratefully accepted the offer to sleep beside the hearth.

'Nay, but it will give my poor wife comfort,' said the farmer, brushing thanks aside. 'She be sorely affrighted of the heathen.'

'Would you not consider moving further down the valley—where there are more people?' asked Boundless.

'I would, but we are settled here, and I do believe the Indians will leave us in peace.'

'He is a brave man,' said Mose as they settled down for the night.

'Or a foolish one—who risks his wife and son for a patch of earth.'

Next morning, they rose to the sound of the woman stirring a pot of porridge that had sat over the embers of the fire. Boundless ate heartily, consuming two bowls of the pottage sweetened with molasses, while apol-ogising for his appetite.

'This is surely the best porridge I ever ate,' he praised, drawing a flush of pleasure from the woman.

'Eat thy fill,' she insisted, ladling more porridge into the bowl. ''Tis rare we accommodate two gentlemen from Maryland.'

'Nay, but you be our second guests this past month,' said the genial farmer. 'Mother, dost thou recall the last?' He smiled at the tight-lipped expression that greeted the question. 'But three or four weeks since, we provided water and feed to a party of Ulstermen as they passed through,' he explained. 'A more contrary tribe you never did see. They refused all offers to hire the boat and myself and son to row it but must build their own raft—in such manner cutting down my finest trees. And when they left, they burnt and sunk the raft so that no one else might use it.' He shook his head wonderingly. 'Did you ever hear of such perversity? I was glad to the teeth when they took off on their way.'

'You have a boat?' Mose brightened at the news. 'If ye could carry us acrost, we would be most obliged. We will recompense you for the trouble, and for your excellent hospitality.'

'Henry!' The father called out to the son. 'Ready the boat.' They were soon taking their leave of the diminutive woman. She stood watching from the doorway clutching her apron, her earlier pleasure at the company replaced by a pale nervousness as she watched them go.

'I had to argue with the Ulstermen to spare the tree,' said the farmer as he untied the flatboat from a large chestnut. 'They thought only of crossing and nought else. Such a truculent and ornery bunch I hope never to see again.'

''Tis their love of potatoes,' quipped Mose as they led the three horses and Prodigal on board. 'It gives them awful indigestion.'

The farmer dug the pole into the water and pushed the boat out from the shore. The crossing was so smooth that Boundless wished they could strap the boat to the backs of the horses.

As they remounted and prepared to depart, the farmer gave them further instructions. 'The soldiers be but thirty miles to the southwest. Follow the trace. And give my regards to that fine tribe of Ulstermen, should you overtake them. Tell them we stuck the pieces of that miserable raft back into the dirt and lo! the trees abounded!'

Mose laughed heartily at the jest and promised to pass on the message. He leant down and pressed a few coins firmly into the man's hand.

'He is a fine fellow,' said Boundless as he turned in the saddle to wave goodbye.

'Aye. 'Tis a pity his wife does not share his enthusiasm for the country.'

THEY CONTINUED IN A south-westerly direction for two days, constantly scanning the distance for sight of the promised fort. The weather had grown exceedingly warm, and they drank frequently from the canteen to remove the dust thrown up by the horses.

'By the bones, what I wouldn't give for one more mouthful of that fine porridge we ate two days past!' said Mose.

In the middle of the afternoon on the third day out from the river, Mose pulled up abruptly. 'The spyglass,' he said, holding out a hand. He put the glass to his eye.

'What do you see?'

'Soldiers!' He passed the glass to Boundless. Putting it to his eye, he saw a stockade rising from amidst a cluster of tents. The Union flag hung limply from a pole on the fort ramparts.

'They will surely have whisky! Har!'

A redoubt of logs and brushwood enclosed the camp. A wooden post at an opening in the palisade bore the etched inscription, *Fort Chiswell*. Beyond the redoubt a semi-completed stockade was visible. The noise of hammering and sawing came from within. A ladder stood against the side of the stockade. A line of men passed cut lumber, hand over hand, to another line of men waiting between an open section of the log wall.

Two sentries raised muskets as they approached. 'Who goes?' challenged one, blocking their path.

'Who in blazes do you suppose?' Mose spluttered with indignation. 'Haven't you the wits to see we are but two Christian gentlemen, as yourselves?'

'Allow them to pass.' A man sitting on a chair in the shade of an elderberry tree put down his book. He was bareheaded and clad in a cream waistcoat and woollen breeches.

'Colonel Byrd at your service, gentlemen. Come, stand in the shade.' He stood up, mopping his brow with a handkerchief as they dismounted. 'Who are you and where are you bound?' He spoke with a cultured voice, his broad face flushed from the heat. His open shirt collar was grimy and soaked with sweat.

'Mose van Zeke and Boundless McLennan,' answered Mose. 'We are travellers, bound for the western plains.'

The Colonel considered this as he dabbed his throat with the handkerchief. 'For what purpose?' he asked.

'To hunt buffalo.'

'Have you passed any French troops?'

'No. But we saw plenty of Indian sign farther back.'

'Oh.' The Colonel seemed disappointed. He glanced at a handful of soldiers who had abandoned work on the stockade to listen. 'Do you have nothing to do but loaf and gawk?' He gave them a sharp look before turning back to the conversation. 'We are here—put elbows into it, damn ye!—to protect the settlers, and travellers such as yourselves.'

'And well settled in, by the looks of it.'

'The fort will be finished within the month—if the weather holds and the men do not perish of idleness!' The Colonel glowered at the snickering soldiers.

'We passed a new fort, up in Winchester,' said Boundless.

The officer brightened. 'Indeed. We intend to deny passage to the damned French. And squeeze the god-forsaken Indians into the bargain.'

'Do you have a scout here?' asked Mose.

'Somewhere. You are certain you saw no sign of French troops?'

'By hearsay and rumour only. But no direct knowledge.'

The Colonel grimaced and fingered a pimple on his throat. 'You are welcome to stay and refresh yourselves.' Sitting down, he picked up the book.

Proceeding further into the extensive camp, they came upon a wide commons area filled with rows of tents and grazing livestock. In addition to the army mounts, a number of mules and oxen foraged the grass.

'See there?' said Mose, pointing at the mules, his voice pleased.

On one side of the clearing, forty or more wagons and carts were drawn up in a double line. Unsaddling the horses and unloading the scant cargo, they left the stock to graze while they wandered around the camp, slightly astonished to be amidst so many people after the emptiness of the road.

Mose stopped a passing Redcoat. 'Can you direct us to the scout?'

'Wick?' The soldier looked around. 'Over there.' He pointed to where a pipe-smoking figure reclined beneath a tree.

'With luck it is the same fellow mentioned by the wagon folk,' said Mose.

The recumbent figure lazily observed them as they approached. He was dressed in buckskin decorated with fringed ties. A knife and a tomahawk were thrust into the broad leather belt around his waist. He was bareheaded, his brown hair tumbling freely about his shoulders as he puffed from a long-stemmed clay pipe, his manner relaxed and carefree.

'Joseph Wick,' he announced after Mose had introduced himself and Boundless. 'Army scout,' he added, the statement seeming to amuse him. Boundless and Mose sat down in the grass. A gunshot sounded from behind them. They turned to see the Colonel berate an unfortunate trooper who had accidentally discharged the weapon.

'Pay no heed to that spark,' Wick advised. 'He is over-anxious to whip the French or some blood-thirsty Indians, so he'll have a valorous tale to enchant the ladies back in Williamsburg.' He held the pipe against his chest. 'Have ye come far?'

'All the way from Maryland,' said Boundless. 'We have been on the road this past six weeks.'

The scout nodded sagely. 'You will be looking to secure land, I expect? If so, better hurry before the darned speculators snatch it all up. They are the lunkheads to blame for this war with the Indians.' He hawked into the grass. 'The Transylvania Company. The Ohio Company. The Loyal Land Company. A plague on all the grasping scoundrels! They steal every inch of land that ain't nailed down. And then the settlers come along and shoot all the game. No wonder the Indians are riled.'

Mose took out the tinderbox and lit up his own pipe with tobacco purchased from the farmer. 'We ain't looking for land. We aim to travel over the mountains and beyond the French country to where we may trap beaver and hunt buffalo.'

The scout puffed agreeably. 'Fine ambition, too,' he said, seemingly unsurprised by the remark as he slowly exhaled a cloud of smoke and watched it hang in the air.

'There is said to be a newly found gap where one may cross the mountains. Do you know of such a place?'

'Know of it? Came within a spit of seeing it for myself.'

Mose and Boundless exchanged looks, Mose's face brightening with triumph. 'Do tell,' he said, prompting the scout.

'Last winter, I and a party of hunters travelled all the way up the mountains—so near we could nigh on touch the gap. But the weather turned foul, and we turned tail. In any respect, your starting place be the fork of the Holston.'

'Is it—the pass—far from here?'

'A fair ways. I suppose I might make a guess if you are keen?'

'It don't matter—' objected Mose.

'I would like to know,' interrupted Boundless, ignoring Mose's frown.

Wick smoked thoughtfully as he considered the distance.

Boundless curbed his eagerness, having learned from observing Mose the rustic habit of reflecting on certain questions as if the reply was of great moment.

The scout blew out a puff of smoke. 'From this spot, nigh on two hundred miles. 'Course, it depends on how far you ride in a day. And, as you'll agree, on the weather, the horses, hostile Indians, snakes, bears, wolves … *ad infinitum*. That's Latin. I learned it from the Colonel who tags it to every darn thing under the sun. 'The road leads that way, men, *ad infinitum*,' he intoned, adopting a cultivated voice. 'The mountains be to the left of us—and to the right, *ad infinitum*. That be a river, snaking off to the west, *ad infinitum*.'

Mose broke into a spluttering guffaw over the pipe.

The scout beamed as he fingered more tobacco into the pipe bowl. 'I suppose you wish for directions?'

'We do,' said Boundless, smiling at the scout's ability to so closely mimic the Colonel's voice.

'Course, your biggest problem be the Shawnee,' continued the scout. 'They are mighty particular about comings and goings through them mountains.'

'How likely are we to run into them?'

'Hard to say. Two weeks back a bunch of our boys tangled with a party further up the valley. I'm a mite surprised you didn't run into them as you came down the road.' Wick raised an eyebrow at Mose.

'We did. They came calling, uninvited.'

The scout laughed. 'They be downright uncivil that way.'

'What about the French?' asked Boundless.

'They be mostly occupied with the Ohio country. But you might run into a fort—or a patrol acrost the mountains. Information is thin.'

'What would they do to us—should we encounter them?'

'Depends. Shoot you, if they're in the mood. Hand you over to the Indians. Offer a glass of wine. You can't tell with the French, any more than with the heathen.'

'The way?' Mose prompted.

'It be an arduous route.'

'Pray, not so arduous as the one so far,' said Boundless, the mock-sigh eliciting a grin from the scout.

'Take a handful of tobaccy—a fine leaf.' Mose leaned forward, offering Wick the bag of tobacco. 'Help yourself, friend.'

'Don't mind if I do.' The scout took a handful and put it in his pouch.

'The directions ... let me cogitate.' Wick pulled himself into a sitting position. Taking the pipe from his mouth, he set it down carefully on a root. He then cast around for a twig or stick, settling for a fallen branch.

'I can point you to it—the pass. Near as a hair lick, anyways.' Wick poked the branch into a patch of dirt. 'Follow the road west of here. 'Taint a road, really, more a mud track. Follow it for a week or so. It will take you to a river. That be the Holston. You will find it past an abandoned house. Follow it down the valley.' He scratched a double line in the dirt. 'You will pass a long island in the middle of the river.' He marked the spot with cross. 'A few miles past the island, the river forks north.' Their eyes followed the branch as it scratched the fork. 'Follow that until you come upon some old Indian houses. That be a good place to ford. On the other side runs an old Indian road. Follow that ... nor'-west to where it twists through a gap in the hills. Acrost that you'll come into some rough country—' The scout grimaced. 'One of our party broke a leg; another got snake bit.' Shaking his head at the misfortune, he continued. 'A mite further on you will come to another stream, the Clinch.'

'Stream upon stream! Is there a ferry boat?'

The interruption drew a guffaw from the scout and an annoyed grunt from Mose.

'Ferry? No. But you will find a ford.'

'Are there any houses?'

'Some few—but back from the path. You'd be hard put to find them without a guide.'

'To return to the *stream*, if you please.'

The scout stopped to think, scratching his head. 'Did I say acrost the Clinch?' He studied the dirt map. 'Through the gap … follow the river—no, before that. The Indian Road will take you through a gap in the hills. Just follow the crick. What the deuce was it? … the Moccasin! Once through the gap, follow the valley to the Clinch. But afore that, you will come upon a troublesome crick. Look for a shelf of rock and use that as a ford. Once acrost, look for the Clinch. That will take you through a gap—there are lots of high hills. The gap—'

'Does it have a name, this second gap?'

'Kane, I recall.'

'Caine?'

The scout nodded. 'That be it. Kane's gap. The trail slopes down to a valley—Powell's Valley. That heads off to the … south-west. It will bring you acrost Powell's River. Stay the course and follow the path up to the ridge. There be your pass.' He poked the dirt with the stick.

'You will know you are on the right trail if you see a tall, white ridge to your right as you proceed down the valley. The gap runs through those peaks.'

'And acrost the gap?' asked Mose.

The scout set down the stick. 'I'm told, by a reputable man, that the path splits off southerly and nor'-easterly. The southerly fork takes you down along a big river that runs back to this side of the mountains. The nor'-east branch is reputed to run clear through to the Ohio River *ad infinitum*, although my informant couldn't swear to it as he had not himself travelled that particular road.'

'How rough is the passage?' asked Boundless, determined to take equal authorship of the route.

'Hellish rough in places. There's brush, gullies, cricks, rocks, water and, when it rains, mud so thick it would swallow a horse. There's also savages, bandits and snakes to watch out for. As to the former, there are plentiful ambush spots that could hide a hundred Indians and you wouldn't spot a single one afore it was too late. But the worst of the road is this side of the pass. Once you're through the rock face, the going is said to be considerably easier.'

'And beside the rivers you mentioned, there are others?'

The scout nodded. 'Cricks aplenty. But you're crossing in summer, so you should have a smooth time of it—although the heat can get considerable. As for the Shawnee, they'll cheerfully lift your scalp come winter or summer. They're not particular, like some folk. The Colonel, for instance.'

Mose grimaced around the pipe. 'He sounds a trial.'

The scout sighed, a tragic expression on his face. 'A tribulation and a sorrow—to Christian and heathen alike. Afore you leave, you might study a petition to take him along with ye.'

'How many have passed through?' asked Boundless out of curiosity. 'Since the pass was found?'

'Hard to tell.' The scout scratched his chin reflectively. 'I can speak with certainty only to the three month or so we've been staked out here. In that time …' He scratched his chin again. 'Mayhap a hundred or more. The ones the Indians don't scalp will likely die of thirst or starvation afore they reach the other side.'

'A hard fate,' said Mose.

'Hellish hard,' agreed the scout, removing the pipe from his mouth. 'Although a party of Ulstermen left here not a week past, bound and determined to find the pass.'

Boundless glanced at Mose. 'The ones the farmer mentioned, back at the river?'

'No doubt.'

'They were an awful hard bunch,' the scout said. 'I almost pity the Indian that tangles with them.'

'It might be as well to travel with another party if the way be as hazardous as you say. Mose?'

'Four miles a day—at most! And wheel-fixing and babes bawling …' Mose spat in disgust.

'Wheels you needn't fret over.' The scout nodded to indicate the line of wagons standing in the grass. 'Abandoned ships,' he said. 'From here on, the trail is too rough and narrow for wagons. Those be the ones sold to the suttler or simply left to rot. The settlers continue on foot, mostly, with mules and packhorses.'

Boundless looked at Mose. 'We should camp here a few days. The stock should rest if the country is as rough as Mr Wick says.'

Mose eyed the scout. 'Any chance your suttler could sell us some mules to replace the ones we lost?'

'Mules, horses, guns, corn, powder, coffee, beans. He operates a regular Philadelphia store. I can't speak as to his prices, but there have been plenty of folk anxious to rid themselves of ballast.'

Mose stood up. 'Where can we find you?'

'Here. Lolling in the shade—away from the noise. I'll enjoy to share a glass of whisky when ye get fixed. But watch out for that Colonel. He'll have you marching up and down in the dust unless you set him to rights. It's a constant struggle to sit and smoke a pipe in peace.'

'He'd have more chance of swallowing his hat!' Mose grunted, irritable at the notion.

They purchased supplies from the suttler to replace that which they had lost crossing the river. Mose examined the mules with great care before deciding to purchase two of the creatures. 'I baptise thee Jacob,' he said of the first. 'After the peerless Mr Gottschalk, patron saint of this here venture. And there is a resemblance, too, in the ears.'

'And the other one?'

'You pick.'

He thought for a moment. 'Patience.'

'Let us join them with good Sir Prodigal.'

After they led the mules back to the horses, Boundless sat down in the grass. 'I should write down the directions. If they haven't flown out of my head already.' He opened the log. 'I counted three passes, and as many rivers. Do you agree?'

'I do. And three mules. We proceed by threes.'

THEY STAYED AT THE fort for several days, resting and grazing the stock. While Mose oversaw the reshoeing of the horses and mules, Boundless took the opportunity to quiz the scout on every detail of the route, the man proving as agreeable as the wagon party had promised. Under the scout's tutelage, he sketched the route in the log.

'A mighty fine map,' praised Wick as he studied the sketch approvingly. 'It looks easier—considerably so—on paper.'

'And the rivers?'

'The Holston, the Clinch, and the Powell.'

'And there—the pass?' Boundless pointed at the sketch.

'Shortly after Powell's River. Remember to look for the ridge of white rock.'

'You mentioned a second gap?'

'Aye. Over Powell's Mountain.'

'Caine gap?' The scout nodded.

'And the very first?'

'The Moccasin. Just follow the crick from the Holston.'

Boundless deliberated over the sketch. 'My companion was right. We proceed by threes. How high is it—the third gap, across the mountains—do you estimate?'

The scout puckered his lips as he considered. 'I heard Mr Martin—one of our party and an educated man—estimate it at fifteen hundred feet and more. How true that be, I cannot say. But it is high. The ridges on either side be that much again.'

'Are there buffalo along the way?'

'Used to be, but hunters shot them all for diversion. The last one perished a few years back. But acrost the mountains, there are said to be scads of them. Plus, deer and wild cats and bears *ad infinitum*.'

Boundless smiled. 'And, once across the gap, how far do you estimate to the Ohio River?'

'I wouldn't dare guess. At least as far as here to the notch, I reckon.'

'You have an excellent memory.'

'I do that.' The scout considered the fact. 'I have not the grace of writing, so must ink each mark in my head or else lose the path.'

Boundless harboured a faint hope that other horseback travellers might come along to accompany them through the mountains. But as the days passed the road remained deserted.

'The Shawnee put the wind up everybody,' said the scout as they watched a family from further down the valley hurry into the safety of the camp—the breathless farmer bringing vivid accounts of fresh Indian attacks.

'And the French?' demanded the Colonel, interrupting the wide-eyed farmer.

'He has French on the brain,' whispered the scout. 'He figures there's more grease in French hair than the Injun variety.'

One morning, Boundless watched a long packtrain of some thirty horses and mules escorted by two dozen heavily armed men stop by the camp on their way south to Carolina. 'We intend to build a church there and establish a God-fearing community,' the leader said when he enquired as to their purpose.

'What sort of church?' asked Boundless, intrigued by the man's quaint appearance and accented English.

The man swallowed from a wineskin, wiping the water from his mouth before replying. 'We are tasked to build Zion in the wilderness.' His eyes took on a glassy look. 'Lord, remember thy congregation, which thou hast purchased of old; the rod of thine inheritance, which thou hast redeemed; this Mount Zion, wherein thou hast dwelt.' He intoned the psalm with a feverish zeal, as if forgetful of Boundless' presence.

'Then I wish you Godspeed, friend.'

'Brother Bořek?' a man called.

His eyes glazed, the man pushed past Boundless as if he wasn't there.

The following morning, they were alerted by the shout of a sentry. Hurrying to where the man stood guard, they watched as the sentry pointed to the distance. The Colonel took out an eyeglass and surveyed the spot for a moment. Muttering in disappointment, he shut the eyeglass.

'Your Indian has no taste for steel,' he complained.

Boundless caught the eye of Wick where the latter lounged against a tree, his arms folded. The scout shook his head as the disappointed commander shut the glass and sat back down.

On the fifth day after arriving at the blockhouse, they took their leave, going over the route once more with the scout before riding slowly forth from the safety of the encampment.

'Look for the high, white ridge,' the scout advised as they rode off. 'And hang tight to your hair!'

34

The Indian Road

THE HORSES AND MULES were in fine fettle, and a breeze kept the gnats and flies at bay. But in spite of the companions' refreshed optimism, progress was slow. The dry, hard track was littered with roots and holes, which made any speed above walking a perilous exercise. In several spots, the woods encroached so thickly upon the passage that brambles and thorns tore at their bodies as they held out arms to protect their faces. As a result, they travelled less than four miles on the first day.

Early in the morning of the second day, they spied a column of redcoats approaching, led by an officer on a spotted mare. The road was exceedingly narrow, forcing them to surrender the path to allow passage. Leading the animals into the trees, they waited for the soldiers to advance to the spot.

'How do!' The officer halted his horse as the soldiers filed past. The men looked exhausted, many of them bandaged or supporting a wounded comrade.

'Captain Franklin of the Virginia Regiment. We are on our way to Fort Loudon.' The officer was drawn and unshaven, his coat ragged and torn.

'You look like you were in a scrap,' said Mose, introducing himself and Boundless.

'We ran into a large Shawnee war party two days northeast of here. Where are you headed?'

'To the Holston. Are we likely to run into your Shawnee?'

'We gave them a good blooding. I don't doubt they've returned to their villages to lick their wounds. But generally, the country is alive with savages. It be prudent to keep a sharp eye at all times.'

'How far is the Holston?' asked Boundless, unable to keep the unease from his voice as the exhausted troops filed past.

The officer gave a wave of his hand. 'Follow this path for six or seven days. You will come upon an abandoned farmhouse. Just past that point, the river cuts the road.'

'Much obliged,' said Mose.

'Good day, gentlemen. I advise caution and vigilance.' The officer nudged the mare forwards.

Boundless felt his anxiety rise further as they waited for the long column to pass. The depleted men trudged wearily one after the other. Some hobbled on makeshift crutches, others were carried on stretchers. He winced at the effort required to carry the wounded over the rough trail. The redcoats were followed by the militia—buckskinned frontiersmen who looked considerably more suited to the woods than their uniformed counterparts. Behind the militia came their Cherokee allies, dressed in breeches and breechclouts, many with bare torsos.

Mose poked Boundless to indicate the fresh scalps hanging from the waists of several of the warriors.

Six redcoats and several of the militia brought up the rear of the column.

'How do, friends?' one of the latter called out as he passed. 'We be looking for the King's Head tavern. D'ye know of it?' The jest brought tired chuckles from his companions and a guffaw from Mose.

'Straight ahead, gentlemen! And pretty wenches to serve!'

'They look the worse for wear,' said Boundless as the column trudged past and disappeared along the trail. 'Maybe we should consider returning to the fort to wait for other travellers? Alone, we wouldn't stand a chance should we encounter a Shawnee war party.'

'Then let us hope the captain be right and that the Shawnee have high-tailed it back to their lodges.' Mose set off, walking Jack. Boundless followed, grumbling to himself at his companion's wanton disregard of the captain's warning.

Eight days after departing the fort, they came upon the abandoned farmhouse described by Captain Franklin. Cheered by the sight, they continued a short distance before coming upon the Holston River. They followed this in a westerly direction for some miles, eventually arriving at where a long island occupied the centre of the river. They halted to stare, confident that this was the same one described by the scout.

'If I recall Mr Wick correctly,' said Mose, 'we are to follow past to where the stream joins with the north branch.'

Boundless nodded. 'Aye. He mentioned a good place to ford, just past the fork.'

Mose got down. 'Let us water the stock, while we may.'

As the animals drank, Boundless eyed a huge elm near the riverbank. He walked around the trunk, estimating it at well over twenty feet. Placing a hand on the warm bark, he felt the rough contours beneath his fingers as he speculated on the age of the tree.

'How ancient must it be to grow so thick?' he wondered aloud as Mose rummaged among the packs.

'Where in blazes did ye hide the jerky?'

Two miles past the island they reined in at where the river split, one arm turning north. 'The north fork,' announced Mose. 'What say we camp here for the night?'

The next day, they followed the fork looking for the promised ford. The heat was intense and the mites were irritating, buzzing in thick clouds about their heads. Boundless wiped the sweat from his face, flapping at the insects and cursing their abundance.

'Where did your Mr Wick say?' called out Mose, equally vexed by the heat and insects.

'He said we would come upon some Indian houses by the crossing.'

'Then we are arrived.'

Five abandoned houses stood a short distance from the river. Much to his companion's annoyance, Boundless insisted on dismounting to examine the ruins. The derelict lodges were built of sticks covered with bark. Lengths of reed matting and broken pots and pans lay scattered in the grass. Several fire pits were still in evidence with many bones visible on the ground. He looked inside the largest house, curious about its former inhabitants.

'What tribe were they—Shawnee?'

'More probably Cherokee, but who the devil can tell? The day wears on.'

'I am coming.' He mounted the bay, making a mental note of the ruined village to enter into the log.

They had barely resumed when they came upon a section in the river where the water flowed over a shelf of rock. 'Hats off to Mr Wick,' said Mose.

They led the train across on foot, the water swirling about their knees. On the other side, the path continued through some sand hills, the passage marked by numerous twists and dense vegetation. They followed this for two miles before the path split. After a brief pause to study the ground, Mose turned to the right fork.

'Are we on the right road?' called out Boundless, wary of the trapper's supreme confidence as to direction.

'He said the road led north-west?'

'I believe so.'

'Then this be the path. It will lead us to the creek your Mr Wick mentioned. What did he call it?'

'The Moccasin. The Indians made this path to cross the mountains?'

'No doubt it was a buffalo trace first, and the Indians followed to hunt the creature.'

He followed Mose along the ascending track while conceiting on the tens of thousands of buffalo that must have trampled the passage over how many hundreds, if not thousands, of years. When they made a brief stop to check the cargo, he crouched down, pressing his palm against the dry mud trail as if it still preserved the warmth of the vanished beasts.

'This must be it—the creek. See for yourself!' called out Mose, considerable satisfaction in his voice.

The creek, no more than a thin, trickling stream, flowed in a westerly direction. To the east rose a series of high peaks—whether properly called 'hills' or 'mountains', Boundless was uncertain. Reaching the top of the incline, he saw yet more hills rolling into the distance. Below, sunlight glinted on a river.

'That must be the Clinch,' he announced. 'In which case, we are standing in the first of our gaps, thank Fortune.

It was late afternoon as they began their descent to the river valley. They passed a number of small salt licks and the tracks of numerous animals. It was growing dark as they made camp by the side of the creek, the area enclosed by laurel and dense thickets of holly and ivy. They lit a fire, confident of the shelter provided by the cane, and passed an uneventful night.

Next morning, they discovered that the stallion had choked on weeds and was in no fit state to continue. 'We must wait until they pass,' said Mose. He urged the horse to the creek even as it tried to pull away. 'The water will help wash them down,' he said.

While waiting for Nature to take its course, they took the opportunity to replenish the food supplies and walked back along the trail in search of a large salt lick they had passed the previous day. The weather was hot and humid as they pushed their way through patches of resistant holly, the spiny leaves catching at their shirts and leggings. 'We passed over this trace but yesterday, and already it is closing back in,' remarked Mose.

Arrived at the lick, they were looking for a place of concealment when they heard a noise in the woods. Thinking it was a deer, Boundless was about to signal Mose when an arrow shot by his shoulder. Too startled to move, he glanced at the undergrowth as another arrow flew past his head.

'Flee!' shouted Mose.

Boundless took to his heels and fled as shrill cries came from the trees. Turning his head, he glimpsed Mose duck into the undergrowth. A party of Indians rushed out from the woods, emitting whoops and yelps as they took up the chase. Breathing hard, he fled down the trail. From behind came triumphant cries as the Indians raced in close pursuit. Panting, he scrambled over rocks and roots as the pursuing cries continued. Arriving at a steep incline, he abandoned the trace, mindful of leaving prints, and plunged into the thickets, badly scratching his face and almost losing a moccasin in the process. The cries grew fainter and he stopped, winded, to catch his breath, He listened for the sound of a musket, fearful lest the pursuers had caught up with Mose.

He heard a cry and fled deeper into the woods, heading away from the camp site. Alternately walking and running, he scoured the brush for a hiding place, too winded to run further. Spotting a tangled bank of fern, he took refuge, concealing himself behind a mossy log. Panting hard, he cocked the musket, determined to sell his life dearly if discovered.

After long minutes of nerve-racking silence, he heard noises from the surrounding trees as the Indians beat the brush for him. Hardly daring to breathe, he peered through the ferns as the savages drew closer. Three or four appeared, communicating by high pitched calls and fluting whistles as they looked for prints. His blood froze as they approached to within twenty yards of where he lay concealed. They stood close enough so that he could hear as they briefly conferred. Their foreheads were painted the same coppery colour as the Indian shot during the attack on the Valley Pike, and the shaven heads bore the same stiff crown of bristles. They wore buckskin shirts as protection against the holly. A gunshot sounded, and they rushed off in the direction. He watched them go, fearful that it may have signalled that Mose had been captured or killed.

He remained stock-still, not daring to abandon his refuge. The air was uncomfortably hot, and a fly buzzed around his perspiring nose. As he deliberated whether to risk unslinging the water bottle to slake his raging thirst, he spotted through the ferns five or six Indians advancing through the trees in a line, peering closely at the ground. They stopped to quarrel among themselves, seemingly enraged that their prey had escaped. One or two clearly wished to continue the search, arguing and gesturing to the woods. The others appeared equally determined to abandon it. Finally, a repeated hooting call from further up the slope seemed to make up their minds. With a final look around that took in the fern bank where he crouched concealed, they gave up the hunt.

He waited until dusk, drinking from the canteen and dampening the neckerchief to mop his neck and brow. Finally, as stars appeared through the gloom, he left the safety of the thicket. No sooner had he done so than he heard an owl hoot in the dense brush. Unnerved, he crept back to his hiding place and stayed there until dawn broke—twice dozing off, to his consternation, in spite of his strained vigilance.

As light paled the sky, he stole cautiously through the trees, expecting an assault at every moment. Taking a circuitous route, he headed back to the camp, concerned that the savages had discovered it. He dreaded that Mose was dead, the camp sacked, and he himself abandoned to the wilderness. He pushed the alarming thought from his mind, treading softly through the undergrowth, musket at the ready, as he made his way through the woods.

It was full daylight by the time he sighted the camp site. To his immense relief, he heard the whinny of a mule. He held position behind a rock, scouring the camp for signs that his pursuers lay in wait. Finally, convinced that it had remained undiscovered, he crept out from behind the rock and advanced stealthily towards the spot. He was almost within reach when he heard a soft hiss followed by a low voice. 'Boundless. Is that you?'

Overwhelmed with relief, he hurried to where a joyful Mose emerged from behind a bush to greet him. 'Thank Christ!'

'By thunder, but I feared you were scalped and hanging from some Indian's belt.' Mose grasped him by the hand, immense relief on his face. 'By thunder!' he repeated, pumping his hand.

The two exchanged accounts, Mose describing how he had fled into the woods expecting to be caught at any moment. 'I was fortunate. The ground was rough, and they were diverted by the noise of a bear.'

The trapper's voice gave full feeling to his profound relief as he recounted how he took refuge inside a small cave, pulling leaves and brush together to hide the opening. 'Three times I heard the devils beat the bushes within feet of where I lay hidden. So close I smelt their hides!'

'It is a miracle they never chanced across the camp.'

'And they would have, had we not led them away.'

'What shall we do now? They may still be lurking.'

'Let us find Jack and quit this cursed spot as soon as we are packed. It be God's mercy that we are safe and unmolested!'

IT WAS SEVERAL MILES before they relaxed their guard, finally convinced that the Indians were not in pursuit or setting up an ambush. Late in the morning, Mose called a halt on the banks of a stream. 'This must be it—the Clinch.' Before them, the stream emptied into a river close to 150 yards across.

'Is it deep?'

Answering his own question, Boundless ventured into the flow, testing for depth. The water barely reached his knees, even when thirty yards out.

'We can cross!'

Fording the river, they picked up the Indian path on the opposite bank. It wound past springs, freshets and steep defiles where the mossy banks closed in on both sides. A mountain loomed ahead of them. To the east and west ran a line of lofty hills.

'That may be the second notch the scout spoke of,' said Mose, indicating a gap in the mountain.

In the afternoon, they crossed over the gap and started down the far side. They stopped to rest and water the animals. Boundless wet another neckerchief and mopped the back of his neck.

'We shall boil in this heat,' complained Mose. They set off again, Mose bringing up the rear while Boundless walked the bay, the mare and mules following behind.

Labouring down an incline, he rounded a bluff. As he did so, he stopped—startled to find himself confronted by three bearded men, muskets at the ready.

'Do not shoot!' He raised his hands in surrender, fearing the men were bandits. They wore linen shirts and buckskin trousers. Their faces were lean and hard looking.

'What be your business?' demanded one, his musket levelled at Boundless' chest. 'Be you cut-throats or thieves?'

'Pilgrims, friend, as yourselves. And meaning harm to none.'

Mose came up behind him, his companion stopping short with an exclamation as he beheld the armed men blocking the path.

The men exchanged alarmed looks. 'How many of you?' demanded the speaker, trying to see past Mose.

'The two of us only.'

The man regarded Boundless with surly suspicion, the musket still aimed at his chest. 'Where be ye from?'

'Late of the soldier camp—and the New River. The farmer there mentioned a party of Ulstermen who had passed by shortly before us.'

'Ha! That old goat!'

'Indeed. We have the same purpose as yourselves, to cross the mountains.'

After a menacing pause, the man slowly lowered the barrel of the musket. 'Then proceed,' he said. 'But be challenged again when you reach the front.'

'We cannot pass. The road is too narrow.'

'Then wait. It is of no matter to us.' With that, the speaker turned away, followed by his two companions.

'A jolly fellow,' Boundless muttered, waiting until the man was out of earshot.

'Aye. They alarm me more than the savages.'

They followed the men for most of the day. Trees and branches had been hacked to blaze a path as the trail rose over bluffs and twisted between narrow gaps in the hills. Late in the afternoon, the road topped a ridge and descended into a long, shallow valley. The ridge afforded their first unconcealed view of the party before them. A long line of men, women and children, close to a half mile in length, toiled over the rough ground. Dozens of pack horses and mules, each heavily burdened with cargo, were strung the length of the column. A herd of goats and pigs followed, driven on by dogs and men with guns.

Mose removed his hat to scratch his head. ''Tis indeed the Scotch-Irish the farmer spoke of.'

'How many, do you think?'

'Ye be better at numbers.'

'I judge two hundred, at least.'

'Then let us pass and put them well behind, ere they shoot us for dinner.'

Mounting the horses, they started forward, overtaking the rear-guard, who regarded them with undiluted suspicion. A pack of the feral-looking dogs growled and snapped at the horses' hooves as they passed.

As they continued up the column, they were assailed by a strong, fetid odour of grease and sweat, the smell mingling with the stench and noise of the livestock. Small children walked barefooted alongside their parents or sat perched on top of the baskets carried by the mules. Many of the women carried infants in their arms, the babes swathed with shawls to protect them from the hot sun.

Boundless touched a hand to his hat as the adults turned to stare. Few returned or even acknowledged his polite greeting. Even the children watched with sharp, curious faces. A number of Negroes trudged amidst the migrants, and he wondered whether they were slaves or freemen.

The adult males were heavily armed with muskets, pistols and knives. In spite of their undoubted hardiness, they appeared exhausted and half-starved. 'It must take a deal of game to feed the entire party,' ruminated Boundless, raising his hat to a young woman clutching a babe as she walked beside a wagon.

It took the better part of an hour to overtake the slow-moving train—their progress continually impeded by the narrowness of the trail or the congestion of livestock. At the head, they were greeted by a short, barrel-chested man who stood squarely in the middle of the road, blocking their path. He wore a loose cotton shirt and canvas trousers. A straw hat, heavily stained with sweat, was pushed back on his head. He was flanked by a group of men, as heavily armed and surly looking as the unfriendly threesome they had encountered at the rear of the column.

Mose raised a hand as he pulled the chestnut to a halt. 'Good morrow, friends.'

The barrel-chested man stepped forward without acknowledging the salutation. His face, pale beneath the hat, shone with perspiration. He studied them, his eyes hard and appraising. 'Where be ye bound?' he demanded, a strong brogue to his voice. He breathed heavily and gave off a rank stench of sweat.

'Why, I imagine the same place as yourselves.'

'And where be that?'

'Along this road and up, over the mountains.'

'Ye be travelling alone?'

'We are, being hunters rather than settlers.'

'Those be fine horses, and mules.'

'Fine, and dearly treasured. Have you had trouble with Indians?' asked Mose as the barrel-chested man appeared to mull on the answer.

'We shot and skinned an even six the day afore yesterday,' one of the men said, the statement drawing no reaction from his companions.

Mose dismounted. 'Baccy?' he said, holding out the pouch, his voice obliging. No one moved forward to take him up on the offer. 'D'ye have news of the way ahead?' he asked, disregarding the snub.

The barrel-chested man gave an imperceptible nod at which the others appeared to relax somewhat. 'We have some news,' he said, 'in exchange for your own.'

As the trail master and Mose conferred, a number of women and children came forward to observe, a mix of curiosity and wariness on their faces. The women looked haggard and fatigued in their bonnets, shawls and heavy woollen skirts. The children were bare-legged and clad in dirty smocks, their faces grimy and distrustful.

'Good morrow to you, ladies,' said Boundless. feeling uncomfortable under the scrutiny.

A young woman attempted a brief curtsey and he half-bowed in return, drawing slack-mouthed looks from the children.

Mose was untying a sack of venison strapped to the lead mule. 'We have spare,' he said, holding out the sack to the nearest woman. She started forward but a sharp remark from one of the men caused her to step back.

'We have food aplenty, thank ye.' The trail master's voice was flat, his face expressionless.

'As you say.' Mose tied the venison back to the saddle. 'I bid you good morrow, ladies, gentlemen. And a fine day it is for travelling!' With a glance at Boundless, he climbed back into the saddle. 'Hup!'

The barrel-chested man stared impassively as Boundless touched his hat in farewell. He felt the narrowed eyes of the man boring into his back as he rode after Mose.

'They were rum fellows,' he said as they slowly left the column behind. 'Were they making sport when they mentioned skinning the Indians?'

'It wouldn't surprise me to learn they ate them as well.'

'Will they be able to cross with all those women and children?' He glanced back at where the party had recommenced its slow, toiling progress.

'In time. If the savages don't kill them, the weather holds, and they avoid the French patrols. If discovered, they will certainly be turned back— or worse.'

'They looked famished. I scarcely know whether to admire their courage or pity their foolhardiness.'

'It be the land that draws them, like flies to honey. The master—the pasty-faced fellow, told me the war with France burns up and down the Ohio. We must needs go carefully once acrost the mountains.'

'One more peril?'

Mose laughed. ''Tis all spice! Would you prefer to sit in your Philadelphia rocking chair and grow fat?'

'At least I should be certain of keeping my scalp. Did you pass on the felicitations of the farmer?'

Mose guffawed loudly, the sound echoing among the bluffs.

Next day, the path split again. One spur led towards a natural recess tunnelled into a formidable wall of rock that loomed high over the trail. 'It must be a thousand feet long,' estimated Boundless, pulling up to admire the sight.

'We have no time to gawk. This way be safer.' Mose set off along the other spur and Boundless followed, regretting he did not have time to explore the rock passage.

One of the mules had incurred a gash in its leg from brushing up against a rock and they made camp to tend to the injury. They took advantage of the hilly fastness to build a fire. While Mose saw to the mule, Boundless ventured a short distance to a lick where he shot a bear. They roasted the choicest portions in the gathering darkness while listening to wolves growling and snarling over the abandoned carcass.

'That good mule William would dance across these hills,' said Mose, still keening the loss of his favourite. He cut off a piece of meat and put it into his mouth. 'Mayhap this bear be cousin to the one that kilt him. In which case his grieving relatives can send letter back to that villainous creature that William is revenged.'

They continued the journey through stands of laurel and beech, the ground rising steadily as the path led deeper into the hills. For three hours, they travelled along a narrow trail, the path hemmed in by crags and wooded bluffs that rose steeply on either side. On several occasions, the trail disappeared altogether, and they were forced to back-track before picking it up again. Fallen trees, swift-running creeks and passages of sharp rock slowed their passage and necessitated walking most of the distance.

On the surrounding slopes, they sighted deer, partridge, bears, wolves and wild cats. Overhead, hawks circled lazily above the pine-covered bluffs, causing Boundless to wish he could sprout wings and fly across the mountains. In the trees, a great mass of warblers, thrush and ovenbirds kept up a constant chorus of song, the noise sufficient to drown out the sound of the mules.

Late the next morning, they followed the trace up a steep defile towards a visible gap in the solid mass of rock. The trail became steeper and rougher as the pass came into view. The high path skirted a precipice—boulders forcing them to step uncomfortably close to the edge. As he cleared the last of the boulders, he heard an unearthly scream. Turning, he saw Mose, mouth opened in shock.

'What happened?' He hurried back to the spot. Mose said nothing but leaned over the ledge. Looking down, Boundless saw the lifeless carcass of a mule where it lay on the rocks far below. Pieces of cargo lay scattered next to it.

'The basket banged against that rock. The blow drove him off balance and over the side.' Mose groaned in frustration. 'It was poor Patience. He was over in a thrice.'

Boundless peered down at the rocks. 'He was carrying food and blankets, and some of the powder. Should we climb down?'

'How would we carry it up again? And the powder is spilled out.'

They departed the spot, disconsolate over the loss of the sturdy mule and the supplies. 'The road is as hard on the animals as it is on us,' he reflected, tallying the loss of five mules.

They toiled upwards, finally reaching the notch—a narrow space bounded on both sides by high, mountainous rock. Boundless halted for breath, relieved to have reached the top. Mose wheezed beside him, exhausted from the steep climb. They looked out over a green landscape crowded with trees and surmounted by mountains to the east and west. A long, broad valley ran to the southwest. Amidst its verdant denseness, the sun glinted on a river that snaked between the trees.

'That must be Powell's River. If so, this be the second gap, and we are on the right path. Thank the gods!'

Mose frowned. 'There be only one. Shall we start down?'

Tired, but cheered by the knowledge they were not lost, they began the rocky descent into the valley. They proceeded carefully, determined to camp in the valley that night. The sun was sinking quickly as they finally struck level ground again. Finding a suitably grassy spot alongside a creek, they set up camp, leaving the horses and mules free to forage and drink from the creek. They decided against lighting a fire, reasoning that the valley was open to scrutiny from any number of places.

Nevertheless, Mose was in expansive mood as he lit a pipe following a supper of salted bear meat. 'By jinks, Boundless, but I scarce believe I be here.' He settled back against a tree to contemplate their journey.

'You do not miss your little cabin in the woods?'

'I do. But it be in nature, to grieve that which was.' Mose puffed on the pipe. 'We have not seen any buffalo. I had expected we might have come across a fair few by now.'

'Mr Wick said they are all shot this side of the mountains.'

'We shall see them without number soon enough.'

'It would not surprise me. The country runs to excess in every branch. How much further, do you think?'

'To the plains?' Mose yawned. 'A month ... two, somewhere in between.' He tapped out the burnt tobacco. 'Take watch, comrade. Wake me in a few hours.'

As he sat by the fire, Boundless pondered the distance they had come, picturing the wagon road and its tortuous length as it wound back to York and, from thence, Philadelphia. The difference between the latter, with its populous streets and taverns, and the Indian-haunted wilderness around him seemed beyond comprehension. *And the true wilderness, sans houses, sans Christian folk, yet lies before us.* He shuddered and added another stick to the fire.

35

The Gap

THE NEXT MORNING, THEY followed the Indian road through the valley. A narrow, trickling creek cut its way through the trees and shrubbery, which they followed, confident it would lead them to Powell's River. The sun was powerfully hot and they moved at a slow pace, glad of the patches of shade and the cooling presence of the creek.

After two hours, they stopped to water the horses. As Mose fussed with the rigging on the mules, Boundless wandered through the many trees that lined the course. He stopped before a tall chestnut, surprised to discover a name cut into the trunk: *A. Powell*. Curious at the find, he examined the nearby trees, discovering the same name, occasionally accompanied by a date, cut into the wood.

Bemused, he reported the find to Mose. 'It must be the fellow the valley is named after.'

'Aye. The river too, and the mountain, if your Mr Wick be a reliable guide. The fellow, whoever he is, has claimed all this land hereabouts, if in name only.'

Boundless pondered the fact as they continued. The unknown Powell had, by the simple act of carving his name, associated himself forever with the formidable valley. Unsure whether the deed represented the idle whim of an idle hour or an act of hubris that dared posterity to forget the unknown author, he looked for the name again at the next stop, finding it carved into several of the trees.

'The fellow was hell-bent on leaving his mark,' said Mose, and chuckled.

'What?'

'A good thing he did not possess a fine old German name, like a merchant I once knew named Knickerbocker!'

'Is this Powell fellow still alive, do you think?'

'Mayhap. The notch be less than ten years old.'

'Then memorialised while yet living! Truly, this country is so new that history invents itself even as we stand watch. Do you not think it a marvel that—'

'See to the mules,' said Mose, climbing up onto the chestnut.

A few miles further on Boundless was shifting in the saddle to relieve his aching back when he glanced up, his eye caught by something. A soaring ridge of white rock gleamed in the distance. 'Mose!'

Mose turned in the saddle, his face shining. 'By the bones! The famous notch!'

Immensely cheered by this irrefutable evidence that they were on the right path, they continued, making good progress over the flat ground. From time to time, Boundless glanced up, reassured by the white ridge.

Towards noon, they stopped for Mose to make water. As he prepared to remount, the trapper stopped, one foot in the stirrup. 'Witness!' He pointed to the sky.

Shading his eyes, Boundless saw a flock of birds circling high above the trees.

'Buzzards,' said Mose. 'They have found something. Stay sharp.'

As they approached the circling birds, Boundless took out the spyglass, but he could see nothing owing to the dense laurel that blocked the view ahead. 'What do you think it is?'

'Something big—with that many birds.'

Soon they were riding within earshot of the buzzards, their harsh cries echoing through the air.

Mose held up a hand and reined the stallion. Climbing down, he unsheathed his musket. Boundless did the same. 'Stay here while I scout ahead.' Leaving the animals with Boundless, he continued on foot.

As Mose disappeared into the trees, Boundless cocked the musket, licking his dry lips as he stared at the woods. A few minutes later, Mose re-appeared. 'Come!' He waved an arm and then turned back again into the trees.

Mustering the horses and mules, Boundless made his way through the trees. To his surprise they opened onto a broad plain, the ground flat and stony and stretching all the way to the mountains in the distance. Mose stood in the open, a grim look on his face.

Perturbed, he followed Mose's stare. 'Mother of God!' Several bodies lay in the dirt, their naked, discoloured flesh obscenely exposed in the sunlight.

'There are more,' said Mose. 'It happened some days ago, I calculate.' He spoke quietly, eyeing the trail for any signs that the attackers still lurked nearby. 'Keep your weapon to hand.'

As they resumed, they found the trail was liberally strewn with corpses, the naked flesh putrefying in the hot sun. Boundless exclaimed in horror at the gruesome sight.

'Keep going,' said Mose. 'Do not stop.'

They continued, passing more bodies with every yard of trail. Many had been shockingly mutilated, the pale, bloated corpses festering in the hot sun. Mules, dogs, oxen and pigs lay scattered among the bodies. Chairs, pots and pans, and items of clothing littered the grass. Buzzards and crows feasted on the banquet, the birds hopping from corpse to corpse while squabbling over the choicest portion.

Shocked at what met their eyes, they made their way along the trail of slaughter—the scenes of wanton depravity so dreadful that several times Boundless was forced to avert his gaze. A woman lay sprawled in the grass, her nose cut off and the eyes gouged from her face. Her hair had been hacked from her head, leaving a congealed, bloody scalp in its place.

A youth sat propped against the side of a small handcart, as if on display, his white flesh dreadfully crimsoned with cuts and slashes. A short distance away the tiny body of an infant lay speared to the ground, a lace cap still tied to its head. Nearby, a naked woman, perhaps the infant's mother, was propped half-sitting against a dead mule. Her lifeless hands still covered her private parts, her head hanging as if in unspeakable shame.

He placed his neckerchief over his nose and mouth to block the over-powering stench of rotting flesh as the trail of carnage continued, the ransacked and swollen bodies gruesome in death. Flies buzzed around the bloodied carcasses—many of which had been fed on by scavengers. A pair of crows flapped up from one body at their approach. Dogs lay along the road, lips pulled back in a snarl of death. He felt a sickening rush in his throat as they passed by the slashed body of a Negro—the entrails torn from the gut and dragged into the grass.

Unnerved by the grisly scenes, neither man exchanged a word as they continued. They stopped only to water the horses and mules before has-tening on again in an unspoken pact to put as much distance as possible between themselves and the place of slaughter.

As the light failed, they made camp in a small grove of hickory trees. They ate a meagre supper of beans and biscuits, staring into the flames of the small fire as they sipped hot tea. Finally, unable to push the grisly images from his mind, Boundless broke the silence, his voice trembling with outrage.

'What manner of creature could so brutishly and wantonly slaughter innocent women and children? They are well named savages! For even beasts do not so wickedly defile the bodies of the dead.'

' They make war as they hunt. We are but deer or wolves to their muskets. Their ways are not ours."

'Their ways be of the devil!' Overcome with bitterness, Boundless cast the remnants of his supper into the flames.

'They are as God made them.'

He brooded on the remark as he stretched out by the fire while Mose took watch. He lay awake, his conscience tormented by images of the mutilated bodies lying pale and desolate in the moonlight. The night was clear and warm, the stars twinkling in bright clusters. At length, sickened and exhausted, he fell into a haunted, muttering sleep.

THEY RESUMED THE NEXT day, eyes vigilant for signs of Indians. But the attackers seemed to have deserted the area. 'No doubt to seek out more settlers,' opined Mose.

For once, Boundless welcomed the hardships of the passage, the many obstacles driving thoughts of the massacre from his mind. Frequent growths of cedar and barberry gave some relief from the sun and the omnipresent mites.

They were crossing a small creek where it trickled through a jumble of rocks when the bell mare gave a sharp whinny and reared up on her hind legs.

'Snake!' Mose dismounted to seize the stricken mare by the bridle. 'Whoa!' He dragged on the rein, attempting to soothe the panicked horse. 'We had best make camp,' he said as the mare calmed sufficiently for him to lead her towards a stand of cedar. 'We may lose her if she is badly bit.'

In the shade of the trees, Boundless unloaded the mules while a worried Mose tended to the mare, uttering dire imprecations against 'the God-cursed tribe of belly-sliders' as he inspected the bite.

'Will she last?' asked Boundless, going over to look.

'Mayhap. The puncture was slight and just above the hoof. The poison may not have taken root. We shall know on the morrow.'

The next morning the mare appeared listless and distressed, refusing to take food. She panted heavily, her neck trembling as she stood beneath the trees. Inspecting the bite, Mose muttered in dismay. 'We will camp here one more night to see if she recovers. If not, she will sicken and die.' He shook his head. 'A plague on all snakes!'

To their surprise and relief, the mare appeared to recover her appetite by evening, accepting oats and nuzzling the mules affectionately as if none the worse for her ordeal.

'Blessed if she ain't cured herself!' Mose rubbed the mare's neck before bending down to inspect her leg. 'She may yet chew grass on the western plains.' He looked up with an expression of great satisfaction. 'Tomorrow, she will be fit to continue.'

His prediction proved accurate as the mare trotted along the next morning as if in fine spirits. Cheered by the sight they continued at a good pace, the path being free of encumbrances.

Early in the afternoon they arrived at Powell's River. The water was clear as glass, and he judged it to be no more than seventy or eighty yards across. They forded without incident. Once across, Mose led off in good spirits, confident that the elusive and long desired pass was at last within reach. 'How far did your Mr Wick say to the notch?'

He searched his memory. 'From here … no more than ten or twelve miles.'

In one of those strange turns of weather to which Boundless had grown resigned, the fine afternoon turned abruptly wet and cold, a gusty wind tearing at their clothes. The ridge became enveloped in grey mist as rain showers swept the exposed ground. They were further delayed by a rushing creek that proved dangerous and troublesome to cross. Buffeted by wind and rain, they travelled for less than four miles before reluctantly submitting to the weather and making early camp.

'Damn and blast all to hell!' Mose muttered angrily as they worked to erect a rough shelter of branches and cane. Thoroughly soaked, they passed a miserable night huddled in their deerskin capes as the wind howled and crashed around them and rain fell in torrents. Mose alternately cursed the gale and tried in vain to light his pipe. When the wind dropped, they were kept awake by the screech of a wild cat and the constant howling of wolves. The latter were so insistent that they had to get up to calm the skittish animals—Boundless catching a glimpse of burning eyes in the darkness as the creatures crept up to prowl around the camp.

Towards dawn, the storm had blown itself out and they made a fire to warm themselves. 'At least we have scads of wood,' remarked Mose as he picked among the fallen branches.

The ground, although soggy, was navigable. Chewing on the remnants of a salted fowl, they set out with the risen sun behind them.

The ridge of white rock loomed above the trail, and Boundless studied it as they rode, struck by its unyielding massiveness. He fancied it to resemble the battlements of some great, medieval castle. The formerly flat path now took a moderate ascent, taking them away from the valley and up into the foothills. In spite of the incline, the road was smooth and passable. He felt his spirits rise as he gazed up at the ridge, impatient to cross it to the other side. 'The plains await,' he told himself. 'And so do the buffalo.'

The climb became steeper. They led the animals on foot, the mules snorting with protest as the baskets banged against the brush. They entered a stretch of dense tree cover and, in so doing, lost the path. Scouting the area, they found it again within a few minutes and continued through stands of oak. In spite of their eagerness, they halted for a rest, well aware of the twin dangers of fatigue and ambush in such thick vegetation. Small spurs led out from the path, and they followed these once or twice before realising their error and returning to the main trail.

Mired in thought, Boundless took little notice as the bay chose an easier path through the stands of hickory, oak and chestnut. He was only brought back to awareness when struck by an overhanging branch. He looked around, uncertain of the way. The trees seemed to have closed in upon them and the trail had become noticeably steeper. *We must be close to the top.* The brush was now so dense he was forced to take out the axe. Walking a few yards in front, he hacked a path, struggling to keep his feet as the trail rose sharply upwards. Within a mile, he was using both hands to climb, clutching at roots for balance, while the weary horses scrambled and lunged behind him. Finally, the ascent grew so hazardous that he called a halt. 'I fear we have lost the path,' he said.

Mose bent to study the ground, his breath harsh and laboured. Straightening up, he wiped his brow, his face disconsolate. 'A plague upon it.' He spat dust from his mouth. 'We must retrace our steps.'

'But we need to be certain,' Boundless insisted, unwilling to contemplate abandoning the ascent when so close to the top. 'Stay here and rest with the animals while I go on ahead. If it is indeed the wrong path, there is no sense in further tiring the horses.'

Mose readily acceded to the suggestion, the trapper looking exhausted as he sat down on a log to open the water bottle. 'Be watchful,' he warned. 'One slip and you will break a leg.'

Boundless set off, shielding his face against thorns and branches. In less than ten minutes, he emerged from the brush to find himself standing on a high, rocky ledge that dropped precipitously to the ground far below. *This cannot be the pass.* Overcome with frustration, he turned and made his way back down the incline.

He found his companion fast asleep, his head slumped to one side where he snored against a fallen branch. He shook the trapper awake. 'It is not the path,' he said, his voice heavy. 'We must go back.'

The trapper groaned. 'Then what in blazes is it—if not the blamed pass?'

'A plateau—with no way down save this one.'

'You are certain?'

'See for yourself if you wish.'

'I do, by thunder!'

A little later, both men stood on the plateau. Mose swore and shook his head as he regarded the sheer drop. 'Samson's jawbone!' In frustration, he kicked a stone over the edge. 'We must retrace our steps,' he said, his voice prickly. 'A moment while I catch breath.' Sitting down in the shade, he leaned back against the rock, his face drained of its normal colour.

Boundless frowned, concerned at the older man's distressed state. 'The day wears on and it is hotter than Hades. What say you we rest here, in this spot, for the night? It is defensible and hidden from view.'

'The horses?'

'Leave them be. There is plenty of tree bark and grass to chew on. They are content and will not stray.'

Mose took a swallow from the canteen. 'Give them some water,' he said tiredly.

While Mose rested in the shade, Boundless collected brushwood to make a fire, confident that the surrounding rocks and high elevation would offer protection from any hostile eyes. He looked up to say something and saw that Mose had fallen fast asleep, his head lolling against his chest. Cross with himself for not noticing his companion's distress earlier, he vowed to keep a closer observation of the older man. *The journey has taken a toll on me,* he reminded himself. *And he is not half as young.*

Feeling the effects of the arduous climb, he walked to the edge of the rocky pinnacle and sat down, dangling his feet over the precipice. Taking off his hat, he allowed the air to cool his head while savouring the heady prospect.

'By the bones but it's a sight, though, ain't it?' Mose had woken up, looking the better for his brief nap. On hands and knees, he crawled forwards to peer over the dizzying drop. 'How high up are we do you calculate?'

'Two thousand feet, I should guess.'

Mose shuddered and retreated back from the ledge. 'You have a head for high places. I am fearful lest a gale swoop me up.'

'It is a long way down.' Boundless stood up to survey the prospect. The late afternoon light bathed the verdant landscape in a languorous haze. Far into the distance, the country blossomed with rolling hills, pine-clad bluffs and deep gorges glinting with water.

'Don't tumble off!'

Boundless laughed, rejuvenated by the bracing elevation. 'Come. Stand by me. See what country it is that awaits us.' Bemused at the trapper's timidity, he held out a hand. 'Come. There is no gale.'

Cautiously placing one foot before the other, Mose made his way forwards. 'By jakes!' His face grew solemn as he took in the full, glorious vista of pine-crowned hills and forested slopes. 'I should shudder to swap such a sight for the whole of Virginny.' He pointed to the rolling peaks. 'And mark. These be but footstools to the mountains that are said to lie beyond the plains.'

'This might stand as the lost Garden—if ever there was such a place.'

'There was indeed such a Garden. I do not doubt it.'

'Then behold, friend. Here it lies, naked before us.'

They stood in silence for a few moments, marvelling at the panoramic view. A bird screeched nearby, and Mose stepped back from the edge. 'I pray that I do not stroll about in my sleep!'

BOUNDLESS AWOKE SHORTLY AFTER dawn. Pink rays flooded the small cavern where they lay. As they waited for full light to better judge the tricky descent, he took one last look out over the precipice. Far below, the landscape was shrouded in mist, the vapour rising upwards like smoke as it warmed in the sunlight. A hushed silence hung over the hills and he fancied the scene to await only the blast of the paradisal trumpet to signal the start of day.

'Are ye fit?' Mose looked refreshed after a sound night's sleep.

'Aye. Ready and able.'

They collected the horses and mules on the way back down, walking them to the foot of the steep incline. As soon as they emerged from the brush, they saw the trace before them. The trail was flat and level in contrast to the thorny ascent to the plateau.

Boundless muttered at the sight, rueful at the wasteful detour.

'I do know not how I lost the path,' he said.

'No matter. We are rested and fit to travel.'

They had barely embarked on the trace when they passed a large cavern set into the hillside. Feeling a draught of cool air as they passed the mouth of the cave, Boundless halted, curious to inspect the interior.

'Perish the cave! Let us finish this jaunt.' Mose's voice was eager, now that the long-dreamed-of notch was at hand.

The trail pitched steeply as they continued. Boundless had to lean forward to counterbalance the incline, dropping the reins of the bay to balance himself. The humid air and loose shale that covered the path made the climb ever more arduous as the horses and mules scrambled for footing. He glanced back at Mose, who had stopped to rest, labouring from the effects of the strenuous climb.

Boundless continued, his breath coming in gasps. To his relief, the top of the ridge at last came into view. Clambering the last hundred yards to the summit, he stopped and stood upright, panting heavily from the effort. Below, and into the distance, the landscape extended in a mazy patchwork of woods and pasture interspersed with streams, creeks and hills.

Jubilant at gaining the summit he let out a tired whoop. 'We have done it Mose—crossed the mountains!'

Wheezing and panting, Mose joined him at the summit, the older man near to exhaustion.

'Behold, Mose—the Western promise!' Boundless gestured to the fertile distance.

Mose nodded, gasping and bent over, too winded to speak.

36

A Country But Newly Found

AFTER THE TRAVAILS OF the climb, the descent proved surprisingly smooth and agreeable—the path unhindered by rocks or entanglements, and the high elevation offering an unobstructed view of the lush country below. As they navigated their way down the grassy ridge—walking to spare the horses—Boundless breathed a little easier, convinced that the most arduous part of the journey was now behind them.

They had not long begun the descent when the girth strap on the first mule slipped, leaving the cargo dangerously lopsided. Calling out to alert Mose, he steered the pack train off the path and into the shade of a laurel grove.

Boundless began tightening the straps and ropes as Mose wandered off into the thicket. He had finished moving supplies between baskets to even the weight when he heard a hail from his companion. He found him standing in front of a beech tree, peering at the trunk.

'We are not the first pilgrims along this path by any means.' Mose pointed to a cross blazed into the tree. 'And see—' He indicated several nearby trees, each similarly blazed with figures, crosses or initials.

Boundless studied the markings, an emotion of fellowship rising in him at these further signs that other travellers had traversed the same wilderness. Mose, meanwhile, had taken out his knife and was busily skinning the bark from a tall laurel that stood neighbour to the beech.

'What are you doing?'

'We ought leave our own mark. It will take but a minute.'

While Mose worked on the blaze, Boundless wandered deeper into the trees, exploring the source of a small spring. The day was humid and cloudy, and the branches provided welcome shade from the sun. He found the source of the spring where it bubbled out from a rock face. He was crouched down, sipping from the cool water when Mose called out to him.

'Come. Witness our mark!'

He went back to where the trapper had blazed the initials *MvD* and *BM* into the skinned trunk of the laurel. Underneath was carved the inscription, *April 1758.*

Boundless rubbed a thumb over the inscription. 'The date is mistaken. How can it be April when we left near the end of that month? By any reckoning we have been on the road for two months. The date ought say June.'

'True,' conceded Mose, looking not the least abashed by the error. 'But April is the Christian month and therefore a more fitting auger of our venture.'

'But surely, the mark ought be authentic to the fact?'

'Pshaw!' Mose waved aside the objection. 'The days are put there for our sufficiency, are they not? Whosoever sees this mark will not think to question its truth but only to admire the fittingness of the moment. What matter a month or two here or there so long as the time be happily suited to the occasion?'

As Boundless continued to argue the point, Mose grunted in exasperation. 'The day is hot. Let us not quarrel over a trifle. We are memorialised by this mark so long as this tree doth last.'

Mose turned and set off towards the horses. 'By jinks. If I had time and tree enough I'd memorialise old Jack too, and the pernickety mules as well!' He slapped the nearest mule on the rump. 'You too, Prodigal, deserve remembrance!'

They continued their descent, entering into a country of surpassing loveliness. The grassy slopes of the ridge gave way to rolling pastures dotted with patches of vivid gentian and pale, pink-flowering shrubs. Numerous creeks and springs watered the rich grass. Mose pointed to where a group of deer browsed the reeds, the animals standing erect to flick their tails and watch as the pack train passed by. The deer sightings became more plentiful as they went along, a herd of two or three hundred feeding on shoots along the banks of a creek. Small bands of elk and antelope foraged amidst the deer, the animals intermingling in the verdant grass.

Shortly before noon, they encountered the largest herd of elk they had yet seen—several thousands of the creatures grazing on meadows of sedge and butterweed.

'We shan't go hungry,' declared a gleeful Mose. 'I never saw such plenty.'

The game became more numerous and diverse as they continued. Fowl were particularly abundant—turkey, grouse and partridge flying up from the grass at the approach of the horses. Mose exclaimed with delight as a plump turkey barely escaped the hooves of the stallion. 'No need of the gun. We shall trample ourselves dinner!'

Within the space of a mile, they spotted a black bear with cubs, a pack of wolves, and several wildcats skulking through the grass, the sharp screeches of the latter unsettling the mules.

'Their durned caterwauling minds me of Indians,' said Mose.

At times, the game herds grew so abundant that they found themselves riding through the midst of the animals—the ranks parting at their approach.

'Should we take one for supper?' Boundless called out as a curious fawn wandered up to inspect the mules.

'Why tote the meat?' Mose replied over his shoulder. 'They are thick on the ground. Let us wait until we make camp.'

Boundless looked around in the saddle. 'Where are the buffalo? I am eager to see the beasts.'

'Mayhap a little ways on. Never fear. We shall encounter them afore long.'

They splashed across a shallow creek, Mose gesturing to where mink and muskrats darted through the reeds. A great variety of frogs, ducks, kingfishers, flycatchers and blackbirds congregated along the banks, their croaks and chirps setting up a constant chorus to accompany the noise of the splashing hooves. Mose halted to observe a line of large rodents where they scurried atop a blockage of logs and branches. 'Yonder skips a dozen, fur-trimmed hats wanting aught but the milliner's hand!'

'These are the beaver?'

'As true as life. It's been a sight since their pelts graced my saddle.' Mose watched fondly for a few moments before nudging Jack forward. 'How long has it been, Jack? Lord, but a time.'

A few minutes later, he pointed to a large grizzly fishing in a creek. 'Watch out for those gentlemen. They be contrary at the best of times and care nothing for courtesy. They will charge man or horse without so much as a by-your-leave. Best to avoid the critter, unless you are fixing to shoot him for supper.'

The weather continued very warm. Boundless took off his hat to let the breeze cool his slicked hair. When they halted by a spring, he dunked a strip of cloth in the water and tied the wet rag around his neck. Resting in the shade, they chewed on fowl salted from the day before. Mose nodded off—to awaken with a start a few minutes later as Boundless made a fuss of tending to the bay.

Sitting up, the trapper yawned and rubbed his eyes. 'Let us continue.'

In spite of Boundless' eager vigilance, the buffalo proved elusive, and he began to doubt the claims of its spectacular fecundity west of the mountains.

'Patience,' said Mose when he voiced his disappointment. 'We are scarce across the notch. 'You shall see them soon enough.'

The following morning, they were bothered by humid, sultry weather and a plague of blackflies that tested the patience of the men and sorely tried the animals. Boundless was forced to restrain the bay as a thick cloud of flies swarmed its ears and eyes. 'Confound them all to hell!'

Mose took off his hat, flapping it wildly in an attempt to disperse the biting insects. At that moment, the bell mare gave a frightened snort and bolted past, the mules in pursuit. 'The devil take it!'

They took off after the spooked mare, pulling her up after a chase. 'She's been badly bit.' Mose inspected her ears as the mare whinnied in distress.

Boundless scratched a bite on his face. 'Let us keep moving and pray for a breeze.'

They abandoned the open pastures, taking to the woods in an attempt to escape the flies. Coming across a small stream, they stopped and bathed the ears of the livestock in an attempt to soothe the stinging bites.

'Why in the name of creation did the good Lord inflict such devilish pests upon us?' grumbled Mose, tending to his own bites.

'The wind is picking up,' noted Boundless with relief.

To their dismay, the breeze died almost as soon as it began. They continued on, suffering in the humid air and slapping irritably at flies.

In the afternoon, hot and discomforted, they came across a river that flowed across the path. They sat on the banks debating whether this was the stream mentioned by the scout that led back across the mountains, or whether it was, as Mose argued, a fork of the Ohio.

'The Ohio! That must be at least a week away.'

'A *fork*, I said! Do you not have ears?'

Boundless stared at the flowing water, irritable in the prickly heat. 'Where the deuce are we, anyway?' he said, dogged by a suspicion that they were proceeding aimlessly.

'We follow the Indian road—to the west.'

'Much lies to the west—which portion of it?'

Mose leaned in the saddle and hawked into the grass. 'The Ohio. Where in blazes do you suppose we are headed?'

Boundless bit his tongue, angry past reason at the flies, the heat, the endless road, and the day in general. 'Then let us at least cross this blasted stream!' He nudged the bay forward into the water.

Once across, a wind sprang up and the weather began to cool. The path led towards a line of hills in the distance, and they rode that way with the intention to make camp at their base.

'Here is a spot.' Mose pulled rein in a stand of trees. 'Perish the day!' The trapper climbed stiffly down from the stallion, his face drawn with fatigue. A bloody swelling on his neck showed where he had scratched at a bite.

Releasing the horses from their tack, and the mules from their baskets, they checked them for bites, fed them and let them graze in the shade. After building a fire, Boundless climbed part-way up the nearest hill to survey the country with the glass. Dusk was already falling, and the landscape was bathed in purple shadow. Apart from a small herd of deer foraging in the distance, the country seemed empty of all save trees, grass, hills, creeks and shrubs.

'There is no sign of habitation,' he said to Mose as he returned to the fire.

'We are beyond the inhabited lands. Here the only denizens be Indians and wild animals.'

Boundless considered this as he sipped a mug of hot black tea while waiting for the venison to roast. Once again, the distinction between his native land and his present abode came back to unnerve him. 'Here there is no civilisation,' he reflected. 'Only unlimited wilderness, wild beasts, *flies*, and savages.' The knowledge that they were beyond the furthest settlements, denied even the consoling thought of a tavern or farmhouse as potential refuge from the elements, gave him sober pause. 'I am as Robinson Crusoe,' he told himself, disconcerted by the notion.

Mose winced as he plucked a portion of burned meat from over the fire. 'Tarnation if I didn't cook my fingers!' He gingerly tested the meat with his teeth. 'By jinks!' He hooted with delight, the earlier fatigue dispelled by his pleasure in the moment. 'We are in the Lord's own country, Boundless. Make me a liar if the meat doesn't taste better this side of the mountains.'

Boundless shook his head in grudging admiration of his companion's rapid powers of recuperation. 'You think that highly of the country—with all its flies and heat?'

'I shouldn't swap it,' Mose took another bite of meat, 'not for all the gold in Spain.'

The next day, they followed the trace as it wound into the hills. The heat increased throughout the morning, but a steady breeze kept away the insects. They were moving along at a leisurely pace when Mose stopped suddenly.

'Hold up.' He raised his arm as he studied the path.

A short distance ahead the trace split into two—one fork continuing up into the hills, the other leading downwards through the trees.

'Which one is the Indian road?'

Mose shrugged. 'Both.' He nudged the stallion towards the second, fainter trail. 'This one will at least take us out of the sun.'

'Will it take us to the Ohio?'

'As good as the other.'

The trail led through a series of rifts and defiles watered by rushing creeks and tumbling waterfalls. The path became narrower as it wound along the foot of the towering hills. The sandstone heights were heavily populated with chestnut and oak which overshadowed the trail and provided some relief from the sun. Turning sharply downwards, the trail skirted a lush, fertile gorge to their right. In the hushed shade of the bluffs, it was easy to fancy that they were the first to ever set foot in this mossy accretion of ancient trees and spongy soil.

The path flattened out as it ran alongside a creek, the bubbling water seeming to cool the air. They were in a small valley, the head of which was formed by a wall of soaring rock.

'Jeremiah if we ain't boxed ourselves in.' Mose halted at a spot where the trace disappeared into a narrow defile in the imposing cliff face.

Boundless groaned in dismay. 'We shall have to turn back.'

'And perish in the heat?' Mose took off his hat and wiped his brow. 'The devil if I will!' He gestured to the cleft in the rocks. 'The path continues through there.'

'What if it also runs into a dead-end? There looks to be scarce room enough to turn round and come out again.'

'Animals would not enter such a trap. Let them decide.'

'Why take the chance? At least we can see the way ahead if we take the road over the hills. Who knows where this may lead us?'

'Then let us discover!' Mose coaxed the stallion forward.

Biting his tongue, Boundless followed, promising that this would be the last time he acceded to his companion's impetuous adventurism. *He goes blindly, trusting only his instincts in disregard of logic or deliberation.* He glanced up towards the wooded heights now towering above them.

'Close up the mules!'

Moments later they entered the shadowy recesses of the gorge—the entrance so narrow that the wicker baskets squashed against the sides as the mules squeezed through. The defile was no more than a split or crack between two solid walls of sandstone—the sheer rock faces on either side and a rift of blue sky high overhead. The air was noticeably cooler in the shade and Boundless took off his hat, glad at least to be out of the burning sun.

'It continues!' Mose shouted from ahead.

They followed a dried-out riverbed that cut between the rock walls. The ground dropped away, the path leading downwards in a pronounced decline. The dazzling variances of light and shade blinded Boundless as he followed his companion deep into the recesses of the gap. The mossy grass underfoot had disappeared, replaced by loose shale and stones that cracked with the weight of the hooves. The dry shale sent up smoke balls of dust as they followed the ancient riverbed between the high bluffs of weathered sandstone. Aeons of wind and rain had polished the overhanging rock face to the smoothness of grey slate.

Patches of blue sky threaded with tendrils of white cloud accentuated the cavernous depth of the narrow canyon. The loud *clop* of hooves on stone, the creak of leather harness, and the snorting sighs of the animals were the only sounds to disturb the heavy stillness of the rocks. Lulled by the cool shadows and cavernous echoes, Boundless had slipped into his own thoughts when he was brought back to alertness by a shout from Mose.

'By the bones but some heathen has left a handshake! Come! Meet your buffalo!'

Squinting to see in the half-light of the canyon, Boundless exclaimed in astonishment as he stared up at the canyon wall. The life-size figure of a horned beast was etched into the grey rock face some twenty feet above the ground. The etching was flanked by smaller images of wolves and birds. A circle, divided into four quadrants, was pecked into the rock to the right of the bison figure. A cluster of stick men holding lances threatened the flanks of the snorting bull. It took him a moment to realise that the image depicted a primitive hunt. To his fancy, the figures seemed captured in the very moment in the dim light of the canyon.

'Jinks if it don't beat all!' Mose shook his head in amazement. 'How in blazes did a heathen get up there to make those marks?'

Boundless shaded his eyes to better study the etchings. What at first sight he mistook for appendages proved, on closer observation, to be lances sticking from the side of the buffalo. The skill of the unknown hand in so vividly depicting the beast confounded him.

'It breathes fire!' he marvelled, spellbound with admiration.

The plain, simple lines scratched and chiselled into the rock seemed like those a child might make, while yet powerfully suggestive in their economy and design.

Mose grunted in disapproval. 'A heathenish image, if ever I saw one. Look there!' He pointed to a faded, dyed imprint of a hand on the rock.

Moving alongside, Boundless stood up in the stirrups, stretching up to place his hand over the mark. 'Exact to the inch!' He sat back down, elated by the discovery. 'Is it not most remarkable? Think, Mose, some savage hand has carved this figure on this rock—eons ago. For what purpose?'

Mose snorted. 'A brag! To scare off enemies.'

'Or mayhap the figure itself has some superstitious meaning? Perhaps the creature—the buffalo, as you say—is an object of veneration, in the way of Aboriginals?' He stared at the artefact as though it might yield up its mystery to scrutiny. The scratched lines were curiously elongated—the artist seemingly unacquainted, or unconcerned with, scale, yet capturing a sense of shimmering breath that imbued the pecked figure with a ghostly presence.

'I have heard of the like in the Scottish Highlands. They are said by philosophers to be of immense antiquity. But never did I expect to encounter such a sight in this godforsaken wilderness. Mayhap it is as old as its Scottish kin.'

'It be drier than Hell!' Mose took a swallow from the canteen. In the silence, they heard a distant rumble echo through the canyon.

'Thunder?' He looked questioningly at Mose.

'Mayhap. Or a rock fall somewhere.' Mose peered up at the high canyon rim. 'We be easy prey for tumbling rocks or savages alike. Hup!' He kicked the stallion forwards, tugging the rope of the bell mare.

Boundless lingered, entranced by the primitive power of the image. The unknown creator had taken the time and effort to detail individual features—a hoof, a barely perceptible tufted tail, and what might have passed as an eye. The great head stared past the rock, the immense body solid and unyielding as it bestrode the stone. He gazed in wonderment—speculating whether he looked upon some ancient heathen god.

Torn between a desire to open the log and sketch the creature and to follow Mose, he reluctantly pulled away from the rock face to catch up with his companion.

They came upon other rocks, similarly adorned. The etchings, set high up in the rock face, depicted bears, wolves and elk, as well as buffalo, the white scrims standing out in ghostly relief against the dark stone. To his immensely curious eye, the works appeared to be of different ages—some so faded by weather that they were almost invisible against the rock face.

He glanced around to find that Mose had again disappeared. He hurried to catch up while bemoaning the trapper's haste to traverse the canyon. 'Who knows but we are the first white men to ever set eyes on them,' he lamented, loathe to abandon the carvings so quickly.

He found Mose halted in a clearing where a spring tumbled down the cliff face.

'Let us pause a spell to drink. I could slake a barrel.' The trapper dismounted and walked, stiff-legged, to the spring. Removing his hat, he dipped it into the rush of falling water. He supped from it before shaking out the water and pulling the hat back down over his head. 'By flint but it be chill!'

Boundless followed his companion's example, thrusting his hands into the stream and gasping at the coldness. He splashed water over his face and hair before drinking. The mules drank thirstily from where the water collected in a pool before trickling into a basin under the rock.

'Jack has picked up a gash.' Mose crouched to inspect the hind leg of the stallion.

Boundless sat on a rock as Mose washed the wound and bound a cloth around the gashed leg. The trapper observed carefully as the stallion nibbled a few shoots of coarse grass that sprouted amid the stony ground. 'The leg is agile,' he said, satisfied. He glanced up at the soaring sandstone bluffs. 'I shall not be sorry when we are quit of this place. Are ye fixed to continue?'

The trail gradually ascended as the surrounding bluffs diminished in height. Boundless scanned the rock face hoping for more etchings, but they seemed confined to the deepest section of the gorge. *If that was indeed the buffalo, then I am doubly eager to witness the creature with my own eyes*, he told himself, vowed to make several sketches as soon as they set up camp.

The stony trail emerged into dazzling sunlight, and he mopped the back of his neck, fervently hoping that his pilgrimage would soon be rewarded.

37

A Mishmash of Singularities

LEAVING THE PASS BEHIND, they found themselves once more surrounded by open, rolling pastures. The heat was overpowering, and they spent the hottest part of the day in a stand of hickory to seek some relief. Unsaddling the horses and removing the baskets from the mules, they rubbed the animals down, Mose expressing renewed concern at the stallion's injured leg.

Boundless marvelled at the phlegmatic equanimity of the mules as they munched contentedly on grass, seemingly indifferent to the oppressive heat that so affected the horses. 'The mules have more fortitude,' he observed, admiring the toughness of the animal. Taking his lead from Mose, he carefully examined the bay for cuts, discovering a bruise above one knee that his companion discounted as 'no more than a knock'.

Taking out the log, he made several sketches of the rock buffalo, dissatisfied with each, the inked lines lacking the primal ferocity and conviction of the original. He did his best to replicate the smaller, geometric designs which, he was now certain, possessed some totemic or superstitious meaning.

Mose had dozed off in the heat, and so he made himself comfortable against a trunk as he pondered the chance discovery. *I was wrong to think that the heathen lacked art, or that art be confined to books and academies. It may be that savages, too, have a lineage, and their own, natural wisdom.* He speculated whether the rock hieroglyphs memorialised the primitive triumphs of their long-vanished creators—the heathen inscriptions as telling and profound to the tribal memory as the stele of Babylon or Persia. Half-dozing in the slumberous heat, he wondered at the savage mind that had taken time from the hunt to painstakingly record their feats for posterity to witness. The notion captivated and perplexed him even as his chin slowly sank to his chest.

When he awoke, it was late in the day and Mose was gone. The trapper returned a little later, fanning himself with a square of bark. 'By the bones, but it be fearsome hot!' They decided to camp in the spot, both feeling enervated by the heat. Wandering down to the creek, Boundless shot a fawn for supper. He butchered it on the spot, cursing the mosquitoes all the while. Mites tormented him as he carried the bloody hams and back straps back to the camp.

They resumed their journey in the cool of the morning, refreshed from the early camp the day before. As they rode, Boundless scoured the hillsides for evidence of buffalo, his eagerness to encounter the creature fired afresh by the rock images. But to his vast disappointment, and despite an increasing abundance of game, the beast was nowhere to be seen. 'Perhaps they populate only the far plains,' he pondered, only to dismiss the notion as he recalled the rock etchings. 'They were drawn from life, surely,' he reasoned. 'In which case buffalo must have once inhabited these parts—even if they are now nowhere to be found.'

The path veered in a north-westerly direction, passing through an oak wood and a number of small hills—the latter sprinkled with an abundance of caves. At one point, they passed under a gigantic stone arch. Despite Mose's grumblings, he insisted on calling a halt to sketch the unusual sight.

''Tis as if fashioned for the purpose,' he marvelled, adding the arch to the astonishing catalogue of natural curiosities that seemed to spring forth at every hand in this inexhaustible New World.

A great variety of trees—familiar and unfamiliar—dotted the landscape, the groves offering shade from the heat as well as a source of diversion. He recognised oaks, walnuts, hickory, maple and elms, but he was unable to put a name to others. A stately tree with large, distinctly shaped leaves caught his attention.

'Do you know what this tree is called?'

'That be a tulip tree. And over there be a honey locust … and beyond is a hackberry, or so I believe. Those shrubs are sumac—best avoided. The berries are poison, although I have heard it said that savages can ingest them without harm.'

It appeared to Boundless that the trees were altogether the largest and tallest he had ever set eyes on, several specimens springing a hundred feet and more into the air. The branches offered welcome relief from the sun as they passed underneath, and the trail seemed to take advantage of this fact, sometimes winding through grove upon grove in preference to the open pastures.

SHORTLY BEFORE NOON, THEY detoured off the trace to avoid a family of grizzlies that lay slumbering in the grass. He kept a wary eye on the somnolent beasts, noting the absence of any sign of fear in the creatures. They continued on for several miles, troubled only by the sun and the absence of a stout breeze to deter the incessant blackflies. After stopping at a creek to refill the water bottles, they came upon a pack of wolves tearing at the carcass of an elk. A dozen of the animals gorged on the feast while as many more lay panting in the grass. He lingered to observe the grisly spectacle until distracted by a whoop from Mose.

'Buffalo, by God!'

'Skit!' He urged the bay to where Mose stared at the distance.

'D'ye see?' The trapper pointed to a grassy slope up ahead.

Shielding his eyes, he stared in the direction. For a moment he saw nothing against the glare of sunlight. Then his eyes picked out a mass of distinctive brown forms milling about the hillside. The herd appeared to be several hundred in number—many with calves in tow. 'You are certain?'

Mose snorted in reply. 'D'ye think I have forgotten the look of the creature! By jiggery if I ain't famished for a taste of cooked rib!'

He was searching for the spy glass when Mose kicked the stallion into a trot. 'This be no time to gawk! Time for your first taste of hump meat. Leave the mules to follow. Har!'

At the approach of the horses, the outlying buffalo broke into a clumsy, lumbering gait—their ponderous bulk at odds with the graceful economy of the short, slender legs. He caught a whiff of gamy musk, like the smell of freshly turned earth after a rainfall. The smell was strong and distinctive, and, allied to the proximity of the huge beasts caused the bay to whinny in fright.

'Whoa!' Mose drew rein within shooting distance of a large bull grazing alongside a female with calf. 'By grip but he's a sight, ain't he? My first sight of buff in nigh on twenty year! Well?' He turned in the saddle. 'Your buffalo stands before you!'

Boundless controlled the spooked horse as he drank in the grazing behemoths—for so they seemed to his astonished gaze. The great bull nuzzled the grass shoots not thirty yards from where he sat. Its peculiar physiognomy—dominated by a monstrously large head and protruded shoulder hump, gave it a grotesque, hunch-back appearance, as though it were part one thing and part another. The mishmash of singularities combined a bulbous head and shaggy forelegs with slim, almost delicate, flanks, as if capricious Nature had fused the hinds of a deer to the foreparts of an elephant—and festooned the miscegeny with the thick, woolly fleece of a ram. The bestiary was completed by the addition of sharp horns that curved out from the massive cranium.

'What say you?'

'As I live and breathe, it is altogether the most curious and original beast my eyes ever did see!' His mind harkened back to the vividly etched rock prototype and he felt a momentary pang of disappointment. 'It seems … tranquil. It lacks the fire of the original.'

'Ha! Never fear. Those horns would gut a bear or slice up a wolf in a shake.'

The prime bull stood taller than the stallion, easily outstripping the latter in bulk and mass. Clumps of partly shed fur revealed a tan-coloured summer coat beneath the blackish-brown wool coating its front quarters. The eyes, and black, velvety nostrils, were partly concealed beneath a mass of dark, tightly woven curls. A tuft of fur hung beneath the slowly munching jaws. The buffalo grunted and trotted forward a few yards, its short, tasselled tail switching at the incessant flies.

'They do not seem to fear us.'

'Mayhap we are the first hunters on horseback they have ever seen. Perhaps they think us kin to themselves.' As he spoke, Mose pulled out the musket from its deerskin sheath.

'Stand ready,' he said. 'The hide be tougher than that of a deer. A ball to the heart is best. The shot must be exactly placed, or it will run half the day.' He set the musket at full cock. 'Hup, Jack.' Coaxing the skittish stallion closer to the bull, he raised the musket and, leaning from the saddle, aimed at a spot just to the right of the front-leg elbow. The buffalo showed no apprehension of danger as it slowly moved forwards, munching the grass. The sudden, explosive *crack* of the musket rang out across the meadow. The bull absorbed the full force of the shot. It gave a bellowing roar, its eye rolling wildly in its head, and took a half step before buckling at the forelegs and collapsing to the grass. Blood bubbled from its nostrils as it struggled to rise. After some moments it gave a great, wheezing grunt and lay still. The surrounding buffalo snorted and backed away, but otherwise showed little alarm. Within moments they had bent their heads to the grass and resumed feeding.

'Thou shalt taste of the flesh this day!' His voice jubilant, Mose indicated the buffalo cow grazing alongside the calf a few yards from the scene. 'Come, try your hand. The specimen there—before you.'

'We have much meat,' he objected. 'Why waste the powder?'

'For the skill, only. Bulls are not best eating. The cow goes better on the tongue. Aim for the vitals—the heart or lungs, just high of the foreleg elbow. See that small patch of bare hide? Let that be your mark. Send the ball there and you will pierce the heart.' Leaning down, Mose poked the dead bull with the muzzle to illustrate the spot. 'You must wait for it to step forward to show the mark.'

Boundless nudged the spooked bay nearer the cow. In imitation of Mose, he leaned forwards to train the weapon on the area adjacent to the foreleg. He held the shot as the cow remained standing in place. She took a step forward and he fired. The buffalo gave a surprised grunt and spun in the grass as if chasing its tail. Slowly, it sank to its knees, blood trickling from the black nostrils. In response to the cries of the frantic calf, it gave a feeble snort and briefly struggled to stand. A moment later, it slumped back to the grass and expired in an explosion of breath. Blood seeped through the tightly curled coat where the ball had pierced the heart.

'Peerlessly done!' Mose dismounted and approached the stricken beast, shooing away the distraught calf.

'Are we making camp? It will take us until nightfall to skin and butcher. And the day is hot.'

'A taste, only.' Mose unsheathed his hunting knife. 'To whet the tongue.'

Boundless got down and held the reins as the horses neighed and shied away from the carcass. 'Stand!' he snapped, as the bay tugged nervously at the rein.

The cow lay slumped on its side. Leaning one knee on its belly and clutching a handful of the curled fleece for balance, Mose stabbed the butchering knife into a spot near the junction of the head and shoulder. Using both hands, he dragged the blade down the spine, towards the tail. He made several 'striping' cuts in the thick hide, folding back the skin to slice away the layer of glistening fat and meat beneath. He then made a cut down to the foreleg. Leveraging the knife with both hands, he worked the blade beneath the cut, flaying back the hide to reveal a layer of wet, pulpy flesh. He laboured in like fashion until he had cut away sufficient fat and meat to expose the foreleg and shoulder joint.

'Fetch me the hatchet!'

He used the hatchet to smash the shoulder joint, partially dismembering it from the carcass. Grunting with the effort, he twisted and wrenched the joint until the bone snapped. 'There is plenty of meat on that,' he panted, dragging it into the grass. The bleating calf had returned to linger by the cow, nuzzling the warm carcass even as wolves and coyotes, attracted by the smell of blood, crept up through the grass to watch.

Mose turned his attention to the rib cage, slicing away the meat to reveal the bones beneath. In the humid heat, the labour proved taxing and he halted, wheezing for breath.

'By gar, but it's a long time since I carved up a buff!' Blood splattered his shirt and leggings. Flies swarmed around the bloody carcass, their buzzing audible in the heavy air. Sweat trickled down from under his hat.

'Git!' He brandished the hatchet at the hovering calf.

''Twould be a mercy to shoot it.'

'The wolves will soon finish it. Git!'

Resuming the butchery, Mose used the knife to gouge meat from between the rib bones while showering spittle and curses on the incessant flies. 'Pass me … the blessed … *sack*.' Stuffing the bloody meat into the jute bag, he handed it back. 'A moment,' he said, and sat on the buffalo, his breath coming in laboured gasps.

'Is this the method of butchering?'

Mose gave a wheezing laugh. 'Butchering! We should be here all day and into the night.' He shook his head. 'Nay, 'tis only to take the choicest meat.' Recovering his wind, he attacked the hump muscle, severing a large portion which he held up for inspection. 'A peerless cut—whether roasted or fried.'

'We have enough for a feast,' said Boundless, with a glance at the circling wolves.

'A moment.' Kneeling by the massive head, Mose slit the throat. 'The tongue is prized by savages above any other part.' Reaching into the throat he pulled the organ through the slit and severed the appendage.

'Hallelujah!' His face shining with triumph, he held the greyish black pulp aloft. 'A morsel to tempt Elisha! Add it to the sack.' His buckskins were soaked and matted with gore. ''Tis a messy business,' he said, regarding the bloodied garments with distaste. 'I ought to have worn the apron but was too a-tremble to wait. Let us find a suitable place to make camp that we may feast on this banquet.'

AS THEY RODE OFF with their bloody trophies, flies descended on the carcass in a thick, black cloud as scavenger birds circled overhead. The waiting wolves loped up to the feast. Two of the pack sank their fangs into the bellowing calf as it stood by the mother's side. It struggled in their jaws as the wolves dragged it to the grass in a frenzy of bloodlust. The surrounding buffalo had moved a short distance away from the carnage, seemingly oblivious to the cries of the frantic calf. A raven alighted on the head of the bull—rising in an indignant flap of wings before the snarling jaws of the ravenous wolves.

'Buffalo rib this night!' Mose's voice revealed his delight at making reacquaintance with the animal. 'It has been well over twenty year since I shot my last in the Pennsylvanny woods. It was a cow, feeding on shoots. Upon my oath if she wasn't the original wearer of that robe you cherish.'

They camped beside a spring, building a fire within the shelter of a grove of white pine. Eager to taste buffalo after so long an abstinence, Mose speared the meat on wood skewers to roast over the fire. Sitting back, he lit a pipe and watched the fat sizzle into the flames.

'Upon my soul, but it smells a treat!' He sucked on the pipe as the fire roasted the meat. Boundless sipped from a mug of tea, his mouth salivating at the smell. Leaning forward, Mose carefully retrieved a skewer, and handed it to him. 'Chaw away, friend. And prove me no liar, but an honest man.'

Boundless nibbled gingerly at the barely cooked rib as Mose observed him keenly over the pipe.

'It tastes like beefsteak—only finer,' pronounced Boundless, savouring the strong, gamy taste before swallowing.

'But finer!' Mose repeated. Taking another skewer from the fire he tore off a chunk of meat with his teeth. 'By the bones!' He smacked his lips. 'May I turn Turk if buffalo ain't the finest plate God ever set afore Adam.' He chewed with relish, stopping to chortle with glee. 'Jinks and jiggery if I ain't dreamed of and *drooled* on the moment.' He tore off another bite. 'By gar! … as the angel said to Mary.'

Boundless helped himself to another skewer, his mouth accustoming to the strong taste. 'I see why you favour it,' he said, savouring the bite. 'Although, in truth, venison runs it a close race.'

'Venison!' Mose hooted with scorn. 'Then try this morsel!' Leaning forward, he retrieved the tongue from the flames. Laying the blackened meat on a flat stone, he sliced off a portion and offered it on the point of the knife. 'Eat and be disproved!'

Lifting the hot meat off the knife, Boundless gingerly placed it on his tongue. Mose watched closely as he made elaborate play of rolling the morsel in his mouth before nodding judiciously. 'The tongue, by a hair.'

'Hooey!' Mose slapped a hand against his knee. 'I knew you'd fold under the taste—as would any Christian.'

Boundless helped himself to a slice of hump meat, chewing as he mulled over the fact that he was now finally in the lair of the creature whose siren call had lured him to this far country. 'Tis a strange, deformed creature— whose physiognomy exceeds my thought,' he mused, thinking back to his first acquaintance with the beast in the Philadelphia tavern. "*As tall as a man, though not so tall as a bear—on its hinds.*"

Propping himself on his elbows, he pictured Humpflinger, arm out-thrust as he described the wondrous beast. His thoughts turned to the dead cow and the stricken calf as he ruminated if it were possible for beasts of the field to feel emotions. 'Undoubtedly, they feel attachment, as, for example, a dog for its master. But these be primal things, inborn in all creatures—the instinct to seek the teat. Such things are part of Nature, arising from the instincts, not the mind. But yet there is a nobility about the creature, in spite of its disproportionate parts. As the mane is to the lion, so too is the great, woolly head crown to the buffalo.'

'One more.' Mose held out another skewer.

He chewed on the rib, grease sliding down his chin. Mose sliced off another portion of tongue, eating it from the point of the knife.

Gorged on the feast, they settled down for the night. Boundless took first watch, falling asleep within minutes under the influence of the heavy meal. He woke with a start, berating himself as he sat up and stared about in alarm. Troubled by the lapse, he allowed Mose an extra hour before waking the trapper, upon which he fell into a prompt and sound slumber beneath the warmth of the buffalo robe.

38

A Desperate Struggle

THEY CONTINUED THEIR PASSAGE, passing many more buffalo as they followed the path in a north-westerly direction. Indeed, the buffalo seemed to grow in abundance as they progressed—the animals browsing the plentiful cane or drinking from the multitude of creeks and springs. Flocks of redwings and magpies perched on the woolly backs to peck for ticks or to swoop on insects stirred up by the hooves. Several times they passed bulls fighting each other, the animals butting heads with a forceful clash that echoed in the air. These jousts continued for a considerable length of time, neither combatant willing to concede to the other. One afternoon, stopped by a creek, Boundless watched as two bulls contested to the point of exhaustion.

He drew sketches at each opportunity, turning to the earlier ones of the rock buffalo and meditating over the differences between the two. 'The rock specimen is finer,' he conceded, readily acknowledging his own limited prowess with the pen. Although box-like in its bulk, and with short legs— the limbs added as though by afterthought—the rock etching caught the latent fire he sensed in the beast and that Mose had alluded to earlier. 'Was it drawn by a single hand?' he wondered, before deciding it was.

Passing a stand of timber, he saw a buffalo writhe on its back to send up a cloud of dust. He saw the same practice repeated several times through-out the day.

'They do so for the relish of it,' opined Mose when questioned on the habit. 'Or, mayhap, to spook bears or wolves.'

They remained vigilant for Indians or French patrols, the bloody slaughter witnessed beyond the mountains never far from their minds.

'They could be Shawnee or Cherokee,' Mose remarked, as they stopped to examine footprints issuing from a creek.

'How fresh are they?'

'Two days, mayhap.' The trapper scanned the distance.

Boundless twisted in the saddle to survey the wooded hills. 'We proceed blindly,' he said, now certain that they were lost.

'The country is wild. Did ye expect a turnpike? Fortitude and these good horses will hie us to the plains.'

Early in the afternoon, they were about to emerge from a stand of buckeye when Mose froze in the saddle. 'Look there!' He pointed across the open meadows to a line of trees in the distance.

Boundless peered at where a column of men slowly emerged from the trees headed in their direction. He groped for the spyglass, certain that the men were Indians.

Mose craned forward to better observe. After a long moment, the tension visibly ebbed from his shoulders. 'White men, I do suspect. But let us hold and make certain.'

The party made directly towards them, clearly unaware of their presence. The men walked slowly, their heads down, as though exhausted.

'I count twenty men,' said Boundless, examining the party through the glass.

The men approached to within shouting distance—still unsuspecting of where they sat concealed by the shade.

'What if they are French?'

'I doubt it. The settlements are along the Ohio, far from here. But best not to unnerve them, whoever they be. They may shoot us from fright.'

Taking off his straw hat, Mose thrust it into the air. 'Good morrow!'

The hunters stopped in alarm, whipping up their muskets as they scouted for danger.

'Hold your fire! We be loyal Englishmen!' Mose started out from the trees, still waving the hat. Boundless followed, leading the bell mare and mules.

The strangers remained where they were, their postures vigilant and suspicious. They conferred amongst themselves before a man advanced to meet the companions, a long rifle cradled in his arms.

'Who are you?' He demanded, his eyes darting past the companions to check that they were alone.

'We be peaceful travellers—headed to the Ohio.'

'You are English?'

'As yourselves.'

The man deliberated for a moment. 'Then let us parley.' Turning, he gestured to his companions.

'I never dreamed to run into another Englishman in these parts.' The man wore a tattered wincey shirt, buckskin leggings and a beaver felt hat with three feathers stuck into the crown. His face was fringed with a wispy beard and drawn with fatigue. 'The boys feared lest you be Frenchies.'

'No more than we did you,' said Mose.

The man took off his hat and wiped an arm across his brow. 'We were in a tight scrap with a party of Shawnee three days past. The devils have been hounding us ever since.'

'We had similar trouble. I am Mose van Zeke and this be my companion, Mr Boundless McLennan.' Mose climbed down from the saddle to offer his hand.

'I forget my manners.' The man, who appeared to be no older than Boundless, brushed lank strands of hair from his face. 'Horatio Curlew, citizen of Virginia.' His youth became more evident as he set the hat back on his head at a jaunty angle. Turning, he urged the rest of the party—who remained in place, wary lest this be a deception—to join them. 'Come! They be friends!'

'Where have you come from?' asked Boundless.

'The backcountry—along the river.' The man gestured behind him. 'We crossed the mountains in pursuit of game. We have been hunting and trapping these past two months.'

'Relax boys, they be fellow Englishmen,' he said, as the other members of the party joined the parley, their faces showing the same signs of pinched exhaustion as their leader.

'You are on horseback?' said Curlew, evidently surprised at the fact.

'We are. Our journey is a long one.'

'We could use a tribe of horses at the moment.' Curlew gestured to the fatigued faces of his companions.

Six mules accompanied the party. Five were heavily laden with fresh hides. The sixth carried a wounded man, white-faced from loss of blood as he sat slumped astride the mule. Another man stood alongside with a bloody cloth tied around his scalp, his haggard face grimy with dirt.

'That must have been some scrap,' said Mose, observing the general distress of the party.

Curlew grimaced. 'They killed Tom and wounded Harry and Frederick in the last rush.'

'The savages damn near kilt us all!' One of the hunters leaned on his long rifle to spit in disgust. The sentiment drew mutters of agreement.

'God-cursed savages!' The speaker, a heavily bearded man trembled with anger. 'They slaughtered poor Tom—hacked him all to pieces!' The distraught man roundly cursed all heathens as his companion patted his arm.

Curlew shook his head. 'That be Mr Ransome. The Indians murdered his brother.'

As he observed the ragged party more closely, Boundless was surprised to see one of the men dressed in a French military tunic. The man appeared injured and wore a dirty cloth bandage around one arm where it dangled free of his jacket.

'Who is that?' he said, motioning to the man.

Curlew followed his gaze. 'That be Johnny French. He was with the Indians. We captured him during the first set-to.'

'Where are you taking him?'

'Back to Virginia so that the authorities may properly question him. What else can I do?' Curlew looked at Boundless as though he might have an answer.

The captive soldier looked the worse for wear, his gaze sullen and defiant.

'Is he the reason the Indians are chasing you?' asked Mose.

The question drew a frown from Curlew even as it evoked angry mutters from the gathered party—the subject clearly a contentious one. 'He may have value,' insisted Curlew. He looked around at the men. 'Do you say differently?'

'I say we hang the French dog!' snarled a lean fellow in tattered buckskins to a chorus of agreement.

'Aye. String the cockerel and have done with him!'

'Dang it!' Curlew took off his hat and scratched his head, his face exasperated. 'We've taken him this far. No sense to hang him now.'

'Are the Shawnee still on your tail?'

Curlew nodded, his expression sombre. 'They are like ravenous wolves after a hind.' As he spoke, several of the party turned to glance apprehensively at the woods.

'Are they close by?' asked Boundless.

'Close enough that we shall have to fight the devils.'

'How many are there?'

'Forty or fifty—less the seven or eight we kilt.'

Taken aback, Boundless glanced at Mose, who seemed equally alarmed.

'Best we deal with them together,' said Curlew, detecting their concern. 'Else you may have to fight them on your own.'

Mose considered this for a moment, clearly perturbed at the turn of events. 'I see no other course,' he said, his voice betraying his unhappiness.

Curlew looked relieved at the answer. ''Tis agreed then. We can make a stand here, in the trees. It gives some refuge and affords a clear view of the meadow. What say you, boys?'

The men dispersed with much grumbling, their discontent readily apparent. One youth, the youngest among them, lingered behind. 'We may not withstand another attack,' he protested. 'We should run away as fast as we can.'

'We are well placed, Hans, and better armed than before. Help set up the redoubt.'

The youth licked his lips. 'Better to run far away,' he repeated, before going off to join his companions.

Curlew glanced at the pack mules. 'Where did you say you are bound?'

'To the plains west of the Ohio.'

'The plains?' Curlew showed surprise at the answer. 'What plains—and why would you travel there anyway?'

'To hunt buffalo.'

'And explore,' added Boundless.

Curlew looked baffled. 'Explore what?'

'You have been there—to the Ohio?'

Curlew shook his head. 'Only this far and a little distance to the south.'

'Far enough, by God,' volunteered a man cutting down brush nearby.

Curlew gave a rueful smile. 'We are most eager to see home again—Virginia, mostly, but some from Georgia.' His face brightened as he remembered something. 'The Frenchie claims to have been garrisoned along the Ohio. Mayhap he can point you in that direction. He speaks English as well as you or me. Although he is a surly character and ill-disposed.'

'Any guidance would be welcome. We proceed blindly.'

'Not so blindly!' Mose cast an annoyed glance at Boundless. 'More by degrees,' he explained. 'As befits cautious men in a wild country.'

'The country is very wild,' Curlew agreed. He turned to his companions and pointed to a spot further within the grove. 'Picket the mules over there!' Hands on hips, he surveyed the patch of trees. 'This is a defensible position. The Indians must cross that open ground if they are to reach us.'

'Would they be so reckless? Surely, they would do better to wait for a more favourable spot.'

'True enough,' Curlew conceded, stroking the wispy hairs on his jaw as he gazed at the men setting up the picket line. 'It depends on how fired up they … *Inside* the trees! Damn it all to hell!' He frowned testily as the men struggled to picket the animals. 'But the Shawnee themselves are in danger from Cherokee war parties. This is contested ground, and the Cherokee despise the Shawnee worse than they hate the French. They may wish to try their hand one more time before fleeing back to their own village. I hope not,' he added resignedly. 'But I fear they have the smell of blood in their nostrils.'

'How far behind did you say?' asked Mose.

'The devils are on our heels.'

Mose gave a concerned look at Boundless. 'Then let us secure the stock.'

They moved the horses and mules into the thickest part of the woods, using a short tether to secure them. 'They ought be safe,' said Mose, testing the ropes. 'Even if the Indians attack from that direction.' He nodded to the clearing behind the grove.

'This is most unfortunate,' said Boundless in a low voice. He glanced to check that Curlew was not within earshot.

'Agreed,' answered Mose, equally cautious. 'But think if we had run into that many Shawnee on our own?'

Boundless nodded, sobered by the prospect. 'A fearful thought.'

Behind them, Curlew strode up and down, busily organising the defences. 'More brushwood!' he ordered one man. 'Trample those bushes to give clear sight,' he said to another. He sent a third man to scale a tree and take watch. 'Holler if you see the devils!'

Boundless watched, impressed by the confident authority of one so young.

'He is a blade, though,' a man beside him grunted, seeing Boundless' admiring glance.

'He is your elected leader?'

'Ha! He jest acts as though he sports a crown instead of that mangy old beaver!'

'Yet you clearly tolerate him—his command, I mean?'

The man looked surprised. 'Horatio? He ain't so bad. He's steered us aright so far.'

As he joined in with the others to construct a breastwork, Curlew spurred them on with advice and encouragement. 'We can finish this once and for all, boys,' he said, patting an anxious looking man on the shoulder. 'We have two extra guns, remember.'

After constructing a redoubt of piled earth and chopped branches, the party halted for a rest. Clearly exhausted from their travails, the men sat together inside the defensive wall smoking pipes. As Boundless looked around at the tired faces, he realised with a shock that one of the party was a woman. Her long, greasy black hair and smooth, dark face betrayed both her sex and her savage blood. Nudging Mose, he nodded in her direction.

'Squaw,' Mose said knowingly. 'They sometimes ride with hunters as a wife. They make excellent guides and smooth the way with their own kind.'

Boundless gazed at the squaw with enormous curiosity. Her skin was very dark, similar to a Negro's, and her features squat and unattractive.

She wore a plain buckskin dress and a necklace of bird bones. She spoke only the occasional word, and then only to Curlew. Her voice was soft, her speech clearly in the Indian tongue.

'What tribe is she?'

Mose poked the man next to him and motioned to the squaw. The man said something in a low voice, glancing at Curlew before speaking again.

'Cherokee,' relayed Mose. He took out his pipe. 'She belongs to Curlew. He purchased her with a sack of sugar and some coffee. She cooks, sews and tends to their general needs.'

'Are they man and wife?' asked Boundless, disturbed by the notion.

'For the duration. It is likely he will abandon her once they reach the settlements.'

'What will happen to her?'

'She will get picked up or sold to another. Or turn to drink, and worse. There are plenty like her in the trading posts and forts.'

Boundless studied the woman as she tended to the needs of the wounded men. 'She deserves better, savage or not.'

Mose rubbed his chin. 'Mayhap. But if you ask her, she might disagree. Life for a woman among the savages is very harsh. They are subject to their husbands in every particular and dare not disobey them.'

They were joined by Curlew, who sat beside them, laying his musket in the grass. 'We are as prepared as we are able,' he said. 'We have twenty reliable shots, thanks to yourselves, and a strong position. With luck, they will try to rush us, thinking our numbers diminished by the earlier scraps.' He glanced at the mules to ensure that they were securely picketed. Satisfied at the preparations, he visibly relaxed, the strain easing from his face. Taking off his beaver hat, he ran a hand through his hair.

'Which part of Virginia are you from, Mr Curlew, if I might enquire?' Boundless asked, intrigued to observe that, hatless, the man seemed even younger than himself.

'Williamsburg.' Curlew sat up and wiped the barrel of the long rifle with a strip of calico he pulled from inside his shirt sleeve.

'That be a ways from here,' commented Mose.

Curlew grinned. 'At times, not far enough. I ran away from home as a lad, looking for adventure. And by God, I found me some.'

'And a wife, too,' said Mose, with a nod in the direction of the squaw.

Curlew flushed. 'She is a great help in these parts. Without her, we should surely have become lost or be decorating some Shawnee lodge pole.'

'What shall become of her?' asked Boundless—the question leaping unbidden to his lips.

Curlew stared defensively. 'She ain't for sale.'

'Sale? I beg pardon. I meant no such imputation. I simply wondered—'

'She'll make do, I expect.' Curlew minutely examined the mainspring on his musket.

'That's a fine load of hides you've secured,' said Mose.

'We had more but lost a mule to the damned Shawnee. And almost our hair, as well.'

The conversation was cut short by a shout from the look-out positioned up the tree. 'Shawnee!' The man pointed to the woods on the far side of the meadow. A murmur of apprehension rippled through the camp.

'How many?' demanded Curlew.

'Twenty-five. Wait. I count … thirty!' the look-out answered. 'Thirty, and no more.'

Curlew grunted. 'We were bloodier than I fancied. Keep your lunk heads down!' he snapped as the men raised up to look.

'Have they seen us?'

'No. They're scouting our trail, though,' the lookout answered. 'Wait!'

A suspenseful pause followed.

'The tall devil is looking this way! He suspects something.'

Peering above the brushwork, Boundless scanned the trees across the clearing but could see nothing other than the shrubs and long grass of the open meadow.

'Where the devil are they?' a voice called out.

'They've retreated back to the trees. They're holding a parley, I expect.'

The minutes dragged by as the defenders awaited further developments.

'Mark now!' The look-out's voice was tense. 'They are disappearing into the grass. Setting up for a rush!'

A profound hush fell over the sun-blown meadow. The weather was warm and sylvan. A gentle breeze rustled the foliage. The defenders began to mutter and fidget as they waited for some movement from the concealed Indians.

'Hold tongues!' hissed Curlew. 'What is their situation?' he called up to the lookout.

'The devils are flat in the grass. Crawling on their bellies, like snakes.' The look-out scrambled down from the tree as the party braced itself for the assault.

'Boys, hold fire until they are on top of us. The initial volley must do harm or we lose the advantage.'

A fox yelped in the long grass, the sound drawing a nervous exchange of looks. 'That be no true fox,' ventured one man, drawing an ireful glance from Curlew.

Still unable to see any sign of the Indians in the long grass, Boundless wondered if the enemy might not be creeping around to their rear to surprise them.

The same thought evidently occurred to Curlew, who sent the look-out back up the tree with orders to keep an eye on the country behind the encampment. 'Harry, Cuthbert, Klaus, crawl over there,' he commanded, strengthening the rear defences.

Boundless slapped at a fly, sweat running down his eyes and onto the stock of his rifle. 'Where the devil are they?' he whispered to Mose, who lay alongside.

'Sneaking up in the grass, no doubt. Making use of the ridges and dips. When they are close enough, they will make the attack.'

'I see one of the varmints!' a man whispered urgently. 'Over there, by the bush!'

'Hold fire!' snapped Curlew as the sighting provoked a murmur of alarm. 'We must reduce their numbers with the first volley.'

In the suspenseful silence Boundless licked his dry lips, suddenly desirous of water. Around him, the faces of the hunters were taut with nerves. He saw the youth named Hans glance in his direction, a horrid grimace on his face. A hawk screamed overhead, the cry drawing gasps.

'Hold tongue!'

Of a sudden, the hush was shattered by a shrill cry that, in spite of Boundless' steely resolution, raised the hairs on his neck. The cry was echoed on all sides as the Indians let fly a sudden volley of arrows. He made himself as small as possible as the arrows thudded into the breastworks or flew low overhead. Just as abruptly as it began, the fusillade stopped, and a tense silence prevailed once more.

'Brace yourselves, boys!'

The command was scarcely uttered when, with shrieks and yells, the Indians leapt up from the shelter of the long grass and rushed the redoubt—intent on overwhelming the defenders in a single assault. Shocked by how closely the enemy had approached, several of the men spontaneously opened fire, drawing a furious oath from Curlew.

'Hold fire, damn ye!'

He heard a burst of musket fire from behind as the Indians attacked the rear in concert with the frontal assault.

'They are upon us!'

'Fire, boys! Give them hell!'

A ragged volley of shots erupted, causing a thick cloud of white smoke to drift up from the redoubt.

Within moments the on-rushing Indians crashed through the breastworks, falling upon the defenders with terrifying yells. The drifting smoke made it hard for Boundless to distinguish friend from foe. He was hastily ramming a ball down the barrel of the musket when an Indian loomed through the smoke, his face a ferocious daub of ochre and black paint. With a shrill cry, he sprang for Boundless' throat.

He had barely time to brace himself before the force of the impact knocked him backwards to the grass. In an instant, he was struggling for his life. The Indian pinned him with his knees and raised a hatchet, the fierce black eyes glittering with triumph. As the hatchet was about to dash out his brains, the savage uttered a strangled gasp and pitched forward on top of him. Almost paralysed from shock, Boundless scrambled out from beneath his attacker, expecting the man to spring up after him. But the Indian lay unmoving in the grass, the back of his head grisly with blood and brains where it had been ripped asunder by a musket ball.

Dazed, he looked around for his saviour. On all sides he heard loud cries as the fighting raged and the desperate defenders fought for their lives. And then, in the very midst of the battle, he felt a strange and profound inertia descend upon him as though he were merely witness to the conflict. He heard indistinctly the shouts and cries of the combatants and saw the hand-to-hand struggles around him. But he was aware also of the stalks of grass as they shook in the breeze and of a scattering of birds high above. He felt the lively warmth of the sun on his face and hands as he walked through the bloody battlefield—part of it, yet immune from its strife. Through the white, drifting smoke he saw a man grapple with a half-naked savage, the two antagonists kicking and clawing for advantage as they wrestled in the dirt. As through a fog, he realised that one of the combatants was Mose—the awareness breaking the trance as the sights and sounds of the battle abruptly returned to flood his senses. The Indian had gripped Mose by the throat, attempting to choke him. Plucking the pistol from his belt, Boundless lashed out with the barrel, catching the savage a glancing blow to the temple. As the stunned Indian released his grip, Boundless smashed the pistol against the greasy black hair—feeling the skull crack under the impact. The Indian uttered a groan and slumped to the grass.

'Mose!' He turned to help his companion.

Taking his hand, the trapper hauled himself up from the grass, gasping for breath, his eyes starting out from his head.

Above the yells and the crack of musket fire, Boundless heard a piercing cry. Hans was cowering in the grass, a terrified look on his face. A Shawnee stood over him, lunging at the petrified youth with a lance.

'Mercy!' The youth cried out in terror as he tried frantically to avoid the thrusts. The Shawnee mocked the boy's fear, feigning with the lance before jabbing the point into Hans' gut with a gleeful cry. The youth shrieked and clutched his belly.

As the Shawnee readied to make a second thrust, Boundless levelled the pistol and blew the Indian's brains out.

He bent over the stricken youth, taking in his deathly pallor and blood-soaked shirt.

Hans looked up, his eyes dazed. 'What day is it friend?' he asked, 'I cannot think.'

The Indians abruptly broke off the fight and, with shrill cries, fled back into the grass, abandoning the wounded in their haste. Within moments, the meadow was empty again—the smell of black powder the only evidence of the ferocious struggle.

'By God, but we whipped 'em!'

'They've turned tail!'

'It's true! The devils have taken to their heels. They're running, boys! Running like scaredy-cats!'

An air of jubilation swept the hunters at the confirmation that the battle was won. 'God in Heaven but I feared we were done for!' A man in a soiled waistcoat dabbed at his eyes with a neckerchief, his voice trembling with emotion.

Boundless turned to look for Mose. To his relief, he caught sight of his comrade sitting safely in the grass, his hair hanging about his neck. The bodies of over a dozen Indians lay scattered under the trees, flies gathering on their bloody corpses.

'See to your weapons!' Curlew strode up from the rear of the camp, his face bruised and streaked with dirt. He held a long knife in one hand, the blade glistening with blood. He carried the other arm tenderly, as though favouring a wound. 'They may return!' he warned. 'Lucas, Virgil—tend to the defensive wall.'

'Do you have eyes? They've turned tail!' the first man insisted.

'It may be a ruse! The devils are cunning beyond description.'

The argument was interrupted by an agonised groan. All eyes went to Hans where he lay tightly curled, clutching his gut in the grass. The Indian woman knelt beside him, wiping his forehead with a damp cloth.

'How badly hurt is he?' asked Curlew, his face grim.

'He is perished hurt.' A stocky man stood over the youth, his face full of dismay. 'A good boy,' he said in a thick German accent. Tears rolled down his face as he gazed at the stricken youth.

'Poor Edward is mortal wounded!' A red-haired man called out from where he sat in the dirt supporting a comrade's head in his lap. 'The fiends hacked his right arm to pieces!' Tenderly, he stroked his comrade's brow. 'Hush now, dearest Edward,' he murmured as the wounded man moaned and rasped for breath.

'What is the full account?' said Curlew, his voice tight as he looked around the encampment.

'Young Tull is done for,' a man answered. 'He was but sixteen years.'

'Who lies over there?' Curlew looked across the grove at where a man nursed another comrade in the shade of the trees. 'Mr Sweetwater. Is that you?'

'It is poor Lemuel. He got pierced in the breast. I shall give him what comfort I can.' Sweetwater shook his head in despair.

The revelation drew angry murmurs.

'Damn'd heathenish brutes! We ought follow and kill every one of the swine!' The speaker, a short, rotund man in a bloodied coat, shook his fist at the meadow.

Mutters of agreement among the survivors were interrupted by an anguished cry. '*Mein Gott! Hans ist tot.*' The German burst into tears, his face wretched with grief.

'Hans is dead?' Curlew strode over to see for himself. 'How? He was alive but this instant!'

The German put his face in his hands, too grief-stricken to speak. Curlew knelt to confirm that the youth had indeed perished. Shaking his head, he stood up. 'It is true, boys. Poor Hans is done for.'

A sombre mood fell over the camp at the announcement, some of the men going over to examine the stricken youth as if to confirm for themselves.

'Boys, through God's grace, we have saved our lives. Now we must tend to our duties.—Elijah.' Curlew addressed a wiry fellow with combed hair and a sunburned face seated in the grass cleaning a musket.

The man looked up. 'What is it, good Horatio?'

Curlew frowned at the appellation. 'Scour the meadow. Take two others with you and count the Indian dead. Stay alert. Some may still be alive and dangerous.'

'William? Shin back up the tree. Keep a sharp watch on all sides. I don't give a damn'd *deuce* if they've turned tail! Keep scout anyway.' Unable to think of anything else, Curlew turned away, wincing at his wounded arm.

As order was slowly restored to the wrecked camp, Boundless walked over to where Mose sat in the grass. From the corner of his eye, he noticed the French captive pacing back and forth, his manner agitated.

'Are you unscathed, Mose?' he asked, crouching down beside his companion.

'Aye, thanks to yourself.' Mose glanced at where his adversary lay dead in the grass. 'That villain was lively as a wildcat, and twice as fierce.' He took the pipe from his pocket. 'By the bones! I was afeared our little jaunt had come to a close afore it had hardly begun.' His fingers shook as he pushed tobacco into the bowl.

'I myself was saved in a most miraculous manner—whether by chance or deliberation I know not.'

Mose listened carefully as Boundless described his own narrow escape.

'There be your certain proof of Providence, friend,' he averred. 'Whether you admit to it or not.'

A pistol shot sounded from the grass. Boundless grabbed the musket as the men sprang to their feet, fearful lest the enemy had returned.

'A breathing devil despatched!' yelled a voice from the meadow where the three hunters scoured the grass.

Shortly afterwards, a second shot rang out followed by a loud, 'Hooray!'

'Another sent to Hell!' the first voice called out.

Boundless sat back and removed his hat. He grimaced as he noticed blood and bits of brain clinging to the front of his shirt. Taking out the canteen, he dribbled water over the buckskin to wash away the gore.

He took a swallow of water and offered the canteen to Mose. 'Do you think it wise to continue? We are just the two of us. Who knows but plenty more savages may lurk ahead.'

'I should be loath to turn tail. We are within reach of our prize. Do you mean to flinch at the last?'

'I merely take stock, as a prudent measure.'

Mose glanced at where the French officer paced up and down the clearing. 'Yonder strides our map to the Ohio. What say you?'

They were distracted by a commotion as the scouting party returned to the encampment.

'One played possum until we were nigh on top of him!' His voice hoarse with excitement, the speaker mimicked the action. 'At which time he leapt up and dashed for the trees! Dashed! But Enoch here drilled him clean through the brain and took his hair.' The man referred to held up the bloodied scalp for all to see.

The others gathered around to inspect the trophy.

'By oath but it's greasy!'

'A fine pelt!'

'See what a fancy woman I be!' The proud owner poured water from a wooden bottle over the bloodied scalp and combed through the bloody hair with his fingers. 'Ain't I jest a catch!' He pretended to fit the scalp over his head like a wig, a preening expression on his face as his companions hollered and goaded him on.

'Thirteen savages! All of them dead.' The sun-burned scout walked up to where Curlew watched the pantomime, a frown on his face.

'Does that include behind, also?' he asked, as the hunter cavorted under the wig to the whoops of his comrades.

'Front and rear, Horatio. Thirteen. None left alive.'

'Thirteen savages, boys,' said Curlew in a loud voice. 'All despatched to Hell!'

Cheers rose at the announcement. Curlew motioned to the side of the clearing where four bodies were laid. 'There are respects to be paid afore we make sport.' The cavorting hunter stopped his antics, suddenly abashed under Curlew's disapproving gaze. 'Fetch shovels. Let us bury our poor comrades.'

'He carries himself like a general,' remarked Mose. 'The youngest general I ever did see.'

As the subdued hunters bent to the task of digging graves, Boundless approached Curlew, who was kneeling beside a wounded man. 'Someone saved me in the thick of the fight. I do not know who.'

Curlew nodded, his eyes bloodshot. 'It matters only that you were saved.' A large, swelling bruise marred Curlew's cheek, and a strip of cloth was now tied around the wound in his arm. He was the image of an exhausted leader as he surveyed the camp, making sure the men were purposefully engaged.

'My companion thinks you might pass as a redcoat general.'

Curlew flushed, clearly pleased with the compliment. 'I am but a poor substitute, I assure you.' He scrambled suddenly to his feet, glaring at something that displeased him. 'Not so close together!'

TWO HOURS LATER, THE men stood hatless in the grass as Curlew recited from a small Bible over the bodies of the four slain hunters. *'And he shall be as the light of the morning, when the sun riseth, even a morning without clouds; as the tender grass springing out of the earth by clear shining after rain.'*

'Samuel,' Mose murmured beside Boundless. 'My poor mother's favourite.'

The afternoon sun was high in the sky and the wind barely a breath in the air as the men stood in a semi-circle, heads bowed as the bodies were laid into the graves. Curlew gave a short speech praising the courage and fellowship of the dead men. 'They were sterling comrades,' he said. 'And as dependable as men ever were.'

They heard a sound. The Indian woman stood under the trees chanting in a soft, ululating voice. Her face was half-raised, her eyes closed as she held up her palms before her.

One of the men muttered, his voice harsh as he glared at the squaw.

Curlew closed the bible. 'She means no harm. It is the Indian custom to sing their dead to the afterlife.'

'They ain't *her* dead!' The man spat out the words. 'She has no business mouthing that heathenish mumbo jumbo here.'

'It ain't Christian,' agreed another.

'It is merely her way of giving respect,' Curlew argued.

'It ain't Christian,' the second man repeated.

Boundless stood silently as the men sat and consoled one another. Simple wooden crosses stood at the head of each of the four graves, the sticks bound by twigs. 'The wolves will dig them up,' he thought.

As the afternoon wore on, the mood inside the camp remained one of sorrow for the dead, leavened with relief at having survived the desperate contest. The men sat around, speaking in low, dejected voices.

'I say we feast our victory.' Curlew stood in front of the men, seeking to raise spirits. 'Mr Sweetwater. Take Fusil, Morgan, young Harry and two others. And the squaw also. Go fetch us a grand side of buffalo for supper.'

'I should like to go too,' Boundless volunteered, glad of the opportunity to escape the sombre atmosphere of the camp.

Curlew nodded. 'Very well. Mr Sweetwater, fetch a mule with you to carry the meat. And remain vigilant. There may yet be Indians skulking about.'

39

The French Captain

THE SUN WAS STILL high in the sky as the small party set out from the camp. They did not have to proceed far before sighting a group of buffalo feeding alongside a small creek. Boundless observed four of the beasts rolling in the dry dirt beside the stream, coating their hides with dust and mud.

'Why do they do that?' he asked Sweetwater, who walked alongside him.

'They favour the mud. It keeps away the flies.' Sweetwater ran his eyes over the herd, searching for the best specimen.

The Cherokee squaw said something and pointed to a buffalo grazing on the periphery of the herd. Sweetwater nodded. 'That be the one, boys,' he said.

Two of the hunters strolled over to the grazing animals, who did not seem overly perturbed by their presence. The first hunter raised his musket and, standing within ten yards of the buffalo, fired. Startled by the noise, the other buffalo splashed across the creek. The shot cow bellowed loudly as she trotted through the grass away from the hunters. The men followed after and shot a second time. The cow turned back and lumbered after the herd as the men hurriedly reloaded.

'Blazes if she ain't getting away!' A man standing next to Boundless rushed forward and discharged his musket at the creature. Another man followed. The first two men had now reloaded and fired again. The cow gave a great bellow before sinking to her knees. She remained in this position for some moments, respiring heavily before collapsing onto her side with a loud grunt.

'It required some artillery,' said Sweetwater as they gathered around the dead cow.

'I suspected you to club her with the musket, Jeremiah,' one of the hunters said, drawing laughter.

'If you are so sharp then come and fire that little piddle-stick you call a gun,' grumbled the other man.

'We shall have to tip her onto her belly,' said Sweetwater. 'Just as well she ain't a giant.'

'Leave her as she is,' another man objected. 'She can take from the top-side only.'

'But if we right her the squaw can take the ribs from both sides,' argued another.

'And the choicest steaks,' added yet another.

'Then let's turn her,' said Sweetwater.

While two of the men stood ready to pull out the legs, the others strained to lift the buffalo and turn her onto her stomach. 'Lift, why don't you!' grunted one man to a companion.

'The devil! Do you think me dancing with the thing?'

Straining every sinew, the five men managed to 'right' the buffalo as the other two tugged out her legs so that she sat on her belly with all four legs distended.

'Lord have mercy!' Sweetwater mopped his brow, panting for breath.

'She must be eight hundred pounds,' guessed one man.

'More like a thousand!' said another.

'Well, she belongs to the squaw now. Make way,' said Sweetwater.

The men walked away further up the grassy bank as the squaw took down half a dozen jute sacks from the mule and set them in the grass alongside the carcass. She wore a hide apron and carried a deerskin bag over her shoulder. Boundless watched as she took several flint knives from the bag.

'Sit a spell,' one of the men called out as they sat down and took out pipes.

'Should we not assist?'

The man guffawed. 'Hell, if she ain't faster on her own!'

Ignoring the offer to sit, he stood watching the squaw as she laid both hands on the slaughtered animal, murmuring as she did so.

'What does she say?' he asked, speaking over his shoulder.

'That? She be praying. 'Tis the heathen habit.'

'What does it mean?'

'Some foolishness or other. It don't affect the taste of the meat, though.'

'Are you not curious?'

'Curious? Why would I be?' The man scowled as though greatly put out by the question. 'Deuced if I care one way or the other!'

'Horatio opines she's asking for favour,' said a broad-faced man.

'I don't see what business it is of mine to be curious,' insisted the first man. 'Why would I be? Answer me that.'

The smoking men watched idly as the squaw used the flint knife to slit the hide from the neck down over the spine to the tail. She then cut down from this line along the outside of the legs. Pausing to swap knives, she flayed the hide back from the carcass—arranging it alongside the animal like a mat. She repeated the process on the other side of the animal. The removed hide revealed a gleaming layer of whitish-yellow fat encasing the meat.

Boundless crouched down, watching her methodical skill as she removed the rich, dark-red meat along the backbone with sure strokes of the flaked stone. The meat was placed on the hide mat beneath the carcass. Working with a swiftness and economy that aroused his admiration, she worked her way along the spine, stopping only to switch knives or shoo away the cloud of black flies that attended the operation.

An hour after she began, the removed meat was still steaming with heat. Turning to the forelegs and shoulder blades, she cut these away from the carcass. She glanced at him, and he went to help, pulling the excised limbs into the grass. The hump meat and rib cage were now exposed. Switching to a hatchet, she started breaking the hump ribs, returning to the stone knife to scrape meat from the bones. She climbed atop the cow to lever meat away from the spine, her apron splattered with blood and gore.

'I guess there is sufficient meat right there,' said one of the resting men.

'Tell her, Henry,' said another.

'Heck no, I want the loin.'

'She hears you!'

'She is mad for the boiled hump,' said another.

'By golly if she ain't at the ribs already.'

'That's the good meat, boys,' said Sweetwater.

'You was always one for the sweetmeat,' said a companion, drawing guffaws.

As the squaw gouged out the rib meat, she popped a portion into her mouth.

'See that!'

'Ain't nothing wrong with that, Harry. It all be buffalo and good for the belly, cooked or not.'

'Well, I ain't a cannonball, so I guess I'll just stick to the cooked bits if you'll pardon!'

'I saw her eat the raw liver once.' A middle-aged fellow in a brown linen jacket gestured with the pipe. 'Tore it right out of the animal and into her mouth, afore God.'

'It was awful to see,' declared the man sitting next to him, his face wrinkling in disgust.

'Eke wasn't too impressed,' said the first man, grinning at his companion.

The squaw stopped to suck her fingers.

'By Gabriel's horn, she's washing down the rib!

The men sat silent for a time enjoying the breeze before the man called Eke turned to Boundless. 'Why would you be headed to the so-called plains? Ain't this country wild enough?'

'It sounds a perilous venture,' Sweetwater agreed. The men looked at Boundless, curious for the reply.

Now that he was asked the question, he felt a little foolish in his response. 'For the sake of seeing them. My companion wishes to explore the country beyond the Ohio River.'

'To *see* them?' Linen jacket looked nonplussed at the answer.

'I hear that the Indians west of here are bloodthirsty as all hell.' Sweetwater chewed on a blade of grass. 'God knows but the ones around here are fierce enough.'

His companion laughed. 'Except where we slaughtered them! Tails atween their legs.'

'How far is it to the Ohio, anyway?' asked the broad-faced man.

Boundless shrugged. 'I do not know. I have hopes that your captive, the French captain, will point the way.'

The other man spat. 'I wouldn't trust a Frenchman to tell the hour! Best take every advice he gives as contrary to Gospel.'

'The Devil's scripture,' agreed linen jacket.

'What in tar is she doing now?'

The squaw was standing, looking expectantly at Sweetwater.

'She wants us to turn it!'

'We must have two hundred pounds of meat. Stop her Henry, afore she takes out the bones to boil.'

Sweetwater shook his head at Boundless. 'She hates to leave the least scrap.'

'She's about to fish out the guts!'

'Finish! *Ha-le!*' said the broad-faced man.

'That ain't the word,' argued linen jacket. '*U-du-lee!*' he said. '*U-du-lee!*'

'What the blazes is that?' asked the first speaker, looking mystified.

'It's the word Horatio uses.'

'I ain't never heard such a word. And she ain't either, by the look of it.'

'*U-du-lee!* Or *Doo-lay!*' the first man said, addressing the woman in a commanding tone.

'Ha! She ain't *doo-laying* for pounds! *Ha-le! Ha-le!*'

Muttering, Sweetwater roused himself and went over to the woman. 'Enough!' He pointed to the sacks of cut meat. 'Enough!'

'Enough?' the woman repeated.

'By thunder, but she spoke Christian all along!'

The men guffawed at the remark as the woman stood up from the butchery. Her hands were bloodied with gore, her apron matted with gobs of flesh and fat. She wiped her hands in the grass, her dark face showing signs of fatigue.

'Someone ought to fetch her some water,' a voice said. 'She done all the work.'

'Then fetch it, why don't you?'

'Never mind the water, fetch the sacks,' ordered Sweetwater.

'Hell no!' he said as the squaw stooped over the carcass again. 'Back to camp. Eat!' He lifted a hand to his mouth.

As if deaf to the command, the squaw cut out the buffalo's eye, which she placed in her hide bag. She bent down to extract its companion from the other side of the head.

'By golly but she won't stir until she has filched every scrap,' complained linen jacket. '*Allez! Allez!*'

The squaw slit the skin off the lower jawbone and reached into the throat, as Mose had done, to drag out the tongue. Cutting the appendage free, she added it to one of the sacks. She then turned her attention to the removed legs.

'Enough!' Sweetwater touched her shoulder as she continued, ignoring him to cut a slab of meat from the foreleg. 'The hell with it!' He turned away. 'Let's get back to camp, boys.'

With the sacks of meat tied to the mule, they set off back for the camp. Glancing over his shoulder, Boundless saw the squaw remove a last chunk of meat before following. Wolves and coyotes had collected in the distance, waiting to approach the remains. The rest of the herd had moved off along the far bank of the creek.

'The buffalo do not seem overly concerned by the wolves,' he remarked.

'Depends. Sometimes they spook and set off like hellfire across the grass. But generally, they don't pay much heed to man nor wolf.'

'Bears irritate them,' contributed another man. 'They can't stand the stink.'

THE SUN WAS DECLINING in the sky as they walked back to the encampment. As they drew closer, Boundless saw the bodies of several Indians lying in the grass. Ravens flew up from the corpses at their approach. The lifeless faces were frozen in a grotesque grimace, testament to the ferocity of the battle. The scalped foreheads were encrusted with dried blood.

'Lord above but it was a close shave,' the man next to him remarked at the sight.

'I shall be glad to get back to Virginia,' agreed another.

As they entered the camp, a man came up to them in a distraught state.

'What is it?' asked the broad-faced hunter.

'It's Jedidiah,' the man answered, his face distressed. 'He has succumbed to his wound.'

The broad-faced hunter angrily slapped dust from his breeches.

'Hell and damnation! He'd have enjoyed a bite of fresh hump meat.'

'That makes five of us,' said another, his voice sombre.

'Six altogether,' a second voice amended. 'Counting poor Edward, that is.'

Sweetwater pointed to where three men smoothed the earth over the freshest grave. Curlew stood beside it, Bible in hand. 'That's half our party that started out from Virginny, kilt,' he lamented.

Supper was a subdued feast, the men eating silently for the most part. The evening was warm, the silence broken only by the sound of the crackling fire and the noise of the men eating.

'For poor Jedidiah!' A man cut off a chunk of meat. He tossed the meat into the flames and watched the fat sizzle and pop.

Curlew stood up and made a brief speech in praise of the dead men—the words evoking tears and fresh murmurs of grief. The atmosphere became less gloomy as first one man and then another recalled the various deeds of the departed, each sentimental reminiscence ending in a toast of water or hot tea. Mose sat to one side, smoking his pipe and quietly listening.

'Upon my word as a true son of Georgia, Lemuel was the best shot I e'er came across,' a man praised. The sentiment drew murmurs of approval.

'What of the German boy—Hans?' someone remembered. They looked to the boy's uncle, who shook his head, tears glistening in his eyes.

'I barely knew him,' confessed Curlew. 'Although he was tireless on the march.'

'He died bravely,' someone suggested.

'To good old Hans!' The toast evoked a half-hearted cheer and another round of eulogies.

'We need a tune, boys, a song to lift us up,' said Curlew. 'Who'll give the air?'

'Bartholomew!' a man declared and slapped the broad-faced hunter on the shoulder.

'Good, gentle Bart, favour us with a melody,' coaxed Curlew as the other man made a show of waving off the request.

'Give us the Barbry Allen!'

'Be it on your own heads, then!'

Noisily clearing his throat, the singer wet his lips and, following a false start, launched into the air, carrying the tune in a hoarse baritone.

As the men listened to the mournful ballad, Boundless sat immersed in his thoughts, reflecting on his earlier suggestion to Mose that they reconsider their venture in light of the Indian attack. *I also should be loath to turn back,* he admitted to himself—the lure of the plains having become as a powerful lodestone to his thoughts. A notion struck him, and he picked himself up and made his way through the darkness beyond the leaping flames.

He found the French soldier seated on the grass warming his hands before a small fire.

'Sir—Monsieur?'

'*Qui va là?*' The captain started as Boundless stepped into the firelight.

'Pardon, sir. I did not mean to disturb you.'

In the light of the glowing embers, the captain's face looked wan and dispirited. His grey *justaucorps* was ripped across the chest and most of the gilt buttons were missing. His white woollen breeches were torn and soiled with mud. He was bareheaded, locks of hair hanging loosely about his face. Around his upper arm he—or someone else, had wrapped a bloody bandage.

He regarded Boundless with suspicion. 'What is it you want with me?'

'I wish only to talk. I am not your enemy, Captain.'

'No?' The Frenchman's face looked comically astonished in the firelight. 'And yet here I sit—your prisoner.'

'Not mine. If it were my choice, I would set you free. I, too, have been a prisoner.'

The captain raised a sceptical eyebrow. 'Of the French?'

'The English.'

'Ah!' After studying Boundless for a moment, the Frenchman gestured to the grass. 'Sit.'

'Obliged, Captain. My name is Boundless McLennan.'

'*Oui.*' The French soldier acknowledged the introduction with grave courtesy. 'Captain François Giroux.'

Sounds of a squabble erupted from the main campfire. Captain Giroux cocked his head to listen. '*Sauvages!* ' He spat the word. 'They quarrel over my neck. It is the same each night.' He shrugged, as if weary of his fate.

'You need have no fear on that count, Captain. Mr Curlew is a civilised man, I assure you.'

The captain gave a humourless laugh. 'You think so? Then you are unacquainted with these fine Virginia *gentlemen*.'

'Hold him!' Curlew's voice rang out in the darkness.

One of the hunters had jumped to his feet, an oath on his lips. A companion sought to restrain the agitated figure as the others spoke to soothe him.

'The war is foolish,' Boundless said, to draw the Frenchman's attention away from the dispute.

The captain was silent, his attention on the fracas unfolding at the fire. As the dispute died down, he muttered scornfully, 'The fools do not even know what it is they fight for!'

Curious at the remark, Boundless volunteered his own understanding. 'The English claim it is because France wishes to monopolise trade with the Indians.'

The captain considered this for a moment. 'Yes and no, as you English say.'

'Then you do not agree—as to the cause?'

Captain Giroux eyed him across the fire as if to gauge his sincerity. 'The truth, *Monsieur*, is that our little war will decide the fate of half the world.'

Taken aback at the claim, Boundless took a moment to respond. 'Surely, you exaggerate?'

'I assure you, *mon ami*, I do not. Whilst we knock heads in this wilderness, our two countries and their allies are at each other's throats in Prussia, Germany, Poland, Bohemia, India, Africa, and elsewhere. I myself was destined for Portugal with my regiment before being despatched to the frontier.'

'But those conflicts you mention, they are half a world away. Surely, they have no bearing on this war?'

The captain stared into the fire but made no reply.

'And what of the Indians?' asked Boundless, pressing the case. 'They claim ownership of this land. Is their claim not more just than either the French or English one?'

Snapping a stick across his knee and placing both ends carefully on the fire, the captain replied, '*La raison du plus fort est toujours la meilleure.*'

'Pardon?'

'A house may have only one master. The war will decide if that is to be England or France.'

'If what you say is true, then more the pity that the quarrels of the Old World should intrude upon a land innocent of such rivalry?'

'Innocent!' The Frenchman seemed bemused by the word. 'Had you witnessed an Iroquois war party butcher a peaceful village you would not say such a thing, I assure you.'

'I am not a fool, Captain. I have seen with my own eyes how the Indians treat their enemies. Aye, and how they are treated in turn.'

A string of vehement curses issued from the campfire. The captain cocked his head to listen 'It may be that, among our countrymen—yours and mine, there are Iroquois, also?'

'I do not doubt it.'

'Then perhaps, you and I, *Monsieur,* are not such enemies after all.' Picking up another stick, the soldier poked the fire, raising a shower of sparks. 'Since the world is on fire, let us warm ourselves before the flames.'

Boundless held his hands over the fire while racking his brains for an excuse to raise the subject that had brought him to the Frenchman. 'You speak English very well.'

'My mother was born in Boston.'

'Indeed!' Boundless was unable to keep the surprise from his voice. 'And you have no divided loyalties?'

The captain bristled 'I am French! And loyal only to France.'

'Pardon. I meant nothing by it, I assure you. Were you yourself born in New France, Captain?'

'*Oui.* Far from here. In a town famed for its artisans.' The Frenchman's voice grew melancholy in the darkness. 'My father was a simple stone cutter, as was his father before him. It was a saying in the town that if you wished to make cheese, ask a farmer. But if you wished for butter, ask a Giroux! such was his skill at softening and shaping the stone. Naturally, he wished me to enter the trade, also. But I chose to become a soldier instead and see the world.'

The sound of singing came from the campfire followed by a bawdy chorus. The captain listened for a moment before making a wry face. 'Better for my neck that they sing!' The soldier frowned, as if suddenly remembering the conversation. 'But what is it you wish with me, *Monsieur?*'

'There is a favour I would ask—as someone who also wishes to see the world. My companion and I are hunters, on our way to the western plains. We are following an Indian path, but I fear we have become lost and go around in circles. I am told you are familiar with the country west of here.'

The captain raised an eyebrow, suspicion returning to his voice. 'You would have me betray my oath as a solider—by giving directions to the enemy?'

'Upon my word. We are but innocent travellers.'

'Hah! Again. *Innocent!*' The captain kicked a burning stick back onto the fire.

They fell silent and Boundless feared the moment had been lost. Casting about for some way to regain the other man's trust, a thought struck him. 'Your hat!'

'What do you say?' The captain looked at him in confusion.

'I meant that when we met—before the fight—you were hatless.'

'What of it? I lost it in battle.'

'A moment, if you please.' Getting to his feet, Boundless went over to the cargo baskets, stumbling in the gloom. In the darkness he rummaged through the contents, muttering at not finding the item readily to hand. After a few minutes he returned to the fire. 'It will keep the sun from your eyes.' He held out the spare straw hat.

The soldier made no move to accept the gift, suspicion on his face.

'You would oblige me by taking it. My own is more than sufficient.'

Cautiously, the captain reached out to take the hat. '*Je vous remercie,* he said, his voice softening.

The noise from the main campfire had diminished as the hunters retired to sleep. Captain Giroux turned the straw hat in his hands, his manner less vigilant as the hunters began to snore.

'You remind me, that, even in war, one recognises the courtesy due to another.' He fingered the brim of the hat and sighed. 'Let it not be said that Captain Giroux departed this world in debt. I shall give what assistance I can for your journey—in repayment for your kindness.'

'Many thanks, Captain. I shall try not to tax your patience.'

The two continued in deep discussion for another quarter hour before being interrupted by a whispered hail.

'Mr McLennan, are you there?' Curlew stood by the campfire, searching the darkness.

'Over here.' Boundless got to his feet.

'Yourself and your companion are to stand first watch.'

'Aye, aye.' He turned to the Frenchman. 'I must take my leave, Captain. I am in your debt, sir.'

The Frenchman stood slowly to his feet and held out his good hand. 'This is the custom, here on the frontier, is it not—the handshake? It is a good custom. *Égalité et fraternité.* Perhaps the New World has something to teach the Old after all.'

The two clasped hands. 'Who knows, *mon ami,* but that we may meet again, under happier circumstances. And, if not, why then, remember the name François Giroux when you stand upon the western plains.'

'I shall, Captain. I promise. But I trust that Fortune may smile upon you and that one day you shall be reunited with your home and family again.'

'*Peut-être.*' A fatalistic look crossed the Frenchman's face. 'If God wishes it so.'

Returning to the campfire, Boundless looked around for Mose. The men were snoring, sated from the buffalo feast. He found his companion standing on the perimeter, the musket cradled in his arms.

'Did you get advice?' Mose squinted in the darkness as he approached.

'I did. The captain was most helpful. He spoke about a great river that runs to the north—the Missouri.'

'I have not heard mention of it. He has seen it?'

'No, but he has revealed some information that will prove useful in finding it. What was the cause of the quarrel—at the fire?'

Mose spat into the grass. 'The hothead—the one with the kilt brother. He was all for slaughtering your Frenchie on the spot.'

'And the others?'

'Some for, and some against. Young Curlew was mostly against.'

'Mostly?'

'Deuced if I could tell. But I wouldn't give two farthings for the fellow's neck. A pound to a penny they string him up afore the mountains. I will be glad to be on our way, I do confess. These Virginians be a cantankerous bunch.'

They departed the camp early next morning, Curlew stretching up to grasp Boundless' hand as he sat in the saddle. 'Farewell, Boundless. It may have gone hard for us had you not chanced along. Remember—you have a friend in Williamsburg should you ever find yourself in that town.'

'Thanks be due on both sides.' Boundless hesitated, searching the other man's face. 'The French officer, he will be safe in your hands?'

Curlew looked uncomfortable at the question. 'The men are angry at our losses.'

'He has been helpful. I would ask—'

'The day awaits!' Mose rode past, the mare and mules following.

'Goodbye. And Godspeed.' Releasing his hand, Curlew stepped back.

As they exited the thicket, Boundless saw the French captain standing in the shadow of a tree. Raising a hand in farewell, he was pleased to observe that the Frenchman was wearing the straw hat. The captain did not reciprocate his farewell gesture, but stood stiffly erect, nursing the wounded arm, his face drawn as he watched them ride away.

The Ohio

FURNISHED WITH THE FRENCH captain's advice, they continued the journey in good spirits. Before noon, they came upon a buffalo trace and followed where it led in a north-westerly direction. The weather was fair, a cool breeze keeping at bay the annoying insects. They rode side by side across a broad meadow, Boundless surprised at the contentment he felt at being under way again.

'Was that our spare hat the Frenchie was wearing?'

'It was indeed. He had lost his own.'

'And what if you, or I, should lose the one on our heads?'

'If you lose yours, then you shall have mine.'

Mose grunted. 'From your mouth.'

'It was a small price to pay for his guidance.'

They had been underway but two hours when they shot an enormous grizzly—the bear being surly and disinclined to vacate the path as they approached.

'Blazes but the fellow was bad-tempered!' Mose lowered the musket. It had taken shots from both muskets plus another from the pistol to bring down the snarling beast. Mose was then obliged to finally despatch the animal as it writhed and growled horribly in the grass. Impressed at the animal's bulk, Mose insisted on measuring the specimen. 'Eleven feet, nose to tail,' he declared, pacing back and forth the length of the animal several times. 'And ten hundredth weight or more, at a guess.'

'That much?' Boundless surveyed the bear doubtfully. 'Though it be monstrously large,' he conceded.

'Those paws would take the head of a mule with one bat. I wish we had the time to skin him. But I am not up to the labour just now.' Mose climbed back into the saddle. 'A banquet for the wolves,' he said.

In the afternoon, they approached a line of tree-topped bluffs running across their path.

'Are those the same bluffs your captain mentioned?'

'I believe so. They run east to west, as described.'

'Then who knows but the fellow may yet steer us to the Ohio.'

'Did you doubt it?'

'I did, I confess.' Mose rode on for a few minutes in silence. 'I did,' he repeated, evidently weighing the matter. 'And yet it was a Frenchie that fetched me here all those years ago.' He took off his hat to scratch his head. 'There be a riddle to things. It sores me to think on it. What say you?'

'Mere chance, no doubt.'

'Chance! That one Frenchie, near half my years ago, should set me on this path and another, just today, should steer me along?'

'What then, if not chance?'

'Providence. That which reckons the fall of a sparrow.'

'Then Providence has a French cast.'

'Jest as you may. But the fall of a sparrow, friend. The fall of a sparrow.'

TWO DAYS AFTER LEAVING the encampment, they lost the bell mare to a falling branch while passing through a pine grove. Without warning, the heavy limb crashed to the ground, crushing the mare as she passed underneath. Mose kicked a shrub in a temper as he stood up from examining the dead animal. 'Neck broke clean as you'd wish,' he lamented. He glowered up at the offending pine. 'By the bones, but how many dozens of years has that limb spread up there waiting for this exact moment to tumble down and kill the poor mare? It distracts the mind to think on it.'

He cast his gaze on Boundless. 'You look pale. Did it whip you on the way down?'

'I felt its passage. A moment either side and I should be lying there, along with the mare.'

That night, as Boundless lay next to the campfire, he dwelt on the incident, shaken at the narrow miss. His thoughts drifted back to the aftermath of the storm at sea and the eerie calm as the yellow flush of dawn illuminated the restless tide. '*For the living know that they shall die: but the dead know not any thing, neither have they any more a reward; for the memory of them is forgotten.*' The words, whispered across the continental vastness, caused him to turn on one side and stare into the fire.

'Up, Boundless. Your watch.'

The next morning, they tied the bell to the bridle of the bay. Boundless mounted and rode in a circle, shaking the bell as the mules stood in place. 'Try it again,' said Mose. 'Lead Prodigal; he has the more sense.'

Riding up directly alongside the mule, Boundless shook the bell as he led off.

'Git!' Mose slapped the mule on the rump. The animal hawed and snuffled but remained in place. 'Git, you doleful, lop-eared punishment!' To their surprise, it was the other mule, Jacob, which suddenly trotted off in pursuit of the tinkling bell. 'How like a merchant!' crowed Mose. 'He answers to the bell! Did I not truly name him?'

Prodigal hawed again before setting off to follow.

'Keep going—for the love of God!' Mose hastened to mount the stallion.

They rode a considerable distance before being halted by a river. Boundless shook his head as he surveyed the turgid water. 'It is as well it is summer,' he said. 'Else would we be in need of a fleet of boats.'

Mose waded out into the stream, which reached up to his waist. 'We can cross here,' he said. 'The flow is tolerable.'

They crossed without incident and spent a day camped on the spot, having laid out the tack to dry.

'HOW FAR DID YOUR captain say the Ohio was?' asked Mose the following day as they again made good progress, crossing three creeks before halting and shooting a plump turkey for supper.

'No more than a week or so.'

'He knows it well?'

'He was stationed there at a fort in the upper stretches of the river. He has travelled down it by boat to where it joins the Mississippi.'

'A week or so?'

'Yes.'

'I shall be glad of it.'

They continued under warm, sunny skies, progressing between eighteen and twenty miles a day. They stopped to hunt and make salt from a lick. Mose was in rare spirits, declaring he could 'smell' the Ohio, and pronouncing each stream or creek a branch of the river. Game was plentiful and Indian signs were few, increasing their feelings that their luck had changed and that the main dangers of the journey lay behind them.

TWO WEEKS AFTER LEAVING the hunting party, they glimpsed the Ohio in the distance. The day was warm and overcast and the river shone dully in the late morning sun. The surrounding country was heavily treed, and the river disappeared from view almost as soon as they spotted it. An hour later, they reined in on the grassy shore to gaze out over the southwestwardly flow.

Taking of his hat, Mose fanned his face. 'Ain't she a sight?', he said, his eyes misting over as he surveyed the wide, glittering flood. 'Gloried indeed be His works.' The trapper seemed overcome as he praised 'the granddaddy of waters.'

'As God be my witness,' he said, his voice choking with emotion, 'I feared never to see it again.'

Under the cloudy sky, the great river emerged from the remote grasslands of one horizon to disappear into the immense wilderness on the other, its serene, unhurried flow undisturbed by house or habitation or any sign of human agency. In the warm, overcast air, sunlight sparkled on the milky surface—the shimmering flood so wide across that they were unable to see to the other side.

Boundless removed his hat, his hair damp with sweat. 'It is a lonesome place, Mose. Why, I feel as if we are the last persons left in the world.'

'And so too was the blessed Garden. But the two companions were embargoed on all sides by the Creator's bounty.' Mose leaned forward in the saddle and took a deep breath as he surveyed the great river. 'D'ye not feel the breath of God?'

'We shall have to build a raft.'

'There is wood aplenty. Do you not see? It be all provided for.' Exultant at reaching the long-desired mark, Mose kicked the stallion forward. 'Hi-yup, old Jack! Let us sup from the Jordan waters!'

After slaking their thirst, they held a brief discussion while looking out over the flood. Picking up a stone, Boundless flung it as far as he could, watching as it dropped into the river with barely a splash.

'It is ten times the width of the New River.'

Mose gazed up and down the bank. 'Mayhap there is a narrow spot. Let us try.'

They rode downstream for some distance, passing through dense brush that grew down to the shore. 'By Jehovah, did you ever see such giants?' marvelled the trapper as they passed through a grove of towering syca-mores. 'Any half-dozen, laid end-to-end, would see us safely across!'

They came upon equally immense specimens of cottonwood and silver maple, Mose opining that, surely, they were trespassing in the abode of giants.

Boundless nudged the bay as they passed under the shade of a spiralling sycamore, suddenly fearful lest it crash to earth with a noise to shake the world. Scarcely had they passed by the gargantuan specimen when they beheld a like giant—one so vast that he felt compelled to stop and take measurements.

Murmuring with astonishment, he paced the circumference, declaring it to be no less than forty-five feet. He stepped back to gaze up at the crown, guessing it to spring 150 feet or more overhead. Huge chunks of bark lay scattered on the grass as if the tree were divesting itself of its woody skin.

Mose stood beside him to gaze up at the profuse canopy. 'It might give shade to an entire tribe of savages.' Reaching out, he peeled off a loose piece of bark and held it up. 'See how thick it grows?'

'This is truly a land of grotesques,' declared Boundless. 'Everything seems of disproportionate height, length or breadth. Such irregularity is surely a breach in the laws of Nature.'

'Fie! It is the handiwork of the Creator. He set these here that we might glory in His works.'

Boundless scratched his chin, eyeing the lowest branches and wondering what it might be like to scale to the topmost heights. *I should probably tumble and break my neck.*

THE SHORE WAS STEEP and muddy, offering no easy access to the river. They noted several islands in the middle of the stream along with numerous snags, sandbanks and floating logs. 'It will be a hazard to cross,' said Boundless, not liking the strong flow or the intimidating width.

'What did your Frenchman say?'

'He advised we wait for a passing boat and pay passage to where it flows down to the Mississippi.'

Mose snorted at the suggestion, the trapper predictably reluctant to entrust their fortunes to anything other than their own legs and horses. 'What else?'

'He said that there are no forts between here and the Mississippi, but that the French occasionally patrol the river and scout the shore from flatboats.'

'Then let us avoid the boats and trust to our own hands.'

A mile further on they encountered a section where the river narrowed as it passed through a series of low-lying flats on both banks. The river appeared no more than half a mile across at the point. An island, dotted with shrubs, stood in the middle of the stream.

'We can float a raft from here. And there is all the material to make one.' Mose pointed to a stand of trees a short distance ahead. 'Let us make camp in those woods.'

The cloud cover had burned away, and the sun beat down upon their heads. Mose tugged at his sweat-stained shirt. 'By jakes, but it be warm.'

Entering into the shade of the trees, they unpacked the mules and turned the horses loose to graze. Fanning himself in the stifling heat, Boundless walked the short distance back to the river and crouched down to splash water on his face. Through the surface, he could see the gravelly bottom twenty yards out from the bank. He wet the neckerchief and laid it across his neck, feeling faint in the suffocating air. From this vantage, the river seemed an impossible barrier to cross, the opposite bank as remote as the shores of a sea.

As he stood up to contemplate the voluminous flood, he felt oppressed by a crushing burden of solitude. So profound was the grassy silence on all sides—disturbed only by the rippling flood—that he fancied it unbroken since the age of the earth. In an unchecked thought, he imagined throwing himself into the mighty stream and surrendering to its ceaseless flow, his bones swept back and forth along the course of the river until time itself did end.

His reverie was interrupted by a splashing sound as a fish leapt from the stream to snap at a dragonfly. The prospect of a variance from the daily diet of meat and beans roused him to go off in search of a suitable branch for a fishing pole. Tying a hook and line to the branch, he baited the hook with a wriggling worm and cast into the water. He immediately felt a tug on the line and drew forth a large fish unknown to him, one with an extremely long snout, shaped like a paddle. The fish struggled mightily as he pulled it into shore. 'Three feet if an inch!' he declared in astonishment. He shook his head at this evidence of originality in the Ohio waters. He baited another worm and threw the line in again, easily securing a large pike.

Returning to the camp with the catch, he unpacked the fishing net and walked back to the river. Venturing out into the stream, he suspended the net in the water as the current rippled around his knees. The bountiful flood soon yielded a catfish, a sturgeon, and a netful of silver herring—the latter eliciting an exclamation of pleasure for its conjuration of Scotland and hearthside suppers.

He explored further along the river, confident of safety in the protective solitude. To his delight, he encountered numerous shoals of mussels clustered together like dark-blue pebbles on the riverbed. The sight prompted him to fetch a jute sack to scoop up the morsels. He waded into the water, taking three-dozen of the coloured molluscs.

Later, over a supper of fish and roasted partridge, he dug the pink-grey flesh from the boiled shells and consumed the meat with great relish. However, nothing in his power could tempt Mose to taste the 'devilish coals'.

'There be such things as are fit for a man to eat and they are not one of them,' insisted the trapper as Boundless swallowed yet another of the plump, juicy mussels.

Following supper, they sat around the fire digesting the meal. As the night closed in and a blaze of stars rose over the broad river, Boundless glanced at his companion, who sat seemingly lost in thought over his pipe. 'You be in a brown study, Mose.'

The trapper grunted a reply, puffing on the pipe as he considered the remark. 'True,' he conceded at length.

'And is there a cause?'

Mose let out a sigh as he stared into the fire. 'Truth be told, my bones be at war with my mind. Long have I waited for the chance to feast my eyes on the plains and now, within distance, my fancy plays strange tricks.' He puffed on the remark for some minutes as Boundless awaited further elucidation.

''Tis a most natural feeling,' he prompted, as Mose continued his silence. 'I feel it as well. The desired gain is often prefigured by trembling and uncertainty. Picture the anxious suitor—bent on one knee and nervously awaiting the outcome of his proposal.'

Mose nodded, his face sombre. 'True. And I be that suitor. 'Tis the consumption that gives fright—to extend your figure. And no need to grin so toothsomely!' He fixed Boundless a testy glance.

'Pardon. I was diverted. We shall soon reach the plains, and you shall see your hopes restored and your fears laid to rest.'

'By God's grace.' Mose tapped tobacco from the pipe.

'If you are bound to be disconsolate—why not take first watch?' yawned Boundless, stretching his arms.

As he lay under the buffalo robe, he reflected on his companion's disquietude. 'We are in the midst of things,' he mused, 'and must now redact our purposes. It is this lonesome solitude. It unnerves the mind.' Turning on his side, he adjusted the rolled-up blanket beneath his head as he heard Mose exclaim and kick a spluttering log back onto the fire.

IN THE MORNING, HE had just stepped out of the dense brush to wash in the river when he glimpsed something upstream. As he crouched, blinking in the morning sunshine, he saw four canoes proceeding downriver towards him. Not daring to stand for fear of being seen, he scuttled back into the brush to alert Mose. Together, the two took their muskets and concealed themselves in the undergrowth, spying from the brush as the canoes drew nearer.

Each canoe contained four Indians. They paddled at a leisurely pace, seemingly without a care in the world as they proceeded. Their passage took them to within thirty feet of where he and Mose lay concealed, close enough that he could see clearly their faces and half-shaven heads.

'Shawnee!' whispered Mose.

The Indians cast lazy looks at the shoreline, supremely confident of being alone. Their voices sounded clearly over the water. One pointed to something in the river and his companion leaned over the side to see. At that moment a whinny sounded from the horses, concealed further in the brush. The occupants of the nearest canoe stopped paddling to listen. Boundless froze. Beside him, Mose cursed. The canoe floated abreast of their position, the Indians scanning the woods along the bank. He hardly dared breathe, his heart in his mouth as the Indians stared directly at where he lay in concealment.

The occupants of the other canoes called out to their companions, wondering what was amiss. At a gesture, the Indians stopped talking, listening hard in the silence. Suddenly, the Indians relaxed, conversing again as they resumed paddling. Boundless peered through the foliage as the rear paddler gave one last searching look at the bank before turning his attention back to the river. Overcome with relief, he watched the canoes continue downstream.

''Tis a reminder not to drop our vigilance,' said Mose, standing cautiously to his feet. 'We are not alone in the Garden. There be serpents here too.'

Perturbed by the near encounter, they spent the day looking for deadwood to make a raft. Finding the available logs unsuited to their purpose, they decided they had no alternative but to fell a tree. Accordingly, they searched the giant trunks, judging even the smallest too formidable a challenge to bring down.

'I fear breaking the axe,' said Mose, dismissing one candidate after another.

Searching for a solution, Boundless hit upon the idea of building a fire at the base of a suitable tree. 'It will weaken the trunk sufficient for the tree to fall by itself or through the axe,' he suggested. 'Otherwise, we must hope to find one levelled by a storm.'

They spent an hour dragging brushwood to the base of a suitable sycamore, carefully piling the brush around the tree before setting it alight.

'Not too high,' cautioned Boundless, as Mose dragged another branch onto the fire. 'We wish to weaken the base only, not bring the Shawnee down on our heads.'

It took two days, and constant replenishing of the banked fires, before they were able to sever the weakened trunk and bring down the tree. 'Stand aside!' Mose hurried to one side as the tree leaned slowly forwards with a loud, groaning sound. The massive trunk hung in the air for a long moment before toppling to the earth with an enormous *crack!* as birds scattered into the sky with indignant shrieks.

'We must work it here,' said Mose, eyeing the distance to the river.

Over the next week they stripped and chopped off branches and split and sawed the trunk into rough-hewn logs. Before they could drag it to the water they had, first of all, to clear a path through the brush. They did so reluctantly, fearing other Indians might pass down the river and spot the clearance. 'We have no choice,' said Mose. 'With luck, any canoes will pass along the western shore.'

Roping the split logs to the mules, they dragged the lumber down to the water's edge, the strenuous toil leaving both men exhausted. 'A respite—a quarter-hour Sabbath,' panted Mose, wheezing from his exertions. 'Would I were but ten years fresher,' he lamented, placing his hands on his knees to catch his breath.

Concerned at the trapper's fatigue, Boundless insisted on extending the rest to the remainder of the day. 'The river will still be there on the morrow.'

After Mose reluctantly conceded, they spent the day dozing in the shade before feasting on cold venison and retiring early to sleep.

Judging the amount of wood to be yet insufficient, they scoured the thick brush for saplings—chancing upon several. They chopped down two, breaking an axe handle in the process. 'Now see the wisdom of carrying a spare,' said Mose as he despatched Boundless back to fetch the handle.

It took another two days to level and strip the saplings and drag them back to the river. The additional toil exhausted the mules and put Mose in a temper as he bemoaned the 'wastefulness of the hour'.

Too tired to argue, Boundless lay back on his elbows to draw breath, half convinced that they were fated never to cross the stream.

His doubts redoubled as the assembled logs multiplied and the raft grew in size. Laid in a square, the logs made up a platform thirty feet long and thirty across.

'Surely, it is too large,' he protested. 'It will be impossible to paddle—and so heavy it must sink.'

'Any smaller and we shall have to make a second trip. And who knows how far downstream the stream will take us? We may not be able to cross back or mayhap the wood will soak up too much water and sink. No, it has to be done once, or not at all. What? I see you doubt me! It will float, do not fear. Come, let us make camp for the night. My poor bones are broke.'

Following a sound night's sleep, Boundless spent the next day driving dove-tail notches into the ends of the logs while Mose fashioned crossbeams to sit in the cuts. They used lengths of wetted twine to lash the crossbeams in place, coiling the twine several times to make certain of the bind. The work was slow and laborious and they paused frequently to drink or visit the shade in search of respite from the heat.

'Many more rivers such as this one and we shall grow old 'ere we reach the plains,' Boundless complained as they took refuge from the sun in a grove of sycamores. Mites buzzed around his face as he mopped the sweat from his brow. He saw that Mose had fallen asleep, a look of exhaustion on his face. He frowned, worried anew at the older man's ability to sustain such a taxing journey. *I must take the lion's share of the work,* he reminded himself as he listened to his companion's rasping snores. Too restless to doze, he examined the palms of his hands for splinters. *These are woodcutter's hands,* he reflected, studying the roughened and calloused skin. He looked around at the trees, a thought hovering on the edge of his mind.

Moving carefully so as not to awaken his companion, he picked up the flintlock and set off to explore the dense brush. He scouted the earth as he went, looking for animal tracks or any sign that others had been there before him. He stopped to admire a robust sycamore that towered so high above that he was unable to see the topmost branches. As he turned to continue, he stumbled against something and pitched forwards—barely able to prevent himself from falling onto his face. Cursing, he rubbed his stubbed toe while casting about for whatever had caused him to stumble. His eye alighted on a knob of bone sticking out of the dirt. Kneeling, he brushed away the earth from the protuberance. Grasping the bone with both hands he attempted to tug it out of the ground. To his surprise, it refused to budge. Taking a branch, he dug around the object, revealing more of the bone in the process. Now intensely curious, he dug alongside where it lay buried scooping away the dirt in disbelief as yet more of the object was revealed. Shaking and tugging the end, and grasping it with both hands, he finally was able to drag the bone clear of the earth.

'What the devil!' Astounded, he beheld the full size of the object as it lay in the grass. The curved bone was ten or more feet in length and as thick around the middle as both of his thighs. He ran his hands over the osseous surface, calculating it as far too large to belong to either a bear or buffalo. 'Then what creature owned it?' he pondered, exceedingly perplexed at the discovery.

An inspection of the surrounding undergrowth revealed several more of the giant bones lying partly or wholly concealed in the grass. One steeply curved specimen, appeared to be a tusk, and he murmured in puzzlement as he tried to imagine what immense creature it signified.

'Jinks if that ain't the rib of an elephant!'

Mose stepped from between the trees—having awakened from his nap and gone in search of his companion. Scratching his head, he stared at the huge tusk. 'Twenty feet if it be an inch!' he declared, pacing the length of the object. Perplexed, he looked at Boundless. 'What leviathan claimed ownership of such an appendage?'

Boundless shrugged, equally nonplussed. 'Could it be some giant animal which stalked these parts?'

The trapper bent down to give the bone closer scrutiny. 'If so, the creature is long dead. This bone is ancient. See, the end is crumbled with age. They have lain here, mayhap, since the Flood.'

The two stared at the object, thoroughly confounded by the discovery.

'Perhaps, in times past, a giant species—similar to the elephant, roamed these plains,' Boundless speculated.

'How is that possible—so far from the torrid zones?' objected Mose. He glanced up at the sky. 'Drag yourself away. Else shall we ourselves form part of this boneyard.'

They spent the remainder of the afternoon finishing the raft and fashioning poles and paddles to propel the platform. As he worked, Boundless brooded on the tantalising mystery of the giant bones. Determined to preserve a record of the find, he returned to the site before supper, making several sketches and labelling the drawings *Giant Bones—Summer 1758, Ohio River*. He deliberated whether to break one of the smaller bones and take it with him for later consideration before dismissing the idea. *What more could I glean if I stared at the artefact for the rest of my days?*

He returned to the campfire to find Mose already snoring beneath a blanket. Lying down, he tugged the buffalo robe up over his chest, still perplexed by the giant skeleton. *Mayhap it belongs to some unknown creature from antiquity. This New World is yet laid crossbeam on ancient footings.* He pondered the conundrum before falling asleep.

They awoke to a cloudless sky—the day already growing warm as they ate cold venison and readied themselves for the river crossing. Following breakfast, he joined Mose on the shore to survey the flood while discussing the passage.

'Why not stay on the river?' he asked. 'That was the captain's advice—to float down to the Mississippi.'

'And did he mention falls or rapids?'

'He did not. But surely, if there were such, he would have said so.'

'I do not trust the raft to take us safely beyond this crossing.'

'The horses are tired. Their hooves are worn. Perhaps it were best that—'

'And what if we encounter more Indians, or the French? We shall be lost.'

'We may encounter them on land, just as well.'

'The hour wastes.' With that, Mose stomped off to collect the mules.

With a sigh, Boundless sat down on the edge of the raft.

It took the Herculean efforts of both men and the mules to lever and drag the heavy raft the remaining few yards into the water. Mose exclaimed in dismay as the front end of the heavy platform promptly slid under the current to rest on the muddy bottom. 'She needs more footage to float. Push that side!'

Splashing into the stream, Boundless grasped the side and pulled manfully, inching the raft further into the river. It required him to stand in water up to his waist before the heavy craft gained sufficient buoyancy to sit, half-submerged, in the shallows.

'How are we to get the animals aboard?' he asked, panting from the strain. 'It will sink again under the weight.' He stepped from the river, smoothing water from his soaked breeches. 'On the Patapsco, we used the bank itself as a wharf.' He pointed upstream 'See that point of land where I caught the sturgeon two days ago? It forms a natural jetty. The water pools beside it to a depth that would cover a man's head. We can drag the raft there and load the animals from the point.'

'Then let us make haste. I am anxious to quit this spot.'

Using the mules to pull the raft, they painstakingly manoeuvred the heavy encumbrance upstream to where the bank formed a small headland. Once positioned, the raft sat squarely in the stream as water lapped the sides. Tying it in place, they carried the cargo baskets aboard. They then led the animals to the spot, the chestnut shying away from the raft. Coaxing and tugging the reluctant animal, Mose brought it onto the rocking platform where it stood nervously, its legs trembling with the motion of the raft. 'We must tether them so they cannot move else will they shake overboard.'

Boundless secured the stallion's bridle to a stake jammed between the logs in the centre of the raft. This done, he led his own horse on board, the bay stepping gingerly across the platform. The mules showed no such reluctance, trotting onto the raft and standing patiently as they were secured next to the horses. The combined weight sank the platform a half-foot deeper into the water. The raft was now crowded with cargo and livestock, leaving scant room for the two companions.

Suddenly doubtful of the entire enterprise, Boundless waded into the shallows. 'If it sinks, we lose everything,' he told himself, reminded sharply of the disaster on the New River. Mose looked visibly concerned, perhaps prompted by the same remembrance. 'Make haste,' the trapper urged, his usual equanimity in the face of danger for once cast aside.

Mose gripped a pole and stood on one side, as Boundless propelled the raft out into the stream with a laboured shove. Pulling himself on-board, he seized a pole, standing opposite his companion.

The raft slowly swung in a circle as both men pushed hard against the pebbly bottom. 'Keep her pointed forwards!'

As they lost the bottom, he exchanged the pole for a paddle, Mose following suit. The flow had caught the raft and began to carry it downstream. Sweeping furiously, they struggled to keep it square to the shore. The air was warm and humid, and Boundless felt sweat trickle down his face and neck as he fought to keep a forward momentum. The river—so placid-seeming from the bank, bubbled and foamed, a breeze casting spray against his face. Even though they paddled energetically, the tremendous flow carried them remorselessly downstream.

Exhausted, he took a break from paddling, noting that Mose had done the same. The raft began to turn in a circle. He resumed sweeping with the oar but was unable to prevent the raft from turning. Already, they were far downstream of their original mark. The raft began to bounce in the waves. To add to his fears, a cross-wind—barely detectable on the shore, scuffed the wave-tops as the raft began to head downstream with increasing speed.

'An inch across for a yard down!'

He glanced over at where Mose was paddling with urgent strokes. The raft, now in the full grip of the current, swept ever more rapidly downstream. The stallion nickered in fear and pulled at the tether, stamping his feet and spooking the mules. Alarmed at the thought of loose animals on board, he stroked with renewed urgency, calculating that they were now two or three miles downstream and in great danger of encountering rapids or some other hazard. Spotting a half-submerged log drifting towards them, he shouted a warning. Moments later the log struck the raft with shuddering force.

'Perish the day, but it almost had me overboard!' Mose guffawed suddenly, the sound incongruous amidst the wind and the noise of the flowing tide. Irritated at first, Boundless slowly joined in, giving way to a belly laugh as Mose whooped with merriment, his hair and beard drenched with spray.

Peering into the water, Boundless was unable to see the bottom. Propelled by fears of capsizing, he swept the oar, his arms aching from the strain. At that moment they struck a cross-current, which floated them appreciably closer to the western shore. To his relief, the ground appeared relatively flat.

'Five hundred yards, no more!' Mose had his hat tucked into his shirt for safety, giving him an oddly misshapen look as he rested for a moment on the paddle.

'Now!' Boundless shouted. 'Give it your all!'

Stroking furiously, they brought the heavy platform into the shallows. The raft struck bottom with a violent thud before swinging around and lodging in some reeds.

Mose flung down the paddle and leapt into the water to grab the raft. 'By Ezekiel's wheels we are across! Chase the horses off! I have her safe! Loosen the dang horses!'

Hurriedly, Boundless untied the frightened horses and stood aside as they splashed ashore and scrambled up the grassy bank. The mules followed closely behind. As Mose fought to hold the raft, Boundless quickly carried the cargo onto the shore, fearful lest the raft spin out into the current again. In less than five minutes, the entire cache sat safely in the grass.

'Stay clear!' Standing in the water, Mose let go the raft. It crushed some reeds and swung out into the river again. Boundless noted with relieved surprise how waterlogged it was, and how low it rode in the current. Waves lapped over the sides. *Another hour and she will sink.* He watched it pick up speed as the tide carried it downstream.

'Creation if I ain't busted through!' Mose flopped to the mud bank, his clothes soaked. 'Lord but it be cold!' He shivered violently in spite of the sun's heat. Stretched out flat in the grass, he wheezed for breath. 'Stir me only if the savages of the world descend upon us!'

Boundless hung his head between his knees, too tired to speak, but exultant to be across the river. The raft was already a distant speck, bobbing aimlessly on the current. He looked back at the eastern shore, barely able to see it. 'We should load the mules and move into the woods,' he told himself, cautious lest anyone pass by and spot them. His limbs ached with the strain of paddling. He looked over at his companion, who was fast asleep. He tried to force himself to his feet to collect the stock but, too tired to move, he collapsed in the grass.

He awoke to see Mose snoring with his mouth open, dead to the world. Uncertain whether to rouse his companion, he looked around, deciding that the country was much the same as it had been on the opposite shore.

'I dreamed I was a fish!' Mose sat up, rubbing his eyes. 'What is the hour?'

'Past noon. We could make camp here for the night.'

'Nay. I am refreshed! Let us load the cargo and move away from this peevish stream!'

41

The Mississippi

THEY HEADED OFF IN a northly direction, relieved to leave the great river behind. They soon came upon a buffalo trace and followed this for three hours until Mose called a halt to rest the stock. Unstrapping a basket on one of the mules, he examined the animal for sores or chafed skin. 'That belt was a mite too tight,' he said, straightening up. 'Are you sure we are headed aright—to the Mississippi?' His voice was testy, the strain of the arduous river crossing showing on his face.

'According to the captain, it flows west of where we now stand. The Ohio is here—' Boundless scuffed a line in the dirt with his foot. 'And the Mississippi, here. They form a rough angle, which we traverse by keeping to this path.' He dragged a line connecting both rivers.

Mose stared at the dirt sketch. 'And I suppose we must cross over it?'

'Aye. We need the western shore. We follow it upstream to where it forks with another river, the Missouri. According to the Captain it is reputedly as big as the Ohio.'

'And that creek will take us to the plains?'

'It will. The captain thinks they start just past the junction of the two.'

'Thinks?'

'He has never ventured so far but has read military reports indicating that to be the case.'

Mose stretched, groaning at the stiffness in his back. 'Is it getting cold?' He glanced up at the sky. 'I do not care for those clouds. Let us continue.'

Leaving the flat bottom land behind, they picked up another trace and followed it for several miles. It led through a landscape of hills and meadows watered by numerous creeks. Game was less abundant than previously, but they encountered groups of antelope, elk and deer. In the afternoon, they stopped to survey the ground where a number of traces intersected, the trails seeming to meander aimlessly.

'Do we have a mark?'

Boundless scanned the surrounding country, trying to recall Captain Giroux's advice. 'An Indian path that runs due west beneath the rim of a high rocky crag topped with trees—like a crown of thorns.'

'A crown of thorns?' Mose pondered the description. 'A certain sign,' he said approvingly. 'Mayhap your Frenchman be a trusty shepherd after all.' He pointed to one trace, broader than the rest. 'Let us try this fellow and see where it leads.'

The country continued smooth and relatively flat as they followed the trace. The day grew hotter, and they stopped for water. The trace ended on the banks of a rippling stream. With no other path to choose from, they followed the stream, stopping briefly to observe a herd of antelope being hounded by wolves. Boundless scratched a troublesome bite on his neck while scouring the horizon for the captain's landmark. His search was arrested by a series of distant rounded hillocks that rose above the flat grass—the contours vaguely puzzling in their symmetry.

Mose had also spotted the mounds. 'Did your captain make mention of such?'

'I think not. He was precise that the marker was rocky and crowned with trees—not smooth and bare.'

'Then what are those?'

Boundless knitted his brow, puzzled by the formation. 'Perhaps they are fortifications of some kind.'

'And your captain made no mention?'

'No, I am certain. I would have recalled such.'

Mose huffed in irritation. 'Then we have indeed lost the path.'

They continued on until they were no more than a thousand yards from the first of the mounds. It rose some fifty feet above the surrounding earth, its smoothly rounded contours suggesting human agency. As they drew closer, Boundless observed the faint evidence of terraced steps—mossed over with grass and cut into the sides, winding up from the base to the summit.

Halting the bay in the shadow of the mound, he sat staring up at the earthwork.

'What the devil is it?' Mose stopped alongside him.

'Whatever it is, someone has constructed it here for a purpose. Perhaps it is a burial mound. Or, mayhap, a monument to the gods in the way of the Egyptian pyramids.'

'Then 'tis both blasphemous and idolatrous.'

'By our standards, Mose.'

'By Christian standards, which is all that aught concern us.'

'How old do you suppose it to be?'

Mose frowned, scratching behind his ear. 'Who can say? A hundred years mayhap.'

'I should think *hundreds* of years. See how the steps are weathered into the sides?'

Mose let out a groan. 'I suppose we must needs study it, then?'

Boundless chuckled. 'It will take but a quarter-hour.'

While Mose checked the rigging on the mules, Boundless paced the distance around the mound, marking off six hundred feet before completing the circuit. Seeing his companion was still busy with the mules, he took the opportunity to ascend the earthwork, clambering straight upwards from the base. Gaining the summit, he surveyed the surrounding countryside. The warm breeze gusted against his face. From the vantage point, it was clear that the mounds formed an approximate circle. 'Perhaps the whole represents a heathen temple of some kind,' he speculated. Crouching, he felt the grass. The notion that bones might lie buried beneath inflamed his curiosity as to the intentions of the mound builders.

'Are ye fit?' Mose shouted up from below, cupping his hands to his mouth. 'Let us find the path and be on our way!'

'I see the captain's pointed bluff!' Boundless pointed to the west. 'No more than a mile that way!'

'Then fetch yourself down and let us proceed!'

He descended, loathe to abandon the mounds so quickly. Mose sat impatiently in the saddle. 'These observations can keep for later. *Later!*' he added sharply as Boundless rummaged through the haversack tied to the bay.

'But one minute.' Finding the log, he held it in one hand as he quickly sketched with the other, eyeing the mound as he drew. He shadowed the sketch to indicate the grass-covered surface and drew a stick figure to reference the height.

'Lord if we ain't sketching our way to the plains!' Mose slapped the chestnut on the rump and led off, his manner techy. 'That could have and *ought to have* waited until camp.'

His mood improved as they arrived at the pointed bluff. 'The captain be a dependable man,' he acknowledged. 'Let us hope those Virginia boys didn't stretch his neck.'

They continued for several more hours until sunset, making camp in a small hollow. While Mose tended to Prodigal, who had acquired a limp, Boundless scouted the brush, shooting a brace of turkeys for supper. He caught the second on the wing after surprising it in the long grass. Pleased with the shot, he returned to camp. The night was warm, and after supper he took out the log, studying the mound sketch by firelight as he wondered at the hands that had fashioned it.

As he turned back the pages, his eye fell upon the printed quadrant set aside for observation of the moon and tides. A tiny table of declination set him to thinking, and he glanced up at the stars, recalling an overhead remark from the *Patience* that Philadelphia lay approximately 39° north of the equatorial line. Setting aside the log, he gazed up at the bright cluster of stars. Finding Ursa Minor, his eye traced the pole star where it shone on the tip of the panhandle. 'Had I a sextant and chart mayhap I could calculate the proximate distance from Philadelphia,' he speculated, in his mind seeing the ship's sailing master 'shoot' the pole star. Pondering the mechanics of celestial mathematics, he fell asleep.

THE PATH CONTINUED SMOOTH and straightforward, passing more rolling bluffs and open meadows. They sighted several Indian villages with clusters of tepees, always keeping their distance.

'I do not know the Ohio Indians,' said Mose, 'else I would be disposed to ride into their villages to trade and smoke a pipe or two. This pestilent war has turned everything on its head. And no one now can tell friend from foe.'

The following afternoon, they forded the 'big clear river', described by the French captain, confident that they were still on the right path. A hundred miles across the river, their confidence diminished as day after day passed without sight of the promised Mississippi. Their uncertainty was somewhat assuaged by passing a third landmark mentioned by the captain—a waterfall splashing down the side of a cliff face into a large pool.

However, it took another two days of steady travelling before they spied sunlight glittering off a distant body of water. 'That surely must be it.' Shading his eyes, Boundless rose in the saddle to stare into the distance. 'It runs to the south as the captain described.'

They lost sight of the river several times over the course of the day as the flat landscape gave way to pine-clad hills. Passing through a defile, they followed a trail up the side of a limestone bluff to where it gave a prospect of the country ahead. They halted, surprised to be presented with rich fields of grain and a thriving settlement in the near distance. A stout fortress caught their attention, its high stone walls seeming to glow white in the sun.

'The road was supposed to take us farther south, below the fort.'
'Mayhap we took the wrong fork, yesterday.'

Boundless surveyed the citadel through the spyglass. A gold-blue *fleur-de-lis* fluttered proudly above the ramparts. Within its walls, he could glimpse the roof of a church along with a row of barracks. On both sides of the fort, cultivated fields stretched back from the river. He saw tiny figures toiling over crops. Herds of pigs, sheep and goats grazed the open pastures. Wagons and carts trundled along a road running alongside the river. The river itself seemed formidably wide, the far bank barely discernible, even with the glass.

As he watched, a company of soldiers marched forth from the fortress gates. The men were clad in long whitish-grey coats—the same as that worn by the French captain. Each trooper wore a black felt tricorn on his head and carried a musket sloped against his shoulder. Once outside, the soldiers wheeled in formation and proceeded to parade the length of the wall. Several men in civilian clothes rode slowly past the fields on horseback, headed downriver.

He offered the glass to Mose. 'I should not like to be the general charged with taking such a fortress.'

Mose shook his head, refusing the glass. He stared at the wide river flowing behind the settlement. 'We are in for more pleasure boating,' he said, grimacing at the prospect.

''Tis said, by the captain, to surpass even the Ohio in depth and flow.'

'How in blazes are we to cross it—given that we must avoid the soldiers to boot?'

'We may have—'

'Look there!'

A detachment of mounted troopers led by an officer emerged from a stand of trees, headed towards the foot of the bluff where they sat. One of the soldiers carried a lance from which fluttered a blue and white pennant.

'They have spotted us!' Mose turned the chestnut.

Faint cries rang out behind them as they hurriedly descended the bluff. Reaching level ground, they spurred the horses, riding as fast as they dared past the thick stands of timber. Boundless glanced to the rear to see the line of troopers descend the bluff in pursuit. 'Skit!' He urged the bay to run faster as the mules galloped behind, baskets shaking and banging against their sides.

A mile further on, Mose reined the blown stallion, attempting to see through the cloud of dust that hung in their wake. 'I do believe they have given up the chase,' he said, twisting in the saddle. 'We had the advantage. They had first to climb the bluff. I doubt they were overanxious to press the chase.'

Taking out the spyglass, Boundless scanned the trail to their rear. 'They have stopped,' he confirmed. Through the dust he saw several of the troopers had dismounted and were walking their horses. 'Why in God's name chase us? They could not tell if we were English or French?'

'Mayhap it was for the sport. They cannot have much excitement in this desolate spot.'

They walked the horses for the next mile, checking over their shoulders to make sure the soldiers had indeed abandoned the pursuit. To be certain, they rode within the shelter of the line of bluffs for the next hour before deciding to risk heading across open ground to the river. No farms or houses were visible as they proceeded across the bottom land towards the Mississippi.

Arrived at the shore, they studied the turbulent river as it swept past.

'Are you certain we must cross it?' Mose sounded doleful.

'If we wish to reach the Missouri.'

Climbing down from the bay, Boundless scooped up a handful of water. In contrast to the clear stream of the Ohio, the river appeared a dullish brown tint, suggesting a thick, silt bottom. 'It is deep,' he ventured, trickling the water between his fingers.

'Aye. And devilish wide. It must be a half mile or more across—and a sight more irksome than the Ohio.' Mose pointed to a floating tree trunk. 'The logs are big enough to upset a boat.'

They rode south along the shore of the river in hope of finding a ferry. The day had grown fiercely hot—the immense flow of water seeming to taunt them with a promise of cool benediction and thirst-slaking refreshment. After a while they sighted a flatboat headed upstream in their direction. As it drew nearer, the sound of French voices carried over the water. A man waved his hand as he stood at the rear oar. *Bonjour, mes amis!*'

'*Bonjour!*' Boundless waved his hat.

Mose grunted. 'Keep *bonjouring* until we find a way across. It may save our hides.'

The unrelenting heat took its toll, and they stopped to allow the horses to drink. Mose took off his shirt to gingerly splash water over his pale chest. 'This sun will boil us to a turn,' he complained.

Using his hands, he threaded water through his hair. He flicked irritably to dispel the swarming cloud of insects. 'Perish, but they latch onto a body!'

As they continued, several more boats passed by, all headed upstream. 'We must be approaching another settlement,' Boundless guessed as they stopped to confer over a course of action. 'Let us hope we are able to purchase our way across. It is worth the hazard. What say you?'

'We have little choice. We must either buy passage or grow wings and fly across.'

Continuing, they entered a thick growth of reeds that stretched back several hundred yards from the river. Dismounting, they led the horses and mules through the tall cane, following a beaten path that held to the shoreline. Within a short distance they chanced upon a large flatboat where it lay partly beached on the shore.

'Zounds, but that would take us across—and with room to spare.'

Boundless stood on tiptoe. 'I see no sign of a house.'

'Then let us press on. Where there is a boat there must be a boatman.'

Before they had a chance to turn from the shoreline, a voice rang out from the surrounding cane.

'*Messieurs, identifiez-vous!*' The command was followed by the unmistakeable cock of a musket.

42

St Genevieve

'WE ARE BUT PASSING travellers.' Do not fire!' Mose held both hands up in the air.

'*Vous êtes anglais?*' The concealed voice expressed surprise.

'*Oui.* Yes. *Anglais.* Do not fire! We mean no harm.'

A rustling in the undergrowth was followed by the appearance of three men—all clad in blue shirts secured around their waists with a red sash. Two of the men wore grey worsted caps. The third was bareheaded. Each carried a musket, the barrels of which were levelled at the two companions. The bare-headed man, a strongly built fellow with a broad face and long black hair bunched back by a length of red yarn, stared at Boundless. His gaze shifted to the laden mules. '*Les voyageurs?*'

'Yes! Travellers. *Voyageurs. Nous sommes amis!*' he said, repeating a phrase he had learned from the French captain.

The man turned to one of his companions. '*Où est Louis?*' The other man turned and disappeared back into the cane. A silence followed, during which the Frenchmen lowered their muskets while still keeping a wary eye on the companions.

'At least they are not brigands,' he said under his breath to Mose.

A noise sounded in the cane and a ginger-haired youth with a tuft of wispy hair beneath his chin stepped from the reeds. He and the broad-faced man, who appeared to be in charge, held a discussion, the youth nodding and glancing up at Boundless. After a moment he stepped forward.

'*Ello,*' he said, in heavily accented English. 'I am named Louis Gibault. This is Monsieur Fournier. What is it you are wishing?'

Boundless introduced himself and Mose, the exchange closely followed by the broad-faced man who observed with a suspicion that Boundless sought to dispel. 'We are travellers only. And we wish to cross the river. We will gladly pay for the privilege. Do you understand?' he said as the youth followed the conversation with wrinkled brow.

'You are wishing to … ah, *traverser*, the river?'

'Yes. We are willing to pay.'

'*Que dit-il?*' Fournier broke in on the conversation, his voice impatient.

After listening to the youth, he leaned on the barrel of his musket, appearing to deliberate. After a moment he gestured to the mule. '*Cela vous coûtera un mulet?*'

'What in tar is he gabbing about?' Mose's voice was agitated.

'I believe he wants one of the mules in exchange for taking us across.'

'Tell him go hang!'

Boundless spoke to the youth while keeping his gaze on the older man. 'Kindly inform the *monsieur* that the mules are not for barter. Tell him we have money to pay for our passage.'

He watched as the two conferred. Fournier grimaced and scratched the back of his neck. '*Deux livre!*' He held up two fingers.

'Do what?'

'We must offer money. What tender do you have?'

Mose went to the saddlebag and fumbled for his purse. 'The scoundrel will take a half Spanish I wager.' He took out a coin and held it up. 'Good silver,' he said. '*Bon!* And sufficient to buy passage twice over.'

'Four *reales*.' Boundless held up his fingers in imitation of the Frenchman. '*Sil vou plat*,' he said, hoping he had remembered it right from the captain.

Fournier considered the offer before holding out his hand for the coin. '*D'accord.*'

'He will to take you, *Monsieur*, for the price you purpose.'

Depositing the coin in a leather pouch secured to his waist, Fournier gestured to a mound of assorted bundles of pelts, snares, cut wood and other supplies lying in the reeds. '*Nous partirons dès que les provisions seront à bord.*'

THE FLATBOAT STRUCK BOUNDLESS as most resembling a ferry—the open, rectangular wood frame being ideal for transporting freight or livestock. The stern end was square, the front narrowed to a more conventional bow. While waiting for the Frenchmen to stow the pelts and snares, he paced the springy deck, estimating the length at forty feet.

On Fournier's instructions, they secured the horses and mules in the middle of the vessel, leaving their saddles and cargo in place. The Frenchmen's own supplies were stacked either side of the bow. Two of the men departed, leaving Fournier and the two youths to make the crossing. As the Frenchmen made ready to depart, Boundless joined Mose at the side.

'Thank Heaven for the boat.' Mose surveyed the wide river. 'I should hate to have had to build a second raft.'

'*Allons-y!*' Fournier had taken up position at the stern next to a long steering oar. The youths positioned themselves on either side of the vessel, long paddles at the ready.

'*Les rames!*' Fournier pointed to a spare pair of oars laying to the side of the deck.

'The devil! Does he expect us to row after paying enough to purchase this tub?'

'What harm if it gets us across quicker?' Picking up the long oars, Boundless gave one to Mose and, with the other, positioned himself behind the English-speaking youth. Mose took up position on the opposite side. ''Tis thievery,' he grumbled.

'*En avant!*' The youths began to stroke the paddles, Boundless and Mose copying the strokes. Fournier picked up another oar to push off from the bank. '*À droite! Assez!*'

A WARM BREEZE BLEW across the deck as they slowly paddled the boat away from the reeds and into the brown Mississippi tide. Fournier kept the vessel pointed into the breeze at a 40° angle to the opposite shore as small waves rocked the boat. Fine drops of moisture sprinkled the deck, giving the impression of rain falling from the cloudless sky.

'It's like the raft!' Mose called as he matched his stroke to that of the youth in front of him.

'But less likely to sink and drown us!'

Although the current was strong, the boat seemed to glide easily across the tide. The youths paddled with slow, relaxed strokes, seemingly content to allow the river to take them downstream. As he stroked the oar, Boundless surveyed the broad reaches of the river, certain that—apart from the Ohio—it was the most voluminous he had yet encountered in the colonies. Curious to learn more, he called to the red-bearded youth. 'To where does it flow?' He pointed downstream as the youth turned his head.

'Where to?'

'*Où? Jusqu'au Golfe du Mexique.*'

'And where does it begin—start?' He pointed upstream. 'The *beginning*?'

The youth grinned. '*C'est le secret de Dieu, monsieur!*'

A partly submerged tree floated downstream on the tide close to the flatboat. As it swept past, Boundless saw a small creature—a possum or woodchuck—clinging to the branches, the tiny body held barely above the flood as the tree floated by.

After paddling for a quarter of an hour, they passed the mid-way mark and saw houses on the far shore, well downstream of their starting position.

'*Arrêtez!*' called out Fournier and immediately the youths stopped stroking.

He lets the river do the work thought Boundless, appreciative of the Frenchman's skill as the boat angled closer to the shore.

More houses appeared on shore as the streets of a sizeable settlement came into view. Carts and wagons trundled along a road. A *fleur-de-lis* blew stiffly from a pole protruding from the roof of a large wood building. He scanned the settlement for any sign of soldiers but could see none. Mose glanced at him and nodded, as if reading his mind.

Four boats of similar construction to the flatboat were lodged on the muddy shore. As they approached, Fournier turned the boat so that the bow drove in towards the bank.

'*Préparez-vous!*'

Boundless braced himself as the keel shuddered up onto the mud.

Within the space of a few minutes, the horses and mules had been led ashore to stand in the grass. They left them there while assisting the Frenchmen to off-load the supplies.

'*Venir!*' Beckoning for them to follow, Fournier set off towards the houses. The two youths had loaded the pelts and snares onto a wooden sled, which they dragged by a rope over their shoulders.

A horde of mites rose up from the grass as Boundless and Mose followed Fournier, walking the livestock. Upon reaching a large grassy common at the edge of the settlement, Fournier stopped and sat down in the grass, motioning for them to do the same. '*Repos! Prenez un moment de répit.*'

Boundless glanced at Mose. 'Should we not take our leave? There may be soldiers.'

'A rest won't harm. We are safely across the stream and have saved a week or more into the bargain. And this may be our last chance to buy supplies.'

'*Dieu merci!*' Louis threw down the sled rope, sweat pouring from his face in the humid air. His companion flopped down in the grass beside him.

'*L'eau!*' Unstrapping the leather canteen from around his neck, Louis began to drink, swallowing loudly. After slaking his thirst, he leaned forward and offered the canteen to Boundless. '*Boisson!*' he said, urging him to take the canteen.

He took a swallow. 'Thank you. *Merci.*'

Mose took out a twist of tobacco and offered it to Fournier, who nodded in appreciation. '*Merci, Monsieur.*'

'Add that to the cost of passage,' muttered Mose beneath his breath.

The Frenchman pulled a black clay pipe and a tinderbox from a fringed bag across his shoulder. As the two youths lounged on elbows to swig from the canteens, Fournier coaxed flame from the tinderbox. Puffing on the flame, he ignited a length of dried reed. '*Non? La pipe?*' He looked quizzically at Boundless as he offered the glowing taper to Mose.

Boundless shook his head. 'A malady,' he said, patting his chest.

'*Ah! La tabac.*' The Frenchman nodded. '*La maladie,*' he said.

Louis looked at Boundless. 'Where are you to go, Monsieur?'

'To the west. To hunt buffalo.' He held up his hands in imitation of firing a musket. 'You understand?'

'*Oui.*' The youth nodded. '*Le buffle.*'

'*Buffle?*'

The youth nodded again and repeated, '*Oui. Le buffle.*' He put fingers alongside his head to imitate horns.

'Ask him for directions,' said Mose.

'Do you know the country—to the west?' Boundless gestured in the direction.

'*Ouest?*' Louis pondered for a moment. 'Go to … ah … *follow* the river to north—three, four days, to the …' He murmured to himself before looking at Boundless and crossing his index fingers one over the other.

'The fork?'

'*The fork!* The fork of … *la rivière Missouri.*' Louis waved an arm. '*Une fleuve grand.* It *takes* to the west.'

'Ask him when we get to the goldang plains.'

'Where do we find the plains?'

'*Pardon?*' The youth turned to his companions for assistance. They exchanged perplexed looks.

'The *plains.*' Boundless tugged at a handful of grass and bunched it up in his fist. 'Grass. *Herb?*' He held out the grass in the palm of his hand. 'Buffalo grass?'

The second youth sat up straight, his eyes widening in comprehension. '*L'herbe de buffle! Le prairie.*'

It was Boundless' turn to be confused. '*Prairie?*'

Louis spread his arms wide. 'The big grass, no?'

'Yes! The big grass! Where?' He pointed. '*Où?*'

To his surprise, the question occasioned a burst of laughter. Fournier, who had remained silent until now, content to smoke his pipe, grinned, his eyes keen with humour. '*Où? Partout!*'

'What does he say?'

'The grass—*le prairie*, is … all the where!'

'Everywhere?'

'*Oui!*' Gibault made a circle with his forefinger and thumb.

'Everywhere!'

'*Partout!*' repeated Fournier, drawing more laughter.

Several more minutes passed in this fashion, the Frenchmen bantering with each other while relaxing in the warmth of the sun.

'Ask him where we can buy supplies,' said Mose after a while.

'Ask him yourself. You speak English as good as I.'

'Supplies? *Oui*,' answered Louis when Mose put the question to him. He gestured over his shoulder. 'In the town. *Il y a des postes de traite et des magasins.*'

'*Soldats? Militaire?*' asked Boundless, repeating the words of the French captain.

'By gar if you ain't snared the lingo!'

'There is to be no danger. The soldiers will think you are to be French 'unters. It is for me to go with you, yes? It is the *occasion* to … *pour pratiquer mon anglais*. For me, the 'abit of the English.' He turned and explained to Fournier, who nodded.

'*Merci*. I am grateful, *Monsieur*.'

'Louis, *s'il vous plait*.'

'Boundless!'

'Eh?' Louis stared, nonplussed.

'Me. *Moi*,' he said and pointed a finger to his chest. '*Bound*-less.' The youth brightened. 'Ah! *Vous êtes* Boundless?'

'I am. Yes. Boundless.' Grinning, the two shook hands, much to the amusement of the youth's companions.

After several more minutes, Fournier tapped out tobacco from his pipe and signalled his companion. '*Alors!*' he said, rising to his feet. He held out a hand to Boundless and then Mose.

'*Adieu, Messieurs! Bonne chance pour atteindre aux prairies!*'

With a nod to their companion, the two Frenchmen picked up the sled ropes and set off towards a large wooden building, dragging the sled behind them.

'We must re-shoe the stock,' said Mose. 'It will be our last chance.'

He bent down and picked up the stallion's hoof, while indicating the same to Louis.

'*Oui. Le forgeron.*' Louis tapped an imaginary hammer to show he understood.

Leading them to a forge situated on the edge of the settlement, Louis entered and spoke to the blacksmith, a burly fellow with formidable arms.

Louis returned with a grin on his face. 'He has promised to *shoe* the 'orses and mules *immédiatement*,' he said, looking pleased with himself at the use of the word 'shoe'.

'I will watch the blacksmith and meet you back where we started,' said Mose. After a brief discussion concerning the supplies, he tapped some coins into Boundless' hand.

Placing the coins in the pouch inside his shirt, Boundless prepared to follow Louis into the settlement. No sooner had they set off than he heard Mose shout out behind them, 'If ye forget all else, do not forget the whisky!'

The town streets seemed largely deserted in the afternoon heat, the only movement coming from a wagon being dragged by a team of oxen.

His companion proved an amiable guide, eager to practise his English as they strolled through the streets. '*Votre ami est vieux*—old, to, ah, *voyage?*'

'Old. But determined.'

'*De-term-ind*. 'Louis repeated the word. 'It is correct?' He glanced at Boundless.

'It is. Where did you learn to speak English?'

'It is to use for the trade. Sometime *les Indiens,* sometime the Spaniard speak *la langue anglaise.*'

Contrary to Boundless' fears, the few inhabitants they encountered proved uniformly polite and welcoming, seemingly not the least perturbed to find themselves in the presence of an Englishman. 'I had not expected so obliging a welcome,' he confessed, following one such introduction.

Louis gave him a look of surprise. 'No? Ste-Geneviève is the *colonie* of the French, the Spanish, the soldiers. Also, the merchants and *le fermier*— of the farms. We wish 'arm to none and *bonne volonté*—good spirits, to all.'

'Ste-Geneviève?'

'*Oui.*' Louis swept out a hand to indicate the town.

They continued up the main street, encountering several oxen-drawn carts and men on horseback. Invariably, the men raised their hats or called out a polite greeting to his companion, who seemed to know each by name. Women hung out washing or collected water from a pump. Children played in the street alongside chickens and pigs.

Boundless noted with curiosity the odd construction of the houses—the roofs seemingly supported by a series of wooden posts sunk into the ground. Many of the houses were surrounded by galleries, the effect lending a pleasing charm to their appearance. He spotted a pretty young girl hanging up laundry behind one house and glanced admiringly as he passed.

The glance was not missed by Louis, who grinned. '*Elle est jolie, n'est-ce pas?*'

Boundless laughed, guessing the meaning. 'Yes, she is. How many families?'

'*Nombre?*' Gibault stroked his chin, thinking, as they progressed. 'Two 'undred, perhaps,' he said, seeming himself mildly surprised by the figure.

Boundless stared as they passed by a group of Indian men and women gathered in the doorway of a dilapidated dwelling. The men smoked pipes, their faces solemn as they gazed back. Two women nursed babes at their bare breasts. 'You have Indians living here?'

'*Les Indiens?* Yes. They come to make the trade and sometimes to … *rester*—stay, *non?*'

They arrived at a street lined with several commercial establishments, including a tavern. A dozen or more carts were drawn up in the street to display assorted vegetables, eggs, cheeses and tubs of butter. Prospective buyers flocked around the various carts to inspect the merchandise or argue with the sellers, their faces animated. Several of the buyers were accompanied by Indian women, whom he took to be their wives or consorts. The women were dressed in plain bodices and petticoats but were unmistakably squaw in their features. Some smoked pipes, watching silently as their menfolk haggled over prices or quality.

'*Par ici!*' Louis pushed through the crowd.

Boundless tensed as he saw a group of soldiers—distinctive in their greyish tunics and crossed bandoliers—lounging on the steps of a church. Some were engaged in a card game while their comrades watched, black felt tricorns tipped back carelessly on their heads. Busily observing the soldiers, he almost stumbled into the path of a wagon.

'*Attention!*' Louis held out a cautionary arm as the wagon lumbered to a halt. Two Negroes dressed in leather aprons jumped down from the back and began to unload barrels in front of a store.

'*Nous voilà!*' Louis led the way inside.

'*Bienvenue, Messieurs!*' The proprietor, a sallow-faced individual dressed in a red shirt tied with the ubiquitous sash, advanced to meet them. His eyes examined Boundless as Louis made the introductions.

'*Comment l'anglais va-t-il payer?*'

'Monsieur Jolliet wishes to discover if you to have the gold or silver?'

'We have good English or Spanish coin.'

Louis turned and spoke to the proprietor, concluding by shaking the man's hand.

'Monsieur Jolliet will prefer the money of Spain. *Reales*. You understand?'

He nodded at the proprietor. 'Spanish coin, it shall be.'

When the prolonged transactions were completed, Boundless was in possession of salt, black powder, lead balls, beans, tea, oats, sugar, a straw hat, biscuits, two loaves of bread, butter, a pound of smoked pork, and six canteens of whisky.

'*Merci.*' The proprietor reached out to shake his hand.

'You 'ave not to worry about the … *things.*' Louis pointed to the supplies. 'Monsieur Jolliet will send his boy to go … um *to took*? Yes? *Ah! Take* the goods!'

'Please Louis, allow me to buy you a drink, for your assistance,' he said. 'The horses and mules will not be ready yet.'

After sharing a bottle of wine, they walked around the settlement as Louis explained something of its history while introducing Boundless to several acquaintances. He found himself much taken with the young Frenchman, reminded of a former companion by the youth's guileless manner. 'A French Humpflinger,' he told himself, pondering the fact that opposing cultures should throw up so distinctive and yet so similar a person. Two hours later, they walked back to the store and watched as a stick-thin Negro boy loaded the provisions onto a hand cart.

'He is a slave?'

'*Pardon?*'

'Slave.' Searching for a way to make his meaning clear, he pointed to his neck to indicate a collar. 'Slave?'

'Ah! *Un esclave.*' Louis nodded. 'Yes. Of course.'

While the boy loaded the cart, Boundless looked around for the soldiers. He saw them still immersed in their card game. His companion followed his gaze. '*Pfff !*' He waved a hand. 'Not to fear,' he said.

MOSE WAS SLEEPING SOUNDLY in the grass, his hat pulled down over his eyes. Boundless shook the trapper by the shoulder. 'Awake, my friend. I have returned.'

'Jack-o'lantern!' Startled, Mose scrambled to his feet, losing his hat in the process. 'Who is this?' he said, staring at the young Black.

'No one. He is delivering our purchases. I trust you slept soundly and didn't lose the mules?'

The trapper bristled. ''Twas between bells,' he protested.

They added the purchased supplies to the cargo and secured the baskets to the mules, the boy assisting.

'Give him our thanks,' Boundless said to Louis, producing a coin after they had finished.

Louis gave the coin and ruffled the boy's tight curls '*Retournez à ton maître. Rapidement.*'

Boundless mounted the bay, the familiar feel of the saddle solid and comforting beneath him.

Louis grasped the bridle. 'Remember. Follow to the north and you … ah, *discover* the Missouri. That waters take you to *les prairies.*'

Boundless shook the youth's hand. 'A thousand thanks for your assistance, *mon ami.*'

'*Dieu t'accompagne, mon ami.*'

'Ask him if there be any taverns or trading posts up ahead.' Louis gave a perplexed stare when posed the question. '*Posts?*

Rien.' He shook his head. 'There is … no thing.'

'Nothing?'

'*Oui.* Nothing.'

43

A Mighty Clash of Waters

'THEY WERE FINE FELLOWS in the end,' said Mose as they set out on the path along the river. 'And most useful. Else it would have taken us a week to cross this stream.'

'It is a great pity we must fight them.' Boundless glanced over his shoulder to where Louis walked back into the settlement.

The day continued fine and warm with a soft, northerly breeze. Sunlight glinted on the dull brown tide as the Mississippi lapped against the grass banks, mere yards from the path.

'You realise that this way takes us back past the fortress?' said Mose. 'Thank God it is on the other side of the river. But be watchful all the same.'

Late in the afternoon, they spotted a party of men on horseback in the distance. Fearful lest they be soldiers, they turned inland with some urgency, finding shelter in the pine bluffs that sat back from the river.

'I doubt they are troopers,' said Mose, as they debated the identity of the men, 'But why chance it? They may equally be bandits.'

They kept to the lee side of the bluffs for the next three days, electing slower progress in preference to the risk of encountering a French patrol along the river. On the afternoon of the fourth day, Mose held up a hand.

'Hark!' He cocked his head to one side, listening.

'What is it?'

'Listen!'

Boundless strained to hear, gradually discerning a sibilant hiss, like the wind rushing through grass. He furrowed his brow. 'The fork?'

'I do believe so.'

They descended the side of the bluff and entered a stand of longleaf pine. The dull thunder of rushing water sounded ever more loudly in their ears as they made their way through the trees. Reaching the edge of the thicket, Boundless brushed aside an overhanging branch. 'God in Heaven!'

'What is it?' Mose reined to a halt beside him. 'By the bones!'

Before their astonished gaze stretched a vast churning flood, as though all the waters of the earth had been gathered together in the one spot. Trees and small islands stranded in the deluge testified to the size and extent of the engulfing tide. The voluminous sea—for so it seemed—whipped up its own winds, the blasts joining with the noise of the immense, rolling waters to produce a muted yet thunderous roar that deafened their ears.

He heard Mose shout indistinctly alongside. The trapper tugged at the bay's bridle and Boundless turned to follow, riding along the shore as if proceeding alongside the blustery Chesapeake itself.

They camped near the fork, dispensing with a watch—both men feeling secure in the embrace of waters. While it was yet light, Boundless attempted to scale a pine on the edge of the thicket. The branches were thin and high off the ground.

Grasping a protuberance, he attempted to hoist himself up to the lowest limb, only to slip and badly scrape his hands and wrists. After several unsuccessful attempts, he wrapped himself around the thin, straight trunk and worked his way up, inch by inch, to the lower branches. Using the branches as footsteps, he managed to hoist himself halfway up the tree. Precariously balanced, he looked out over the turbulent flood to where the two streams converged in a momentous clash of waters. To his eyes, the Missouri appeared the larger and more energetic of the two—its foaming tide carrying it across the darker strata of the Mississippi like a huge wedge. The point of land where their campfire now flickered in the dusk seemed the only speck of solid ground amidst the vast, alluvial riches of the floodplain. The sun began to sink in the western sky and he thought he heard Mose call out. But he lingered—compelled to watch as the glowing red sun liquefied into the dusky sea.

'YOU RISKED BREAKING YOUR neck,' Mose chided as he re-joined his companion by the campfire.

He used grass and water to rub the sticky pine resin from his hands while Mose added tea leaves to the pot. 'Well?' Mose asked. 'What did you see up there that you cannot see just as well from here?'

Boundless picked tar and needles from his shirt. 'A tide that might easily float the combined navies of England and France. The pastures and rivers of old England—and I daresay Europe entire—be altogether insufficient yards for the superlatives of this New World.'

Mose nodded as he sucked on the pipe. ''Tis indeed a rare sight—sufficient to persuade the heretic that old Noah's flood still laps the corners of the earth.'

'Missi-*ssip*-pi. Miss-*our-i*.' Boundless rolled the words on his tongue, the sibilant vowels seeming to resonate with the sound of the swirling waters. 'What is their meaning?'

Mose tossed the tea leaves into the dirt. 'Who can tell? They are heathen, no doubt.'

Later, as he lay beneath the buffalo robe, Boundless felt himself still in the thrall of waters. *Surely, the rivers be misnamed seas.* He lay awake, listening, scarcely able to comprehend the voluminous flood gathered less than a hundred yards from his head. As he finally closed his eyes, he heard Mose snore, the sound barely audible above the ceaseless swell and flux of the conjoining tides.

THEY FOLLOWED THE MISSOURI north for a week, sticking close to the shore. The early summer weather continued hot and humid, the flies and mosquitoes a constant source of annoyance. Game was plentiful and fish from the river were available in abundance. Grizzly bears were a constant menace, the beasts so numerous that they were forced to maintain a vigilant watch—occasionally firing the muskets to scare off the beasts if they ventured too close.

The rugged landscape of hills, trees and valleys slowly began to flatten out as they continued in a north-westerly direction. To avoid any possible contact with French patrols, they travelled a short distance inland while yet retaining sight of the river.

One afternoon, they halted before an immense buffalo trace—the shallow trough so vast that they could not see its perimeters.

'By the saints!' Mose gazed at the churned-up earth. 'I calculate we may come upon the plains by the hour!'

'How will we know them?'

'Why, when we look to the east and see grass, and to the west, north and south the same, then are we arrived.' Jubilant, Mose gestured to the immense trace. 'The signs are before us. Look to the signs!'

They camped that night beside a small spring in a stand of oak and hickory. Mose was in a pensive mood, smoking and murmuring to himself as he stared into the fire. 'Stay where put!' He kicked a spluttering log back into the flames.

'How far do you judge we have come?'

'Mayhap a thousand mile or more.'

Boundless ruminated on this while fidgeting with a tea cup.

'Something on your mind?' Mose regarded him over the pipe.

'I was thinking …'

'Yes?'

'We rode maybe a thousand mile to get here. And before us is God knows how much more country—all bare, save for savages and grass.'

'And buffalo.'

'And buffalo.'

'What of it?'

Boundless frowned and set down his cup. 'What now—now that we are here?'

Mose spat into the fire. 'We ride onto the prairies and harvest pelts and robes.'

'Agreed. That was the purpose. But who will we sell to? There are no more settlements—not even a trading post.'

Mose stroked his chin. 'Why, we do as the Frenchies do and store the pelts until we ship the entire cargo downriver.'

'How? And to where? And even so, the French may seize any cargo of fur.'

'By Pharoah's nose! Must you tie the tail of every fox afore the chase has even begun?'

'I simply wish—'

'Is it not enough that we are here—that we have almost reached our destination after a most arduous journey?'

'And no man would say different. But still, a reasonable hope—'

'Reasonable? *Pshaw!*'

Boundless sighed and set another log on the fire.

'I hadn't studied on all the particulars,' said Mose after a while, his tone conciliatory. 'The mules will carry a goodly cargo of furs. Perhaps if we head up to the Canada country ...' His voice trailed off as he stared into the fire. 'By *thunder*, but I wouldn't trade what we have seen. Not for Old England itself!' He eyed Boundless, his expression fierce. 'Think on it! The voyage of a lifetime! In a day or two at the most, our eyes will feast on the very buffalo plains. Think on it!'

'I do, Mose. I do.' He stretched out his arms. 'Who knows? We may strike gold into the bargain.'

He took first watch, allowing the fire to die down to glowing embers as he listened to the yelps of a coyote above the snores of his companion. All at once Mose uttered a furious shout. 'Who passes!' The trapper sat bolt upright in his sleep. He remained vigilantly erect for a moment, staring at some unseen foe, before sinking back again to the grass where he resumed a loud, rasping drone.

THE MORNING DAWNED, WARM and cloudless. After watering the animals, they set off at a slow walk, the river a mile to their right. They had just skirted a crag, following a fresh elk trace, when the bay suddenly shied in fright, almost tipping Boundless from the saddle.

He heard a grunting roar and turned to see a large grizzly charge out from the trees. Before he could react, the panicked bay took off at a run that had him clinging to the saddle. As he fought to control the frantic horse, he heard a sharp cry from behind followed by an unearthly scream. Hauling on the reins, he brought the bay to a halt. As he turned, the mules rushed past, eyes wide with terror. His heart constricted with fear as he saw Mose gripped in the jaws of the huge grizzly. The big stallion lay on its side in the grass.

Whipping the frightened bay back to the scene, he sprang from the saddle and grabbed the musket from its sling. The snarling bear still had Mose in his jaws, flinging him about like a raggedy doll. Dropping to one knee, he aimed and fired. The ball struck the bear in the shoulder, drawing a roar of pain. With a bloodcurdling snarl it dropped Mose and turned its ferocious eyes on Boundless.

He froze as the bear charged, rushing through the grass with the speed of a horse. He barely had time to discharge the pistol before the bear abruptly wheeled away into the meadows, having passed by so close that he felt the blast of its hot breath on his cheek.

'Mose!'

He rushed to where his companion lay moaning in the grass.

Gasping in horror, he saw the mauled and bloodied entrails spilling through the ripped buckskin. The trapper's face was deathly pale, and he trembled violently as Boundless knelt to cradle him.

'Lord, but he has kilt me.' Mose stared wildly, his hand clutching Boundless' wrist. He coughed, blood mixed with the spittle. His breath was laboured as he struggled to breathe.

'Hush now Mose, let me bind your wounds.' He soothed his stricken comrade even as his voice betrayed his distress.

'How is old Jack?' Mose tried to turn his head. 'Is Jack kilt?' he said hoarsely. His fingers tightened where they gripped Boundless' wrist.

'Hush, Mose. Everything is alright.'

The trapper moaned in agony, his weathered face now blanched to the colour of snow. He gave a faint gasp and was still, his eyes fixed on Boundless.

'Mose? Mose!'

HE BURIED HIS COMPANION beneath the grassy crag, erecting a rough wooden cross made from two branches. Retrieving the hide map, now smudged and water-stained, from the saddle bags of the dead stallion, he cleaned the surface as best he could. Beneath the faded imprint of the arrowhead mountains, he wrote Mose's name and the month and year. Beneath the date he added the words, *Trapper, Pilgrim, Friend.*

Gouging holes in the top and bottom of the hide, he secured it to the cross with twine. He placed rocks and stones on top of the mound and then sat slumped in the shade, staring into the distance. Towards evening, he roused himself sufficiently to make a small fire. He sat there, unable to eat, staring into the flames until dawn pinked the eastern sky.

IT WAS THE WOLVES that brought him back to his senses. The snarling pack descended on the carcass of the stallion at daylight, rousing him with their frantic yelps and grinding teeth. Disgusted by the noise, he flung a smouldering branch at the frenzied animals. They backed away, snarling and snapping their teeth. Rousing himself, he set off in search of the mules. He found the half-eaten remains of Jacob lying in a gulch. A few yards distant, Prodigal stood trembling in the grass, his flanks bloody with claw marks.

He walked back to the fire, leading the mule by the rope. To his anger, he saw that the wolves were once more feeding on the carcass. Cursing, he picked up a rock, and flung it at the pack, driving it off a short distance. There they remained, just out of range, lying down, panting, to watch as he tended the wounded mule.

He sat by the extinguished fire for another hour, unable to summon the will to continue. The horse and mule grazed close by his side, terrified of the lurking wolves.

As the new day grew hotter, he released a heavy sigh and stood up. He walked over to the rock pile. 'Goodbye, old friend.' He racked his memory for a suitable verse but could think of nothing. 'Rest in the bosom of your wild plains,' he said, tears coursing down his cheeks.

HE LED OFF THE two remaining animals on foot, holding the reins of the horse as he trudged through the grass. Behind him, the wolves crept back to the stallion carcass to resume their feast, growling and snarling over the remains.

When he glanced back, he was scarcely able to pick out the grave in the billowing grass. He walked for another hour before climbing into the saddle. 'Skit, Buck!' He flicked the reins as the puzzled horse awaited direction. Prodigal kept close, not needing a rope.

From habit, he continued on a northerly path, his mind heavy with grief for his absent companion. Several times, he fancied that Mose was following just behind and half-turned in the saddle, only for his heart to sink at this fresh reminder of his loss.

Late in the afternoon, he was consumed by a ravenous hunger and stopped to make camp. Hobbling the animals, he walked out into the grass and brought down a quail for supper. He cooked the flesh over a blazing fire, adding branches carelessly as the flames leapt higher into the darkening sky. As the logs spluttered and burned in a cascade of sparks, a belated sense of caution overtook him and he hastily reduced the blaze, standing to scan the dusky horizon for the presence of Indians.

Later, lying under the buffalo robe, he tried to focus his thoughts—his mind torn between an urge to retrace his steps back to the Ohio and a fatalistic determination to continue the journey until weariness or some other intervening agency caused him to abandon it. 'I shall continue for your sake, friend,' he murmured as a restless sleep claimed him.

The landscape of hills, ridges, and gulleys gradually gave way to smooth, rolling swells of grass that undulated into the distance as far as the eye could see. Following a buffalo trace, he moved entirely away from the river, tired of its meandering course. It dimly occurred to him that he had left civilisation behind and that before him lay an immense emptiness. Only the numbness of grief prevented him from being overwhelmed by a profound loneliness as he continued ever deeper into the trackless wastes.

Late in the afternoon, he reined in the bay and turned in the saddle to survey his whereabouts. On all sides, the grass billowed limitlessly to the horizon, the wind flattening the stalks as cloud shadows raced over the sunlit expanse. For a dizzying moment he experienced a sensation of being marooned in a vast and terrifying sea—sole human tenant of the windswept world. He scanned the blowing solitude for any signs of life amid the muted roar of the wind as it swept the grass in long, curving swathes, seemingly to the ends of the earth.

'I am entirely alone,' he told himself. 'As alone as any man might be.' Weighed down by despair, he nudged the horse onwards, voyaging ever deeper into the boundless sea of grass.

Acknowledgements

The transatlantic crossing that opens the novel is based on contemporary accounts, in particular Benjamin Franklin's detailed journal of his voyage from London to Pennsylvania in 1726. The description of Boundless' eventful journey across America is likewise informed by contemporary accounts found in letters and memoirs. The depiction of the arduous trek through the mountains to Cumberland Gap draws from the works of Thomas Walker and the historian and pioneer John Filson. And finally, Boundless' shock at the biblical abundance of wildlife he encounters across the mountains is a precursor of the astonishment voiced by many later explorers including Lewis and Clark in their journals.

Exile concludes the first part of *Monuments of Grass*, a five-book series charting the creation story of one man's epic vision and its unfolding over time. The five books in the series are *Exile*, *The Fur Post*, *The Claim*, *New France*, and *Voyages of Discovery*. Print copies can be ordered online through bookstores, libraries, online retailers such as Amazon, and are also available as ebooks.